ELENA MARIKOVA

A HISTORICAL NOVEL OF AN EPIC CONSPIRACY AGAINST STALIN IN PRE-WAR RUSSIA

ELENA MARIKOVA

A HISTORICAL NOVEL OF AN EPIC CONSPIRACY AGAINST STALIN IN PRE-WAR RUSSIA

HERBERT EGGIE

iUNIVERSE, INC.
NEW YORK BLOOMINGTON

Elena Marikova
A Historical Novel of an Epic Conspiracy
Against Stalin in Pre-war Russia

iUniverse books may be ordered through booksellers or by contacting:

iUniverse
1663 Liberty Drive
Bloomington, IN 47403
www.iuniverse.com
1-800-Authors (1-800-288-4677)

ISBN: 978-1-4401-6392-0 (sc)
ISBN: 978-1-4401-6393-7 (ebk)

Library of Congress Control Number: 2009933568

Printed in the United States of America

iUniverse rev. date: 7/29/2009

CHAPTER 1
WEDNESDAY, 8 JANUARY 1939

Captain Timo Koskinen was to remember that day for the rest of his life. But, at 0530, braced against the bitter morning cold of a Finnish winter, walking east on Hameenkatu, the main thoroughfare transecting the center of Tampere, Finland's second largest city, Koskinen was preoccupied with thoughts of considerable resentment toward his superior officer, Colonel Lars Blomquist.

Blomquist had telephoned him Monday morning from military intelligence headquarters in Helsinki and instructed him to meet at 0545 hours Wednesday at the Hotel Tampere. Koskinen was rankled ever since. As he walked the quarter-mile from his office in the huge Finlayson manufacturing complex to the hotel across the street from the Tampere railroad station, Koskinen turned Monday's telephone conversation over and over again in detail in his mind. It is what one does when one is confronted with an injustice over which one has no control. And Koskinen felt that he had been dealt with unfairly.

"That's a helluva early hour, Colonel. Is there a possibility you can make it later?" he had asked.

"No. I have to be back in Helsinki by noon."

"Are you coming up Tuesday evening and staying overnight at the hotel?"

"Yes."

"Can we meet that evening? We could have dinner together."

"No. I'm coming up late and I want to get some rest. Things have been a bit strenuous down here lately."

"My reason for mentioning the time, Colonel, is that there is no transportation from my home at that hour. I'll have to sleep in the office Tuesday night."

"Well, we all have to do that on some occasions," said Blomquist, unmoved by Koskinen's prospective inconvenience and discomfort.

Koskinen knew it was futile to protest further. The Colonel had, in effect, issued an order. "Is there anything I need to do to prepare for the meeting?" inquired Koskinen, hoping to get some clue as to the purpose of the meeting.

"No, nothing. I'll explain when I see you."

As he hung up, Koskinen had muttered to himself, "That damned inconsiderate, arrogant Swede!" It was that resentment that lay at the basis for his aggravation.

It was not the fact that he would have to sleep in his office for the night. He had, indeed, as the Colonel had pointed out, done that before, usually in the event of some emergency situation that required his around-the-clock attention. Irregular hours and personal inconvenience were expected as part of Koskinen's job as Chief Intelligence Officer for District III, which included the City of Tampere and an area generally of fifty kilometers radiating from the City. Likewise, it was not even the early hour of the meeting that had him fuming. That, too, went with the job.

No, Koskinen had analyzed his feelings. He recognized why he resented Colonel Blomquist. He resented Blomquist because Blomquist was a Finnish-Swede and Koskinen had little use for Finnish-Swedes. These were people born in Finland of Swedish ancestry. The Swedes had colonized and ruled Finland for six hundred years up to 1808 when they lost it to Russia. Although many families of Swedish origin had been in Finland for centuries, Koskinen still considered them as foreign interlopers.

Koskinen considered himself as a true Finn, a Tavast Finn who traced his origins to a tribal people who settled in central Finland a millennium or more earlier. Like other "true Finns," Koskinen was aware that the Swedes had long treated the Finnish people as inferior, had imposed the Swedish culture on the native peoples and had made Swedish the official language. While much of this had changed by the time Koskinen was born in 1896, the Finnish memory was long and

Finnish-Swedes were still regarded as haughty and aloof, arrogant and condescending and inassimilable to the Finnish culture because of their Swedish clannishness.

Yet, there was another and more immediately personal reason why Koskinen resented Blomquist, one which, however recent and personal the experience, nevertheless, confirmed to Koskinen the historic conflict between Finn and Swede. Koskinen felt that he should have received the promotion to Commander of Military Intelligence for the southern half of Finland, which went instead to Blomquist. And the only reason it was given to Blomquist was because he was a Finnish-Swede and the top people at headquarters in Helsinki were a majority of Finnish-Swedes. A true Finn didn't stand a chance, according to Koskinen.

As he neared the Hotel Tampere, Koskinen suddenly realized that he had to quickly dispel from his thinking the malevolence he felt for the Colonel. If he allowed it to persist, he knew it might become apparent to the Colonel and affect their professional relationship which up to now had been quite free of any expressed personal conflicts. While Koskinen and Blomquist were by no means "buttonhole buddies" in a social sense, they had worked well in tandem on some military intelligence matters and, professionally, respected each other's talents.

With these more positive thoughts in mind, Koskinen entered the dismal hotel lobby with no inkling of what to expect and no information upon which to even speculate. No one was in the lobby. The lobby was, for Koskinen, about as cold as the outside weather. He kept his greatcoat closed and the fur collar raised about his neck. The only adjustment to his outer wear that Koskinen made was to remove the wool scarf from around his face and to raise the ear protectors of his fur hat so that he might hear better.

Koskinen rang the bell on the clerk's desk. In the lonely silence of the room, the bell sounded harsh and unpleasant. Waiting a few moments and there being no response, Koskinen rang the bell once more. With that, he heard someone seemingly stumbling about in a back room. After a few moments, the heavy maroon colored curtain behind the desk parted and there appeared a small stature, thin, pallid man dressed in a night shirt that, at one time, must have been of white muslin, but which now had the look of a well-used table cloth upon which coffee and potato soup had been spilled simultaneously. The stubble of a beard on the old man's wizened face at once reminded Koskinen of a kind of bread mold he had seen on old loaves tossed to the pigs on somebody's farm. Koskinen was repelled by the unkempt appearance of the man and wondered how the hotel owner could tolerate such a fellow as a representative of the hotel.

"I am Olavi, the managing clerk here. Do you want a room?"

"No, I do not want a room. I am here to see Herra Blomquist, one of your guests, I believe. I am Herra Koskinen. He is expecting me."

"Ah, yes. He left your name. You can go up. He is in Room 317. Can you operate the elevator?"

"Yes, of course."

After a slow, creaky ride to the third floor on the ancient elevator, Koskinen stepped off and proceeded down the hallway to Room 317. He knocked on the heavy, mahogany painted door.

A voice from within the room inquired, "Who's there?" Koskinen recognized the high-pitched voice of Colonel Blomquist.

"Koskinen."

The door, restrained by a security chain, opened only sufficiently to allow the occupant of the room to see who was on the other side of the door. Koskinen saw the partly obscured face of Blomquist staring at him for a quick survey. The door closed, the chain rattled as it was released and the door reopened fully, revealing a smiling and half-dressed Colonel Blomquist.

"Ah, Koskinen, come in please." The Colonel with a sweeping motion of his arm beckoned Koskinen in.

"Of course, I knew you were coming, and, of course, I recognized your voice when you announced yourself, but we always have to be careful," said Blomquist, referring apologetically for the door chain. Koskinen shrugged as an indication that he considered the incident as unimportant, but said nothing as he entered.

Blomquist continued, "I'm sorry that I had to set this meeting for such an early hour, but, as I explained to you over the telephone, I had no choice. I must return to headquarters by noon. There is an important meeting, a meeting which will include discussion of our meeting this morning."

Again, Koskinen said nothing but simply nodded his head to acknowledge that he had heard the Colonel. What could he say, he thought to himself? He was still mystified as to the reason for this meeting. He knew, intuitively, that, whatever was afoot, it must be of considerable importance to be called on such short notice, in the early hours of the day and in Tampere and not at headquarters in Helsinki. Nevertheless, Koskinen knew he'd have the answers within the next few minutes. The Colonel, he knew, was not one to spend much time on social trivia.

"I am sure it is quite cold outside and you had a distance to walk. Shall I order some hot coffee from the office downstairs?" Koskinen, with visions of the unkempt Olavi and what his kitchen must look like, hastened to decline the offer. By this time he had removed his coat, hat and scarf and had taken a seat on one of the two wooden straight back chairs in the room while he waited for the Colonel to carry the conversation.

"How is Anna?" Blomquist inquired, referring to Koskinen's wife.

"Fine, thank you."

"And your two fine sons?"

"They are also quite well, thank you."

"They are still going to school?" Blomquist finished putting on his shirt, sox and shoes while he continued his inquiry regarding Koskinen's family.

"Yes," replied Koskinen. "The older, Aari, is studying engineering and Pauli, the younger, is--well, he doesn't know yet what he wants to do. He's primarily interested in sports." Koskinen thought it quite odd that Blomquist should be inquiring about the family. The Colonel had never done so before this, but had always gotten right down to business at prior meetings. Koskinen suspected that there was some purpose to Blomquist's delay of coming to the reason for the meeting

Blomquist had sat down on a small sofa, which with the two wood chairs, a brass framed bed, a diminutive round table in front of the sofa and a floor lamp behind the sofa about filled the room. The common bathroom, or water closet, was at the end of the hallway. Next to the W.C. was a sauna without which no public or private residence was considered complete in Finland. From the single window in Blomquist's hotel room, Koskinen could see the Tampere Railroad Station across the street. There was no one in the vast pedestrian area in front of the entrance to the building. In any event, in the bitter cold it was unlikely that anyone would have loitered outside the station.

For a few moments neither man spoke. Koskinen was scrutinizing Blomquist. Blomquist was looking at the floor as if to avert Koskinen's gaze. Koskinen thought that Blomquist appeared to be both nervous and hesitant. Koskinen was sure that it had something to do with the business of the meeting.

Koskinen broke the silence by asking, "What time does your train leave, Colonel?" Koskinen thought his question might spur the Colonel to come to the purpose of the meeting.

Blomquist looked at the large, gold-plated pocket watch that was on the table in front of him.

"The Helsinki train leaves at seven forty seven. I have about an hour and a half yet. Yes, I guess we had better get down to our business." The Colonel was again silent for a few moments as if thinking how he might start explaining the reason for the meeting. Koskinen waited while trying to suppress any manifestation of impatience.

Colonel Blomquist finally began:

"The Chief and the rest of us at headquarters have had some very lengthy and quite serious discussions over the past several weeks about what we all consider as an enormously important and urgent mission and who might be best to lead it. We all concluded unanimously, I might add, that you were the most qualified for it. To initiate the matter with you, the Chief felt it was best for you and all concerned that I come up here rather than have the first conference at headquarters."

Koskinen was not at all flattered by having been selected as "the most qualified." He had been assigned many times before this to head projects and missions and it had generally meant intensive and arduous work frequently under difficult conditions. Koskinen sensed, however, that this meeting at an early hour in a hotel away from headquarters or in his own office and the reticence of Blomquist was different from past meetings and mission appointments. To Koskinen the whole set of circumstances now indicated that something unprecedented was happening. Nevertheless, being professional, he felt able to deal with whatever had to be.

Using the short pause again by the Colonel, Koskinen asked, "What, specifically, might the mission be, Colonel?"

"The mission, Captain, is to neutralize the influence of Stalin in the Soviet Union." Blomquist looked directly at Koskinen and awaited his reaction. Koskinen was imperturbable.

"What is meant by 'neutralize?'" Koskinen thought the Colonel was being deliberately obscure.

"It means what it says, Captain. It means to render Stalin ineffectual."

Koskinen thought to himself, "the damned fool is still being vague." Koskinen was becoming irritated and frustrated by Blomquist's lack of candor. His impatience with Blomquist was beginning to evidence itself. Koskinen painfully concluded that the Colonel was playing games with him, trying to force him to guess at what headquarters expected of him. He decided he had to clarify things.

"And what does 'render ineffectual' mean, Colonel? What I am asking is what it is that I am expected to do. Perhaps I'm stupid. So perhaps you should spell it out for me!" The tone of Koskinen's voice clearly evidenced his growing annoyance. He stared impatiently at Blomquist.

Blomquist averted Koskinen's eyes by turning his face towards the window. He appeared to be thinking how to answer. After a few moments he turned back to Koskinen.

"I suppose whatever it takes, Captain. Anything from A to Z." He shrugged his shoulders to indicate that he could not be more definite.

Koskinen retorted, " 'A' can include Abduction and Assassination."

"Yes, I know." Blomquist hesitated. "We're assuming you'll know what to do when the opportunity to act presents itself. That's why we chose you for this mission."

"I take it then that there are no guidelines, no parameters on how, when and with whom, if anyone, I am to act. Is that it?"

"Perhaps not exactly. When you get to Helsinki and meet with others in the office there will be further consideration of these things and you'll have a better idea of the details."

In a soothing voice, Blomquist continued, "I truly spoke the truth when I said that your choice of action was from A to Z. Right now, we really don't know what solution there might be as to how to accomplish the mission. We have never faced this sort of crisis problem before. So we have no answers specifically. We suspect that it could very well be a solution by assassination. I know that may be an act that may be repugnant to you. It would be to me, that is, unless and I say, 'unless' there was a supreme compelling reason such as a matter of life or death. We at headquarters believe that there now exists such a compelling reason. In the time I have left before I must leave, let me explain it to you."

Koskinen interrupted. "Before you start your explanation, I have a very simple question." Koskinen then pointed to himself and said, "Why me? I am aware that you said headquarters decided I was the most qualified. That tells me very little. Qualified to do what? I have had no experience in assassinations or in neutralizing a head of state as you have put it. Based on lack of experience in these matters, I would say there are several other people in the department, including you, who are just as well qualified as I am. So I ask, why me?"

Colonel Blomquist smiled. "A fair question, Captain. First, you speak and understand some amount of Russian. That carried some weight with us. Admittedly, some other of our agents also speak Russian in one degree or another, but we considered your record of having successfully completed other important assignments. There is no question, Koskinen, that your talents, competency and reliability are held in very high regard by all of us at headquarters. You should know that another factor is that you are Finnish and will fit in with official delegations to Russia much better than a Finnish-Swede. You mentioned that I am qualified for this mission, but I have a Swedish name and a Swedish heritage and I'm sure you know that, historically, the Russians have not been very fond of Swedes, to put it mildly."

Koskinen thought to himself, "Here we go again. A Finn is being asked to bear the brunt of what could be a very dangerous mission. When Sweden ruled Finland for some six hundred years prior to 1809, the Swedish kings were frequently engaged in wars of one kind or another. Invariably, they used the Finnish farmers and workers as soldiers. Rarely, were any Swedes drafted for military service except for the higher ranked officers. It was the Finns who died in these military excursions of Sweden. And now, here was Blomquist, born in Finland, using his Swedishness to avoid a dangerous mission." To Koskinen it was an all too disgustingly familiar scenario. No wonder he had a passionate dislike for Finnish-Swedes.

It was obvious that Captain Koskinen was not at all happy about his prospective assignment.

"Colonel, this mission appears to me to be exceptionally dangerous and will probably require me to be away from my family for a considerable time. You know that I'm married and have two children. Having a family to be concerned about could very well influence my decision as to whether to act as boldly as I should in a life-threatening situation. There are some single people on the department staff who might welcome an opportunity such as this for an exciting experience. Why not ask one of them?"

The Colonel replied sympathetically, "Captain, we were aware of all that when we discussed this mission. We decided to select you and, unless you can persuade the Chief otherwise, the die is cast. Now, since the time for my leaving is getting short, I want to explain the reasoning behind this mission."

Koskinen understood that further protestation would avail him nothing, at least not with Blomquist. At the moment, he was not sure of what he might do to get out of this assignment, if at all. His immediate duty was to listen to the Colonel expound on the mission.

"Go right ahead, Colonel."

"Good! Thank you, Captain."

Both replies sounded slightly caustic.

"Captain," Blomquist began, "Finland may be shortly in mortal danger, danger from Russia. I cannot go into a great deal of details at this time. The Chief wants you at headquarters next Wednesday at about 1130 hours. At that time, all the specifics will be given you. I can tell you, nevertheless, that reports coming into headquarters over the past several months and some of it is rumor only just now, indicate that, if events in Europe continue to develop as they seem they might, then we are in deep, deep trouble."

Koskinen was startled upon learning for the first time that he was to be in Helsinki the following week. Events were moving far too rapidly for his emotional digestion. He was not at all pleased.

Blomquist continued, "Ever since Hitler's invasion of Austria in March 1938, certain Soviet government authorities have let our embassy in Moscow know that their government is seriously concerned about a German invasion of Russia through Finland and on to Leningrad. While you have not read the reports, we all know from newspaper articles that last October the Soviet government has made several demands of Finland. Even though you know what they were and still are, I'll repeat them quickly as they are part of the reason for this mission."

Blomquist paused, looked at his watch while Koskinen remained silent.

Blomquist continued, "The Soviets want a thirty-year lease of our port at Hanko, cession of certain islands in the Gulf of Finland which are part of Finland, demilitarization of the frontier on the Karelian Isthmus, and cession of part of Fisherman's Peninsula near Petsamo. They may add more demands as time proceeds. Who knows?"

Koskinen interrupted, "To your knowledge, are we going to yield to these demands?"

"I cannot speak for our government," Blomquist answered, "but, knowing the characters of both President Kallio and Prime Minister Ryti, I would think not."

"And if we don't give the Soviets what they want, then what?" further inquired Koskinen.

"They'll probably try to take them," said Blomquist grimly.

"And that will mean war between Finland and Russia."

"In all probability, yes."

Koskinen and Blomquist looked at each other with consternation expressed on their faces as the reality of a potential horror struck them.

"Yes, Captain," Blomquist said softly, "For the first time since we achieved our independence from Russia in 1917, our big, brutish neighbor is again knocking at our door threatening to once more subjugate us. Now, you know the reason for this mission of which you will be a very important participant. The thinking behind the mission is very simple. If we can liquidate Stalin, the Soviet Union, without its formidable leader, will fall into disarray. When it does, it will become vulnerable to Hitler and we believe Hitler will seize the opportunity to invade Russia. Under such circumstances, Russia will no longer be a threat to us."

"What about Germany?" queried Koskinen. "Are you in headquarters at all concerned that Hitler will, in fact, send his army through Finland to attack Leningrad?"

"No," replied Blomquist, "we are not fearful of Germany. Germany is not interested in us, except to use our waters and land routes to get at Russia, perhaps. That does not bother us. They will not remain permanently and our sovereignty is not at risk with them. There is some talk in some European countries and even in the United States, that Hitler should be assassinated. We, in Finland, are and very well should be against that. We are certain that if Hitler remains alive, Russia is doomed. Getting rid of Stalin will facilitate that. Do you now understand?"

"Yes, but I still wish you'd assign someone else," said Koskinen, still testing the waters for relief. Blomquist said nothing, but smiled tolerantly.

Colonel Blomquist began to gather up his personal belongings and pack them into his small carrying case. As he busied himself, he continued to talk.

"Since you have been in this business many years, Captain, I know I need not stress that our meeting and what was discussed must be held in utmost confidence. No mention is to be made of it, not even to your wife Anna and your family."

Captain Koskinen broke in. "Colonel, Anna knows of this meeting. When I called her and mentioned that I would have to remain in the office overnight because of the early meeting with you, I, of course, told her that I did not know what the meeting was about. At the time, that was the truth."

"Fine," commented Blomquist, "but, for the moment, don't mention the nature of the mission we discussed. I realize you'll have to tell her eventually, because of the possible length of your absence from home."

Koskinen nodded his assent.

Blomquist then said, "That brings me to another matter, Captain. How does Anna take your being away from home for periods of time?"

Koskinen answered, "Anna has adjusted her life to the requirements of my work but she has never fully accepted it. There is a distinction between adjusting and accepting. I'm sure she is not going to be very happy about this new assignment."

"You're fortunate, Captain. My wife, Erika, has neither adjusted nor accepted my being away often for several days and nights. When she asks where I'm going and what I shall be doing, I have to tell her, frankly, 'I can't tell you because it's secretive or confidential.' As a result, Erika becomes suspicious and oft times says she thinks I have a girlfriend somewhere. She thinks that I use the demands of my job as a cover for having an extramarital affair. Of course, it's not true. Does Anna suspect you like that?"

Koskinen was taken somewhat aback by the confession and revelation of his personal life by the Colonel. This, again, was someone who had never behaved before like this and, in fact, during the entire meeting. The Blomquist with whom Koskinen was familiar was, generally, formal and distant with an impermeable outer shell of dispassionate reserve. Blomquist was, normally, a very taciturn individual.

Koskinen answered Blomquist's question with some reserve of his own. "Anna has never said she suspects me of any unfaithfulness. I'm sure she trusts me even as I trust her. If I had any girlfriend, I'm sure my actions with Anna would reveal it. Women have an uncanny ability to read men and it is very difficult for a man to hide emotional secrets from a woman, especially a wife who has lived with the man for years and knows all about his feelings and actions. Anna and I love each other dearly and deeply and I would not jeopardize that relationship by having an extramarital affair."

"Good, I'm glad to hear that for your sake. We men get tempted from time to time to stray and some surrender to the forbidden fruit while others do not." The Colonel closed his traveling case.

"I must leave in a few minutes, Captain. I'll see you in Helsinki next Wednesday morning. I believe you'll want to take the same train that I'm taking. It will get you to Helsinki in time for the 0700 meeting at headquarters." Blomquist then added, "Reverting back to the mission, Timo, I want you to know that you will not be alone on this assignment. You will get help."

Blomquist came over to Koskinen, shook hands and put his arm around the Captain's shoulder. And as Koskinen put on his coat, hat and scarf, he could not help but conclude that the interaction between their two personalities during this unique meeting had been like a seesaw oscillating between unfriendly and unsociable to warm expressions of camaraderie. To Koskinen it was an experience of incomprehensible inconsistency. He knew he'd never forget it.

It was close to 0700 hours when the two men parted. Rather than take the creaky elevator down, Koskinen used the stairway to the lobby. Olavi, the clerk, was already behind the desk apparently busying himself with all sorts of paper records. He smiled at Koskinen as Koskinen entered the lobby from the staircase. No one else was in the lobby.

"Ah, good morning, Herra Koskinen."

"Good morning," replied Koskinen, nodding his head in acknowledgment as he walked past the desk. Koskinen observed that the clerk was now wearing a rumpled suit and shirt and tie although he still appeared not to have been in a sauna for some time. And the beard stubble was still there.

Outside it was still dark and bitter cold. In Finland, the winter nights are long. There may be three or four hours of daylight. Mental depression and a general malaise affect many Finns during this time of the year. Also, the birth rate in Finland increases sharply during the months from June through August.

The streets had become considerably busier when Koskinen emerged from the hotel. Under the light from the street lamps, people could be seen hurrying to wherever they were going. The buses were operating and lights that showed through the windows of buildings disclosed that a city had resumed its life for another day.

As Koskinen walked back to his office and blended in with others on the street his thoughts turned to these individuals hastening toward their respective destinations and to get out of the cold and there came over him a sudden feeling of intense empathy and compassion for each and all of them. How totally unaware they were of a possible cataclysm that might descend upon them at any moment and that their lives might be violently changed forever.

These were the innocents, Koskinen thought. These were his people and they were the ones who would be called upon to sacrifice with their lives and the lives of their loved ones in the event of a war. They would all become a part of a conflagration not of their making and the purpose and reason for which they would probably never understand. How unfair and how unjust!

Yet, Koskinen, acquainted as he was with the history of his country, knew that it had been ever so over the centuries. A few kings and a few dictators and their henchmen had periodically dragged the farmers, the working people, the young as well as the elderly into major wars and into small skirmishes alike solely for political purposes or to feed their egotistical need to express their power. The citizens, most of whom wanted to be left alone to go about their daily lives, had no choice. Kings and dictators could be ruthlessly and cruelly punitive if not obeyed.

Koskinen's thoughts then turned to his own family. His two sons would, of a certainty, be called on to fight in such a war. Their lives, too, would be disrupted. They could very well be killed or badly wounded. Koskinen realized now that Blomquist and his superiors at Intelligence Headquarters were right. It was clear that Stalin had to be stopped; he had to be destroyed. There was no other answer if Finland was to be saved and a terrible, destructive conflict averted. Koskinen began to have a feeling of being crushed by an overwhelming sense of enormous responsibility for the welfare of his country and its good people. So much depended upon his success in the mission that had been outlined to him by Blomquist.

With these thoughts, by the time he reached the Hameenkatu Bridge over the Tammerkoski River several blocks from the Hotel Tampere, Koskinen became aware that his resistance to becoming involved in the mission had quite evaporated leaving, nevertheless, some residual concerns and reservations. The latter centered about considerable doubt about his competency and ability to accomplish his part of the mission. At that moment, he had not the faintest idea on how to proceed to dispose of Stalin. That, he realized, was the ultimate issue to be resolved. Perhaps the meeting in Helsinki next week might provide the answer or answers.

After reaching the other end of the bridge, Koskinen continued walking past the Keskustori, the open-air market center, thence north on Alexis Kiven Street a short distance to the Finlayson Manufacturing complex where his office was located.

The uniformed guard at the gatehouse at the entrance to the company buildings checked him through with a smile and wave of recognition. At Finlayson, Koskinen was known as an export specialist. The company and his job title were covers for his intelligence activities.

Finlayson had been founded about 1820 and had become one of the oldest and most respected industrial plants in Finland. It was recognized in Europe as one of the major producers of cotton textiles and was a significant employer in the region. Its huge spread of buildings was situated on both sides of the Tammerkoski, a rapidly flowing river that bisected the center of downtown Tampere. Just south of the Finlayson buildings a large dam controlled the flow which, when the dam was closed, created two levels of the river. Even when closed, water would cascade over the top of the dam and fall to the lower level of the river that would then proceed to pass under the Hameenkatu Bridge.

During the warm and dry days of summer, Koskinen liked to sit and eat his lunch on one of the benches in the strips of parkland reserved by the City on both banks of the river. The beauty of the dam and the power of the river enthralled him. Sitting and watching the natural spectacle, Koskinen would gain a great sense of peace and of harmony with his surroundings.

Now, arriving at his office on the second floor of the main building, Koskinen sank down wearily in his chair behind an ordinary appearing wood desk. Both his room and his secretary's outer room were still quite chilly from the turned-down heat during the night. He kept his heavy coat and fur hat on, put his hands in the coat's deep pockets, and in a huddled position, closed his eyes and almost immediately fell asleep. It was close to 0730 hours and his secretary was not due at the office for another hour.

Later, when he was with his wife Anna, Koskinen told her of the strange dream that he had while asleep that morning in his office.

"I was walking across the plowed field of your family farm. The early morning sun was bright and I felt its warmth. I was feeling quite happy and I began to sing an old Finnish folk song, one my father liked so much, I can't recall the name. Suddenly, a seagull appeared in the distance and, as it neared me, I heard a gunshot and the gull fell to the ground, flapped its wings a few times and died. As I watched, I saw the spirit of the gull arise from its body. The spirit was in the shape of the gull and as it stood on its former body that was near me, its black eyes stared at me accusingly. I shouted to the gull spirit that I had not shot its body, that I would never have killed it, that it was not I. But the gull spirit continued its piercing stare at me and then, as I stood and watched with my heart beating wildly, the gull spirit just evaporated and I saw it no more. And the mortal, material body of the gull had also disappeared from the spot where it had been lying."

Koskinen paused and then, after a few moments said, "Can you make any sense out of that, Anna?"

Anna shook her head hopelessly and replied, "No, I have no idea what it means or portends."

Koskinen awoke in his chair to a gentle prodding on his shoulder and to the soft voice of his secretary, Kirsti Rantala.

"Captain Koskinen! Captain Koskinen!"

Koskinen stirred slightly, opened his eyes reluctantly and acknowledged the presence of his secretary.

"Ah, yes, Kirsti. What time is it?"

"Shortly after eight thirty. Perhaps you should go home and get a good rest," Kirsti suggested.

Koskinen remained silent for a short time and then laboriously stood up and stretched.

"You are probably right, Kirsti. I am exhausted. I guess it's the result of trying to sleep in my office and the early hour of the meeting. Perhaps I should take the day off. I'll put the office in your charge for today. You know how to reach me by 'phone if you have to. There are a few things I want to go over with you, though, before I leave."

When Koskinen was scheduled for the early morning meeting with Colonel Blomquist, he had informed Kirsti. He now told her of the meeting in Helsinki the following week, but refrained from telling her of the purpose or of the mission. In this, he was following the instruction of Blomquist to tell no one.

Kirsti Rantala had been with Koskinen for the past six years. Although her official designation in the Finlayson Export Department was that of Secretary, Kirsti was more than that. In fact, she served as an Assistant Intelligence Officer in the Tampere office of the Department. Like

Koskinen, however, she was on the payroll of Finlayson that enhanced and assured the cover for the Intelligence operations. Kirsti had been trained in the operations and procedures, the rules and regulations and in the rudiments of intelligence gathering. Her experience in working with Koskinen had augmented her knowledge of the system and, for Koskinen, she had become an invaluable adjunct of his office.

Kirsti was tall, blonde, with a slim figure and a lively featured face set with large blue eyes that were captivating and disarming. Her whole demeanor evinced friendliness and sociability. Her engaging personality drew people to her and even the most casual of acquaintances would open up and tell her of their personal and business problems. Kirsti was a good listener. Koskinen had once told her, in all seriousness, that she had all the ingredients to seduce the secrets from any male foreign agent.

The relationship between Kirsti and Koskinen was nothing more than that of good friends and of a harmonious partnership in a business in which the virtues of trust, loyalty, dependability and professional detachment from personality were the rule. Both Kirsti and Koskinen understood, intuitively, the location of appropriate behavioral boundaries and the limits of decorum. Kirsti had been a welcome guest at the home of Koskinen and his wife, Anna, many times on a purely social basis. There had grown up over the years a deep affection between Anna and Kirsti. Each admired and respected the other.

Kirsti, at age 32, was divorced. There were no children. The marriage had lasted five years; until Kirsti had become convinced that her husband's philandering conduct was more than just rumor. Her husband was that kind of man, of which, perhaps, there are too many, who feel shackled by marriage.

As he rode the bus to his home in the Pyynikki section on the western outskirts of Tampere, Koskinen, in his mind was totally occupied with the implications of the new mission he had been ordered to lead. He felt the need to share his thoughts and his concerns with someone. Who else but Anna? Anna had always been his confidante and, Koskinen would readily admit, his comforter in times of stress.

Although Blomquist had admonished him not to speak to anyone not even Anna about the mission, Koskinen decided to tell Anna about it and to seek her opinion about what he should do. He resented that his superior officers could extend their authority to instructing him as to what he could and could not say to his wife. His relations with Anna were none of their business and he had no intention of complying with that part of the instruction involving what he said to Anna. Anna would not talk about the mission realizing that if it got out to the wrong person or persons, his life could be jeopardized. Anna had understood early in their marriage of twenty-two years that as the wife of an Intelligence Officer her lips had to be sealed on everything concerning her husband's work. She had observed that rule strictly.

Upon arriving home, Koskinen found no one at home. Anna was at work and Aari and Pauli were at school. None would be back to the house until late in the afternoon. The empty house would give him a chance to rest. He felt totally exhausted. The short sleep at the office had, apparently, been of little benefit. He got out of his street clothes and into his bedclothes, but before getting into bed, Koskinen made coffee and ate several pieces of herring on some Finnish flat dark bread.

As he sat alone at the kitchen table in the silence of the empty house, Koskinen began to have a numbing feeling of acute depression. True, from the first, he had not been happy with his assignment and he had left Blomquist's room quite disturbed and agitated. But, now, Koskinen became aware of an escalation from mere unhappiness to feelings of anger and alienation, to a sense of hopelessness and a lack of control over his life. When walking to his office this morning from the meeting with Blomquist, Koskinen had concluded that it was right for him to participate in the mission; his country needed him to step up to a threat to all Finns. But, that was a cerebral conclusion. His heart and soul dictated a converse conclusion. And therein lay the reason for the inner conflict.

Koskinen lay down on his bed and, utterly fatigued, was soon in troubled sleep. He did not awaken until shortly before Anna was to arrive home at 1600 hours. Koskinen had to force himself to get out of bed in order to greet Anna. Before sitting down again at the kitchen table, he got a deck of playing cards, thinking that a game or two of solitaire might help to distract him from his distressful state of mind. But, it was not to be. Laying aside the cards before completing the first game, Koskinen simply leaned back in his chair and allowed his thoughts to run rampant.

For Koskinen there was no easy answer whether to accept or reject the assignment to Russia. His initial reasonable and understandable concern about his competency to handle the mission had now become amplified into a colossal fountain of irrational fears and anxieties. This was so unlike Koskinen, so uncharacteristic of him. Those who knew him well have described him as a clear, logical, hardheaded thinker capable of making the difficult decisions and, above all else, having an abundance of "sisu," the Finnish term for having "guts" and perseverance. Close friends knew that Koskinen had little or no tolerance for foolishness, irresponsibility, lack of self-discipline and cowardice.

Koskinen, himself, was much aware of the change that had taken hold of his usual stoic frame of mind. Though aware, he was perplexed and puzzled by what might be the cause. He understood that it was related to his new assignment, but what was there about the assignment that had so affected him? Was it the idea of assassination? He was not sure. Was it that he might be killed in the operation? No, he had faced that risk before in a few other assignments. Was it the possibility of a long separation from his family? It could be, but he wasn't certain about that either. Perhaps it was the knowledge that the fate of Finland and all of its innocents rested on his shoulders, on the success of the mission. Yes, that could be the reason, but, again, he was not convinced that it was.

While he was pondering all this, Anna arrived home. Koskinen arose and greeted Anna with a hug and kiss and his usual warm smile.

"How did things go today, Anna?"

"Oh, as normal. Nothing different. The students had their lessons prepared for a change. Brrr, it's really cold outside, and it isn't very warm in here either." Anna proceeded to add some wood to the kitchen stove fire, kept her heavy coat on but pulled off her boots and stepped into slippers.

"When did you get home?" Anna inquired.

"Oh, about eleven this morning," Timo replied. "I was absolutely exhausted. I had to get some sleep. I got very little sleep in the office last night, and the early morning meeting didn't help any."

"Have you had anything to eat?" Anna asked with some concern.

"Just some herring and bread before I went to bed."

"Oh, you poor dear. I'll see what I can put together for you and I'll have something to eat too."

"No, I'm really not hungry. But, you go ahead and heat up something for yourself." Koskinen's depression which up to now he had fought to suppress so that Anna would not notice began to surface. Anna, in fact, sensed that something was wrong. Timo appeared troubled.

Anna said nothing, but continued to heat up some potato soup and to make fresh coffee. As she put bread and butter on the table she stopped momentarily and looked directly at her husband.

"Something is bothering you, Timo. What is it?" Anna's face showed her concern.

With that question, Anna revealed that she had seen through his pretense of normalcy. Koskinen surrendered to his depression and his whole demeanor shifted to dolefulness. At first he looked down at his folded, clasped hands on the table and then back up to Anna who still stood at the table.

"Why don't you finish cooking and then we can talk about it," Timo said. He wanted to unburden himself to Anna, but he wanted to wait until there were no distractions. He knew that Aari and Pauli would not be home from school for another couple of hours.

Anna waited for the soup to heat and then filled a bowl and placed it in front of Timo. "Here, eat this. You need it. You have to eat even if you have to force yourself."

Timo smiled appreciatively. "You always mother me," he said in mock protest. "Alright, I'll eat it." Timo lightened up a bit. It was the beginning of his unburdening. Anna joined him at the table with her bowl of soup and bread and butter. Timo ate quickly, not from hunger, but from the need to tell Anna about his meeting with Blomquist and he did not want to talk about it between spoonfuls of soup.

Timo began his description of the meeting while Anna continued to eat slowly.

"You know that I had an early meeting with Colonel Blomquist this morning."

"Yes, you telephoned me and we talked about it. What was it about?

Timo hesitated a moment. It was going to be painful to tell Anna about the mission.

"Headquarters has given me an assignment in Russia."

Anna abruptly stopped eating.

"In Russia?" Anna exclaimed incredulously. "What will you be doing in Russia? How long will you be gone?" Anna's voice portrayed anxiety. It was the reaction that Timo had expected.

"Don't get upset, Anna," Timo said in a soft, soothing voice, trying to assure his wife that it was not as bad as it sounded.

"Well, it does come as a shock to me, Timo, and I have noticed that you are somewhat upset yourself. What are you to do there?" Anna was insistent that he get on with his story.

"I am to be part of a mission to try to avert a war between Finland and Russia."

"I wasn't aware that there was supposed to be a war." Anna's remark was sharp and she was still incredulous.

"It is a distinct possibility if we do not give in to the Russian government's demands. You've read about some of them in the newspapers. Hango, Karelia."

"But, I thought that was all being discussed and negotiated in Moscow," Anna said.

"Well, it is and it isn't, apparently," replied Timo. "Stalin and his henchmen are making demands for concessions which our government does not believe are reasonable and, therefore, cannot be met. We would lose parts of our country."

"You still haven't said what part you are to have in this assignment and how long you will be gone." Anna was trying to get an answer from Timo, which she felt he was reluctant to give. "Whatever the mission is about, you know I can keep it confidential."

"Yes, I know that," Timo said. He realized that he could no longer circumvent Anna's questions.

"My job will be to try to get rid of Stalin and, if that is done, Russia will have no leader and will be in no position to attack Finland."

"What do you mean 'getting rid of Stalin'? Are you going to assassinate him?"

"Yes, if necessary."

Timo got up from the table. He put a couple of pieces of wood on the stove fire and poured himself a cup of coffee.

"I can't believe what I'm hearing!" Anna said, shaking her head in her disbelief.

"Would you like a cup of coffee?" Timo asked. He hoped the mundane question would relieve the tense atmosphere.

"Yes, thank you." The question did seem to have a calming effect. Anna acted a bit more relaxed. For Finns, coffee is a universal palliative. Coffee eased every problem without curing it.

After setting the cup of coffee before Anna, Timo resumed his seat at the table. Anna was still inquisitive.

"How do you expect to accomplish the assassination?"

"I don't know yet. I imagine I'll have to wait until I get to our Embassy in Moscow and have some time to evaluate the situation."

"How long do you expect to be gone?" Anna had a worried expression on her fact.

"I imagine it will be until the job is finished, possibly, a couple of months."

"Oh, for goodness sake," Anna said in a voice that sounded with hopeless despair. "Why were you picked for this assignment? Why you?"

"I asked Blomquist the same question, Anna, and the answer I received back was that I was the most talented and trustworthy. Other than that was my basic understanding of the Russian language."

"Do you have to accept this assignment?"

"I suppose not. But, if I refused it, I think that would be the end of my career. I have never before refused an assignment. Anna, I feel I must accept it. From what I have been told by Blomquist, and I imagine headquarters will confirm it, the fate of Finland depends on the success of the mission. Knowing that, how can I refuse it? Would you want me to refuse it?"

"Timo, you do not understand what is in a woman's heart. We are not like you men who require tests of strength and courage and risk-filled challenges to prove you are men. I love you and I don't want to lose you. Frankly, I fear for your life in this undertaking. What if you get caught over in Russia? We know how brutal they can be. A dead hero-husband does little for me and for Aari and Pauli, for that matter. You know that I am as patriotic as you are, but the fate of Mother Finland ought not to rest on one man's shoulders. That, to me, is absurd. Do you see what I am saying, Timo?"

"Yes, of course, Anna dear. It is obvious that you do not want me to take this assignment." Timo expected Anna to not like the idea of this assignment, but he had hoped that she would have been more sympathetic to his dilemma than she was.

"Anna, do you want me to resign from the military service? Is that the answer?" Timo put the burden of a decision directly on his wife.

"Yes! That is my answer to this intolerable situation into which your headquarters has placed you. The whole project is not fair to you and your family. You will be at great risk while the people at your headquarters are enjoying life and going home to their families at night." Anna spoke in a strong, determined and forthright tone that resonated with resentment.

"Anna, Anna," Timo implored, "you are not making it any easier for me to make a decision on what to do." Timo spoke softly trying to assuage Anna's anger.

"What decision, Timo? You either accept the assignment or you do not." Anna was clearly upset.

"That is precisely the decision that must be made, Anna. 'To go or not-to-go'. The question is simple; the answer is very difficult."

Anna's answer encouraging him to resign from his position in the military had surprised and shocked Timo. Anna was not a timid person, but she was normally gentle, thoughtful and artful in expressing her views. Timo now saw another side of Anna, a side that was aggressive and combative when confronted with a life-threatening situation and the perceived need for a desperate defense of family; a family that was being put at risk.

Although Timo was startled by Anna's forceful protest, he was, nevertheless, delighted to see that Anna was willing to fight for her convictions. Timo admired a fighter whether man or woman. He had known all along in their marriage that Anna had that quality, but he was pleased to see her exercise it.

Anna decided to use another ploy to persuade Timo not to accept the assignment.

"If you succeed in assassinating Stalin, Timo, then if you return to Finland and that 'if ' is what concerns me, you will bear the tag of an assassin. That is a label that becomes a stigma."

"Anna, this is a secret, confidential mission. The public, our friends, will never know who liquidated Stalin - only a few people at headquarters and you. Not even Aari and Pauli will know."

"Yes, but I will know, Timo. And it will affect our relationship. I will find it difficult to live with an assassin. How can I sleep with an assassin? How can I be expected to make love to an assassin? It goes against everything I believe in. Do you understand, Timo?" Anna looked at Timo sternly and waited for his answer to her challenge.

Timo's response was immediate and his voice showed he was irritated by Anna's remarks.

"No, I don't understand, Anna! Would you feel that way if I were a soldier in a war to defend our country and killed soldiers of the enemy?"

"Well, that is different," replied Anna.

"How is it different?" demanded Timo, now clearly annoyed.

Anna could see that her ploy was rubbing Timo in a way she had not intended. She knew it would serve no purpose to persist in this route. It would only be counterproductive to her attempt to influence her husband to accept her view. Anna was clever and she would extricate herself from her predicament without losing Timo's respect.

"Timo, the difference is that a soldier on the front line facing an enemy has no choice but to kill or be killed. In your case, you have a choice. You can choose to accept or to refuse the assignment. Do you see that?"

"No, you are quite wrong, Anna. A soldier does have a choice. He can stand and fight or he can throw down his rifle and run away from the confrontation. And if he ran away he would be stigmatized as a coward. Would you be able to sleep with a coward?" It was Timo's turn to look sternly at his wife. From Anna's reaction, he knew he had won the intellectual argument. But, he also recognized that he had not won the emotional or spiritual one. Timo knew intuitively, that Anna, in her heart, would never change her feeling that he should not go to Russia on this assignment.

"Anna," said Timo resuming his soft and soothing tone, "let's not have discord between us over this. We've been married too long not to understand each other. I can fully appreciate that your fears for my safety and the future welfare of our family are very real. If I didn't share these concerns with you, I would not be in this terrible state of mind, this terrible dilemma. This is something that I must resolve as soon as possible. I am scheduled to go to Helsinki headquarters next week and I must make my decision before then." Anna appeared to have given up any further attempts at persuasion and to have lost the fire that had moved her to so passionately express her view.

"Timo, knowing you, I am resigned to the idea that you will accept the assignment. You have always loved the difficult challenges. You have a crusading spirit. That is what attracted me to you and that is one of the reasons I love you. But, to me, this mission is fraught with far more danger than any others you have been involved in. In fact, I think it has little chance of succeeding. But it's for you to decide. I cannot say any more than I have said already."

"I think we can agree Anna that Aari and Pauli need not be told about this as yet. Is that right?"

"Yes, of course," Anna replied.

Anna was, by nature and upbringing, a very independent person. She was also a religious woman who practiced the virtues of honesty, truthfulness, and loyalty to the immediate family, fidelity to one's spouse, a love of mankind and a general belief in the goodness of most people. She was a member of the Pispala Lutheran Church choir and a ready volunteer in many of the Church's social programs. Although she was insistent that her sons Aari and Pauli be taught to abide by the same virtues, she was not what may be termed a "religious or moral fanatic." She encouraged her two boys to be independent thinkers, to challenge ideas, but short of being dogmatic.

Anna was of medium build, about five feet seven inches in height. Her finely featured face reflected the beautiful virtues of her soul. Those who met her liked her immediately because of the warmth of her personality, her friendliness and her willingness to accept people as they were and without pretense.

Anna had been born in 1897 to Matti and Kaisa Peltola on a farm near Vammala in Southwestern Finland. Three years before her birth, her parents had migrated to the United States and had located in Ironwood, Michigan as did many Finns at that time. Like others, the Peltolas had gone to America in the widely accepted belief that America offered a life of comfort and prosperity, a land where jobs were plentiful and the pay substantial enough to allow one to grow rich and, perhaps, to buy a farm of one's own after accumulating savings. The Finns, of course, were not alone in having this euphoric dream. Gathered in Ironwood, Michigan and surrounding communities were Germans, Poles, Italians, Norwegians, Swedes and a mix of other immigrants.

When Matti and Kaisa Peltola arrived by train at the Ironwood Railway Station, they found a place to live in a boarding house. Matti, in need of a job, found work within a few days at the Aurora Mines. A farmer by occupation, he had no experience or skills at mining. He had to rely on a few words of advice from a supervisor and the instructions on what to do from fellow Finnish miners while working in the underground shafts and tunnels.

Disillusionment came quickly to the immigrant mine workers. The work was hard and dangerous. Accidents were frequent and fatalities all too numerous. The injuries to miners were usually severe and the circumstances of the deaths horrible and violent. The mining companies did little or nothing to make the work safe for the miners and when miners were injured and perhaps were unable to work, the company provided no financial assistance either for what minimum medical care was available or to help sustain the family during the time the worker was disabled. If a married miner was killed, there was no company compensation to the widow and any children. Such widows, under the urgency of need, were compelled to promptly marry another miner in order to survive. The living conditions were primitive even by the standards of that era.

After almost two years in the mines and their dream of a better life having faded from the ever present red iron ore dust that persistently hung over their home and infiltrated their lives, Matti and Kaisa Peltola decided that they'd had enough. They resolved to return to Finland. By scraping together some money of their own and borrowing the balance needed from relatives and friends, Matti and Kaisa were able to buy passage back to Turku, Finland, a main port off the Baltic Sea. They then rented and later purchased a small farm near Vammala.

The lessons learned by Matti and Kaisa from their experience in America were consistently passed on to their children as the children grew up. Anna, who was one of seven children of Matti and Kaisa, often spoke to friends in reverential terms about how her parents had instilled in her and her siblings certain immutable values.

"My parents," Anna once told a group of churchwomen, "taught us children that if we recognize that we have made a mistake, then we should correct it as soon as possible and get on with our lives. Brooding over a wrong decision made and failing to take corrective action, my parents told us, showed we had little faith in God to help guide us." Anna added, "When my parents realized that they had made a mistake in going to America, they told me they prayed together every night to God to show them the way out of their predicament. They received their answer and, in unexpected ways, the financial means to enable them to return to Finland was made available. And so, their lesson has been my lesson." Anna told the churchwomen. She continued, "Whenever I have a problem for which the solution remains obscure, I pray God to reveal it to me. He always does, although, sometimes I don't always like His answer, but I accept it, of course." The churchwomen had applauded Anna's statement. Later, Anna had related this event to Timo.

"I think it was a marvelous testimonial to your philosophy," Timo had said. "It is a belief I willingly accept as right morally and spiritually." Timo recognized and was proud of his wife's inner convictions and strengths. However, he did not have the same degree of piety that possessed Anna. His beliefs were akin to the philosophy of naturalism. He believed that events or happenings could be explained in pragmatic and scientific terms. Nevertheless, Timo believed that the Bible was a basis for moral and ethical conduct and should, to that extent, be followed. Both Anna and Timo were, like 97 percent of Finns, Lutheran. The Lutheran Church is the state-supported church in Finland.

Timo and Anna had met while Timo was visiting a friend for several weeks during the summer of 1916. The parents of the friend had a summer home on the shore of the Liekovesi, a bay area just southwest of Vammala. The parents knew the Peltola family through membership and activities in their same church. During a church social gathering, the friend had introduced Timo to Anna. At the occasion, Anna looked so unassumingly lovely and innocent in her crinoline skirt that Timo fell in love with her immediately. Anna, who had only casual contact with boys in school and a few from neighboring farms, was quick to feel a strong attraction to Timo. To her Timo was handsome and possessed a charm and an intellect that the local farm boys lacked. She found him to have a steady temperament, easy to talk with and considerate and respectful. Anna felt comfortable with Timo.

Anna received permission from her father to invite Timo to their farm while he was visiting in Vammala. Father Peltola could hardly deny Anna's request when he perceived her ebullient look and her unusual expression of interest in a boy. The Peltolas were a close-knit family of parents, four boys and three girls. Their relationships within the family were loving, open and honest. Father and mother Peltola were firm but not stern in raising their children. Work on the farm was hard and demanding and each child, commensurate with his or her age and abilities, was required to assume some responsibility for the day-to-day tasks. Nevertheless, the family atmosphere was, generally, cheerful and, among the children, animated and playsome. It was the prevalent pleasantness and the easygoing interdependency of the family members that deeply impressed Timo when he visited. It was so unlike his own experience.

During the year following and as the months went by, Timo and Anna saw each other with increasing frequency until it became apparent to Peltola family and friends that something quite serious had developed between the two young people. Anna's parents were, at first skeptical of the wisdom of their daughter's continuing interest in Timo. Timo was a city boy and from a working class family. Such families had a reputation of being politically 'left-leaning' and farm people, generally at the other end of the political spectrum, did not readily accept his kind. Nevertheless, Matti and Kaisa Peltola grew to like Timo as they perceived that he had admirable moral qualities, was ambitious and conservative in his views.

Timo had returned to Tampere after the short summer visit to his friend's home near Vammala. From Tampere to Vammala was a train ride of about an hour and a half. Father Peltola or a farm hand would pick up Timo at the railroad station with a horse and buggy. Timo would spend the weekend and some holidays on the farm with Anna and would always pitch in to do some of the chores.

28

As the love for each other grew, and their happiness in each other's company developed, Timo and Anna came to understand that they would some day marry. Timo and Anna spent long hours talking and getting to know each other. Nothing sexual, however, occurred during the visits. They both respected each other's moral integrity.

During their talks, Timo told Anna about himself and his family.

"I grew up in what might be termed a dysfunctional family," Timo confessed to Anna. "I have two brothers and a sister. I am the oldest. My father was always, as long as I can recall, an alcoholic and very abusive of us children, in fact, of my mother as well, poor soul. He worked at the Finlayson factory as a machinist. After work he would always stop at some gin mill and then come home drunk. It was a regular ritual. It was terrible." Timo paused and a frown came over his face as he related what he would have preferred to forget. The memories were bitter ones. Anna said nothing, but listened with a disquieting sense of sadness and sorrow for this young man for whom she had a growing love.

"All of us lived in constant fear of my father's arrival home at the end of a workday. There was no happiness, only an expectancy of violence. We trembled when we heard him at our door. We children, even as we got older, would cringe in some corner of a room. Father would come staggering in, shouting, swearing and demanding his supper and whatever else, in his stupor, he could think of. He would glower at us children and say, 'You don't like me, do you, you little monkeys' and, if one of us were close enough, he'd swat him on the head. We were all relieved when he, soon after eating, went to sleep. I'm telling you this, Anna, because there is nothing you should not know."

In his recounting of these details, Timo had become morose and was, to Anna, reliving his suffering. And Anna, sensitive Anna, was by now in tears.

"Timo, please, do not go on. It is not necessary. I would rather not hear any more."

"I must tell you something else, as it will explain my views."

"Well, if you must," Anna said reluctantly.

"My father, in the early nineteen hundreds, became a fanatical Communist. Finlayson, where he worked, was a hotbed of Communism. In fact, it is still so. You know, the appeal to the working class. Turning them against their employers and against everything in Finland that did not favor a government of and by workers, meaning factory people and non-intellectuals. I heard so much of this at home in the last few years that I have turned against everything that even smells like Communism. Of course, coming from my father, it was not at all persuasive. I have come to hate my father and, so much so, whatever he supports or espouses, I would oppose. That isn't very nice, is it Anna?"

"No, it isn't," responded Anna softly but reprovingly. "I hope all this has not scarred you. You must not let it dominate you and destroy your joy in life," Anna then added with a sly smile, "and mine."

At the time of this conversation, they had been sitting in a swing seat on the porch of the main building on the Peltola Farm. It was an unusually warm September evening and they had taken advantage of the outdoor privacy.

Responding to Anna's admonition, Timo said, "It is impossible for one's experience as a young person at home not to be influenced by it. However, conversely, it is possible, I believe, to control whether the experience will have a good or an adverse result in one's life. I intend that my experience will point me in a good direction."

"I am glad about that," Anna said. "Are you still living at home?" she asked.

"No, I moved out a year ago. I had to get away from the constant tension and violence. Besides, the area in which we lived was a frightening one. Perhaps you have heard of the Pispala section of Tampere." Timo paused and looked inquiringly at Anna.

"No, I have not," she replied innocently.

"Pispala is a working class section of the city, but it is also a haven for all sorts of criminals, thieves, pick pockets, drug dealers, you name it, and a sanctum sanctorum for prostitutes. Almost every night there are knifings and shootings. The police stay away from the place. My mother wanted to move away from it, but my father insisted on remaining. I guess he felt that his own conduct would go unnoticed as an acceptable norm by the neighbors."

"When you left, where did you go and what did you do?" Anna further inquired.

"I went to live with Aunt Helevi, one of my mother's sisters who lives right in town. She's a widow and no children. I'm still living there and going to technical school."

"Are you working? Do you have a job?"

"Yes, I've gotten a job with the City Parks Department doing maintenance work. It's flexible work and allows me to schedule my school classes around it."

Anna was impressed. She thought to herself that here was a young man determined to overcome adversity and to make something of himself. She liked and admired his character.

Timo and Anna were married on a Saturday afternoon in July 1917. He was twenty-one and she a year younger. The ceremony took place in the Tyrvaa Old Church, some distance northeast of Vammela and overlooking the Rantavesi, a large body of water extending north to south many kilometers. The church had been built in the 1300's and, except for some repairs from time to time, had retained its original structure. It had about it, a romantic mystique that comes only with a long history. As Timo and Anna stood inside the church, they both remarked how they could almost feel the presence of all the people who had celebrated services, births, marriages and deaths within its walls for the past 600 years.

The church had thick stone walls with few windows. The pews were of wood, narrow and straight-backed with little legroom. Timo remarked that they were not meant to be comfortable. They were designed to keep people awake. The floor was of crude, hand-sawn wood planks quite well worn. On the border of the overhang around the room were hand-painted portrait panels of biblical persons of interest.

As they walked down the aisle toward the altar where the Lutheran minister awaited them, Anna whispered to Timo, "There are ancient church people buried beneath the wooden plank boards, a custom in the early days."

Timo whispered back, "Good Lord, we're getting married in a cemetery."

Timo's mother, Hertta, and his brothers and sister had traveled from Tampere by train to attend the wedding and would stay overnight at the Peltola Farm. Timo's father, Ville, was left at home, drunk and cursing farmers, in general, for charging such high prices for food products that the workingman was unable to properly feed his family. He vowed that when Communists came to power farmers would be collectivized and forced to produce food at government set prices. Hertta explained, with some embarrassment, that her husband was unable to attend because "he was not feeling well."

After the church wedding ceremony Timo, Anna, the Peltola family and relatives and friends wended their way to the Peltola Farm for a grand "pidot" or banquet. Some of the guests at the wedding had traveled by boat from their homes and proceeded to the Peltola Farm by the same means. In Finland the older churches had, traditionally, been built near the shores of a lake or other waterway to accommodate the parishioners who found rowing a boat to church more direct and considerably less time-consuming than following circuitous narrow dirt roads around impassable woodlands. Large farm families conventionally used long boats to go to church with anywhere from four to six strong males manning the oars. Anna's family had such a long boat that was used until the waterway froze over in wintertime. Anna's father and some farm hands did the rowing until her brothers grew up and could manage the heavy wooden oars.

At the banquet that evening, Matti Peltola got Timo aside and asked him if he'd be interested in staying and working on the farm.

"You know, Timo, our family has all come to love and respect you and, now that you are a member of the family, you are welcome to stay here and work and live with us," father Peltola said. "It's hard work, as I'm sure you know by now, but, it is good and secure work. I think you would be happy here."

Timo stood in respectful silence for a few moments as if considering the offer seriously. He then replied, "Father Matti, I appreciate what you have said. I, too, love my new family. You are very fine people. However, I do want to further my education and there are no higher education schools here. I hope you will understand. Farming is a very worthy and honorable occupation. I am not opposed to it. It is just that I have other plans, objectives and goals for myself and Anna is a part of them."

"I understand, Timo, and I respect your decision. However, if, at any time you should change your mind, the offer shall always be there."

"Thank you, father Matti."

Lurking behind Timo's decision was also the knowledge that joining the Peltola Farm operation could very well be a dead end since the farm would eventually on the deaths of the parents, devolve to the eldest son according to the Finnish inheritance laws.

Timo and Anna remained at the Peltola Farm for a week after the wedding. Other than having a small room to themselves, there was little privacy. Both accepted the conditions graciously. At the end of the week they departed for Tampere where Timo had rented a room with a family on Vainolankatu in the Tammela section of the city. It was a block east of the railroad tracks and not far from both the Finlayson factory and the city government buildings. The room and its location was not a paradigm of exquisite surroundings. For Timo and Anna it would do until they could afford better. Besides they were in love and independent of their families and their prevailing attention was to each other rather than to their immediate exterior conditions. At this time in their lives, the outside circumstances were superficial and tolerable.

Timo continued his work with the City Parks Department and Anna, in August, was hired as a grade school teacher beginning with the new school term in September.

During their first year of marriage, the times in Finland were tumultuous. Five months after their marriage, Finland declared its independence of Russia. That event was aided and abetted by Lenin whose Bolsheviks had overthrown the monarchy of Tsar Nicholas II that very same year. The Bolshevik government was the first to recognize the new independent country of Finland. Thus, one hundred and eight years of Russian rule over Finland was ended.

Most Finns rejoiced and celebrated the casting off of the noose of foreign rule, first by Sweden for six hundred years and by Russia from 1809. However, hanging over the festive occasion was a dark, ominous and menacing threat to the newly acquired freedom. Civil war was about to unfold and to envelop Finland.

While under Russian rule, Finland was a Grand Duchy of the Tsarist government. However, it had considerable autonomy and, except for matters of foreign and military policy, Finland was pretty much in control of its own institutions. It had its elected Parliament that passed laws subject to the ratification or veto of the Tsar. In early 1917 the Parliament was dominated by a Socialist Party majority, which, while labor union oriented, nevertheless, like most Finns, had growing aspirations for freedom from Russia. With events in Russia being uncertain as a result of the revolution, the Finns decided that the time had come to strike out on their own and in October 1917, new Parliamentary elections were held. The Socialists lost their majority and the new non-Socialist legislature voted for independence.

Almost immediately after the election a radical group formed with the intention of preparing a revolution to bring down the new government in Finland and to replace it with a Marxist administration with close ties to the Bolsheviks in Russia. This radical group formed a Central Revolutionary Council and, in November 1917, called for a general strike which lasted about a week. During that week lawlessness and violence spread throughout much of Finland. In January 1918, extremists took control of the Socialist Party and organized their own military force called the "Red Guards." On January 28, the Red Guards began armed rebellion and quickly "conquered" much of the Southern half of Finland.

At the time, the Finnish government had no military or police force with which to combat the Red Guards. The government leaders fled to the City of Vaasa off the northwest coast of the Gulf of Bothnia. Finnish Premier P. E. Svinhufvud persuaded General Gustav Mannerheim to organize an army that became known as the "White Guard." Mannerheim called for volunteers and the response was overwhelming. The majority of the Finns saw the Reds as a threat to their new independence and freedom.

The City of Tampere had been captured early in the civil war by the Reds and had become a crucial control point for them by reason of its locality in central Finland and its large population of workers in its industrial economy.

For Timo Koskinen, the crisis in Finland, especially the situation in Tampere with the Reds, had become alarming. The Red Guards were going through the city neighborhoods and out into farming areas and arresting people on the slightest suspicion of lack of sympathy for the Reds. When farmers had advance notice of the Red Guard coming into their area, the men, at least, would take refuge in nearby woods. Some of those arrested were shot on the spot. Others were imprisoned and maltreated.

During late December 1917 and early January 1918, it became obvious to both Timo and Anna that a violent uprising was developing rapidly and the social order was nearing collapse. Mobs of Reds and Red sympathizers were on the city streets exhorting citizens to join in the overthrow of the government. It was no longer safe to give even the appearance of not supporting the cause of Marxism.

"Anna, you must leave here. You must go back to your parent's farm until this political situation is resolved and things settle down," Timo urged Anna. Anna was already five months' pregnant.

"No, Timo, I'm going to stay here with you. I will not allow you to face this danger alone," Anna declared.

"In fact, Anna, you must pack up your bag and be ready to leave on the train for Vammala tomorrow. There is no time to lose. You must leave while the trains can get through without being stopped for passenger inspection."

"What will you be doing, Timo, once I leave?" Anna's face mirrored her concern and solicitude for her husband's welfare.

"I am going to be leaving here also. I have heard that the government is forming and organizing a police force to oppose the Reds. I am going to volunteer for that. I am convinced that we must do everything possible to protect our new independence and freedom." As he spoke, Timo took Anna's hands and drew her close to him while looking into her eyes in his usual calm and assuring manner.

"Then, I will not know where you are." Anna's fears for Timo's safety rose.

"I'm sure that I'll be moving about quite a bit, but I'll do my best to keep in touch with you, perhaps by telephone if I can. My job is gone, anyway. There will be no park work. The City government has ceased to exist already. These Reds are treacherous people, Anna."

"Yes, I know you're right, Timo. I just hate to admit it," Anna conceded. "I'll get ready to go. Shall I pack your things, too?"

"That would be a good idea. I'll be leaving in a couple of days. There is an extra traveling bag you can put my clothing in. I'll help you get to an early morning train. You can call your parents when you arrive in Vammala. I wouldn't call from here. You can't be sure of who is listening in."

Anna proceeded to prepare a supper of eggs and potatoes on the wood stove in their room.

"The last supper," Anna said mournfully referring to the biblical story.

"What do we do about the landlord here?" Anna asked while they were eating.

"I intend to say nothing to him," replied Timo. "I don't trust anyone right now. Our room rent is paid in advance, so we owe him nothing. The landlord is the least of my concerns. Your safety is paramount at this moment."

At six-thirty the next morning after a quick breakfast of coffee and Finnish dark bread, Timo and Anna left the boarding house and walked the short distance to the railroad station. Timo was carrying Anna's traveling case. Having been married but for a short time, they had not yet accumulated many material possessions: clothing, a few toilet articles and some photographs of the family.

Except for one or two other pedestrians, the streets were empty. No Red Guards were present or seen. Both Timo and Anna were considerably relieved when they reached the station and bought Anna's ticket without incident. Nevertheless, the train for Vammala did not leave until seven fifty nine and as Timo and Anna sat in the waiting room of the station, they confided their anxiety to each other. They attempted to look nonchalant and casual, but they looked furtively at each person who entered the building trying to determine if the person might spell trouble. A rough looking character of middle age with a heavy beard and, obviously, a workingman sat down next to them and proceeded to read a small brochure. He said nothing to Timo and Anna, but they felt uncomfortable in his presence. His presence stifled their conversation. So after a few painful moments of silence, Timo addressed Anna, "Perhaps we should get some cheese and crackers at the station kiosk." This was said in a voice loud enough for the bearded stranger to hear.

Timo and Anna arose from the bench and walked over to the kiosk in the station lobby. Timo turned his head quickly and caught the bearded man staring at them who, when he saw Timo looking at him, averted his gaze back to his brochure.

"I don't like this bearded fellow," Timo mentioned to Anna. "I have an uneasy feeling that he may be one of the Reds."

Timo and Anna took their cheese and crackers and moved to another bench, but still within view of the bearded stranger.

The train Anna was to take to Vammala finally pulled into the station a few minutes late. Timo walked with Anna along the platform to a passenger coach that they both entered. Timo placed Anna's traveling bag on an adjoining seat and they then embraced.

"Anna, remember I love you dearly."

"Yes, yes, Timo and I love you and shall be thinking and praying for you every moment." There were tears in their eyes. Timo quickly left the car on hearing the voice of the conductor announce a momentary departure.

When Koskinen reentered the lobby from the train platform, he observed that the bearded stranger was nowhere to be seen. He hoped that he had not gotten on the same train as Anna. Now that Anna was on her way, Koskinen relaxed and felt more at ease. Anna was relatively safe and he now had himself alone to be concerned about. He felt ready to confront any untoward circumstance. His immediate intention was to return to his room at the boarding house, but by way of some main streets. He was curious to see what if anything, was happening as a result of Red Guard activities.

Leaving the railroad station area, Koskinen proceeded to walk north on Rautatien Street toward Kongan Street that ran east across the railroad tracks in the direction of his boarding house.

Koskinen had gone only a short distance on Rautatien Street when two men came from behind him and accosted him. They ordered him to stop. Koskinen turned and saw that one of the men was the bearded stranger who had been in the railroad station. He did not recognize the second man who was of medium height, of thin build, clean-shaven and with sharp facial features. Now that the bearded one was standing, Koskinen observed that he was tall and heavyset. Like Koskinen, the two men wore heavy coats and fur caps as protection against the bitterly cold January weather. The two men's attire was, however, quite shabby.

"Young man, do you have a card?" the bearded one asked.

"Before I answer any questions, I want to know who you are." Koskinen put the question with a hard, cold direct scrutinizing look into the faces of the two men. Koskinen's imperturbable outward expression belied his inner emotional trepidation.

"We are members of the Safety Committee of the Central Revolutionary Council and we expect you to answer our question, young man." The bearded one did the talking and his tone of voice was threatening.

Koskinen could see that he was in a difficult situation and that he had no choice but to deal with the men and to answer their questions.

"What card are you referring to?" Koskinen asked.

"Obviously, you can't have one or you would know what I'm talking about," said the bearded fellow. "The card is issued by the Council to those who are sympathetic to our cause. You will come with us to our headquarters for investigation." The men took positions on either side of Koskinen and escorted him south about three blocks to the Tuomiokirkan Street near Hameenkatu. Headquarters of the Council was an architecturally baroque wood building with some boarded-up windows and the exterior of which appeared to have been bombarded over the years by microscopic meteorites. A guard at the entrance apparently recognized the bearded one and his slim companion since he allowed them to enter the building without challenge and with Koskinen sandwiched between them.

The three walked down a dim corridor with small rooms on either side until they came to a door with a paper sign tacked to it that read "Command Post-CRC." Without first knocking, the bearded one opened the door and entered telling Koskinen and his slim captor to wait in the hallway. Koskinen had noticed a common washtub in the hallway along with a common wood stove both of which, he assumed, served all residents of the building.

The building, itself, to Koskinen, had a dank, musty odor that he concluded was the result of a long vacancy after generations of human effluvia had impregnated the interior of the building. The odor was unpleasant.

After a few minutes the bearded one came to the door and beckoned them to enter.

When Koskinen entered the room his attention was immediately seized by a small, wizen faced man seated behind a plain, straight-legged table upon which there was a notebook and some papers and several pencils. The man glowered grimly at Koskinen from two cold, unblinking large eyes set over a sharp, pinched nose and an open, puckered mouth that, at first, uttered no sound but expressed impatient disdain. The man reminded Koskinen of a fledgling hawk with a hooked beak and a constant open mouth ready to devour anything fed to it.

Koskinen's anxiety rose. This fellow behind the desk, whoever he was and whatever his title, appeared to be a prototype of evil, someone who would shoot his own grandmother upon the slightest provocation. Koskinen surmised that the fellow was an old-time, rabid Communist to whom ideology was more important than human compassion. Koskinen knew that people like this could be merciless and vindictive and that his future could be determined in the next few minutes. He couldn't even guess what that would be.

The two security guards who had brought Koskinen here stood respectfully silent behind Koskinen and near the door. It was obvious that they were deferential to the little man at the desk. Finally, the man addressed Koskinen. His voice was stern and arrogantly officious.

"Do you know why you're here?"

"I have the impression it is because I do not have a membership card of the Revolutionary Council," replied Koskinen.

"You were stopped because you were observed sending your wife out of the City. Obviously, neither you nor she are sympathetic to our cause. If you were, you both would have stayed to work for us. We have many young women who are doing work for us. The fact that you have no card shows you have no intention of signing up to help us." The fellow pointed an accusing finger at Koskinen.

"No, sir, that is not true," said Koskinen, feeling that he had to offer a defense in order to survive this inquisition. "My wife is five months pregnant and she wanted to stay here, but I felt she ought to go back to her parents' home until the birth where her family could look after her in case of a problem. As concerns my failure to have a Council card, frankly, I intended to apply for one, but I didn't think it was urgent to do so and so I put it off. In fact, I really didn't know

39

where to make an application for a card." This explanation was the best that Koskinen could think of at the moment.

The man at the desk paused as if to evaluate Koskinen's statement. Koskinen thought he detected a slight relaxing of the man's stern and forbidding look. The man then asked, "What do you do for a living?"

"I do maintenance work for the City Park Department."

"Ah, so you are a worker, a laborer, then," the man concluded.

"I suppose you could call me that." Koskinen thought he was making some progress in getting accepted.

"What is your name?" the man asked, his voice a bit softer.

"Timo Koskinen."

"Koskinen, Koskinen, that's a common name. What is your father's name?"

"Ville Koskinen."

"Has your father been active in the Communist movement?"

"Yes, for years."

"Ah, so, you are his son." The man at the desk became suddenly friendly.

"Yes, I know your father very well. I have known him for years. He has been one of our staunchest leaders, a great organizer. Of course, sometimes he drinks too much, but we overlook that because of his work for our cause. I admire him immensely. So, you are his son. Of course, you can have a card. You are one of us. What else do you do?"

"Well, I'm a student. I am hoping to become an engineer, but, I'm neither working nor going to school right now due to the present upheaval."

The man at the desk nodded at the security guards and told them they could leave. When they had left the room, the man stood up, offered his hand to Koskinen and introduced himself.

"I am Toivo Niskula. I'm the Senior Secretary of the Central Committee for the Tampere area. We are looking for several intelligent, physically strong young men for espionage work. Would you be interested?"

"I have no experience in spy work," replied Koskinen. "I wouldn't know what to do. What would it involve?" Koskinen was enjoying the confidential relationship that had developed so swiftly as a result of his being the son of Ville Koskinen. Koskinen thought to himself, "What a stupid fool this Niskula is. He has asked nothing about my beliefs politically. He has assumed that I think like my father. Well, I'll play along and let him think it."

"Your espionage missions will vary from time to time depending upon what is needed. However, your primary mission will be to infiltrate the opposition ranks to get information about what the enemy is planning. We are not concerned about your inexperence. We are all learning our jobs as we go along. None of us has been involved with a revolution before this. We learn very quickly just to survive. You will learn quickly or be at risk of dying. It's quite simple."

"Herra Secretary, I don't know what to say" Koskinen wanted to think how he could use this offer as an opportunity to serve the opposition as he had intended when he sent Anna to her parent's home.

"Herra Secretary, I can give you my answer tomorrow. This is all very sudden. If I do not accept the espionage assignment, I perhaps can serve in another capacity."

"Of course," replied Niskula, "give it some thought. We want you to be convinced and willing to accept the risks of such an assignment. In the meantime, let me issue you a Party Card so that you are free to come and go."

When Koskinen arrived at his room in the boarding house, he lay down on the bed and, with hands behind his head, stared up at the ceiling and thought about what he should do. From what he had read and from what he had heard, Koskinen knew that engaging in espionage is a dangerous occupation. But, he reasoned, for that matter, being a soldier on the front line was also dangerous. The difference was that as a spy, he would be on his own with no back up or reserve in support in case difficulties arose.

Koskinen thought of Anna and the birth of their child. He had to consider them when risks were to be taken. But, he reasoned again, in the present tumultuous times, every day's events were fraught with danger. There was violence and lawlessness all around him. He could be a victim of it at any moment.

Koskinen's thoughts cascaded through his brain oscillating from one option to another regarding the course of action to take. One thing was certain: he would do nothing to help the Red cause. Then like a thunderclap, a majestic thought struck him. It was an inspiration that awed him with its grandeur. He would conduct espionage for both sides. For the Reds he would submit false information. For his government, he would search out and get essential and useable information. The idea excited him. In fact, he was ecstatic. He would be of service to one side and a disservice to the other. Koskinen then and there made the decision to accept Niskula's proposition to serve the Reds as an espionage agent. Under the guise of getting intelligence information for the Reds, he would go into the government camp and offer his services to it. Koskinen, usually a forthright, unsophisticated and candid man, went to sleep that night satisfied that he had made the right decision and that the duplicity of roles he was about to adopt was justified under the threat to his freedom and his country's independence. Accordingly, he decided to keep his room at the boarding house as evidence of his intent to maintain Tampere as his permanent base. This would please Senior Secretary Niskula.

At 0900 hours the next morning, after a cup of coffee and some cheese on Finnish dark bread eaten in his room, Koskinen appeared at the headquarters building of the Revolutionary Council. The guard admitted him after an inside telephone call to Secretary Niskula.

The Senior Secretary greeted Koskinen at the office door.

"Good morning, Timo, did you sleep well?"

"Yes, sir," replied Koskinen.

"Can I offer you some coffee?"

"Yes, thank you. It's very cold outside and I could use a hot cup of coffee to warm me."

Niskula poured coffee for himself and Koskinen and then asked Koskinen to be seated. Niskula took his seat at the desk. Looking directly at Koskinen, Niskula asked, "Have you arrived at a decision about the espionage assignment?"

"Yes, I have," Koskinen replied. "I have decided to accept."

Niskula smiled broadly. "Good, good. I'm glad you've decided to do it. It will be exciting and a challenge. I'm going to refer you to our Intelligence Section where you will be tutored on our rules and given guidelines within which to operate. You will henceforth be responsible to that Section. You will report today to Agent Commander Kostari on the Second Floor of the Kauppahalli Building on Hameenkatu Street."

Koskinen nodded, "Yes, I know where it is downtown."

"I will let them know you are coming. So, good luck, Timo, I expect to hear good things about you."

"Thank you and good day to you, sir," said Koskinen as he left the Secretary's office.

In a way, Koskinen was glad he did not have to report to Niskula who gave the impression of being an insidious person. Niskula was friendly enough and had accepted him in good faith based on the highly respected reputation of Koskinen's father, but Koskinen could not be sure that Niskula would not contact his father and learn the truth of his son's political stance

The walk from the Council Secretary's office to the Kauppahalli building in the center of Tampere was several long blocks including crossing on the windswept bridge over the Tammerkoski River. The weather was bitter cold and some light snow was falling. At about 0930 hours, daylight was only just to reveal itself. There were only a few hours of daylight in a Finnish January. The long spread of darkness day in and day out resulted in a general malaise among the Finnish people. Mental depression was common. For Koskinen, at this moment, there was no depression but a grand sense of euphoria laced, however, with an underlying feeling of apprehension and anxiety over the possibility of having his true political beliefs exposed. He tried to put this concern out of his mind so that his actions, his facial expressions would not reveal fear to an especially acutely perceptive person.

As he reached the second floor of the Kauppahalli, he observed a long corridor that commenced at the head of the stairs and along both sides of which were office rooms. Koskinen saw nothing unusual in this design as older public buildings in Finland had this type of interior layout.

Most of the doors to the rooms had some sign with the name of the occupant. On one of the doors was a cardboard sign tacked to the outside with the name "L. Kastari." Nothing else. Koskinen assumed this was the person Secretary Niskula had referred to him.

Koskinen knocked on the door and, in a few moments, a woman came to the door.

"What can I do for you?" the woman asked.

"A Herra Niskula referred me to a Herra Kastari. May this be his office?" Koskinen asked, beginning the intelligence game that avoided using titles, status or agency names.

"Come in," the woman said, "So, you were told to report to Herra Kastari. What is your name?"

"Koskinen. Timo Koskinen. No, actually I was told to report to Agent Kastari."

"Young man, you will have to learn to be more accurate," the woman admonished Koskinen. "I am Agent Kastari." The woman paused and watched for Koskinen's reaction and then asked, "Does that surprise you?" The woman smiled as if enjoying Koskinen's evident embarrassment at the error in his assuming that Agent Kastari was a male.

"Well, yes," Koskinen replied in a very humble and apologetic manner. "Please accept my apology."

"Herra Koskinen, I exonerate you by saying that you are not the first to make that mistake. Sit down, please." As she beckoned to a chair, Kastari continued to speak.

"You must understand that under Communism, women have equal status with men. There is no discrimination between the sexes. If a woman is qualified for a job, she is allowed to compete for it with an equally qualified man. Under capitalism, as I'm sure you well know, women are treated as chattels, like bondsmen. That is why I believe in Communism and why I am a member of the Socialist Party. That is why I am in this fight to bring Finland into close ties to the new Bolshevik government of Russia."

Koskinen listened and said nothing. He felt it best not to debate the issue with Agent Kastari, but he thought that he certainly did not consider Anna as a chattel. Maybe he was a good Communist because he thought of Anna as his equal intellectually. He was bemused by that thought. He knew that Communism had other features about it that repelled him.

"I understand your father is Ville Koskinen. I have not met him, but he has a respected reputation in our Party as one of the early organizers of our movement. You are following in good footsteps. Incidentally the 'L' in my name is for 'Liisa.'" She paused and regarded Koskinen and then said, "Timo, I want to spend time with you today discussing your background, that is, your education, your work, your hobbies, your preferences in sports, your religious affiliation, and so on. This will help me to decide what mission you are best suited for. I am in charge of all of the intelligence agents in this part of Finland and I have to know the talents of each agent. Then I will give you our rules and a statement on our policies. Nothing will be in writing. It will be all oral and you must commit what I say to your memory."

Koskinen nodded that he understood.

"Would you care for a cup of coffee?"

Koskinen declined, "Not right now, thank you." The usual and customary pot of coffee without which Finns seemingly could not function, was sitting on the small wood stove that heated the room.

"May I suggest that you go downstairs to the Halli and, if you wish, get something to eat and return here in about an hour. I have some matters on my desk that must be given attention and there is no point in your just sitting here. In any case, we shall work through lunchtime so it is best that you have an early lunch now. I have my lunch with me." Liisa Kastari then began to shuffle some papers on her desk. Koskinen arose from his chair saying, "I'll be back, then, in an hour," and he left.

The Kauppahalli was just that, a hall of shops. It was, in fact, an indoor marketplace devoted primarily to the retail sale of food products. The Halli was divided by two long walkways for the public and on either side of each walkway was a row of open stalls vending bakery goods, meats, seafood, and, in season, fruits and vegetables. In the center of the building was a small area set aside as a mini-restaurant where customers could purchase a simple meal and sit at tables. On most days, the Halli was a lively place with crowds of people moving slowly from one shop to another. Koskinen was very familiar with the place as a native of Tampere, having visited it many times in the past. The restaurant chairs and table were often occupied by some seedy looking characters that appeared to gather there to socialize and, with no doubt, to use the place as a haven from the severe weather.

Koskinen's lunch consisted of a plate of musta makkara, Finnish dark bread and coffee. The musta makkara or Finnish black sausage was Koskinen's favorite dish although it resembled the contents of an outhouse. As he sat and ate, his thoughts dwelt on the role he was about to undertake as a spy for the government.

Returning to the office after lunch, Koskinen began his session with Kastari.

"Your name will be changed to Tommi Salo. While your name, Koskinen, is quite common, there is a risk that someone will relate you to your father who is a well-known activist in Socialist circles. That could create problems. Do you understand?"

"Yes, of course."

"Also, you are to grow a mustache and a goatee to make your detection more difficult."

Koskinen smiled. He had never cultivated that sort of facade before. It would be interesting to look in the mirror.

The rest of the day was spent in instructions on the rules and specific modus operandi of the work.

"All the rules and regulations will not help you in tight situations," Madam Kastari pointed out. "You are on your own and will have to use your wits in most situations."

"When do I start a mission?" Koskinen inquired.

"In four or five days," Madam Kastari replied.

Koskinen looked startled. "So soon?" he asked rhetorically. "I can't grow a mustache and beard in that time."

"Yes, I know it is quite hasty, but time is very important. Mannerheim has gone up to Vaasa to form an army for the government and we must know how he is proceeding and what his plans are. Your mission will be to go to Vaasa and get the information we need."

Kastari was referring to General C. G. Mannerheim, a Finn who, nevertheless, had had a distinguished career in the Russian army before the Bolshevik revolution and who had returned to Finland only six weeks before the Socialist revolt on January 28, 1918. Finnish Premier P. E. Svinhufvud had named him Commander-in-Chief to organize an army to maintain law and order. Mannerheim left on January 18, 1918 for the city of Vaasa, a provincial city of 22,000 on the west central coast of Finland to form a fighting force. Vaasa quickly became the legal seat of the government when the Reds seized control of the Capitol, Helsinki, and forced the government leaders to flee.

"We are assured of victory," Madam Kastari told Koskinen. "The Russian garrisons already here are helping us in supplying arms and the Russian officers are helping in leading our military action."

"Are there enough Russians to make a difference?" Koskinen asked. He intended already to get information to pass on to the government in Vaasa.

"There are about one thousand Russian soldiers in Tampere alone. There are garrisons in northern Finland as well as in the south numbering totally about ten thousand Russian troops. Our own Finnish worker forces number about one hundred thousand. So, you see, we should be in control of all of Finland within not more than two months. But, we need information about the government's plans and forces so that we do not miscalculate our own plans and strategies. Do you understand?"

Koskinen knew that Madam Kastari was unsuspecting of his intentions. So far, so good, he thought.

For the next two months Koskinen shuttled back and forth between Tampere and Vaasa, often stopping in small villages near where fighting was going on. His credentials read that he was a businessman and that he was to be allowed to pass through the Red Guard lines. On his first trip to Vaasa by train, he had contacted Colonel W. Holmberg, the adjutant on General Mannerheim's staff and revealed his true name and what his mission was for the Reds. Although Koskinen did not, of course, know it at the time, the Civil War would end by April 13, 1918 with the capture of Helsinki, the Capitol, by German troops specifically sent to help the government forces.

Colonel Holmberg was skeptical, at first, of Koskinen's story.

"You come here and tell me that you have been hired to spy for the Reds and that, what you really want is to spy for us and to give the Reds misleading information. How can I believe you? I don't know you. You have confessed to being a spy for the Reds. I could have you shot right now. Are you aware of that?"

"Yes," replied Koskinen. "If I didn't feel quite sure that you would believe me, do you think, sir that I would confess to being a spy? That should be your proof." If Koskinen felt threatened by the Colonel, he didn't show it. He did think, however, that the Swede-Finn was acting arrogant and aristocratically condescending, a trait Koskinen had come to recognize in Swede-Finns even at his young and social inexperience. Finnish families had passed this disparagement from generation to generation as if it were an inherited property right.

"Colonel, I am loyal to the Finnish government and I want to participate in the fight to regain Finnish independence and democratic freedoms. I came here for that purpose and if you are suspicious of my motives, why not put me to the test and give me an assignment?" Koskinen felt himself becoming exasperated with the Colonel's apparent unwillingness to accept him and his offer.

Colonel Holmberg did not reply for a few moments as, apparently, he was thinking the matter through. He was still suspicious of Koskinen's true intent and, yet, could not just summarily ignore an opportunity to obtain important information about the operational plans of the Reds.

Finally, he said, "Alright, Koskinen, I'll do just that. Here is what I want you to do: We believe that at the headquarters of the Russian military garrison in Tampere they have a telegraph communication operation with a telegraph center at the railway station in Helsinki to telegraph units with Russian troops stationed in other parts of Finland. I want you to verify the existence of the Tampere operation and, if it does exist, then to seek one or more telegraph operators who are loyal to us and to get them to send us information about what is going on in Tampere and in the outlying Russian troop units. You should try to do this as quickly as possible."

"Are the telegraph operators Russian?" asked Koskinen.

"No, we believe they are Finns hired by the Russians who have to communicate with the Finnish Reds throughout Finland. The Reds, apparently, have no telegraph operators of their own and have to rely on those Finns who were telegraph operators prior to their revolt."

"When I return to Tampere and report on my mission here, I am expected to bring importation information about your operations. What can I offer?"

"You can tell them that we expect a German expeditionary force to help us and that they will reach Finland in about three to four weeks. We have been negotiating with the German military command and they have agreed to send substantial relief."

"Is that information true or false?" asked Koskinen.

"It is true," replied Holmberg. "I am sure that the Reds can verify it. Since it is true, it will help you to establish yourself as an efficient and credible agent for the Reds. I give you this information because the German assistance will not remain a secret for very long and may have an effect of panicking the Red command. When the leaders in Tampere know you are reliable, it will help you with getting information for us. Do you understand?"

"Yes, yes, of course." Koskinen's enthusiasm was obvious to the Colonel.

The Colonel continued, "I am not going to tell you where the Germans will land in Finland. You can tell them that it will be somewhere in the South part of Finland."

"Good," Koskinen said elatedly. "I'll get the train back to Tampere tomorrow morning."

"We can set you up with a bunk bed here," said Colonel Holmberg.

Upon his return to Tampere, Koskinen reported to Agent Liisa Kastari concerning the German expeditionary force.

"Good?" Kastari exclaimed. "That confirms what we suspected might happen. You've done a good job already, Timo, or shall I say, Tommi." Kastari smiled at the use of the pseudonym. Koskinen felt that he had established his credibility with Kastari, at least.

Within the next ten days Koskinen established contacts in the telegraph office in the Russian headquarters in Tampere. The Finnish operators were enthused about serving the Whites as the government came to be known. Like their peers in other Russian units throughout Finland, they had served in the Russian military prior to the Russian revolution and had continued to serve after the Bolsheviks took control of the Russian government. They continued their jobs after the Finnish Reds had formed to establish a Marxist government in Finland. The Finnish telegraphers reasoned that they were not disloyal to the Finnish government since they were only sending and receiving messages. Koskinen had enlisted them to transmit, surreptitiously, information to Vaasa.

As the civil war progressed, both sides engaged in unrestrained cruel acts against each other. Reds, taken by the Whites as prisoners, were often shot forthwith. The Reds performed equally without mercy for

Whites taken prisoner. The hatred on both sides was intense. Prisoners taken by the White Guard, if not summarily executed, were placed in prison camps where they languished in unrelenting squalid, intolerable conditions. The camps were filthy, food inadequate, medical care nonexistent. Prisoner deaths from dysentery, pneumonia, malnutrition, wound infections, and other assorted ailments were in daily profuse numbers.

By the end of the Civil War it was estimated that the Whites had executed from two thousand to three thousand Reds. Another 95 died as war prisoners of the Whites. The Reds are estimated to have murdered 1365 Whites. While both opposing forces were disdainful of human life during the war, the Whites continued their vengeful actions by maintaining the inhuman prisoner camps for months after the Civil War ended with the defeat of the Reds. More than eight thousand Red prisoners died in prison hospitals and about twenty-seven hundred died in the prison camps due, for the most part, to the scarcity of food and inadequate medical care. About 12,000 Whites were killed or wounded in the struggle.

The Civil War of 1918 in Finland had profound and, in some respect, disastrous long term effects on Finnish society. It had a personal traumatic experience for Koskinen. After the Civil War was over, he told his wife, Anna, and some of his friends of the painful event that occurred during the bitter siege of Tampere by the White Guards.

"I was on a train returning to Tampere when, about twenty miles east of the City, the train stopped and a White Guard soldier came aboard and told us the train would not be allowed to proceed further because of heavy fighting and troop movements up ahead. This happened about two weeks before the war ended in April 1918. It was about 1300 hours and a chill was in the air. It was a dreary day, I recall.

"There was a White prisoner of war camp about 500 feet from where the train was stopped and, with little else to do, I wandered over to the camp. The guard at the gate permitted me to enter when I told him I was a courier for General Mannerheim. Strangely, he didn't ask for any proof. But, then, Colonel Holmberg once complained to me about the lack of discipline among the volunteers of the White Guard."

Koskinen would continue his story. "The prison camp compound was a quite small area considering that there were several hundred prisoners held within it, probably about 300 by 500 feet. There were many small individual tents scattered about within the compound; each one could contain two men. I talked with some of the prisoners who told me they took turns sleeping in the tents. However, there were still not enough tents even for that process and some men had to sleep on the ground regardless of weather conditions.

"I saw at once that conditions in the camp were absolutely deplorable. Some of the prisoners were standing about either by themselves or in small groups. Others were either sitting or lying on the bare ground. Some huddled about a few wood fires.

"All of the prisoners looked haggard and filthy. They were unshaven, their clothes stained and dirt covered. They were coughing a lot and spitting up phlegm and sometimes, blood. I asked a prisoner about sanitary provisions and he pointed to a corner of the camp where a large hole in the ground served as a latrine. The drinking water was in two large wood tubs. I was told that no prisoner would dare use it for washing. If he did, other prisoners would beat him severely. Food, I was told, was sparse. Potato soup and potato soup.

"As I walked about the compound, there were some hostile stares of resentment since it was obvious to the prisoners that I was one of the 'enemy.' However, my safety was not threatened. The prisoners told me that the White Guards would regularly take out seven or eight prisoners. Those prisoners never returned; the other prisoners assumed that they were shot."

Koskinen would pause. "And now I want to tell you about the one experience I had at the camp that will forever cause me anguish and feelings of guilt." This time there was a perceptible labored pause as if Koskinen had to call up some reserve of inner strength to relate the incident.

" I saw off to one side a prisoner sitting somewhat in a crouched position staring into space forlornly, and frequently putting his hand to his face as if wiping away tears. I tell you even though these prisoners were an enemy who had tried to overthrow the government and to take away freedom and independence, my heart went out to them in compassion for fellow human beings who were living worse than farm animals. In particular, this crouched individual with the vacant stare and trembling with some kind of emotional inner turmoil seemed to represent the horror into which all of the prisoners had fallen.

"I guess I walked over to the man drawn by a desire to console him, although they could all use consoling. As I drew near to the man, he looked up at me with an expression of pathos I shall never forget. There was immediately something familiar about him. And then the next moment I experienced shock beyond description. My god, it was my father. Through all the grime and gaunt, unshaven face I recognized him. He had aged terribly since I last saw him sometime before the Red revolt. I spoke to him gently. I said, 'Papa, this is Timo, your son.' He looked at me incredulously, as if not comprehending. He, obviously, did not recognize me because of my moustache and goatee. I repeated, 'Papa, I am Timo. I am your son.' He must have then recognized my voice because in almost a whisper, he said, 'Timo, Timo.' He reached out his hand to me and I took it. It was an emaciated hand, thin and bony. I knelt next to him and he began to cry.

"In a weak, barely audible voice, Papa said, 'I am so sorry for everything. Please forgive me. My life has been one of wrongdoing. I feel so terrible. My family should have been important to me. I was a brute. This whole Socialist revolution is wrong. I should never have supported it. I see that now. Can you forgive me? This is the end for me.' His words did not come easily and it took time for him to speak while weeping. Tears came to my eyes too when I saw how he was suffering not only physically, but spiritually, as well. All the abuse my family and I had endured and tolerated from my father in earlier years seemed no longer of any importance and the hate that I had borne for my father then and there evaporated in a sudden surge of a feeling of love for him. I am sure now that it was love and not just being sorry for him."

Koskinen struggled to contain his latent emotions at the remembrance of that day with his "Papa." But he continued to relate what followed. "I said to Papa, 'Papa, I shall see if I can get you out of here. I know the people who can order it.' Papa looked at me so pathetically, still holding my hand. I could see that he had no fight left in him. In that respect, he was no longer the Papa I had known."

"Papa said, 'No, Timo, don't do it. I don't care to live any longer. I have no purpose in life any longer. When you leave here, just know that I now realize I love you, Mama and your brothers and sister. I wish I could do things over in my life, but that is impossible.'

"'Papa, let me try,' I said. 'If you want to die, at least, do so at home and in dignity.' Papa said, 'Timo, I have no home. I never treated my home as a home. It would be hypocrisy for me to do so now. No, Timo, you must go now. I am happy to see you once more.'

"Papa released my hand and got up. He said he would walk with me to the gate. My soul was absolutely torn when I left him at the gate. As I walked away toward the railroad station, I turned once more. Papa was standing inside the gate. He waved to me. I never saw him again. We don't know what happened to him. We can only guess that because he was a ringleader in the Communist cause he may have been taken out and shot and buried in a mass grave. We just don't know. This whole revolt, this Civil War was so unnecessary and cost so many lives. It was a catastrophe for Finland.

"I feel so guilty about Papa. I should have gone to Colonel Holmberg or one of the other superior officers I had come to know and gotten Papa out of there whether he wanted it or not. It was my childhood ethic all over again. I did what my father ordered. I obeyed him, right or wrong. It's terrible."

By the time of the end of the Civil War, Koskinen had come to be highly respected for the work he had accomplished for the victorious Whites. Colonel Holmberg, who at first had been so skeptical of Koskinen, now praised him unreservedly. Whereas, at the commencement of the War, the Finnish government had no army, no military establishment at all, now, at the end of the war, it had an organized army in the White Guard with paid staff and personnel.

Colonel Holmberg summoned Koskinen into headquarters.

"Timo, would you like to make the military your career?"

Timo replied, "Colonel, I hadn't given it any thought. It might be interesting, but I have to finish my schooling."

"I'm glad you want to complete your formal education. That is very important. I am going to suggest this: the staff and I think highly of your talents. We need to establish a permanent Intelligence Section operating throughout Finland. We would like you to take over the

Tampere area. We'll set up an office for you in the City. You can be part-time until you finish your schooling. How does that sound?"

"It sounds wonderful, Colonel. It would be difficult for me to reject such an opportunity. But, I would like to ask my wife, Anna, for her opinion. I can do that within a day or two. Anna is now with her family on a farm near Vammala. I can telephone her."

Colonel Holmberg appeared slightly surprised. In his world, it was customary for men to make decisions without reference to wives. But, he said nothing and accepted what to him was Koskinen's unorthodox behavior.

Koskinen had been in touch with Anna during the war whenever he had found a telephone line that had not been either destroyed or controlled by the Reds. But, until the war ended, the contacts had been infrequent. Now, in talking with Anna who was still in Vammala and explaining the offer of Colonel Holmberg, Anna had said that, in her opinion, Timo should accept the offer, but, to confirm that the job was subject to his completing his schooling. Anna was adamant that Timo's education must be a priority.

Thus it was that Timo Koskinen began his career in the Intelligence Section of the Finnish military service.

The Civil War of 1918 in Finland when he was twenty-two years of age had had a tremendous influence on Koskinen. By being a member of the Socialist revolution organization and, especially, of their Intelligence group, Koskinen had been privy to the plans of the leaders in the inner circle and what he learned of those plans to subvert the independence of Finland by establishing a Marxist government with close ties to the Soviets caused him to resolve to do whatever he could to prevent any restoration of Russian influence over Finland with the loss of freedom.

Now, twenty-one years later, as Timo and Anna were conversing in their kitchen, Timo continued to explain to his wife why he would probably decide to accept the Stalin mission.

"You recall, Anna, how thousands of our countrymen died in 1918 to preserve freedom and democracy for themselves and future generations here in Finland. I was a part of that struggle and, when it was over, I vowed that I would do everything possible to see that never again would I permit, through inaction, our country to come under

Russian control or, for that matter, under the control of any foreign government. I feel that way still today. I am not saying that my family is unimportant to me in relation to our government. It is precisely because you and our sons are important to me, your freedoms, their freedoms, that I may choose to undertake the mission. For the time being, Aari and Pauli can be told that I am going on a trade mission to Moscow."

Anna said nothing further, but still appeared to be disenchanted with the entire idea. And Timo discarded talking about the subject entirely. He felt enough had been said and that there were more pleasant things to talk about.

In the week that followed and before going to Helsinki for further conference on the mission, Koskinen regularly went to his office in the Finlayson complex, but had little on his mind except the decision he must make about the assignment to Moscow. The truth was that he had pretty much made up his mind to accept, but wanted, nevertheless, to still think about it before informing Anna of his decision. But Anna was quite right.

Timo chuckled to himself with the thought that Anna knew him so well as to predict that he would accept the assignment. Anna had always had unusual talent for discernment.

During the weekend following their initial discussion of the assignment to "take care of Stalin," Timo told Anna of his decision.

At home while sitting in their parlor, Koskinen spoke gently.

"Anna, you probably already know that I have decided to accept the assignment, unless, of course, something should be outlined next Wednesday that will be entirely unacceptable to me."

"Yes, I expected it, Timo," Anna said with an air of weary resignation. "Well, you must do what you want to do. I don't at all like your decision, but you have my support and love, nevertheless."

"And I love you too, Anna." Koskinen came over and sat down on the sofa next to her, hugged her and kissed her on her cheek. She turned and looked at him with love and appreciation for his affection

CHAPTER 2

Bill Chance sat in his large leather upholstered executive swivel chair staring gloomily out of his office window on the fourth floor of the Federal State Office Building in Washington, D.C. It was the last week of January 1939, the weather outside was a damp cold with a heavy gray, cloudy pall hanging over the city. A light snow was falling; a wet snow that left no imprint of the beauty on the landscape that normally occurs from frozen flakes. The snow covered nothing and, because it became only slush on the streets, it washed away nothing. The grime of the city was still exposed and, perhaps, under the conditions appeared even more intrusive. But, at the moment, Chance was completely introspective. What he saw was in his mind's eye and the images were dark, foreboding and ominous.

Bill Chance was head of the Soviet Union Section in the U.S. Department of State. He had held this position for the past seven years, since 1931. A career diplomat since graduating from Georgetown University, he had served in a variety of positions at "State," as the Department was referred to. He reported directly to the Secretary of State. Among his responsibilities was that of making policy recommendations to the Secretary vis-à-vis U.S.-Soviet issues and relations. Those recommendations were generally the result of his and his assistants' evaluation of reports from a variety of sources, of conversations with representatives of foreign countries including the Soviets and, on infrequent occasions, of visits to the Soviet Union.

For much of the past year, reports from both the U.S. Embassy in Moscow and from the National Intelligence Authority that had come across his desk described the horrendous purges that were taking place in the Soviet Union. Mass arrests and executions of thousands of Soviet citizens of all walks of life, men, women and children, had become daily events. Those who were not executed were sent to labor camps everywhere; conditions were appalling. Very few, after a summary trial, were set free.

These reports were very disturbing to Bill Chance who, by nature, was a nonviolent, compassionate person. He found it incredible that one human being could, in cold blood, take the life of another, let alone thousands. But, from the standpoint of his job, he found even more disquieting the reports, however meager and inconclusive, that had recently come into his office that Stalin might seek an alliance of some sort with Hitler. If that came to pass, his entire appraisal of the relationship between the United States and the Soviet Union would have to be reevaluated and, in all probability, revised.

Chance pressed the interoffice buzzer for his secretary. "Charlene, call Wagner and Stolz and tell them I want to see them in here." Gene Wagner and Randy Stolz were assistants to Chance with offices a few doors down the corridor.

A few moments later Charlene got back to Chance. "Mr. Wagner and Mr. Stolz said they'd be with you in a few minutes." While awaiting them, Chance continued to turn over in his mind what implications there might be for the United States if Stalin and Hitler entered into an agreement of any sort. He didn't have any ready answers.

Wagner and Stolz entered Chance's office and sat down around his desk. The relationship among the three was very informal since they held office conferences with each other several times a week on various matters.

"I've been getting some information lately about a possible agreement between Stalin and Hitler. I'd like to get your thinking on what you think should be done," said Chance.

"What are the terms of the agreement?" inquired Randy Stolz.

"As I gather, there is no agreement of any kind yet," said Chance. "All that comes to me is that Stalin might try to negotiate some kind of agreement of cooperation between himself and Hitler."

"Well," observed Gene Wagner, "until you know what they've agreed to, it's a little difficult to determine what we have to do about it."

"Then it might be too late to do anything," said Chance. He added, "The information that has been sent to me speaks about Hitler and Stalin dividing up Europe between them. That's all I know at this point. The reports have been very vague on the whole subject."

"An agreement between Stalin and Adolph Hitler is unbelievable," remarked Stolz. "These two guys hate each other. They'd just as soon slit each other's throats."

"I agree with Randy," added Wagner. "Where are these reports coming from?"

"From within our Embassy in Moscow and from our National Intelligence Authority," replied Chance. "I haven't checked with either of them to determine how reliable their sources are. They may be just reporting rumors. I will run it down, however. But, my guess is that there is some substance to the information. We have some fairly reliable informants over there judging by past experience."

"I question why Stalin would want to enter into any agreement with Hitler. I don't see any basis for it," said Wagner.

"The reason I would guess is that Stalin wants to make sure his western borders are secure," said Chance. "Stalin is no fool. This past September 1938, he saw Hitler enter and take over the Sudatenland of Czechoslovakia and also of Danzig in northern Poland. I think he realizes that this is just the beginning and that Hitler will want more territory and take it by force of military arms. Stalin wants to get and keep what he can while making sure Hitler does not invade the Soviets. That's my guess."

"Well, what do you suggest we recommend doing about it?" inquired Wagner.

"That's what I got you in here for," said Chance. "I want your ideas on how to handle this now, even before we know there is an agreement."

"You're asking us to come up with possible answers to thwart such an agreement, is that it?" said Stolz.

"Yes, I think you could put it that way," said Chance.

"There are several options that could be used," Stolz offered. "First, have our Ambassador urge Stalin not to enter into any agreement with Hitler. Now, I understand that you have to offer an incentive or an inducement for Stalin not to do so. So, I suggest that we agree to supply

Stalin with substantial military hardware and with economic support to get his country ready for an invasion by Germany. If he can defend himself, Stalin won't be in a hurry to align with Germany."

"That sounds good," observed Wagner, "but, first, giving Stalin economic and military help will take considerable time and, if the rumors about an agreement are right, there may not be time. Stalin has to deal with Hitler right now. Secondly, if we start supplying the Soviets, the effect may be that it will force Hitler to invade Russia. He's not going to wait around until Stalin gets prepared to fight. In addition, the United States will no longer be able to claim to be neutral."

"Yeah, I think you may be right, Gene," Chance told Wagner.

"Randy, you mentioned several options. What others did you have in mind," Chance asked Stolz?

Stolz replied, "The United States could offer to mediate between Germany and the Soviets to try to settle their claims and to allay their fears."

"Yes, we could offer," said Chance, "but you must recognize that you're dealing with two egomaniacs, if I can use the word, and they're not going to allow their peoples to think that outsiders have laid out terms for them to adhere to. Hitler is getting his people worked up into a war frenzy and he won't change that. It's what he wants. It's how he stays in power. We can offer, but I don't think it will go very far."

"I know what would probably work," chimed in Wagner, not waiting for Stolz to offer any more options.

"And what's that?" queried Chance.

"If we could get both of these guys assassinated that would probably solve a lot of international problems. Both Germany and Russia would be leaderless and rudderless. The shock to both countries would be so great that everything would come to a standstill." Wagner stopped and the look on his face was one of huge satisfaction, the look of a child who has just solved a mathematical problem or of a scientist who has just discovered a long sought after principle. One might say it was the "Eureka" expression.

Chance smiled at his assistant's suggestion. "You are jesting, of course."

"Maybe, maybe not, but you'll agree, won't you, that it would solve problems."

"The President would never go for it and neither would the Secretary. The United States has long ago adopted the policy of not encouraging or participating in assassinations. It presents an image of a government that is lawless, one that solves problems through violent acts."

Wagner was sarcastic in his reply to Chance's arguments. "Assassinating heads of State or high officials is illegal, but, it's legal to assassinate hundreds of thousands of young soldiers and civilians in a war. It's wrong to assassinate one or two government leaders to save the lives of thousands of innocents, is that what you're saying?" Wagner had become suddenly emotional and challenging.

Chance answered, "I'll be very blunt and say 'yes', but that is not what I'm saying. All that I'm saying is that it's government policy not to sponsor an assassination. I have to agree with you that, on principle, taking one life to save thousands might or should be acceptable."

"Well," continued Wagner, "we could try to arrange it without involving the government officially and without the President knowing about it."

"How to arrange an assassination is the big 'if'," said Stolz, who, up to now, had been listening closely to the discussion between Chance and Wagner. "How do you expect to assassinate either Stalin or Hitler or both? These fellows have more security people around them than our own President has."

"There are two possible ways," said Wagner. "Either a sniper at long range when they're outside at some public function, or by a trusted person who can get physically close to either dictator and not arouse any suspicions. That is, someone who sees the dictator frequently and, yet, a person who hates Stalin or Hitler and would like to get rid of either one."

"How do you find such a person or persons?" asked Stolz.

"Either our Embassy people or our Intelligence people may have some knowledge about persons who have a grudge against Hitler and Stalin. We'd have to make discreet inquiries," answered Wagner.

"How are you going to do something like this without the people at the White House, at the Intelligence Authority and in our own State Department knowing what we're up to and once they know about it they'll probably nix it?" asked a skeptical Stolz.

Replied Wagner, "I think NIA and our Secretary should be brought in on the proposal. I believe NIA will endorse it surreptitiously and I believe we can sell the idea to our Secretary if we can show him that people in Russia, a Russian citizen, will carry it out. I don't know about the White House. I don't trust those guys over there. Everything the President's advisors do is based on how many votes will it get the President, how will the public and the newspapers react. In addition, I wouldn't put it past someone at the White House leaking something like this to the press or to some Congressman. If that happens, then you might as well forget it."

Still challenging Wagner on the idea, Stolz asked, "Suppose the Secretary feels obligated to tell the President, assuming the Secretary himself approves of the idea, and then the President says, 'no', then what are you going to do? Don't forget, the Secretary is in a different position from us. He has responsibilities to the President as a policy advisor that we don't have. He's ultimately accountable to the President for what State does. We don't have that sort of relationship."

Wagner felt himself getting irritated by the questions Stolz was asking. Wagner had already convinced himself that he had struck on a solution to very serious international problems. Nevertheless, he was smart enough to recognize that Stolz was raising issues that had to be met and answered.

"I think that is something we have to discuss with the Secretary. I think that if Bill here can persuade the Secretary that this project can be undertaken quietly and unobtrusively and with minimum involvement by State and Intelligence except for seeking out one or more Russian citizens to carry out the plan, then the Secretary may go for it. What do you think, Bill?" Wagner turned to Chance.

"I've been sitting here listening to you two fellas debate this," said Chance. "I find it very interesting. As I listen and think about the proposal, I don't like it one bit, but I think, at this moment at least, that it is the only solution. I haven't heard anything or thought of anything else that would stop the madness that both Stalin and Hitler are about to impose on Europe and, perhaps, the world. I share Randy's questions. I think Randy has raised legitimate points that must be addressed. On the other hand, I think that Gene may have a proper approach to answering those questions. One problem you haven't covered is that we in this Section are dealing only with the Soviets. That's our expertise and specialty. But you're suggesting that we include Hitler in the assassination plot. To me, that means that we have to bring in the German Section. Let's assume we manage to take Stalin out of the picture and this results in a Soviet government rendered impotent and floundering. If Hitler is still intact, won't that be perceived by him as an opportunity to invade the Soviets? If that happens, then what have we accomplished? Don't Stalin and Hitler have to be taken out at the same time or almost the same time?"

"Yeah, I guess you're right about that. But, again, if we raise these questions with the Secretary," said Wagner, "I think we'll get an answer to that problem also. If the Secretary goes for the idea, then the German Section will have to do their part if the Secretary tells them to do so."

"Well, let's do this," said Chance. "This is a pretty radical idea, maybe even a crazy one, and I'm saying that with no disrespect to you, Gene, let's give it some thought for a couple of days and then talk about it further. The Secretary is out of town until next week, Tuesday. That's a week from now. Suppose we get together this coming Friday morning about 10:00 a.m. In the meantime, of course, you understand that none of us is to mention this idea to anyone. It's a very confidential matter."

Both Stolz and Wagner nodded in agreement and got up to leave.

"See you Friday, gentlemen," said Chance.

After Stolz and Wagner had left, Chance pivoted his chair so that he could again stare out of his office window. It seemed to him, over the course of years, that he could always think things through better when looking out of his window at nothing in particular. He was thinking about the discussion on assassination that had just taken place and he was astounded that he had permitted such a discussion to take place.

Bill Chance was not a violent man. His approach to a problem was to reject violence as a means to a solution. Yet, now, in his mind he had concluded that the problems created by Stalin and Hitler could only be solved by some form of violence. At another time and under different circumstances such a conclusion would have been unthinkable to him.

Now, at age 44, Chance had risen through the ranks at State quite rapidly in a Department that traditionally promoted personnel when vacancies occurred through deaths or rare resignations. His considerable success in this regard was due in part to his friendly and warm personality. He was one of those persons who people liked almost immediately upon first meeting. He had an inherent quality of making people with whom he dealt feel important and that he sincerely cared about them. In addition, however, his line of superior officers had come to respect his judgment in State matters, knowing that his recommendations were based on thorough and exhaustive research of the facts and that he demanded the same meticulousness of his assistants. The Secretaries of State under whom Chance served had universally found early on that his advice was reliable and could be considered seriously.

Bill Chance was married to his high school sweetheart. He and Melissa had three children, two girls and a boy, now in their teens and at different levels of formal schooling. Chance enjoyed the opportunities, however infrequent, of taking the family on short bird watching trips in the surrounding Virginia countryside. He and his wife thought of these excursions both as peaceful communications with nature and as a means of firming the family bonds with their children. The children, in turn, seemed to enjoy this family hobby. At the very least, they did not protest about going on the walks. Connie, age 17, was a high school senior, Fabian, 13, had just begun high school and Bill, Jr., 10, was in a private elementary school.

Chance tried to play handball two or three times a week. He felt that it kept him physically fit, counteracting his sedentary desk job. At six-foot two with a solid, muscular frame, he welcomed the competitiveness and the demanding quick action of the sport. Chance liked winning, but accepted losing graciously. Primarily, he enjoyed the camaraderie and association with men who possessed similar qualities.

Turning away from his office window and back to his desk, Chance pressed the interoffice button to talk with his secretary.

"Charlene, get Madeline on the line and see if she can schedule a conference with Roth as soon as possible after he returns next Tuesday. She should allow about forty-five minutes and with just Roth and me, no one else."

"She'll want to know what it's about so the secretary can prepare. What shall I tell her?" asked Charlene.

"Tell her it's something I can't discuss over the phone. She'll understand. Madeline's a bright lady. She's a good personal secretary for Roth," said Chance and then added, "Just like you are for me."

"That's because you're so congenial to work for." Charlene threw the exchange of compliments back to her boss. She and Chance had a good working relationship. From years of being Chance's personal secretary, Charlene had come to know his personality traits and his work habits quite well. She was divorced. No child or children. A frequent visitor to the Chance home by invitation, Charlene had become close to the Chance family. She adored the kids and they reciprocated by accepting her as one of the family. At work Charlene retained her formal and professional position as Chance's secretary. She recognized that her closeness to the Chance family did not translate into overstepping the limiting boundaries of appropriate behavior on the job.

A few moments later, Charlene called her boss over the intercom. "Madeline says she can schedule you for Wednesday morning at 0730. That would be February 3. However, she'll have to verify it with the secretary when he returns and she'll confirm on Tuesday."

"Seven-thirty!" exclaimed Chance. "That's an ungodly hour. Alright, let me know as soon as you hear from Madeline." He hung up and turned his attention to a pile of papers on his desk. There was much administrative work to be done.

Chance had decided not to wait for the conference with his Assistants on Friday. After the discussion with them, he had concluded very quickly that it was imperative that he take the matter up as soon as possible with McKinley Roth, the Secretary of State. There was a very real threat to the interests of the United States if Stalin and Hitler were to agree to divide up Europe into respective spheres of control. Chance had come to the conclusion that maybe getting rid of the two dictators was the answer to peace.

At dinner at home with the family, Melissa observed that Chance was unusually quiet and pensive. Ordinarily, he would be ebulliently engaging the kids about what they had done that day or about some news item that he thought they might be interested in or whatever. The children may have noticed also, but neither they nor Melissa said anything about it. The family had a rule that if some one of them appeared to be troubled, the other members would not pry or intrude by asking questions, unless the troubled condition continued for an unreasonable length of time.

Later that evening when they were sitting alone in their bedroom, Chance suddenly asked his wife, "Melissa, what do you think of assassination of an important person in government?"

A bit startled, Melissa replied laughingly, "Who are you thinking of assassinating?"

"I'm not thinking of assassinating anyone. I just want to know what you think of it."

"Well, as a matter of general principle I'm opposed to it," said Melissa recognizing that her husband wanted her to be serious. "On the other hand, I suppose there may be occasions when it is necessary. I can't give you a good answer unless I know what the circumstances are or what the problem to be solved may be. The real issue that would have to be answered is whether an assassination would truly solve the problem and you wouldn't know that until afterwards."

Chance commented, "Then what you're saying is that under certain circumstances assassination may be justified if it appears to be the only way to solve a problem, a major one, and you have to take the risk of whether it solves it."

"Yes, that's what I'm saying, but I'm also saying that may be an oversimplification of the subject. Really, Bill, I just can't give you an answer or an opinion. This is a case of where one size doesn't fit all, if you know what I mean."

Then Melissa added, "I noticed you were very quiet at the dinner table and you seemed to be withdrawn into your own thoughts. Is there something you'd like to talk with me about?"

"Melissa, you know I have great respect for your opinion on matters. We've talked about things many times and I have frequently sought your advice. But, right now there is really nothing I can talk about. I was just turning over the general idea of assassination in my mind. Nothing specific and there is nothing for you to be worried about." Chance smiled at his wife and assumed a relaxed appearance. Melissa accepted his decision not to talk further about the subject, but she was inwardly disturbed. She knew her husband wouldn't mention such a subject unless there was some substance to it. She wondered who, if anyone, might be a target for which Bill was concerned.

Sharply at 10:00 a.m. on Friday Gene Wagner and Randy Stolz appeared at Bill Chance's office for the scheduled conference. Chance invited them to be seated. After a few ritualistic remarks about the weather, Chance said, "I presume you've given some thought to the subject we discussed at our meeting last Tuesday and I'd like to hear what you have to say. How about you, Gene?" said Chance turning to Wagner.

"Yes, of course I've given it considerable thought. In fact, I haven't slept since we discussed the subject." Wagner smiled teasingly knowing no one would believe that part of it. He had the reputation for sleeping through Department seminars and training sessions. "Frankly, I could come to no conclusion other than that the elimination of Stalin is the only way to prevent a European catastrophe sometime soon. I also, after thinking about it, concluded that the United States should not be directly involved in the elimination, or, if you will, the assassination."

"Why is that?" interrupted Chance.

"Well," continued Wagner, "In the first place, I don't think that we'll convince the Secretary or the President that the United States should undertake an assassination, either covertly or overtly. Secondly, the United States, at this time, is not perceived as being threatened or even having its interests significantly threatened by Stalin or, for that matter, Hitler."

"Don't you think that if Stalin and Hitler divide up Europe that our economic interests are threatened?" Chance interjected again.

"No, I don't," answered Wagner. "We'll continue to do business with Europe no matter how it is divided up. It's always been that way. Europe after every war is constantly being reshaped and the United States goes on dealing with the new configurations."

"So, what I'm saying," Wagner added, "is that there are countries which have a great deal to lose by Stalin and Hitler dividing up Europe and those are the countries whose independence and sovereignty will be lost. Those countries, which, I assume, will be placed in the Stalin camp, are the Baltic States of Lithuania, Latvia, Estonia and Finland. It is my suggestion that we, the United States government, should attempt to get one of those countries to undertake the elimination of Stalin and that we'll give them our covert support."

"What do you include as covert support?" Stolz asked. He had been listening intently up to this time and, from his expression, with agreement with what Wagner was saying.

"By covert support, I mean making our Intelligence information and sources available, by making available our contacts in the Soviet who can work surreptitiously with the other country's agents, and to help, indirectly, of course, to plan a set up of the elimination."

"What do you think, Randy?" Chance turned to Stolz.

"I think it's an excellent idea. In fact, I was thinking along the same lines. I think a country with a great deal at stake, with a great deal to lose should be the one to carry this plan out."

"What are your ideas as to what country should be approached to involve itself?" Chance now addressed his two assistants.

Stolz replied, "One of the Baltic countries. Understand! I'm talking about Stalin. I'm not talking about Hitler. That's not our department. If there is a division of Europe, Hitler will get the countries of Poland, Czechoslovakia, and most of the rest of middle Europe. That's my guess. He'll leave the Baltic to Stalin. Estonia, Latvia and Lithuania are, to my mind, very weak countries. Latvia has a big population of Germans and Russians. It may not be trustworthy. Estonia is right in the path of the Russians and very vulnerable. It may not want to cause trouble. On the other hand, Finland is a larger country and with about three times the population of each of the others. All of these countries, as you know, have had independence for only twenty years. However, Finland, even though it was a Grand Duchy of Russia since 1818 had pretty much its own self-rule. So, they're used to independence for a longer time than the others. They've gotten used to it and I think will be more willing to do whatever is necessary to keep their independence. They're a very rugged, independent people. From what I understand the Finns hate the Russians intensely and their government leaders are very firm in dealing with the Russian government. I'd opt for Finland to do the job we have in mind."

"I'd go along with that," said Wagner. Then he added, "With Stalin's Soviets and Hitler's Germany, it is my opinion that we are dealing with two cults, however different, each of massive proportions. You can't reason with cult people. They're fanatics who believe that what they are doing is right. There is no compromise. That is why I am of the opinion that diplomacy won't work and you have to cut down the leaders of the cults."

"I think you are right, Gene," said Chance. "We have the cult of Stalin and the cult of Hitler. Each of their peoples regards them as a deity. As virtual deities their peoples worship them and follow mindlessly. I agree that if you eliminate the so-called deity, the cult will collapse. I think we all agree on that, right?"

Stolz and Wagner shook their heads in agreement.

"I'll present all this to Secretary Roth when he returns. I'll have to do a good selling job."

Chance thought for a moment. "By the way, neither of you has said anything about eliminating Hitler. At our last meeting, I thought we agreed that for Europe to be safe, both Hitler and Stalin had to go."

"That's true," said Stolz, "but we decided or, at least, discussed that the German Section had to take care of that. Actually, Bill, I'm more concerned about Stalin as a threat to us than I am about Hitler."

"Why is that?" Chance inquired.

"Frankly," Stolz replied, "I don't care if Hitler gets eliminated. The Germans are more like us, whereas the Russian people seem so different, their culture, their way of thinking. Most of them are peasants. Their leaders from Stalin on down are old revolutionaries who care nothing for human life. They've eliminated all the intellectuals, all the people with any class. The Germans, on the other hand, have a Western culture. They're intelligent, educated, innovative and ambitious. I can go to Germany and feel at home with them. I can feel very comfortable in their country. After all, over half of the people in the United States are of German origin. When I go to Russia I feel like I'm in an entirely alien land. I don't meld with them. So, if Hitler takes over some of Europe, maybe he can instill some good Germanic qualities in the peoples of those countries."

Stolz, having said this, seemed to have momentarily lost his relaxed, easygoing manner and to have acquired a stern and fervent expression.

Chance appeared somewhat surprised and even incredulous. He had never seen Stolz quite that animated about anything. Chance thought to himself that Stolz was clearly showing his German roots. Stolz was obviously a strong Germanophile. Chance had to keep that in mind when evaluating Stolz's opinions when Germany or Germans were involved.

Chance again turned to Wagner. "What about you, Gene? What is your opinion?"

"I agree that we should get one of the threatened Baltic countries to spearhead this project and Finland is fine with me. However, as far as Hitler and Germany are concerned, I do not go as far as Randy does. I am of the opinion that for our project to be successful, we should deal with both Stalin and Hitler. This is nothing against the German people as such; it is against Hitler. I think if we get rid of him, the German people will settle down. However, our Soviet Section is not concerned with that. Hitler, as we have stressed, must be dealt with through our German Section. And that's where I think we should leave it."

"Well, I guess I get your opinions," said Chance, "and we agree that I shall recommend to Roth that Stalin must be eliminated, but that a country such as Finland should carry it out unless we can find a Russian to do it, and we shall work out the implementation with them and help with our sources and resources. We also will ask that the German Section take care of Hitler, but our Soviet Section will coordinate and cooperate with them. Does that summarize our position to be presented to Roth?"

"Yes, that's quite right," said Wagner. Stolz nodded in agreement.

"Fine," said Chance and indicating that the meeting was concluded. "I'll keep you informed. Enjoy your weekend."

Chance remained in his office for much of the rest of the day. He had Charlene bring him a sandwich and coffee from the employees' cafeteria in the building. There were other matters demanding his attention and he wanted to get away early. Right now, the office seemed oppressive and Chance hoped that if he was home he could relax and think of something other than the Stalin project. In his mind, however, he knew better. For the past week it had become difficult for him to think of anything else but the idea of eliminating Stalin. The whole proposal had quickly become an obsession with him. He told himself that he had to try to put the subject aside, otherwise his weekend would be an unhappy one and the family would be affected. His wife and children were very important to him. He and Melissa had decided when their first child was born that the weekends and holidays belonged to the family unless there was some unusual demand on Chance's time.

As he drove home, Chance began to ask himself why he should become involved in such an enormous, complicated and risky project like getting rid of Stalin. It was his job at State to evaluate reports coming in about the Soviet Union, summarize those he determined to be important and informative and, where necessary, make recommendations to be presented to the Secretary. Did his job require that he recommend doing away with Stalin? If the information coming to him required such a recommendation, he, of course, should not shy away from making it. On the other hand, Chance reasoned, he could just give the Secretary a summary of the information and let the Secretary come to his own conclusions. Chance decided to talk over the matter with Melissa sometime appropriate during the weekend. He knew his wife could keep confidences.

At the dinner table, Chance acted his usual cheerful self. He complimented Melissa on her delicious Swedish meatballs and mashed potatoes. No one could ever make them better. The gravy was just of the right texture. "Hey, do you agree, kids?" Chance turned to his children.

"You bet! Mom, it's excellent," said Connie. "I'm going to have to take the time to watch how you make them. When I get married, I'm going to have to appeal to my husband's stomach, just like you have to Dad's."

"Yeah, if it hadn't been for your mother's cooking, I'd never have married her." Chance smiled mischievously while looking at Connie. Connie simulated shock. "I thought you married Mom because you loved her."

Bill, Jr. chimed in, a frown on his face, "Oh, come on. This is boring. Mom, the dinner is great."

Melissa beamed in appreciation. "It took me a couple of hours to make this meal and all of you are gulping it down in five minutes, but that's alright." Melissa was resigned to her family's disposing of meals in quick fashion. The family had told her that it was a sign that the food was excellent.

After the remaining food had been put away and the dishes washed and dried with Connie and Fabian helping their mother, the kids retired to their second floor rooms to do their schoolwork. Outside, it was dark and damp cold. Inside, with a fire in the fireplace adding to the heat of the coal furnace in the basement, it was warm and comfortable.

Sitting in the living room and out of earshot of the children, Melissa mentioned to her husband as she had previously that he seemed to have something on his mind that was weighing him down. "Bill, I know you made the effort to appear jovial in front of the kids at dinner, but I could see that it didn't sound true. There is something that is bothering you and I'd like you to share your problem with me, whatever it is. You can trust me to be discreet."

"Yes, of course, I know that," replied Chance. "I was going to talk the matter over with you this evening."

"Has it something to do with that assassination idea that you spoke about a few days ago?"

"Yes, let me explain it to you and get your thinking after you know the details."

Bill Chance then described the proposal and the conversations that had occurred with Randy Stolz and Gene Wagner, both of whom Melissa knew very well from frequent socializing of the families. When he had completed, Chance asked, "Now what do you think?"

Melissa sat quietly and did not reply for a few moments as she thoughtfully mentally digested what Bill had said. Bill waited, fidgeting a bit while anxiously waiting for Melissa to say something.

"Bill, my immediate reaction is, 'Wow!'"

"What do you mean, Melissa? That doesn't tell me very much. In fact, nothing." Chance frowned. He had expected a better answer than that.

"Well, what I mean, Bill, is that I'm overwhelmed by the enormity and complexity of what you're proposing." Melissa shook her head slightly and her raised eyebrows indicated a sense of disbelief that such a project was being given serious consideration by her husband and his assistants.

Chance felt dismayed that Melissa didn't react more positively to the proposed project. He was so convinced that he was right, that he wanted Melissa to also enthusiastically embrace the idea, to encourage him and to urge him to push for it at the Department. Yet, Chance knew that it wasn't fair to expect that from Melissa. Deep down, what he wanted from Melissa was her usual candid, objective and honest opinion and advice. He knew that he could count on her for just that sort of evaluation of the proposal in spite of her initial incredulousness.

Melissa and Bill had both been born, grown up and gone to school in Reedsburg, Wisconsin, a small farming community about sixty miles northwest of Madison, the State capitol. Neither of them had any desire to stay on the farms after graduation from high school. Melissa went on to the University of Wisconsin in Madison where she received her degree in Education with a major in History. Bill, interested in making a career in government, hopefully in the diplomatic field, left for Georgetown University in Washington, D.C. Both he and Melissa got together on extended holidays and during part of the summer vacations.

Bill and Melissa knew in their senior year in high school that they would get married. They were physically attracted to each other, but, beyond that, Melissa liked Bill's easygoing, relaxed and gentle manner. He had a good sense of humor and, yet, was serious and determined to make something of himself. Melissa wanted that in a husband. It meant future stability and the creation of a sound and secure family life.

For his part, Bill viewed Melissa as a sensible partner in life, a good and virtuous girl who loved him and would encourage him in his career and who could help establish a respectable family. She loved the outdoors as he did and both had an interest in personal athletic sports. When living at home, both helped their families with farm chores. Both families knew each other well and often got together for picnics and games at one or the other's homes. Both parents of Bill and Melissa approved of their being serious about each other, although both of their parents urged them to get college educations before getting married and assuming family obligations.

Bill and Melissa decided to get married while they were seniors at their respective universities even though they would live apart while completing their undergraduate studies. Both felt confident about their futures together. With a degree in Education, Melissa felt she could get a teaching job almost anywhere. With his degree, Bill believed that he, too, could get work fairly soon after graduation, perhaps, as an aide to a Congressman to begin with while he explored the possibility of opportunities in the State Department.

Their marriage had taken place on August 7, 1919. County Judge Cyrus McMahon who had been a Judge for as long as anyone could remember performed it. Neither Bill nor Melissa wanted a big wedding ceremony. They were too practical to spend money on a wedding when it could be used to buy the things needed to start a home and to tide them over while they looked for jobs. Bill was hired almost immediately by the State Department upon his graduation. Melissa, on the other hand, was unable to find an opening for a teacher job in the Washington, D.C. area. She spent her time putting together a household for Bill and herself. The marriage started off well. Bill and Melissa discussed and advised each other on various matters and decisions were made together.

"I would like to know what you think of this project." Chance pressed for an answer from his wife.

"My immediate reaction, Bill, is that I wouldn't do it. I mean I don't think the United States should get involved in something like assassination. Neither Stalin nor Hitler threatens us. It is my opinion that if you think either or both of them should be eliminated, that it should be done by a Russian or by someone in one of the countries that are threatened."

Chance shook his head in disagreement. "But, the United States is threatened, Melissa. Not so much from Hitler, but from Stalin. Stalin wants to export Karl Marx throughout the world and he'll first take over Europe and then will try to instill Communism here by military action or by infiltrating our government operations."

"Well, instead of you or some other country undertaking the elimination of Stalin and Hitler, why don't you let them, eventually, kill each other. They may decide how to divide up Europe, but it will be only a matter of time before one or the other will disregard the agreement and will attack the other. I agree with you, Bill, that, from what is pretty much common knowledge, Stalin wants to spread communism throughout the world. But, if you're concerned about that, won't Hitler checkmate him? And, perhaps, we should be helping Hitler to do just that."

Chance smiled and showed that he was once more /pleased with and respectful of Melissa's reasoning. Nevertheless, he continued to persuade to his view. "Don't you think that your suggestion is too indefinite,

Melissa? It leaves the control of world affairs to two egomaniacs. We are guessing that Hitler may take the action against Russia or that Russia may attack Germany. It leaves everything up in the air. The United States is powerful enough to control events and should do so, because we're a democracy and should try to bring peace to the world."

"I understand what you're saying, Bill, but, it is still my opinion that we should not get involved in a project of this kind. Let's see what Secretary Roth thinks when you present your ideas to him." Melissa indicated that she thought that they had said enough on the subject for that evening. Bill did not persist further, but, for the remainder of the weekend he turned over and over in his mind the options that were open to him. For a while he would conclude that Melissa was right: the United States should not meddle in this matter and should let someone else do the job if it should be done at all. He would soon turn back to his original thinking: that the United States should participate in getting rid of Stalin, but to do it covertly. Then, the most challenging question would enter his mind: assuming the Secretary approved of the mission, how was it to be accomplished? Chance had no answer to that at this moment. His first step was to persuade Secretary Roth that the project was necessary and not unreasonable. How it would be implemented could be determined later. Chance had made up his mind that if it appeared that Roth could not make a decision within, at the most, ten days, then he, Chance, would try other avenues or means to get the project rolling.

Fortunately for Chance, Roosevelt in January 1939, about two weeks before, in fact, had remarked that he recognized that Germany, Italy and Japan wanted to dominate the world and there was always the hope that someone would assassinate Hitler and that someone would kill Mussolini. Roosevelt had not mentioned Stalin, nor had he said that the United States would be a party to that sort of thing. Yet, Chance regarded Roosevelt's comments as making it easier for him to persuade Roth that the proposal to eliminate Stalin was not some outlandish fantasy.

In addition, the Secretary, Chance thought, must be aware that there were those in government and, especially, in the State Department who preferred Hitler to the domination of Europe by Communists. Roth might not share this sentiment, but it would lend weight to the argument for focusing on Stalin as the major threat to European stability.

President Franklin Roosevelt appointed McKinley Roth Secretary of State in 1933. At the time, Roth, then age 62, was serving in the United States Senate representing the State of Tennessee. Both Roosevelt and Roth were Wilsonian Democrats encompassing a world view of the interdependency of nations. Aside from this, however, the personalities of the two men were contrastingly different, so different, in fact, that many involved in the Washington scene wondered why Roosevelt had even considered Roth for Secretary of State. As an answer, at the time, to this perplexing question, it was rumored that Roosevelt wanted to be his own Secretary of State and needed someone who would neither put up resistance to nor a fuss about Roosevelt's dominating intervention in foreign policy matters.

Whereas Roosevelt was charismatic, flamboyant, imaginative and innovative, flexible and willing to compromise in seeking solutions to significant issues, Roth appeared dull, slow, plodding, inarticulate and with such a grim tenacity to principles that allowed little adaptation to changing circumstances.

Indeed, one observer reported, "Roth was inept and passive, tongue-tied at press conferences, incapable of making a reasoned presentation of a subject. He relied on stock phrases, such as, 'We are looking into all phases of the situation.' "

During Roth's term at State, morale was bad within the ranks at all levels of the Department. Roth was, to his employees, maddingly indecisive, providing little firm guidance on policy and enforcement of rules. His procrastination on matters of importance was legendary. He was once asked to provide names of individuals to serve in ministerial posts at legations throughout the world. After several months, he submitted the name of one person, a friend in Tennessee, to serve as Minister to Finland.

Yet Roth had admirable qualities of a personal nature that circumscribed him as a truly unadulterated icon of American character. He was born in a log cabin in the Tennessee mountains where primitive living conditions, perpetual poverty and social and economic isolation from "the rest of the world" were accepted norms among a people whose extreme individualism was defined by strict, narrow and unyielding unwritten rules of conduct among themselves as well as a distrust and suspicion of anyone and anything outside of their immediate geographic circle of family and neighbors. Roth early recognized that to escape from these circumstances he had to get an education and to become involved in politics. He accomplished both. He went to college and law school and, in his early fifties, rose to become Chairman of the National Democratic Party as well as a Congressman. Yet, Roth did not wholly escape the early experiences of his life in the Tennessee mountains. They continued to influence his performance as Secretary of State and to shape his foreign policy decisions.

Although he supported Woodrow Wilson for President, Roth did not fully subscribe to the world of international relationships proposed by Wilson. Roth, to the contrary, had narrow and dogmatic views of the place of the United States in relation to world events. He was suspicious of the motives of other countries while, perhaps inconsistently, promoting free trade among them. His innate individualism was so predominant that, except for the President, Secretary Roth resented the intervention of anyone else in the decision making process within the Department even when he, himself, failed to make decisions. Nevertheless, he relied heavily upon the recommendations of his department and section heads in formulating policy.

It was in this context that Bill Chance met with Secretary of State Roth to discuss the matter of disposing of Stalin and Hitler as a way to achieve world peace and to avoid war. Chance had no way of knowing what Roth's reaction might be. The subject had never been discussed or, for that matter, even been considered in the Department until just now. Events in Europe were developing rapidly and ominously toward military conflict. To Chance, a crisis was at hand; there was precious little time left for definitive action to dispel the war clouds. Chance was well aware of the Secretary's propensity for procrastination in making decisions however urgent the need to do so promptly. Chance was reasonable and realistic; he could not expect the Secretary to make a decision forthwith on an undertaking of this magnitude. Nevertheless, there could not be months of delay.

When Bill Chance entered Secretary Roth's office for the appointed meeting, he found the Secretary standing and looking out of the office window in apparently quiet contemplation. Then he turned partly toward Chance in acknowledgment of his presence.

"Come over here, Bill. I want to show you something." Chance walked over and joined the Secretary at the window.

"Look down there at the street, all of those people bustling in different directions; all of those automobiles being driven by people headed for jobs or whatever."

Chance looked down. Although it was still early in the morning, the street below was already busy with crowds.

The Secretary continued his observation. "All of those people are concerned with only their personal lives, their individual problems they may have at home or at work. They are seemingly totally oblivious of the enormous events that are developing in the world, especially in Europe, events that may very well change their lives forever. The President and a few of us here at State, you and I, for example, are responsible for their lives. It is a very great responsibility, a very great burden to bear. They depend on us to make decisions that are best for them and their way of life. They expect the government to have information that they don't have and to use that information wisely. And you know, Bill, I'm only human and I can make mistakes and if I make a wrong decision I am accountable to all these people, both here and throughout our country, if not the whole world. It is an awesome responsibility, wouldn't you say?"

"I agree with every word that you said," replied Chance. "But, I hope that you will pardon and forgive me if I express the opinion that your position requires you to make decisions regardless of the enormity of the problem. We are here to help you with information and studied recommendations, but the final decision is yours. As you know, I am sure, those decisions frequently must be made on the spot, so to speak, before events change and you lose control of them. I think it is our job, at least in the State Department, to try to control events rather than have events control us."

Chance regarded Roth intently to perceive any sign of resentment or of annoyance with what Chance knew could be considered by the Secretary as a blatant overstepping of the line between superior and inferior in the kind of advice Chance had just propounded. He saw none. In fact, Chance sensed that the Secretary was looking for that very sort of bolstering from a trusted employee in order to arise out of the persistent doldrums of equivocation in decision-making. It had occurred to Chance on other occasions that the Secretary was afraid to make a decision on a controversial issue. Chance now saw not only the opportunity, but also the need to prod the Secretary into action and his advice was given to lay the groundwork for his proposal on Stalin.

"Yes, Bill, you are quite right. I do not dispute what you say.

Decisions, however troublesome, must be made." The Secretary was speaking almost contritely. Roth went on, "I have always relied on prayer and on God to lead me to make right decisions. I cannot and would not change that. I believe that what I should do in any given situation will be duly revealed to me. It is my duty to listen and to wait for an answer. My mother instilled that in me and I know she was right."

Chance knew that if he argued that point with the Secretary, he would accomplish nothing. Instead, he said, "Yes, I agree, Mr. Secretary, that more spiritual inspiration such as yours is badly needed in government. I, too, have Christian principles and I firmly believe we should boldly confront those who would seek to destroy those principles in favor of atheistic materialism. If Marx and Engels were to prevail in this world, our freedoms and our way of life would be gone forever."

"You speak most eloquently, Bill. And now that we have had this conversation, what is it you wanted to see me about?"

With that question Chance inwardly cringed and he felt that he was facing the day of reckoning. But he knew that he had to be bold and assertive, straightforward and convincing and to demonstrate confidence in the rightness of what he was about to propose. He could not be hesitant.

Secretary Roth suggested an informal atmosphere by indicating that they sit down on a couple of comfortable leather chairs in a part of the room away from his desk where they could converse in a close and casual manner. To Chance, the Secretary appeared tired and subdued. Chance wondered whether the Secretary was becoming overwhelmed by the swirling events in Europe.

"Mr. Secretary," Chance began, "my Assistants and I have been giving close attention to information that has come across my desk in the past few weeks. We have evaluated this information and have concluded that Europe is on the brink of war and that, unless some specific action is taken very shortly to avoid it, we will have another World War on our hands and the United States may very well become involved whether we like it or not."

"Bill," said Secretary Roth, "I have been aware that we have been on the brink of war ever since Hitler's tanks rolled into Austria in March 1938. Aside from encouraging the competing parties to try to settle the issues peacefully, there is little or nothing I can do. The President simply does not want to get involved in a war, especially in Europe. He wants to avoid any entanglements. In view of that, my options are very limited if not nonexistent." Chance then remarked, "Doesn't the President know and understand that if war comes to Europe, the United States will not be able to stay out of it. How can he allow, for example, Europe to become Communistic? How could the United States possibly coexist with a system whose purpose is to destroy democratic capitalism? Chance sounded frustrated by a leader, the President, who could not see the reality of what he was facing.

"I know, I know," replied Secretary Roth. "The President thinks that if he could talk one-on-one with Hitler and Stalin that he could bring about peaceful solutions to the problems among governments in Europe. He believes he is a great persuader. But you and I know that will not happen. It's pure fantasy. Britain and France are so desperate for peace that they're willing to concede to all sorts of demands by Hitler. That Munich Agreement of Chamberlain's signed on September 30 last year isn't worth the paper it's written on. It allowed Hitler to annex the Czech Sudetenland without a shot being fired. And so Hitler will go on grabbing other parts of Europe. You know that and I know that. But what can I do?"

Chance saw the opening he needed. "Mr. Secretary, there is something we can do and I stress the "we." It is true that, at the moment, Hitler has taken the initiative in land grabs. Perhaps that is wrong. But my assistants and I have concluded from all the information we have that Stalin presents a far greater threat over the long term to our interests and the focus should be on him rather than Hitler."

"I don't understand," Secretary Roth said. "Stalin isn't giving us any trouble. It is Hitler who is on the move. What is it that you see that I don't see?"

"What I see," replied Chance, "is what many in the Department see, namely, that Stalin, a Communist, wants to control and rule the world, whereas Hitler, a Fascist, wants to control Europe. Hitler will accomplish this goal through military force if necessary; by taking over surrounding countries and maintaining control through military occupation. This type of expansion is clear cut, definite and easily and readily understood by everyone. There is nothing subtle about it. The need to occupy countries with German troops and German civilian administrators is a limiting factor on the extent of the expansion. There are, after all, just so many occupational forces that are available and can be supported. The Germans will not be able to trust the native peoples to enforce the control. Since we can see what Hitler is about, we can then make our own plans and moves accordingly and we can then deal with him in international relations."

"And Stalin?" Secretary Roth asked.

"Stalin's method of expansion will be quite different," continued Chance. "He will take over countries by subterfuge, by 'boring from within' as it were. Takeover by military force will be an exception. Instead Stalin will employ agents and fellow Communists in the country to be taken over. Strikes, protest movements, parades, and propaganda of all kinds will be used to cause a government to fall and to be supplanted by a sympathetic Communist group. The people in the subverted government will neither recognize nor understand what is happening until it is too late to do anything about it. This process of expansion of Communism will take far longer than a quick military takeover. But it will be far more efficient and durable over the long term. There will be no need for occupational forces that will limit expansion. Over the years, one country after another can be subverted in this manner. In the case of Hitler's occupational forces, the native peoples can hopefully and eventually rise up to cast out the occupiers. In the case of Stalin's system, the native peoples will not rise up against themselves. It is one thing to rise up against a foreign force. It is quite another to rise up against foreign ideas once they have taken a foothold in the native culture. I could go on, Mr. Secretary, and present other additional reasons for considering Stalin the greater menace, but you have, at least, my basic thoughts."

"You have made a remarkably articulate and well-reasoned argument for your proposition to focus on Stalin rather than Hitler, but you have not told me what I need to urgently know, that is, what must be done to avoid an imminent war. Do you have a recommendation and if you have, what is it?" The Secretary had been brought by Chance to the very point where he, Chance, wanted him to be. Chance was now ready to drive home the wedge of finality to the proposal.

"Mr. Secretary," Chance said, "if you agree that what I have just said is valid and sound and realistic, then I hope you will agree that the recommendation we in our Section propose will be considered as equally valid, sound and meritorious. We recommend that immediate steps be taken to plan and carry out the disposal of Stalin. Time is of the essence to do this."

"You mean 'assassination', don't you?" the considerably startled Secretary asked.

"Yes, probably," Chance replied forthrightly and determinedly.

"I would normally verbally spank you and send you out of the office with the observation that such a proposal is ridiculous, but since the recommendation comes from you and your capable Section people whom I respect for their and your professionalism and mature analyses of circumstances, I will give it serious consideration. You know, of course, Bill, that the United States government has, since time immemorial, taken the policy position that it will not become involved in assassinations of any head of any government. So, I don't know how you will get around that policy. I am, as Secretary of State and a member of the Cabinet, bound by the policy."

"Mr. Secretary," countered Chance, "I would not suggest and am not suggesting a violation of that policy. What I shall suggest is that we work clandestinely to get one or more people of another country to do the job, even some citizen of the Soviet Union itself, perhaps. To that extent you might say that we are involved, but such a policy, like any policy, ought to be sufficiently flexible to be adaptable to circumstances. Any policy ought to be subject to the higher policy of doing what is in the best interest of the United States. I am going to suggest that you send one of my assistants and me to our Embassy in Moscow, ostensibly on a trade mission, as soon as possible. No one is to be told of the true purpose of our visit so that there will be no information about our objective that will find its way to the wrong people and put us at risk. When we get to the Embassy, we shall reveal our true purpose only to the First Deputy Secretary at the Embassy and he will be sworn to secrecy. Consequently, the only individuals who will know about this will be you, my two assistants and I, and the First Deputy Secretary at the Embassy. Should, for any reason, our mission somehow be revealed to the Soviet government, our government will deny any knowledge of what we are doing except for the trade mission. You can be sure that we shall be very furtive in how we conduct ourselves. The plan for how we shall carry out our mission will depend upon the opportunities that will present themselves after we have been in Moscow for a time. Nothing is to be said to the President and to the Ambassador in Moscow about this. We shall stay at the Embassy as long as it takes to accomplish the mission or, of course, until we are called back by you."

The Secretary was silent for a few moments. Finally, he said, "Bill, I want to think about this for two or three days. I will then let you know of my decision. I'll want you to come back here when I do so. I suggest you bring your two assistants with you since they are already privy to the proposal. I know that you deem the matter urgent and I shall not delay the decision. The decision will be mine alone. Is this alright with you if we handle it in this manner?"

"Of course, Mr. Secretary," Chance replied. "I might add that once Stalin is disposed of, we would expect that his government will fall into disarray for lack of a leader. When that happens, a major threat to us and to Europe will have been summarily removed. I might also add that the President just recently said he hoped someone might assassinate Hitler and kill Mussolini. So, the policy against our government becoming involved in assassinations is apparently not altogether rigid."

"I understand," said Roth as he arose to signal an end to the meeting. "You will hear from me shortly. In the meantime, carry on."

As Chance was leaving the Secretary's office, he thought he detected a certain sadness in the countenance of the Secretary. Perhaps it was the realization that the anti-Christ was as prevalent in professed Christian countries as it was in Communist countries.

When Bill Chance returned to his own office he immediately had Charlene contact his assistants, Gene Wagner and Randy Stolz, to have them come to his office. When they arrived, Chance related to them his conversation with Secretary Roth.

"I expect absolute secrecy from both of you in this matter," he told them. "Nothing is to be said to anyone, not even your wives and close relatives, not even to your secretaries." Both Wagner and Stolz gave Chance their assurances of confidentiality.

"Should Roth decide to accept the proposal, have you decided which one of us is to accompany you?" inquired Wagner.

"No, I haven't given it any thought," replied Chance. "Either one of you is acceptable to me. Perhaps you should talk it over between you, if you wish. If not, then I'll talk with you about it when we receive the Secretary's decision if it is favorable."

When Wagner and Stolz had left the office, Chance leaned back in his chair, hands behind his head, and closed his eyes as if to screen out the other paperwork that lay on his desk and to focus solely on the discussion with Secretary Roth. Chance felt exhilarated. He had gotten through a difficult presentation to the Secretary. He felt he had done his best to convince the Secretary and that the Secretary had not rejected the proposal outright led Chance to conclude that there was hope for a favorable decision.

Then Chance's thoughts drifted to his family. If the Secretary decided to send him to Moscow for an indefinite time, what effect would this have on Melissa, his wife, and the children. Melissa was used to his occasional assignments away from home or even staying at the office over the weekends for urgent work. But this would be different, perhaps for several months. Bill Chance considered himself a family man, a husband and father who considered the interests of his family a priority. He asked himself why he was concerning himself with whether there would be a war in Europe. Why couldn't he be like other people concerned about their immediate personal needs with little else but curiosity about Hitler ranting and raving about the wrongs imposed on Germany by the Versailles Treaty at the end of World War I or about Stalin's massive purges of the Russian population. The world would little know or thank him for his sacrifices of family and risks of his own life and career.

Bill Chance thought he knew himself and he knew that his responsibilities to his family included his responsibilities to the community, in this case, the United States and Europe. He understood that the kind of world his children would inherit depended, in a great measure, how he, their parent, met his responsibilities to the community both in a large and small sense. He recognized that in his position at the State Department he had the opportunity to influence world community events, an opportunity that the people on the street did not have. He knew he could not be like some of the street people because, inherently, he had concerns and caring beyond his own personal needs.

Although he tried to remain calm, the next few days were agonizing emotionally for Bill Chance. Waiting for the decision from Secretary Roth, Chance found it difficult to concentrate and give attention to his other work. Three days, four days and then a week passed and he had not heard from the Secretary. Finally, on the eleventh day, word came from the Secretary that he wanted to meet with Chance and his assistants.

Charlene signaled her boss on the intercom. "Madeline called and said the Secretary wants to see you, Gene and Randy at 1:30 this afternoon. We are to let him know only if there is some reason you cannot make it."

"No, we'll be there. Call Gene and Randy and alert them and tell them to be in my office at 1:00."

Chance concluded that the decision of the Secretary must be favorable else he would not have asked that Gene and Randy also come along. Instead of feeling ecstatic about this, Chance became apprehensive. He was shortly to receive the most important assignment of his career and he hadn't the slightest idea of how he was going to carry it out. Nothing like this had been ventured before. There was, at least at the moment, no one to turn to for suggestions or for any kind of help. The Intelligence Department was, to a large extent, ineffective and didn't have a good handle on Soviet inner workings or have agents within the Soviet government who could be of some help. Chance knew this from his frequent contacts with the Intelligence people. One of them had told Chance some time back, "Hell, we don't get enough money from Congress to run our operation except to shuffle papers around." At any rate, he could not talk about it to anyone; the more people who knew about the project, the more risk that it would be revealed to the wrong individuals. Chance was aware that he was on his own.

He had Charlene bring him a sandwich and coffee for a quick lunch. At 1:00 Gene and Randy came in and sat down opposite Chance at his desk.

"Did you get some news?" Randy asked.

"Yeah, the Secretary wants all of us to meet him at his office in a half hour. The fact that he asked for you to be included leads me to believe we'll get a favorable decision and we'll be on our way."

Neither Randy nor Gene looked to be enthusiastic.

"In case the decision is favorable, have you two talked about who will be going?"

Wagner spoke up, "We talked about it a bit, but came to the conclusion that you should make the selection. Now that reality has set in and we're faced with a possibly long stay away from our families, neither of us is as enthusiastic about the idea as we were when the idea first came up. However, either of us will do our job and do it as well as we can, as always." Stolz shook his head in agreement.

"I understand how you feel because I feel the same way, but we'll have to look at this as another assignment that is part of our work here."

"Geez," Stolz exclaimed, "part of our work! We don't assassinate people every week!" His voice sounded sarcastic.

They all laughed at the obvious truth. "Yeah, you're right, Randy," Chance said. He accepted Stolz's remark graciously.

"Anyway, I've got to let the Secretary know who will be going with me in case there is a favorable decision." Chance looked at Wagner and Stolz to see what reactions they showed. He had a good-natured smile on his face as if enjoying the suspense being felt by his assistants.

"Well, to come to the point, I'm leaning toward Gene to go and the reason is that Gene is more fluent in the Russian language. I think both of you will acknowledge that."

Wagner swallowed hard, but showed no signs of emotion one way or another.

Chance continued, "Gene, if there is some substantial reason that you cannot go, such as health problems either with you or someone in the family, or if there is some other personal problem, please speak up and be candid about it. I don't want you to be overseas operating under anxiety and stress except what is normal under the circumstances."

"No, there is no real reason that I cannot go. Of course, my wife and family are not going to be dancing with joy about it, but they'll take it in their stride, I'm sure. How long do you think we'll be gone, just as a guess?"

"It could go to June, about four months. If we can't get the job done by then, I'd say that it can't be done and we might as well pack up and return."

Wagner nodded acceptance.

"Well," Chance said, "I guess we should be on our way to see the Secretary. It's almost one thirty.

There was silence as the three proceeded to the Secretary's office. The gravity of what was before them did not allow for small talk or the usual bantering.

Madeline, Roth's secretary, was not aware of the proposed project and the reason for the serious expressions on the faces of Chance and his assistants.

"Oh," she said in jest, "I see the three of you just came from the undertaker's convention."

"Yes, Madeline," countered Chance, "we need a fourth pallbearer for the State Department and we thought we'd ask you!"

Madeline, in good humor, repressed her laugh at Chance's rejoinder and gave Chance, instead, a mock killing look.

"The Secretary is on the telephone and he'll be with you as soon as he finishes, which may be an hour. In the meantime, you all can sit and relax." Madeline's banter helped somewhat to relieve the tension of Chance and his assistants.

They had hardly sat down when Roth's telephone line light on Madeline's desk went off indicating he had completed his call. Madeline arose, knocked on the Secretary's door, entered and announced that Chance and the others were waiting.

"Have them come in," they heard the Secretary say.

"Good morning, Mr. Secretary." The three spoke almost in unison.

"Good morning, gentlemen," and Roth indicated the chairs on the other side of his desk for them to sit down.

"Well, I think you know why you are all here." Roth wasted no time in getting to the subject. His mien was as serious as was those sitting before him. Addressing Wagner and Stolz, Roth said, "Am I correct in assuming that Bill has gone over with you the gist of what he and I talked about at our meeting a week ago?" Both Wagner and Stolz nodded and replied, "Yes." Chance chimed in with, "Yes, I have."

Roth continued, "My decision is to approve your proposal, but on certain conditions which I shall outline to you. There will be nothing in writing and you are to make no notes either now or at any time. Everything about this mission will be verbal and committed to memory. That is the first absolute requirement. The second requirement is that no one and I stress, 'no one', is to be told about this and the knowledge about the project is to be confined to me, to the three of you and, when you arrive in Moscow, to the First Deputy at the embassy. If there is any leak in the information, it won't be difficult to trace its origin. I might add that I have spoken to the President about this project. When Bill and I last met, we mentioned not telling the President about it. However, after thinking it over, I decided that a mission such as this was too fraught with ramifications that I could not undertake a decision on my own without discussing it with the President."

Roth continued, "The President was quite surprised by my presentation to him. His reaction at first was the same as mine had been when Bill proposed the project to me; that is, that the real threat was Hitler and not Stalin and that Stalin could be a counterweight to Hitler's expansion efforts. However, when I related Bill's analysis of Stalin and the Soviet's objectives, the President seemed convinced. However, he did not say 'yes' or 'no' to the mission; that is, he did not approve or reject it. He said he wanted me to make the decision, but that he did not want any United States official or citizen to be directly involved. By that, I assume he meant that our part would be confined to facilitating information to foreign sources willing to carry out the liquidation of Stalin. I certainly subscribe to that limitation. I think we can count on the President to keep this confidential. In fact, I got the impression that the President will put the whole matter out of his mind as if it was never discussed with him. I shall desist from any further mention of the matter to him. So the decision was mine to make and I have made it. Now, is there any question so far?"

Roth looked at the three men for a few moments. They all shook their heads indicating they had no questions. Roth then proceeded.

"I want to outline the conditions on which my approval is based. If you have any questions as I go through them, stop me and raise the question as I proceed rather than wait until the end of my instructions. First, let me ask who will be accompanying you, Bill?"

"Gene will. He speaks Russian more fluently than Randy. Randy will remain and will run our Section while we are gone."

"Fine. Now the first condition is that at all times this is to be considered a trade mission. You will talk and act to promote this impression with everyone you contact or deal with. I talked with Pat Lonergan over at Commerce about using you for a trade mission and he jumped at the idea immediately. His budget is such that he can't send people all over to carry out trade negotiations. He will draft some proposals for you to negotiate in Moscow and, perhaps, in other areas of the Soviets. He will give you the names of the trade people in the Soviet to contact to discuss negotiations. Pat doesn't know what your real mission is. I did not tell him a thing about that."

"Will we have a chance to sit down with Pat or someone at Commerce to get an idea of how he wants us to proceed?" asked Bill Chance.

"Yes, I'll arrange a time for you and let you know."

"The second condition is that you shall absolutely not get directly involved in the disposal, if you know what I mean. That is, you will not do the disposing. You must work through foreign sources. That is, through a Soviet citizen or an agent of another country. You know which countries are likely targets of Russian expansion and of Russian threats. Those are the countries' agents you can work through. However, you are to be very cautious and very circumspect about whom you deal with. You cannot be too careful. That is something I cannot instruct you on. You will have to exercise your sixth sense on each occasion that arises and seems to offer an opportunity to advance your mission."

Roth paused for a few moments for any questions. There were none. He continued.

"The third condition is along somewhat the same lines. You are not to fraternize. By that I mean you are not to get involved on an intimate, personal relationship with any women, Russian or other foreign agents or our own embassy staff. I do not mean you cannot socialize in a non-intimate way. You can still have a pleasant time in your social relations, but keep it at arms length. What I am saying, in effect, is that your conduct must be such that you will never allow yourself to be in a position which may compromise our country, your integrity and the project itself." Secretary Roth paused again and scanned the faces of Chance and Wagner.

"Need I say anything further on that rule?"

Wagner spoke up. "Mr. Secretary, since our mission is to obtain and dispense information, I have heard that often excellent information can be obtained through developing intimacies with the right persons. Are you saying that we should avoid that method even though we would do it in the sole interest of the United States and for no other reason?"

Roth, ever straight-laced, looked at Wagner sternly and unsmilingly.

"Mr. Wagner, I suggest you ask your wife that question! If anyone feels that being deprived of sex for a few months is something that he can't handle, then perhaps he is not the right person for this assignment."

Wagner felt himself cringing in his chair. He realized he had spoken out of turn and had used poor judgment in raising the question. He sat silently suffering at the Secretary's sharp rebuke. He glanced at Chance and saw immediately that his boss was embarrassed and agonizing over the incident.

"Let me go on," Roth continued. He appeared disturbed and annoyed by Wagner's question and his attitude had lost its warm and friendly expression.

"You should be aware that the NKVD might try to bribe you to reveal information to them that they should not have. They may even try to recruit you to work as an agent for them while employed by us. If you allow yourself to be subverted and we discover it, you know the personal consequences for you will be severe legal punishment. Now, in all that I am saying here concerning my outlining the rules, please understand that I am not assuming you are weak men who cannot be trusted with a very important mission. If I did not trust your judgment, you would not be here this morning. I feel it is a necessity to rehearse the rules for this mission. The rules are few and simple. Since this is a mission without precedent, I have to leave you pretty much on your own."

Roth continued. "In your reports to me, you are always to couch them in trade negotiation terms. For example, 'trade negotiations proceeding slowly' or 'trade negotiations have reached a stalemate', or 'trade talks are proceeding satisfactorily', or since you will be engaged in some legitimate trade talks, then to distinguish between the legitimate and the clandestine, use the words, 'instruct Commerce trade negotiations are etc., etc.' I shall know that, 'instruct Commerce' means the legitimate."

Roth again stopped speaking as if for further questions. There were understandably none.

"I want to add that your personal welfare is paramount to me and to the Department. If you get into a tight or dangerous situation, for example, if you are arrested or even accused of improper or unacceptable conduct by the Soviet authorities, we shall abort the mission and, while we shall deny your clandestine actions or deny knowledge of them, we shall do whatever is necessary to get you back here safely. We are not going to abandon you. If such an event should occur, the Deputy will inform us and the full pressure of the United States government will be brought to bear on the Soviet government."

"Now, can you leave in about two weeks? That should give you enough time to make your personal preparations and give time to you, Bill, to arrange to temporarily turn over the Section operation to Randy during your absence. You will meet with Pat Lonergan at Commerce and we will have an additional conference before you leave. We'll take care of all the travel arrangements through our Transportation Section. You are relieved of your usual duties commencing tomorrow morning. If you have any questions, please call me directly. So I guess that is about all at this time. You're now on your way." The Secretary arose and shook hands with the three men. His warm and friendly manner had returned and he showed that he was genuinely interested in the success of the mission assignment.

As the three walked back to Chance's office, Wagner remarked, "I really goofed in there today, damn it."

Stolz, who hadn't said a word during the entire meeting rubbed it in on Wagner. "Yup. That wasn't your brightest moment, Gene!" Stolz laughed at Wagner's discomfort.

"Hey, listen," Wagner retorted, "you're staying at home. You can afford to laugh, you sonofagun. Now I know I should have tried to flunk that course I took in Russian instead of breaking my back to get an 'A'."

"Aw, come on, Gene," interceded Chance. "It's not going to be bad. It'll be a great adventure you can tell your grandkids about."

"Yeah, if I come out of it alive."

Still ribbing Wagner, Stolz said, "I wonder what Siberia is like. Ha, ha!"

"O.K., Randy, break it off," Chance remonstrated thinking the joking would get out of hand.

"For today, I think we should take care of clearing up as much as possible of the unfinished business on our desks and, then, tomorrow morning we'll sit down in my office and think through what has to be done in preparation for the changeover. Let's count on 10:00 a.m. in my office. In the meantime, how you break the news to your families is up to you. Knowing your families, I'm sure there won't be any hysterics. See you tomorrow, but you can call me before that if you have to."

Chance entered his office while Wagner and Stolz proceeded to theirs.

Randy put his hand on Gene's shoulder assuringly. "Actually, Gene, I would not have minded going. In fact, I sort of envy you. It'll be exciting and I'll back you all the way. There may be some things my wife and I can do for your family while you're gone. We'll be in close touch with them and see that they're taken care of and okay. Don't worry about them."

"Thanks, Randy, I appreciate that."

After dinner that evening and when the kids were in their rooms, Bill Chance broke the news about the trade mission to Melissa. He said nothing about the Stalin project. He had agreed that there was to be no talk about it to anyone except the few who were or would be in on the plan.

"It seems like an awfully long time away for just a trade mission," Melissa said, her face clearly reflecting her concern and displeasure.

"Yes," agreed Bill, "normally it would be, but this is a special mission because events that are shaping up indicate a war in Europe could break out at any time." He went on to fabricate a credible story for Melissa. "In view of that, the Secretary and the Commerce Department felt that we had to negotiate certain trade arrangements ahead of time in case that happened. Since events are changing quite rapidly, we will have to be constantly changing those arrangements and receiving new instructions from the Department on how to proceed. The State Department is involved because the mission is not solely economic, but requires a background of foreign policy information on our part in addition."

"Well, I guess so. Besides there is nothing I can do about it anyway," said Melissa in an air of quiet, resigned nonacceptance of the whole idea of an extended absence.

"It's all part of the job," added Bill. "I expected this sort of thing when I took the job. But, please, there is no need for you to worry. I'll be alright. Time will pass quickly."

"If your stay depends on the constantly changing circumstances, then you could be overseas forever or, perhaps, until a war starts."

"No, there will be a time that we can stabilize the trade arrangements to be flexible enough to adapt to changes and when that point is reached, we'll be home. True, it's somewhat indefinite, but that point should not take too long to reach, probably a little longer in Russia since they're unpredictable hard bargainers."

Fortunately for Bill, Melissa did not refer to his earlier discussion with her about assassinations; probably having dismissed it as unrealistic and something the State Department wouldn't go for, anyway. Furthermore, she trusted Bill to tell her if it did come to pass.

As he sat with Melissa and talked about his going away, Chance experienced a deep sense of guilt in not telling his wife the truth about the mission. They had not kept anything from each other in all the time they knew each other. When Melissa found out, as she would eventually, that, in fact, he had lied to her, would she ever trust him again. Would she respect him as she did now. A part truth is also a part lie, Chance thought.

By not revealing the truth about the mission, Chance knew he was saying that he could not trust Melissa to keep a confidence. He knew better. He knew he could trust Melissa completely, yet he had agreed with Secretary Roth that he would reveal nothing even to his wife. Chance was in a terrible dilemma. He felt trapped. His mind was racing in a panic with all sorts of flash thoughts. Was his country more important than his marriage? He loved Melissa deeply, passionately, and unreservedly. He would give his life for her in a moment if necessary. His love for country was abstract. It was patriotism and loyalty and a remote sense of appreciation for the principles America stood for, hardly the same thing he felt for Melissa.

Chance wondered what Gene Wagner was going through. How was Gene handling the situation with his wife? He remembered that he and Gene had failed to talk about and agree on the story they would tell their wives. If their wives got together, as they did frequently, and compared what their husbands told them of the mission, the wives might know immediately that there was something going on that they were not supposed to know about. And that included Randy Stolz, too. He'd have to talk to them both in the morning.

Then Chance began to rationalize. What he was doing or about to do on this mission was, after all, for the good of his family, for their protection, for the preservation of his kids right to freedom to live in a democratic America. If he didn't tell Melissa the whole truth, it was because he loved her so much that he was willing to jeopardize his life so that she would not have to experience the horrors that many women in Europe had and would experience under the rule of dictators. Surely, Melissa would see his motives and understand.

"We'll talk to the kids tomorrow," Chance said. "In the meantime, let's sleep on it. We're pretty tired now, both of us, and things always appear worse when we're tired."

Melissa said nothing, but nodded in agreement. Neither slept well that night.

When Chance arrived at the office the next morning, he immediately had Wagner and Stolz come into his office.

"Well, fellows, how did things go last night when you broke the new to the wives?"

"I didn't discuss it at all with Ann," Gene Wagner replied. "Ann was out to a woman's club meeting and got home late. I didn't think it was the time to talk about it. I'll break it to her this evening."

Chance felt immense relief upon hearing this.

"What about you, Randy?"

"Likewise. I didn't mention it to Grace. I realized that we hadn't talked about what we were to tell our families and I thought we ought to decide on that. I was going to take that up with you this morning."

"You're absolutely right. It would have been terrible if there were three different explanations of the mission."

Chance then recited what he had told Melissa. When he had finished, Wagner and Stolz agreed that the explanation was credible and that they would use it at their respective homes.

Chance was candid and forthright. He went on to describe his own feelings when he had talked with Melissa and how he had rationalized the matter. He had known Gene and Randy for years and was close to them. He felt he could confide his personal feelings to them. He also wanted to prepare them for what might be similar feelings on their part.

The next two weeks were hectic in making preparations for the departure and the changeover in the Section. Several meetings with Roth and with Lonergan in Commerce were held. Lonergan gave Chance the items to be negotiated and a list of the Soviet trade representatives.

"What do you know about any of these Russian trade representatives?" Chance asked Pat Lonergan offhandedly. He thought he might as well start getting information about the contacts he might need.

"Well, a couple of them have been in the business for a number of years and are probably more flexible in negotiations than the younger ones who feel they have to impress their bosses with tough bargaining. The older representatives are wise to the give and take and know when to stand firm and when to yield. You might want to look up those two fellows. Their names are on the list I gave you. David Kandelaki and Eugeny Babarin. Kandelaki was chief of the Soviet trade delegation in Berlin in 1935. He is back in Moscow now, as far as we know. Babarin has been on a number of trade delegations. Both are still doing trade commission work. I believe you'll find you can do business with them."

"Are they loyal to Stalin?"

"I can't tell you. I've seen nothing to the contrary. The reports we get from our delegations have never mentioned it."

At one of the meetings with Secretary Roth, Roth relented somewhat on the rules he had propounded earlier. He told Chance and Wagner, "I've rethought what I have told you. I think I have been too restrictive in placing parameters on your mission operation. Instead of limiting you to providing information to those who may carry out the removal of Stalin, I have decided that, short of performing the removal yourselves, you are to do whatever is necessary to help bring about a successful result. The other rules, however, still apply such as fraternizing, keeping the operation secret and seeing that your conduct does not compromise the project, yourselves, and the United States. So, in effect, do what you have to do."

"Thanks, Mr. Secretary," said Chance, "that does help us. We were wondering how we could accomplish the objective with the restrictions placed on us. You can be sure that we shall use our best judgment."

"Although every foreign official is under surveillance by the GPU, there is less suspicion of United States representatives, especially since Roosevelt signed the Neutrality Act in May 1937. Consequently," Roth added, "you can move around more freely than some of the representatives of other countries. However, you will have to be very cautious."

"Yes, we know," acknowledged Chance.

As Chance and Wagner walked from the Secretary's office, Wagner remarked, "I feel a lot better about the mission now that he has loosened the reins on us. I think we can operate more efficiently."

"Yes, but you still can't sleep with the enemy," Chance ribbed Wagner hearkening back to Wagner's remark at the earlier meeting with Roth.

"Ok, ok," Wagner replied good-naturedly.

During the preparations for the departure of Chance and Wagner, several reports came across Chance's desk, (now Stolz's desk) concerning serious talks about possible German-Soviet commercial negotiations that might lead to political rapprochement between the two countries.

The reports from the American Embassy in Moscow indicated that Stalin was convinced that Britain and France would continue their desperate policies of appeasement of Hitler's expansion in Europe. Stalin, it was reported, wanted to assure himself that he would be safe from a German invasion of Russia if there was no restraint on Hitler by British and French action. Furthermore, Stalin might want to have an agreement with Hitler to divide up Europe.

These reports, especially those hinting at the breakup and division of Europe, made the mission of Chance and Wagner all the more urgent.

Chance was right. Hitler was limited in his expansion and could possibly be evicted by local forces over the next few years after occupation of countries by his troops. But, if Stalin acquired any countries, like the Baltic States and part of Poland, he would be in them permanently. Stalin must be stopped. United States long-term interests were at stake

CHAPTER3

Vladimir Kovalenko sat on the plush sofa in the small, ornate reception room of the United States Embassy building near the center of Moscow. He was so obviously nervous that the receptionist, Helen Morgan, later remarked to her boss that Kovalenko seemed almost in a panic. His eyes seemed to blink uncontrollably, his hands on his lap clasping and unclasping continuously with one hand frequently lifting to rub his face, and one foot tapping in a tense, quick rhythm. In fact, Helen Morgan was becoming nervous herself just from occasional glances at the man in his emotional state. She hoped that the First Deputy Secretary would soon call her to send the visitor into the Deputy's office. Kovalenko had been waiting almost a half hour. The wait did nothing to relieve his anxiety.

Vladimir Kovalenko had contacted the Embassy through a source that could not be revealed until Kovalenko thought it safe to do so. The source had talked anonymously on the telephone to First Deputy Secretary Fraser Addison and arranged an appointment at a date and time certain at the Embassy.

The source, a female voice on the telephone had said, "It will be of benefit to you and your government to see this man. He has much to tell you about his government."

Addison asked the caller, "Who is this speaking?"

"I cannot tell you," the source replied, "and it is not important who I am."

"What is the man's name?" Addison inquired.

"I cannot tell you that either," said the source, "but he will use the code word 'Koba 2!'. You will please inform your guards at the gate of this so that this man can be passed through."

Addison immediately recognized the name "Koba" as one used by Stalin for years and by his intimates as an affectionate name for the ruler. Addison surmised "Koba 2" must be someone close to Stalin.

The Deputy Secretary advised the anonymous caller that regardless of the use of a code name, the person for whom the caller spoke would have to be searched at the Embassy gate.

Addison also told the caller that he, Addison, would have to take the matter up with the Ambassador as he was sure that the Ambassador would not want to do anything to antagonize the Soviet government.

"Will you call back in a day or two and I'll let you know?" Addison told the caller.

"I cannot call back. I'm risking my life right now, as it is. Either you accept now and arrange an appointment or the whole thing is off. There will be no further contact." The caller sounded annoyed.

Secretary Addison thought a moment. Perhaps the man had something of importance to inform the U.S. government. Perhaps he should take the risk, assume personal responsibility. Later, if the Ambassador would not agree, he (Addison) could instruct the guards at the gate to deny entrance to the man.

Addison advised the caller that he agreed to see the man. It was suggested that the man arrive at the Embassy two days hence in the morning. It would then be March 6, 1939.

*****

So many thoughts were rushing through Kovalenko's mind as he sat and waited. The same thoughts he had had on the way to the Embassy and even before. Thoughts that arose out of fear, anxiety, and concern. Thoughts that had one recurring theme: Am I doing the right thing? Am I a traitor? What will happen to my dear wife and my child? Will the Ambassador believe me? Will what I have to say be of value to the United States government? Will they give me asylum? Did the NKVD know I was coming here and did they follow me? Poor "Nitchka." Did they pick up her call to the Embassy? Will she be arrested? Was I really on Yezhov's list for arrest and trial? Could Stalin possibly suspect me of disloyalty to him? What have I done to make him suspicious if he is? Was I too hasty in deciding to come here to the Embassy? If they don't give me asylum, I'm a dead man! And his family and Nitchka will also be arrested and probably tortured.

The last two answers were the only ones of which he was certain. Kovalenko had no answers to all the others. He would, perhaps, get some answers when he spoke with the Deputy Secretary. He was in such a state of mind that he was both hopeful and despairing at the same time about the outcome of his meeting.

Helen Morgan answered the buzzer on her desk telephone. She turned to Kovalenko.

"The Secretary will see you now, Mr. Kovalenko." She arose and led the way down the corridor to the large, paneled door that opened to the Deputy Secretary's office.

"Mr. Secretary, this is Vladimir Kovalenko." Helen then left.

"Sit down, Mr. Kovalenko. My secretary, Helen, tells me you speak English, probably far better than I speak Russian." Deputy Secretary Addison smiled warmly and, trying to put Kovalenko at ease, asked, "Can I give you a cup of coffee?"

"Yes, I would like that. It has been some time …" Kovalenko did not finish his sentence, as he knew the Secretary was probably aware that coffee was in short supply in the Soviets. The Secretary personally served the coffee to Kovalenko from a hot plate nearby in a further effort to create an informal, friendly atmosphere. As a result, Kovalenko could feel himself beginning to relax a bit.

Secretary Addison began the more serious conversation. "I have talked with the Ambassador and I have received his approval to have you visit here and to discuss whatever it is you wish to say. The Ambassador, nevertheless, wants it understood that the United States government will not, at this time, make any commitment to you as a result of our discussion."

Kovalenko's heart sank. The tension and fear within him returned like a large ocean wave suddenly rising up and pounding the shore. Kovalenko implied from this that he would not be given asylum if and when he requested. He decided to speak out and to lay his cards on the table forthwith.

"Mr. Secretary, in order for us to have a basis for our discussion, I want to disclose to you at the beginning why I am here in the first place.

If you can agree with my conditions, then we can proceed further. If not, then there is little point in my continuing to take your time."

"Well, Mr. Kovalenko, tell me what those conditions are and then I can, perhaps, give you my response," replied Addison.

"Good," Kovalenko exclaimed.

"First," Kovalenko began, "I want to explain that I have been a personal secretary to Stalin for many years and, because I have some knowledge of languages, I have also served as an interpreter and translator when the occasions arose. My family and I have always been loyal supporters of Stalin. We have never given him any cause to doubt that."

Kovalenko, though still considerably tense, continued, "I was born in 1895 and in 1915, when I was 20 years old, I joined the Party under Lenin. I became active immediately and when Stalin entered the picture, I supported him unequivocally. I knew when I first met him that he was destined to become a great leader in the mission to establish communism in our country. I was not wrong in that observation. You can see for yourself."

Secretary Addison nodded affirmatively.

Kovalenko continued on, "As Stalin grew in the Party hierarchy, so did I. Finally, eight years ago, Stalin made me his personal secretary and office translator. I also had other duties, but I won't describe them at this time. It's not important.

"I saw Stalin daily for these many years. He even insisted that I come with him to Sochi, his vacation spot in the Caucasus. He told me many things that he told no one else, about his boyhood, his early years, his first run-ins with the Tsar's police, his first marriage and so on. In a sense, I was his confidant, perhaps his sounding board, perhaps, also, someone who would listen and to whom he could unburden himself."

The Deputy Secretary began to wonder what all this recitation had to do with why his visitor had come to the Embassy. As if sensing this thought in the Secretary, Kovalenko then said, "I am now in fear of my life and I fear for my family, my wife and child. I have described my relationship to Stalin because it describes similar experiences of hundreds of others who have been Stalin's loyal supporters. They have been arrested, tried and either executed or sent to labor camps. They have all been as innocent as I am of any wrongdoing or of plotting against Stalin. I have known many of these poor souls."

"How do you know that you are being targeted for arrest?" queried Secretary Addison.

"I have a lady friend who works in the NKVD office who told me confidentially that she saw a file on me that had been left by an agent on a nearby desk and there was a note attached signed by Nikolai Yezhov that I was to be investigated for possible charges of spying for foreign interests."

"Yezhov is the head of the NKVD, the State Police, is that correct?" asked Addison.

"Yes, that is so."

"And was the lady in the NKVD who informed you, the same one who called here on your behalf?," asked Secretary Addison.

"I would rather not tell you that. It's a matter of protecting her," replied Kovalenko. "I am very concerned for her safety."

"In any case," continued Kovalenko, "because of my close association with Stalin, I have a great deal of information about him and his plans that is not known to others. It is information that I believe will be of interest to the United States. However, in exchange for this information, I am requesting asylum in your embassy. I am also requesting it for my family if they are still free to move about. If we cannot be granted asylum, then there is little reason for me to give you this information. Frankly, Mr. Secretary, I am using my personal knowledge of Stalin as a bargaining tool for the safety of my family and me."

"There are hundreds of Russians out there who are being arrested who would like to come here and have us grant asylum," pointed out Addison.

Addison then added, "I am sure that you recognize that we don't have facilities here at the Embassy to take in all those people, even though we might like to."

"I understand," Kovalenko replied, "but none of those people have the knowledge of Stalin and his plans that I have. That is the difference."

"You've caught me by surprise, Mr. Kovalenko. I did not suspect that you were going to ask for asylum for yourself and your family.

Consequently, I have not discussed that with the Ambassador. I will have to present that to him. I cannot make that decision on my own."

Secretary Addison could see that Kovalenko was becoming agitated again. The delay on the matter of asylum was cause for his consternation.

Kovalenko, his voice evidencing the strain, asked, "When can there be a decision?"

Replied Addison, "I will take it up with the Ambassador in the morning. That is the earliest. He is not here now. By the way, how do you expect to get your wife and child here?"

"I have arranged with an old and trusted friend who will see that she gets here. I cannot tell you more than that. If I do not return to our apartment this evening, that will be the signal for my friend and family to leave the apartment by noon tomorrow and come here. I have asked for a couple of days off from my work at the Kremlin and that will help to make it less suspicious."

"But you said you were under investigation. You and your family movements may already be under surveillance," said Addison.

"That may be true," answered Kovalenko, "but that is the risk that we take. We are living in a very dangerous time. Too many individuals think that they are safe, that nothing will happen to them. These people believe that because they have done nothing wrong, nothing to offend the authorities, that the NKVD will ignore them. They delude themselves. The NKVD has to please Stalin; and the NKVD knows that only seeing long lists of people who are considered 'enemies of the state' who are to be disposed of pleases Stalin. Stalin gets those lists almost daily and goes over them meticulously. He removes very few names. On the other hand, there are those who, like me and my friends, realize that we are doomed in any case and our arrests are only a matter of time. We believe that we should do what we can to let the world know what inhuman, monstrous practices are going on here in the Soviets."

While Kovalenko was talking, Secretary Addison was studying the man. Was Kovalenko sincere? Was he perhaps a "plant" by the Soviet government to embarrass the United States? Could he be a mere imposter seeking a safe haven? Was the information he would bring factual or fabrication? Addison felt unsure of any preliminary judgment he might make of the man who sat before him.

Vladimir Kovalenko was a heavyset person of about five feet eleven. He had the appearance overall of having come from a peasant or lower-working class stock: a broad, round face, heavy jaws, puggish nose, large blue eyes overhung by bushy eyebrows and a thick head of hair with beginnings of speckled gray scattered throughout. Addison noticed that Kovalenko's hands were large and beefy, reminding the Secretary of a blacksmith he had known as a boy growing up in Red Granite, Wisconsin.

Addison found a certain fascination with the deep, basso profundo voice of Kovalenko. Whenever Addison had occasion to hear the male bass singers at the operas or at classical music presentations, the sound would send tremors through him. Those voices sounded with such force as if to say, "I am invulnerable, don't trifle with me." Addison had always secretly wished that he had such a voice.

Secretary Addison addressed Kovalenko. "You have taken it upon yourself to assume that our Embassy will take you, your wife and child in and keep you here indefinitely." Addison's voice sounded annoyed and scolding. "By doing so you have put yourself and us in a very precarious position."

The Secretary went on, "I'll tell you what we shall do. We'll have you stay here overnight. I'll discuss this with the Ambassador either later this evening when he returns or early tomorrow morning. If he decides against granting you asylum, then you will leave here immediately and see to it that your family and friend do not come here. If the Ambassador decides to grant you asylum, then you must understand that it does not obligate us to keep you for any length of time and that it can be revoked by us, if we decide to do so, at any time.

"In the meantime, I'll have one of my orderlies show you to a room which you can occupy. Then, in about an hour, I'd like you to return here so that we can talk a bit more.

"There are a few rules and conditions we ask that you abide by: you are to make no telephone calls; you are not to go outside of the building and you are to keep the drapes over the room windows drawn shut; we prefer you talk with our staff as little as possible and certainly do not mention why you are here. When you are not in my office or at meals, you are to remain in your room."

Kovalenko nodded in assent. "I understand. Thank you for your patience and consideration. I understand all this that you are doing."

The Secretary pressed a button on his desk and, shortly thereafter, a male orderly appeared to guide Kovalenko to his room.

After Kovalenko had left, Secretary Addison swiveled his chair toward the large window overlooking the Embassy courtyard. Deep in troubled thought he wondered if he had done the right thing in allowing the visitor to stay even overnight. The Ambassador, fortunately, left the decision making to his Deputy Secretary whenever the Ambassador was gone from the Embassy compound. There were occasions, however, when Addison felt that the Ambassador should make a final decision. The matter of this Kovalenko was in a sort of gray area for decision-making. He, Addison, had made the decision to allow Kovalenko to stay at the Embassy overnight. However, he had made no decision as to asylum.

Addison felt that he could not let Kovalenko get away. The man just might have important information of interest to the United States government. Addison reasoned that Kovalenko could be sent away tomorrow, but he could not be brought back once gone. The more he thought about it, the more Addison became convinced that he had made the right decision.

Addison pressed the buzzer button on his desk for Helen. "Helen, will you leave a note for the Ambassador stating that it is important for me to see him as soon as possible. He'll probably be back the latter part of the evening."

Kovalenko looked around the second floor room that had been assigned to him. Through the floor to ceiling window he could see the street and the guard gate. Two soldiers with carbines stood guard. As instructed, Kovalenko drew the heavy drapes closed. Turning on the one table lamp to give light, Kovalenko saw that the room was plain but comfortably outfitted with a bed, sofa chairs, end tables and a dresser. A small bathroom was set off at one end of the room. There were a half-dozen American magazine publications in a magazine rack next to one of the two sofa chairs. A telephone and telephone book lay on top of one of the end tables. Pulling open the drawers of the dresser, he observed some blank stationery and a couple of pencils, a deck of playing cards and a list of the extension numbers to various personnel in the Embassy.

Kovalenko placed his coat over a sofa chair, took off his boots and lay down on the bed. Staring up at the ceiling, he thought of his wife, his son Alexi, Nitchka, his old friend and of the people at his office in the Kremlin. For some reason, he gave only a fleeting thought to the "Boss," Stalin. Now that, for the moment at least, he was in the American Embassy, Stalin seemed so distant, so remote, and so less powerful.

Kovalenko's concern was no longer for his country, for the promotion and expansion of Communism, or for loyalty to Stalin. These had all very suddenly become irrelevant in the face of a certain challenge to his personal survival and that of his family and a few close friends. The enthusiasm and the emotional intensity with which for years he had fought for the ideology of Lenin and the conceptual objectives of the Party were gone.

Kovalenko now understood how all the sophisticated rules and all the cultural refinements and niceties that man had developed over millenniums for living in an orderly, organized civil society yielded to the powerful primitive instincts for survival when an individual is cornered in a life threatening circumstance. At that moment, man reverts to the level of all animal creatures. But, he mused, as in all animals there are differences. When cornered, some sought to flee, some were passive and, though fearful, stood and waited to be killed. Others charged out of their corners fighting savagely. Similarly, these differences found expression in humans. Kovalenko did not dwell on why this is so.

While thus musing, Kovalenko had dozed off in a troubled, superficial sleep. He was aroused by a knock on the door. It was the orderly reminding him of his appointment to continue his interview with the Deputy Secretary.

Once more Kovalenko sat across the desk from Deputy Secretary Addison. This time there was more of an understanding between the two men with regard to the expectations of each. However, both knew there were issues to be resolved that would have to await the decision of the Ambassador.

Addison addressed Kovalenko. "Why don't you begin by telling me what might be of interest to the United States government?"

Replied Kovalenko, "Mr. Secretary, I don't want to play games especially since you have been so hospitable, but I don't want to reveal crucial information until I have an assurance of asylum. I think you can understand that. If that is a condition that is not acceptable to you, then there is little I can do about it."

Addison perceived that it would be pointless to insist. He wanted to keep the man at the Embassy until the Ambassador had decided. Nevertheless, he felt that Kovalenko should give some indication of what he knew so that he could advise the Ambassador who would rely considerably on Addison's recommendation.

Kovalenko had no wish to irritate or antagonize his host. Nor did he feel it wise to create a stalemate. He understood that he could not expect a favorable decision if he did not give some evidence of his having information beyond what was public knowledge.

Kovalenko spoke up. "Mr. Secretary, may I begin by giving you some background information about Stalin, some of which you may know already and some of which I am sure will be new to you. As I have said, I have been with Stalin for a long time, in fact, almost since he became a protégé of Lenin."

Kovalenko proceeded, "You must understand Stalin if you are to understand what is going on in the Soviet Union today. And if you understand Stalin, you will have a key to the future of our country. Stalin is Russia. Stalin is the Soviet Union. He controls everything. He decides everything. All those around him from the Generals in the military to the managers in the factories to the teachers and scientists in the schools and universities, all are mere pawns. None of them think, speak or act independently. If they did, they would be quickly liquidated."

Listening intently to this dissertation, Addison wasn't sure whether Kovalenko was speaking with pride and adoration about Stalin or with condemnation. He could see that Kovalenko spoke, in any case, with a passion.

"I am interested in what you have to say," said Addison. "Go on!"

Encouraged, Kovalenko settled back in his chair and seemed to relax a bit. For years he had been storing information in his brain and, now, for the first time he had before him someone who would listen and someone with whom he felt secure in talking. He began to feel important again, much as he did when Stalin first brought him in as his personal secretary.

Secretary Addison interrupted. "Do you have an objection to my taking notes as you talk?"

"No, not at all."

Kovalenko proceeded. "It is quite strange. Stalin was not always the cruel, iron-fisted person that he is now. Stalin told me in our informal talks together that as a young boy growing up in Gori in the Caucasus in Georgia he was very pious and was involved in church and school activities. It was his mother, Stalin's mother, Ekaterina Geladze, who insisted he must become a priest and she saw to it when he was nine years old in 1888 that he entered the Gori Ecclesiastical Seminary."

Kovalenko went on, "Stalin's mother called him affectionately, 'Soso.' Soso had a good singing voice and he sang at church services. He completed his schooling for the priesthood, but instead of becoming a practicing priest, he became involved in revolutionary activities.

"I must perhaps tell you," Kovalenko said to the Secretary, "Stalin's father, Vissarion Dzhugastilvili, was a drunkard and a brawler. His nickname was 'Beso.' He was a shoemaker by trade, but earned very little, so Stalin's mother had to work at homes of the wealthier people in town doing cleaning and laundry. Some of these rich families were Jewish merchants. Stalin told me when he saw his mother working so hard for these people he began to hate Jews. As you may know, Mr. Secretary, Stalin has been and still is very anti-Semitic."

"No," replied Addison, "I wasn't aware of that. That's interesting."

Kovalenko added, "As I think about it, another childhood experience influencing Stalin's attitude and behavior was witnessing the constant brawling and fighting of his father. I believe it led the impressionable young boy to conclude that brute force and violence were the means of getting his way. Stalin did not say that to me, but I think it explains much of how he has conducted himself."

Kovalenko continued, "You are aware, are you not, that in the last couple of years Stalin has been engaged in massive arrests, trials and either executions or exile to labor camps of those convicted of one thing or another?"

"Well," replied Addison, "we have some information of arrests of a number of people and that, on conviction, they have received prison terms. But, it is our understanding that these people were plotting against Stalin and the government. So, we can understand that it was appropriate for Stalin to take action."

Kovalenko raised his bushy eyebrows to express his astonishment at the Secretary's opinion. He gave a weak smile and shook his head at what he thought was the incredulous naiveté of the Secretary.

"Nothing could be further from the truth, in all due respect, Mr. Secretary," said Kovalenko. "I wish what you said were so, but it isn't. The Soviet newspapers and the radio dwell on a few high profile cases, but they do not report about the millions of innocent, ordinary people who have been arrested, tried summarily, convicted and disposed of one way or another. Husbands are arrested, disappear, then the wife and the children are also arrested. The young children are usually sent to children's homes. The wife and older children are usually shot or exiled. I would tell you about the high military officers who have been liquidated. It will affect the evaluation that your government makes of the Soviet military power. But, that is one of the things I hold in reserve until I know what you plan to do with me."

"I suppose that's fair enough," commented Addison. He looked at his wristwatch.

"It's 1130. We'll be having lunch in about a half-hour to forty-five minutes. You can join me. But, at lunch there is to be no mention of the real reason you are here. For the present, I'll introduce you to whoever is around as Mr. Boris Ivanov, a history instructor at the Moscow Academy. I'll lead the conversation by talking about the United States."

"I understand," said Kovalenko. "I might observe, though, that professors and teachers are an endangered class these days."

"How's that?" asked Addison.

"Stalin thinks that the professors, including all instructors and teachers, are in a position to subvert the government with their teaching of young students. Stalin thinks that teachers can influence the students through criticism of the government and by proposing political ideologies other than Communism. So he has a continuing assault on the centers of learning and many professors and members of the academies have been arrested and liquidated."

"That's incredible and terrible," exclaimed Addison. He shook his head in utter dismay.

"Since there is some time before we go to lunch," said Kovalenko, "would you care to have me describe an incident that will help you to understand the kind of man Stalin is?"

"Yes, I am interested," replied Addison. "Go right ahead."

Kovalenko, now quite relaxed and feeling that he had begun to win over Secretary Addison to accepting him as authentic, proceeded.

"My wife Lidia and I attended an anniversary party at the Moscow apartment of Voroshilov. It was the night of November 8, 1932. I will never forget it. There were at the party, Stalin, his wife Nadezhda Alliluyeva, Nikolai Bukharin and his wife, Anna Larina, Vyacheslav Molotov, Anna Sergeevna Allihuyeva, Marshall Yegorov and his wife, some other notables and, of course, Voroshilov. Voroshilov was a full member of the Politburo and a close and trusted associate of Stalin."

Kovalenko paused. His eyes were half closed and he had turned his head toward the window. His voice had acquired a soft monotone and Addison got the impression that Kovalenko had, for the moment at least, become lost in the nostalgia of the event almost as if he was living the experience again. But it was just for a fleeting moment and Kovalenko again turned his attention to Addison and continued.

"Stalin was in an exceptionally good mood, joking and drinking a bit heavily. In fact, he began to show the effects of the alcohol.

"Marshall Yegorov's wife started to unabashedly flirt with Stalin. It was quite obvious to all of us. Yegorov's wife was a passionate woman whose flirtations and love affairs were well known and certainly to Stalin. She was attractive and Stalin responded by giving her attention. The flirtations between the two of them were not only obvious to the guests, but also to Nadja. 'Nadja' is the name her relatives and close friends used for Nadezhda.

"Stalin became abusive and insulting to Nadja, cursing coarsely even as he continued to play up to Yegorov's wife. The Marshall himself could do nothing about the spectacle that his flirtatious wife had started. He did not dare to remonstrate with her or with Stalin.

Appearing outwardly calm and seemingly indifferent, the Marshall told me later that he was inwardly seething. His wife he could beat when they got home, but against Stalin he was utterly without recourse. I am sure that Yegorov left humiliated and embarrassed even as the rest of us felt embarrassment for him. But we all continued the affable socializing as if nothing untoward was happening."

"Shall I go on, Mr. Secretary?" Kovalenko inquired.

"Yes, of course, it is very interesting. Something we here at the Embassy never knew about. Yes, go ahead. There is still time before lunch is served."

"Well, then," continued Kovalenko, "Nadja had had enough of Stalin's disrespectful and rude conduct toward her at the party and she left accompanied by Anna Larina, Bukharin's wife. Larina returned to the party somewhat later and mentioned to me that she and Nadja had walked in the garden outside for a while and that she, Anna, tried to comfort and reassure Nadja. She said she told Nadja that her husband was drunk and that he did not know what he was saying and doing. She further told Nadja that if Stalin were sober, he would not do this, that he is a good man and he loves you, Nadja. You know, she said to Nadja, how men are and the flirting doesn't mean anything. Besides, it was the Marshall's wife who started it. Anna said she advised Nadja to go home and forget it.

"Anna said that Nadja was very upset and Anna's words didn't seem to have much effect. Nevertheless, Nadja had said, 'Thank you, Anna, it is very difficult. I don't know if I can continue to live this way. It is not just tonight. It is the accumulation of so much unhappiness.'

"Nadja and Stalin had married when she was sixteen and he was about twenty-five years older. She had borne him a son, Vasily, and a daughter, Svetlana. Stalin's and Nadja's married life was one of tension, constant violent arguments and long absences on his part. Stalin admitted as much to me during one of our conversations. It seems that they loved each other while at the same time reviling and hating each other. I see, Mr. Secretary, you are shaking your head. But, it is possible. Most of us humans portray emotions that are quiet and peaceful one moment and violent the next. I think we can all love and hate, but it is important which one is dominant most of the time."

Continued Kovalenko, "Stalin was not faithful to Nadja. Believe me, I know this personally. The women in his life were many. Nadja's suspicion of this was the hot steel of jealousy that was the cause of many of their wild arguments. But she got nowhere. Stalin continued his amorous escapades.

"Stalin's ego was fed by the attraction women had for him. Women are apparently attracted to powerful men. Stalin loved this adoration. In fact, beautiful women were Stalin's Achilles heel. It was where he was most vulnerable. The hard shell of this man was impenetrable by all who sought his favor except for the soft spot in his armor for female companionship. I believe much of Stalin's hardness and his cruelty can be explained by the fact that in his daily life he was surrounded almost entirely by male associates, most of whom were rough, tough and ruthless themselves. This male environment brought out his coarse and brutal tendencies and accentuated them. So it was only natural, I suppose, that he welcomed retreating, from time to time, into the gentler world of the female, the non-revolutionary kind."

"Am I boring you, Mr. Secretary?" Kovalenko was testing again his effectiveness with Addison.

"Not at all, not at all. Please go on," replied Secretary Addison. This time he sounded almost eager to hear the rest of the story. He had even stopped looking at his watch.

Kovalenko instinctively felt he was winning points. He continued his recitation.

"A few hours later, rather in the middle of the next morning, it was November 9, 1932, I was at home when I received a telephone call from Stalin's and Nadja's housekeeper, Karolina, telling me of Nadja's death. I have known Karolina for years. I immediately went over to the Stalin apartment. Stalin was there and was a picture of shock and grief. Tears were running down his face even as he tried to control himself. There was nothing I could do, but to await any instructions Stalin might give me. A few others who had been notified arrived shortly after I did, Molotov and Voroshilov among them.

"The story as I got it at that time, was that Nadja had arrived home alone from the party, gone to her bedroom, locked the door, wrote a note to Stalin, and sometime later shot herself with a small revolver.

I did not see her body as we were all kept at the other end of the apartment from her room."

Addison interrupted, "What about Stalin, didn't he go to her room when he arrived home later?"

"Apparently not," Kovalenko replied. "Stalin generally slept in his own room. He either got home after Nadja had shot herself, or he was already asleep when she did, because he told all of us that he had heard no gunshot.

"At the funeral gathering for Nadja, Stalin, I observed, seemed to be in tears and deeply grieved. It seemed to me that he was remorseful as if he now, for the first time, recognized the result of his years of neglect of Nadja and of the unhappiness that he had caused her.

"I could not help but think that this sorrow, this grief, this remorse, this deep sense of personal loss had personally struck this man who had for many years sent thousands of other human beings to their deaths with no feeling or understanding or even caring about the sorrow and grief of the loved ones of his victims. Did he even now relate his personal grief to all those others now that it had hit him personally? I cannot answer that except from the evidence that I observed. His personal grief did not change Stalin one bit from the steel-hard, impersonal and indifferent executioner of all whom he suspected of any disloyalty to him. Did Nadja's death make him more compassionate for his fellow humans? Absolutely not! In fact, as later and more recent events proved, he became crueler."

"I shall finish this story by briefly relating about the funeral," Kovalenko said.

"The reason that I'm relating the funeral is because it reveals more about the man, Stalin.

"As the funeral cortege proceeded from the Kremlin to the Novodevichi Cemetery on the other side of the City where Nadja was to be interred, Stalin walked beside the horse drawn hearse. But he did so only for a short distance. He knew that he was in an exposed position to an attempt to assassinate him. He understood that he had many enemies and he understood that it would take only one vengeful individual with a high-powered rifle to kill him. So, with this in mind, he climbed into an automobile to complete the trip to the cemetery."

"So, what we have here," Kovalenko opined, "is a man who has created in a vast country, as is the Soviet Union, an obsessional, universal fear, even, one could say, a national hysteria that everyone and anyone could be arrested for no reason at all and quickly dispatched either by being shot or sent to a labor camp.

"This same man who has made the Soviet Union a country of fear, lives daily with his own fear, a dreadful fear of assassination. Although Stalin has made elaborate arrangements to forestall the possibility of an attempt on his life, nevertheless, he is pragmatic enough to recognize that there are occasions when his vulnerability to attack could not be avoided. It is indeed ironic that the man who controls the lives of millions cannot control a possible threat to his own life. He really never knows for certain in what form and from what direction and by whom the attempt on his life will be made, if at all."

Kovalenko paused, waiting for Secretary Addison to comment or to ask a question. Although considerably intrigued by what Kovalenko was relating, Addison, looking at his watch, called a halt to the interview.

"Suppose we go to lunch now. You must be hungry. We can continue after lunch."

The Secretary took Kovalenko by the arm as they walked down the long hall to the dining room.

Said Addison, "I am curious as to how you have come to speak English so fluently."

"Yes, of course, you have every right to ask," replied Kovalenko.

"My mother, now deceased, was English. My father, also deceased, was Russian. They met sometime in the late 1880's at some social event in St. Petersburg, which, as you know, later became Leningrad. My father was a student at the St. Petersburg Academy of Sciences and my mother had come from England to study music under the tutelage of the noted composer, Sergei Chernovsky. She came from a wealthy family in London. They saw more of each other, fell in love and later married. My mother went back to England for a year and then came back to my father and it was then that they married. My mother was twenty-two and my father twenty-seven."

Addison and Kovalenko arrived at the dining room, selected a table and sat down. During the meal, Kovalenko continued to explain his fluency in the English language.

"While I was a young child, my mother insisted on speaking in English to me. My father did not object. He thought it was a good idea to learn a language in addition to Russian. He himself learned some English this way. I also was taught by my mother to read English."

"Good! You have satisfied my curiosity," said Addison. Addison had begun to warm to Kovalenko although he still had some reservations about how Kovalenko could help the United States beyond revealing information about Stalin as a person. Addison understood that knowing as much as possible about the personality and character of Stalin might be helpful in dealing with him, but was it enough to grant asylum to Stalin's personal secretary and his family? Addison was still troubled by the potential for creating a political schism between the two governments.

* * * * *

Deputy Secretary Fraser Addison had been in the diplomatic service of the United States government since 1924. His latest assignment to the United States Embassy in Moscow had been made in 1936. Prior to that he had been assigned to the "Russian Desk" at the State Department in Washington, D.C. Through the latter assignment he had acquired an invaluable knowledge of background as well as current and ongoing information about the Soviet Union. This inherent intelligence was such that he was able to quickly assimilate and evaluate the information that came across his desk and to send summary reports and memoranda to the Secretary of State that included the essentials needed by the Secretary to make decisions. Addison had gained a performance record of efficiency, reliability, and excellence. That record had led to his promotion to Deputy Secretary at the Moscow Embassy.

Addison was a tall, rather slim man, light complexioned, blue eyed with a shock of unruly brunette hair. And except for the unruly hair, he was rarely other than well groomed, at least while on the job. Off the job, he was casual; casual in his case defined as a reluctant concession to wearing a sport shirt and no tie. He was outwardly in appearance always calm. His words were precise and well chosen to articulate what he wished to say and he had disciplined himself to focus on and speak to the issue at hand and to not digress into collateral side subjects. In short, he wasted no words and, therefore, as he was proud to avow, wasted no time. Addison had little tolerance for someone who was needlessly verbose or who failed to convey reasonable and logical thoughts in discussions. Being a diplomat, Addison did not show his displeasure when faced with that type of person, but his opinion of the person and the decision on an issue were subtly and, perhaps, adversely influenced by these "ranters and ravers," as he called them.

At age forty-four, Addison was reasonably content with his life at the Moscow Embassy. His wife, Julia, lived at the Embassy compound with him. His two children, Jim, age 21 and his daughter, Mavis, 19, were students at college in the United States. Although he and Julia missed their children, they accepted the fact that being at school in the States was in the best interests of the children.

Addison and Kovalenko walked slowly back to Addison's office while conversing.

Addison said, "You have told me a great deal about Stalin, things I did not know. I have seen Stalin on only two occasions. The one was when he granted a meeting with about a half-dozen American journalists and writers. I had accompanied them as a sort of liaison between them and Stalin. The other time was at a State dinner for foreign Embassy officials."

Addison continued, "I was not very impressed with Stalin when I first saw him. He is a short stocky person, with a pockmarked face and with rather overly long arms and legs. He shook hands when we arrived, a handshake that was strong and firm.

"At the journalists meeting he wore a khaki jacket and pants with the pants stuffed into high black boots. Frankly, had I not known he was Stalin I would have thought he was a peasant farmer or an ordinary working man."

"Yes, I know that is the impression that strangers get of Stalin, an impression he deliberately fosters," commented Kovalenko. "But, those of us who know him intimately and who work for him on a day-to-day basis know differently. He is highly intelligent, but very shrewd, generally cold as steel and cruel and ruthless."

When Addison and Kovalenko arrived at the reception room to Addison's office, Helen was busily filing folders in the filing cabinet behind her desk. Hearing them enter the reception room, she turned and addressed Addison.

"Mr. Secretary, while you were at lunch, a message came through from the State Department. I thought you should see it before the Ambassador arrives."

Helen handed a note paper to Addison. Addison took the note and, without reading it, turned to Kovalenko.

"Mr. Kovalenko, will you come into the office," said Addison.

Once inside his office, he opened the note and read:

> *"Bill Chance and assistant, Wagner, will arrive at the Embassy on March 14, 1939. Purpose is to promote trade. Arrange, if you can, a conference with someone close to Stalin who can speak for Stalin's eco. policy."*
>
> *Signed,*
> *McKinley*
> *Secretary of State*

Addison pondered a few moments. The fact that someone from the State Department was coming to the Embassy was not unusual. It happened frequently. But, for the purpose of promoting trade with the Soviets was somewhat of a surprise since the Embassy had trade and economic experts on its staff. Nevertheless, Addison shrugged the question off.

As for getting someone close to Stalin, Addison knew that would be impossible or, at the most, very difficult. Stalin had a penchant, Addison knew, of not permitting anyone on his staff to discuss policy with foreign visitors. His foreign minister, Molotov, would perhaps be an exception to the rule.

Then, suddenly, the thought came to him like a flash fire. Kovalenko! Why, of course, if Kovalenko were everything Kovalenko said he was, then Kovalenko would be the natural person to start with, at least. Addison knew that he'd have to take this up with the Ambassador.

Turning to Helen, Addison said, "Helen, you've read the note. Do what you have to do to prepare for Chance and the assistant accompanying him. You've done this before." Helen nodded in assent.

"However," Addison added, "don't do anything about getting someone from Stalin's staff. We probably couldn't get anybody anyway, but I want to take that subject up with the Ambassador."

Helen suggested, "Would Mr. Kovalenko serve the purpose in this case?"

"Yes, I have thought of that," Addison replied. "That is also something I want to discuss with the Ambassador. In the meantime, we'll keep Kovalenko here. But don't mention that he might play a role when Chance arrives. Kovalenko's status with us is still up in the air."

When Kovalenko had settled into the chair on the other side of the desk from Addison, Addison said, "Mr. Kovalenko, I had intended to continue our discussion this afternoon, but something has come up which I must get done. I know you appreciate that we get assignments on the so-called 'spur of the moment' and we have to drop what we had planned to do." Addison wanted to put off further discussion with Kovalenko until the Ambassador arrived. Kovalenko had suddenly acquired new importance in view of the message from State.

"I would like to have you remain in your room under the same conditions as we earlier had discussed. I'm sorry to have to restrict your movements and activities here, but that is the way it has to be for the present."

"I understand," Kovalenko replied.

"If there is anything you need, just ring Helen. Helen will give you the schedule for dinner, but I'd like to be with you when you go. I'll be in touch with you before that."

"Thank you, Mr. Secretary. You have been very kind and thoughtful," said Kovalenko as he arose from his chair and proceeded to leave the office.

Addison leaned back in his chair and thought of how he would prepare his remarks and opinion about Kovalenko to the Ambassador. He felt sure that if he, Addison, presented the case in a persuasive manner for giving asylum to Kovalenko and his family, the Ambassador would agree to it. Addison had pretty much made up his mind that Kovalenko had information that might prove of value to the United States to be worth the risk of antagonizing the Soviet government once they were aware of Kovalenko's residence in the Embassy.

But, would the Ambassador approve ultimately? That is the question that bothered Addison even though he felt assured that the Ambassador would probably agree. It was not definite, not certain.

Secretary Fraser Addison awaited the arrival of the Ambassador.

When Ambassador Harrison Hayes arrived back at the Embassy at 7:30 p.m., later than expected, he saw the note from Rose, his Secretary, stating that Addison had a matter of urgency to discuss with him when he returned.

Rose had earlier left the office for the day, so the Ambassador called directly interoffice to Addison. Addison was still in his own office awaiting the Ambassador, in the meantime working on routine matters.

"Fraser, I've just gotten back and I have a note here that you have something urgent to discuss with me. Can't it wait until tomorrow morning?"

"Well, it could, but I really think you ought to hear about it now. The matter is quite important in my estimation."

"Alright, come on in."

Settling into a chair in the Ambassador's office, Addison related the coming to the Embassy of Vladimir Kovalenko and, for the Ambassador's benefit, recited, in brief, some of the things that Kovalenko had talked about.

"Normally, if this fellow had been an ordinary Russian citizen, I'd have had him leave the Embassy immediately, but this fellow claims to be a personal aide to Stalin and, from what he told me, he appears to know the inner workings of Stalin's office and to know quite a bit about the way Stalin thinks. I thought he might be of use to us and didn't want to get rid of him before I had spoken to you."

"I appreciate your reasoning, Fraser, but even if it is true that he could be of value to us, I don't see how we can possibly keep him here alone or with his family." Ambassador Hayes' face expressed a troubled frown.

"When Stalin finds out, as he surely will, that we have given asylum to his personal aide, all hell will break loose and we'll all be called on the carpet to explain why we created an international crisis in order to save one person from possibly being shot."

Ambassador Hayes continued, "There are thousands of Russian individuals and families out there who would love to have asylum in our Embassy in order to escape arrest. We don't have the physical facilities to harbor even a handful of them."

"Yes, I understand," said Addison, "but this fellow is someone we should make an exception for, perhaps."

"What Stalin is doing to his countrymen with arrests, imprisonment and executions is absolutely sickening," declared Hayes, "but there are larger political issues to consider even though I'm sympathetic to this Vladimir Kovalenko."

Ambassador Hayes went on to say, "Yet, what you say might be true. He could be of considerable value to us considering the turmoil Europe is in just now and the fact that Stalin one day seems to be on the side of Britain and France and the next day trying to make friends with Germany. I think that I should not make the decision on Vladimir without first getting word to Washington and asking for their advice. What do you think of that?"

"I think it would be a wise step," replied Addison.

"Well, tomorrow morning I'll get a message out to Secretary Roth," Hayes said. "In the meantime, keep Vladimir here and if his family shows up, tell them to go back to their home and wait for our decision."

"They may either never get home or, when they are there, they'll be arrested," observed Addison.

"Well, that's the chance and risk that they'll have to take," Hayes said, throwing his hands up in a gesture of hopelessness. "It's a terrible environment we're in, but that's the way it is."

The conference ended and both the Ambassador and Fraser went to their respective apartments in the Embassy conclave. Both were troubled by the recognition of being confronted by competing interests, the moral interest of saving a life and the political interest of doing what is best for the United States. As officers of their government they understood that the latter interest was the most compelling.

The coded telegram sent to Secretary of State McKinley Roth was, of necessity, long and detailed sufficiently to allow him to make an informed decision. Ambassador Hayes, himself, made no recommendation, leaving the matter entirely in the hands of the State Department.

Within hours after the telegram was sent came the reply. The quick response surprised both Hayes and Addison. The contents of the reply telegram surprised them even more. It read (in code):

> "*Give asylum to K and wife and child. He may be of great value. Bill Chance and Gene Wagner on their way to Moscow on trade mission will want to question K on their arrival. Refuse demand by Soviet for their release. End.*
> *R*"

"Well, we have the answer," commented Ambassador Hayes to Addison. Both appeared relieved that a decision had been made at the highest level.

"I'm happy about the decision, but I'm curious to know the reasoning and the motivation behind it and why Chance and Wagner want to question Kovalenko if they're truly on only a trade mission," remarked Addison to the Ambassador as they sat together in the latter's office after receipt of the telegram from Roth.

"Yes, I'm curious about that too," said Hayes. "Well, we'll just have to wait for the answer until Bill and Gene get here. In the meantime, why don't you let Kovalenko know about the decision. I'm sure he's quite anxious. And let the gate know to admit Mrs. Kovalenko and the child when they arrive. As a matter of fact, it's two p.m. and I thought they were supposed to arrive here this morning."

"Yes, that was my understanding," said Addison. "Maybe there has been a cautious delay on their part for some unforeseen reason."

Back in his office, Addison sent Helen to get Kovalenko and guide him back to Addison.

When he arrived at Addison's office, Kovalenko appeared visibly distressed. Addison guessed the concern. Kovalenko's wife and child had not yet gotten to the Embassy.

"Mr. Kovalenko, your wife may have decided that it was best to delay coming here. I'm sure she and your child will show up as soon as she and your friend who will guide her feel confident in coming." Addison tried to reassure Kovalenko, although Addison, himself, was beginning to feel fearful about Mrs. Kovalenko's situation. The NKVD was, if nothing else, an efficient and ruthless arm of the Soviet government. Since Kovalenko had not shown up at Stalin's headquarters this morning, the agents might have become suspicious.

Addison informed Kovalenko of the decision to grant him and his wife and child asylum.

"I'm glad to hear that, Mr. Secretary." Kovalenko nevertheless remained distressed. "I am sorry to behave this way, Mr. Secretary. I am grateful that you are allowing me to stay here, at least, for a while. But, I'm very concerned for my wife and child. I know these people in the police. They are suspicious of everybody and will make an arrest without proof of any wrongdoing. I think now that I should have brought my family with me when I came. But, I didn't want to involve them until I was sure we would be accepted by you." The tension in Kovalenko was mounting moment to moment and there were tears in his eyes as his thought dwelt on what might be happening to his wife and child.

While Addison and Kovalenko were thus sitting in the office, an intercom call came from Helen in the outer office.

"Fraser, there is a call from the gate. Will you take it?"

"Yes, of course, put me through." Addison knew almost instinctively that this concerned the Kovalenko family.

"Secretary Addison here, what is it?"

The guard at the gate said, "There's an elderly Russian man here who says he wants to come in and see you and a Mr. Kovalenko. He looks like the man who was here yesterday with the Russian fellow. He's quite excited. What shall I do?"

"Is there anyone with him?"

"No."

Immediately, Addison sensed that his own fears for Mrs. Kovalenko may have come true.

"Send him in to see my secretary, Miss Morgan."

As soon as he hung up on the guard, Addison contacted Helen on the intercom, "There is a gentleman being admitted to see me. Keep him waiting until I buzz you."

Addison then turned to Kovalenko, "The gentleman who brought you here yesterday is coming in now through the gate. He is alone.

Your wife and child are not with him. Do you want to be here when he comes in?"

"Yes, yes, of course! Oh, my God! Something terrible has happened!" Kovalenko began to sway back and forth in his chair, burying his head in his hands and partly moaning and repeating, "Oh, oh, oh."

"Vladimir, try to calm yourself for the friend of yours when he comes in here. Let's hear what he has to say. Please, Vladimir."

Kovalenko raised his head. His face was ashen and tears were rolling down his cheeks. He straightened up a bit and ran a large, rough hand over his eyes and face to remove the traces of his crying. But, it was obvious to Addison that Kovalenko was completely unnerved in anticipation of the worse.

"Helen, is the gentleman there yet?"

"Yes, he's standing here."

"Escort him in, if you will."

Moments later, with Helen leading the way, there entered a tall, slim man who Addison estimated was in his middle sixties. Addison also noticed that the man carried himself with some military bearing. Addison speculated that he had probably been an officer in the military service at one time, maybe even in the Tsarist army, although Addison was aware that Stalin very early in his Communist Party career had had almost all Tsarist officers shot or sent to prison camps.

Addison turned to Kovalenko who was too distraught to be thinking of the social civilities.

"Vladimir, will you introduce me to your friend?"

Kovalenko quickly came to himself and jumped up from his chair. "Of course, I'm sorry."

"Mr. Secretary, this is Pavel Vasilevski." "Pavel, this is Deputy Secretary, Mr. Addison"

Addison approached the new visitor and shook his hand. Vasilevski bowed slightly, emphasizing that he was a very formal, socially correct person. However, in spite of Vasilevski's conservative reserve, Addison could not help but perceive that the man was extremely agitated. Addison beckoned the man to a chair, while Kovalenko remained standing, too tense and upset to relax in any chair. Addison took his seat behind his desk.

"Mr. Vasilevski, do you speak English?"

"Some, yes."

"Can you tell us, then, why you are here?"

"I would like to begin in a nice way, but I can't. I must come to the point right away. Vladimir, they have come and taken away Anna and Alexei." Vasilevski looked at Kovalenko with an expression of great sorrow and sadness. Kovalenko was again swaying back and forth and again holding his head and moaning, "Oh, God! Oh, God!"

Addison could not help but think that here was a man undoubtedly steeped in godless, atheistic Communism who at the ultimate peak of anguish over his family, was calling on God. This, Addison remarked to himself, demonstrated, at least for this person, that Communistic ideology was only superficial in some people's lives and there was a deeper need, emotionally and spiritually, to seek out a higher, universal power which could not be quenched even by threats of punishment.

Kovalenko stopped moaning and sat down, prepared to hear out Vasilevski, but with an expression of utter despair.

Vasilevski began again. "I was walking about 0730 this morning toward your home, Vladimir. As I got near your apartment building in view about a block away, I saw two black limousines in front. I think we all know that a black limousine is the trademark of the NKVD. I sensed that something was wrong and that I should not proceed further. I pressed myself into a doorway and stuck my head out just far enough to observe what was going on. After about ten minutes, I saw two men come out your building doorway followed closely by another two men in dark jackets and caps. One of these last two men had Anna by the arm and the other had Alexei by the hand. Neither Anna nor Alexei looked up as they were both put into one of the limousines. Both cars then drove off. The men did not handle Anna and Alexei roughly. They were not pushing and shoving the way they sometimes do."

Vasilevski stopped for a moment as if to decide whether to go on. He had related the facts of what he had seen. He decided to speak about how he felt and his reaction, as if Kovalenko could care about that.

"I tell you, I felt an immense urge to rush up to those men and to beat them and grab Anna and Alexei and run for it. But, I am an old military man and I know when to charge ahead and when to hold one's fire and I knew well enough that it would do no good to throw myself at those people. Anna and Alexei could not be rescued and I, myself, would only become a prisoner. I feel great shame at my own impotence and the impotence of the Russian people to stop these persecutions. Think of it! A few thousand organized individuals control millions of unorganized citizens. It's incredible."

"Is there any way to find out where they have taken Anna and Alexei?" asked Addison, who had now been taken up somewhat emotionally by the story told by Vasilevski and the terror he knew Kovalenko must feel.

Kovalenko answered, "Perhaps through the family lady friend who works in the NKVD office headquarters, the one who tipped me off that they were beginning to look at my personal file. But, I don't know how to get in touch with her now and I don't want to put her at risk, either."

"Yes, and I don't know just what to do now," Vasilevski said. "Actually, I fear going to my home. The agents might force Anna to tell about me and my involvement with the disappearance of Vladimir here; about bringing him to this Embassy. I don't know what I shall do. No matter where I go, I might be spotted by those police agents."

Addison wondered whether he should ask Vasilevski to stay at the Embassy. Whether Wagner and Chance would want to question him, too, would depend on what he knew, how valuable he could be.

"Did you have a position in the government?" Addison asked Vasilevski. "I was a Colonel in the Tsar's army. I was in the army from 1894 to 1917 when the Tsar was overthrown and the Bolsheviks took over. After that, I was rounded up with other Tsarist officers and sent to a labor camp in Eastern Russia. I was there five years. Believe me, conditions were terrible. A few of us survived. For some reason, I was singled out and brought back to Moscow where I was given the job of training recruits for the new Soviet army. Believe me, so many Tsarist officers were killed or died in the camps that the Bolsheviks did not have many experienced people to make an efficient army. Believe me, they didn't bring me back as an act of kindness. I did my job and I stayed clear of any involvement in politics. I think that is why I'm still here. I was training recruits for twelve years. They retired me in 1935. I got married in 1900. My wife died six years ago. I was very lonely. I was glad to make friends with Anna and Vladimir. They are very good people."

"What do you know about the Russian military today?" Addison pressed for information to determine what value this ex-military officer might have.

Vasilevski was silent a few moments as if not knowing how to answer the question. Then he said, "Of course, I have not been involved for several years, but in talking with some of my friends in the military, I get the impression that the army is very efficient and competent."

"Efficient and competent and strong enough to handle the German army?" queried Addison.

"I really don't know that," Vasilevski replied.

"Is there dissatisfaction in the army with conditions?"

"I haven't heard of it or seen any of it. Of course, everyone is very cautious about complaining. It isn't good for one's health."

Addison decided that Vasilevski really had no hard information that would be of any value to the United States government and that there would be no point in giving Vasilevski asylum except from a humanitarian view. And as the Ambassador had said, "We can't take everyone in who is fearful for his or her life. We'd be overwhelmed."

"Is there anything, Vladimir, you'd like to ask your friend here?"

"Yes, just one thing. If you can manage to get information about Anna and Alexei, please let me know what you find out. I must know." Kovalenko implored Pavel.

"Well, I'll do what I can, but you know how it is out there. I've got to let things quiet down for a few days and get attention off myself, if Anna has said anything about me."

"I understand," Kovalenko said.

"Mr. Vasilevski, my secretary will see that you get out of the Embassy safely." Addison rose and shook hands with the man. If Vasilevski had any hope of remaining in the Embassy, that hope was now dashed.

Addison explained to Kovalenko why Pavel was not asked to stay at the Embassy. The reason: not enough space.

"There are two men coming from the United States Department on a trade mission. They will need rooms. Incidentally, they would like to talk with you after they arrive. In the meantime, we'll try to find out about Anna and Alexei. You understand that we cannot do it directly. The Soviet government would wonder why we have an interest in your wife and child and, because you're missing, they might just guess that you have some connection to us. We'll have to work through some of our contacts. Now, for the next few days, you will have to remain in your room. You can come to our dining room, but you will either eat with me or alone, not with any of our staff. The Ambassador will probably want to talk with you as soon as he can find the time. You will have to try to adjust to being alone a good deal of the time. Do you have any questions?"

"No. And thank you and your Ambassador again for keeping me here."

Addison buzzed Helen on the intercom. "Have one of the aides come down and escort Mr. Kovalenko to his room."

Kovalenko having left the office, Addison leaned back in his chair and wondered where all of this with Kovalenko was leading. Was Kovalenko the real thing? Was he a clever plant for the Soviet government to get into the Embassy and get information? Addison considered that a possibility. Yet, Kovalenko seemed honest and sincere. "Well," Addison said to himself, "time will tell."

CHAPTER 4

Captain Timo Koskinen boarded the train at Tampere bound for Helsinki at 0700 hours one week after his meeting with Colonel Lars Blomquist at the Hotel Tampere. He was tired even at the early hour. He hadn't slept very well since that meeting. His almost every thought was about the Stalin plan (he refused to call it a "plot" since that term implied something insidious and less than professional). He retired to bed each evening thinking about it and arose every morning mulling it over and over. In between, what little sleep he got was troubled. The lack of proper sleep showed in his actions toward his wife, Anna. Although he loved her dearly, he was irritable and short with her. Captain Koskinen had had stressful assignments before this and it did not affect his behavior, at least toward Anna. But this proposal by Blomquist was different. He saw it as life-threatening, complicated and, for once in his professional life, as unachievable.

Koskinen took off his coat and hat along with a small bag containing an overnight change of clothing, if needed, and placed them in the rack above his seat on the train. The car he was in had only eight or ten other passengers, leaving a substantial number of vacant seats. The straight backs of the seats were not very comfortable, but they could be reversed depending upon which direction the train was traveling. Taking advantage of the empty seat in front of him, Koskinen had pushed the seat back, providing him with a seat on which to place his feet. The train had proceeded about fifteen kilometers when Koskinen dozed off.

He was awakened by the clang of the hookups on each car and the screeching noise of the train brakes as it lurched to a stop at the scheduled station stop. Koskinen peered out of the window and saw that he was in Hameenlinna, a city of about sixty-five kilometers south of Tampere and another one hundred eight kilometers north of Helsinki.

Koskinen got up and stretched a bit and then decided to step outside for a breath of fresh, but cold, air. He retrieved his hat and coat from the basket and at the steps down from the car he asked the conductor how long the train would be at Hameenlinna. He was informed about "ten minutes." Koskinen spent a couple of minutes outside the train observing the people boarding and then walked to the end of the station and back to his car, standing at the steps for a few minutes before boarding again. It was quite cold outside but the walk had revived him.

As Koskinen walked down the car aisle, he quickly noticed that a young woman was occupying his seat. "Well," Koskinen thought, "these are not reserved seats, so I suppose she has a right to sit there. Anyway, I'll just mention it to her."

Koskinen faced the young woman, "Young lady, I got on at Tampere and I believe you have my seat. My bag is on the rack over your head." Koskinen said this quite gently and yet with feigned sternness. He really didn't care where he sat, but he thought that, in striking up a conversation, it would take his mind off the concerns that he had regarding the "plan."

Startled, the young woman apologized profusely. "Oh, I'm sorry. I didn't notice your bag." She started to get up.

"No, just stay there. It doesn't matter. I'll sit here on the opposite side of the aisle and I'll leave my bag where it is," said Koskinen and he proceeded to sit opposite the young woman. Koskinen had noticed a distinctive accent as she spoke even a few words.

The young woman, according to the observation and appraisal of Koskinen, was, he guessed, in her late twenties or early thirties, very attractive but not ravishingly beautiful. She had placed her fur hat on the seat alongside her, thus revealing a shoulder length flow of black hair. Koskinen saw that she had fine facial features: high cheekbones, a small upturned nose set between large dark eyes that seemed to him to catch the sparkle of the early sun reflecting through the car windows.

The young woman still wore her heavy long coat, testimony to the not so very warm condition inside the car. The coat prevented further appraisal by Koskinen of other physical features of this lady.

Koskinen, ever mindful of his love for Anna at home, was nevertheless attracted to the lady. She seemed to him friendly, gracious and expressive, without words, of natural warmth of personality.

Koskinen turned to the young woman. "I presume that you got on the train at Hameenlinna. How far are you going, if I may inquire?"

"Yes, of course," the young lady replied without hesitation. "I am traveling to Helsinki. And you?"

"I am also going to Helsinki. I am on a business trip for a couple of days. I live in Tampere." Koskinen thought that by describing, without her asking, why he was on the trip and where he lived, the lady might feel freer to reveal similar information about herself. To reinforce this purpose, Koskinen said, "I notice you have a slight accent. Could I speculate that you are from Karelia?"

Koskinen knew very well that it was not a Karelian accent, but he used it again as a ploy to lead her into being specific in her reply. Karelia was in the area of Finnish territory that lay in the Southeastern part of the country and bordered the Soviet Union not too many kilometers from Leningrad. Koskinen had been to Karelia many times, had friends there and was well acquainted with the Finnish dialect of the people.

"No," the young lady replied demurely, "I'm from Leningrad. I'm Russian. If you wonder how it is that I speak Finnish," and she added with a smiling laugh, "with an accent. I am a translator. That is my job. You know, I am sure, that Finnish is a very difficult language with all of its different case endings." Koskinen nodded in agreement.

"When I was eighteen, my family sent me to the University at Turku, as they felt that I would get a better education there than in the Soviets. I was there three years except for summer vacations. I made many good friends at the University and they helped me to learn Finnish. So, there you are, Mr.-----. What is your name?"

"My name is Antti," replied Koskinen. Koskinen thought to himself, 'I don't know this young lady and I must be cautious in my job. There is no reason for me to reveal my name of Timo.' "Well," he said to the lady, "you do have some roots branching from Russia to Finland.

I might tell you that, to the contrary, I have no roots branching from Finland to Russia. So, I cannot share the 'roots' with you."

Koskinen was not a little surprised that the lady had offered as much information about herself as she had. But, he concluded, what she revealed did not, after all, say much about her. Koskinen did get the feeling, while the lady talked, that this young lady was pretty much in control of herself with a great deal of self-discipline, perhaps, he mused, a lady with a soft exterior and a hard and determined character. He could see that she was probably not one to be easily intimidated.

"Now that I have given you my name, perhaps you would care to tell me yours." Koskinen's voice and bearing were easy, soft and cajoling. He wanted to give the appearance of being a gentle person, which, he admitted to himself, he generally was, at least in personal and private relations.

"Certainly," replied the young lady, again without any hesitation or reservation. "My name is Elena. Elena Marikova." By giving her last name, Koskinen wondered whether it was now she who was leading him to give his last name and, perhaps, other information about himself. "Well," he thought, "I am not about to, at least not yet." However, Koskinen found himself having a growing interest in this young lady, not sexual, but because she seemed to present an unusual and intriguing challenge to him.

Sensing that Elena was quite willing to talk, Koskinen asked, "Will you be in Helsinki for very long?"

"Only two or three days. I'm going to do a bit of shopping before I return to Leningrad. Your shops here in Finland have so many things that we do not see in our Russian shops. The government allows us to bring back some small items."

Koskinen nodded in assent. "Yes, so I have heard. Do you mind if I ask how long you have been in Finland?"

"Only two days," Elena replied. "I have been here as an interpreter for some Russian officials on a trade mission. They are traveling in their limousines. They had me return by train. They are going shopping tomorrow morning in Helsinki and I have to assist in interpreting for them. They'll be leaving to return to Russia in the afternoon." Elena made a facial expression and hand gesture which Koskinen took to mean that she'd be glad when they left.

Elena looked directly at Koskinen. "Now that I have told you so much about myself, may I ask what business you are in?" Her warm smile encouraged an answer.

"I'm in the export-import business. I am in the regional office in Tampere. I live in Tampere with my wife."

"Oh, so you're married!"

"Yes, quite happily."

"Well, that's nice. Any children?"

"Yes, two sons. They're both in school."

If the information about Koskinen's family had any effect on Elena, she didn't evidence it. Koskinen thought that it was either because she had no great interest in him or as he had previously concluded, that she was very much in control of her actions. Nevertheless, he continued, "I travel to Moscow and Leningrad on occasion on business, not very frequently. My company is headquartered in Helsinki."

The train was pulling into the station at Riihimaki, a small city a little more than seventy kilometers north of Helsinki. Outside on the station platform were two or three food vendors peddling musta makkara, juusto, pikkuleipa and kahvi.*

Koskinen arose to go outside and asked Elena, "Would you care to have something to eat or drink? I'll bring it in."

"I would like some coffee and a cookie, but I'll go out with you," Elena replied.

They both hurriedly donned their fur hats and descended to the station platform. There were several people leaving the train and a few boarding it. They approached a peddler selling musta makkara.

"Would you care to have one of these sausages?" Koskinen asked Elena.

"Ugh! No. They look like something from an outhouse. But, please have some yourself, if you wish."

Koskinen proceeded to buy a black sausage that the peddler placed in a piece of newspaper.

"I admit it doesn't look very appetizing, but it has a wonderful rich taste. Here, just try a piece of it."

Elena did and, with a surprised and pleased expression, agreed that it was a very tasty morsel.

"Yes, it's excellent, but I'll just stick with a cookie and coffee."

"I might inform you," offered Koskinen, "that this city, Riihimaki, is famous for its glass works, for its manufacture of art glass and glass implements. Their products are truly exquisite. We have some items in our home."

"Oh, I would just love to see some of the craft work and how they're made. Perhaps I can get back here some day."

The warning signal came from the train and Koskinen, with his black sausage and Elena with her cookie and coffee, proceeded hurriedly to board the car. Settling down in their seats, they ate and carried on with small talk, including a bit of banter back and forth. Whatever social barriers may have existed between them were further eroded by the friendly humor and the comfort that they found building up in a more relaxed relationship.

Koskinen's growing interest in Elena also caused him to have some concerns for her. After the train had traveled south a few kilometers, Koskinen was prompted to ask Elena, "Do you think it is safe for you to be talking with me? We've heard that there are mass arrests of all sorts of people being conducted in the Soviets, sometimes on suspicion only. Am I right?"

Elena replied in a somewhat painful tone of voice, "Yes, there are such arrests, but we have been told that those who have been arrested are counter-revolutionaries plotting to overthrow the government. We've been told that they are proven traitors."

Elena added in response to Koskinen's concern, "I don't think I'm in any peril, but, of course, one can never be certain. As a translator, I come into contact with many foreigners, you for example." Elena laughed and said, "Anyone keeping me under surveillance might think I'm talking to an intelligence agent of Finland and giving you information about Russian preparation for war or some other security information."

Koskinen smiled at Elena's reference to the possibility of his being an intelligence agent, but he made no comment. Instead, he suggested, "Perhaps you should seek asylum here in Finland. Why take the risk of arrest? I'm sure that you would find a safe haven with us."

"Thanks for the thought," Elena said. "I could not remain here even if I wanted to. I live with my mother and mother, poor soul, God bless her, needs me so badly."

"Oh, I see," said Koskinen.

"No, you don't see and couldn't possibly see," replied Elena in a now remonstrative tone. "Only someone who has experienced what we have gone through can understand."

"Well, what is it that I don't see or understand," said Koskinen in a gently soothing voice.

"My father was arrested almost a year ago," Elena replied. "It was the night of February 19, 1938. I remember it so clearly. I was in bed reading. There were several loud knocks on our apartment door. Mother opened it and, without waiting to be invited in, they brushed past mother. Three men came in and went over to the table where father was writing and told him he was under arrest and to get dressed to leave immediately. Mother began to scream, 'No, no, no, he has done nothing wrong! You cannot take him! I beg you! He is my husband! I love him.' She kept repeating, 'He has done nothing!' Tears were streaming from mother's eyes. She was beside herself. She apparently sensed what might happen to my father."

Elena continued to describe the scene. "I had come from my bedroom when the men first entered. It was a very traumatic experience. My brother who was living with us also came into the living room. He asked the men what my father was charged with. They said they didn't know, that all they knew was that they had arrest orders."

Elena's usually lively, ebullient face had by now assumed a dark, clouded visage as she seemed to be turning inward in reliving the tragic event. But she went on with her description.

"Father, dear Papa, all through this, while at first surprised, remained calm and kept telling us not to worry, that everything would turn out alright, that when the authorities realized that he had done nothing wrong, they would release him. After Papa had dressed, the men took him away. We last saw him as they put him into a large, black limousine. We have not seen Papa since. He has just disappeared. We have heard nothing. We inquired, but no one seems to know anything or they will not tell us. Was he shot? Is he in some labor camp somewhere? We just do not know."

Elena was tearful as she related this experience. And then she added, "Two weeks later, they came and took my brother away. And he has disappeared also. He was two years older than me. We have heard nothing. We know nothing of his fate either. It is so terrible. As you might know, it was devastating to my mother. And that is why I must return."

Elena leaned back in her seat as if she were exhausted from the ordeal of reliving and retelling the story. Her face was pale. Her eyes closed. She was breathing heavily.

Koskinen saw the situation and said nothing. He felt that anything he would say, under these circumstances, would neither comfort nor reassure Elena. For these few moments, at least, Elena had to suffer alone and in her own world. But as Koskinen had listened to Elena recite the event he felt her pain and her anguish. He was shocked at her story and he was suffering with her. Indeed, his heart went out to this lovely young woman and he wondered how she could have been so cheerful and lively up until now on the train trip. Koskinen was impressed on the inner strength that Elena demonstrated.

After about five minutes, Elena opened her eyes, looked at Koskinen and smiled that very warm smile that Koskinen had noticed since he first met her.

"I'm sorry," she apologized, "I didn't mean to become so overwhelmed in telling you these things. But, I guess it is all so fresh in my mind. Please forgive me."

"No, no, there is absolutely no need for you to apologize," said Koskinen in protest. "You may not believe me, but I do understand your feelings. I am glad you told me about it. It is remarkable that you have stood up so well. However, I am angry and outraged by what you have described. Your experience confirms what we have been hearing. I wish we could do something about these atrocities going on in the Soviets."

"I was very angry too, for some time," Elena commented. "But I have gotten past that point. There is nothing I can do except to get on with my life. I have been trying to get mama to accept that she, too, must try to adjust to the future, but she says there is no future for her and that she lives to die. I feel so bad for her."

"You must have hatred for the government that does these things to its people," Koskinen ventured.

"I suppose I should hate Stalin and the government, but, like anger, I no longer hate; I do resent the government and I would like to put a stop to the way it treats its citizens and to reform the way it operates as a Communist state. But, I am only one person. What can I do?"

"What did your father do, what was his occupation?" Koskinen asked.

"He was a chemistry professor at the Gorki Pedagogical Institute in Moscow. He enjoyed his work. But, the government has arrested almost the entire professional faculty. There are very few left. My father was not the only one. Even some of the junior instructors have been arrested. The government believes that these teachers are indoctrinating the students with treasonous ideas. Of course, that is not so, at least, not so in my father's case. But, innocent or not, they were all classified as traitors or counter revolutionaries."

"What about your brother? He was a teacher, too?" Koskinen inquired further.

"No," replied Elena, "he was arrested because he was my father's son. My brother, Sergei, was working as a skilled mechanic in a factory in Leningrad. He was not interested in politics and didn't belong to any subversive group. Nevertheless, that didn't matter to the authorities."

The train was by now on the outskirts of Helsinki. Homes and factories were beginning to become more numerous alongside the train tracks. Frequent road crossings were appearing. The train was slowing down, a sure indication that the Helsinki station was just minutes away. Koskinen felt that he somehow had to preserve his relationship to Elena. He could not just say, "Goodbye" and allow both of them to walk out of each other's lives. There was something that compelled him to say to her, "Since you're going to be in Helsinki for a few days, I think it would be nice if we could have lunch or dinner tomorrow. What do you say?"

"Yes, that would be fine. I cannot make it for lunch as I may still be with the Russian people. But, dinner would be best for me."

"Where are you staying?" asked Koskinen.

"I am staying at the Hotel Klaus Kurki where the trades mission men are staying. Are you familiar with it on Bulevardi?"

"Yes, I have been there many times. This time I shall be staying at one of the company officer's home. I can call you sometime tomorrow afternoon, let's say about 1600 hours. Will you be in your room at that time?"

"I'll make it a point to be there at that time," replied Elena.

"I know of a nice little restaurant near the Hotel on Bulevardi Street," Koskinen said. "They have good food. I've eaten there before." Added Koskinen, "When we leave the train, for your safety's sake, we shall do so separately and act as if we do not know each other. Do you agree?"

"I am not really concerned," replied Elena, "but if you wish it that way, I'll do so."

"Also," continued Koskinen, "I'll meet you at the restaurant, rather than at your hotel, for the same reason. I am concerned about you."

"Again," Elena said, "if that is what you want, then that is acceptable to me. But you will call me at about 1600 tomorrow."

"Yes, of course."

As the train pulled into the station, both Koskinen and Elena arose, gathered up their bags and stepped into the aisle. Elena turned toward Koskinen, extended her hand, which Koskinen grasped and momentarily gave it a gentle squeeze. They smiled at each other and proceeded to the car steps and, as the train came to a stop, descended to the platform and walked separately to the station waiting room and on out to the street.

Elena hailed a taxi cab. The Hotel Klaus Kurki was only eight long blocks southwest from the railroad station, but it was too cold to walk if not necessary.

Koskinen turned and walked toward the Parliament House a short distance northwest of the station on Mannerheimentie. Headquarters of Finnish Intelligence was located in the building that was referred to by the Finns as the Eduskuntatalo.

At the meeting with Colonel Blomquist the week before in Tampere, Blomquist had asked him to give some thought about how he would organize and plan for the "Stalin Project," as Koskinen called it. Koskinen had struggled in his mind during the intervening week to develop such a plan and the best he could come up with was to work through the Finnish Embassy in Moscow using whatever resources and personnel available there.

When Koskinen boarded the train at Tampere, he had intended spending the time on the trip refining his thoughts on a plan and formulating its presentation to the staff at Headquarters. That intention was disrupted when Elena appeared on the scene.

Now, as he walked from the station to the Parliament House, Koskinen's thoughts were about Elena. Although he welcomed the lively conversation with Elena and her description of the family ordeal with the arrest and disappearance of her father and brother, Koskinen was still puzzled as to why Elena had been so unabashedly open and exposed so much about her personal life. Her revelations seemed to just gush forth. Normally, Koskinen mused to himself, one does not do this with a stranger such as he was. Did Elena suspect that he was not who he said he was, a businessman? Had Elena's story been truthful or fabricated for some reason? Was she playing a game with him? Was she, perhaps, working with Russian Intelligence? Why she and her mother were spared from arrest and why, if her father and brother were arrested, was Elena still in the employ of the government? Surely, translators were not that scarce in Russia that she was irreplaceable.

These questions disturbed Koskinen. He had no answers to them. He hoped that when he saw Elena on the morrow that he might find the answers and, because he had allowed himself to develop a personal attachment to her, he hoped the answers would show that she was honest, sincere and forthright.

A tall wrought iron fence surrounded the Parliament House with a main gate opening to an expansive, landscaped yard with a walkway to the front building entrance. At the gate entrance was a wooden check station manned by a soldier.

Koskinen showed his identifying credentials to the soldier who, satisfied at their validity, waved him through the gate. Two more military personnel stood at the massive entrance door to the building, but did not challenge him.

Koskinen took the elevator to the third floor headquarters of the Finnish Intelligence Department. He was a familiar figure to the reception and secretarial staff and was greeted by the usually friendly personnel.

"I have an appointment with Colonel Blomquist," Koskinen announced to Marjatta, the receptionist.

"I'll call him and let him know that you're here," Marjatta said as she lifted the phone and buzzed the Colonel.

"He said for you to come right in," Marjatta said.

"Thanks, Marjatta." Koskinen proceeded down a long hallway on either side of which were several offices with their doors closed and without any identification tags to show who the occupants were. But Koskinen knew which office was that of the Colonel, having visited with him on prior occasions.

"Good morning, Captain Koskinen," Colonel Blomquist greeted Koskinen with a large smile.

"Good morning, Colonel." Koskinen thought Blomquist was surprisingly and especially gracious and friendly, maybe even overly disarming. "Probably wants to soften me up for this ordeal," Koskinen said to himself.

"Sit down, Captain. Did you have a good trip down here?"

"Oh, yes, thank you."

With that preliminary short ritual having been danced through, Blomquist got down to the business at hand.

"Captain," said Blomquist, "in a few minutes we'll meet with General Mahlmgren and a couple of the staff to discuss this project which we talked about last week in Tampere. Of course, the General will speak for himself, but you should know that he is determined to go ahead with it. He will want to be assured of your commitment to participate as a key person. We picked you for this job because of your absolute dedication and dogged perseverance in past undertakings. We respect your talents and your ability to intuitively select the opportunities to accomplish your missions."

Koskinen did not respond to these accolades of his abilities, nor did he show any reaction. However, inwardly, he grimaced at what was an obvious attempt by Blomquist to stroke his ego and he, Koskinen, resented it. Koskinen considered egotism as a character flaw, a symptom of self-importance. Like arrogance, egotism was a veneer that covered over a person's sense of insecurity and made the person vulnerable to others' blandishments.

Koskinen considered himself to be a plain man, direct in speaking, forthright in expressing his opinions, analytical at arriving at decisions based on all available facts, and clearly aware of his abilities and talents as well as his limitations. He did not need Blomquist's cajoling or his proselytizing and he resented that Blomquist didn't recognize that after the many meetings and conferences he had had with Blomquist. Of course, Koskinen acknowledged to himself, maybe he just resented Blomquist.

Colonel Blomquist buzzed Marjatta. "Let me know if the General is ready for us to come to his office."

A few moments later a ring on the intercom and Marjatta said, "The General said he will see you now."

Blomquist and Koskinen walked to the end of the corridor to the General's office and entered.

General Aarne Mahlgren rose from his chair behind his massive pine desk to greet them.

"Good morning, gentlemen. It's good to see you again, Captain Koskinen. How is the family?"

"Fine, thank you, sir," replied Koskinen.

"Please be seated, gentlemen." Mahlgren gestured to chairs on the side of the desk opposite to him. "I expect Colonel Lindforst and Captain Annala to be here shortly. As soon as they arrive, we'll discuss what I have in mind." Mahlgren remained standing.

General Mahlgren was a dominating figure of a man. At six foot four inches, with a large and broad muscular frame, rugged facial features, high cheekbones, square, determined jaw and large blue charismatic eyes, one received an immediate impression that here was a man of great courage, forceful character, exuding confidence and a quick intelligence. One's attention became riveted upon the General to the almost exclusion of anyone else in a room, like a powerful magnet drawing and concentrating to itself.

At age 44, General Mahlgren had risen quickly in the Finnish military system. His organizational and administrative abilities along with his military prowess had been early recognized by his superiors both in the civil government and the military establishment.

In the early 1900's, a small group of men organized a secret organization to gain independence for Finland from the oppressive Tsarist regime of Russia which then controlled Finland. The group called themselves the Activist Opposition Party. To them, Russia was an enemy to be cast out of Finland's affairs.

When World War I began in 1914 some of these Finns were residents of Berlin, Germany and, with Germany at war with Russia, they recognized that Germany could be an ally of Finland in overthrowing the Russian grasp on Finland. The Finns managed to successfully persuade the German General Staff to accept 200 young Finns to be given limited military training. Finland up to that time had no military establishment of its own. Russian soldiers occupied the country.

The secret activist organization began to recruit volunteers for the training in Germany. Forty percent of the volunteers were university students who were rabidly anti-Russian and intensely devoted to bringing about the independence of Finland.

At the age of twenty-one, Aarne Mahlgren was among the first of the student volunteers for the German training. He arrived at the German camp in Holstein, near Hamburg, in February 1915 where training for potential officers and noncommissioned officers was given. The volunteers grew in number to about 2,000 and in 1916 they were formed as the 27th Royal Prussian Jaeger Battalion. The Finns training in Germany became known in Finland as the "Jaegers" and, on return to Finland in 1918, they served as the officer cadre basis for the new Finnish military. The young "Jaeger" officers who showed exceptional promise were promoted rapidly. And among those who demonstrated exceptional promise was Lt. Aarne Mahlmgren.

On December 6, 1917, the Finnish Parliament formally declared Finland to be an independent, sovereign nation. Events in Russia with the turmoil caused by the Bolshevik revolution and Lenin's conciliatory attitude toward Finland had presented the Finnish leaders with the opportunity to realize their long held dream of nationhood.

Shortly after the declaration of independence, in January 1918 a radical, revolutionary Finnish Socialist workers party, later called the "Red Guards," attacked the government and seized control of Helsinki. The objective of the Red Guard was to establish a Communist, Marxian type of government in Finland. The Red Guard was aided and abetted by the Russian military and, especially, by the Russian soldiers still in Finland.

Under the leadership of General Gustav Mannerheim, a new Finnish army was organized. In the civil war that ensued, the army was known as the "Whites." Many of the "Jaegers" played prominent roles in the battles against the "Reds." Mahlgren distinguished himself in the vicious, brutal battle to regain control of the City of Tampere in central

Finland. Tampere was the center of the Reds power and had become a hotbed for the so-called "Workers Movement."

Mahlgren and his company had been in the vanguard of the Whites' attack on the City. In a daring and ruthless assault from the western perimeter of the Red forces in the City, he and his men had quickly pushed to the center of the City, causing disarray in the Red ranks and making it somewhat easier for other White units to advance in their sectors. Mahlgren took few Reds as prisoners. He had ordered his men to shoot on the spot the Red soldiers including the Russian soldiers helping them. The Reds were doing the same to the Whites. Mahlgren took no pride in these executions, but, to him, Finland had to be saved from Communism and order had to be established out of the anarchy that then existed.

The Reds were defeated in Tampere on April 6, 1918 and Helsinki fell to the Whites by April 13. By the middle of May the Whites had taken the rest of the areas held by the Reds and the Civil War came to an end. Mahlgren received an immediate promotion to Colonel and was personally induced by General Mannerheim to remain in the army and to make the military his career. He was given the task of organizing an Intelligence section, which up to that time, was nonexistent. It was Mahlgren who had recruited Koskinen to head the Tampere Intelligence Region.

Colonel Anders Lindforst and Captain Helena Annala entered the office together and the General waved them to chairs.

"You all know each other, so I'd like to get down to the business at hand," Mahlgren stated. Mahlgren took his seat and sat silently for a few moments as if pondering how to start the discussion.

General Mahlgren turned and addressed Koskinen, "Colonel Blomquist discussed a proposal with you last week, Captain. So I'm assuming you understand the task at hand. I believe Colonel Lindforst and Captain Annala can be of great help to you. I want to express our objective, the reason for the plan and how we may accomplish the objective as soon as possible."

"First, let me say that I expect absolute, and I mean 'absolute' confidentiality in this matter. This is something that must not go beyond you here and a few people in the government with whom I have discussed the plans we are proposing."

"If anyone breaks that confidentiality, there will be severe consequences to the person who broke the confidentiality and consequences for the country, our country."

The General then proceeded to explain the substance of the project. His manner was that of professional detachment, coolness, and objectivity devoid of any emotion except that of determination to do what he felt had to be done by whatever method would get the objective accomplished.

"We all understand, I trust, that the objective of this project is to eliminate Stalin from his position as head of the Soviet government. If you do not understand that, please speak up now."

Koskinen spoke up, "Sir, what do you mean by 'eliminate'?" Koskinen felt that he had a right to ask that question since it had become apparent that he was to be the point man in this project.

"By that I mean," Mahlgren replied, "anything that will remove Stalin from power and decision making. That implies assassination; drug induced physical or mental incapacity, a revolt engineered to overthrow his government, or whatever. I personally favor assassination as the ultimate resolution of the matter. Does that answer your question, Captain? Perhaps you have some other ideas."

No one in the group said anything, but sat ready to hear the General out.

The General went on. "Stalin is an absolute ruler. His word is law and his commands and orders are obeyed without question. Those who do or might question him do not live very long thereafter. He rules with an iron fist and through fear, not his fear but the fear held by every one of his subjects that they will become victims of his psychopathic passionate need to punish. The Soviets are held together by Stalin's rule of fear. If you eliminate Stalin, the Soviets will disintegrate and the influence of the Soviets in international matters will be destroyed."

General Mahlgren then went on to reveal his feelings in the matter. "Do I care if Stalin is undertaking mass executions of his people? Absolutely not! Do I care if every Russian person lives in fear? No, not at all! Do I care if Stalin is ruining the economy of his country? I could care less!

"What then do I care about? I care that Stalin will seek to seize Finland, my country, my people, that we shall again become a vassal state as we were only too recently under the Tsars. I want to make sure that that will not happen and the only sure and certain way that I know of to see that it does not happen is to eliminate the dictator, Stalin. If he is eliminated, the Soviets will fall into a confused mass with all sorts of individuals entering into a struggle for power. That will render the government impotent to do any mischief to Finland."

As General Mahlgren spoke, Koskinen became entranced by the transformation that the General displayed. From what was a cool, almost cold, initial recitation of the objective to what could only be described as a passionate crusading fervor of a man who was again caught up in the heat of a battle he was determined to win at all costs.

The General must have realized that he had allowed himself to become too emotional for he stopped talking and permitted a few more silent moments. Then, more calmly, he addressed the group before him.

"The reason that we have originated this project is because we have received some evidence, not much, admittedly, but some evidence that Stalin may have some designs on grabbing Finnish territory. We have received some information, and we cannot confirm its reliability, that Stalin and Hitler may be working towards an agreement between them to divide up Europe. Finland and the Baltic States of Estonia and Latvia and possibly Lithuania will presumably go to Russia. Hitler will get parts of Czechoslovakia, Poland, Romania and Bulgaria. If this is true or not true we cannot wait to find out. We must stop it before it develops, and again, the only way to stop it is to get rid of Stalin."

Koskinen raised the question, "But what about Hitler? He's another dictator."

"We are not worried about Hitler," Mahlgren replied. "Hitler has his hands full with Poland and the rest of the Eastern European countries. Besides, Hitler hates Stalin and the Russians. Any agreement he makes with them won't last very long. Hitler won't attack us. He wants us to remain neutral so he can concentrate on bigger fish. I don't know this officially, but it just seems common sense."

"But wouldn't Russia also want us to be neutral?" further inquired Koskinen.

"No," Mahlgren answered, "Stalin is shrewd enough to know that if Hitler wants to attack Russia, he may send troops through Finland to attack Leningrad which as you know isn't very far from the Finnish border to the South. So, to make it difficult for Hitler to use that route, Stalin will want to be in control of Finland, and Finland would, in either case, no longer be neutral."

General Mahlgren paused, looked at the people in the room as if to let what he was saying sink in. No one said anything. Each felt it appropriate to let the General have the floor to express what he had in mind.

To break the session for a few moments, General Mahlgren suggested that if anyone cared for a cup of coffee to feel free to help themselves. It was close to the noon hour and, except for the black sausage he'd had at the train stop in Ruhimaki, Koskinen had not had much to eat that day. He was getting hungry. In addition, he had not yet checked in at his hotel. He thought that he'd sound out the General's plans for the day.

"Sir, are you planning to reconvene this afternoon, that is, after lunch?"

"Yes, I think we should get most of this resolved today. I take your hint, Captain." Mahlgren smiled at Koskinen's not too subtle suggestion that they break for lunch.

"Why don't we break for lunch now and get back here by 1400," declared the General.

Colonel Blomquist spoke for the first time since the meeting with the General started. "Perhaps the four of us can have lunch together in the cafeteria downstairs." He referred to himself, Colonel Lindforst, Captain Annala and Koskinen.

Koskinen begged off. "I'd very much like to but I have to check in at the hotel where I'm staying. I'd like to get settled there."

"Of course, I understand," replied Blomquist. "Where are you staying?"

"At the Hotel Torni on Yrjonkatu."

"Yes, it's not very far from here. Well, we'll see you a bit before 1400 hours."

Koskinen picked up his suitcase at Blomquist's office where he had left it on entering the Parliament House. He then proceeded to his hotel, about a ten minute walk.

As he walked, Koskinen mused over what General Mahlgren had said. But these musings were interlaced with thoughts of Elena. He wondered about her shopping with the Russian bureaucrats. He wondered if she would keep her dinner appointment with him. He also wondered if he should keep the appointment. Koskinen decided that he would discuss his experience with Elena when the Section reconvened at 1400 hours. As much as he was attracted to Elena, his job and the Stalin Project required that he exercise extreme caution. Someone's life, even his own, could be at risk unless everything went smoothly and without warning to the Russian government leadership. Koskinen realized that the slightest mistake would very likely result in a crisis between Finland and Russia.

After checking in at the hotel, Koskinen went to the small restaurant in the hotel and ordered potato soup and two "piirakka," a type of Finnish meat pie. On his way to his room, he picked up in the hotel lobby a copy of the Helsingin Sanomat, Finland's largest newspaper. Lying on his bed, he began to read, but the news was of little interest to him. His thoughts were of Elena. She had become a pervasive, or better still, he had allowed his thinking of her to take control. He had not given one thought to the Stalin Project.

"This is ridiculous," Koskinen said to himself. "I'm acting like an adolescent school boy. Until I call her, I will have to concentrate on my job." As the saying goes, "It's easier said than done." But he tried, anyway.

When the group reconvened at 1400 hours, everyone seemed more jovial, more relaxed. "Perhaps," Koskinen thought, "a little Vodka at lunch had created a more convivial atmosphere." Even the General joined in some banter back and forth. But, after a few moments, the General looked at his watch, sat down in his chair and became quite serious in demeanor. Those in the room fell silent. Only the General spoke.

"Captain Koskinen, our plans for the moment, at least, are for you to be attached to our Embassy in Moscow for a short time so that you can get a 'lay of the land' so to speak and, perhaps, make necessary contacts. You will be given a free hand to do what is necessary to accomplish the Project."

Koskinen's heart jumped when he heard the General speak of a "free hand." He'd better ask what the parameters were.

"Sir, what do you mean by my having a 'free hand?'"

"Just that! You must decide from day to day, perhaps hour to hour what to do."

"I assume, then, that there is no necessity for me to get prior approval of the measures I might take, is that right?"

"Yes, that's right. And that is why we have chosen you for this mission. We have trust in you to do what is right and of benefit to Finland. We know you to be sensible, realistic, yet imaginative and resourceful. You're the kind of person we need in this matter. You will receive help from Colonel Lindforst, our liaison officer to our Embassy and Consulates in Russia and from Helena here, who is our Specialist on Russia."

The General paused for a moment and then said to Koskinen, "Have you given any thoughts about how you are going to proceed?"

Koskinen hesitated, his mind racing to come up with some answer.

"Well, I had come to the conclusion that I would have to start at our Embassy in Moscow, but as for any specifics, no, I have, at this moment, no ideas. I am of the opinion that I will have to evaluate what opportunities arise as I go along. It is impossible to outline a course of action in advance in a matter such as this."

"I suppose I'll have to agree," said General Mahlgren. "This is not something we have had to deal with before and so there is no prior experience to fall back on."

Koskinen thought the time had come to reveal to the group his experience with Elena and to see what their reactions were.

"There is a matter I'd like to tell you all about and to have you tell me what you think."

Koskinen then proceeded to relate how Elena and he had met, her job as translator, her traumatic experience with the arrest and disappearance of her father and brother, and her wish to do something about the mass executions going on in Russia.

"I have arranged to have dinner with her tomorrow evening."

The others in the room all looked startled.

"Why did you do that?" asked Colonel Blomquist, a deep frown on his face indicating to Koskinen a sense of disapproval.

"I thought that she might be useful in this undertaking of ours. I am almost certain she might welcome the opportunity to revenge her father and brother. I cannot, of course, be sure, but that is why I arranged to see her, to sound her feelings out and whether she, in fact, might be of help."

"I think you should go ahead with your plan to meet her tomorrow evening," General Mahlgren said, "but you might exercise extreme caution. Sitting down to dinner with this lady and talking with her is not a very good test of whether she can be trusted. She can say anything she thinks you may wish to hear. In any case, you must continue your facade as an import-export businessman and you must continue to use your pseudonym. If she is not trustworthy, we cannot afford to give any slightest hint of our plans."

The General then suggested that Colonel Lindforst and Helena might just wander into the restaurant after he, Koskinen, and Elena had been there awhile.

"Perhaps they can evaluate this Elena, sort of size her up. Anders and Helena can sit at a nearby table, but continue to act as strangers to you. What do you think, Captain?" the General asked.

"Sir, I don't think that I can endorse it. In the first place, in all due respect to Colonel Lindforst and Captain Annala and their competency, I cannot imagine how they can evaluate anyone by seeing that person from another table and by not talking with her. In the second place, Sir, as long as you are trusting me with spearheading this project and will, necessarily, have to rely on my judgment, especially when I'm in Russia, I would prefer that you rely on my judgment here. I welcome Colonel Lindforst's and Captain Annala's help, but not in this immediate situation with this young lady."

General Mahlgren chuckled good-naturedly, "Yes, you've convinced me. So Lindforst and Annala will stay home."

Koskinen knew in his heart that he had not completely leveled with the people in the room. He had not mentioned that he had a certain attraction for Elena. It was something he was not about to reveal anyway. After all, he was not at all certain just what his feelings were. Koskinen wondered whether General Mahlgren might not have sensed something about his feelings, maybe in the way he had talked about Elena. Maybe that's why the General had suggested that Lindforst and Annala drop in at the restaurant.

These thoughts were running through Koskinen's mind when General Mahlgren continued with plans for the project.

"In about two weeks, our new Foreign Minister, Eljas Erkko, may go to Moscow with Vaino Tanner, the leader of the Social Democrats, to discuss and clarify some of the rumored demands of the Soviets regarding the Aland Islands. We'd like to have you accompany them as part of the delegation. When they return to Finland, you can remain at the Embassy. Going as part of a delegation will enable you to enter Russia more easily and it may give you an opportunity to size up the situation when you attend the discussion group."

Koskinen nodded in agreement.

General Mahlgren added, "Of course, you understand that these plans are always subject to sudden changes. We'll have to adjust if there are any. Tomorrow, we can work out some necessary details and, thereafter, you can return home and await further instructions, but to be ready to move on short notice. Do you have any questions, Captain?"

"Yes, I'm curious. Do President Kallio and Prime Minister Cajander know of this project?"

"I could say that is not your concern, but I'll answer you because I know you and all of us here can keep confidentialities. President Kallio does not know. The Prime Minister only knows that we are considering it and he has not offered any objection, although, when I discussed the hypothetical case with him, I got the impression he'd rather not know anything about it. You know, if the Soviet government should later protest, he could always say that the action was unauthorized and that he never would have allowed it, had he known. It's part of the diplomatic game, I suppose."

"It's also a safeguard for the country, I would imagine," offered Colonel Blomquist.

General Mahlgren arose from his seat as an indication that the meeting was being adjourned.

"We'll all meet here tomorrow morning at 0930. We'll work out the details. In the meantime Captain, remember, at your dinner appointment with the lady be very, very careful. You know, not too many drinks to loosen the tongue." Mahlgren smiled and patted Koskinen on the shoulder as he guided him to the office door. It was 1530 hours.

As the group walked down the corridor from the General's office, Colonel Blomquist said to Koskinen, "Captain, perhaps we can talk a few minutes in my office."

"I thought everything will be covered tomorrow at the meeting. What would you like to talk about?"

"About your young lady."

"No, Colonel, I would rather not discuss it any further. The General has given his approval of the dinner."

Blomquist detected a tone of annoyance in Koskinen's voice and so he dropped the subject. "Well, we'll see you tomorrow, Captain."

"Good day, sir, and good day to you, Colonel Lindforst and to you, Captain Annala." Koskinen left the group standing in the corridor in front of Blomquist's office.

Captain Koskinen walked hurriedly to his hotel. He had decided to call Elena and ask her to have dinner with him tonight instead of tomorrow evening. When he reached his room and immediately called the Hotel Klaus Kurki, he asked the clerk at the hotel to be put through to Elena Marikova. He experienced a moment of anxiety during the silence that ensued as the clerk checked the register. Was Elena at the hotel? Then he heard the telephone ring and he relaxed to know that, at least, she had registered. So she was being truthful about staying at the hotel.

When Elena answered the telephone, he recognized her voice.

"Elena, this is Antti, your train companion."

"Yes, of course, but I was not expecting your call."

"How did your buying trip go?"

"Well, enough. But, of course, they bought everything they saw."

"Have the trade mission people left for home?"

"Yes, earlier this afternoon after lunch."

"Then you are free to have dinner with me this evening?"

"Yes, I'd be delighted."

"Good. Can you meet me at about 1800?"

"Yes, where shall I meet you?"

"Are you familiar with the Ravintola Kreisi?"

"No, I'm not."

"It's a small restaurant on Bulevardi, the same street your hotel is on and just a short distance from the hotel. I'm sure the clerk at the hotel desk can direct you. It would be simpler for you to ask him than for me to try to give you directions. I shall have a table ready and be there when you arrive."

"Thank you, and I'll see you at six. That is 'Kreisi?'"

"Yes, 'K-R-E-I-S-I.'" Koskinen spelled the name out.

When he had hung up the telephone, Koskinen remained standing at the table as if immobilized. He felt a surge of multiple emotions, of excitement, of confusion, of doubt, of fear, and of considerable anxiety. After a few moments he walked over to the sofa chair and sat down as if exhausted already from the conflicts going on in his mind. Where, prior to his making the call, he had eagerly anticipated seeing Elena again, he now had some reservations and reticence about the whole event.

Koskinen began to wonder what he might be getting into, whether he had been too impulsive, too aggressive in pushing the relationship with Elena. He recognized a confusion of feelings. Was he truly interested in Elena only from a professional stance or was he attracted to her physically or was it a combination of both. In any case, he wasn't able, for the moment at least, to sort it out and maybe that was because he didn't want to be totally honest with himself. Koskinen was not used to allowing his emotions to seduce him. He valued his ability to detach himself from the emotional aspects of his job and to perform objectively and dispassionately. But, somehow, he recognized that this was different.

While he sat mulling over the impending dinner with Elena, he finally resolved that he would go ahead as if it was just another social casual dinner that he had participated in many times before and that he would put aside any personal feelings. After all, there was Anna at home and he would be seeing her in a day or so. He hadn't given much thought to Anna in the last several hours. He was probably taking Anna for granted; she was always there for him. Wonderful, devoted, loving Anna. And he still loved her dearly.

Feeling relieved at having resolved how he would handle his dinner with Elena, and the tenseness having left him, Koskinen dozed off for about an hour, awakening at close to 1700 hours as if he had preset an alarm clock for just the right time. He washed face and hands, put on a clean shirt which, as he reminded himself, Anna had laundered and ironed for him just before he left for Helsinki. Putting on his great-coat, fur hat and gloves, Koskinen walked down the hotel stairs, nodded to the clerk as he passed through the lobby and proceeded out to the street.

It was still January and still very cold. The chilling wind that swept in from the Baltic Sea added to the penetrating chill. Helsinki, situated on the northern shore of the Baltic, had no immunity and no insulation against annual winter deep-freezes. Those few Finns who could afford financially to do so traveled south to Cyprus and other warm areas at the beginning of winter and did not return until spring. Koskinen did not have that luxury.

It was dark when Koskinen arrived at the restaurant. In Finland in January there are only a few hours of daylight, a couple of hours on either side of the noon hour.

Koskinen approached the headwaiter and asked for and received a corner table at the far end of the dining room. Koskinen checked his coat and hat and proceeded to his assigned table and sat down. It was about 1745 hours. He ordered a brandy and soda and told the waiter he was awaiting another person.

The restaurant, at that time, had only one other table occupied by a couple, a young man and woman. Koskinen observed the couple for a few moments and concluded that they were too busy talking with each other to be of any concern to him. He sipped his drink only occasionally, preferring it to be a prop, something to do than to just sit like a lump on a log. Waiting for Elena increased somewhat the tension he felt about the impending visit with her. He had to remind himself from moment to moment that he had to relax and suppress his anxiety. He would hate to have Elena sense his anxiety or tension. He had been so much in control of himself during the train trip, casual and friendly and at ease. He felt that that was what had attracted Elena to him. Koskinen reasoned that women like to feel comfortable with a man, a man who was in control of himself, as well as the circumstance of the moment.

At a few minutes before 1800 hours, Elena entered the restaurant. Koskinen arose to greet her and to walk to the front of the restaurant to help her with her coat as well as to guide her to their table.

"Hello, Elena. Did you have any trouble finding this place?"

"Hello, Antti. No, I received good instructions from the desk clerk at the hotel. But, it's cold out. Whew!" Elena shivered. Koskinen helped her with her coat and checked it with the coat-check Madame.

"I already have a table. Shall we go back?" Koskinen took Elena by the arm and gently guided her to their table.

"Can I order you a drink?" Koskinen inquired.

"What are you having?"

"A brandy and soda."

"I'll have the same."

While awaiting her drink to be served, Elena initiated the conversation. "Well, how did your day go, Antti?"

"Very well. My company informed me that they want me to go to Moscow in about two weeks to firm up an order for some textiles placed by the Russian Foreign Commerce Department some months ago."

Koskinen smiled and looked a bit facetiously at Elena. "You know, I might need a translator."

"I know a couple of them who live in Moscow. I can give you their names and you can contact them."

"I appreciate that, but I would like to work with someone I can trust." Koskinen's facial expression clearly indicated that he was referring to Elena. "My company has trade secrets to protect," he added.

Elena quickly caught on as to what Koskinen was referring to and continuing her smile, said, "I would love to serve, but I would need to get the permission of our regional regulator. If there was no assignment pending at the time, he probably would approve of my request to travel to Moscow."

"By the way, Antti, I don't think I know your last name and what work you do. I probably should have asked earlier."

Koskinen replied, "My last name is Salonen and I work for the Finlayson Company in Tampere. They are manufacturers of textiles. A very large company in Tampere."

Elena's brandy and soda having arrived, she and Koskinen proceeded to order dinner from the menu. Koskinen helped a bit by translating the Finnish entrees offered by the restaurant.

Koskinen, at this point, felt that he should open the conversation to a more serious vein. He didn't want to spend the evening talking about trivia and, consequently, perhaps miss the opportunity to enlist Elena in his project. But, he knew that, while he had to be cautious, it was inevitable that crucial questions had to be asked unless he was willing to write Elena off as a potential participant in the project. He was not willing to do that, at least at this time.

Koskinen observed that Elena appeared to be somewhat tired and less lively than on the train trip, although she still had the warm, disarming smile and the attractive vivacious eyes. He reasoned that she'd had a tiring day shopping with the trade mission people. She was dressed in the same outfit that she had worn on the train, a plain, navy-blue coat jacket with a white blouse underneath and a matching navy blue skirt. Around her neck Elena wore a long gold chain with a large pendant at the end nestled at her breast line. The pendant was of gold laced edging with a porcelain oval center bearing a colored painting of what appeared to be some noble woman. A very fine piece of art jewelry, Koskinen thought.

"Who is the lady on your pendant?" Koskinen asked. "It's a very attractive piece of jewelry."

"This pendant belonged to my great grandmother and has been handed down through the family. The portrait is of Empress Catherine the Great. It's one of the few things of value we were able to salvage when we moved to Leningrad."

"It's very lovely," commented Koskinen. "You know, Elena, I fail to understand how you can work for a government that brought so much distress to your family by the arrests of your father and brother."

"Antti, I don't have any choice. I am told what to do with a threat that if I refuse, my mother and I could not be assured of our safety."

"Are translators that scarce in Russia that they had to force you into the job? I would think that after the arrests of your father and brother, the government would consider you unreliable."

"Translators, as such, are not scarce," Elena answered, "but translators of Finnish are a bit hard to find, so I'm told. You know, Finnish is a very difficult language with its many different word endings which can change meanings."

"Yes, I suppose you're right," Koskinen remarked. "You said on the train that you wished you could change the system in the Soviets, less fear, arrests, executions and so forth, perhaps, to move toward a democracy."

"Yes, I said that and I still believe it and hope for it."

"I understand," Koskinen said as nonchalantly as he could, "that there are groups outside of the Soviets, perhaps even governments, which would like to bring about that sort of change."

"Yes, I have heard there are groups which would like to do that, but I am not aware of any governments wanting to get involved." Elena looked sharply at Koskinen as if she was wondering why he was raising this issue. Koskinen sensed that and changed the subject of discussion, but not before explaining why he was asking the questions.

"I mention this only because I realize that, if you are serious about changing things, you cannot do so alone. You will need help."

Elena did not reply, but just shook her head thoughtfully.

"When I am on my visit to Moscow," Koskinen said, "I may be able to stop in Leningrad either on the way to Moscow or on the return."

"If you can manage that, it would be nice if you could stop in at our home and visit for a while."

Koskinen got the feeling that Elena was not very interested in talking about the politics in Russia and that the conversation was dragging and, perhaps, getting boring for her. So he asked her about her interest in music and the arts and about the museums she had visited. He talked about his interest in sports, of how he had competed in long distance track competitions when he was younger and of how he enjoyed skiing as most Finns do.

Koskinen could see that talking about these personal things had rescued the dinner table conversation from being submerged in boredom. But he also recognized that he had not gotten very far, if at all, in the matter of ferreting out Elena's interest in helping the project in some way. At that moment he was at a loss as to just what to do or say to arouse her interest without revealing his true role in the undertaking. He decided that it was appropriate to continue the more personal subjects.

"If I may ask, Elena, have you been married or are you married?"

"I was married when I was twenty, but the marriage lasted less than a year. I got a divorce. We were just not compatible."

"Do you have any children?"

"No, but some day, perhaps."

"Do you have a boy friend?"

"I do go out with different men, from time to time, but nothing serious. Russian men, that is, those still around, are not interesting. They're mostly Communist Party members and their primary intent when they take you out is to drink, get drunk, get boisterous and want to have sex at the end of the evening. I find that unacceptable, so, I don't go out very often. When I do, I think that this time it will be different. But, it never is, except for minor variations."

Koskinen chuckled at the description Elena had just painted. He thought that that description could fit some of the Finnish men he knew. But he said nothing.

Then Elena spoke and volunteered, "Do you know, Antti, after I left you at the railway station and during the shopping trip with the trade people, I kept thinking about why I had agreed to have dinner with you, because, after all, you are married and I have gone out with several married men and it is quite a dead end for me. Married men are generally so self-centered. By that I mean, they tell me about how miserable and how dissatisfied they are with their married life and how they might get a divorce. They don't seem interested in me as a person, except as a bed partner, and so, with that type, I never see them again. Why should I?"

Koskinen perceived that Elena had become rather sad, not bitter, just sad. He suddenly realized that his lively, ebullient lady was really very lonely and, probably, quite unhappy with her way of life. Life had not been good to her. She had her share of tragedy, Koskinen mused. And Koskinen felt sad, too, sad for Elena. He had come to have tender feelings for her. He felt bad, guilty about deceiving her about himself, using pseudonyms. He knew that he could not take advantage of her or to use her. He felt he had only two choices, to either kindly let Elena drift out of his life or to reveal who or what he really was. He could not bring himself to continue the deception for much longer. Elena was too nice a lady to lead her on.

Koskinen addressed Elena, "Elena, I am married. I told you that on the train. Do you think I have been self-centered as those others you just described?"

"No, you have not. And you have seemed to be genuinely interested in my welfare. And you have said you are happily married. Then, what puzzles me is why you asked me to dinner. Is it that you expect sex as a payback for this lovely dinner? Frankly, you seem like a nice guy who wouldn't have that as an objective. Perhaps, that is why I'm attracted to you. I feel comfortable with you, Antti. I feel I can trust you and that you have no motive but friendship."

Listening to Elena say this made Antti wince inwardly as he realized that Elena was being so candid and trustful with him.

"Yes, that's about it, Elena. I want to be your friend and I want to be helpful to the extent that I am able. I must confess that, yes, I am physically attracted to you, but I am also attracted to you as a person I perceive you to be, intelligent, forthright, strong character, a good sense of humor, honest and trusting, good emotions and other virtues."

"Thanks, Antti, I appreciate your sentiments." Elena looked lovingly at Koskinen, reached across the table and placed her hand in his. He gave her hand a gentle squeeze. They looked into each other's eyes and they were silent. A silence and a look that said much.

Koskinen, after a few moments, looked at his wristwatch. "It's going on 2100 hours. Perhaps, we should get you back to your hotel. You've had a long day."

"A good idea," Elena replied.

"I can get you a taxi," Koskinen suggested.

"No, it's only a couple of blocks. I'll walk it."

"I'll walk you back, if you don't mind."

"Of course, I don't mind."

Koskinen paid the bill and retrieved the coats and hats.

It was cold out on the street and the wind had become stronger. Elena walked closely to Koskinen as if for protection from the elements.

And Koskinen, reflexively, took Elena's arm and pulled her close to him in a reassuring gesture.

In a few minutes they arrived at the entrance to the Hotel Klaus Kurki and entered the well-lighted lobby. Koskinen released his hold on Elena's arm. Elena turned toward him as their coats touched and, looking wistfully at him, stood silent for a moment and then said softly with her warm, gentle smile, "Would you care to come up for a short time? The evening is still young."

Koskinen hesitated to answer, but Elena's look was so compelling that he found himself saying, "Yes, of course, for a short time. I'd love to." He took her hand and they entered the elevator to the third floor.

Elena's room was not the usual hotel room of a couple of chairs, a sofa and a bed. The rooms in the Hotel Klaus Kurki were more luxurious as befitted an older hotel designed for the upper class, paneled walls, crystal lamps, plush carpet, and well-upholstered furniture. Art pictures decorated the walls. Koskinen had stayed at the hotel on a few rare occasions. It was expensive and the Department budget, generally, did not allow for the higher rates.

Entering the room and being alone with Elena made Koskinen feel a bit awkward. Yet, he was glad Elena had asked him to visit her because he still wanted to learn whether Elena could and would be of some help in the project to which the Department had assigned him.

"Why don't you take your coat and hat off even if you will be here for a short time," Elena suggested. Koskinen did so.

Elena sat down on the sofa and pointing to the additional space said, "Please, sit down here. The sofa is more comfortable." Koskinen could not refuse the invitation and, as he admitted to himself, he had no thought of refusing. In the soft light of the table lamps, Elena looked very pretty to him, maybe even a bit seductive. They engaged in some small talk for several minutes.

Elena looked down at her hands in her lap as if she wanted to say something, but was hesitant to do so. Finally, she looked up at Koskinen.

"You probably sensed that I like you, Antti. I would not have asked you up if I did not."

"Well, I assumed that you didn't find me obnoxious." Koskinen had a twinkle in his eyes and a humorous smile. "And, if I did not like you, I would not have accepted your invitation to come here. So, that makes it quite mutual, doesn't it?"

"Yes, it does."

Elena appeared pensive and after a moment, said, "Even so, I don't know you for very long and I know very little about you and the little you have told me, I don't know if it's the truth."

"Well, that is something that is also mutual," Koskinen said.

"I'm not at all distrustful of you, Antti. Quite to the contrary, as I have already said, you seem to be different from the other men I have been with. I apologize. I should not have implied that you might have lied to me. Please forgive me, won't you?" Elena placed her hand on Koskinen's arm.

"There is nothing to forgive. I can understand that you should be wary in these situations. You know, in a way, I feel a bit wary of you, too. And I don't like that sort of thing. I think it's horrible that two people who like each other must necessarily have reservations about each other."

"Perhaps," Elena said, "it is because we come from such different cultures and such different philosophies."

"No, I don't think that's it so much as it is a gender difference. Men and women are not only physically different, but they are emotionally and intellectually different. Each perceives things from a different basis. Each could live in the same culture, same politics, same community, and, yet, there would be an invisible barrier between them. And, no matter how long you knew each other, the difference in perceptions is still there."

"Well, perhaps so. But where does that leave us?"

Koskinen thought a moment. "It leaves us with something that is common to everyone, man or woman. It leaves us with something we all share and that is a need for love, a need for reciprocated love. Can you agree to that?"

"Yes, of course, I can agree. You are very perceptive. That should dispel our concerns. Except that love should be sincere and without reservation. Can you agree to that?" Elena and Koskinen both chuckled as each realized that they were, in a sense, challenging each other.

"Look, why don't we relax a bit, forget about being so serious," Elena smiled her warm smile. "I don't have anything to drink here, vodka, brandy, that sort of thing. But, I can call down to the desk and order a pot of coffee. How would that be?"

"Sure, fine. I wouldn't care for any liquor right now anyway."

Elena called the clerk on duty at the desk and placed the order.

Koskinen got up and walked casually about the room, admiring the artwork on the walls. He turned and walked over to Elena, who was still standing at the desk phone looking at him, but not saying a word. Koskinen took Elena by the arm and gently kissed her on the lips. Elena placed her hand on Koskinen's shoulder and her lips parted as she reciprocated the kiss. The kiss was not a long one, nor was it one of surging passion, but it had the meaning that previous millenniums of men and women had instinctively understood, the rite of initiation to a love relationship.

The emotional moment was interrupted by a knock on the door. The bellboy had brought the coffee. Koskinen paid and tipped the young man who quickly left after placing the tray on the telephone desk. The kiss had cracked the barrier between Elena and Koskinen. The coffee was no longer needed.

Alone again, Elena and Koskinen embraced. The one dispassionate and brief kiss now graduated to several, longer and more fervent kisses and gentle caresses. Like the pounding waves rising higher and higher in the primitive stormy seas from which evolutionists tell us man's ancestors had come, the tides of an emotional storm were beginning to roll in on Koskinen and Elena. And emotional tides like the ocean tides cannot be stopped until they are satisfied they can go no further and must retreat. How far the tide will roll in will depend on the intensity of the storm.

Even as the intensity of the physical proximity of Elena began to build in him, Koskinen had thoughts racing through his mind; thoughts of Anna, thoughts of fairness to Elena, thoughts of his professional mission, thoughts of where all this might end. These thoughts created a conflict with his physical impulsions.

Releasing Elena from his embrace, Koskinen took her by the hand saying, "Let's sit down on the sofa for a while." Elena complied but with a puzzled look on her face.

"Is there something the matter?" she asked in a voice that showed some concern.

"I would like to talk with you," replied Koskinen.

They sat closely and turned slightly toward each other, her hand in his.

"Elena," began Koskinen, "if we are to continue as friends and in our newly found relationship, I feel that there are things you ought to know about me. I like you very much and, for that reason, I want to be fair and as open as I can be with you. I don't look upon you as someone who is here today and gone tomorrow."

"Are you saying that you have not been honest with me in what you have told me since we met?" Elena frowned with a troubled look.

"I have been very honest about my feelings for you, but I have not been honest or forthright about my background and that may or may not have an effect on you. It is something that goes beyond you as a person."

"I don't understand. Can you be more specific? I'm willing to listen."

"Elena, you are a Soviet citizen employed by the government. I am a Finnish citizen employed by my government. The relationship between the two governments has not always been harmonious and peaceful and perhaps may get worse. I do not know, at this moment, whether you have other duties when you come to Finland beyond just translating." Koskinen was speaking kindly and softly and as a friend.

Elena smiled, "Do you mean that I might be a spy?"

"I don't know. That is my point because my government work requires that I be very cautious, especially, with Soviet citizens. I won't ask you to swear on a bible, but can you be honest with me in answering my concern?"

"Antti, if I gave you an honest answer, one which I knew to be honest, would you trust that my answer was honest? I mean, how can I prove to you that my word is true?"

"Yes, I suppose I would need some demonstrative proof beyond mere words. But, until you proved otherwise, I would have to assume your honesty."

"Well, let me be candid with you. I am not a spy and I have not been given any duties by the government beyond those of translating. Does that convince you?"

Elena paused for a moment. "Well, then you are not in the export-import business."

"No, I'm not."

"Well, then, what is it you do?"

"Elena, my job is to let my government know what is going on in other countries, for example, in the Soviets and to do what I can to see that no harm comes to Finland."

"Ah, then, you are a spy!" Elena said this in a put-on mocking voice. "No, seriously, let me guess. You are in intelligence work."

Koskinen knew then, as he had observed all along, that Elena was no fool. She had put two and two together very quickly.

"Yes, but all governments are constantly trying to find out what is going on in other countries. We all know that and there is nothing wrong with it. It's to be expected by every government." Koskinen tried to play down his role.

"Are you hoping that I will help you? Is that why you asked me to dinner? And now up here?"

Koskinen felt he was being trapped by this sharp- minded lady. What could he say without revealing his current project and still be honest with Elena.

"Elena, I want to tell you again, I like you very much. I was attracted to you when you sat down in my seat in the train and, during the trip, I developed a strong feeling for you. I would have invited you to dinner regardless of my position. I am still attracted to you and I still think you are a very fine person, one with whom I hope to remain friends. However, yes, the thought has occurred to me that if you can be of help in my work of the moment, I would welcome it. But, if you'd rather not, then I hope we can still be good friends."

"What is it that you think I might do to help?"

"I don't know, frankly. I'll know more when I get to Moscow. However, I know that if the troubles in Russia can be stopped, then that will mean that Finland will be in less danger."

"Do you expect to stop them by yourself?" Elena was inquisitive, but being sweet about her demeanor. She was not prodding, not sarcastic, not demeaning. She was merely trying to get a better understanding of what Koskinen was all about. She sensed so much hesitation on Koskinen's part.

"No, of course not," Koskinen said. "That is where you might come in. I know it all sounds very mysterious, very secretive, but it will just have to be that way for now. It is something I would not even tell my wife. I hope you will believe me. Also, now that we know each other better, my first name is not Antti. It is Timo. And my last name is not Salonen. I cannot tell you my last name either. Please forgive me. I have feelings for you, but you will just have to accept what I am saying and doing."

Elena could see that Koskinen was feeling very wretched and she decided not to pursue the questioning.

"Yes," she said, "I'll accept that. I believe that you're being sincere and as open as your situation allows. Suppose we have that cup of coffee."

"That is a good idea," said Koskinen, thankful that Elena recognized his predicament. He felt that he had handled the situation adequately. He had been honest and forthright up to a permissible point.

Koskinen arose from the sofa and as Elena poured coffee into the two cups, he put his arm around her waist.

"Thanks, Elena, for your understanding and for your compassion."

"On, it's really nothing. Don't be concerned." She turned fully to him "You can kiss me again if you'd like."

"How can I say, 'No'," and Koskinen drew her closely to him and kissed her gently. And Elena pressed her lips to his. They stood there for what must have seemed like an eternity, kissing and caressing. The tide came in again, as it always does and there was no stopping it.

Elena and Koskinen, still holding each other, walked to the edge of the bed and sat down. Quickly, what was a smooth and even tide became a storm. The waves rose higher and higher and pounded the sands on the shore until they parted and revealed below the surface a crevice into which the waters poured relentlessly. The storm lasted only a short time. As quickly as it had arisen, it subsided. The sands washed back into the crevice and covered it once more. The tide retreated and, as it withdrew, the shore became peaceful and quiet. In a short time nature had demonstrated its two sides, one of fury and irresistible forces and one of a return to a healing calm.

When Koskinen awoke the next morning, he found that Elena was already dressing and moving about. He looked at his wristwatch. It was close to seven. He remembered his appointment with General Mahlgren and the others at nine-thirty. There was no need to rush.

"Good morning, Timo," Elena came over and sat down on the bed next to him.

"Good morning, Elena. How are you feeling?"

"Fine, and you?"

"I feel very good. How long have you been up?"

"Only about twenty minutes."

"I didn't expect this, you know," Koskinen said this in a not very convincing voice, referring to the previous night.

"I didn't either. That is proved by the fact that the coffee is still untouched in the cups."

They both laughed. They both recognized that the coffee was a mere amulet to facilitate the exorcism of the emotional ritual that was to follow. The coffee was like a key to open the door to a room that needed to be explored for hidden treasures of the heart.

"You know, Elena, you're so sweet. So delicate, so feminine, so loving and lovable. What more can I say." Koskinen needed no answer to his rhetorical question.

"Well, you're a lovely guy," Elena responded. "I suppose I could say, 'it was a wonderful one night,' but, I would like to know if I shall see you again."

"I would hope so. I do want to see you again," said Koskinen. And his voice sounded sincere and truthful. "Why don't you give me your address and telephone number in Leningrad and I'll keep in touch with you. When, I cannot say. I will probably be back in Tampere for the next two weeks before I leave for Moscow. Even that has not been firmed up yet. I'll know more, possibly, after today. However, for your world, I am Antti Salonen in the export-import business. And if I call you, I shall use that name. Eventually, you will know more about me."

"I understand." Elena leaned over and kissed him and Koskinen held her firmly yet gently. Koskinen then arose and began to dress.

"I have to get back to my hotel and pick up my things and then get over to the office. I have a 0930 appointment."

Koskinen paused, "Do you think you'll be safe? Do you think you've been watched?"

"No, I am such an insignificant cog in the wheel that the government would not waste manpower by having me trailed. I'm sure of it."

"But, you get into foreign countries like Finland. Doesn't that create a basis for suspicion? Aren't you a valuable source to look for certain things while you are in Finland?"

"The Government hasn't asked me to do that up to this time," replied Elena and a bit upset that Koskinen was going over the same sort of questions he raised the night before.

"Elena, before I leave you, can I ask you if you will help me get information in your country?"

"Timo, I can't answer that until I know what you want to know and whether, in any case, I can help you will depend on the circumstances at that time. You see, we all in Russia are in a state where we never know what will happen next. You must understand that. It is not like it is in Finland where, I assume, there is some stability in your day to day life and you are able to forecast what you will probably be doing next month or the next six months."

"Yes, you're right," Koskinen said. "I should not expect immediate answers. But, whether I need your help or not, I shall keep in touch with you."

Koskinen was ready to leave. Elena wrote her address and telephone number on a piece of Hotel Klaus Kurki stationery. Koskinen gave it back to her. "I think you should write the information on a piece of plain paper." Elena got the import of his request, smiled and tore off the printed letterhead.

"There you are. You now have your plain piece of paper."

Koskinen laughed. "I should have thought of that."

"Well, Elena, as they say in Finnish, 'Nakemiin!' goodbye. I hate to leave, but I must. And you'll be leaving shortly, too."

Koskinen and Elena kissed and hugged for a few moments and Koskinen detected tears in the corners of Elena's eyes. He felt grieved. They looked lovingly at each other for another few moments. And then parted.

Koskinen had a mission to accomplish and he understood that he now had to concentrate on that. He did not look back.

Walking back to the Hotel Torni, Koskinen's thoughts ranged over a wide spectrum, primarily and recurringly to Elena, to the project to be discussed shortly at the Intelligence Office and to Anna, his wife. He had never been unfaithful to Anna before this. In his thoughts he compared Anna to Elena. Anna, like Elena, was a very attractive woman, but where Elena was usually smiling and with good humor, lively and expressive, Anna more taciturn and, like so many Finnish women, especially those from the central part of Finland, like Anna, quite serious and mundane, not given to displays of emotion. Anna, Koskinen admitted, was, nevertheless, good-hearted and considerate and attentive to his needs as he was of hers. There was no problem between them that was not discussed and resolved. Yet, what attracted him to Elena was the "fire" in her. Anna was not "fiery." Maybe that was the Russian temperament that Elena had.

Checking out of his hotel, Koskinen proceeded to Parliament House arriving at about 0915. He told the receptionist to announce his presence to General Mahlgren when the time approached 0930. In the meantime, he'd just sit and wait. Koskinen did not feel like visiting with Colonel Blomquist again.

At 0930, precisely, Koskinen entered the General's office. The others had not arrived as yet. Mahlgren told Koskinen he'd like to talk a few moments alone before calling Blomquist, Lindforst and Annala.

Mahlgren addressed Koskinen, "Captain, about your dinner tonight with the young lady."

Koskinen interrupted the General. "Sir, I had the dinner last night."

The General looked surprised. "Did you come to any conclusions about her helping us?"

"Not specifically. I told her that I might like to use her for getting some information about some Russian issues and she said she'd have to know what, specifically, I wanted her to do before she could say. Under the stringent and unstable conditions now prevailing in Russia, I can understand her position."

"You didn't reveal anything to her about the project we have in mind?"

"Absolutely not."

"You know, Captain, I tried to reach you at the Hotel Torni last evening about 2230 and again this morning at 0730 and the hotel clerk said there was no response from your room" The raised eyebrows and skeptical look on the General's face hinted to Koskinen that the General suspected that he had spent the night with the lady. Koskinen felt his face flush and his uneasy reaction must surely confirm the General's suspicion. He said, "I'm sorry you couldn't reach me. I hope it wasn't inconveniencing."

Mahlgren stated, "I called to ask you to come in a half-hour early so I could talk with you before getting the others in here."

General Mahlgren stared at Koskinen a few moments and than said, "Captain, I'm not going to ask you how you spent your time last evening and night. What you do personally is of no concern to me unless, and I emphasize 'unless,' what you do will compromise our Department or adversely affect a mission we may have. Anything like that would result in severe disciplinary punishment and your disgrace. To be more precise, if this lady can help the mission without compromising it, then fine. If she cannot or, if there is a possibility of compromise, then I suggest you drop her and get on with other solutions."

The General paused. "I know I must sound like I'm scolding or that I'm already accusing you of some dereliction. Neither is the case." Mahlgren appeared to Koskinen to be displeased, maybe even worried that the Captain had possibly told the lady too much.

Koskinen felt a rush of anger, but he managed to control his feelings. Koskinen felt the General was doubting his judgment. And he felt the General had no business involving himself in his personal life.

"General, I assure you that I have used good judgment in this matter and that I shall continue to do so. Nothing has been compromised up to now and nothing will in the future to the extent that I can control the project. However, you must know that I cannot give guarantees that everyone who becomes a contact will prove trustworthy. We all do the best we can in checking people out, but in a place like Russia, checking out a person can be difficult."

"I understand what you're saying, Captain, but, in this case, it wouldn't be the first time some sharp, enticing female has been able to loosen the tongue of a trusting male operative." Mahlgren's voice and visage had become less severe as he accepted Koskinen's assurances.

"Now," Mahlgren said, "I wanted to talk with you about the aspects of this project. You know that the reason we have for getting rid of Stalin is that we perceive it as the only way to secure the safety, integrity and sovereignty of Finland. An incidental benefit will be the lessening of tensions in Europe as a whole. There will be only one remaining dictator to deal with, namely, Adolph Hitler, and, as I have explained before, we are not overly concerned that he is a threat to us.

"There is an urgency to get this project underway and to get it done. It is January 1939 and a crisis for Finland could come any day. We have had rumors that Stalin wants to protect his ass by cuddling up to Hitler. Stalin, we understand, is mortally afraid of Hitler and is going to take whatever step he thinks necessary to protect the Soviets borders. I explained this yesterday.

"If all goes as planned, you will go to our Embassy in Moscow in about two weeks. Our Ambassador will be here in Helsinki for a few days at about that time and you will be able to meet and talk with him before he returns to the Embassy. We shall explain to the Ambassador when he is here what your purpose and mission is. However, officially, you will be going as a foreign trade specialist.

"The Embassy already has contacts within the Soviet government that provide some information about what is going on in the country and what the government is planning. When you get to the Embassy you will be briefed on who the informants are and how to work with them. However, you'll have to develop your own contacts as well because we are not sure whether our informants will go so far as to participate in an assassination."

"Will there be a code name to this project that I can use for communication back there?"

"Yes, there will be. We'll give it to you when you come back in two weeks. The Embassy will continue to use the established code in sending and receiving messages. We have our code specialists at the Embassy."

General Mahlgren added, "As far as working out the details as to how you're going to accomplish the mission, that is something you will have to establish when you have been at the Embassy for a while. Before you leave for Moscow you will talk with Captain Annala. She can answer a lot of questions you may have."

"I detect that I'll probably be in Russia for several months," Koskinen said in a rather obvious observation.

"I would hope that whatever you do will be done as soon as possible," replied Mahlgren. "However, the objective is to get the job done efficiently and irrevocably and so, even though time is of the essence, the goal is not to be hasty at the risk of failure."

"I might add another caution," and Mahlgren took on his commanding look again. "I would not tell your wife, Anna, or anyone else, relative or friend, what your ultimate mission is. I suggest you tell Anna that you have an important fact-gathering assignment in Russia and you may be gone for a while. Tell her that, officially, you are on a trade mission. Tell her that you will call her from time to time, but that the conversation will have to be small talk, like, how are the kids, the weather, and your health Tell her that we'll keep in touch with her to keep her informed of your well-being. Incidentally, you might be coming back here from time to time, and when you do, Anna can join you down here in Helsinki."

"Well, I'm sure all of this will help to comfort her a bit," Koskinen ventured.

Added Mahlgren, "As far as your other relatives and friends are concerned, most know you're in Intelligence, so just tell them you are on an important assignment and can't discuss it. People understand that."

Koskinen nodded in agreement to these instructions from the General.

"Let's call Colonel Lindforst and Captain Annala in now and outline what is expected of them." General Mahlgren buzzed his Secretary and gave her instructions to have the two officers report to his office.

While waiting for the arrival of the two, General Mahlgren in an aside to Koskinen said, "We won't need Blomquist in this any further. He'll be involved in covering for you in Tampere in case something may need attention up there. He understands that. If he's needed, we can call him into the project anytime."

Koskinen felt elated to hear that. Colonel Blomquist was not one of his favorite persons.

After Lindforst and Annala had arrived and been seated, General Mahlgren reviewed some of the discussion he had had with Koskinen.

"Captain Annala, I will expect you to advise Captain Koskinen on the structure of the Stalin government, that is the various agencies and departments, how they operate and where they're located. Also, acquaint him as much as possible, with the key people around Stalin, what their functions may be, how often they see Stalin, their positions in the Politburo and, very important, whether they've lost any relatives in the purges that have been going on. You should have some intelligence information on these matters. If not, then do what you can to get it, maybe through other country's Embassies."

Captain Annala replied that she would research the matter and see what she could come up with. Mahlgren told her, "Captain Koskinen will be back here in about two weeks. You will need to give him help on this project. You're our Russian expert."

At that moment the General's telephone rang. Answering it and listening for a moment, he said, "Bring it in now." He then hung up. Moments later, his secretary entered the office and handed him a piece of paper. The General read it.

"I have received information that the Soviets have asked our government for trade talks in Moscow. Our government will accept. It is expected that a commercial delegation will be going from here about the middle of February. Erkko, Tanner and Juho Paasikivi have delayed their trip in order to go with the trade delegation. Captain Koskinen, we'll arrange for you to be included in the trade delegation. It's a natural opening for you."

Koskinen nodded his approval of the idea.

General Mahlgren went on to say, "However, this only points up the urgency of our project. The Soviet government is not really interested in resuming trade talks. We know from their methods of the past that this trade talk will devolve into their demands that Finland give up some of its autonomy. Their newspapers, which everyone knows are controlled by the government, are already saying that Finland has a secret agreement with Germany to place our Aaland Islands in the Baltic Sea at the disposal of Germany in case of war. So, this is a prelude to the Soviet government demanding that Finland lease some of these islands to the Soviets. We know that is what is coming and the trade talks are a Soviet ploy to begin these demands."

"Do you think we'll accede to the Soviet demand?" queried Koskinen.

"No, absolutely not," replied Mahlgren firmly and with a look of determination. "Prime Minister Cajander and Foreign Minister Erkko are opposed to any such proposal either from the Soviets or from Germany. In fact, they went to Sweden just a few days ago and signed an agreement for Swedish and Finnish cooperation in the defense of the Islands. But, you know the Russians. They're going to insist that we do as they demand. That is why I again repeat, our project must succeed and soon. If we don't get it done, it may mean war between Finland and the Soviets."

"As for you, Colonel Lindforst, as liaison to our Embassy, you will arrange for the Ambassador when he returns here in about ten days to meet with me. He is going to have to know what our plans are. Captain Koskinen will be in touch with you from the Embassy from time to time, by code of course, and you will immediately see that I get his messages and that he gets mine, if I have any. You will arrange with the Embassy for Captain Koskinen to have the usual use of the facilities as his base of operations. Also, you are to set up a special communication code between Koskinen and our Department. I don't know if the Russians may have broken our general use code and I don't want to take any risks that they might be warned by eavesdropping our present code."

"General, I shall get to work on it immediately so that Captain Koskinen can carry the special code with him when he leaves with the trade delegation," replied Lindforst.

"General, I have a crucial question," inquired Koskinen, "what method do I use to get rid of Stalin?"

"That is something we are leaving up to you after you have organized yourself at the Embassy and have lined up reliable people. The only admonition that I have is that Stalin must be killed. If he is only wounded or gets over being poisoned, or whatever, our cause will be lost and he'll be more psychotic than he is now. He must be killed if Finland is to remain safe and a sovereign nation. There are no other options open to us."

Mahlgren was silent for a few moments to allow any other questions or comments.

"Since there are no questions, I'll adjourn this conference. If you think of something that we haven't covered or if you have any questions, please feel free to contact me. We want as much certainty and clarity on this project as possible." Mahlgren arose from his seat at his desk as a signal that the meeting had concluded.

As Koskinen, Lindforst and Annala walked down the corridor toward the reception room, Colonel Lindforst remarked to the others, "This is going to be a most difficult mission. There is no room for mistakes. I don't think I shall be sleeping very well for quite awhile."

Koskinen observed wryly, "Hey, I'm the guy at the vortex of this project. I'm the one who should not be sleeping very well." They all chuckled at the obvious humor.

In the large reception room of the Department, Koskinen used a telephone to call Anna. It was about 1115. The next train for Tampere would leave at 1310 hours.

"Hello, Anna, this is Timo. I'll be home this evening about 1600 or 1630 hours. I may stop at the office on the way and if I do, I'll call you from there. How has everything been? … That's good. Yes, I know you love me. I share your feelings, sweetheart. See you soon."

Koskinen felt a deep sense of remorse about his affair with Elena. Would something about his actions give any hint to Anna that he had not been faithful to her. Would she suspect something. Women had an instinct about such matters that men could neither fathom nor understand. He would be making love to Anna when he got home and, for once, he wished he didn't have to. The conflicting thoughts and emotions ran rampant through Koskinen's mind as he got out on the street. It isn't that he did not want to make love to Anna. It was just that he was afraid to do so. The affair with Elena was so recent that he really had not had time to put it behind him so that he could be more comfortable with Anna. Nevertheless, Anna would expect him to make love to her. Naturally, he would have to go through with it.

If Anna suspected anything or the truth would come out eventually, he could always say that he did it to promote his mission to the Soviets, to find someone who would cooperate in the project. But then, Koskinen immediately knew that it was a ridiculous excuse. Anna was no fool to accept such an explanation. No, there was nothing to do between now and when he arrived home except to put Elena out of his thoughts completely and to persuade himself that nothing had happened which could impair his marriage with Anna. Elena did not exist. He would treat the affair as a dream from which he had now awakened to reality. Koskinen reasoned that reality is what you make it. And the reality was that there never had been an Elena.

Koskinen felt satisfied that the long train ride would allow him to be self-mesmerized into a convincing denial of the reality of Elena and what had occurred the night before. He would be able to respond to Anna as he always had. There was nothing to fear. In Koskinen's case, one could easily conclude that the contortions and distortions of fact by the human mind when seeking to avoid the truth were amazingly convoluted.

Koskinen was glad that neither Lindforst nor Annala had suggested having lunch with them. He preferred to be alone until train time. He went to a small nearby restaurant and had a combined breakfast and lunch. Thereafter, he returned to the Parliament House and its library and sat down to read some of the current magazines. He still had about an hour before train time. He was tired, but he could not sleep, not even doze. Too many things were racing about in his mind. In fact, he could not read consistently. Too many distracting thoughts. Laying down the magazine, he put his head back on the sofa chair, closed his eyes and left reality for a while.

A short time later he opened his eyes, glanced at his wristwatch and saw that it was time for him to leave for the railroad station. He would not see the inside of Parliament House again for two weeks. Thank goodness for that, he thought.

Arriving at the station, presenting his ticket and boarding the train, Koskinen vowed that if there were any young ladies sitting nearby, he would avoid them as if they had the plague. In fact, that would be true of anyone on the train. No more striking up acquaintances with strangers. He had to resume being a professional.

Koskinen's train ride proved to be uneventful. No one spoke to him and he spoke to no one except for the train conductor.

When he alighted from the train he found that it was still bitterly cold outside and that there was a slight snowfall going on. And it was already dark with intermittent streetlights symbolizing some small element of human warmth.

Koskinen was glad to be back in Tampere. Nothing had changed since he left and he felt at home and comfortable. Helsinki was a world away and he was quite able to divorce himself from the whole experience. He walked down the Hameenkatu Avenue toward his office at Finlayson feeling jaunty and rejuvenated. He was himself again. And he was thinking of Anna and eagerly looking forward to seeing her

CHAPTER 5

When Bill Chance and Gene Wagner arrived at the American Embassy in Moscow in the late afternoon on March 14, 1939 and had a casual walk around the inside of the facility, one of the first things they observed was the number of Russian citizens employed at the Embassy. They were both surprised and alarmed.

"Good Lord, Gene, have you seen the number of Russians on the Embassy staff?"

"Yes," Wagner replied, "and I don't like it."

They were in the sitting room of the suite to which Chance had been assigned and were talking about their initial experiences in coming to the Soviet Union. Chance raised the point on the "locals" on the staff.

"I suspect, Gene, that the Russians make up about 80 percent of the people employed here. In my opinion, it's not a healthy situation."

"Yeah, I agree, Bill. Any one of these people could be passing important information to Russian intelligence. I don't understand how either the Ambassador or Addison could allow this."

"It's certainly something that should be corrected as soon as possible. I'll talk to Addison about it when we see him," further commented Chance.

Wagner had a worried expression on his face. "Maybe, Bill," he said, "we have to be very cautious about our real mission. Maybe we should not mention it even to Addison until we learn more about the Embassy personnel."

"I think you're right, Gene. So far as anyone here at the Embassy knows, you and I are on a trade mission. Secretary Roth instructed us to tell Addison our real purpose in coming here, but maybe we should wait to tell him until we are sure of the security here at the Embassy. That goes for the Ambassador, as well."

"I think that is a wise approach," Wagner said. "Let's hold off and see what develops."

Chance then added, "By the way, we have to let our families know that we've arrived safely. We'll send a message to Randy tomorrow and he'll contact Melissa and Ann."

Wagner nodded in agreement.

When Chance and Wagner had arrived at the Embassy and been passed through at the gate entrance by the American military guard, they were met in the lobby by Helen Morgan, secretary to Deputy Secretary Addison. Helen was her usual friendly, gracious and warm personality which tended to disarm and put at ease anyone who might feel tense and anxious in a strange environment for the first time. However, both Chance and Wagner and Helen were no strangers to each other as they were in frequent communication by reason of their work with the State Department.

"Gentlemen, we're delighted to have you here and we'll do everything we can to make your visit pleasant and comfortable. Ambassador Hayes and Deputy Addison have asked me to express their regrets at not being here to greet you. They are at a dinner meeting with Maxim Litvinov, the Soviet Foreign Minister, and representatives of some of the other missions here in Moscow. The invitation was received only a few days ago and so the Ambassador and the Deputy had to change their plans rather abruptly."

"That's quite alright," responded Chance. "We can use the time to get settled in and rest up."

"I'll have Yakov take you to your rooms and one of the staff will bring your luggage up," Helen stated. "Yakov will explain the facilities and the dining schedule to you."

"Who is Yakov?" asked Chance.

"Yakov," replied Helen, "is Managing Director of the Embassy. He is, in a sense, our 'man Friday'. He is in charge of running the detailed day-to-day operation. He supervises the 'locals' as we call our Russian staff, takes care of the work schedules, sees that the staff does their jobs, and so on."

"Sounds like a pretty important guy," commented Wagner.

"Does he hire and fire the locals?" inquired Chance.

"No, we do that," replied Helen. "But Yakov makes his recommendations. Being Russian, he knows how and where to get employees we may need. He's quite knowledgeable in that regard. And he does speak quite well in English," she added. "Why don't you wait here and I'll go into my office and locate him? It shouldn't be long."

About ten minutes later, Yakov strode into the lobby from an adjoining hallway and proceeded to greet Chance and Wagner with firm handshakes and a slight, ingratiating bow from his hips.

"Welcome, gentlemen, to our glorious American Embassy. I am Yakov. Would you tell me who is Mr. Chance and who is Mr. Wagner, please?"

Chance and Wagner introduced themselves.

"What is your last name, Yakov?," inquired Chance.

"You mean my surname, Mr. Chance?" Yakov gave a saccharine smile that Chance thought was intended to be condescending. Chance took an immediate dislike of the fellow. He sized Yakov up as an arrogant self-important boor.

"No, I mean your last name, Yakov," countered Chance, who quickly demonstrated his irritation with being corrected by a Russian who, apparently, felt he had to prove he knew the complexities of the English language.

"My last name, gentlemen, is Strinovsky."

Wagner who, up to that moment, had spoken nothing after having introduced himself, said, "That sounds Jewish. Are you Jewish, Yakov?" The question was blunt and unfeeling. Wagner, too, had an initial unfavorable impression of Yakov.

Yakov hesitated an almost indiscernible moment, but then replied, "Yes, I am a Jew. Now then, gentlemen, I shall show you to your rooms. Would you follow me, please?" Yakov turned and walked toward a wide staircase at one end of the lobby. He said nothing further as he mounted the stairs followed by Chance and Wagner.

Chance looked at Wagner, smiled and winked as if to say, "We've let this guy know he can't intimidate us." Wagner nodded and winked back.

Although Yakov was dressed in western style clothing, business suit, white shirt and tie, nevertheless, he had, in Chance's opinion as later expressed to Wagner, the appearance of the stereotypical Russian peasant. Yakov was about five feet ten in height, broad and heavyset in his frame, albeit, apparently very muscular, a square, high cheek-boned yet fleshy face with bushy eyebrows and an incrustation of a large moustache that, again, in Chance's opinion, had the appearance of a piece of muskrat pelt. Nevertheless, both Chance and Wagner agreed that there was about Yakov a considerable engaging, though ominous, quality of personality that might reasonably captivate an unsophisticated person. Chance and Wagner decided that they had to be wary of what they said and did when Yakov was around, at least until they knew more about him.

The two rooms assigned to Chance and Wagner adjoined each other and were among several on a second floor corridor that ran the width of the building. From their rooms Chance and Wagner could see the street outside the Embassy compound as well as the guard gate.

"Who else is on this second floor, Yakov?" Chance inquired.

"Primarily the Executive Staff, that is, the Ambassador, the Deputy, the Commercial Attaché, the Military Attaché, the Agricultural representative and a few other officers."

"Where do the minor members of the administrative staff stay?"

"Either on the first or third floors," Yakov replied.

"Does that include the locals?" Chance continued.

"Some stay here, some go to their homes and some stay here part-time, depending on their work schedules."

"I see. Well, thank you, Yakov." Chance began to open his luggage and Yakov left the room, but not before advising Chance that dinner in the Ambassador's dining room would be at 1800 hours.

Chance interrupted his unpacking to telephone to Wagner's room through the Embassy switchboard.

"When you finish unpacking, Gene, come into my room. I'd like to talk a bit with you."

"How about in a half hour, Bill?"

"Fine, Gene."

It was about 1700 hours when Gene and Bill sat in Chance's room and they both discussed the number of Russians employed at the Embassy and the need for caution about their mission.

"We'll probably meet with Hayes and Addison or maybe just Addison alone tomorrow morning," said Chance. "I think we should talk strictly about trade matters. Perhaps, we can get some information that will help us in our real mission without revealing our main purpose in being here."

"I agree," said Wagner. "Also, I thought we were going to mention security here at the Embassy."

"Yes," replied Chance, "I'll take that up at the meeting. It's very important."

"What's your opinion of Yakov?," Wagner asked and the expression on his face showing that he knew what Chance's answer would be.

"I don't usually pass judgment on people until I get to either know them better or have facts sufficient to arrive at a conclusion. But on Yakov, my impression is that he is not to be trusted." Chance frowned over the breach of his own practiced principles. He disliked, in any event, being judgmental. He added, "There is just something about the fellow that makes me very uncomfortable with him. I can't put my finger on it. How do you feel about him, Gene?"

"Yeah, I've got the same impression," said Gene.

"You know, Gene, I winced inwardly when you asked him if he was Jewish. Why did you mention that?"

"It was probably because of certain mannerisms that he had that gave me the impression that he might be. You know, the expression in the eyes, the movement of the arms and hands. Maybe it was the sarcasm of his reply when you asked him for his last name."

"But that doesn't answer, 'why'," Chance persisted. "I got the feeling that because he was a Jew that it added to your dislike of him."

"I probably should be honest and admit that it didn't help me like the guy. I'm not anti-Semitic, Bill. I have some Jewish friends and get along with them fine. But, by and large they're a race of people I'm not particularly fond of. They're different from us, from the Christians. Their culture is different. Their way of thinking is different. They are clannish. They are arrogant, pushy, noisy, and, as far as I'm concerned, you can't trust them. And those little beanies they wear are ridiculous. What are they for?" Wagner stopped talking to get his breath. It was quite apparent to Chance that Wagner's prejudice was aroused.

However, Chance chuckled and remarked, "I would say, Gene, that you're rather dogmatic about the subject." Chance seemed amused by Wagner's unusual effusive and fervent articulation of his disaffection for the Jews in general. Chance was aware of the considerable anti-Semitism in the State Department and was aware of Gene Wagner's indifference to past and current Jewish pogroms in parts of the world. But, Chance now, for the first time, sensed the depth of Wagner's antipathy. Nevertheless, Chance was neither bothered nor concerned about it. However, Chance did agree that the Jews, as a people, were different. That difference was sufficient for him to be indifferent to their problems, their sufferings or whatever might befall them. Based on his experience with American Jews, Chance had long ago concluded that the Jews took care of each other, helping each other financially, in schooling, in building careers and in meeting the needs of other Jews. Therefore, Chance believed that he could be indifferent because, as a Christian, the Jew did not need him and, in all probability, would reject any offer to help in a distressed circumstance.

"Gene," Chance said, "I believe that you have a constitutional right to have an opinion and to express that opinion, nevertheless, I would caution you to be discreet on the Jewish question while we are over here. There may be some Jews in high places and we don't want to alienate them unnecessarily if they can be of help to us."

Wagner nodded his head and said, "Understood."

At shortly before 1800 hours, Chance and Wagner made their way down to the first floor dining room for dinner. Helen Morgan met them at the door to the main dining room.

"Gentlemen," Helen said, "you will dine in the Ambassador's dining room. Some of the other officers will be there and I'll introduce you."

Helen led them past the tables in the main dining room and through a high, paneled doorway into a smaller room which was normally reserved for the Ambassador and some of the staff officers and guests of the Embassy. Helen stopped at an elegantly set round table at which two young men were already seated. They both arose and Helen introduced Chance and Wagner. "This is Leonid Milchakov, our commercial assistant. And this is Valentin Pavlovich, our economics assistant." Chance and Wagner were introduced as on a trade mission from the State Department. Formal handshakes were exchanged.

"I expect a young lady to join us shortly," Helen said. "Ah, yes, here she is now."

Chance and Wagner, whose backs had been toward the entrance door, turned and saw a strikingly attractive young woman approaching the table. She was introduced to the two visitors from the United States.

"May I introduce you to Sofia Kameneva," Helen said. "Sofia is our chief translator. When you meet with the Soviet officials, either Sofia or one of the other translators, will go with you. Also, Leonid and Valentin speak English fluently. Secretary Addison asked that I arrange to bring you all together this evening so that you might get acquainted. Leonid and Valentin will be able to discuss current trade issues with you from the Soviet point of view. They can also direct you to the officials of the Soviet government who deal with foreign trade matters. The Secretary felt that they could be helpful to you."

"Yes, I'm sure they can be," replied Chance. "I know Gene and I will have questions."

The dinner proceeded pleasantly with small talk about families, schooling, work background, and entertainment spots in Moscow. Helen Morgan had joined the group in place of Secretary Addison. The feminine presence helped to modulate a relaxed and soft milieu at the table. In fact, Chance observed Wagner looking frequently at Sofia. Wagner was not ogling Sofia. He was much too urbane for that. But, Chance wondered whether Sofia could translate the language expressed in Wagner's eyes as he glanced at her. When Sofia spoke, she directed her conversation to all at the table, but Chance thought he noticed that when Sofia turned her head slightly to look at Wagner as she spoke, it seemed that her gaze lingered an almost imperceptible moment longer than on the others at the table.

By the time the dessert was served, Chance had become convinced that some interactive interest had begun to brew between Wagner and Sofia. Knowing Wagner's propensity for sacrificing himself on the altar of love in order to carry out his mission for his country, Chance decided that he'd better remind his co-worker of Secretary McKinley Roth's stern admonition not to get involved intimately with the opposite sex while on this mission.

Sofia was admittedly and manifestly an intelligent, educated and attractive woman. Chance understood that it would be neither difficult nor unexpected for a man to have an interest in Sofia. Her hair was dark blond and was drawn tightly back, giving an accentuation to her face. The hair, falling somewhat below the shoulder line, was tied together at the back with a bejeweled ring. Her face was delicately featured with large, expressive blue eyes. Chance thought it was a very strong face with its finely sculpted bone structure. Chance casually estimated that Sofia was about five feet nine and, possibly, in her late twenties.

Neither Chance nor Wagner wanted to question the three local staff members too closely at this first meeting. To do so might convey the impression that, as visitors from America, they were suspicious of the integrity of the Russian employees.

As they were leaving the dining area, Chance asked Helen to schedule an appointment with the Ambassador and the Deputy or either one as soon as possible. Helen agreed to do so.

"We have a movie we're showing this evening if you gentlemen would like to attend," Helen advised. "At times, there is not a great deal of entertainment here in Moscow and so we try to provide a little something."

Chance demurred, saying that he was somewhat tired from the trip and would accept the invitation another time. Wagner likewise said he'd retire for the evening.

Chance invited himself into Wagner's room. "I'll just come in for a short time, if that's O.K. with you, Gene."

"Of course, come on in. I'm tired, but it's too early to go to bed. If I went to bed at this hour of 8:15, I'd be up at 4:00 a.m. unable to sleep any further." Between themselves, Chance and Wagner used the American measure of time.

Wagner brought out a bottle of brandy he carried with him from the States.

"Have an after dinner drink, Bill." Wagner got a couple of water glasses from the night stand.

"Sure, that's a good idea, Gene."

Chance raised his half-filled glass in a toast.

"Here's to Stalin! Long live Stalin!"

Wagner chuckled as he raised his glass in a mocking gesture.

"Gene, what did you think of the dinner?" Chance began.

"The food was good," Wagner replied. "But, I still don't understand why all the Russians on the staff. That puzzles me."

Chance came to the point. "I noticed that you developed an interest in Sofia."

"Yes, she's quite an attractive gal," Wagner conceded.

"As long as it remains a casual friendship, there is no problem," Chance said.

"Oh, come on, Bill. Do you think I'm going to bed with her?"

"Yeah, you might. Just remember what Secretary Roth said about getting involved with a woman over here." Chance spoke in a remonstrative voice.

"Well, I think the Secretary was referring to a possible enemy," Gene said. "Sofia is certainly not the enemy."

"I wouldn't be too sure about that," responded Chance. "I'm serious, Gene. These people are Soviet citizens."

"Well, Bill, trust me. I'll be very careful. Here, have a little more brandy. It's good for the soul."

"No, thanks," Chance declined and added, "I'm going to turn in. Good night, Gene. See you in the morning."

"Sleep well, Bill."

It was about 2100 hours when Chance got into bed. The day had been a long one considering the arduous changing of trains on the last leg of the trip and the fact that catching sleep on the train was impossible, what with the bumping, rocking motion of the cars, the noise of the passengers at the frequent stops and the almost constant sounding of the train's horns to get people and animals to move off the tracks.

Chance fell asleep almost immediately. He was awakened by the loud sound of voices coming from the other adjoining room. Lying awake in the dark for a few moments and listening, Chance determined that a couple of men were arguing bitterly and strenuously about something. Chance snapped on the lamp light on the night stand next to his bed. Looking at his watch which lay on the table, Chance saw that it was close to eleven-thirty p.m. He arose and walked over to the wall separating the two rooms. He recognized that the men were talking in Russian, but the voices were not clear enough for him to understand what they were talking and arguing about. But Chance was struck by the vehemence of the exchanges between the two men whoever they were. Surely, he thought, these people should know that the walls between the rooms were not soundproof. The arguing went on for about ten minutes and then suddenly stopped and Chance heard the door to the corridor of the adjoining room close sharply.

Chance went to his own door and, out of curiosity, opened it and stuck his head out to see who might have been in the room. As he did so, he came face to face with Yakov. Yakov was startled to see Chance, but quickly regained his composure, smiled ingratiatingly, and in an unruffled calm voice said, "Good evening, Mr. Chance. I hope you have not been disturbed." Yakov sensed that Chance had heard him arguing with the occupant of the adjoining room. Yakov added, "I had to talk with one of our employees about not getting his work done on time." With that and before Chance could say anything, Yakov continued walking down the hallway. Chance closed his door and went back to bed, accepting Yakov's explanation of a minor dispute between the manager and an employee on the staff.

Breakfast at the Embassy was served from 0700 to 0830 hours. The dining room was closing when Chance and Wagner entered. The waiter, who was cleaning up, said in English with a heavy Russian accent that he would gladly bring them coffee and some Russian dark bread and cheese.

"The chef will be upset if you place an order now. I'm sorry, gentlemen."

"Quite ," said Chance. "We'll take the coffee and we'll try some bread and cheese." Chance turned to Wagner. "Is that alright with you, Gene?"

"Sure. I'll try anything. I'm a bit hungry."

The waiter was obviously one of the locals working at the Embassy. When he returned from the kitchen with a large silver pot of coffee and with the bread and cheese on a tray, Chance struck up a conversation with him.

"Tell us, what is your name?"

"Yuri."

"Yuri, this is Mr. Wagner. I am Mr. Chance. Will you be our waiter while we are here?"

"Perhaps, Mr. Chance. It depends on our schedule. There are other waiters employed here, of course."

"Mr. Wagner and I just arrived yesterday from the United States. We're on a trade mission," Chance said. He wanted the word to get around to the locals at the Embassy of why he and Wagner were in Moscow.

"We don't know much about Moscow. Perhaps, Yuri, you can help us. You know, where some good restaurants are, where the entertainment is and where some of the interesting sights are located."

"I'll do what I can," replied Yuri.

Chance continued, "How long have you worked here, Yuri?"

"About two years."

"Do you have a family?"

"Yes, my wife, Nadezhda, and my sons Anton and Boris."

"I'm curious, Yuri," said Chance. "How do the local people like yourself and the other Russians get jobs at an Embassy?"

Yuri replied, "Most of the time an Embassy officer will request our Foreign Office to send over people needed at the Embassy. Our Foreign Office keeps a list of Russians who are interested in working at another country's Embassy or Mission. On some occasions someone already working at an Embassy will recommend some friend to the Embassy officer. However, such a person has to register and go through the Russian Foreign Office Agency in order to get approval for the job."

"So, the Soviet government then knows where you are at all times. Isn't that so?" Chance thought he'd press for as much information as he could without seeming to be more interested in details than someone on a trade mission might normally be.

"Yes, of course," responded Yuri, who seemed surprised that that might be considered as something other than a usual and customary practice by a government.

"You speak fairly good English. Do all the locals who work at a foreign mission have to speak the particular language of the foreign country?" inquired Chance.

"No," replied Yuri while looking furtively toward the door leading to the kitchen. "No, some jobs like janitor, repairman, room maids, gardeners, and so on, those who, generally, do not come into contact with the officials of the Embassy. Those of us, like myself, do have to speak the foreign language in order to get approval for the job."

Yuri waited a moment and Chance sensed that he wanted to get on with whatever he was required to do.

"Gentlemen," Yuri said in an apologetic voice, "I am sorry, but I must get my clean up work here in the dining room completed and I must help out in the kitchen to get ready for lunch. If you will excuse me, please."

"Of course, Yuri, you've been very kind to answer my questions," said Chance.

As Chance and Wagner arose from the table, Chance said to Wagner, "Gene, let's walk over to Helen Morgan's office and find out if she has arranged a meeting with Addison and, perhaps, the Ambassador."

"Sure, of course," agreed Wagner. As they walked toward the other end of the Embassy building, Wagner said to Chance, "When you were asking Yuri those questions, I was tempted to ask him whether he had to report to his government what was going on in this Embassy. However, I felt that it might be prying too much for this first conversation."

"I'm glad that you didn't ask him. It might have put him into a difficult position as well as embarrassing. Also, he might get a bit suspicious about our being here and that is the last thing we would want to create."

When they entered Helen Morgan's office, Helen informed them that she had arranged a meeting with her boss for 1330 hours in his office.

"The Deputy had a few errands to run this morning. If he gets back for lunch he will want you to join him in the dining room," Helen advised.

"Will the Ambassador be at the meeting?"

"No, he sends his regrets. He apparently has to visit with some Japanese bigwigs at the Japanese Embassy."

"Well, we may walk over to the Kremlin and see if there is anything interesting going on. We have plenty of time before lunch." Chance seemed a bit anxious to get out of the Embassy.

Helen smiled at Chance's naiveté. "I don't think you'll want to walk there in this cold weather. The Kremlin is about two miles from here.

I'll see if I can locate our chauffeur, Gregor. He can drive you there. If he isn't driving, he generally does odd jobs around here."

After putting on their fedora hats and winter coats, Chance and Wagner proceeded to the Embassy gate and signed out with the guard. Gregor had the Embassy car waiting. Wagner had put his camera in his overcoat pocket to keep the film warm. As they drove south on Novinskey Boulevard and to the east on Novy Arbat, they passed several old buildings, some of wood, others of stone. Many had obviously seen better days. Wagner remarked to Chance that buildings, generally, did not appear to be well-maintained and that the shops had unattractive and drab window displays. In fact, the shops looked foreboding.

"However badly I might need something, I wouldn't venture into one of these shops," Wagner remarked. "Do you agree, Bill?"

"Yes, I agree. However, I read on the information sheet that the Torgsin store for tourists and foreign visitors is recommended for shopping. Apparently, it has goods not available to the average Russian citizen. We'll have to go there sometime."

Gregor left them off at the entrance to the Alexander Gardens and said he would wait nearby for them. Chance and Wagner walked casually into the government complex area, past the Palace of Congresses and the Kremlin Theater.

"These buildings are awesome," remarked Wagner. "You get the feeling that you're in another world, that there is a living history here."

They proceeded through the main entrance to Red Square. The entrance was known as the Gate of Salvation according to the information sheet Chance carried with him. At the south end of Red Square, Chance and Wagner looked with fascination at the huge, stately grandiloquent Church of St. Basil with its several minarets. Their information sheet stated that the church had been completed in 1679.

"I have to take a picture of that church," exclaimed Wagner enthusiastically as he opened the camera case he was carrying. After focusing rather painstakingly he had snapped three pictures from slightly different angles when he and Chance noticed a policeman approaching them hurriedly.

"Oh, oh, here comes trouble," warned Chance. "You'd better put the camera back in the case and under your coat."

Wagner fumbled with the camera and had not even closed the camera cover when the policeman reached them and in a gruff voice and with a menacing stare said in Russian, which Wagner interpreted as, "No, no. You cannot take pictures. It is forbidden. Give me the film from your camera." The policeman, a heavy-built fellow, held out his gloved hand.

Wagner retorted in his best Russian, "No, I will not give you the film. I have taken pictures of only the church which you can see and I can see. The church is a church, not a military establishment."

The policeman showed anger with Wagner's reply. His voice became louder and more threatening. He drew closer to Wagner. "You will give me the film or must I use force to take it?"

Wagner was adamant. "This gentleman," pointing to Chance, "and I are members of the United States government at the American Embassy. I'll show you our papers."

"Don't bother," ordered the policeman. "It does not matter who you are. You cannot take pictures here. Do you understand?"

Chance had said nothing up to this point in the altercation, but he now took Wagner by his coat sleeve and said in a soft and calm voice, "Gene, give him the film. We don't need an incident to draw attention to us."

"It's a matter of principle, Bill." Wagner had become belligerent by this time.

"I know, I know," Chance persisted, trying to quell the agitation and pacify and soothe Wagner's vituperative attitude. "You can probably buy a postcard picture of the church, if you really want a picture of it. Give him the film."

With a flare of indignation, Wagner removed the film and tossed it at the policeman, who stuffed it into his coat pocket. The policeman glared icily at Wagner and, pointing his finger at him, said, "No more pictures. You take anymore, I'll arrest you."

Wagner and Chance turned their backs on the policeman and strode away to the Gate of Salvation.

"Whew! I'm glad that's over," declared Chance. "Gene, remember our main mission here. You must realize that this is the Soviet Union and try to accept their customs and rules. In any event, control your temper. We have more important work to do."

Gene, still upset, said nothing.

However, after a short time of silence, Wagner finally muttered in a tone of disgust, "What a lousy country! Not even a picture of a church. Policemen watching every move. Look at the people on the street; I haven't seen anyone smile yet. They don't even look at you. Everyone looks like they're afraid of something, of being arrested. Look how they dress. Their clothing looks like it has been worn and patched over forever. Look over there. A couple of more policemen." Wagner drew Chance's attention to the officers standing on the street corner. "How can people live this way?"

Chance listened patiently to Wagner's contentious generalizations and thought the incident provided a good lesson for both of them.

"Now you should understand, Gene, why we're here and why our mission is so important. Stalin wants to export this system throughout the world and that, of course, includes the United States. Now you know why he has to be stopped. We don't want this kind of thing for our children and their children."

"Yes, I understand," Wagner replied, his tone of voice a little less ruffled as he began to calm down. "However," he added, "I'm afraid some of our high officials back home are not aware of the threat."

"I agree with that, Gene. Stalin is regarded as a kindly grandfather type by some people in the administration who have apparently not read our reports." Chance was referring to the classified, confidential memoranda the State Department Russian section had been issuing from time to time over the past three years. Those memoranda reported in some detail on Stalin's purges carried out from 1936 to the present early 1939.

When Chance and Wagner arrived back at the Embassy, they stopped in briefly to see Helen Morgan. They related their problem with the policeman at Red Square.

"Oh, I'm so sorry," said a contrite and sympathetic Helen. "I did forget to tell you that you should not take your cameras with you and, in any case, not to snap pictures. The Russian government bans photo taking unless you first get a permit to do so. I certainly apologize for not telling you."

"Your policeman friend didn't even ask if I had a permit," complained Wagner.

"Well, he should have," Morgan said. "Perhaps he was in a bad mood. Who knows? He, at least, did not take your camera."

"We'll see you later, Helen, when we come to the meeting." Chance and Wagner made their way back to their rooms to review some of what they would talk about with Deputy Secretary Addison at their meeting after lunch.

Fortuitously, Addison met them at the dining room and the three sat down together at Addison's dining table. Their conversation was about certain mutual friends in the State Department in Washington, about relations with the President and with Congress and about their families. It was tacitly understood that more serious discussion would be reserved for their post-lunch meeting. Addison explained that the Ambassador was not able to attend, but gave no reason.

Lunch having been concluded in a very friendly and jovial atmosphere, the three returned to Addison's office. Addison instructed his secretary, "Hold the calls, Helen. I'll be with these good gentlemen for a while."

As they took seats around Addison's large, impressive desk, Addison addressed Chance and Wagner. "I understand that you are here on a trade mission of some kind."

"That is right," said Chance. "I think what we need is some direction and advice from you as to the Russian officials to see on this subject."

"Well, I know who to suggest for you to see, but the problem is whether they will see you."

"Why is that a problem?" asked Chance, his face mirroring puzzlement.

Addison regarded the two men for a few moments and then, in all soberness, said, "As you know from the reports I have sent to you, from time to time, Stalin has been conducting some devastating purges over the past several years and Moscow, as well as the entire country, is one great boiling cauldron of intrigue, treachery and duplicity in true Machiavellian sense. People everywhere are living in fear of being arrested, imprisoned, tortured and even executed for no reason at all. Anyone having contact with a foreigner or with an Embassy official of a foreign country will be under suspicion. So, I imagine some Russian trade officials, for this reason, will be very reluctant to see you."

"Yes, but there are trade matters to be discussed in an ongoing practice between the United States and Russia. They have to have someone whom we can talk with and who can make decisions. How can that be done if people are afraid to talk with us?" Chance was incredulous about the situation.

"The trade people are required to go through channels to get permission to deal with you," replied Addison. "They may even have to get permission from Stalin himself. You might not believe it, but the guy makes a lot of decisions himself on details that our President would never think of bothering with. I'll put together some names of trade officials for you to try to see and, if you wish, I'll make some introductory calls to pave your way."

"That will be fine," replied Chance. "Before you make the calls, we'd like to go over the names."

Chance then addressed the Deputy, "Gene and I could not help but observe the number of locals you have working here. Isn't that a considerable security risk given the present penchant of the Soviet government to pry into everything and everybody including, probably, the foreign missions?"

"Yes," answered Addison, "we are aware that there is some risk; however, we think it's minimum. We are quite certain our local employees are required by the Soviet bureaucrats to report regularly as to what goes on here in the Embassy. However, they have no contact with classified material or with policy information. Our American employees handle the high priority stuff including coded messages."

Addison paused for a moment and then added, "I don't like the idea of having to hire all these locals, but I have no choice. Congress has cut our budget to the bone. We don't have enough money to operate this Embassy with solely American help. For that reason we have to get cheap labor. Another consideration is that if we restrict ourselves to American employees, we'd have to bring their families over as well. That would be a substantial expense for travel, housing and schooling for children. Congress will have to allocate more money to us if they want us to eliminate the hiring of locals."

Chance said, "I'm well aware that using locals is a traditional practice of the Embassies and missions. But, this is not London or Paris or Brussels which are reliably friendly to us and have democratic systems we know and can trust. This is Moscow, Russia, Stalin, unpredictable, unreliable, not democratic and, in my opinion, not to be trusted."

Wagner spoke up. "If the Russian citizens are suspect if they have contact with foreigners and foreign Embassies, then I would think these Russian employees would be in fear of their lives."

"The Russian employees have all received permission from their government to work here," commented Addison. "Of course, even then there is no assurance that they will not be suspect. But, by Russian standards the work is pleasant and pays well and our locals are willing to take that risk."

Chance changed the subject. "Last night I had a peculiar experience. I was awakened at about eleven o'clock by some shouting, loud arguing and some thumping going on in the room adjoining mine. I got up and went to the door and as I opened it, your employee, Yakov, came out of the room next door and walked down the corridor. When I spoke with him, he said he was just admonishing another local employee about doing a better job. I didn't think any more about it, but I am wondering who the fellow is in the adjoining room." Chance looked at Addison quizzically. Addison's face flushed slightly and he shifted in his chair, obviously uncomfortable with the question.

Addison studied his folded hands on his desk for a few moments and did not immediately answer Chance's seemingly innocuous question. But, he finally said, "Bill, what I have to say is to be kept confidential. The person in your adjoining room is an important defector to whom we've given asylum. He has been a personal Secretary to Stalin and, as such, knows a great deal about not only Stalin, but also about other higher-ups in the government as well as how their system works. We think he will be invaluable to us by giving us a better understanding of how to deal with the government and with the individuals in leading positions of control and policy making."

"What is his name?" asked Chance.

"Vladimir Kovalenko," replied Addison.

"Does the Soviet government know he's here?" inquired Chance.

"I don't know for certain, but I'd guess that it does," answered Addison.

"Has the Soviet government asked or demanded that he be sent back?"

"No, we haven't heard a word. However, it is reported that the police arrested his wife and child just before they were getting ready to come here. Nothing has been heard of them or from them since and that has been about a week ago."

"Does this Yakov know the identity of Kovalenko?" Chance persisted. "He referred to the occupant of the room as an employee."

"The staff has been told Kovalenko is an employee, but I'm sure Yakov knows his true identity. I don't know what he was doing up in Kovalenko's room and I surely will ask him."

"Gene and I would like to meet and talk with this Kovalenko fellow," Chance remarked. "He might be able to advise us on the culture and customs of dealing with bureaucratic officials, such as our Russian trade people."

"Sure, I'll arrange it," Addison said obligingly. "Let me know when you'd like to see him. You can use our conference room."

"Tomorrow morning would be fine," suggested Chance. "But I think I'd prefer to interview him in his room. That will avoid attention from others here. I suggest you call him and tell him it's alright to talk with us and we'll see him in the morning about nine-thirty in his room."

"Good, I'll do that. In fact, I'll call him now and you can talk with him on the phone and make your own arrangements."

Addison got Kovalenko on the Embassy telephone and, speaking in Russian, explained the arrival of Bill Chance and Gene Wagner, their trade mission and their desire to talk with him and that he, Kovalenko, could do so. Chance, also in Russian, spoke with Kovalenko, introducing himself and arranging to visit with Kovalenko the next morning.

Addison observed, "I see you're struggling with your Russian language," he laughed good-humoredly. "This fellow does speak some amount of English."

"Yeah, my Russian needs considerable brushing-up. I don't get much occasion to use it back in Washington." Chance continued, "You know the Department's policy. You have to be familiar with the language of the country you are going to serve in and in the foreign section you're working in like Gene and me. The problem arises that, if you work in Washington there is very little opportunity to talk in the foreign language except, perhaps, when you talk with someone in the Soviet Embassy. And those people talk pretty good English, so there is a tendency to use English."

"Well," Addison said, "you'll get some practice here. Use it when you can."

Chance then said, "I'm curious about this fellow, Yakov. He seems to have considerable authority and to have the run of the place."

"Oh, he's alright. He supervises the locals. You need someone like him, someone who understands the locals and can be tough on them if they slack off or if they begin to be absent more than an occasional day or so. We can't have one of our American officers spending time on that sort of thing."

"Is Yakov trustworthy?" Chance was anxious to know more. "Is he a possible security risk?"

"No, I am confident he's not a risk," Addison replied. "He's been here a little over a year and we haven't had any problems with him. Of course, I'm sure he has to report to the government from time to time what goes on here just as the other locals probably do. Anyway, he's no risk to your trade mission." Addison seemed to shrug off Chance's possible concern and neither Chance nor Wagner pursued the questions about Yakov any further.

As they left Addison's office and were walking through the lobby, Wagner remarked to Chance, "Bill, don't you think we ought to tell Addison about our true mission here? We can waste a lot of time going through this charade of a trade mission. If we talk to Addison about our true purpose here, he might be of some help getting us started in the right direction."

"I'm just as anxious as you, Gene, to get started," Chance answered, "but, I think we ought to hold off for another day or so until we get a better feel for security here."

"You sound like you don't exactly trust Addison," Wagner countered.

"I trust him," Chance replied, not wanting to appear to doubt the integrity of the second in command of the Embassy operation.

"However, he does seem quite casual about security. Maybe he does have good security measures in place, but we don't know that since we have been here only a short time."

Wagner persisted, "He's probably casual because he doesn't think a trade mission needs much security about its activities. If we explain to him what we are up to here, he'll understand our concerns and tighten the security for us."

"Well, let's talk to this Kovalenko first," Chance continued. "He may know something about how the government controls the local employees in an Embassy, methods used to breach security and he might even have some knowledge about some of the locals here including Yakov."

"Well, alright." Wagner resigned himself to Chance's senior status.

As they approached their rooms, Wagner suggested they stop and say "hello" to Kovalenko.

"It will break the ice," Wagner said. "At least Kovalenko will know what we look like and that we are friendly."

"Good idea, Gene," Chance replied approvingly.

Wagner knocked on Kovalenko's door. After a few moments, the door opened and Kovalenko stood framed in the doorway and appearing somewhat surprised and quizzical.

"I am Gene Wagner and this is Bill Chance. Mr. Chance spoke with you over the telephone and made arrangements to have both of us meet with you tomorrow morning."

"Yes, we just stopped by to say 'hello' and sort of get acquainted first. You are Mr. Kovalenko, are you not?" Chance asked.

Kovalenko replied in fairly good English, "Yes, I am Vladimir Kovalenko. I'm glad to meet you, gentlemen. Would you care to step inside?"

"No," responded Chance. "We have to get some work done in our rooms, but we'll see you tomorrow morning about 900 hours."

"Fine. I shall see you both then. Good day, gentlemen." Kovalenko closed his door before Chance could say that he was an adjoining roomer.

"He's quite businesslike," observed Wagner with a sardonic grin. "See you for dinner, Bill." They each entered their respective rooms.

Once in his room, Bill Chance lay down on his bed and with hands under his head, stared up at the ceiling and began to ponder on the dilemma that he and Gene Wagner were facing, needing to get started on their mission and yet not revealing it to anyone, not even Deputy Addison. To eliminate Stalin by one means or another was crucial to the best interests of the United States if not the world. The mission required the utmost secrecy and there was no room or allowance for mistakes of any kind in prosecuting the intent of the mission. Bill Chance knew that it was critical to exercise the greatest caution before each step along the way was taken. As he focused his thinking on the question of what first step to take to commence the operation, he arrived at the inescapable conclusion that he and Gene had to get information about the daily fixed and customary habits of Stalin. Their plan of elimination had to be shaped around those habits. This, then, is where, perhaps, Kovalenko could help. Kovalenko, the personal secretary of Stalin, would surely know better than anyone the daily routine of his boss, Stalin. To Chance, Kovalenko was the key to initiating their mission. Chance thought of how fortunate it was that Kovalenko had decided to defect and to seek refuge at the U.S. Embassy. Chance felt that in getting Kovalenko to talk, it might not even be necessary to reveal to anyone the nature of their mission, at least, not just now.

Bill Chance decided he would discuss his thinking on the subject with Gene Wagner. Perhaps Gene was thinking along the same lines and they could evaluate each other's ideas. But Bill Chance did not know, of course, that his friend and Assistant was sitting in his room gazing out of the window and thinking not of the mission but of Sofia Kameneva and of how glorious it would be to bed down with her. Gene Wagner was pondering about what his first step would be to achieve this goal. The more he thought about it the more he was led to conclude that he would have to start by being friendly and using opportunities as they arose.

To say that Gene Wagner gave no thought to the mission was, on the other hand, not entirely true. For a fleeting moment, the transient idea occurred to him that, perhaps, as their relationship grew he could obtain important information from Sofia that would help the mission. By the time Bill Chance knocked on his door to go to dinner, Wagner had convinced himself that his sole motive to pursue Sofia was to use her as an informant. He certainly could not be censured for that, he thought.

As they entered the staff dining room for dinner, there were then only a few people in the room and Chance and Wagner both saw Sofia Kameneva sitting at a table by herself. They intended to walk on through to the Ambassador's Dining Room, but stopped at Sofia's table to say hello and exchange a few pleasantries. Wagner was tempted to tell Chance that he would have dinner at Sofia's table, but thought better of it in view of Chance's earlier admonition to not get entangled with any female while on the mission.

Chance was already near the entrance to the Ambassador's Dining Room when Wagner, in turning to leave Sofia's table, addressed her directly saying, "Sofia, I'd like you to show me a good restaurant in Moscow."

Sofia nodded and said, "Why, yes, I'd love to, anytime." Wagner winked at her in a jovial manner and was elated as he entered the Ambassador's dining room and sat down at the table with Chance. Chance sensed why Wagner was so joyful, but he pretended not to notice. He felt that as long as his Assistant remained at a platonic distance from Sofia, he would not interfere.

Yuri, the Embassy waiter, was again serving their table. Chance and Wagner found themselves alone at their table. Neither the Ambassador nor the Deputy Secretary had yet appeared for dinner. Chance thought he would use the absence of others at the table as an opportunity to put a few questions to Yuri.

Adopting a very casual mien, Chance asked, "Yuri, have you ever seen Stalin sort of up close?"

Yuri smiled as if he welcomed the moment to tell of his intimacy with the great leader. "Oh, yes! On occasion Stalin has banquets with one hundred or more people dining and his staff has to get extra waiters by borrowing from the various Embassies. The staff knows that Embassy waiters are experienced and don't require training. I have served at several of the banquets. Of course, extra waiters don't get to serve Stalin himself or those near him. He has his regulars who wait on him."

"You know," Chance continued, "I have often wondered how a head of government, whether it be Stalin or the President of the United States or the Prime Minister of England or any other head, can avoid someone poisoning his food in order to kill him. After all, every leader has enemies who would like to dispose of them if they could, isn't that so?"

"I'm sure you're right," replied Yuri. Then, to both Chance's and Wagner's surprise, their waiter became quite voluble in an all too apparent desire to impress his two customers with his knowledge of the inner sanctum of the government.

"I am told by a friend of mine who works in the NKVD, that Stalin's meals are prepared under the watchful eyes of a couple of NKVD men and, when cooking is completed, the food is placed in a steel container that is sealed and delivered to Stalin who is the only one who can break the seal." Yuri continued, "The same friend of mine has stated that each dish of food comes with a certificate which says, 'No poisonous substance found.' So, you see that it isn't likely anyone could intentionally introduce a poison to Stalin's food and not be observed and held accountable."

"Well, I agree it isn't likely," Chance countered, "but there is never any guarantee that it cannot be done."

To this, Yuri said nothing, but smiled, turned and departed for the kitchen.

Chance turned to Wagner and, with a sly look, said, "Well, that is an interesting revelation. What do you think?"

Wagner replied, "I never thought our job would be easy, but this information means it is going to be damned hard to accomplish. The guy is, obviously, surrounded by security."

"Yeah, I agree. It won't be easy. Maybe this fellow, Kovalenko, will have some information we can proceed on. After all," Chance observed, "if he was a personal secretary to Stalin, he should know a lot more detail than this Yuri."

"I hope so," Wagner said. "We'll find out tomorrow."

They continued to eat in silence, each engrossed within his thoughts about their predicament. They were startled by a cheery voice of greeting. It was Helen Morgan, the Deputy's secretary.

"Fellows, do you mind if I share your table?"

"No, not at all. Please, sit down. We're delighted to have you." In a way, both men were glad to have their reverie interrupted and to talk about something other than their mission. Nevertheless, thoughts about the mission kept intruding into their minds.

After Helen had placed her order with Yuri, Chance, on the spur of the moment, addressed Helen with a more serious demeanor. He had not discussed with Wagner what he was about to say, but felt that the time was ripe to express himself and that, in all probability, Wagner would agree with him.

"Helen," Chance began, "Gene and I have been concerned about security here at the Embassy ever since we arrived. The reason for our concern is that, in addition to our trade mission, we have another matter that we have been asked by Washington to take care of that requires the utmost secrecy and confidentiality. I cannot go into that matter at this time. But the number of local Russians working here does worry us. We know that their government requires them to report what goes on here and if any one of them gets wind of this special matter that we have to undertake, then we might as well go home. We haven't even talked to your boss about this for fear that somehow there may occur a security breach. Do you understand, Helen?"

Wagner told Chance later that he was absolutely taken by surprise by what Chance said to Helen, but he strove not to show his astonishment. Helen, for her part, said nothing for a few moments as she thought about her answer to Chance's inquiry.

Finally, she replied, "Bill, what you say about the locals is true. We try to do the best we can about security. But, we can't guarantee that a confidential matter will remain confidential. We think we have trustworthy employees, but we realize that they are under pressure from their government, especially the police, to report on what they see and hear here. All of our American staff has been instructed not to discuss anything with any of the locals. And they have been ordered not to let documents lie around when they leave their offices, that is, documents of a confidential matter. Each office has a small safe for the very purpose of keeping the documents that require their non-disclosure. Frankly, I think you should take this matter up with the Deputy. You can certainly trust him as well as the Ambassador."

"Well, we've mentioned our concern to Fraser when we first met him on our arrival and he said pretty much the same thing you have just said. But, we'll talk with him again and perhaps we can make arrangements to tighten security in regard to our mission." With that Chance let the matter drop for the time being except to ask, "Can you arrange for us to see Fraser tomorrow either late in the morning or the afternoon?"

"Certainly," Helen replied. "I'll let you know after I've talked with him in the morning. He and the Ambassador are at the British Embassy this evening. They're talking over something having to do with the relationship of Germany and the Soviet Union."

"Yeah," Chance commented. "I understand that Britain is trying to get Moscow to agree to respond to requests for aid from neighboring countries if attacked by Germany and Washington is trying to get Germany to agree not to attack the neighboring countries."

Wagner added his comments, "I don't think any of that is going to work out. Hitler has his agenda and he's going to follow it through regardless of what others may think, do or say."

"You're probably right," added Chance.

After dinner, Chance and Wagner spent some time in Wagner's room chatting about their families, some of the people in Washington and about the next day's schedule.

"Bill," offered Wagner in a tone of undisguised frustration, "we are still in a state of never-never land. We don't seem to be able to capitalize any plans or procedure for carrying out our mission. I'm getting discouraged, frankly. I think we just have to open up with Fraser, tell him our real purpose here and ask for his help. If we can't trust him, then there is no one else we can trust."

"Yes, Gene, I was fast coming to that conclusion myself. We'll lower the boom when we see Fraser tomorrow. Since we're not supposed to do the so-called 'execution' ourselves, our first objective is to find someone willing to do it and give him or her our assistance as best we can. That person may be somebody who has a grudge against our target person and is willing to take a life-threatening risk. The second objective is to find the way to carry out the project."

"Maybe we should just hang it up for the night, get some sleep and start fresh in the morning," Wagner suggested.

"Right on," Chance agreed. "We'll get breakfast at about seven-thirty and then see this Kovalenko chap." Chance arose from his chair and walked toward the door. "See you in the morning, Gene."

Wagner laughed. "Sowbelly and eggs!"

Chance joined the laughter. "Yeah, covered with Russian borscht. Good night!"

"Good night, Bill."

When he got back to his room, Chance turned on the radio. There was an announcement of news spoken in Russian. Chance knew some amount of Russian, but was not fluent. He could read it, better than to speak it. He understood enough, however, to learn that Hitler had entered the City of Memel in Lithuania in a colorful display of triumph. Hitler had annexed Memel just four days earlier. In exchange for Memel, Germany guaranteed Lithuania's independence, according to the radio announcement. Chance had already concluded that Hitler would expand his control over all of Europe peaceably as either in the case of Memel and Czechoslovakia or by military force. Chance believed having Germany control Europe was preferable to having the Soviets in control. If Hitler was ruthless, he, at least, did not exhibit the malevolent savagery of the crude and primitive Stalin.

Chance turned the radio off and was shortly asleep.

When Chance and Wagner entered the Embassy dining room for employees the next morning they saw only four people at one table having breakfast. They assumed them to be locals who were either coming off or going on shifts. Chance and Wagner had their breakfast in the employee section.

"Let's not bother going into the Ambassador's Room," said Wagner. "We aren't going to be here long enough to justify getting special attention." Chance acceded.

They had a different waiter. Yuri was nowhere in sight, probably not on duty they surmised.

Kovalenko, likewise, was not in attendance. This did not cause any surprise to either Chance or Wagner since sometimes people forego eating breakfast.

After finishing breakfast, both men walked out into the courtyard at the rear of the Embassy. They didn't remain long as the air was damp and cold and they had not brought coats or sweaters with them.

"Here it is at the middle of March and it's still like winter here. I'll bet it's close to sixty in Washington," said Wagner.

"Let's not get nostalgic," cautioned Chance. "You'll only get depressed. Let's go on up and wait for the time of our appointment with Kovalenko."

Wagner joined Chance in his room. It was eight-forty and their appointment with Kovalenko was scheduled for nine. They wanted to be neither early nor late, but precise. They wanted to impress Kovalenko with their American efficiency.

"When we go into this Kovalenko's room," said Chance, "let's act informal and relaxed, as if we're old friends. I think in this way we'll get him to talk more freely."

"I understand some of these Russian guys are hard drinkers," said Wagner and added, "maybe we can all get relaxed and friendly-like, if we had a bottle of Vodka."

"Nah, we don't want to do that," said Chance. "It's probably against the rules anyway. No drinking in the rooms, you know." They waited for a few minutes to pass.

"Well," observed Wagner, "it's a minute before nine. Let's get started."

Outside in the corridor, Chance knocked on Kovalenko's door. No response. He knocked somewhat more vigorously. Still, no answer. He waited a few moments and then virtually pounded on the door without result. Kovalenko did not come to the door.

"Wait here, Gene. I'll go into my room and see if I can get him on the telephone." Chance entered his room and got the switchboard operator on the telephone.

"Will you ring Mr. Kovalenko's room?" Wagner out in the corridor could hear the telephone ring several times in Kovalenko's room.

Chance came out into the corridor. "No answer. Frankly, I'm puzzled. Maybe he left the Embassy. I'll give Fraser a call and let him know we're having a problem. Back in his room, Chance got Fraser in his office on the telephone."

"Fraser," Chance said, "Wagner and I had an appointment at nine with Kovalenko. I've knocked on his door and I've called him on the telephone and there is no answer."

"I'll come up. I have a pass key. Just wait there." The Deputy hung up and Chance went to join Wagner in the corridor. Shortly, the Deputy Secretary arrived.

"On the way up, I checked in the Dining Room to see if he was having a late breakfast, but he wasn't there and the waiter said he had not seen him this morning. I had Helen call the guard gate and the guard reports that no one has signed out since last evening."

"Well, I'll knock once more," Chance said. He knocked several times, but no answer.

"I'll just have to use this pass key and get in," said the Deputy. "I don't see any alternative. Maybe he's sick."

All three of the men had suddenly become apprehensive. They shared a sense of foreboding. If Kovalenko was in the room he surely would have answered by now unless there was something dreadfully wrong.

Fraser Addison inserted the pass key and slowly opened the door just a crack, enough to call out, "Mr. Kovalenko! Are you there?" There was only silence. He threw open the door and took a few steps inside, followed by Chance and Wagner. Abruptly, as if in unison, they stopped. They had found Kovalenko.

Kovalenko lay on his back on the floor at the side of his bed. His legs were spread-eagled, his right arm flung out, his left arm leaning upright against the bed. His eyes were open, staring dully and sightlessly at the ceiling. His mouth was partly open with teeth slightly bared.

Addison, Chance and Wagner just stood as if petrified, momentarily stunned by the scene. Addison was as white as a sheet. Chance uttered, "Oh, my God!" It was immediately obvious to all that Kovalenko was dead. "Look at his face!," Wagner exclaimed. Kovalenko's face was a peculiar bluish color.

Looking around the room quickly, Chance commented, "It doesn't look as if anything has been disturbed or that there was a struggle."

Wagner added, "It looks as if he got out of bed and then collapsed on the floor."

Addison, recovering from his initial shock, took command of the situation. He turned to Chance and Wagner. "Let's not touch anything. In fact, let's leave the room and lock up. One of you stay in the corridor and keep anyone from going in, the cleaning maid or whoever. Just say that Kovalenko isn't feeling well and doesn't want to be disturbed and that the doctor will be coming soon. I'll have to call the police, of course, but I want to first get our doctor in here to take a look and give us his opinion. Once the police come in and take the body out, we'll never know what the cause of death is. I'll also have to let the Ambassador know and Washington as well. Bill, I'm going to use your phone to get Helen to call the doctor."

The three men left Kovalenko's room, closed the door and Addison and Chance went to Chance's room while Wagner stood outside of the door to Chance's room to keep an eye out for anyone who might want to go into Kovalenko's room.

Addison got his secretary on the line. "Helen, call Dr. Kulikov and tell him it's an emergency and to get over here right away. If you can't get him, get his associate, Dr. Boyarsky. Let the guard at the gate know to let them in and when either arrives will you please escort them to Bill Chance's room."

"Is there something wrong with Bill, Mr. Addison?" Helen asked.

"No, Bill and Gene are quite alright. It's something else and I don't want to get into it right now. If the doctor asks you what the problem is, tell him you don't know, but it is an emergency."

Addison then had the switchboard operator ring for Ambassador Harrison Hayes in the latter's room.

"Harrison, I'd like to discuss something important with you right now. Can I come over to see you?"

"Yes, of course, Fraser, come on over to my room."

As Addison prepared to leave, Chance asked, "I noticed you called Russian doctors. Aren't there any American doctors available?"

"No, not in Moscow," Addison replied. "We've been using Dr. Kulikov for the Embassy for several years. He's very good, very competent, very trustworthy and highly respected in local medical circles. He speaks English fluently. We can't get any American medical doctors to come here, so we have little choice. I think there's an American doctor in Leningrad, but that doesn't do us any good."

Addison added, "If I'm not back from the Ambassador's when the doctor arrives, please contact me in the Ambassador's quarters as I want him and me to be here."

Chance nodded and said, "Will do." When Addison had left, Chance sauntered over to Wagner who was standing in the corridor outside Chance's door.

"No one has shown up yet," remarked Wagner.

Chance observed the obvious. "I guess our plans to interview Kovalenko are dead." Both he and Wagner smiled cynically at the metaphor.

Wagner said, "I can't help but think it is an odd coincidence that Kovalenko should kick the bucket just before we are to talk with him."

"I was thinking the same thing," said Chance. "However, there may be no relationship at all. The only persons who knew we were going to speak to Kovalenko were us, Fraser and Kovalenko himself. I don't think Fraser would have mentioned it to anyone except, perhaps, Helen. Of course, we don't know if Kovalenko said anything to anyone. Gene, are you thinking that we may have a case of murder on our hands?"

"Well," replied Wagner, "in an atmosphere that prevails in Russia today, one of suspicion of everyone, anything like this can stimulate the imagination. I really think we have to see what develops with the doctor and any additional investigation."

A half-hour had passed when Fraser and Ambassador Hayes came down the corridor walking toward Chance and Wagner. The Ambassador appeared calm but worried.

"Good morning, Bill, Gene." The Ambassador offered a handshake. "Fraser has told me about Kovalenko and I agree that we should wait for the doctor to come to get his opinion before we or the doctor calls the police. We might as well wait in your room, Bill, if it's alright with you."

When Dr. Kulikov arrived about a half-hour later with Helen Morgan by his side, Wagner ushered them into Chance's room to join Chance, Addison and Ambassador Hayes.

"Well, gentlemen, what is the problem?" Dr. Kulikov inquired.

Fraser answered, "Doctor, about 0930 hours this morning we found the occupant of the room next to this lying on the floor dead. I decided that we should have you give your opinion on the cause of death before we called the police. We can go next door now and have you take a look. Mr. Chance, Mr. Wagner and I have already been in there, but we left after discovering the body. Nothing in the room has been touched or disturbed, not even the body."

"Alright, let's go next door." The doctor motioned for the others to lead the way.

Addison turned to his secretary, "Helen, will you go back to the office and, if people call or ask for me, just tell them I'm out and will return after lunch. And make certain to say nothing about this to anyone." Helen agreed and left.

When the group entered Kovalenko's room, Dr. Kulikov immediately began his examination of the body. After several minutes of the procedure, the doctor turned and addressed the others.

"In my opinion, this man has died of an overdose of a drug known as Scopolamine hydrobromide. It is a drug that, with other drugs combined, is generally used in the treatment of irritable bowel syndrome. In proper dosages it is also used as a sedative when combined with other drugs. However, a large overdose can induce coma and respiratory failure. I think that is what happened here. The bluish color of the face seems to support this."

Dr. Kulikov continued, "I have seen several similar cases. Sometimes, prostitutes will use this drug to knock out their customers so they can rob them and disappear before the guy wakes up. However, the women don't know really how much to give and sometimes they slip too much into food or drink and then they have a murder on their hands. However, I'm sure that's not the case here. Do any of you know if this man was taking the drug for any disorder?"

Chance, Wagner, Addison and the Ambassador all shook their heads and each replied, "No, I don't know whether he was or not."

"Well," the doctor continued, "I am obligated to report this to the police. I can put down the cause of death as an accidental or negligent overdosing by the victim and, actually, I don't know that it wasn't that. By the way, who is he?"

Addison who took on the job of being the spokesman for the others said, "He was a private and personal Secretary to Stalin, but he defected because he felt that he was going to be accused of being a plotter against the government like so many others. So, he asked for asylum and we granted it, at least for a while."

At this disclosure, Dr. Kulikov raised his eyebrows and pursed his lips. His facial expression gave clear meaning to his thoughts. It was obvious that he was having second thoughts of how the overdose had occurred.

Ambassador Hayes, cognizant of his responsibility as head of the Embassy, thought he should be direct. "Do you think, Dr. Kulikov, that this man was poisoned by someone deliberately?"

"I cannot answer that," replied the doctor, "my job is to determine the cause of death, not the reason or reasons for the motive behind the death. I will still report this as an accidental overdose. That may be satisfactory to the police and deter them from climbing all over the Embassy for clues and questioning everyone. Right now, I shall have to call them and they can come for the body."

Addison asked the doctor, "Is there any medical clue we can use in an investigation of how he died?"

The doctor replied, "If you can find a relative or friend of his, you might ask if this chap was taking this medicine. If he wasn't, then it would seem that someone administered the overdose either deliberately or carelessly."

"Is this a prescription drug?" Chance inquired.

"No, it's a proprietary drug, that is, one that can be bought without a prescription. It should be a prescription drug because of its potency, but, as yet, it isn't." The doctor then asked to use the telephone in Addison's office. The doctor, Addison and Ambassador Hayes proceeded to the first floor. Chance and Wagner remained behind and went into Chance's room. The door to Kovalenko's room was locked and Addison had hastily tacked a sign on the door that read, "No admission."

"I think this is a homicide, Bill," Wagner conjectured. "I don't for a moment believe that Kovalenko took an overdose of the drug knowingly and intentionally. If he was a user of the drug, he would know how much of a dose was safe. And I don't believe that he used the drug to commit suicide. His coming here to the Embassy for asylum indicates that he wanted to stay alive. It's my firm belief that someone for some reason fed him the drug overdose."

"You could be right, Gene," said Chance, "but on the other hand, I understand when he came to the Embassy seeking asylum, he had hopes of bringing his wife and son here. Now, they have been picked up by the police and, to him that spells disaster for his family. Maybe it was too much for him to bear and he committed suicide."

"No, Bill, I don't subscribe to that theory. Somebody wanted him dead. After all, he had been a personal aide to Stalin and knew a great deal about the great leader himself."

"Well, alright, Gene. Our next step is to talk with Fraser and Ambassador Hayes about our main mission and try to get some help from them."

"What about this guy, Yakov?" Wagner posed the question in a tone and manner that did little to obscure his dislike of the fellow. "You heard him arguing loudly with Kovalenko a short time ago. Maybe an investigation ought to start with him."

"That is up to Fraser and Hayes, Gene," said Chance, attempting to mollify Wagner. "We have no concern with all this or anything else that may take place in the Embassy unless something interferes with or intrudes upon or compromises our secrecy and security."

Wagner was adamant. "How do you account for the death of Kovalenko just when we were about to talk with him? I think someone got wind of our arrangement to see Kovalenko and decided to do away with him to prevent our talking with him."

"I'm more apt to think that Kovalenko's death and our appointment to talk with him was just a coincidence. First of all, Gene, Kovalenko has been here long enough to have talked to Fraser or other staff members. If someone wanted to keep him from talking, they should have done so a long time ago. I do agree that someone wanted to kill him, but for a reason other than our plan to talk with him."

At that moment, Chance and Wagner heard the voices of several people outside their door in the corridor. It was probably the police. When they opened the door and went into the corridor they found Ambassador Hayes, Dr. Kulikov, Sofia Kameneva, Yakov and two of the male locals on the staff with an old canvas stretcher. Ambassador Hayes, seeing Chance and Wagner, said, "We're waiting for the police. We will wait out here until they get here." With that said, everyone became silent and solemn in apparent agreement that the occasion was so fraught with complexities that there was little anyone could say that would have any meaning. Wagner, however, made it his business to scrutinize each of the players in this melodrama, but in a way that was scrupulously unobtrusive.

Wagner glanced quickly at Sofia and she at him, and when their eyes met there was a vibrant but inexpressible message of mutual admiration along with an understanding that this was not the time for anything but a restrained and vicarious interchange so momentary that no one else present would notice.

Looking at Yakov, Wagner could clearly see that the man was quite agitated by the turmoil that had come upon the Embassy with the death of Kovalenko. Yakov looked at no one. Rather, his eyes were cast downward toward the floor with an occasional glance at the stretcher that had been placed upright leaning against the wall. The constant contortions of his mouth and the persistent small shifts of his body forced Wagner to wonder why Yakov seemed so perturbed. Wagner was convinced that somehow Yakov was involved in Kovalenko's death. But, as Chance had said, "It was none of our business."

Wagner's eyes wandered to Dr. Kulikov. He liked the man immediately when the doctor first came to examine the corpse. The doctor was about five foot eleven of heavy, stocky build. His clean-shaven face was square with prominent cheekbones with lines of determination around the mouth. The doctor's composure was relaxed as he waited for the police. He struck Wagner as a man of great moral and ethical strength, perhaps even fearlessness in the face of possible adversity. Wagner felt that Dr. Kulikov could be trusted to speak and to do what was right and fair. Wagner estimated his age to be in the early or mid-sixties.

Ambassador Hayes also appeared quite calm. Wagner knew that he was an appointee of President Roosevelt and a heavy contributor to the Democratic Party back in the States. Nevertheless, he was considered a competent, able diplomat who could be depended upon to make firm decisions on behalf of United States interests. This was reflected in the respect that the American professional career staff had for him. At the moment, standing in the corridor, the Ambassador appeared immersed in his thoughts as if trying to decide how to handle the situation at hand.

Slightly more than an hour after Dr. Kulikov had placed his telephone call to the police, the police finally arrived. They could be heard coming up the stairs from the lobby to the second floor. Addison led the officials down the corridor to where Ambassador Hayes and the others were standing. There were three policemen in uniform and two plain-clothes men.

Addison spoke. "These three police officers are from the district police department which includes the Embassy. The two gentlemen in civilian clothes are from the NKVD. We're going to need Sofia. None of these people speak English."

One of the police officers took on the role of spokesman for the group. He had a deep, guttural voice when he spoke. Sofia translated, "He says that we should open the door as he and the others would like to get into the dead man's room." Addison complied and unlocked the door to Kovalenko's room. The police officers and the NKVD men walked into the room and followed by the others except for Chance and Wagner who remained at the open doorway from which they could see and hear most of what took place.

The spokesman for the district police looked at the body on the floor as if studying it for a few moments, then turned to one of the other policemen, said something in Russian, whereupon the second policeman took a camera from a valise he was carrying and proceeded to take pictures of the body and of portions of the room.

In the meantime, the two NKVD men were rummaging about the room, opening dresser drawers, examining lamps, going through Kovalenko's clothing and, presumably, his papers left lying about, the bedding and, generally whatever, apparently, struck their fancy. They said nothing and what they were looking for they did not reveal to anyone else. They appeared grim, businesslike, and intimidating.

The police spokesman addressed Dr. Kulikov and Kulikov replied.

"What did they say, Sofia?" the Ambassador asked.

"The policeman asked the doctor for his opinion on the cause of death. The doctor said he thought it was a drug overdose, but that he didn't know where the drug came from." Sofia continued to translate the further conversation from Russian.

"The policeman is asking the doctor about the drug and the doctor is explaining that it is his opinion that it is scopolamine and that he doesn't know how it became to be ingested by the dead man. The policeman says he is familiar with the drug."

One of the NKVD men approached the doctor and engaged him with several questions. Sofia continued, "This gentleman wants to know if the doctor thinks this is a homicide. The doctor said that he doesn't have any facts to make any such conclusion and that is a matter for the police based on whatever investigation is made."

The NKVD man seemed to accept the doctor's statement. He then conferred with the other NKVD man, but in such a low tone that Sofia could not understand what was said. The first NKVD man then approached and spoke with Ambassador Hayes and Deputy Addison who were standing together with Sofia translating:

"This gentleman says he wants to examine the other rooms in the Embassy and to talk with all of the employees and staff. He says it is part of the investigation which he is required to make whenever there is a question about the cause of death."

The Ambassador responded without hesitation but in his customary polite and urbane manner that belied the resolute and uncompromising position that he decided to take immediately with the government officials. Looking directly at the NKVD man, he spoke to Sofia who was at his side. "Tell the gentleman that I understand the gravity of this situation and his desire to investigate, but this is United States property and I cannot permit him to rummage about the Embassy rooms. He can make an inspection of the dead man's room here, but that is all." After Sofia had finished translating that for the Russian, the Ambassador continued, "Tell him also that he can interview our local Russian employees and, if he wishes, I shall provide a conference room for him to conduct the interviews. However, Deputy Addison here will have to be present with this young lady translator when he does so. However, he is not permitted to interview our American staff members or any American citizen in this Embassy."

Upon hearing this from Sofia, the NKVD man's face reddened and his demeanor bristled with anger and belligerency. Obviously, boiling with indignation, he snarled a guttural reply. The moment had become tense and confrontational. Sofia, herself, showed signs of being alarmed and intimidated by the bellicose defiance of the NKVD fellow. However, she continued bravely though somewhat tremulously to translate.

"The gentleman says that he must make his investigation without any restrictions or limitations placed on him. He says he represents the Soviet government and that you have no authority to tell him what he can do or can't do to carry out his duties. He also says that you Americans are guests in his country and you must abide by the laws of the host country, that is, the Soviet. He says he wants to start immediately his investigation here in the Embassy."

The Ambassador, remaining quite calm, replied, "Say to him that we understand that we are in the Soviet Union, but that this Embassy is an extension of American soil and American sovereignty and if he does not understand that he should confer with his government authorities. We will conduct our own investigation and, when completed, we shall be happy to report the results to his government. Ask him if he wishes to use our conference room to interview the local employees."

Listening to the translation and glaring at Ambassador Hayes, the NKVD man growled tersely. "He says," Sofia translated, "that he will take this matter up with his superiors when he gets back to headquarters and you will hear promptly from his government. He says he expects the Soviet Foreign Minister will order you to comply with his demands."

Sofia, who up to now had retained a professional aloofness from the crosscurrent of personality discord in carrying out her duties as translator, became quickly uncomfortable with what she perceived as a developing acrimonious relationship between the principal actors in the situation. It was the hostile and caustic conduct on the part of her fellow-Russian, the NKVD man that caused her growing consternation. Sofia was well aware of the vindictive and harsh punitive measures the Soviet government all too often inflicted upon the Russian citizens who had contact with foreigners. Even though her government had issued her a permit to serve as a translator at the American Embassy, that, in itself, she well understood, provided no unlimited immunity from insufferable harassment by constant questioning by the authorities or a not unimaginable arrest at the worst. Sofia, nevertheless, did her utmost to keep her consternation under control and to continue to translate the conversations with a veneer of detachment.

"You can tell the gentleman," Ambassador Hayes instructed Sofia, "that he may take the matter up with whomever he wishes, but my decision stands unless my government orders otherwise. Tell him that even before he gets back to his headquarters, the United States State Department will have my report on this conversation."

Sofia repeated the Ambassador's statement to the NKVD man who then turned abruptly to the uniformed policemen and ordered them to remove the body of Kovalenko for transport to the city morgue. With that being done, the police and the NKVD officials departed from the Embassy.

Ambassador Hayes turned to the others. He looked exhausted and pale from weariness. "I think I need a teaser or brandy with coffee. Would you all like to join me in the dining room? I mean we can all go downstairs together and try to relax a bit."

Addison, Chance, Wagner, Sofia and even Dr. Kulikov almost in unison nodded their heads and said, "Yes, an excellent idea." The experience of sharing a common stressful event had served to draw them closer to each other and had created a mutual feeling of camaraderie that would, in all probability, never have been otherwise achieved.

As they sat around the table in the Ambassador's dining room, Addison raised his brandy glass in a toast. "I think we should all pay our respects to Ambassador Hayes for the magnificent way in which he handled the situation upstairs. So, I raise my glass to honor him."

The Ambassador accepted the plaudits with gracious humility. "I accept your good words, not so much for me, but as a tribute to all of the loyal and devoted people who work here at the Embassy, especially those who risk much by being here. We have seated here with us two individuals of immense courage and dignity in the face of potential danger to themselves. I refer to Sofia and Dr. Kulikov." The Ambassador became silent for a few moments as he turned and smiled amicably at the two Russian citizens. Then he added, "American employees here are afforded the protection of the United States government both within the confines of the Embassy compound or outside of it. Our local Russian employees have that protection only when they are inside the Embassy. We cannot shield them when they are not within our compound. Outside of the Embassy these fine employees are vulnerable to the capriciousness of government agencies. For that reason I worry about them."

Dr. Kulikov spoke up for the first time since entering the dining room. "I shall speak for myself. I appreciate your concern for my safety and well-being, but I am not concerned and, therefore, you need not be. I have survived several purges throughout the years, purges of the intellectuals, the doctors, lawyers, educators, scientists, engineers, or whatever. I have long ago become resigned to the fact that today I am a survivor and tomorrow a prisoner designated for torture and then to be shot because the government fantasizes that I have committed treason because I have expressed my thoughts verbally. Perhaps, even now these walls have ears and have heard what I have just now said. It does not matter to me. What does matter to me is that when I die it shall be as a free man. A man is free when he has refused to allow threats to his life to cow him into yielding his inherent right to think and speak freely to the repressive forces of evil men."

"You are indeed very unusual, Dr. Kulikov," Deputy Addison said. "I truly admire you for your integrity to the principles of right. Do you have a family?"

"Yes, my wife and an adult son and an adult daughter," replied the doctor.

"Aren't you jeopardizing their safety by your stance?" Addison asked.

"Yes, probably," Dr. Kulikov responded. "But in my family, we all understand that life is not worth living unless we are free to think, speak and act as we believe to be right within, of course, the parameters of reasonable civil laws."

"Do the authorities know of your position as you have expressed it here?" Addison continued to inquire somewhat fascinated by the doctor's apparent disdain and contempt for a ruthless, pitiless government bureaucracy that could banish him to a miserable camp in the Siberian wastelands or have him shot after a brief trial that made a mockery of justice.

Addison continued his questioning. "If the authorities know how you feel about them, then how do you explain why you were not arrested as a traitor or on some other ground. After all, I understand that people are being arrested for much less offensive talking than you have expressed here."

"I have been questioned several times by the NKVD, but they have always let me go on my way. They gave me no reason for releasing me, except that, in my opinion, it was because I had the gumption and temerity to stand up to them and tell them I did not care if they fed me to the lions or not. I think they respected me for that. They are so used to interviewing people who are sniveling, whining and begging, spineless individuals who will confess to anything illegal as long as it saves their lives. People like that are disgusting."

The doctor took a deep breath and then continued. "Besides, what would they gain by arresting and disposing of me?" Again, a pause. "When they are criticized for suppressing freedom of speech and silencing opponents of their tactics, they can point to me and declare, 'Oh, no we don't. Look at this fellow Kulikov. He's going around protesting in public our policies and we haven't arrested him and had him shot. We allow people to speak their minds.'" Another pause. The others at the dining room table were listening intensively to the doctor, seemingly mesmerized by what he was saying.

Dr. Kulikov continued. "It is like Stalin with the Jews. He is fanatically anti-Semitic. If he could, he would wipe the Jews off the face of the earth. He has sent thousands of them to labor camps and has separated husbands and wives and parents from children. Yet, he is smart. He is shrewd. He appointed some Jews to a few high positions in government and then he can say to his world critics, 'You are wrong. I am not anti-Semitic. Look! The Secretary of the Executive Committee of the Comintern is Meer Trilisser, a Jew. There is Yakov Agranov, First Deputy of the NKVD. He is a Jew. And then there is Lazar Kaganovich, a Jew, who was appointed as Commissar of Transportation.'"

Dr. Kulikov regarded everyone at the table and perceived that they were completely engrossed by what he was saying. The doctor concluded by adding, "Of course, the world generally does not know that all these Jews in high position are or were, themselves, intensely anti-Semitic. They want to curry favor with Stalin and they think that by persecuting other Jews they can accomplish that." The doctor sipped at a brandy.

"So, you see, I am in the position to speak freely and yet I have no freedom. I am in a self-imposed prison. How so? Let me explain." Another sip of brandy and then, "If I spoke freely to my friends in criticizing the regime, they would say to themselves, 'Ah, Kulikov speaks with criticism of government policies and he is not arrested. So, I shall feel free to do the same,' and then they speak out and the next night the black limousine of the NKVD stops at their doorway. I would feel as if I had betrayed my friends like a Judas. I would be the means of condemning them to death as surely as if I had shot them myself. That is why I have no freedom to speak." The doctor lapsed into silence, but continued to sip at his brandy as if it were an elixir to the poison in a society gone mad.

There was silence from all the others at the table as if no one knew what to say. Wagner looked at Sofia, the other native Russian in the gathered group. She was the picture of being in deep thought as she stared at her brandy glass and turned it back and forth and back and forth.

Finally, Chance addressed the Ambassador in a very restrained, soft and almost muffled tone, "Sir, are you planning an investigation?"

In an equally subdued voice, the Ambassador answered, "I don't know. I'll talk it over with Fraser."

Then Wagner, seeking to change the atmosphere abruptly, asked, "By the way, where is Yakov? He was upstairs with us when we were waiting for the police to arrive. But, I can't recall seeing him afterwards. But, I wasn't paying him any attention."

The people in the group each shook their heads and shrugged their shoulders to indicate that none had seen Yakov for some time.

Addison said, "He's probably in his room. I'll contact him later."

Ambassador Hayes arose. "I have some matters that need attention. So, I'll have to leave. I suppose I'll be getting an indignant note from the NKVD about my refusal to allow their agents to conduct a room search."

Dr. Kulikov spoke up. "No, I don't think you'll hear from them. They care nothing about the death of a Russian employee in a foreign embassy. Furthermore, the officials in charge know the rules about the sanctity of Embassy compounds. They are not fools to start a crisis with the United States government over something like this."

"Perhaps," said the Ambassador, "but I'll make my report, nevertheless, to my government."

The others took their cue from Ambassador Hayes and also prepared to leave.

Chance and Wagner accompanied Hayes and Addison toward their offices. On the way, Chance asked the two Embassy officers about having a meeting with them. The Ambassador suggested about 1530 that afternoon. Chance, Wagner and Addison agreed that they would all meet in the Ambassador's office.

When they were alone in the lobby, Wagner said to Chance, "There isn't anything to do between now and three-thirty. I think I'll ask Sofia to lunch at some restaurant outside the Embassy. I've already asked her about outside restaurants."

Chance, with a clear look of disapproval, said, "I think you're using unwise discretion just now, but I don't want to stop you, if you want to do this. However, don't you think you might be placing Sofia in a very precarious position by having her, perhaps, seen dining with a foreigner? You've just heard what the NKVD is capable of. They may have their agents watching the comings and goings of this Embassy especially just now after what happened."

"You may be right, Bill, but I'll give her a call and see what she thinks. It's up to her."

Chance shrugged, as if to say that there was nothing further he would add.

Back in his room, Wagner put in a call for Sofia. Mindful, however, that there was a switchboard operator between him and Sofia, he had decided on an innocuous conversation that would arouse no suspicions. Sofia answered the phone.

"Sofia, I hate to bother you. This is Mr. Wagner. I have a paper that needs to be translated. Could you meet me in the lobby in a few minutes?" Wagner's voice was businesslike.

"Yes, of course." Sofia's voice portrayed no excitement and seemed to Wagner, who was filled with expectations, almost lifeless.

The two arrived almost simultaneously in the lobby. Wagner had a couple of papers in his hand that he had snatched up from the table in his room without even looking at their contents. He greeted Sofia with a warm, friendly smile. Sofia likewise smiled, but appeared pale and wan. Wagner concluded that she had obviously been quite shaken by the events of the morning. They sat down on a sofa in the lobby.

"How are you feeling?," Wagner asked in a manner that showed his concern for Sofia.

"I'm a bit unnerved by what occurred this morning. How about you?"

"I'm alright. But I cannot help but notice that you've taken the events rather hard."

"Well, the NKVD fellow was very vindictive and with someone like that, we Russians get somewhat fearful for our own fate. A fellow like that if he cannot get anywhere with the Americans can very easily take his frustrations out on we locals. He can tell his superiors any lie about us interfering with his investigation and they will believe him. Then we, a person like me, are in deep trouble."

"Yes, I see," said Wagner. "I don't have anything for you to translate. I really intended to ask you to lunch in some restaurant outside the Embassy. I thought it might be a welcome diversion for you. I didn't want to ask it over the phone because I have no assurance the switchboard operator might not listen in. She's a local, I gather."

"Yes, she's a local," said Sofia. "But, Nadja is alright. She would not listen in. She can be trusted. About lunch, though, I think it would be unwise just now for me to be seen with you outside the Embassy. You're a foreigner and the NKVD is very suspicious of their locals who are in contact with foreigners, even though working at the Embassy means constant contact with foreigners. It's all very crazy."

"Well, I understand," Wagner said. "Perhaps, when this thing blows over … "

"I have a suggestion, however, " Sofia smiled. "Why don't you get a couple of sandwiches and some tea and we'll have lunch in your room. That will be a diversion for me. I'd like to talk to you about life in America."

Wagner was momentarily taken aback at Sofia's offer. He hadn't expected that. And with the common American casualness, he readily agreed. "Sure," he said. "I'd be delighted. What kind of sandwich would you like?"

"Whatever you choose for yourself, I will have also. I'm not fussy."

"Come over in a half-hour," Wagner proposed. "I'll leave my door open. Just come in."

They parted and Wagner went back up to his room. He wanted to make sure that the room was in an orderly condition. On the way, he stopped in to see Chance.

"Bill, I spoke with Sofia and she says that it would be best for her not to go to a public restaurant with a foreigner just now. That's in agreement with what you said. However, she'll have lunch with me in my room. I felt that I should let you know. We're just going to talk. She said she'd like to know about life in America. Frankly, I can't see anything wrong with it."

Chance showed his irritation. "I still don't like it, Gene, but you do what you want. Remember, we are here on a trade mission. Don't go beyond that."

"Of course. I'm well aware of that, Bill. You can trust me."

Wagner had left his door open as he had told Sofia he would. When she arrived at his room, she stood in the doorway and gave a gentle knock in a hint of formality and feminine modesty. Wagner arose from the chair where he had been reading and greeted her. "Come in, Sofia." Wagner's voice was soft and reassuring. They exchanged smiles and, as they met in the room, Wagner embraced her gently for a moment, then took her hand and led her to a sofa chair. Sofia responded willingly.

To Wagner, Sofia seemed less distraught, more relaxed than she had been earlier when the met in the Embassy lobby. Nevertheless, Wagner was aware that she did not exude the charming vibrancy that had first attracted him to her. He sensed that she was troubled.

"Sofia, I have a couple of sandwiches and a container of coffee. Would you care to eat now?"

"I will have some coffee, but I'd prefer to wait a while with the sandwiches. I'm not very hungry at the moment," Sofia replied. "Is that alright with you?"

"Certainly," Wagner answered obligingly. He felt a strong compassion for this young and beautiful woman. He wanted to help her, to protect her, to commiserate with her. His physical attraction for Sofia was still there, but, now there was something else. It was an obscure feeling that she needed someone to confide in, to comfort her, to console her, perhaps to admire her. He wanted to take her in his arms and to tell her tenderly that he was there for her, to stand between her and whatever may threaten her. For the moment, however, he would encourage her to talk about her fears.

Wagner spoke soothingly. "Sofia, I know something is troubling you. I want to help you if I can. Shall we talk about it?"

Sofia did not respond immediately, but looked down at her hands as if in embarrassment to entrust her intimate thoughts with this man whom she really didn't know for very long and very well. Yet, in her distress she felt the need to turn to someone. She liked Gene Wagner and sensed that he liked her. Sofia recognized that, as in all cases of initial meetings between the opposite sexes, the conversation tended to be superficial and, generally, meaningless and was not to be taken seriously. However, with Gene Wagner it was somehow different. She knew instinctively that Wagner had quickly acquired an emotional link to her. She, in turn, had an intuitive perception that she could trust him with her feelings.

Sofia looked up and her eyes met those of Wagner's and, in that moment, they both knew that there was a deep-felt bond between them. It was a sense of closeness that needed no words to express and to understand.

Sofia began with, "Gene, I have reached a point where I feel I can no longer live in Russia. The conditions here are so terrible and the stress so great that life has become intolerable. I know of no one who does not live in persistent, constant fear of their government. The fear is pervasive at all levels of our society. I must get out of this environment, but I don't know how to do so without great risk."

"Are you in fear for your life?," Wagner asked with concern.

"Yes, of course. I am no exception. Like everyone else in Russia, I do not know from day to day whether I will be arrested. People are arrested and punished on all kinds of trumped-up charges. People are arrested for being traitors or enemies of the State for making some innocent or naive offhand remark."

"You seem to have become upset only since Kovalenko's death. Why is that?" Wagner thought he should ask questions that would focus on Sofia's problem.

"Once a person comes to the attention of the NKVD, whether as a mere bystander or, in my case, as a translator in an Embassy, they have the reputation of conducting a malicious inquisition of that person and usually ending up with an arrest. So you see … " Sofia did not finish her obvious answer.

"However," Sofia continued, "it is just not this one incident that is the reason for my wanting to get out of Russia. It is the accumulation of many stresses and strains, of continued economic hardship, of not having sometimes the necessities of life. Look at what I have to wear!." She gestured to her clothing, a plain, one-piece dark-brown muslin dress with long sleeves and a black belt around the waist and a high collar.

"I think it looks fine." Wagner was sincere in his observation.

Ignoring his remark, Sofia continued her explanation for wanting to leave her country. "In this Russia of ours, if a woman wears nice attractive, fashionable clothing with even a minimum of better quality jewelry, there is an immediate suspicion that she must have an illegal source of money to buy these things or that she has some insidious foreign contacts or that she is a prostitute or a thief. Instead of appreciating a woman's pride in her appearance and her desire to improve her femininity, the authorities always conclude the worst about her. Stalin started that attitude. It is common knowledge that his wife committed suicide because he belittled her appearance and embarrassed her in front of all the high officials and their wives at a dinner party."

"When was that?" Wagner was suddenly alert to the possible implications of Sofia's reference to Stalin.

"It was in November 1932. Everyone remembers the date. Stalin and his wife, Nadezhda Alliluyeva, were at an anniversary party at some official's home. She had put up her hair in a stylish manner and was wearing a fashionable foreign made black dress and high-heeled black patent leather shoes. We understand she did this to make herself attractive to Stalin who was always flirting with other women at these parties. Instead, when others at the party said how lovely she looked, Stalin became furious and told her, in front of everyone, that she looked like a street tramp. Nadja went home and shot herself. They found her the next morning. Stalin had this terrible incident covered up for a long time, but the truth finally leaked out."

Wagner was amused by the emphasis that Sofia placed on clothing as an important reason for wanting to leave her country, but he understood that she was still a young woman in whose life experience being physically attractive was eminently important. But, he also figured that there were more serious reasons for wanting to leave. Perhaps, these would be revealed in due time. He was, nevertheless, startled by her criticism of Stalin and the seeming blame she attributed to him for the conditions in Russia. He hoped the walls did not have ears.

There was a silence for a few moments as they pondered what had been said up to then. Sofia broke the silence. "Gene, do you think you could get me into the United States?"

Wagner smiled good naturedly and replied, "I think I could probably get you into the United States without much difficulty. The biggest impediment is managing to get you out of Russia. I can't give you an answer on that, at least not now. Perhaps, you yourself have some ideas on how to go about it."

"I thought that if I could get into an adjoining country I would be able to get asylum to remain there. I'm thinking of either Estonia or Finland. I would rule out countries that border both Russia and Germany that are in the paths of invasion from either one or both of them. That would be too risky. What do you think of that idea?" Sofia looked at Wagner rather skeptically about the feasibility of such a project. "It's only an idea," she added.

"I think it's a good idea, but it doesn't resolve the question of how you are to get into the other country."

Sofia thought a moment. "If I can get to Leningrad, it may be that I can arrange to get on a Finnish freight boat that sails out of Helsingfors to Leningrad and back. From Finland perhaps I can get to America. There is a constant flow of boats across the Gulf of Finland to Leningrad."

"How would you get on board a freighter?," Wagner asked. "Would you sign on as a member of the crew?" Wagner was neither incredulous nor sarcastic in asking that question. He merely wanted to lighten the conversation. In fact, he admired Sofia's innovativeness and the audacity of her proposal.

"You are making fun of me, Gene," commented Sofia.

"No, not really. I'm just leading you on."

"There are several ways of getting on board a ship. I could bribe a crewman to smuggle me on and hide me until we had left port. Or, I could promise the Captain to sleep with him while making the crossing back to Finland."

"Are you serious?"

"Yes, of course, anything to get out of here." Sofia was adamant. "However, there is a problem," she added. "I would have to get a travel permit to travel to Leningrad and I would have to demonstrate a good reason to get such a permit. If you were going to Leningrad on your trade mission, you could request that I accompany you as a translator. The government would grant your request I'm sure because of your Embassy status."

"Sofia, I don't know if our plans will include Bill and my going to Leningrad. Bill's the head of the trade mission, so I'll have to await developments. However, you know I'd like to help you. In the meantime, how about getting after these sandwiches? Some more coffee?"

As they were finishing their lunch, the phone rang. Wagner answered. It was Bill Chance.

"Gene, the Deputy wants us down in his office right away. I'm going immediately. You can meet me there, but don't take too long."

"I'll just be a few minutes, Bill." Wagner turned to Sofia. "The Deputy wants Bill and me in his office immediately. I'll have to go. I'm sorry to cut our visit short, Sofia. I'll see you at dinner and maybe we can continue our meeting for later or for tomorrow. I'll be in touch with you." Wagner got up to leave. Sofia did likewise. Wagner gave her a gentle hug and they kissed with just a pittance of passion before they left the room together and then parted in the outer corridor. Wagner was disappointed. He had not anticipated that his visit with Sofia would end so abruptly. But, he had no choice. He knew that. Sofia lingered a few minutes more in the corridor and then left for her room on the first floor. It would cause gossip if they were seen leaving together.

When Wagner entered Addison's office, the Ambassador and Chance were already there sitting around the Deputy's desk. He quickly noted that each was the picture of abject consternation. Wagner concluded that some sort of crisis had erupted. As he sat down with them, he assumed he would be informed.

Addison addressed Wagner. "I've already informed the Ambassador and Bill and I want to let you know, too. We have another death on our hands. Yakov has apparently committed suicide. I tried to contact him in his room and when I did not get an answer, I went to his room and found him hanging with a rope around his neck from the corner of his highboy clothes closet. I've called Dr. Kulikov again and we'll have to get the police involved for the second time today. I'm sure they'll wonder what's going on here in the Embassy. Anyway, we'll have to cancel the meeting for this afternoon. We'll reschedule for tomorrow some time."

Wagner was stunned as were the others. Wagner asked the logical question. "Do you know why Yakov committed suicide?"

Addison replied, "No, not at all. He left a note on his table, but none of us here can understand it. I have it here. It says, 'We are deceived by an appearance of right. I am casting my burden aside.' That's all it says." Addison shook his head to express his feeling of utter futility in trying to understand and decipher the message intended in the suicide note.

Ambassador Hayes mirrored his despair. "It's really getting to be too much. These two people, Kovalenko and Yakov, were locals. I think we should let the doctor and the police handle both of them. I don't believe it is our job to worry about reasons or motives for these deaths." The Ambassador directed himself to Addison. "When the police come, get Sofia again for translations."

"Are you saying that you do not want us to investigate these deaths?," inquired Addison, somewhat startled by the Ambassador's precipitous dismissal of the two tragic events.

"Fraser, you can do what you think is necessary. All that I'm saying is that it is my opinion that we should not waste any time probing into the whys and wherefores of these deaths. With Stalin ordering the executions of thousands, perhaps hundreds of thousands of his countrymen, how can we justify being concerned about the deaths of two Russians? It would have been only a matter of time before these two fellows would have been shot anyway."

Chance and Wagner exchanged glances of incredulousness with the Deputy.

Chance spoke up. "Mr. Ambassador, I would hope that you are not equating us with Stalin. In America, each individual's life is considered precious and of great value. The taking of a life is considered as an assault on our democratic society. Are we supposed to change our values when we enter another country with a different culture?"

"No, I'm not suggesting that you have to change or give up your values, but when you, as a foreigner, visit another society which is rooted in different cultural practices, then I think you have to acquiesce to those differences. The trouble with Americans is that they don't recognize and admit that they cannot force their values and lifestyles on people whose habits have been developed and followed for centuries. Do you understand?"

At that moment, Helen, Addison's secretary, came to the door and announced that Dr. Kulikov had arrived.

"Have him come in," Addison instructed.

"Well, gentlemen, we meet again today. I was told it was urgent and to come immediately," said Dr. Kulikov as he entered the room. "You all look very healthy to me. What is the problem?"

Addison responded with a grimace generally typical of someone with a tumescent gumboil. "We have had a suicide. Yakov Strinovsky, our Director of Embassy Personnel, has hung himself in his room."

Dr. Kulikov was professionally cynical. "Well, the government has saved a couple of bullets. I'll take a look, if someone will lead the way."

Yakov was still hanging. No one had cut him down. A cadaver is not, in most cases, an object of beauty, especially one with a stretched neck, a purple face and bulging eyes, along with trousers dripping with body fluids.

Dr. Kulikov took one look and, without the benefit of a medical textbook, declared the cause of death as self-imposed strangulation. "Notify the police immediately and I'll wait until they arrive. Let's leave the body hanging until there has been a viewing by the police." Dr. Kulikov began to write out a report on the incident while Addison went back to his office to call the police and to greet them when they arrived. Chance and Wagner, likewise, walked back to the lobby. Ambassador Hayes remained at the scene with the doctor.

While waiting, Ambassador Hayes thought it might be an opportunity to get some thoughts of a Russian from a Russian intellectual, the doctor.

"Doctor," said Ambassador Hayes, "do you have an opinion about when Stalin's purge will end, that is, the arrests, the sending people to camps and having others shot?"

"It will end," replied Kulikov, "when the last peasant has been shot and Stalin can stand alone and, for once, not feel threatened. Or sooner, if Stalin is assassinated. That is when, in either case, the bloodletting will end."

"Then Stalin is the key to all of this miserable fear being inflicted on the Russian people. Is that what you imply?"

"Yes, of course. The man is absolutely paranoid about the idea that people are conspiring against him. Not only are strangers being liquidated, so also are Stalin's close friends and relatives. No one is immune to the head-chopper's axe!"

"You know, Doctor," said Hayes in a reflective tone, "speaking of assassinations, I find it beyond understanding that no one has even attempted to assassinate Stalin, let alone actually assassinate him. Here he is; one man places a whole vast country in universal fear; one man so controls millions of lives that he can order imprisonment, torture, placing in slave labor camps or execution of thousands of individuals and not one person has done away with him. It's simply incredible." The Ambassador shook his head in mind-boggling perplexity.

Dr. Kulikov's response to this was to smile at what he thought was the naiveté of the Ambassador. "Mr. Ambassador, you cannot judge our circumstances here by your American standards. You must try to understand the Russian psyche. They have been oppressed by their government since time immemorial, whether it's by a Tsar or by a Communist Party head. They have accepted harsh treatment from the government as a way of life. A Russian is born into tyranny, lives under grinding, draconian rules and dies from the crush of a relentless iron heel." Dr. Kulikov paused as if enamored of his own eloquence. Ambassador Hayes stood silent and fascinated by the doctor's candid dissection of the Russian soul. He admired the doctor. The police not having yet arrived, the doctor continued with his diagnosis of the marrow of Russian character.

"You ask, 'Why is there no mass protest or an attempt to overthrow the government or to assassinate Stalin?' The answer is fear, apathy, and hopelessness. Those three things together produce paralysis whether in an individual or a whole society. I call it paralysis of the soul. What benefit have the Russian people gained from the Bolshevik Revolution of 1917? The people were filled with a hope for freedom and better living conditions. What they got in place of Tsar Nicholas was Stalin. The Russian people, in effect, exchanged a chronic but non-lethal microbe for a deadly virus."

"Perhaps," observed Ambassador Hayes, "in order to bring about change you don't need a mass uprising. Perhaps one individual or a mere handful of individuals can change the course of history by assassinating the head of the government. Although neither I nor my government approves of that method, nevertheless, I mention it as a possible solution. What do you think?"

Before Dr. Kulikov could answer, both men heard loud voices out in the lobby. The police had arrived. Deputy Addison led the two officers to Yakov's room. Sofia accompanied them. They were not the same officers who had been at the Embassy earlier for the death of Kovalenko. This time there were no NKVD people, much to everyone's relief. Addison had called an ambulance to take Yakov's body away.

One of the police officers said in Russian, as translated by Sofia, "Obviously, a suicide." He turned to the other officer. "Take some pictures!" The second officer took a small camera from a bag he was carrying and proceeded to snap several photographs of Yakov's body and the room itself.

The ambulance crew had arrived and, on orders of the first officer, took Yakov's body down, placed it on a stretcher and, not bothering to cover it, carried it to the lobby and out to the ambulance.

The officer began to write out his report, asking questions and getting information.

"Why do you think this fellow committed suicide?"

"We have no idea," answered Ambassador Hayes. "He did not seem to be worried about anything and he never spoke about having any personal problems. To the contrary, Yakov seemed quite happy and content to be working here."

"Did he leave a suicide note?," the officer inquired.

"Yes, he left this note," said Addison and handed the officer the note Addison had found upon first entering the room.

The officer looked at the note and shook his head. "What does it mean? It seems meaningless. It's not worth much. It explains nothing." The officer threw the note on the table with obviously no further interest in it.

As the officers were leaving Yakov's room, the one officer said to Ambassador Hayes, "We have a record of the man's relatives from the time he applied for a permit to work here. We'll notify them."

Ambassador Hayes said, "We have a record of the relatives also. We'll contact them to express our regrets."

The officer nodded to express his understanding, when Sofia translated for him. "Tell the Ambassador that I shall report this as a suicide, but if he obtains any information indicating otherwise, I would appreciate his calling our office." With that and escorted by Addison, the two officers departed. Before closing up the room, Ambassador Hayes picked up Yakov's suicide note that the police officer had tossed on the table. As he put the note in his coat pocket, he turned to Dr. Kulikov who was still standing by. "What Yakov wrote on this note is a puzzle. Maybe some day we'll find out what it means. Well, thank you, Doctor, for coming again. By the way, I found your explanation of the Russian people and conditions today remarkably interesting. We shall have to continue that discussion some time."

As the two men walked toward the lobby, the Doctor said, "Mr. Ambassador, if at any time you need a prescription drug to take care of a deadly virus, let me know." The doctor winked at the Ambassador and smiled shyly. Hayes gave a knowing smile. Both men understood what was meant.

Chance, Wagner and Addison were standing in the lobby as the Ambassador and Dr. Kulikov joined them. Chance remarked, "Well, that police investigation didn't take very long this time. Maybe it's because the NKVD were not involved."

"No, it's a different case from Kovalenko," countered Hayes. "Yakov is an obvious suicide."

After Dr. Kulikov had said his goodbye to the group in the lobby, the Ambassador spoke up. "I think we should reinstate the meeting originally scheduled for this afternoon. We have the time before dinner. Bill and Gene have been patient and understanding, but, I'm sure they want to get on with what they came here for. So, we'll cancel tomorrow morning's meeting and all meet in Fraser's office in a half-hour. How will that be?" The others agreed and each left the lobby. Chance and Wagner walked to the dining room for coffee, Addison and Hayes for their offices.

At three p.m. sharp, Chance and Wagner appeared at Deputy Secretary Addison's office reception room. Helen, his secretary, appeared dejected. "Today has been a rough day. In fact, I haven't been able to concentrate on my work at all. It's been terrible. First, Kovalenko and then Yakov. I simply don't understand either of them."

Helen announced the arrival of Bill and Gene over the interoffice intercom. Addison told her to have the two men come into his office. "The Ambassador called to say he'll be a few minutes late," Addison told Chance and Wagner as they entered his office.

"Have seats, fellows." Addison gestured to some chairs.

"Well, what do you think of today's events?"

"Is it possible that Yakov poisoned Kovalenko and then took his own life because he knew that an investigation would reveal his guilt?," Wagner asked thoughtfully.

Addison replied, "We can surmise any number of things. Perhaps, we should be guided by what the Ambassador said earlier. Perhaps, investigating the cases is a local job and we should not get involved, especially when there is considerable work to be done by us on other matters. As for Yakov murdering Kovalenko is concerned, I'd have a difficult job trying to uncover something like that."

"I still remember from the first night we were here, a loud argument at the adjoining room where Kovalenko roomed and Yakov then coming out of the room," Chance said. "That's what leads me to believe that there was some antagonism between the two, perhaps enough to cause Yakov to want to get rid of Kovalenko."

Addison interrupted, "Well, while we're waiting for the Ambassador, let me tell you about Yakov and Kovalenko. Since they are both dead, I think I can tell you the background without fearing getting them into trouble. The Ambassador knows all about it and I think it explains why he doesn't want to proceed with any investigation." The Deputy leaned back in his chair and began his account.

"Kovalenko was not an employee. As I mentioned to you earlier, shortly before you two arrived here he came with a friend to the

Embassy and asked for asylum on the grounds that he feared for his life. Normally, we would not grant asylum for the obvious reason; that we would soon be overwhelmed by Russians who fear for their lives. In Kovalenko's case, however, he said he was a personal assistant or aide to Stalin and he told us enough about Stalin that caused us, at least me, to believe him. I thought he was a person who might be valuable to us and the Ambassador approved granting him asylum. We told the staff that he was a new employee.

"However, in Russia today you have a tendency to be suspicious of every Russian you deal with. So to put Kovalenko to the test of his sincerity and truthfulness, we gave him the job of quietly and surreptitiously looking into the backgrounds of our local Russian employees to see if there might be one or more who might be what is called 'plants' by the police or NKVD to spy on us and get information for them. Naturally, he had to do this by casual conversation with the employees, that is, in a way that would not cause any alarm among the employees. Remember, Russians are just as suspicious of each other as we may be of them."

Addison paused a moment. Chance and Wagner showed intense interest in what the Deputy was relating. Addison continued, "Almost at the start of his project, Kovalenko got a tip from an employee that Yakov was a homosexual and that Yuri, the waiter, was his lover. You can understand that we don't want 'those kind' of people in our Embassy. So the Ambassador and I called Yakov into my office and confronted him about the information we had received. At first he vehemently denied it. He wanted to know who told us such an outright lie. We didn't reveal our source right away, but, finally, to prove we were not fabricating our story, we told him it was Kovalenko and when we told him that we would call other employees in and question them about it, he relented and admitted the affair with Yuri. However, we at no time told him that Kovalenko was other than an employee."

Addison continued, "I gather that Yakov went to Kovalenko's room and that was the argument Bill heard. I assume also that Yakov told Yuri that he admitted to the truth. We called Yuri in and he quickly affirmed that he and Yakov were carrying on a homosexual relationship. We told both Yakov and Yuri that they were fired and their job termination would be effective in two weeks."

"So, Yuri having access to the food he served could easily have put the poison in Kovalenko's food," Chance commented. "He had an excellent opportunity for revenge."

"Yes, that is something we thought about," Addison said. "But, we're not going to pursue it. Whether Yakov was involved in the poisoning or whether he even knew about it before it took place is unimportant now that he is dead. As far as Yuri is concerned, he's out of here and that is all that matters to us. We have also sent the message to our employees that we won't tolerate homosexuality in this Embassy. If we find out about it, they're fired."

"Does that policy apply even if the practice takes place outside the Embassy?," asked Wagner.

"Yes," replied Addison. "It's a disgusting, abnormal and unnatural practice. I have no respect for anyone participating in homosexual activities. I would refuse to deal with such a person regardless of his title or standing in the community."

"I don't know about you, Gene," said Chance, "but I agree wholeheartedly with Fraser."

"I do, too," Wagner replied. "Homosexuality is an abomination. People who practice it are a scourge on society. They're moral lepers and like lepers they should be banished from decent society perhaps to a commune of their own on some uninhabitable island."

Addison and Chance laughed at the vividness of Wagner's antipathy.

At that moment, Helen announced the arrival of Ambassador Hayes whom she then escorted to the door of Addison's office. Hayes sat down among the others.

Addison addressed the Ambassador. "I've told Bill and Gene about Kovalenko and the project we assigned him regarding our local employees and how he discovered Yakov and Yuri were carrying on a homosexual liaison with each other. I told them we had fired Yuri and we were not going to follow up on any investigation. I told them that you knew all about it."

"Yes, that's correct," said the Ambassador. "You know, I couldn't understand the suicide note that Yakov left. But as I think about it, I believe the note does explain his suicide. I have the note here with me and I want you, Fraser, to put it in the file you have on Yakov. But, let me read it to you all and you shall see what I mean." Hayes then read the note aloud: "'We are deceived by an appearance of right. I am casting my burden aside.'" To me it means that Yakov recognized that he had deceived people by appearing to be normal while all the time being abnormal and that he tired of the deception and of having to hide his true feelings and that became an unbearable burden to him. Possibly, the fact of disclosure to his fellow-workers that he was homosexual and the accompanying embarrassment and ostracism might have been the precipitating cause of committing suicide. One has to be in a very extreme emotional condition in order to kill oneself. Suicide goes against every animal instinct."

"Yes, it could mean what you say, Mr. Ambassador," said Addison. "Anyway, could we get on with our originally intended meeting?"

Addison looked toward Chance and Wagner. "Well, Bill and Gene, you requested this meeting. I'll turn it over to you and you can tell the Ambassador and me what you have in mind."

Wagner pointed to Chance. "You carry the ball, Bill."

Chance began. Addressing both the Ambassador and the Deputy, he said, "It is your understanding that Gene and I have been sent here on a trade mission. Isn't that correct?"

"Yes, of course," Addison said. The Ambassador nodded in agreement.

"Well, that is not true. The trade mission thing is a blanket or cover for the real reason we were sent here."

"And what is that?," inquired Ambassador Hayes with evident curiosity.

Chance was silent for a moment, although he had decided some time before as to how he would break the news about the real purpose of coming to Moscow. Both he and Wagner had some trepidation about how Addison and Hayes would react to the announcement. Nevertheless, it had to be divulged if they were to accomplish their goal.

"I shall be very forthright," Chance said. "Gene and I have been sent here to help bring about the elimination of Stalin as head of the Soviet Union."

Chance looked at Addison and saw that the Deputy's eyes had widened almost to bulging and that his jaw had dropped. A sudden blow to the head could not have startled him more. Then looking at the Ambassador, Chance observed him with a frown of incredulity on his face. To Chance it was obvious that his statement had shocked the two men.

"I can see that you both are surprised," declared Chance in an understatement. "However, before you have me and Gene committed to an insane asylum let me give you some background." Hayes and Addison sat silent and motionless, seeming frozen in a torpid state.

Chance continued his explanation. "We in the Russian Section of the State Department some time ago came to the conclusion that the greatest threat to the United States interests both at home and in Europe is the Soviet Union. We see the Soviet's goal is to establish and expand the Communist movement in the world beginning with Europe. The Communist ideology is the antipode of our democratic tenets; it is the antithesis of every value to which we adhere. I don't think I have to go into details. You two have lived here long enough to know whereof I speak. There is another and more urgent reason for our so-called secret mission and that is that we have the same information that you, presumably, have about Russia and Germany possibly carving up Europe between them and each taking over certain countries or portions of countries. If this were to happen, it is almost a certainty that a second World War would start. Britain and France would go to war with Germany and Russia and the United States would be drawn in. We believe that getting rid of Stalin would go a long way to solving the problems. If Stalin goes, the whole Soviet Empire will become disorganized and rendered impotent. Stalin is the force holding the Soviets together. Secretary McKinley Roth has approved the idea unofficially and very privately. He took it up with the President who did not object but would want to know little, if anything, about the mission. In other words, while the President and Roth are giving their tacit approval, they do not want to be publicly identified as having any part of it. I will add that we are not to undertake the actual elimination of Stalin but merely to lend support to some person or group that is not American who will execute the elimination. That aid and assistance from us will have to be of the utmost secrecy. This is why we are using the trade mission as a cover."

Chance paused in anticipation of some comment from the Ambassador and the Deputy. By this time as Chance had been explaining the background of the secret mission both men had seemingly recovered from their initial shock.

"Bill," said the Ambassador, "you have concentrated on Stalin, but what about Hitler. He's the other part of this possible agreement to divide up the European Continent. In addition, even if you got rid of Stalin and thereby neutralized Russia, Britain and France would not sit idly by and let Germany take over the Continent. So, you would not avoid war anyway."

Replied Chance, "Of course Hitler presents a problem for us. But we are not as concerned about him as we are of Stalin. In fact, if Germany were to invade the Soviets it would be just great. It would probably topple Stalin because right now the Soviet army is no match for the German Wehrmacht. When Hitler marched into Austria in March 1938 no one got excited and protested. We in America believed that he was right to want to unite German-speaking people. The same is true of the Sudatenland of Czechoslovakia and the Danzig area of Poland. Those are all German ethnic conclaves and there is nothing wrong in his wanting to bring them into Germany. Not only that, but we in America think Germany is a great nation, advanced in science, of hard working, educated, intelligent people. Can we say that of Russia?"

"Well, alright," said Ambassador Hayes, "whatever we think, you have been sent here for a specific purpose and we have to do what we can to help you accomplish it without involving the United States except indirectly. We'll continue to use your cover of a trade mission and line you up with some foreign trade officials of the Soviet government. In the meantime, we'll have to work out a plan for you to follow for your special mission. Accomplishing what you have in mind won't be easy. I'm sure you're aware of that," said Hayes, looking directly at Chance and Wagner.

"Agreed," acquiesced Chance.

"I don't think you're going to have a lot of time to achieve results," the Ambassador pointed out. "From what we hear, Hitler will take over Czechoslovakia by the end of this April and then he'll send his troops into Poland. Britain and France will probably not go to war over Czechoslovakia, but they probably will over Poland. And the nice part for Hitler is that by that time he will have a mutual pact with Russia whereby Russia, that is, Stalin will do nothing about these invasions except to share in the booty."

Ambassador Hayes turned to Addison. "Fraser, do you have any ideas?"

"No, this came up so suddenly that I have not had the time to think about it at all," responded the Deputy. "However, I do know that if any peoples other than his own countrymen exist who would like to see Stalin dead or, at least, removed from power, it is the Estonians and the Finns. Stalin has made demands on both of those Baltic countries to yield land to the Soviets and both have resisted those demands to date. Unlike other European countries coveted by both the Russians and the Germans, the Germans have no designs on either Finland or Estonia and Finland and Estonia know that and do not anticipate trouble with Germany. Their problem is with the Soviet Union and Stalin. The representatives of those two countries have been negotiating furiously with the Soviet government to forestall any takeover action on the part of the Soviets. Frankly, since you're prohibited from any direct involvement, then you might want to explore getting someone from those two countries to carry out the coup de gras, so to speak."

"That might be an idea we can pursue," said Chance, "but we'd have to be very circumspect about approaching and inquiring of them."

"Wait. I have another thought," exclaimed Wagner. "How about getting Yuri the waiter involved. He told us that he works as an extra, on occasion, at the big dinners staged by Stalin from time to time. Perhaps he'd be willing to drop some poison into Stalin's food in exchange for our keeping him on here as an employee of the Embassy."

"That would be distasteful and against my principles as I explained earlier about homosexuals," declared Addison. "However, we could try it if we had to, but I don't know if we could trust Yuri not to divulge the secret mission to the NKVD. I have no idea how he feels about Stalin. I'll talk to him before his job termination date becomes effective."

The Ambassador spoke up, "I'll do this tomorrow morning as a starter. I'll call both the Finnish and Estonian Embassies and tell them we'd like to meet with their trade's specialists and at the same time I'd like to visit with their respective Ambassadors, if available. If either or both of their missions can see us in a few days, then I'll go with you.

The whole subject has to be handled at the highest level and supremely discreetly. Anything less will spell huge trouble for everyone including the countries involved. I'll let you know as soon as I have been able to make arrangements. How does that sound?"

"As you said," stated Chance, "it's a starter. If you or Fraser come up with any other ideas, please let's discuss them. Every avenue of approach to this mission should be explored. The biggest problem has been and remains, 'How do we get to Stalin to carry out what we have to do?'"

Addison looked at his watch. "It's close to dinnertime. Why don't we meet in the dining room in a half-hour and sit together?"

All present were in agreement. Chance and Wagner left Addison's office. Ambassador Hayes said he'd stay behind for a few moments.

As they passed through the reception room, they observed Helen typing in a lethargic manner. "How are you feeling now, Helen?," inquired Wagner with a voice expressing concern.

"Oh, a bit better. I took a headache powder. It seems to have helped me to relax," said Helen.

"Good," declared Wagner, "maybe we'll see you at dinner."

After breakfast the next morning, Chance and Wagner repaired to Chance's room to talk over the previous day's frenetic events and to await word from the Ambassador. Shortly after eleven a.m. the telephone rang. Chance answered. It was Fraser Addison.

"The Ambassador is in my office. He has some information for you and asks that you come down now."

"Gene and I will be right down."

A quick greeting to Helen, Chance and Wagner entered Addison's office and took seats as they bid good morning to Fraser and the Ambassador.

Ambassador Hayes got to the business at hand immediately. "I telephoned and talked with Ambassador Pentti Peltonen of the Finnish mission here in Moscow. He says that there is a delegation of officials due in from Finland sometime in the middle of this afternoon and he is of the opinion that there is someone with the Finnish trade section coming with them. He says they're a negotiating group that is to meet with Max Litinov, the Soviet Foreign Minister. Ambassador Peltonen wanted to put off a meeting with us for a couple of days, but I told him it was urgent that we meet with him. So he has invited us to dinner at the Finnish Embassy this evening at seven p.m. I accepted the invitation on the assumption that you would approve. I'd like to have Fraser there also. Is that agreeable?"

"Yes, we'll be there," Chance answered.

"Fine, then meet me in the lobby at six p.m. The dress is business suits in case you're wondering. We won't require a translator because most of these people speak fairly good English. When we arrive at the Finnish Embassy you can get together with the Finnish trade representative while I'll try to have a private meeting with the Finnish Ambassador."

"Are we to discuss with anyone about our Stalin mission?" asked Chance.

"No, hold off on that until I've talked to the Finnish Ambassador. I'll get his reaction if I have the opportunity. I'd suggest you confine yourself to the trade mission talk until further notice from me. I almost forgot. You'll both ride with me and Fraser."

CHAPTER 6

This is one of the most depressing of major cities that I've been in," remarked Gene Wagner as he, Bill Chance, Ambassador Harrison Hayes and Fraser Addison rode in the Embassy limousine to keep their appointment at the Finnish Embassy.

It was already dark and as they drove south on Novinski Boulevard and then turned somewhat southeast on Kropotkinski Avenue, the headlights picked out what, seemingly, was one after another old, drab buildings. Although the street pavements were clean and free of refuse, the buildings of apartments and stores appeared to need a good hosing down and scrubbing to remove the grime of years of inattention.

"I don't understand why these people cannot put some bright paint on these buildings," continued Wagner with a tone of disgust in his voice. He added, "Mr. Ambassador, I don't see how you can live here for very long."

Ambassador Hayes chuckled. "One gets used to it. Besides, I keep busy along with social activities that relieve the monotony."

Chance spoke up. "Just to review: Gene and I will be talking trade matters with the Finnish trade officials while you, Mr. Ambassador, will speak with the Finnish Ambassador possibly about our main mission."

"Yes, that's correct," replied Hayes.

Both Hayes and Chance were cautious about mentioning anything about the main mission in the presence of Gregor, their Russian driver.

Arriving at the Finnish Embassy, the military guard at the entrance gate passed them through after identifying them as American diplomats. Gregor drove into the courtyard and parked the limousine. The three

Americans entered the anteroom of the Embassy building where an Aide to Finnish Ambassador Pentti Peltonen greeted them.

"The Ambassador will be with you shortly," advised the Aide. "In the meantime, would you come with me to the conference room and, perhaps, you would care to have some coffee to help warm you up."

Ambassador Hayes knew that it was in the Finnish tradition to have a pot of hot coffee at the ready at all times and that it was not appropriate to decline the offer of a cup of the brew.

"Yes, of course, we'll all have some," Hayes replied.

The four Americans were joined in the conference room by the Aide, whose name they learned was Kalle Nevakivi and that he was a native of the City of Viipuri.

The Aide had gone to the Embassy kitchen and brought back a steaming pot of coffee from which he served the coffee. As the Americans discovered when they drank the coffee, the coffee grounds had been left in the pot and some went into their cups.

"In Finland," said Nevakivi, "we keep the pot heated continuously and if the grounds are left in the pot, the coffee gets blacker and stronger which we like."

"So I notice," said Ambassador Hayes good-naturedly.

"By the way, Herra Nevakivi," remarked Hayes, "I hear that the Soviets want to have Finland cede the Karelian Isthmus to the Soviets, which borders the Soviets off the Gulf of Finland."

"Yes, that's true," Nevakivi confirmed. "Viipuri is on the Isthmus and my family and I would find such a demand as unacceptable. We would never live under the Soviets. We would abandon our lands and move out to another part of Finland."

"But, can you blame the Russians if they want to protect Leningrad which is only twenty-five miles from the Karelian border?," Hayes inquired. "They want to prevent an attack through Finland directed at Leningrad."

"I can understand their concern," replied the Aide, "but, that is no reason we should give up a big part of our country which, by the way, is quite industrialized."

"Do you think the Finnish government will yield to the Soviet demand?," Hayes persisted.

"No, my government will never yield voluntarily. We shall propose that we will guarantee that we shall not allow any country to use Finland to get to Russia. The Soviet government should be satisfied with that."

"But, how could little Finland prevent the German army from using Finland as a bridge to Russia? The Germans have a pretty powerful military force," continued Hayes.

Before Nevakivi could answer, Wagner broke in. "Isn't Stalin the problem? If, somehow, he was no longer in the picture, these matters could be resolved."

Hayes and Chance both, simultaneously, shot a reproving look at Wagner that clearly conveyed the message that he had overstepped himself and should get off the subject. Wagner, on his part, averted their looks.

"Yes, some of us have mentioned that. But, of course, it's a pipe dream." The Aide looked hopeless in considering the subject. One would judge Nevakivi to be in his early thirties, vigorous, aggressive, patriotic, but not yet fully matured sufficiently to make important decisions on political issues. The Finnish authorities must have felt that he was adequate as an Aide to the Ambassador.

Nevakivi paused for a few moments while the Americans remained silent while regarding the Aide with a surprised interest. Nevakivi then resumed speaking and with considerable and noticeable fervency. "I would do anything to save my homeland from being taken over by these Russians." His reference to "these Russians" was said in a tone of contempt and despisement. Bill Chance thought Nevakivi's passionate love of country had loosened his tongue beyond what was appropriate for one in the diplomatic service. Yet, Chance was pleased to have met this young man. Nevakivi might be useful in the American undertaking.

Ambassador Hayes looked at his watch. It was close to seven p.m. They had been waiting about twenty minutes for the Finnish Ambassador. Nevakivi, noticing that Hayes was checking the time, arose and started to walk towards the conference room door saying, "I'll see what may be delaying our Ambassador." As he said this, Ambassador Peltonen strode into the room.

"Welcome, gentlemen. I apologize for keeping you waiting, but I have been with some people from Finland. As I explained to you, Ambassador Hayes, they arrived this afternoon."

"That is quite alright," replied Hayes. "We appreciate your arranging to see us on such short notice. Let me introduce these gentlemen from our State Department who, as I mentioned on the telephone, are here on a trade mission."

Ambassador Peltonen shook hands with Chance and Wagner. The latter commented while riding on the return trip to the American Embassy that they liked the Finnish Ambassador. He was, they remarked, not the usual stiff and formal diplomat with a chilling impersonality but an unpretentious and unassuming "regular guy" as they put it.

"I think dinner is ready to be served, so perhaps we should go to the dining room. Would you be good enough to follow me? The other guests are already there, I believe." The Finnish Ambassador spoke in a soft and cordial voice.

hallway towards the dining room with the others following, Hayes said to Peltonen, "I hope I can speak privately with you before I return to our Embassy this evening."

"Yes, we'll go to my office immediately after dinner. There is no need for me to remain with the Finns. Three of them are here on some preliminary discussions about the Aland Islands at the southern end of the Gulf of Bothnia between Finland and Sweden. The Russians are raising a fuss about militarizing the Islands to protect the entrance to the Gulf of Finland. They want protection for Leningrad at their end of the Gulf. If we Finns don't stand up to them, the Russians will gobble up the whole of Finland. They're some arrogant bunch, these Russian leaders. I have to be nice to them. I am, after all, a diplomat."

When they arrived at the dining room, the other guests were standing in a corner talking among themselves but broke up when Ambassador Peltonen entered.

Peltonen introduced the Americans to the Finns. He gave especial attention to introducing the fourth Finn to Chance and Wagner. "Mr. Chance and Mr. Wagner, this is Antti Salonen, who is here on a trade mission just as you are. You might like to sit together at dinner to discuss your mutual interests." Chance and Wagner nodded affirmatively.

Antti Salonen then turned to a young woman who was standing by his side. "This is Elena Marikova. She is a Russian translator for the Finnish men here who will be meeting with some Russian leaders. The Russians don't speak Finnish and the Finns don't speak Russian. So Elena is very important in the discussions." Antti smiled warmly at Elena as he said this.

Elena spoke up. "And I speak a little English too." Her accent was quite heavy. "However, if I have some difficulty this evening with some of my English, I will depend on Antti here to translate for me." Elena well knew that Antti Salonen was, in truth, Timo Koskinen, but she played along with the deception.

As they talked, Gene Wagner was studying Elena Marikova intensely. She was very attractive he thought and he was intrigued by her charming accent. He thought back to Sofia Kamineva. There was no question in his mind. Young, educated Russian women had considerable captivating allure. They seemed to exude a sensual carnality. Gene Wagner liked that. It was exciting.

At the dinner table, Wagner managed to sit between Salonen on his right and Elena on his left. Chance was relegated to the other side of Salonen. Wagner, during the dinner, carried on an almost exclusive conversation with Elena while ignoring Salonen. Chance, for his part, engaged Salonen in discussion of trade matters. Chance, however, felt embarrassed by Wagner's lack of civility in seemingly snubbing the Finnish trade representative and giving his attention to the young translator. Indeed, Chance was smoldering inwardly about it and resolved to firmly remonstrate with Wagner later.

The conversation between Wagner and Elena, by any measurement, was harmless and innocuous. Each spoke about themselves yet intentionally revealed little. Each sensed a prudent caution in the other. In that place and time and under the circumstances of different nationalities neither one expected much more at their initial meeting.

After a plain dinner of baked codfish, boiled potatoes and cabbage with side dishes of Baltic herring and hard rye bread and crisp bread and a rice pudding dessert, both Ambassadors excused themselves and went to Peltonen's office for discussion.

Ambassador Hayes remarked that the Embassy building must be new and freshly outfitted.

"Yes, it is a new building and, in fact, was just dedicated this past December 1938. It is so much more comfortable and efficient than our old building."

After settling down in comfortable chairs in the office, Ambassador Peltonen inquired, "Ambassador Hayes, what is it you wanted to talk about?"

"What I have to say, Ambassador Peltonen, requires a pledge from you of utmost confidentiality and secrecy. If the information I shall present to you gets out somehow, there will be very serious international consequences. It may even start a war."

"Well, we may have a war anyway. But, I promise that I will maintain the confidentiality of what you tell me. Please feel free to go on."

"First, let me ask you how you feel about Stalin." Ambassador Hayes felt he had to use a stratagem of getting Peltonen to reveal his position before disclosing his own proposition. It would be more comforting to know that they were both on the same side.

"Do you want a diplomatic answer or do you want the unvarnished truth?," Peltonen asked facetiously.

"The truth, of course."

"Ambassador Hayes, what does anyone feel or think of a madman who slaughters hundreds of thousands, if not millions of his own countrymen for little or no reason or cause and who threatens the existence of my country?" Ambassador Peltonen's face had taken on a glowering look as he asked the question that begged the answer. It was clear that he was contemptuous and disdainful of Stalin.

"I can tell you," Peltonen continued, his voice resonating scorn, "I believe the world would be better off without Stalin, certainly his countrymen would. You know, Hayes," Peltonen said in warming to the subject, "Stalin reminds me of Robespierre, the assassin of the French Revolution in 1793."

"I'm familiar with Robespierre, but what is the comparison with Stalin?," inquired Hayes.

"Robespierre," explained Peltonen, "Was the leader in France of a Reign of Terror. He had thousands of his countrymen executed on the guillotine on the slightest pretense. No one in the country felt safe or was safe from him. Intellectuals and peasants alike felt the blade. The major charge against the person arrested was 'Enemy of the people, a traitor.' In the end, Robespierre was, himself, killed by the guillotine. I see a strong parallel."

"Up to this point," argued Hayes. "The difference, as I see it, is that Robespierre's own supporters in the Jacobin party turned on him because of his excesses, had him arrested and executed. I don't see that happening with Stalin. Stalin has been either executing or sending to labor camps his supporters and those who have worked with him in the party. No one is given the opportunity to rise up against him and get rid of him. Stalin knows how to survive."

"Yes, I guess you're right about that," Peltonen conceded.

"Do I conclude, then, from your remarks that you'd like to see Stalin gotten rid of?," queried Hayes in reverting to the reason for which he had requested this meeting.

"Confidentially, between us, the answer is 'Yes'," admitted Peltonen. "Of course, I would not say that publicly and if it was rumored that I believed that, then I would deny it."

"I would agree with you that both of our countries would be better off if Stalin, somehow, was either neutralized or eliminated," said Hayes. "I think Finland has far more at stake in that regard than does the United States and, therefore, has a greater need to get rid of Stalin than the United States." Ambassador Hayes was shrewdly trying to remain noncommittal while determining whether Finland was sufficiently motivated to work with the United States to plan and carry out Stalin's elimination. Hayes, at that point was not aware that Finland had already made the decision to get rid of Stalin. Consequently, Hayes could not know that Ambassador Peltonen, as a result of their conversation, had, quite abruptly, become interested in determining if the United States would perhaps collaborate in the project. Had both men realized the position of the other, the game of cautionary probing would not have been necessary.

"I don't, for a moment, doubt that the Russians could invade Finland and take it over physically and that this could not be done with the United States. But, Russia could take over the United States by insidious infiltration of its Communist principles and politics. So, you do have a stake and a risk," replied Peltonen.

Hayes felt it was time to bring the matter to a head. The parrying had gone on long enough in his opinion.

"Assuming both of our governments are persuaded that it is in our mutual interests to eliminate Stalin, would you be willing to determine if your government would collaborate with mine in such an undertaking?" Hayes asked.

Peltonen remained silent for a few moments as if pondering how to reply. Finally, he said, "Finland has already made that decision." He paused to see how his confession affected Hayes. Hayes gave no outward sign or expression of any reaction, but inwardly, had an immediate tension of excitement over the prospect of cooperation in the mission.

Peltonen continued, "That fellow out in the dining room, Antti Salonen, has been sent here for that very purpose, to try to carry out the elimination. So now you know what Finland has decided. What about the United States?"

"That is why I requested this meeting with you," said Hayes. "My government is unofficially interested in pursuing the same objective that your government is. We believe that in the interest of promoting peace and democracy, Stalin should be deposed in one manner or another. The two gentlemen who came with me this evening, Mr. Chance and Mr. Wagner, are here for determining what can be done to accomplish that mission. Their trade mission is only a cover."

"I am pleasantly surprised," said Peltonen, unable to conceal his elation that the powerful United States might be a confederate in what was, obviously, a difficult and dangerous undertaking. "I hope we can work together. But, why did you select Finland as a possible accomplice?"

"Our intelligence sources informed us that Finland was a likely target to be taken over by the Soviets as a security measure against Germany," replied Hayes. "We knew that the Finnish people were fiercely independent and would probably resist such a takeover. But, we also were aware that Finland is a small country with limited manpower and that in the long run it could not succeed in holding back a Russian military invasion. We reasoned from that that Finland would want to take the desperate step of doing whatever was necessary to thwart a takeover before it could begin. We also felt that probably no one would suspect that Finland would undertake such a risky plan. We thought we should, at least, approach you on it. We had a pretty good idea of how Finland felt about the Russians, a fearful contempt."

"Well, you guessed quite accurately," commented Peltonen.

Ambassador Hayes then added, "I want to make it clear, however, that my government has one condition to all this. That is, we'll assist in such an undertaking, but we will not actually administrate any coup de grace. That would have to be done by some other party."

"I understand," responded Peltonen. "Frankly, we don't know just how we are going to go about this. Do you have any specific ideas?"

"No," replied Hayes. "That is something we have to yet determine."

"We don't have much time to set up a plan," cautioned Peltonen. "Perhaps the best way to handle this is for me to talk privately to our man, Salonen, and to let him know about our discussion. On your part, you can do the same with your two men. Then we can have both sides meet to try to work out a plan. What do you think of that?"

"Yes, it's a good approach," replied Hayes. "By the way, can you guarantee confidentiality? Do you trust your man?"

"Absolutely," assured Peltonen. He added, "Incidentally, the name, Antti Salonen, is not the man's true name. It does not really matter, though."

"We also have to continue the trade mission cover and to promote that publicly," Hayes advised.

"Of course," agreed Peltonen. "I guess we should get back to the dining room. We can discuss our meeting with our respective people tomorrow and, then we can proceed from there. We'll be in contact with each other. However, something like this should not be mentioned on the telephone. We'll talk on the phone about trade matters but we'll understand what we mean. Is that agreeable?"

"Yes, by all means," said Hayes.

When Hayes and Peltonen returned to the dining room, they found the guests had moved their chairs away from the dining table and were sitting in a circle, each holding a cup of coffee while listening to Bill Chance describe some of the culture of American Indians. The Ambassadors drew up chairs and joined the group in a display of congenial informality.

Peltonen immediately joined in the conversation. "I think I can say that most of the Finns are fascinated by American Indians. A few years ago, we had an international music festival in Finland and brought over a small group of Indians from America, probably about twelve or fifteen. I attended a couple of days of the week-long festivities and I recall that the Indians were the main attraction for the festival goers. The Indians gave an explanation through translators, of course, of some of their history and cultures and then conducted their tribal dances dressed in full Indian regalia. I found it extremely interesting. The crowd reacted very enthusiastically to the performances."

Chance asked Ambassador Peltonen, "Are the Finns aware of the relations between the Indians and the white man?"

"Yes, a great many Finns know about the persecution of the Indians by the white people who were settling the country. We have read about how the Indians suffered and were massacred. It makes us very sympathetic for the Indians. We don't understand how you Americans could treat the native peoples so miserably." Ambassador Peltonen appeared sincerely concerned and incredulous.

Ambassador Hayes joined in with an explanation. "I agree that our treatment of the Native Indians was terrible and is a blot on our history, but you have to understand the reasons behind it. As more and more white Europeans immigrated to America there was a need to expand into the countryside. Land was needed for farming, cattle raising, and for some industry. The whites were in a hurry to spread out and the Indians were in the way. The whites had neither tolerance nor patience with Indian resistance or delaying tactics. The Indians occupied the land that the whites wanted and the whites were ruthless in taking it from the Indians.

"Nevertheless, the explanation for our treatment of the Indians, even today, is much deeper and more fundamental than merely economic needs for land. In my opinion, the brutality the whites practiced on the Indians can be understood as based on an attitude of racial superiority. The whites were Christians and regarded the Indians as heathen, untutored savages, in fact, as subhuman. The white settlers with their so-called advanced civilization and Christian principles felt so superior to the Indians that they, the whites, had not only the right, but the obligation, to rid the land of these godless, soulless people."

"But, wasn't that just outright prejudice without any basis in fact?," suggested Peltonen.

"Yes, of course," answered Hayes, who had taken over the discussion. "But, isn't the belief in racial superiority the basis for Hitler's treatment of the people in the countries he is invading and in his practices against the Jews and Slavic peoples? Isn't racial superiority an explanation for Stalin's anti-Semitism? Isn't racial and religious superiority behind the churches sending Christian missionaries into areas occupied by native peoples who the church leaders feel should be educated and introduced to the white man's culture and religion?"

Bill Chance then spoke up. "The idea of racial superiority also explains the practice of slavery in the United States."

The others seated about in the dining room had been silent during this discussion between the Ambassadors. Finally, Hayes observed, "Well, it's getting a bit late and we should be heading back to our Embassy. The purpose of our getting together here was to have you meet and visit with each other. Some of us will meet again in the near future. Ambassador Peltonen and I have discussed certain matters that we'll take up with you when we are in our own privacy. I hope you got to talk about trade matters." The Ambassador said the last remark with a roguish smile. He was aware now that no one of the group present was even plausibly interested in trade issues.

In accordance with arrangements made on the way back to the United States Embassy from the Finnish Embassy the evening before, Chance and Wagner, after breakfast, met with Ambassador Hayes in the Ambassador's office the next morning, March 10, 1939.

Hayes began the conversation. "I had a very interesting private and confidential visit with the Finnish Ambassador last evening."

Chance and Wagner kept a respectful silence while awaiting a report on the results of the Ambassador's conversation with Ambassador Peltonen.

Hayes continued, "I think we have struck pay dirt. Finland is after the same thing we are except that they're willing to be more direct. The Ambassador made it clear to me that they want to get rid of Stalin in any way they can and soon. Finland has a lot at stake. They suspect that Stalin will invade Finland unless he gets what he wants from them. Of course, the Finns want desperately to avoid that. They're trying to accomplish it by diplomacy, but they don't have a lot of hope in that process. The Finns believe if they cave in to Stalin and give him what he demands they'll lose their sovereignty and their independence. They're probably right. I think that the next step is for you two fellows to get together with Antti Salonen, the gentleman you were talking with at the Embassy last night. The Finnish government will be advised of our interest in the matter, but, like us, will want to be discretely in the background. Consequently, while your first meeting can be at the Finnish Embassy, I suggest, thereafter, you meet, if possible, in an open air park or in some remote and inconspicuous place. Do you understand?"

"I can understand up to a point," said Chance. "We were sent here to facilitate, through indirect means, the liquidation of Stalin. How much clandestine help can we expect from you or from this Embassy? We may need funds. We may need your cooperation in whatever we do. We need some guidelines."

"I'm sure I can arrange for you to get the funds," replied Ambassador Hayes. "As for cooperation, bring me a plan and I'll consider it at that time." The Ambassador then added, "I am certainly going to help you, because my government wants to do so. But, I want you to know that I am a devout Christian and I don't believe it is right to kill someone. I have been raised to believe that life is precious and that the Sixth Commandment, 'Thou shalt not kill' is a strict and unalterable mandate."

"Mr. Ambassador," Chance said, "we must regard Stalin as the devil in human form. I think we can agree that he is the epitome of evil. I recall somewhere in the New Testament it is said, 'Put on the whole armour of God, that ye may be able to stand against the wiles of the devil. For we wrestle against powers, against the rulers of the darkness of this world, against spiritual wickedness in high places.' Doesn't that justify what we have in mind?" Chance was emotional in the challenge on principle to the Ambassador.

Ambassador Hayes smiled upon hearing Chance's counterpoint. "I see you are versed in the Bible, Bill. I think you are quoting from Ephesians. I suppose one can interpret the admonitions in the Bible in justification of most of our actions as Christians. We can rationalize in order to fit the Bible to our conduct. History proves that. In any case, we'll respect each other's beliefs. In this world, to survive we must always compromise our beliefs. I am an example of that. I do not believe that there can be any reason to take a life and, yet, here I am helping you to do just that. So, I am an accomplice to murder. That thought is revolting to me as a Christian. As an Ambassador, I must follow orders and my orders are to assist you in liquidating Stalin. If my country orders me to kill, then, regardless of my beliefs, I must kill or aid and abet a killing." The Ambassador paused as if to collect further thoughts. The silence that ensued presented Gene Wagner with an opportunity to interpose a few ideas.

"Mr. Ambassador, if I may, I was brought up in a strict, Catholic family. My parents lived by the rules that the church laid down. We children were indoctrinated with the idea that the Catholic Church provided the structure within which we were to live our daily lives. Everything we did or did not do was to be determined and judged by whether it was a sin and what was sinful and to be avoided was told to us by the priests and the nuns. The edicts of the church were not to be challenged ever."

The expression on the faces of Hayes and Chance mirrored their surprise at Wagner's sudden personal divulgement. It was obvious to them that Wagner had some strong feelings about religion and religious upbringing.

Wagner, unrestrained by feelings of modesty or interruption from his listeners, continued. "When I was about fifteen years of age, I began to resent being told how to think and act. I had come to know, through church teachings, that Jesus was a very simple man, a totally spiritual man who gave little or no thought to material needs. He lived humbly and without fanfare. He expressed and taught the simple truth that man is made in God's image and that since God is Love man could only express love. Yet, the church that taught me this was, at the very same time, engaged in all sorts of complex rituals with grandiose physical adornments and accouterments. It didn't make sense I had begun to think independently and I began to reason that the Catholic Church was interested only in perpetuating itself by holding on to generations of members through fear, fear of condemnation and excommunication by the church if church tenets were not adhered to strictly. All of the ornate trappings of the church had become for me just so much festooned buffoonery, actually an insult to the simple, spiritual teachings and lifestyle of Jesus. To make a long story short, I just left the church. I think I have become a better Christian because of my leaving. So, what I am really saying is that Christian principles are quite simple, but it is the churches that have distorted the teachings of Jesus, complicated the principles and discouraged independent thinking by their parishioners. I believe that a good Christian will and must exterminate the devil and I agree with Bill that Stalin is the embodiment of the devil."

"Hey, Gene, that was quite a dissertation you just made. But, I'm proud of your independence. I admire you for your beliefs," Chance said.

"Yes, I likewise respect you for your independence," joined in the Ambassador. "I think, however, we have to now get back to the job we have to undertake. Although the digression was interesting, we need to concentrate on the mission we have been assigned."

Ambassador Hayes continued, "I'll make the arrangements with the Finnish Embassy for you both to have a meeting with that Salonen chap. I'll let you know as soon as I have the necessary information. It may only be a day before I know. In the meantime, you should try to figure out some sort of a plan as a basis for discussion with the Finn."

Hayes began to shuffle some papers on his desk and it was obvious to Chance and Wagner that the conference had ended.

As they left the Ambassador's office, Chance suggested, "Why don't we take a walk outside for a short distance. I could use some fresh air after the conference we just had."

"You mean my discourse made it stuffy in there?," Wagner laughed. "I did lay it on pretty heavily, didn't I?"

"No, it was not you, Gene. I think you demonstrated that you had a lot of insight into the Catholic Church's fetishism. I'm not Catholic, but I have always thought that much of its ritual, religious ceremonies and exhortations were nothing more than sorcery. No, my complaint is with the Ambassador. I had to sit and listen to him profess what a devout Christian he is while I knew all along that the guy built his business by being absolutely ruthless and merciless in driving competitors out of business. He had absolutely no compassion for his employees. He had or has mining interests in Upper Michigan. Miners were treated like expendable animals. If a miner died from a mine accident or was injured badly and could not work, that was too bad. The family of the miner had to shift for itself. No compensation, no caring, no sentiment, no human sympathy or condolence. Christian? Ha!." Chance was derisive.

Wagner said, "I understand that the Ambassador has done a great deal of philanthropic good for charities."

"Of course," Chance replied. "Fellows like Hayes who make millions on the blood, sweat and sorrows of working people always salve and placate their consciences, if they have any, by philanthropy. They buy the respect and the plaudits of the community through generous donations to perceived noble causes. And the people running the noble causes are always willing to forget or overlook how the philanthropist made his money."

Walking down the street near the Embassy, Chance suggested that they should talk about how they would deal with the Finns when they met. "We should formulate some ideas on how we can help them in our mutual mission regarding Stalin. What do you think?" Chance addressed Wagner.

Wagner replied thoughtfully. "There are a number of methods that can be employed. The first would be to shoot him. There are several ways of doing it. When Stalin makes an appearance on the balcony overlooking Red Square on some event, a sniper some distance away could shoot him. Or, at some meeting with a foreign delegation attended by Stalin, one of the people in the delegation could shoot him point blank. Or when he's in his car going to his dacha on the outskirts of the City some group could ambush the car and fire a volley at him."

Chance reacted by giving a cynical shrug of his shoulders. "With any of those methods you'd have to find someone ready and willing to commit suicide. Any individual or group shooting at Stalin would be arrested within minutes and either shot immediately or tortured in prison horribly before he died. No. We'll have to find a more subtle method."

"Say, the thought just occurred to me," Wagner exclaimed with an apocalyptic fervor, "perhaps, somehow we could feed Stalin some of that poison which killed Kovalenko. That could probably be done without much risk to the person administering it." Wagner was enthused by the idea.

"That might be a possibility," Chance observed. "Let's explore that further. Someone would have to be recruited to do it."

Chance and Wagner had by this time walked about a half kilometer down Novinski Bulvar and were preparing to return to the Embassy when a young man walked past them and then abruptly stopped, turned around and approached them. In faltering English and with an ingratiating smile revealing a missing tooth, the young man said, "I hear you speak English. I speak a little. I like to talk to you. No people here speak English much. Are you American?"

"Yes," replied Chance. Both he and Wagner were startled by this sudden and unexpected intrusion. They looked at each other with astonishment. Both knew that Russians were very cautious about speaking to foreigners in public. To do so might invite a harsh visit from the State police. Chance and Wagner regarded the young man acutely trying to get his measure. They waited for him to speak again.

"I see you come out of American Embassy. You visit there, yes?" The young man continued to smile in a friendly way.

"Why do you ask?" Chance had become suspicious of the young man's motive.

"I like to show you good bakery, good bread, good cake, good coffee. Near here. You come with me, yes?" The expression in the young man's eyes was compelling and insistent. It was at once obvious to Chance and Wagner that the young man was making a point that it was in their interest to accompany him.

"Aren't you afraid to be seen with us?" Wagner asked.

"No," the young man replied. "You ask me where a good bakery. I say I show you. That is all, yes?"

Wagner addressed Chance, "I'm curious. Let's go and see what this is all about. Besides, I would like to try some Russian cake."

Chance nodded his approval. "I'm game." He spoke to the young man, "We'll come with you."

"Good. Follow me." The young man led them to Pryamoy Pereulok, a side street off the boulevard. There were several storefront shops along Pryamoy, but as Chance and Wagner had come to expect, the shops were drab and the window displays appeared not to have been changed for years judging by the dust and dead flies lying about. Relying solely on the window display, it was difficult to know what a shop was selling.

The trio finally reached the bakery near the end of the street. In contrast to the other shops, the bakery window display exhibited cleanliness and refreshment. The elaborately decorated cakes in the window were artificial and inedible but appetizing in appeal to one's gastronomical demands. Pointing to the cakes in the window and noticing the American's interest in them, the young man laughed and said, "No good to eat. Real ones inside. Come in."

Entering the narrow doorway and heading straight to the back of the building, Chance and Wagner observed a long hallway. Immediately to the right of the entrance doorway was another door that opened into the bakery shop. The customer front of the store was quite small with a wood counter on which at the near end stood a cash register. Behind the counter were wood cabinets on top of which were three levels of shelves containing several varieties of bread. At the far wall was hung a large poster picture of Stalin in a plain peasant jacket and looking benevolently at whoever happened to be in the store.

When Chance and Wagner entered there were already two Russian women at the counter buying each a loaf of dark Russian bread. They paid little heed to the Americans and the young Russian man. Chance, Wagner and the young man stood by silently while the women completed their purchases and then left the store.

Waiting on the customers from behind the counter was a youngish woman whom Wagner judged to be in her early thirties. She obviously knew the Russian for she spoke to him in Russian asking, "Who are these gentlemen?" Both Chance and Wagner knew enough Russian to understand what she said.

The young man replied in Russian, "They are American tourists who would enjoy having some cake and coffee. Can we use the back room?"

"Of course." The woman motioned to an open archway at the far end of the counter.

The young man apparently knew his way around the store for he turned to Chance and Wagner and said, "Come with me." Although Both Chance and Wagner had become somewhat apprehensive about the situation they had gotten themselves into and not knowing what next to expect, they nevertheless followed the young man mostly out of continuing curiosity.

They passed through the open archway into a large room containing the baking equipment. Chance and Wagner observed three men busily preparing bakery products. The men looked up as Chance and Wagner entered, but continued with their respective chores and showing little interest in the visitors. The young man led his guests to a small portioned off room at the rear of the production area. The room was quite bare except for a plain wooden table and a half-dozen cane chairs.

"Be seated, my friends," said the young man. "I go for coffee and cake. Only a moment."

"If we mention this to Fraser, he'll say we were out of our minds to do this," said Chance referring to the First Deputy Secretary at the Embassy. He added, "I would just as soon clear out now, but I suppose we'll have to be courteous and have coffee and cake."

"I wonder if this young guy was watching the Embassy. He says he saw us leave and followed us. It puzzles me," said Wagner. "Why would he watch the Embassy and why would he want to pick us up like this?"

"Yeah," replied Chance. "It is a bit unusual. Here he comes with the coffee and cake."

The young man entered the room with a tray of cups of steaming coffee and a plate containing several varieties of pastries. "Gentlemen, you take what you like." He sat down at the table and began to sip at a cup of coffee. Chance and Wagner helped themselves to coffee and some pastry.

"It smells very good in here," Chance remarked to the young man. "The baking bread stimulates my appetite. By the way, young man, what is your name?"

"I give you first name only," replied the young man. "It is Boris." His smile was like a permanent amenity; it never left his face. It reminded Chance of a court jester that he's seen performed by some college drama group. But this fellow was obviously no fool or comedian. Sitting across the table from Boris, Chance had his first real opportunity to scrutinize and try to take the measure of the young Russian.

Chance judged Boris to be in his early twenties. He was a very friendly sort. Someone you could warm up to quickly upon a first meeting. Chance's first impression of the young man when he and Wagner had first encountered him on the street was that the young fellow was a likeable, easy going, simple but honest person, a sociable person wanting to use what English he knew. Yet, even then Chance had noted the compelling, almost importunate look in the young man's eyes that had to be the explanation of why Chance had put aside his normal caution and agreed to accompany the man. Now, with a closer examination of Boris, Chance was startled to see a noticeable transformation in the expression on Boris' eyes. The smile and the little wrinkles it induced at the outer corners of the eyes could not hide the steely cold penetrating look. To Chance, the smile was now perceived as a cover to a deep, passionate fire burning within this young man.

Boris' face was almost Lenin-like with its high cheekbones, deep-set eyes and small goatee, a somewhat oriental configuration in Chance's opinion.

"What do you do?," Chance inquired of Boris.

"I work here. Help bake. Never starve here. Always can eat bread." Boris laughed at the irony of working in a food shop in a country of persistent food shortages.

At that moment, a stocky, heavyset man about five feet ten wearing a soiled white apron and white baker's hat entered the room bringing his own cup of coffee. As he sat down at the table, Boris introduced him. "This is Petrov. He main man here, main baker. He speaks no English, but you can talk some Russian to him. I help translate too."

Petrov, unlike Boris, was unsmiling with a serious, businesslike appearance. It was clear to Chance that Petrov was not there merely to be sociable with a couple of tourists from America. In fact, his whole body language was that he wanted to avoid wasting time and to get on with some business at hand. He had apparently been cued in on the street encounter and the fact that Boris had seen Chance and Wagner leave the Embassy.

"Let me tell you why you are here." Boris now spoke in Russian as he looked directly at Chance and Wagner. Refreshing his English was no longer a priority with Boris. The smile also was gone. The steely gaze had become more intense and resolute and his overall facial expression grim and stern.

Boris continued, "We know who you are and why you are here in Russia."

Chance looked quickly at Wagner and both reacted immediately with alarm. But they sought to outwardly show an undisturbed composure to conceal their anxiety. "That is interesting," replied Chance speaking in Russian. "Tell us who we are and why we are here. We are curious to know about your information." Chance did not know what to expect from this new development, but he was determined to resist any intimidation or to reveal anything about their mission.

Boris continued to carry the conversation while Petrov sat by silently watching the scenario evolve.

"You are William Chance and Gene Wagner of the United States State Department. You are both over here to help to get rid of Stalin as soon as possible. Is that not correct?"

"We acknowledge nothing," Chance answered. He again looked at Wagner who had now lost his stoic composure and appeared appalled and aghast at this revelation of a breach of confidentiality. Chance himself was dismayed. This must have evidenced itself to Boris.

"Don't be concerned, gentlemen. We will protect your cover." Boris tried to be reassuring to the Americans. "You see, we are a part of an underground group which is working to bring down and destroy Stalin. There are many of us, but only a handful of our leaders know about you. We will not disclose your mission to anyone else and we will do nothing to harm you or to interfere in your mission. We share your objective. We brought you here because we want to work with you, not against you. We wait to work out the details with you. We want to help each other. Do you understand?"

"How did you come to know about us?" Chance was challenging Boris to reveal what he knew.

Boris replied equivocally, "We cannot reveal our sources. And it really doesn't make any difference on how we obtained our information, does it?"

"We can only conclude that you got your information from someone in our Embassy and if you want to work in cooperation with us, we expect you to tell us who your informant is." Chance demonstrated his anger and frustration at the evasiveness of Boris and Petrov.

"We are sorry, but we cannot tell you that. You must understand that knowing our source will not be necessary to work together." Boris was equally adamant.

"Mr. Chance," Boris persisted, "we are so sure of who you are and what you are here for that we are willing to risk telling you who we are. Do you think for a moment that we would reveal our underground group to you if we were not quite confident that we are allies?"

Chance could see that there was no purpose in demanding the source of information that these people had. He looked at Wagner. Wagner nodded in a way implying that Chance should pursue the overt offer of Boris and his group.

Chance, still speaking in Russian, addressed both Petrov and Boris, "Assuming that we do have the mission you say we have and we don't admit that we have, how do you think you can help us or we help you?"

Boris studied Chance and Wagner sharply. Petrov motioned to Boris that he should continue to carry the conversation. Petrov said in Russian to Boris, "I think you should speak in English. There is less risk."

Boris nodded in agreement. "Petrov knows what our plans are and knows what I shall say. So, there is no need for me to speak in Russian for his benefit." Boris then spoke in English.

"We have some women willing and anxious to carry out our purpose. They lose relatives or friends. They do anything to strike back. Stalin like women, beautiful women. He takes them to dacha, sleeps with them. Many times Stalin choose woman in a party or dinner group. We want you, your Embassy, to arrange party or dinner for Stalin and include one or two our women, yes?"

Wagner nudged Chance and said in a low but perceptible voice, "I'm beginning to see a good idea."

Chance seemingly ignored Wagner's comment and asked Boris, "So Stalin might take one of the women to his dacha. What then?"

"Ha? Can't you guess?" Boris simulated surprise at Chance's naiveté.

"Poison, my friend! Poison!"

Chance did not reveal that he was startled by the simplicity of the plan. But he was immediately aware of the risks to his government. "If the woman fails and is caught, she will be arrested and she may confess that the United States was an accessory to the attempt to kill Stalin. We could not have that."

"If the woman is arrested," Boris replied, "she be tortured until she confesses and after that, she be killed. Women know that. They very brave. If arrested, they kill themselves. But, we try to rescue them at dacha first. You see?"

"Yeah, I see," said Chance, his voice sounding sarcastic. "You guys play it safe while you put the women in danger."

"No! No! No!," exclaimed Boris as if offended by Chance's remark. "We men in great danger, too, if we must rescue women. Yes?"

Chance looked at his watch. Mindful of the appointment possibilities with the Finns if Ambassador Hayes could arrange it for that day, Chance told Boris that he and Wagner had to return to the Embassy.

"You come here when you make arrangements. Do not take long. We want move ahead soon, yes?"

"We can't agree to anything right now," said Chance. "We'll have to talk this over. We can let you know in a day or two."

Boris with that cold, steely look in his eyes, but still smiling, said, "If our group is disclosed to Russian government by what you do or say, then you and your Ambassador be killed. Understand? Nothing done to put us in danger, no?"

Chance, bristling with anger at the explicit threat, said in equally unambiguous language, "We guarantee nothing. We shall cooperate with you if we think it is to our advantage. Again, we'll let you know."

As he arose to leave, Chance added, "By the way, when we leave here, we should be carrying some loaves of bread. That's what we came for, isn't it?"

Boris translated the request for bread to Petrov. They both roared in laughter although everyone understood that strange eyes might be watching to see if the Americans went to the bakery to buy bread or cake.

"Of course, some bread and some pastry," said Boris. "You must pay, of course."

"We'll do that," replied Chance.

As they walked back to the Embassy, Chance asked Wagner, "What do you make of all this?," referring to their experience at the bakery.

"I think it's authentic," Wagner answered. "But I don't like the idea that they had information about us and why we're here."

"Then, you don't think it's a trap by the Soviet government to embarrass the United States?," inquired Chance.

"No, I don't think it is a trap. I think they're legitimate. As much as I dislike the idea that they knew about us, I still think that we should put that aside and go along with them on their idea of getting a dinner put together for Stalin."

"Who in hell could be informing on us? Obviously, it's someone in the Embassy. Probably, a local," Chance was turning the matter over and over in his mind.

Wagner was equally puzzled. "As far as I'm concerned, Bill, except for you and me, everybody at the Embassy is a suspect, everybody."

"Including the Ambassador and the Deputy?"

"Absolutely."

"Well, I wouldn't go that far. That's somewhat over burn." Chance sought to control his consternation. "I think our approach to this should be to avoid being stampeded into a panic. We have to talk this matter over with both Hayes and Fraser. We can't make any arrangements without them. We just have to assume that the Americans at the Embassy are not guilty of being in contact with this underground group."

"Maybe it's Yuri, the waiter," Wagner speculated. "You know homosexuals can't be trusted. They can be easily manipulated by someone who knows about their moral weakness and threatens to disclose it."

"I agree," said Chance. "But Yuri, I understand, has either been fired or will be shortly. So we don't have to worry about him anymore. However, we still have to find out who gave out the information. We can't have a spy in the Embassy."

"All the locals are, in effect, spies," Wagner retorted. "The NKVD is constantly visiting the locals to ask what they have learned about Embassy activities. The locals are expected to report."

"Yes, that's exactly what I said when we first arrived here, if you'll recall. I said there were too many locals employed to help run the Embassy." Chance was noticeably perturbed by that condition in the Embassy.

"Did you notice," Wagner asked, "that Boris said nothing about the Finns? They probably didn't know about our visit to the Finnish

Embassy. Which means that their informant is Yuri who is gone or someone who is not always at the Embassy, probably lives at home."

"In my view," Chance said, "we'd better proceed with our plan to meet with the Finns regardless of what we do about this underground group. The Finns may have some ideas that can link all parties together to make sure the job is done. We'll have to talk that over with Hayes and Fraser and we should do it as soon as possible."

Wagner, in a sarcastic tone, added, "It looks like we'll have to hold our conferences on some park bench outside the Embassy to be sure we're not being eavesdropped."

Chance did not reply, but smiled wanly and shrugged his shoulders as if to imply that it might not be a bad idea.

By this time, they reached the gates of the American Embassy and, entering the lobby, Chance went immediately to Fraser Addison's office and spoke with Helen Morgan, Fraser's secretary. Wagner waited in the lobby.

"Helen, will you arrange a conference with the Deputy and Ambassador Hayes as soon as possible. It's quite urgent." The serious demeanor of Chance conveyed the urgency.

"Why don't I try to do that right now while you're waiting here?" Helen did not wait for Chance's answer, but proceeded to lift her telephone and ask the operator to put her through to the Ambassador's office. Helen expressed the urgency to Rose Orlov, the Ambassador's secretary who said the Ambassador would be available in mid-afternoon of that day.

Helen said, "Deputy Addison will be in the office this afternoon, so I'm sure he can attend also. You'll meet in the Ambassador's office."

"Fine, Helen, I always knew you were a woman of action." Chance smiled his appreciation of Helen's efficiency.

Out in the lobby, Wagner was sitting on a sofa with the bag of two loaves of bread next to him. Although he was elated to hear of the prompt conference, he was, at the moment, more concerned with the bread.

"What do I do with these?"

"You can have them for lunch. No, I'm just kidding. Take them into the kitchen and let them use them. It's near lunchtime, anyway."

That afternoon, about two-thirty, Chance, Wagner and Deputy Fraser Addison gathered in Ambassador Hayes' office.

"Well, Bill, you asked for this urgent meeting." The Ambassador was quizzical. "What is it all about?"

"Mr. Ambassador, someone in this Embassy has learned of our true mission and has revealed it to an underground group of Russians who, like us, want to do away with Stalin." Chance then proceeded to describe their encounter with Boris and what occurred at the bakery. He added, "I don't think our position or our mission has been or will be compromised or become known to the Soviet authorities. We have a common goal with this underground group and they want our help, so I don't see them as disclosing us to the authorities. I think they will keep what they know about us as confidential. What bothers Gene and me more than anything else is the fact of someone gaining information about us and revealing it."

As Chance recounted the story, both he and Wagner watched, closely, the faces of the Ambassador and the Deputy for whatever clue might be revealed that they may have known of the breach of security in the Embassy. The Ambassador's usual taciturnity had given way to unmistakable agitation. He appeared grim and his face was flushed crimson with anger. Except for the drumming of his fingers on the arm of his chair, Ambassador Hayes sat rigidly and unmoving as if in shock as he listened to Chance's improbable story.

Deputy Addison, on the other hand, appeared about to become unhinged as, one moment slumped over in his chair holding his head and the next moment with his head rolled back and eyes rolling, clasping and unclasping his hands while shifting constantly in his chair.

Finally, when Chance had finished his description of events, Ambassador Hayes muttered, almost inaudibly, "Impossible, impossible." His first reaction was one of denial that there could be any disloyalty among his staff. After a few moments of agonizing silence, Hayes said, "I cannot believe that we have anyone who would do such a thing as this." He turned to his Deputy. "Fraser, you have a list of all of our staff and employees. Maybe if we reviewed the list, we could come up with some suspects and then proceed with an investigation."

"Mr. Ambassador, if I may say," Addison replied, "I don't think that will tell us anything. Anyone and everyone could be a suspect. The person who has been an informant has been obviously very shrewd in being able to conceal his or her activities."

"Well, then, what shall we do?," Hayes inquired of Addison who had gotten control of his emotions by now.

"I would do nothing. Fortunately, this underground group is on our side and as Bill has said, they're not likely to let the information about our mission go any further. Eventually, if we work with them, we'll learn who the snitch is. We'll just have to be more careful about how we talk about our plans."

Chance asked, "Mr. Ambassador, have you been able to make arrangements with the Finns?"

"Yes. You and Gene will meet at their Embassy tomorrow morning about nine-thirty. I suggest that, for the time being, you not mention the underground group to them. Just get their ideas."

"Mr. Ambassador, I disagree with that," Chance said. "I think they should know so that we can resolve how all three parties can work together to get done what we came to do. It would be, in my opinion, a waste of time to discuss plans that would be irrelevant if we decide to coordinate with the underground group."

Ambassador Hayes thought a moment and then addressed Deputy Addison. "What do you think, Fraser?"

"I agree with Bill. Let the Finns know about the underground group. We are all in this together. Why play games?"

"Alright. I'll concede," Hayes said. "Go ahead and tell them the story. Let me know, of course, what their ideas are."

Both Hayes and Addison had quickly regained their composure as they discussed the details. Both, however, remained perturbed and very concerned that someone had been able to break through the high priority secrecy of the Stalin mission.

"We have to reexamine our system of security here. There is no question about that." The tone of Ambassador Hayes' voice was one of urgency.

Deputy Addison commented, "As long as we employ locals, we shall be vulnerable to having our security violated. It's no different in any country; England, France, Belgium, Sweden, you name it. Every country wants to know the secrets of every other country. Every one of our foreign Embassies, no matter where located, has the same problem we have. As long as locals are used in working at our Embassies, high level decisions and activities are pregnable. The answer, of course, is to be staffed only by Americans. We know that is not possible for two reasons: the lack of supply of Americans willing to spend years in a foreign country and a tightwad Congress that won't appropriate money to staff Embassies with Americans even if they are available. So, there you are. But, I agree, Mr. Ambassador, we should review our security procedures to see if they can't be tightened. I'll get to work on it immediately. Some of our own people here may have some ideas."

"Good, Fraser. Now, Bill and Gene, you are going to have to come up with some plan very quickly on how to accomplish your project. We must get moving on it before the wrong people get wind of it. I'm leaving the details up to you."

"Right," Mr. Ambassador," Chance exclaimed.

The meeting broke up and as Chance, Wagner and Addison walked back towards the Deputy's office, the Deputy in a low voice said to the others, "I stressed the locals at our meeting, but you know we Americans are also all suspect. That's the frustrating problem. I'm not accusing anyone of intentionally betraying secrets. It's more a case of saying something carelessly, of talking too much, of talking without thinking about the implications of what one is saying. Especially here in Russia there are eager ears all over the place, people who pick up on what is said. This is a country of spies."

CHAPTER 7

The two weeks that Timo Koskinen spent at home after his conference in Helsinki and before returning there to join a trade delegation to Moscow was very stressful for him and Anna. Especially Anna, whose every waking thought seemed ruled by a foreboding fear of the dangers and hazards of her husband's new mission. It adversely affected her work as a teacher so much so that she was on the verge several times of requesting a leave of absence. She had explained to her students that she was not feeling well for she was aware that surely they must notice that she was not herself. She did not remain after class hours, as she usually did, to talk informally with one or two of her students who might need some counseling or comforting. Instead, she left immediately upon the closing school bell to rush home only to lie on the bed and allow herself to be convulsed by unremitting thoughts of what might happen to her beloved Timo. He would be killed. He would be caught and tortured. He would disappear and never be heard from again. She would never see him again. She had heard the Soviet police were brutal with prisoners.

Two days before Timo was to return to Helsinki and then on to Moscow, Anna was in a panic. She had come home from school so overwrought as to be on the verge of hysteria. By the time Timo arrived home from his office, Anna was so unnerved that she rushed to him even as he entered the doorway, threw her arms around his neck and sobbed repeatedly, "I don't want to lose you, Timo. I love you. I don't want to lose you!"

Timo, for his part, tried to calm and reassure Anna. "Anna, don't worry so much. I've always had some risks in my job and I've always survived. This is just another job with some of the usual risks."

"But, Timo, this is different. I just feel it." Anna shook her head in despair.

"Anna, you have always been strong in your faith in God. Your faith has been tested many times in the past. Each time you have found support in knowing that all would be well in relying on God. This is another test. If it seems to be a more severe test, then you must be just that much more strong in your reliance on God who has always seen us through the rough times. You and I know that it is easy to have faith when the problems are minor." Timo paused. "Why don't you make some coffee and we'll sit down and I shall explain something to you, although I suspect you may know it already." Timo removed his hat and coat, hung them up and then took Anna by the hand as they walked to the kitchen. Timo knew that to comfort Anna, he had to appeal to her spirituality. There was no other way with Anna in her present emotional state.

Sitting at the kitchen table with their cups of coffee before them, Timo reached across the table and gently touched Anna's hand. "Anna, I have long ago come to the conclusion that there are three stages in our relationship to God. The first is a belief that there is a God. We acquire this belief very early in life by being told by our parents that there is a God and by going to church and being indoctrinated by the minister and others. There is no question that you and I believe that there is a God."

Anna nodded her head in agreement as she calmed down somewhat while listening to Timo.

"The next step or stage is a faith in God," continued Timo. "This is a faith that God is always there when we need Him and that he will not abandon us and that whatever happens to us, good or bad, is God's will. Most of the time this is a blind faith. We don't know how or why God acts the way He does. We rely on Him, but we really don't know how to appeal to Him and therefore we often are not sure He is listening. That is why our faith frequently weakens when confronted with what we think is a life or death situation. You and I, Anna, are probably in this stage in our relationship to God, but I like to think that, perhaps, I have grown into the third stage."

Anna did not nod in agreement at this point, but said quietly, "And what is the third stage, Timo?"

"The third and final stage, Anna, is understanding God. When you understand something you accept that something without question and as a totally normal occurrence. For example, two plus two equals four. The sun rises and the sun sets. We know these things as fact and accept them as true. So, what is it that we must understand about God?" Timo paused to see if Anna had any questions. Anna said only, "I'm listening, Timo." Being with Timo and hearing his voice was enough to calm her at least for a while.

Observing that Anna had calmed somewhat and that by talking about God he had chosen the right path to reassure her, Timo continued, "To understand God is to know that God is good, that God is love, that God is life and that God is everywhere and ever present. He is All in All so to speak and because he is All in All there can be nothing else for us to experience but the qualities of God, that is, Good, Love, Life. And when we understand this, then we accept it as a perfectly normal state and we don't think twice about it. Knowing this, then we can confidently know that we are safe in every situation." As Timo finished speaking he and Anna found themselves looking deeply into each other's eyes as if to exclude the material world about them and to silently communicate to each other that they shared a common bond with God. This was a moment when all the superficialities of everyday living vanished and Timo and Anna discovered, quite suddenly, that through their eyes, they could perceive in each other the profound expression of the human soul.

But this spiritual tranquility lasted only a few moments. Anna was again gripped by her fear of what might happen to Timo during his mission.

"I appreciate what you have said, Timo, but it is all so very intellectual. How to understand God is just a theory that needs to be proved." Anna's thinking had become confused by the weight of contradictory feelings. She had, she knew, always been so strong in her religious and spiritual faith and now, faced with what she perceived to be a major threat to her and her family's well-being, fear had seemingly so engulfed and submerged her that faith had become strangely irrelevant and an ineffective resource to which to turn for comfort. Anna actually felt terrible about succumbing to such abject fear.

"It was never just a theory, Anna," replied Timo soothingly. "Jesus proved it. He said, 'I and my Father are one' and he also said, 'The things that I do, shall you do also.' But, each person must prove it for himself, using Jesus' example and instructions. It is provable if you once understand your relationship to God."

Anna was pensive for several minutes, saying nothing, but turning her head to gaze out of the kitchen window. She then turned and addressed her husband. "If there is nothing else but God, nothing else but love, how do you explain this evil man Stalin and how do you account for your mission to kill him, a mission hardly expressing love?" Anna knew that her question would pose a real dilemma for Timo.

Timo was quick to respond, having, apparently, anticipated such a question. He had, in fact, thought through years ago what his relationship to God might be. The interplay between good and evil was a necessary component of seeking answers in his quest for the truth.

"Stalin," explained Timo, "is an atheist. He denies the existence of God and, therefore, does not express God's qualities. The only alternative, except for living in an insensate vacuum, is to express the opposite of God's qualities. What is the opposite of expressing God? It is to express evil. That is exactly what Stalin is expressing. What do we do about human beings who express evil?" Timo continued to answer his own questions.

"Normally, we ignore evil conduct. Except where the evil conduct is of such a magnitude as to threaten to undermine the established moral and ethical values of our social system. Society punishes those who violate those values. As far as Finland is concerned, perhaps even as far as the world is concerned, Stalin is the greatest threat to our values of living in peace and harmony with our neighbors. He has violated all the values we hold dear by persecuting his own people. We cannot expect anything different from him if he decides to take over Finland. Society cannot punish his evil conduct in the usual way of punishing the common criminal. He cannot be arrested. He cannot apparently be deposed by a coup. So he must be punished by extreme and unique measures to remove him from society. God is Love, it is true, but God does not love evil. If God were to excuse or even tolerate evil, God would not be God. I hope you understand, Anna."

Timo then added, "I have been chosen to be the instrument through which Finland and its democratic social system will be saved from the evil that Stalin has imposed on others. In that view, I suppose you and I and our children should be honored that I have been selected for this highly important mission."

Anna gave a weak smile. "Timo, as a wife and a mother, I am not interested in being married to a hero, perhaps a dead one. You will forgive me if I take a narrow and selfish view that I prefer a living husband and father. My priority interest is my family, not the world. You know I am concerned for Finland, but I am not so patriotic that I am willing and happy to sacrifice the life of my husband, especially, for a cause or a war that has not yet come about. I will not say anymore except to say that I shall try to concentrate on my religious faith. In that respect, you have helped me to see the importance of doing that."

"That's fine, Anna. I'm sure you will succeed." Timo got up from the table, walked over to Anna and gave her a gentle kiss on the cheek. Anna responded by giving a loving touch to Timo's arm.

Captain Koskinen used his two weeks in Tampere getting his office and personal affairs organized. He had informed his secretary, Kirsti Rantala, that he would be in Moscow on a trade mission for a month or so and that she would be in charge of the office during his absence. Colonel Lars Blomquist, the Regional Chief, would be in touch frequently with her.

Kirsti thought it strange for her boss, an intelligence officer, to be on a trade mission. Nevertheless, she said nothing. She had learned over the years of service in the Intelligence Section that things were not always what they were purported to be. Above all else, she had learned not to question and not to talk about what went on in the office.

Koskinen also made out his Last Will. He had wanted to do that for a long time and the obvious risks inherent in the Stalin mission provided the motivation. He willed everything to his wife, Anna. Without a Will, part of his estate would have gone to Anna and part to his children. In case anything happened to him, Koskinen wanted Anna to be cared for and he knew she would, in turn, care for the children.

Koskinen decided to leave the Will in the custody of Kirsti. He mentioned nothing about it to Anna. He knew that telling Anna that he had executed his Will might only fuel the fears she already had. To many people, possibly Anna included, making a Will meant that death was imminent and that, in his case, it might indicate his own estimate of the high degree of danger.

Anna accompanied Timo to the railroad station in Tampere. She had regained, at least outwardly, her composure. She had come to the conclusion that it was inevitable that Timo would be leaving on the mission and there was nothing she could do to stop it. She realized on this day she had to demonstrate to her husband that her earlier emotional distress was a transient, fleeting departure from her usual self-control. She could not let him leave with a picture of her as a hysterical woman. She knew Timo well enough to know that he did not respect weaknesses in people's characters. As a woman she instinctively understood that if he lost respect for her, he might also lose his loyalty and faithfulness to her and more readily succumb to some other woman.

Anna also had her two sons to think of. They had not been told of their father's true mission. If she were to break down in front of them at any time, they would question the reason and she could not avoid telling them the truth.

As Anna and Timo stood on the station platform awaiting the boarding signal neither said much. Just being together, feeling each other's presence and touching each other was enough at this moment. "Timo, please be careful," Anna said in almost a whisper while clinging to his arm and looking into his eyes. "I love you."

"I shall, Anna. I want to return to you and our children. I love you, too." What more could they say to each other that would not sound superficial and trivial.

The train whistle blew signifying that departure was imminent. Anna and Timo hugged each other and tears welled up in their eyes as they gently kissed, a kiss that was meant to be remembered, cherished and that would bind them forever. Timo pulled away, picked up his bags and strode quickly to the train's boarding steps. He turned once more on the train car steps, looked at Anna, smiled lovingly and then disappeared into the car. The train moved off even before he could reach his seat to wave to Anna. Anna remained on the platform looking after the train until it disappeared into the distance. Then, unhappy, heavy-hearted and despondent, she walked down the stairs, through the waiting room and out to the street. Anna's thoughts were totally concentrated on Timo and the danger inherent in his mission. She was oblivious of everything going on about her. As she was crossing the street from the railroad area, she was startled to hear an automobile horn. So deep in her thoughts was Anna that she had looked neither right nor left and had not noticed the auto bearing down on her. Fortunately, the auto driver had been able to stop his vehicle before it might have struck Anna. The driver had a few unkind words which he shouted at Anna. Anna ignored the driver. She felt lost, abandoned, alone. She had always been a patriotic, staunch supporter of her government. Now, suddenly, she hated the government for giving Timo an assignment that was almost certain to fail and to risk her husband's life at the same time. She resolved that the only recourse left to her to remain rational was to pray for Timo. Timo was right. She would place the safety of Timo and the security of the family in His hands. Anna was somewhat comforted by this thought.

As he sat looking out the window of the train as it headed for Helsinki, Timo's feelings became clouded over with a great sense of sadness and sorrow. He dearly loved Anna and he knew how she must be suffering with her fears and concerns. He felt guilty and blamed himself for having put this burden on her. He could have stood up to his supervisors and refused to accept the assignment even if it meant being discharged from his job. He could still refuse. He could stride into General Mahlgren's office, head held high and, defiantly, say, "No, I will not accept this assignment. Do with me what you want." And, yet, Timo knew, even as he thought these thoughts, that he would not do such a thing. It would not be him. It would be out of character to refuse to do what Finland, his country, asked him to do. Besides, he was a fighter who was easily stimulated and energized by unusual and unfamiliar challenges to his talents.

As the train rolled on and the distance from Tampere grew longer, Koskinen's thoughts gradually turned to his previous ride to Helsinki and his meeting Elena Marikova. The thought of her, never quite far from his mind in any case, kindled a rush of excitement in him. He had thought about her frequently during his past two weeks while at home and in the office. In the atmosphere of gloom that had pervaded the environment, the image of Elena yielded the one source of pleasure for him. His resolve to put Elena out of his mind upon his return to Tampere from Helsinki was unsuccessful, primarily because he really did not want to put her out of his mind, a fact he admitted to himself. Koskinen loved Anna and, yet, he was thinking about Elena. How could that be? Koskinen found himself very confused by this apparent contradiction. He sought answers. It was a very perplexing condition to be in. Koskinen pondered about it and the more he tried to analyze himself, the more his thoughts oscillated from one explanation to another, rejecting each as they arose in his mind. Was his love for Anna waning? Of course not! That thought was waved aside almost as soon as it occurred. Was his attraction to Elena merely sexual? Perhaps. She was young and alluring. But, no, it could not be simply sexual for he had a feeling for her that went beyond the physical. Was it pity because she had to live in constant fear of her own government not knowing when she might be visited any night by men in a black limousine? True, he felt sorry for her that she had no experience with freedom, but that was not why he wanted to be with her again. It could be that he had fallen in love with her. To Koskinen it meant that it was possible for a man, some men, at least, to love two or more women at the same time.

That thought neither surprised nor shocked Koskinen. In the animal hierarchy, the single male often had a harem of females. It was just nature's way for the survival of the species. Biologically, man is an animal. Koskinen understood this. It could be that under the thin veneer of human civilized behavior there were still the primitive, instinctive emotions and urges that identified the kinship that man had with all animals. But, did animals, other than man, experience love? That would probably never be known. Did a dog love his master or mistress? Perhaps. But, there again, without communication there could be no understanding between species.

Koskinen tired of this train of thoughts. It was, he realized, an endless tunnel that led nowhere. He decided to just let events develop and act accordingly. He knew that he had to begin concentrating his thoughts on his new Stalin mission. After all, his superiors expected him to have some ideas on the subject. Here again, however, he soon concluded what he had all along recognized: how could he plan anything when he had so little facts? What were Stalin's everyday habits? Where did he live? How was he guarded? What were his customary public appearances? What opportunities might arise so that he could kill Stalin? What about his own escape plans? What help would he receive? Even though he was in intelligence work, Koskinen had never had a need to know these things. He had never been involved in a masquerade of this immensity, acting as a trade delegate when, in fact, he was an emissary of death. He decided he would have to talk this whole thing over with the people at headquarters. They would realize that there was no precedent for what he was to undertake. No guidelines established.

Having resolved these dilemmas by admitting he had no answers to any of them, Koskinen dozed off until awakened by the clanking of train brakes and the jerking motion of the train as it switched from one track to another in the Helsinki station.

When Captain Koskinen arrived in Helsinki the international world was in political turmoil and disarray. The rise of the charismatic Adolph Hitler to power in Germany with his unpredictable and seemingly insatiable demands for Germanic hegemony in Europe presented European governments with an enigma the meaning of which they failed to grasp. During 1938 and for most of 1939 both British and French leaders, with a mere few exceptions, suffered the illusion that they could deal rationally and diplomatically with Adolph Hitler. Hitler, in turn, was sufficiently astute to understand that he could offer all nations the mirage of peace while craftily expanding German land acquisitions from his neighbors in piecemeal fashion on the pretext that he wanted to absorb into Germany the Germanic populations in the countries contiguous to Germany.

The British and the French found this argument perfectly plausible and consequently did nothing when Germany annexed Austria in March 1938 and annexed the Czechoslovakian Sudatenland in September 1938. The reaction was the same when Hitler demanded that Lithuania cede its City of Memmel to Germany because of the large German population in that city.

If Neville Chamberlain, then Prime Minister of Britain, and Edouard Deladier, then the French Premier, were lulled into a somnambulant state by Hitler, Stalin, on the contrary, had no illusions about Hitler and the threat he posed to the Soviet Union. On numerous occasions, Hitler had spoken both publicly and privately about his absolute opposition to communism. He perceived Russia as a threat to Germany because of the former's malevolent support for the spread of communism through world revolution. Hitler had his own ideas for the German domination at least of Europe. Occasional cordial contacts between representatives of both countries seeking some sort of rapprochement were but a veneer over the fundamental and innate distrust which Stalin and Hitler had for each other. The undeniable reality was the inevitable physical, violent clash between two antithetic political and moral ideologies each seeking to be the dominant force in a predetermined sphere of influence. Both leaders were fully cognizant of this reality. Both took steps to assure their own survival and success.

Immediately after the German Anschluss in Austria in March 1938, the Soviet government became seriously concerned about a German invasion through Finland. The major city of Leningrad was only eighty kilometers from the southeast border of Finland. It was obvious to Stalin that something had to be done to prevent that potential. That something was to get the cooperation of Finland.

Stalin may have had the ultimate objective of annexing Finland. On one occasion he spoke about having to "resettle the Finns." The Baltic States of Estonia and Latvia after they had succumbed to Stalin's military forces discovered painfully and bitterly what "resettlement" meant. Stalin's labor camps became the new home of the exiles. At first, however, Stalin had his Second Secretary at the Soviet Legation in Helsinki, Finland, Boris Yartsev, meet with Finland's Foreign Minister, Rudolf Holsti, in April 1938 to explore ways of improving Soviet-Finnish relations. This included guarantees by Finland that Finland would not side with Germany and that Finland would resist any use of its land by German troops on their way to Russia.

The talks between Soviet and Finnish authorities languished for several months thereafter. However, two events brought this quiescent condition to an abrupt end. In August 1938, Hitler called up 750,000 men for military maneuvers and in September Germany annexed the Czechoslovakian Sudatenland on Hitler's standard claim that the population of the area was overwhelmingly German and needed to be incorporated into Germany. The Czech government, intimidated by Hitler's threat of military force, caved in and did nothing to resist the annexation.

Stalin, at the time, understood that he could not depend on England and France to take forceful action to deter Hitler's expansionist ambitions. Those governments, he knew, were reluctant to act militarily, preferring to try to keep Europe at peace through diplomatic negotiations with Hitler. Stalin undertook a number of steps to checkmate Germany's covetousness. With regard to Finland his demands became specific. Finland was to allow the Soviet military to establish an air and naval base on the Finnish island of Hogland located in the eastern part of the Gulf of Finland. In addition, the Soviets would agree to the militarization of the Finnish owned Aland Island but on condition that the Soviet government would control the military forces there. The Aland was located at the western end of the Gulf.

The Finns rejected these proposals as a violation of Finnish sovereignty as well as a conflict with the Finnish policy of neutrality. The Finns are a sensible people, by and large, and the Finnish government understood that it could not summarily reject a Soviet demand with impunity. So talks continued between the representatives of both the Soviets and Finland to find a means of granting the Soviets some sort of compromise while at the same time assuring Finnish neutrality.

In December 1938, Finnish delegates went to Moscow ostensibly to attend the opening of a new Finnish legation building, but, in reality, for discussions with the Soviet government. In March 1939, a trade delegation was scheduled to go to Moscow but, again, the purpose was discussion of the demands of the Soviet government. All of the conferences were inconclusive on the subject of what was expected of Finland.

Stalin understood the Finnish character. At one occasion he spoke of them as a "remarkable people." Is it possible that he admired them? Did he see in the Finns a reflection of his own determined struggles to overcome personal hardships and economic poverty? Finland by this time in 1938 had attained, through sheer hard work and resolve, an enviable economic prosperity and lifestyle. How else does one explain how this ruthless and generally uncompromising tyrant who created a system of Soviets by unmitigated brute force and who with an iron hand and Draconian measures trampled and crushed all those whom he suspected of resisting his rule, would now sit down and over months of negotiation try to persuade the Finns to allow him to use some of their islands in order to defend his country? No one could think that Stalin could not have marched in and abruptly seized what he wanted and that would be that.

Stalin was well aware that the Finns hated and despised the Russians, a feeling that existed since the early Tsarist days. He also knew that there were strong pro-German sentiments in Finland. This partisan warp favoring Germany was vividly brought to Stalin's attention by the forced resignation in November 1938 of Rudolf Holsti, the Finnish Foreign Minister, when Holsti publicly pronounced anti-German remarks which others in the Finnish government concluded might irritate the Germans. With all this, Stalin in 1938 and early 1939 continued to show uncharacteristic monumental patience with the Finns. Stalin even went so far as to guarantee the integrity and security of Finland from German aggression if Finland acceded to his demands. This, the Finns knew, meant the occupation of their land by Russian troops. This, of course, was unacceptable to the Finns who cherished their independence and freedom.

The Finns did not fear a German invasion. What they dreaded most was Russian "protection." Generally, to the Finns, Austria, Czechoslovakia, Poland, Romania, Italy and the other mainland western countries were remote. The Finnish concern was concentrated on the Soviet Union, their colossal next-door neighbor. If Stalin had no illusions about Hitler, the Finns had no illusions about Stalin.

Captain Timo Koskinen was fairly well informed about these events and matters. Like many Finns, he was a habitual reader of the daily Helsingin Sanomat, an independent, liberal newspaper that reported on the major developments. In addition, he received frequent briefings from Intelligence Headquarters in Helsinki on matters not generally revealed to the public for reasons of security. The one intimation that kept coming through from informant sources over the past months before Koskinen was to leave for Moscow on his mission was that, in the long run, Finland could expect a takeover by the Soviet government no matter what concessions the Finnish government made to Stalin's demands. If this was true, and Koskinen did not doubt their verity, then it was absurd for the Finns to try to placate the Russians through negotiations. To Koskinen it would be far better to start to build up

Finland's military, especially its defenses. Perhaps, even to the extent of asking Germany to come to Finland's aid if Finland were to be invaded by Russia. Yet, how could Finland, a small country with a population of three million five hundred thousand hope to defend against the vast manpower that Russia could throw at it. Finland would not have enough bullets for beating back the hordes of soldiers that were in unlimited supply. Koskinen knew this. He was no thick-skulled simpleton. But, he also understood that the tough, hard-nosed, obstinate character of the Finns would never yield to the arrogant ultimatums of the Russian bully. The Finns were no cowards and would fight to the last man, that is, except for the despised and contemptible Finnish Communists. Koskinen realized that it was precisely to prevent such a debacle that he had to succeed in his mission to assassinate Stalin. For Koskinen the matter was not debatable. He was ready to go. Of course, it did help that he anticipated that he might see Elena Marikova again when he got into Russia.

In accordance with prior instructions, Koskinen, with his luggage, proceeded by taxi to Intelligence Headquarters where he would receive information as to his lodging arrangements while in Helsinki. At Headquarters he was greeted by Colonel Blomquist.

"Ah, Captain, glad to see you again. How is everything at home?"

Koskinen for a fleeting moment stared at the Colonel incredulously. What a stupid question, he thought. Did Blomquist think that Koskinen's family would be jumping with joy at the prospects that this mission could turn deadly? Nevertheless, Koskinen gave the usual vacuous answer.

"Fine, thanks, Sir."

Koskinen still harbored his long-felt dislike of Blomquist. There was something about the Colonel that expressed imperious insincerity. Try as he would to accept the Colonel for what he was, Koskinen found it impossible to overcome the antagonism.

"We shall talk in my office, Captain."

Koskinen followed Blomquist down a corridor leaving his luggage under the careful eye of Marjatta, the congenial receptionist.

Entering the office, Koskinen was surprised to find Helena Annala, the specialist in Soviet affairs, sitting in the room. She was holding a short-stemmed cigarette holder with a burning cigarette sending a thin waft of bluish-gray smoke into the room. She arose, shook hands with Koskinen and sat down again while uttering "Welcome, Captain" in a matter of fact tone. Her face was expressionless.

Observing Koskinen's surprised look, Colonel Blomquist explained, "I have Captain Annala here because you will be staying with her and her husband in their apartment while you are here in Helsinki. Captain Annala has agreed to this arrangement."

Captain Annala nodded her head in confirmation although Koskinen sensed that she was not altogether happy about it. And neither was Koskinen. For fear of offending Annala Koskinen did not want to object or to ask why in her presence. However, Blomquist must have felt a footnote was necessary.

"I explained to Captain Annala that General Mahlgren felt that since she would be advising and discussing with you important information and intelligence about Stalin and Russia that is not known outside of our narrow circle, it should occur in a private place. The reason is that your meetings with Captain Annala, if they were in our offices, might stir up some curiosity among the employees. In a private home there would be less risk from inadvertent gossip. It is true, our employees are trained not to discuss what they see or hear at this office, but we recognize that they are human and could casually mention something and then we'd have rumors on our hands. You'll spend some time during the day with the trade department so that you'll appear authentic when you accompany the trade mission." Blomquist smiled at his own concept of "authentic." "Does that explain why you're staying with the Annalas?"

"Yes, yes," Koskinen replied. But he still was not happy with the prospect of staying with the Annala family. Koskinen liked his privacy.

"We'll have a taxi take you, your baggage and Captain Annala to her home." Blomquist was unusually ingratiating.

"Colonel, before we leave, I would like to talk with you privately. Perhaps, Captain Annala will excuse us." Koskinen looked directly at Annala, leaving her no choice.

"Of course, Captain Koskinen, I shall await you in the reception room," Annala said.

When Annala had left, Koskinen turned to Blomquist. "In all respect, Colonel, I object to staying with the Annalas. It is unacceptable.

The whole arrangement is absurd and the General's reason for it is, in my opinion, ridiculous. I am being asked to undertake a very dangerous mission and I think I ought to be allowed to make the more personal decisions like where I am to stay while in Helsinki." Koskinen was plainly angry.

"I'm virtually a stranger to the Annalas. I have never met her husband and I have had only a casual conversation or meeting infrequently with Captain Annala. I don't feel comfortable staying with them, especially when it's not necessary. If you don't want me to meet here with Captain Annala, we can arrange some other place, perhaps her home during the day."

"Timo," Blomquist said in a soothing voice, "your staying with the Annalas is an order from General Mahlgren. Do you want me to overrule his order? You know I cannot do that. I will take the matter up with the General and perhaps he'll change his mind. Unfortunately, however, he is out of town for the next two days. Why don't you try it for a couple of days?"

"No," replied Koskinen, his frown evidencing his continuing agitation. "I'll tell you what I shall do: I'll get a hotel room at my own expense until the General returns. At that time, the General will either rescind his order and allow me to stay where I wish at reasonable cost and will have the Section pay my expenses or I shall return home and the General can get someone else to perform the mission." Koskinen realized that he was using strong language, but he intended to be forceful and to leave no doubt about his position on the matter.

Koskinen would admit frankly, if asked, that he was tired of people in the government telling him what to do and what not to do, where he could live, where he could dine, whom he could see or not see, what clothing to wear, what to say and all that sort of thing. He thought he had the ability for mature judgment and common sense and that the bureaucrats should recognize it and give him the necessary latitude to exercise those talents.

Surprised by the intensity of Koskinen's objections, Colonel Blomquist responded softly, "Captain, you can do that if you wish but I cannot agree to your disregarding the General's order. You will have to do this on your own and at your own risk. I'm not going to compel you to follow an order but you understand that there may be disciplinary consequences for your refusal."

"Yes, I'm willing to take whatever comes," Koskinen replied.

In Koskinen's mind, he was almost certain that the General would cave in to his demand and rescind his order. He would see that it was an absurd, senseless order. The General would also recognize that he, Koskinen, was indispensable to the success of the mission regarding Stalin.

Koskinen had always had considerable respect for General Mahlgren and his professional competency and he could not comprehend why the General would issue such an order. What neither Captain Koskinen nor Captain Annala knew at this time was that the General had instructed Colonel Blomquist to tell both Captains that it would save time if Koskinen and Annala could confer at the Annala home for the few days before Koskinen was to leave for Moscow. If either were to object to the home arrangement, then Blomquist was not to insist, but rather to allow Koskinen to stay where he wished and at the government's expense. Koskinen was to later learn of Blomquist's distortion of the General suggestion. Blomquist, however, had not counted on Koskinen's defiance.

As Koskinen turned to leave, Blomquist remarked slyly and not very artfully, "I suppose if Captain Annala were a slim, attractive and sexy-looking young girl, you wouldn't mind staying at her home." Colonel Blomquist smiled and winked suggestively.

Koskinen glared at the Colonel.

"I resent that, Colonel!"

Koskinen left the Colonel's office clearly showing his indignant displeasure. The old wounds between the two were still festering.

Koskinen met Captain Annala in the reception room.

"Captain, I have decided that I shall stay at a hotel during the time that I'm in Helsinki. I intend no offense to you and your generous offer of hospitality, but I believe that we both shall be more comfortable if it is done this way."

To Koskinen, it seemed that Annala was perceptively relieved by his decision. Nevertheless, this was suffused with a noticeable apprehension.

"But, Captain Koskinen, it was the General's order ..."

"I know. I have decided not to abide by that order because I think it's foolish. Don't worry about it. I shall take the blame. You are exonerated."

"Captain, I think you are a very brave man. I respect you and I don't want you to get into trouble. It will not be a burden for me and my husband if you come to stay with us for a relatively few days."

"No, Captain, this is such an obvious ridiculous order that I simply will not obey it. I shall not be told where I shall sleep at night when it does not interfere with a mission."

"Captain--may I call you Timo--in government and especially in the military, there are often silly, incredible orders, but in the chain of command we are required to follow them however unwise and stupid."

"Captain Annala, please don't preach I have made up my mind. I am aware of what you're saying and, in my opinion, that is precisely what is wrong with government. I do not include military operations. Everyone must go by the book. There can be no independent thinking. If you challenge an order or a rule because you believe there may be a better way of accomplishing something, then you are disciplined. It is a situation that stifles new ideas, innovative thinking and, in fact, progress. I am not going to allow myself to be stultified."

"But, Timo," Annala persisted, "you have been with the Intelligence Section many years. In that time, there surely were some silly orders. How is it that you are now rebelling for the first time?"

"I have been rebelling inwardly for quite a long time but I have been hypnotized by the thought that I have no choice but to follow orders. I have now concluded that I have a choice. I am not a slave."

"What led to that conclusion?" Annala found herself caught up in the volatility of the subject. The conversation had taken a new dimension in interest for her.

"This mission has altered my perspective. I have quite suddenly realized that the danger inherent in this mission and my willingness to undertake it to help save my country from possible tyranny has placed me a cut above in courage and in character to these so-called leaders. I am superior to these gutless, arrogant pencil pushers like the one down the hall." Koskinen motioned in the direction of Blomquist's office.

In response to Koskinen's answer, Captain Annala's facial expression had lighted up with a broad smile of glee and exhilaration. "Timo, come over here. I want to whisper something in your ear."

Koskinen, who had been standing, bent over to listen to Captain Annala as she sat on a small sofa.

"That's wonderful, Timo. Continue to stand up to these guys. More of us should be doing that. If the word gets out, and I'll spread it, maybe a few more of us will follow your example. We need some changes around here."

Koskinen wondered why she thought she had to whisper that testimonial to his disobedience of an order. Her caution obviously did not peg her as a ready volunteer to follow his example.

"Timo, even though you are staying at a hotel, we should consider that we use my home to discuss Stalin and the Soviet situation as it relates to your mission. The General feels it best that we do not meet at the office and I cannot think of any other place for privacy. What do you think about that?"

Koskinen thought a moment. "Yes, I suppose it is alright. By the way, what about your husband? Has he agreed to the use of his home?"

"Oh, Risto. Yes, he had no objection. If it is what I want, he'll go along. I want you to meet him. He's a very nice man."

"What does he do?" Koskinen asked.

"Risto is a professor of electrical engineering at the University of Helsinki."

"Have you mentioned the mission to him?"

"No, I have merely said that you will be on a trade mission to Moscow and the General thought that we could get more accomplished discussing the Soviet Union if you were to stay with us. As I said, Risto had no objection."

"Good. Shall we start tomorrow?" Koskinen was businesslike.

"Certainly. How about eleven in the morning? I'll make up some sandwiches for us at lunch. Where will you be staying so that I can give you directions to our home?"

"I'll call the Hotel Torni right now to see if they have a room available."

Koskinen called the hotel from the reception desk, obtaining a room reservation and informed Captain Annala. Annala gave him directions to her apartment on Jaakarin Street, a considerable distance south of headquarters as well as the hotel.

"There is a bus which runs about two streets from the apartment or, of course, you can take a taxi. The bus goes by about once every hour, but there is no guarantee."

While Captain Annala went back to her office, Koskinen gathered up his two suitcases, went outside and hailed a taxicab.

After settling in his hotel room, Koskinen lay down on the bed and stared at the ceiling. He turned the morning's events over and over in his mind. Later, he spent a restless mostly sleepless night thinking. His mind flitted from one thought to another in a disorganized jumble. The next morning when he got out of bed, he was exhausted. He went down to the hotel lobby where a pot of hot coffee was kept brewing for the guests. Koskinen drank three cups as fast as the coffee cooled a bit. The coffee would keep him going and, hopefully, keep him alert at the Annala home.

Koskinen took a taxi to the Jaakarin Street address provided by Captain Annala. He observed an older building of about a half-block in length of two stories with a rather drab cream-colored stucco exterior. Koskinen was familiar with the type of building that was quite common in the larger Finnish cities. The entrances were at the rear of the building rather than fronting on the street. Walking around one end of the building to the rear, Koskinen saw six separate entrances spaced along the length of the building. In the small lobby of each entrance was a panel on the wall containing the names of the tenants in that part of the building with the respective apartment numbers.

Captain Annala had apparently forgotten to give Koskinen the entrance and apartment numbers locating her apartment in the building. After going into the lobbies of four entrance-ways and reading the tenant lists, Koskinen finally found the Annala listing in the fourth lobby and the apartment, itself, on the second floor. He used the knocker on the door to announce his presence. It was a few minutes before eleven hours.

In response to the knock, the door was opened by a man Koskinen assumed was Captain Annala's husband, Risto. Koskinen was momentarily startled by the Leninesque features of the man. The bald head, the arched eyebrows, the piercing eyes, high cheekbones, a moustache that drooped and curved slightly around the ends of the mouth and a small, pointed goatee.

"Ah, you are Captain Koskinen, of course."

"Yes."

"I am Risto Annala. Please come in. We were expecting you."

As Koskinen entered the vestibule of the apartment, Captain Annala appeared wearing an apron and wiping her hands on a small kitchen towel.

"Welcome, Timo. You will excuse my appearance, but I am in the midst of preparing some sandwiches. You have already met my husband here, Risto." Annala gestured towards her husband.

Risto, all smiles and jovial, said, "Yes, yes, we have met. Please, Captain, come into our living room and make yourself at home."

Before she disappeared into the kitchen again, Captain Annala said, "I asked Risto to remain home to have lunch as I wanted him to meet you."

The living room, as Koskinen observed it, was neat and tastefully furnished and decorated. A sofa along one wall was long enough to seat four. Two overstuffed chairs were placed one at each end of the sofa and at a right angle. A long pine wood cocktail table was situated in front of the sofa. A bookcase with glass door enclosed shelves was against the opposite wall. It contained as many knickknacks as it did books, among the latter of which appeared to be a large Bible. At an end wall stood an oversized sewing table of mahogany color. On it were placed several framed family photographs. On the walls were a number of framed prints and oil paintings. An oil painting over the sofa portrayed a lake with pine trees growing almost to the shoreline and among the towering trees the artist had introduced a log sauna. Koskinen recognized the typical Finnish lake scene. The far end of the room had doors that opened on a balcony overlooking the rear courtyard. Koskinen felt he was in a well organized and self-disciplined household. Every object seemed to have its proper place.

"I understand that you will be leaving for Moscow soon on a trade mission, Captain," Risto Annala began the conversation.

"Yes, that is true," Koskinen replied.

"Helena is to advise you on the Soviet-Finnish trade relations. That is my understanding." Professor Annala went on. "I cannot understand why she is not advising the others in the trade mission group, as well. Why you alone?"

"I suppose," answered Koskinen, "because the other members who are in the group have already participated in previous missions and do not require the information. Also, the others will only be in Moscow for three or four days, whereas I shall be staying for a month or more." Koskinen had fabricated quickly an answer to his host's right to question a dubious situation.

While they were talking, Koskinen studied the Professor intently. Professor Annala was relatively short in stature and neither noticeably thin nor heavy in body structure. He was dressed in a business suit with shirt and tie. As the Professor continued to speak, Koskinen became impressed with his courtly politeness and civility. Good breeding emanated from Professor Annala accompanied by an early display of a vigorous intellect.

Koskinen wondered why the Professor had chosen to embrace a Lenin-like facial appearance with the moustache and goatee adding to an already similar facial structure. Perhaps the Professor would reveal the reason if the conversation could turn to Russia.

"What is your impression of Stalin?," Koskinen asked.

Professor Annala took the bait and answered without hesitancy. "Stalin is a monster, an utterly amoral, malevolent, savage brute. No other words can better describe him. From his early beginnings and continuing to the present he has had the character of a ruffian, a hoodlum and a terrorist. He is a scourge worse than Attila the Hun. That is my opinion of him."

Koskinen smiled at the Professor's articulate description. "I can agree with you," he said. "Stalin has principles, but his principles are all of the devil." Professor Annala, having started on the subject, became more animated. Apparently, it was a favorite subject as he was galvanized into further remarks.

"You know, Captain, if Lenin had lived, none of the terrible purges going on in the Soviet Union would be happening. Stalin is a threat to Finland. We should be, if we're not, terribly concerned about him. Lenin would never have been a menace to us. Lenin respected and admired the Finns. Lenin understood the Finns. He was an intellectual, not an uncouth, loathsome creature like Stalin."

Professor Annala paused for a moment, then continued, "I met Lenin in Tammerfors when he was in hiding from the Tsar's security police. His name, of course, was not Lenin at the time. He was using his birth name of Vladimir Ilych Ulyanov. A few of us who were active in the Social Democratic Party had gone to meet with him. He told us then that when he overthrew the Tsarist monarchy he would give Finland its independence because he believed that every peoples had the right of self-determination under Communism. He kept his word after the success of the Bolshevik Revolution in 1917. That is why I admire and respect him, he kept his word. He granted us our independence."

Koskinen then said, "I hope you will excuse me if I say that your appearance is very much like the photographs I have seen of Lenin. There is a very close resemblance."

"Yes. You are not the first to tell me that. I intentionally conform my appearance. It is my way of honoring Lenin. He was a very great man. And because he gave us our independence, he was good for Finland. I tell my students that. I tell them we should celebrate him."

Observed Koskinen, "We have an annual holiday to celebrate our day of independence. We don't have a holiday to honor Lenin."

"We should have," replied Annala.

Koskinen was saved from further pursuit of the subject by Madam Annala coming into the room and announcing that lunch was ready. Lunch was served at a small table in an alcove adjoining the kitchen. Nothing further was said about Lenin, Stalin or the Soviet Union. The conversation was about family, education and the quality of students today as compared to "our generation."

After lunch, Professor Annala left for the University. He did not appear to be concerned about leaving his wife and Captain Koskinen together in the apartment. The age difference between Captain Annala and Koskinen apparently lulled the Professor into believing that there could not possibly arise any amorous peccadillo between the two Captains when left alone in the apartment.

Koskinen was to spend two or three hours a day for the next ten days receiving instruction on the Soviet Union and Stalin from Captain Annala, the expert on such matters. After Professor Annala had left for the University, Captain Annala and Koskinen sat at the kitchen table and Annala outlined the topics and points she intended to cover to prepare him for his mission.

"I am going to cover such matters as Stalin's family and personal history and background, his early political activities and his early rise in the Bolshevik Party and how he accomplished getting to the top." Captain Annala added, "We of course have some limits on what we know on some of these items. On some we have validated confidential information. On others we have only hearsay and unsubstantiated rumor. I shall tell you which is which as we go along."

Captain Annala continued, "I shall also describe the people in Stalin's inner circle and those few in whom we believe he places his trust and reliance. I will also give you information on Stalin's personal habits and peculiarities to the extent that our Intelligence has that information. You can make written notes on all this if you wish, but I advise against taking the notes with you when you leave for the Soviet Union. If the Soviet police find such notes on you, they will undoubtedly conclude that you are a spy and your life will not be worth one Finnmark."

"What about information that will help me as a member of the trade mission?" Koskinen inquired. "I have to know something about trade relations between Finland and Russia so that I'll have some legitimacy to being a member of the trade group."

"You will be getting some background information on that from one or two of the old hands in the trade group which is to go to Moscow. My understanding is that you will be sort of in an apprentice status in the group and you won't have to be concerned about acting as an expert." Captain Annala then concluded, "Well, shall we end our discussion for the day? I will see you here tomorrow at nine hours and we'll start on the lessons."

As they stood in the vestibule of the apartment with Koskinen about ready to leave, Captain Annala said with a warm smile and an inquiring look, "Would you mind if I hugged you?" She waited for Koskinen's answer. Koskinen was taken by surprise and, for a tense moment, was voiceless. He felt his face flush and obviously flustered, said rather weakly, "No, if you wish, I suppose it's alright."

Captain Annala then embraced him for a few seconds, gave him a light kiss on his cheek and, still smiling and with a sparkle in her eyes, said, "I think I should explain that I am a member of a church group that believes that hugging demonstrates love for one's fellow man. We practice it among the members of the group and we are urged to do the same with whomever we come to know but with consent, of course. We believe that hugging overcomes all the human, social negatives like hate, suspicion, anger, resentment, jealousy, destructive criticism and so on."

"Well, that's quite interesting," commented Koskinen, still somewhat uncomfortable with this sudden display of spiritual fervor. He quickly thanked Captain Annala for the lunch, her hospitality and information and departed. As he descended the stairs, he remembered that he had failed to telephone for a taxi. Embarrassed, he returned to the Annala apartment, knocked on the door and explained his forgetfulness when Captain Annala opened the door and with some jollity showed him the phone.

Back at his hotel room, Koskinen became lost in thought about his day with the Annalas. Professor Annala was an interesting, likeable gentleman albeit a bit odd. Koskinen judged him to be in his late fifties. Koskinen judged Mrs. Annala to be in her mid-fifties. She was pleasant looking, probably quite attractive in her younger days, but now had let herself become quite plump. She had a boyish haircut set over a chubby face with large, pretty blue eyes, a straightforward nose and thin, unpainted lips. When she had hugged him, Koskinen sensed a perfume that smelled like bay leaf. It reminded him of his wife's homemade chowder.

In the evening of that first day in Helsinki, Koskinen telephoned his wife. He described the day's events but omitted mentioning that he was getting his briefing on Stalin and the Soviet Union in the Annala apartment and, of course, prudence dictated that he say nothing about Captain Annala's religious compulsion for hugging. After all, Koskinen realized, it would only create anxiety in Anna who then could imagine all sorts of goings-on. Anna didn't distrust Timo but, then, Anna knew how women could tempt men, even those who held to the principle of marital fidelity. Koskinen, however, was not physically attracted to Captain Annala but he saw no reason to even mention that to Anna.

It was on the third day of their instruction session that Koskinen became uneasily aware that there might be more to Captain Annala's religion than mere hugging. The session had hardly just begun on Stalin and his penchant for flirting at social parties with attractive wives of some of his inner council officials, when Annala diverged into observations about her husband.

"Talking about Stalin and his love life, I cannot help but say that my husband, Risto, is just the opposite. I never have to worry about Risto. He is so involved with his teaching and work at the University and his writing that he does not seem to be emotionally interested in women. Sometimes I think he would have been better off remaining single." Captain Annala paused and looked at Koskinen as if closely studying his reaction to her remarks.

From the manner in which Captain Annala looked at him, Koskinen felt intuitively that she was leading up to something more personal. Koskinen knew and understood that in the relations between men and women, generally, there can be considerable implicit, unspoken communication that can be as comprehensible and intelligible as if voiced. The eyes, the facial expression and, frequently, the rest of the body can serve as a virtual bulletin board with a message pinned to it. Koskinen was getting a message from Captain Annala, a message he did not welcome. Nevertheless, he tried not to reveal his reaction, judging it better to show a passive interest in what Captain Annala was saying about her personal life.

The pause ended and Captain Annala continued, "Risto is a very fine person. He and I get along well together. I can pursue my interests and he does not object. If I protest at times that he gives too much attention to his work and neglects me, he agrees but does nothing to correct it. He makes no sexual demands of me and I wish he would." Captain Annala smiled wanly as if the situation was hopeless. "Sometimes I am tempted to find someone who can give me some love, something physical. You know, we are all human, male or female." Another pause, but this time Captain Annala stared miserably at her hands folded together on the table as she exposed her unheeded needs to Captain Koskinen.

Koskinen felt embarrassed, uncomfortable. He searched his mind for something to say. Finally, he spoke up. He addressed Captain Annala by her given name for the first time, thinking that formality, under the circumstances, was not appropriate. In a soft, soothing and reassuring tone of voice he said, "Helena, I appreciate how you feel, but, if Risto is good to you in every other way, then you can be grateful. So many wives, as I'm sure you know, are very abused by their husbands. Sex to those wives is often not pleasurable but a duty to perform. Marriage is putting in perspective the good compared with the bad. It is not perfect. How many married people find complete fulfillment? Few, if any. There are gaps. A happy marriage exists when each is mature enough to reach, within him and herself, a compromise with their dreams. The dreams we have of married life when we first get married are usually not realistic." Koskinen, in turn, regarded Helena for her response. He hoped they could get back to discussing Stalin.

"I know, I know," Helena replied. "I'm sure you are right, Timo." She lifted her eyes and looked at Koskinen. "Timo, do you find me attractive?" She appeared so hapless that Timo felt a deep sense of sympathy for her. Nevertheless, he had no intention of becoming intimate with Helena in order to satisfy her needs. Helena, after all, was no youthful Elena Marikova.

"Of course you are attractive, Helena. An older woman sometimes exudes more beauty in her way than younger women. Of course, I find you attractive, but I remind myself that I have a wife and children and I must be faithful to them." Koskinen felt that if Helena was suggesting an intimate relationship, he had to anticipate and forestall it. Helena smiled sweetly. "I accept your advice, Timo. I should not have said all this. Perhaps we should get back to the instruction about Russia." Koskinen nodded in agreement.

They spent the next two hours in discussion about Stalin's personal habits in so far as known to Finnish Intelligence. Koskinen was surprised at the amount of information Captain Annala possessed on the subject and which was not known by the public. Koskinen, not unlike the public, thought of Stalin as an enigma, an inscrutable despot.

As Koskinen was about to leave the apartment, there was the usual hug by Helena. Koskinen took it good-naturedly in stride. After all, he was happy that the morning session had not gone beyond a hug. Nevertheless, it was a distressing situation and Koskinen had determined that it had to be corrected. He decided that he would see General Mahlgren who had ordered that the conferences be held at the

Annala home. Early that afternoon Koskinen was in Mahlgren's office sitting across from the General at the latter's desk.

"General, I am very uncomfortable with your order that I stay at the home of Captain Annala and that conferences with her be conducted in her apartment. I am here to request that you change the order so that I can stay at a hotel and that conferences be held here at headquarters. In fact, I hope you will forgive me, but I have already taken a room at the Hotel Torni."

General Mahlgren was startled. "Captain Koskinen, I am surprised. I did not issue such an order. Before I left for a few days, Colonel Blomquist and I discussed your coming here and at the time I merely suggested to Colonel Blomquist that because you had a good deal to learn about your mission you might have more privacy and fewer distractions if you were at the Annala apartment. But, it was only a suggestion. And I told the Colonel that if you and Captain Annala objected to them, then to make arrangements here at headquarters."

"Sir," replied Koskinen, "that is not what Colonel Blomquist told Captain Annala and me. He said it was your order and that he could not change it and that if I went to a hotel I would be violating your order at my risk."

"Well, Captain, I assume that Colonel Blomquist felt I had issued an order. You know, when a General makes a suggestion, his staff will more often than not construe it as an order. A suggestion can be ignored, an order cannot and staff members are not prone to ignoring whatever their Commander may say. In a way that is unfortunate, but that is how it is in the military. I think you know that. Every officer below the Commander in rank fears having an independent thought or making a decision that does not conform to a military manual. I don't know how to change that without weakening the whole chain of command structure. So, I believe that is the rationale for Colonel Blomquist's instruction to you and Captain Annala. In any case, Captain, continue your room at the hotel and I'll get one of our aides to allocate a conference room here at headquarters for you and Captain Annala. Will you notify Annala?"

"Yes, of course. But one more thing, if you please, General."

"General, when I'm in Russia on this mission, I would rather not report to Colonel Blomquist. Anyone else would be preferable. This incident that we have just discussed confirms what I have long felt. I have no rapport with him, no confidence in his judgment. I might want to seek advice from my contact here. I don't feel very comfortable with Colonel Blomquist's advice. I hope you understand what I am saying, General."

General Mahlgren did not reply for a few moments, but swiveled his chair so that he faced the side of the room away from Captain Koskinen. He was obviously thinking about what to say. General Mahlgren was a military career officer. In his rise to a top ranking, he had always been a staunch and undeviating believer in adherence to rules and regulations and that included never questioning the authority and competency of a superior officer. Now, here was a Captain, an inferior officer, asking him to depart from the rules because he, the Captain, didn't like his superior officer.

General Mahlgren recognized that Captain Koskinen's mission was no ordinary intelligence project. The mission, the General knew, was delicate and dangerous and everyone involved had to have the utmost confidence in everyone else. The operation had to run smoothly and with everyone concentrating and focusing on each step towards the successful conclusion and attainment of the objective. The General had two choices. He could insist that Captain Koskinen follow the rules regardless of his personal feelings, or he, the General, could bend the rule to suit the Captain. The General quickly came to the conclusion that if Koskinen was ill at ease with Colonel Blomquist, then the General would have to opt for bending the rule as much as the General abhorred doing so. Captain Koskinen was vital to the mission. Colonel Blomquist was not.

General Mahlgren turned back to face Koskinen. "Captain, if you prefer not to report to Colonel Blomquist, then you will report to me directly. Does that resolve the problem for you?"

"Yes, General, it does." Koskinen was relieved. He had scored a victory. He had gotten Blomquist eliminated from the mission. The message would get back to Blomquist that he, Captain Koskinen, had the influence and the power to get the Colonel displaced from the mission. Koskinen savored the thought. He arose from his chair, saluted the General and left the office.

For the next nine days, Koskinen met intermittently with Captain Annala, Colonel Anders Lindforst, the Liaison officer with the Finnish Embassy in Moscow, and some trade negotiation people who would be in the group going to Moscow on the trade mission. Each evening Koskinen telephoned to his wife, Anna. There was just small talk, neither of them wanting to arouse further fears about the pending mission. Yet despite the tone of assurance and confidence that acted as a veneer to their underlying feelings, Koskinen, at least, could detect the spirit of desperation and anxiety in Anna's voice. He understood very well the depth of her alarm.

On the last weekend before he was to leave for Moscow, Anna came to visit with Timo. General Mahlgren and his wife, Seri, invited Captain Koskinen and Anna to dine with them at the Hotel Klaus Kurki in downtown Helsinki. The Hotel was a luxury facility, a gathering place for the upper echelon of society and high government officials. It had catered to generations of the hauteur classes. The dining room exuded a grandeur found in few other places in Finland. With its heavy, dark, carved wood paneling, the large floor to ceiling arched windows with heavy, elegant drapes, the enormous crystal chandeliers and the white linen tablecloths set with fine silverware and china together with service by ingratiating waiters in formal wear, all conveyed an impressive atmosphere of magnificent splendor and an ostentatious pomposity. This environment and the presence of the General's rank were not conducive to a feeling of ease on the part of Timo and Anna. Both, however, strove to be cordial and interested in the conversation at the table. Both would have preferred to have dined by themselves in some small, cozy and out of the way restaurant where they could have nourished their feelings of warmth and intimacy between them.

The visit of Anna had been a hastily arranged decision of the moment during the telephone call that Timo had placed as usual of an evening. Timo had mentioned it casually to General Mahlgren. The Mahlgren's immediately made the dinner invitation out of a sense of thoughtfulness, kindness and grace for this couple who would soon have to part. Timo could not refuse the Mahlgren's well-intentioned gesture.

A good part of the conversation at the dining table concerned the crisis in Europe, of Hitler grabbing countries or parts of countries, of the threat of Stalin to the Baltic States and to Finland. At one point, General Mahlgren was highly critical of the United States.

"They should be getting involved in these upheavals in Europe," he declared.

"The American policy of non-intervention in Europe's affairs is totally unrealistic. They think they can isolate themselves from the rest of the world. That is an impossibility. They will wake up some morning and find that they are involved whether they like it or not. President Roosevelt could be of enormous help to us right now by letting Stalin know that the United States will not tolerate any invasion or grabbing of Finland or any Nordic country. Instead of being a world leader and making hard, but right decisions, he is proving to be just another politician playing up to the uninformed masses." General Mahlgren shook his head in frustration. His wife, Sari, said nothing but commented by nodding in obvious agreement.

Koskinen's only pronouncement was, "Well, we, at least, must be realistic and do what must be done and not wait for someone else to help us."

"Yes, of course, you're absolutely right," said Mahlgren.

Returning after dinner to Koskinen's hotel room, Timo and Anna were able to relax and embrace with all the passion that results from a long absence from each other although it was but a few days. This was different. Their ardent caresses now came from a realization that their absence from each other was not ending but just beginning and that this was probably to be their last intimate blending for a long time to come. In these remaining hours of privacy, Timo and Anna experienced a resurrection of the profound and deep-rooted love for each other that had enveloped them as a young couple, but with the passing of years of daily living had fallen prey to the common notion that with marriage love no longer needed to be nurtured and everlastingly cultivated. Timo and Anna both appreciated that now was the time to say the words of endearment that should have been spoken between them each and every day of their lives together. Yet, they did not have to speak in order for them to understand at this moment that their love for each other was the only reality, the only true substance and that all else, except for their children, was but a transient ephemerality, a series of worldly experiences necessary only for survival and which, in importance, would fade away and count for nothing in the long term.

In his arms, Anna softly whispered, "Timo, no matter what happens, I shall remember and hold onto these moments forever and I shall be sustained by them as I wait for your return. This will give me the strength to go on. I love you so much."

Timo's gentle response was, "Yes, my dear Anna, I know. I, too, will hold on to these moments as memories to be cherished. I love you also, Anna."

The next day, about the noon hour, Anna boarded the train for a return to Tampere. Timo accompanied her to the railroad station. Little was said as they held hands and kissed goodbye. Their eyes communed their thoughts and feelings. Somehow, their love had suppressed and overcome their fears. Anxiety had seemingly evaporated and, in its place, Timo and Anna both found a peaceful tranquility. There were no tears as the train pulled away, only a sense of spiritual fulfillment. Timo walked towards headquarters building with energy and exhilaration. His perspective of his mission in Russia was one of confidence that all would turn out well.

The next two days were spent in final preparation for the trip. He could not take much clothing and personal items with him. However, the Intelligence Section provided him with money to purchase in Helsinki additional clothing and personal items that would be shipped to the Finnish Embassy in Moscow. In addition, Koskinen was given new identification papers. His passport and visa identified him as Antti Salonen. Fabricated correspondence addressed to Antti Salonen was to be carried by Koskinen to further reinforce his identity should Russian authorities require it. A spurious letter from Koskinen's wife, Anna, "Salonen" written and signed in feminine handwriting was included in the packet. The "Dear Antti" letter spoke of their children and the hope that "Antti" would not be away too long on his trade mission. Koskinen was amused by it all.

He was not amused, however, by the three capsules of cyanide given him. But as an Intelligence Agent he understood that they were meant for his use in the event that he was arrested by the Russian police if they discovered his real mission and his deception. It was well documented in the Section of the methods used by the NKVD to force people to talk. There was no guarantee that the Russian authorities would recognize diplomatic immunity.

On the morning of February 17, 1939, Koskinen joined the small entourage of diplomats, political leaders and trade specialists at the Helsinki railroad station for the train trip to the Finnish city of Viipuri where they would transfer to another Finnish train to Terijoki and on to the Russian border inspection and customs station. Viipuri was an important city about ninety-six kilometers from the border. Terijoki was a village about sixteen kilometers from the Russian border.

There were rumblings from the Kremlin that the Finns should cede Viipuri to the Soviet Union in order that Leningrad would be better protected in the event of a German invasion of Russia through Finland. Viipuri was only about one hundred twelve kilometers from Leningrad. That, according to Soviet leaders was too short a distance from Finland for ease of mind for proper defense of Leningrad. The Kremlin was not certain whether the Finns could or would put up a resistance to a German assault from that area.

As the train pulled out of the station, Koskinen had an acute feeling that he was cutting away from everything that linked him to his way of life, his family, his friends, the familiar places, the very culture of the country he loved. For a while he had a daunting and depressing sense of inevitable doom, that the mission to assassinate or somehow eliminate Stalin was insane and impractical and could not possibly succeed. As the train rolled on from Helsinki to Viipuri, Koskinen aroused himself from these unhappy thoughts realizing that he had to maintain a positive, aggressive and optimistic attitude to the job for which he was chosen. Talking with other members of his entourage helped to alleviate the initial sense of despair simply by diverting his attention to other subjects.

It was not that Koskinen was a person given to despair or trepidation when confronted with complex and challenging Intelligence projects. But, in the past, the operations had always been planned with attention to detail and anticipated situational changes as a project progressed. Generally, the results met the expectations of the Intelligence Section.

However, with the mission now at hand, Koskinen had become aware that neither his superior officers nor anyone else in the Section had any plan or any specific scheme or plot on how he was to approach and accomplish his assigned task. He had been given vague suggestions by those who knew about the mission, such as using a sniper, planting poison in food or drink, an ambush, shooting Stalin and those around him point-blank, injecting with a slow-acting fatal chemical, and so on. Nothing specific. The only information Koskinen had about Stalin's habits and routine were what he was told by Captain Annala and, in Koskinen's opinion, that was interesting but of little help. So Koskinen had come to the conclusion that he was given a dangerous mission and impliedly told that he was on his own to develop his own plan as he went along. Koskinen was to become reconciled to the fact that this was the way it was to be.

The train finally arrived at the Russian border station. It was here that the Finnish delegation was to transfer to a Soviet train. Since neither Finnish trains nor Soviet trains went beyond their respective sides of the border, passengers from either direction were required to walk along a wood platform that extended into both sides until they reached the custom buildings of whichever country they were entering.

The contrast between the Finnish and Russian facilities was remarkable and a comparison travelers could hardly fail to make. On the Finnish side, the building, while small, was nevertheless well maintained both inside and outside and the appearance of cleanliness and orderliness was at once noticeable. Surrounding the building and along the wood platform were decorative pots for flowering plants during the warmer months. Inside the building was a well lighted and airy waiting room with a kiosk that sold newspapers, magazines, candy, sandwiches and coffee. There were several tables and chairs as well as plain wood benches for the travelers. At one end of the waiting room was an enclosed check-in room through which passengers from the Soviet side had to pass for custom inspections before entering the waiting room. Koskinen was able to observe that the uniformed custom inspectors seemed to be pleasant and cordial although formally businesslike. Passengers destined for the Soviet were, of course, not required to pass through Finnish customs but were required to fill out a form giving information as to where they were from and their destination in the Soviet Union as well as their expected length of stay. Having completed this task, the Finnish trade delegation left the building to walk to the Soviet side of the border.

The members of the delegation who had been quite lively while in the Finnish building, talking and joking animatedly among themselves, now became suddenly silent and solemn as they traversed the short distance to the border with Russia. It seemed to Koskinen that a sense of gloom and unhappy anticipation of what lay ahead had come over all in the delegation. Those who had been to Russia before were, perhaps, justified in their feelings by previous experience. Those who had not been to Russia before were infected by what they had heard and read about conditions in Russia. As a result, these "newcomers" easily shared the somber mood.

As he crossed the border and continued walking towards the Russian custom building, Koskinen had a deep touch of heavy oppression. The very air seemed different. The atmosphere was almost funereal, Koskinen thought, he could sense the pervasive malodorous stench of evil. He felt he had just left behind him a world of happiness, joyful lightheartedness, freedom and security and entered the realm of some sinister, satanic society of fear. For a few moments he was not sure whether it was all in his mind as a result of all the stories he had heard about Russia, but upon entering the custom building on the Russian side, fact and fantasy merged. There were a half-dozen grim-faced, uniformed officials either standing about or seated at a table staring in an almost threatening manner at the travelers from the Finnish side and acting as if impatient to get the registration process done with and annoyed that the travelers' arrival was forcing them to even work at the procedure.

One of the Russian officials standing near the entrance door motioned the travelers to a table at the far end of the room where another official with some smattering familiarity with the Finnish language was seated and handing out registration forms. The forms, Koskinen noted, were printed in Russian, Finnish and English presumably all stating the identical instructions.

The room in which the travelers were to have their first contact with Russian officialdom was small in size, sparsely furnished with a few tables at which travelers could sit while completing the required papers. The paint on the walls and ceiling, Koskinen observed, was a dirty, faded cream color with peeling at numerous places. Two unshaded light bulbs hung from the ceiling. Dirt from the floor had, apparently, been swept into the corners of the room and several layers had been there long enough to have become permanent fixtures.

Although the place was distressingly cheerless and woefully lacking in any human esthetic touch, it was the stern, scowling Russian officers that made Koskinen uncomfortable. As Koskinen remarked to several of the trade delegation later, these Russian fellows seemed ready to pounce if some unfortunate attempted to erase something written in error on the form. No one dared to ask what a question on the registration form meant for fear of creating further suspicions on the part of the Russian officials. The fact that the trade delegation was an official representative of the Finnish government evidently meant nothing to the Russian custom people. Koskinen concluded that every foreigner entering the Soviet Union was treated the same, miserably and distrustfully. From here on in Koskinen realized that he had to be constantly on guard not to act in any way that would attract more than the usual attention to himself. His comportment had to be scrupulously in conformity to Russian expectations that foreigners abide by the Russian rules of behavior. In this regard, Captain Annala's counseling would prove to be of considerable help.

When Koskinen had completed the form he arose from his chair and walked over to the official at the table who had handed out the forms initially. Koskinen gave him the paper and remained standing.

"Give me your passport." The official was gruff.

Koskinen handed the passport to the custom official who paged through it, stopping on occasion to read something. Koskinen did not know what. The official stared at the photograph in the passport for a few moments and then looked up at Koskinen as if to compare the two. The official then took the registration form and read the information that Koskinen had written in response to questions.

"Antti Salonen, ha. We have several Salonen's come through here lately. Your relatives?"

"I wouldn't know," Koskinen replied. "Salonen is a very common name in Finland."

Koskinen acted nonchalantly. Inwardly, he felt himself tense. What if the official pulled out some registration papers of Salonen's already on file and asked about his knowledge of them. It was a delicate situation.

After another moment and without further word, except for a grunt, the official stamped the passport and the registration form.

"We keep passport. You get it back when you arrive in Moscow." The official waved Koskinen on and turned his attention to the next person waiting in line. Koskinen took a deep breath and rejoined some of the other travelers awaiting the order to proceed to the Russian train. Koskinen seemed suddenly beset with a feeling of anxiety and foreboding. "Maybe," he thought, "it was because he had something to hide."

It was at this point, while standing with other travelers, that Koskinen remembered a part of "The Kalevala," the national epic folk poem with which all Finnish school children became acquainted in one manner or another. It was the part where the mythical figure, old Vainamoinen, was considering how to fell the great oak tree, an evil tree that because of its spread blocked out the sunshine and the moonbeams. The old man called on the water folk to fell the tree and a small man arose from the sea and said he had come to break the oak. Seeing the size of the folk-man, old Vainamoinen said, "I do not think you were made to be the great oak's breaker." But the little fellow struck the great tree three times with his axe and the great oak fell and the sun was free to shine and the moon free to gleam.

Koskinen mused that this part of Elias Lonnrot's collection of folk tales in 1849 aptly fitted his situation. Koskinen imagined that Vainamoinen was the Finnish Intelligence Section that had called upon him, the small man from the sea, to fell Stalin, the great oak who was blocking out the sunlight of freedom for all people. The Intelligence Section probably doubted that he, Koskinen, could accomplish the mission, but he, an insignificant small man in the vast structure of government, would show that he could fell this great oak, Stalin. Koskinen smiled as he developed the comparison.

While the Finnish trade delegation continued to stand by in the customs building awaiting the signal from one of the Russian officials to proceed to board the train, a short, heavyset fellow approached and addressing no one in particular in the group said in a loud, bass voice, "I am from the foreign service. I will accompany you and be your guide as far as Leningrad. Someone else will then take charge from there to Moscow."

The Russian from the foreign service was dressed in a heavy dark winter coat that hung almost to the floor. It fitted quite snugly so that the man's corpulent build was starkly outlined. His face, peering out from between a large fur collar and a huge fur hat, was burdened with cumbrous jowls that seemed to vibrate ever so slightly as he spoke. Small, stern brown eyes scrutinized the Finns closely with a look that was as frigid as the outside air. The man was clearly unfriendly and unfeeling. Koskinen thought he was probably an agent of the NKVD secret police. Although the Russian spoke in abused Finnish, the Finns understood enough to be able to follow directions in spite of the man's corruption of their language.

"You will follow me." The Russian then led the way from the building to the train on the tracks outside. The air outside seemed to Koskinen to have gotten considerably colder since they first entered the Russian customs building. A few flakes of snow were falling and adding to the dampness that permeated the atmosphere. There were no lights on the station platform, but the light from inside the cars was, at least, sufficient for the group to see where they were going. The Russian guide stopped at the third car from the rear of the train and beckoned the group to start boarding. In the faint light given off from the cars, Koskinen estimated that the train had about eight cars plus the locomotive and coal car. The locomotive was rumbling and hissing as it awaited the order to get underway.

The Russian guide walked the Finnish delegation down the car aisle and then pointed to three of the several enclosed passenger compartments that lined one side of the aisle. "You will use these." The Russian continued to speak with a harsh, authoritative gruffness. Koskinen thought that since the Finns were officials of a neighboring country, the Russian guide could have been more polite and respectful. Koskinen concluded that Russian officials were not given to social niceties and amenities and, obviously, not as civilized as Finns. He'd have to make allowances for Russian crudity.

Koskinen shared a compartment with two others of the trade delegation, Mikko Korkala and Petri Hiltunen. Koskinen guessed that they were both in their mid-forties. He knew nothing about them except that he was told that they were bureaucratic specialists in foreign trade matters and were to act as advisors to the negotiating team leaders.

While at the custom station, Koskinen had observed that there were few other travelers, about twenty-five or thirty at the most. These people were guided to other cars on the train. Koskinen mused that they must have urgent business to want to travel in Russia.

The train gave a sudden lurch with much clanking and jerking as it started to move. Getting underway was ever so slow as if the train was reluctant to depart and to Koskinen, it did not seem to gain much speed as it proceeded through the countryside. He could hear the locomotive puffing and chugging like some great exotic beast of burden gasping for breath.

The train had traveled for about two kilometers when suddenly two uniformed Russian soldiers barged into the compartment and ordered Koskinen and his two Finnish compatriots to stand up. They promptly obeyed without question or protest. The soldiers immediately went through an inspection procedure of the compartment. One of the soldiers stood on the seats while he felt around on the overhead storage shelves and finding nothing of consequence stepped down and began a search under the seats. The other soldier, in the meantime, conducted a search of the baggage brought on board by Koskinen and his two countrymen. The whole procedure lasted about four minutes when the Russian soldiers left as abruptly as they had come. The Finns resumed their seats.

"I suppose," Koskinen observed, "That they thought we had some guns or bombs that we had brought on board and hidden."

Petri added, "Mikko and I have been through this before. Yeah, they're probably looking for weapons, but they probably were looking for booze. If they found any bottles of liquor they would have confiscated it and, in short order, they'd have emptied the bottles down their throats. Right, Mikko?"

"Yup, that's right," Mikko replied obligingly.

"Gad, I'd hate to live here in Russia for very long," said Koskinen. "A person lives in fear every moment of his life that he may be violating some law, rule or regulation and that, if he is in violation, his punishment can be very severe. What a helluva way to live! Thank God we live in a democracy. In Finland, if we break a law or regulation, we know we are not going to prison for years or for life or be tortured or shot."

"That may be one of the disadvantages and flaws of a democracy," rejoined Petri. "You can't have an orderly society if people know that laws will not be strictly enforced. In a democracy the country is always teetering on the edge of being somewhat out of control to being totally out of control. It seems to me that in Finland we are in a constant state of bedlam created by the clamor and pressures of competing interests. Everyone wants something for himself. In my opinion, democracy promotes selfishness. I may not like everything that goes on in the Soviet Union but at least there seems to be a sense or orderliness and of a people acting and working for the good of their society." Petri paused to let his ideas sink into his companion's minds.

Mikko and Koskinen looked with astonishment and raised eyebrows at each other. Mikko said nothing; he was apparently a person who never said much and, except for his professional advice required by his job, generally kept his thoughts to himself. Koskinen, on the contrary, felt he had to take up the challenge to the Finnish ideology and democratic way of life. After all, he was about to risk his life with his mission to preserve and protect that ideology and democratic freedom. If the ideas expressed by Petri Hiltunen were to spread and prevail, he could possibly die for nothing.

So Koskinen countered, "Petri, at what expense and cost to the human race does this Soviet orderliness come?" Koskinen did not wait for an answer, but continued, "Aren't you aware that hundreds of thousands of Soviet citizens are being arrested, imprisoned and either shot or sent off to so-called labor camps? Don't you know that fear is the basis for the apparent orderliness of their society? Don't you know from all of the reports that people in the Soviets go to bed not knowing if there will be a midnight knock on their door by the police who will cart them off to a potentially, almost certain disappearance? Do you admire that sort of condition? Would you want Stalin to come into Finland and have his soldiers and police impose that kind of rule on us?" Koskinen stared sternly at Hiltunen and awaited an answer. Hiltunen remained silent for a few moments, but knew that he had to justify his remarks.

Finally, Hiltunen replied, "It is my understanding that no one who obeys the law in the Soviets need fear a knock on the door. It is only those who conduct themselves in such a way as to threaten the existence of the State."

At this, even the quiet Mikko jumped into the conversation. "That is not true, Petri, and you know it. In the Soviets, you can get a knock on the door for no reason at all, perhaps because some relative in the next town or province said something that some neighbor reported to the police that the neighbor felt was against the government or because the neighbor wanted some revenge against the relative. In the Soviets, you're accountable not only for yourself but for anyone connected to you, however remotely." Mikko said no more, but looked incredulous and disgusted with Hiltunen.

Hiltunen for his part smiled and said, "Well, I guess I'd better drop the subject. I don't find much sympathy here. But, what I was really trying to say is that both systems have their advantages and disadvantages."

Koskinen thought that was a pretty weak retreat, but did not persist in the discussion on the subject. But from that time on he felt uneasy about Petri Hiltunen and whether he could be fully trusted.

During the relatively short trip to Leningrad the Russian guide overseeing the Finnish delegation appeared only once at the compartment occupied by Koskinen, Korkala and Hiltunen. The guide entered the compartment and, uninvited, sat down on the empty bench next to Koskinen. The three Finns had no idea of what to expect of the guide.

In impaired and adulterated Finnish, the guide spoke. "You all go to Moscow on a trade mission?"

"Yes," replied Koskinen.

"What you want to sell to Russia?"

"We hope to buy and sell." It was Koskinen who again replied. He was being cautious in not saying any more than politeness required. In the Soviets, Koskinen reasoned, saying as little as possible to government agents would avoid being trapped into conflicting statements and creating suspicions.

"You know, I like Finland and I like the Finns," the guide continued. "I was in Finland a few years ago. Very beautiful country. Very beautiful women, too." The guide rolled his eyes and puckered his lips to form a kiss. The three Finns nodded in agreement, but said nothing, riveting their attention on the guide.

"You know," the guide said, "when Stalin takes over Finland, I shall come and make my home in Finland. That would be nice, wouldn't it?" The guide looked around at all three of the Finns.

Mikko spoke up. "Yes. We would welcome you and your countrymen with our arms."

Koskinen tried to contain a chuckle at the double-entendre. Later, he would mention to Mikko that he appreciated the use of the word "arms."

"You did mean 'firearms,' right, Mikko?"

"Yes, of course," Mikko replied with an air of satisfaction. "However, my comment was wasted. The dumb Russian didn't get my point. He thought we would actually welcome him."

The guide said, "Thank you, thank you, comrades." His heavy jowls seemed to tremble with excitement at the thought of living in Finland.

Koskinen was puzzled by the Russian's sudden loquacity. There was this gruff, stern, cold and taciturn official who had met them at the custom building and accompanied them to the train now demonstrative and voluble. Quite a turnabout, Koskinen mused. Koskinen saw this as an opportunity to get some information from the man, still using precaution, however. He could not be sure of the guide's motive in showing friendliness.

"How can you be certain that Stalin wants to come into Finland?" Koskinen asked. "We are a small country. We are not a threat to the Soviets."

"It is a rumor," the guide replied. "In our foreign service department we hear things that others do not hear about. Even in our department it is difficult at times to distinguish fact from rumor. Maybe, the head of the department knows but he usually doesn't pass the information down to us. So, it is only a rumor." The guide shrugged to indicate that there was no need to talk about it further.

Koskinen persisted. "Russia is a very great country. Why would you want to leave it to live in Finland?"

The guide was quick to respond. "The Finns don't have black limousines." The guide gave a sardonic grin. Koskinen knew instantly what the Russian meant. It was a subtle reference to the police coming to one's home in the middle of the night and arresting one or more of the occupants to be taken away in a black limousine automobile for questioning.

Petri then joined in. "Today you were only few meters from the Finnish border. You could easily walk across into Finland."

"I cannot do that." The guide shook his head in frustration. "I have a wife and two children in Leningrad." The Finns understood that the family would almost certainly suffer grave consequences if the guide defected.

"Why are you telling us this?" Koskinen asked abruptly and still mystified at the unexpected and unusual discourse.

The guide looked disconsolate and was silent for a few moments. Koskinen sensed that the Russian was seeking an offer of help from the Finns. Before the Russian could answer, Koskinen interjected. "You must know we cannot help you. We are here on a trade mission from our government. We are limited to that." The guide nodded his understanding.

"I have already said too much," the guide said. "I must be going. I thank you, comrades." He stood up and prepared to leave.

Koskinen stopped the man by inquiring, "I will probably remain in Russia somewhat longer than these other gentlemen here. If I get to Leningrad, how do I reach you?"

"You can call the foreign service branch in Leningrad and ask for me. My name is Leonid Petrof. If they ask why you want me, you tell them I was good guide on this trip and you need a guide in Leningrad. Perhaps they will assign me to you, but there is no guarantee." The guide then left the compartment.

"What do you make of that?" Petri asked of the other two.

"It's quite strange behavior for a Russian agent," observed Koskinen. "I think we have to be very careful. It might be some sort of trap. You never know in Russia."

The three Finns sat in silence for a considerable time, mulling over the meeting with the Russian guide. Koskinen filed the experience in his mind with the thought that perhaps some day he might make some use of it.

The train clattered, groaned, and swayed on its run to Leningrad. It stopped frequently at isolated groups of houses along the road for some purpose for which the Finns had no interest except to brace themselves for a sudden and back-wrenching lurch in starting up again. Koskinen mentioned to his companions that the Russian train stock was just another peril that one had to face when coming to the Soviet Union. The others agreed.

As the train drew closer to Leningrad, Koskinen began to think more about Elena Marikova. She was never very far from his thoughts most of the time. She lived in Leningrad with her mother and he wondered if she was at home at this time. He was tempted to try to telephone her home when he arrived in Leningrad. Although his desire was great, he decided against it. To call her could put her at risk if government agents had her telephone line tapped as they might because of her position as an interpreter. Calling might very well jeopardize his mission by alerting the authorities to his possible interest beyond that of trade. The agents would wonder why he was telephoning one of their government's employees. This was Russia where, as Koskinen knew, everyone was regarded with suspicion. Conduct, which Finns looked upon as normal and usual behavior in a free society, was viewed all too often in Russia as abnormal and unusual and subject to severe scrutiny by the authorities. Maybe, Koskinen pondered, maybe that explained why their guide, Leonid Petrof, broke down and confessed to wanting to live in Finland. He may have reached a point, however temporary, where he was fed up on the rigid strictures of Soviet society and his yearning to be free was a force greater than the fear that normally inhibited his expression of opinion. Like many others who visited Russia, Koskinen thought, "How can people live like this?"

Although Finland lived under Russian rule for about one hundred years before getting its independence in 1917 when the Bolsheviks under Lenin released the Finns, Finland, under the Tsars had been generally autonomous. The Tsars had not been repressive for the most part. So Finns were familiar with a sense of freedom much longer than the twenty-two years since independence would indicate.

The train finally pulled into the rail terminal of Finljandskij near the mouth of the Neva River in Leningrad. The guide, Petrof, announced to the Finnish delegation that they would have to get off the train and walk to another that would take them first to the Moskovskij station and then on to Moscow.

"I will take you to the Moskovskij terminal and then another guide will be with you to Moscow."

With luggage in hand, the delegation followed Petrof and, what seemed to some in the group, an interminable walk, arrived at the transfer train. The advice from Petrof was that the transfer train would leave in about an hour. Koskinen and the others decided that they would catch up on a quick nap, sitting up, of course. Koskinen awakened from a shallow doze when the train lurched as it started up on its circular trip to the Moskovskij terminal. There the group was again instructed to get off and proceed to the train on the Moscow line. This unanticipated transferring caused considerable grumbling from members of the delegation who were under the impression that the train they boarded at the Russian customs near Terijoki would take them to Moscow without having to change trains.

At the new terminal, Petrof turned the travelers over to the new guide. "This is Maxim Timashuk. He will be your guide to Moscow. He does not speak Finnish but some of you speak some Russian so you will get along, I'm sure. I now say goodbye to you. Enjoy the rest of your trip." As he turned to leave, Petrof's eyes rested momentarily on Koskinen. Koskinen got the impression that Petrof was conveying a message of friendliness.

Having been assured by Petrof that the train for Moscow would not leave for another forty-five minutes, the members of the delegation went to a kiosk in the station where some simple food and drink were available. They gathered around a large wood stove for warmth while eating and joking about their experiences on the trip up to this point. Finns, as a people, are, generally, serious, reserved and laconic. However, they are quick to see humor in an otherwise stressful circumstance. And they laugh easily. The new guide, Maxim, who had accompanied them and who understood nothing of what the Finns said, stood by unsmilingly and seemingly quite bored. Koskinen judged him to be in his late thirties and, unlike his predecessor Petrof, Maxim was short and thin of body. His face was, likewise, thin with high cheekbones, a thin, aquiline nose that appeared to be disproportionately long and shaped at its end with a hook slightly less than that of a falcon. His upper lip and the sides of his mouth and his chin bore a narrow moustache and beard on the order popularized by Lenin in the latter stages of his tumultuous career. Maxim wore the traditional Russian fur cap which on his narrow face looked like one of the bulging, Byzantine towers on Eastern Europe churches.

As the group stood about the stove they were approached by a young woman and a young man. Koskinen had his back to the couple as they neared, but, noting the sudden, diverted gaze of some in the group towards whatever was behind him, he turned and saw the two young people.

"My god! Elena Marikova!" This was said solely to himself. But there she was. He was totally surprised. Nevertheless, he was elated and excited to see her. Koskinen immediately surmised that she had been assigned by her government department to interpret for the members of the Finnish trade mission. Elena saw Koskinen almost at the same time that he saw her. Their eyes met in mutual recognition, but Koskinen observed Elena shake her head ever so slightly, almost imperceptibly, to indicate that he was not to speak of or show any prior relationship between the two. Considering the circumstances, Koskinen would have wanted it that way. It was, he thought, less risky for both of them. He hoped there would be a time when they could be together in private.

But who was the young man with Elena. He wore a military uniform and appeared to hold some officer rank. To Koskinen, he was quite good-looking, well built, about six feet tall, rather dark complected, clean shaven and with a pleasant, friendly expression, certainly, not severe or intimidating.

Elena spoke up. "Gentlemen, I am Elena Marikova. I have been assigned by our Foreign Service Department to serve as an interpreter for your trade mission while you are in the Soviet Union. I shall be with you during conferences you have with our government officials and I shall be available at other times if there is a need for an interpreter or translator. I shall let you know how you can reach me." Elena paused to await any question from the group.

One of the members of the trade delegation asked, "Is the young officer who is with you also a part of the interpreter team?"

"No, he is not." She introduced the young man. "This is Lieutenant Sergei Valentnikov. He is a friend who is going to Moscow on a new assignment."

Koskinen became somewhat perturbed at this. The thought that someone else might be close to Elena was repugnant to him. He had a puerile feeling that he didn't want to share her with another man. However, his mind told him that it was ridiculous for him to feel this way. He was, after all, married and Elena was younger than he and single. She did, he knew, have a right to a life of her own and, realistically, had no obligation to him. Nevertheless, in spite of the impossibility of the relationship amounting to anything, Koskinen became aware that he had deep feelings for Elena. So he decided he would see her alone as soon as the opportunity arose.

As the train got underway to Moscow, Koskinen shared a compartment with two new members of the trade delegation, Eino Partola and Raimo Niemi. When they talked, it was primarily about matters of trade between Finland and the Soviet Union. Again, soldiers came into their compartment and searched every nook and cranny for whatever it was they were looking for. Koskinen could not figure that out. The new guide came around on occasion during the trip and looked in the compartment supposedly, Koskinen thought, to make a head count and to see that everything was normal. The guide never said anything and was not at all animated. He gave the appearance of someone who had a job to do and was doing it in a robotic manner.

The train made an agonizingly number of stops at villages along the route. To the trade group, the train seemed to gradually slow down several kilometers before coming to a stop and seemed to require more kilometers to get up to an acceptable speed only to have to slow down again to stop at another village. The jerking, jolting and clanging that accompanied the whole process while basically annoying to the Finns became a topic for disparaging and uncharitable joking as each stop became anticipated. The Finns were accustomed to the comparatively smooth operation of the Finnish rail system. The contrast between the Russian and their own was beyond parallel. Although the Finns were able to visit other compartments of their car, they were prohibited from venturing into other cars of the train. Occasionally, their guide would put in an appearance to seemingly check on them.

The guide, Elena and her friend, Lieutenant Valentnikov, occupied one of the compartments of the Finn's car. There were no other passengers on their car. The authorities, apparently, wanted no intermingling. Although Elena would have liked to have talked with the members of the trade mission, she thought it would be unwise. There would be time after everyone got settled in at Moscow and she could visit them at the Finnish Embassy.

It was during the casual visits among the members of the trade group that Koskinen had the opportunity to talk informally with the Finnish leader Juho K. Paasikivi, special envoy to Moscow, and Vaino Tanner, leader of the Social Democrats Party, who were leading the delegation. Both leaders were less a part of a trade mission and more on a diplomatic mission to dissuade Stalin from making impossible demands on Finland. Both were strongly opposed to making any concessions to the Soviet government demands that would involve Soviet troops in the Finnish mainland or that would mean ceding or leasing to the Soviets any area belonging to Finland. That position was the official position of the Finnish government and hence left little room for negotiating a compromise. The Finns were interested in buying time until the international conditions might present a solution to their dilemma. The events in Europe were rolling on and, from moment to moment, the decisions and actions of Adolph Hitler in Germany were producing surprises, consternation, and counteractions among the nations most closely affected. That included the Soviet Union.

About the time Koskinen was getting started on his mission, that is, February 1939, Great Britain was discussing with Poland and Rumania whether they should ask Soviet Russia to agree on mutual assistance among them in case Poland and/or Rumania were attacked by the German military. Eventually, Poland and Rumania decided against it since such an agreement, these governments felt, might only serve to provoke the very attack they feared. Furthermore, Prime Minister Neville Chamberlain of Great Britain was personally opposed to any cooperation with the Soviet Union. However, his Cabinet looked with considerable favor on forming an alliance with the Soviets. Interestingly, Stalin favored collaboration with Hitler to one with the other Western nations since he had the impression that the West was unreliable and unpredictable as well as weak in taking any aggressive action against Hitler's depredations.

The Finnish leaders were well aware of all these vacillations. Such irresolution's by the other nations played to the advantage of Finland. Nevertheless, they were not dreamers and recognized the threat to Finnish security posed by an inscrutable Russian leader, namely, Stalin who could strike at anytime it pleased him. Hence the urgency of Koskinen's mission.

The three men, Koskinen, Paasikivi and Tanner, were standing, informally, in the car passageway just outside the doorway to the leaders' compartment. They were merely exchanging pleasantries and trivia conversation. Koskinen had introduced himself again using his pseudonym, Antti Salonen. He thought they might have forgotten who he was since the initial meeting of the group in Helsinki.

"Oh, we know who you are, Herr Salonen." Tanner smiled knowingly, leaving the impression with Koskinen that they were aware of his true personage.

Koskinen thought he would use their visiting together as an opportunity to get some information perhaps useful to his mission.

"Will you gentlemen be seeing Stalin during this trip?"

"We hope so," replied Paasikivi. "After all, a personal conference with him might bear results which we could not get from his foreign minister, Maxim Litvinov. However, we never know. In the past, Stalin would put in an appearance at our consultations or he would not. At the occasion of his presence he most often would say very little but, at least, we could observe his reaction to what was being said."

"In addition to trade issue discussions, would it be possible to include me in your more diplomatic meetings?" Koskinen asked.

Both Paasikivi and Tanner understood the reason for the question. They knew Koskinen was representing Intelligence covertly.

"We shall see what we can work out. We'll be available at our legation to decide the matter," Paasikivi replied.

"Yes, perhaps we can talk more there," Koskinen added.

"Probably." Paasikivi indicated by his expression that the matter could be dropped for now. They continued their lighter conversation for another few minutes. Koskinen excused himself and walked to the compartment occupied by the guide, Elena and the Lieutenant. He wanted to just look at Elena again.

Koskinen saw Elena reading a book of some kind and the guide and the Lieutenant appeared to be sleeping. Elena looked up when Koskinen appeared in the open entrance. She looked quickly at the other two occupants of the compartment and verified that they appeared to be sleeping. She put a finger to her lips to indicate that Koskinen was to remain silent. Then she quietly and carefully arose so as not to disturb the sleepers and motioned to Koskinen to go down the passageway. Still holding the book, she followed him a short way and joined him where he had stopped.

"Antti, I cannot talk with you very long. I should not be seen talking to just one person in your group. It will arouse the guide's suspicions."

"How about the Lieutenant?" Koskinen asked.

"No, he's alright. There is no risk from him. I'll explain to you some other time, not here. Please don't try to contact me. I expect to be at the Finnish Embassy from time to time. I'll be able to talk with you there. Do you understand? I still think you're a dear. We'll work out some arrangement for privacy. Just leave it to me for the time being." Elena gave Koskinen a warm smile. "I must go back now." She turned and left, but not before giving his hand a gentle squeeze.

Koskinen felt elated by what Elena had said. He knew he would be impatient until she came to the Finnish Embassy. He returned to his compartment and relaxed in his seat with his thoughts totally on Elena.

The rail trip from Leningrad southeast to Moscow some six hundred and sixty-six kilometers should normally have taken about ten hours considering frequent stops at villages along the line. Instead, the journey consumed almost forty hours. To Koskinen and his contingent of Finns it seemed that almost every half-hour there was a major halt and prolonged delay. This was accompanied by, apparently, rail employees running about outside and shouting to one another. There was the usual and customary clanging and jerking of the train as it backed up, moved forward and backed up again. At a place called Bologoye about halfway to Moscow, a conductor came through the car occupied by the Finns. Koskinen stopped him for a moment. In the rudimentary

Russian that he was able to use, Koskinen asked, "What is the trouble that we stop so often?"

"Repairs, repairs," replied the conductor. He too showed exasperation. "Something always breaking down on these trains. Every trip is like this. It's terrible. I apologize." The conductor then moved on.

About then, Vaino Tanner was walking down the passageway to stretch his legs. He overheard Koskinen's question of the conductor. He stopped at Koskinen's compartment.

"Ha! You are wondering why we are stopping so often. The conductor is right. Repairs. Let me tell you why these constant repairs. It is the result of Stalin's purges over the past few years. He has arrested and either imprisoned or shot almost all the older and experienced railway personnel. The people who knew how to operate and maintain the rail lines have all been liquidated. In their places have been installed inexperienced people who know little about running a railway."

"Why were the rail people arrested?" Koskinen asked.

"Why is anyone arrested in the Soviet Union?" Tanner replied rhetorically. "The charges were usually 'sabotage' or 'intent to sabotage' the rail lines. The rail lines in the Soviet Union are near collapse. All because of Stalin's phobia about almost everyone being a threat to him." Tanner then advised, "Be patient. We'll get to Moscow eventually."

At the City of Kalinin on the Volga River, everyone on the train was ordered off and directed to another train. The one they had been on had its locomotive break down.

Kalinin was the last leg of the trip. Relatively, it was not far from Moscow. While the Finns waited for the replacement train to get organized, they seized the opportunity to buy some food at the kiosk at the station. It was the usual hot soup, dark Russian bread and cheese. Food had not been available on the train they had just left. Consequently, the travelers were dependent on kiosks situated at certain station stops. It seemed to the Finns that the national meal in Russia was hot soup, bread and cheese. Coffee, also, was generally available.

The Finns, however, did not complain. They could plainly see why the food fare was so limited. All along the way to Leningrad and to Moscow, Koskinen and his teammates passed village after village containing run-down dwellings very much in need of repair. Frequently at train stops, the villagers or some of them, had gathered at the station or platform that acted as a station and had stood silently and morosely watching the train and its passengers. The peasant villagers generally wore drab and somewhat tattered clothing. To Koskinen all of the Russian natives he saw on the trip seemed to be in poverty. He could understand why even the operators of the kiosks had little to offer in the way of food. Koskinen had a great feeling of sympathy for these Russian peasants. He knew they were victims of a vicious system of unfeeling, inhumane government both under the Tsars and the Communist rulers. He knew that these people in the villages had virtually no control over their lives. Koskinen contrasted these conditions with those of the Finns in Finland with their prosperous farms and their democratic institutions. He didn't complain about the soup, bread and cheese. If he wearied of the monotony of the food, he nevertheless knew it was only a temporary discomfort. The Russian peasants had to deal with the tediousness of their meals as a permanent condition. Koskinen felt grateful to be a Finn. He understood that if he were to succeed in assassinating Stalin, the plight of the Russian peasant would not change. There would always be someone else to oppress them. The assassination would benefit Finland, not the Soviets, and the benefit to Finland, Koskinen understood, was the sole reason for his mission.

Arriving at the Moscow station, the Finns with their omnipresent Russian guide entered the station building. While alighting from the train, the Finns observed about two or three Russian policemen dragging a man out of a car of the train. The man was being held by one officer on each arm, while the third officer led the way through the people on the station platform. The fellow being arrested was resisting and yelling. The police proceeded to beat him on the face with their fists in an effort to control him. He soon became a bloody mess. The guide to the Finns looked at the spectacle and shrugged his shoulders to indicate that there was nothing to do but to proceed into the station house. Other people coming off the train or those already on the platform merely looked and then ignored the situation, hurriedly walking away.

Koskinen was amazed that not one person tried to intervene on behalf of the hapless fellow. Koskinen thought that if all the Russian people were like those who showed no indignation at the brutality being exercised, then surely the intimidation of the populace was complete. But the thought occurred to him that somewhere in Moscow and its environs there must be someone or some group that was ready to protest or rise up against this repressive regime. Human beings have always revolted, eventually, against a tyranny that sought to shackle them physically as well as mentally. The revolution in 1917 of the Bolsheviks, the Mensheviks, and the Trotskyites against the Tsarist system was a prime example of this. So reasoned Koskinen.

Inside the station, the Finns gathered around their guide who proceeded to return their passports to them and then directed them to administrative officials who would stamp them after a cursory examination of the information in the passports. The guide without further word then departed. The group was left to arrange their transportation to the Finnish Embassy. They managed to bribe with some extra rubles a couple of grubby-looking taxis to take them to the Embassy. On the ride to the Embassy and for several days thereafter, Koskinen was haunted by the episode of the fellow being arrested and beaten at the train station. Although he had witnessed much violence in his lifetime, for some reason Koskinen was especially troubled and offended by the incident.

Arriving at the Embassy in the morning, Koskinen, as did others of the entourage, spent the first day washing in the Embassy sauna and resting from the trip. Koskinen shared a room with Eino Partola, one of the members who occupied a rail car compartment with him on the trip from Leningrad to Moscow. Partola was a congenial fellow and Koskinen had come to like him while on the journey through Russia. Partola was considered to be a specialist in the foreign trade department in the ship building industry of Finland. His expertise required that he be included in the trade mission since the Soviets were a substantial buyer of ships built in the Finnish shipyards. The Soviet government was woefully lacking in professional talent to build their own ships and, apparently, had little interest in promoting the industry. The Finns, for example, had established a worldwide reputation in building quality icebreakers, that is, ships that could effectively and efficiently open up waterways otherwise frozen over during the winter months of the northern climates. Ice breakers, warships, large freighters, fishing vessels, cruise ships and ferry boats in use in the Soviet Union were primarily produced in Finland and sold to the Soviets. Consequently, the Finnish government felt that its shipbuilding ability was an important bargaining chip when dealing with the Soviets on most any issue between the two countries. Koskinen and Partola talked about this on several occasions during their time together.

When Partola inquired of Koskinen, (Antti Salonen) what his function was in the trade mission, Koskinen replied that his interest was to develop contacts with the commercial attaches in the Embassies of other countries in the hope of creating a means of interchange of information on trade issues regarding the Soviets and the respective countries. That is, establishing a sort of clearinghouse of information for the benefit of all concerned countries. The answer seemed to satisfy Partola.

Two days after Koskinen arrived at the Finnish Embassy he saw Elena Marikova in a conference room of the Embassy talking with Paasikivi and Tanner, the leaders of the trade mission. Koskinen was excited to see her. He had been thinking of her often but had not expected her visit to the Embassy this soon after arriving in Moscow. Elena saw Koskinen as he hesitated a moment at the open door to the conference room, but she gave no sign of recognition as far as Paasikivi and Tanner would notice. But her quick glance at Koskinen told him that she would like to see him before she left the Embassy. There is a sensitivity between two individuals in a vibrant relationship that, inexplicably, allows them to convey thoughts and to communicate without having to utter a sound. This, quite graphically, was the case just experienced between Elena and Koskinen.

Koskinen proceeded to the reception room and sat down to await Elena. No one else was in the room and he started to read a magazine to occupy his time. The words in the magazine blurred as his mind wandered off to anticipate Elena's arrival. After an interminably long approximate half-hour, Elena walked into the room, smiled warmly and extended her hand to Koskinen as he quickly arose from his chair. He reciprocated in grasping her hand, whereupon they embraced and kissed. The hugging was but for a few moments as both realized that the reception room was not an appropriate place for demonstrating a physical expression of affection.

"I have missed you, Timo." They both looked deeply into each other's eyes as if to see through them into a sparkling tunnel leading to the soul and to emotions for expression of which words were completely inadequate.

"I have missed you more than you know, Elena." Koskinen, still holding Elena's hand, led her to the sofa chair in the room. "Perhaps we can sit and talk here for a while. Do you have time?"

"Yes, of course. I am not scheduled for anything other than having the conference here."

"If I may ask, what was the reason for the conference with Paasikivi and Tanner?"

"Our foreign trade department here in Moscow asked that I come out to establish a schedule for meetings between your people and ours. You have your own interpreter but our department wants me to be involved at least for translation purposes. Apparently, they don't trust your interpreter to interpret correctly. I think that they're afraid your interpreter will put his own agenda, whatever it might be, on translations and thereby corrupt the negotiations. I don't agree with them, but they make the decisions." Elena shrugged as if to say, 'she couldn't really care one way or another.'

Elena then said, "Timo, I called you Antti on the train. I was aware that you wanted me to refer to you with that name when we were in public."

"Yes, you did right, Elena. That's my pseudonym and it must be used whenever you and I are not alone together, even here among the Finns."

"Which leads me to ask, Timo, why you have to have a pseudonym?"

"It is because my mission here must be kept secret. It is known only to a handful of people."

"Can't you reveal it to me?" Elena inquired.

"Elena, even though I feel very deeply and close to you, I have known you only a very short time. How could I really know if you might not be an agent of the police and inform them of my mission. I don't want to offend you, but I have to be real cautious." Koskinen showed that he was disturbed by having to assume two conflicting roles, one of not endangering his mission, the other to show that he trusted Elena. It was a difficult situation for him to be in.

"What about your friend, the Lieutenant?"

"Timo, he is just a good friend of mine. In fact, his family and mine were long time and close friends. I have virtually grown up with Sergei. If you are asking if we are lovers, no, we are not. He is of no risk or danger to you. He is one of us."

Koskinen was startled. "What do you mean, 'one of us?'"

"Timo, even though you seem reluctant to confide in me, I'll confide in you. I understand your doubts about me, even though I think that you should have no doubts knowing how I feel about you."

"The difference, Elena, is that in confiding to me, you can feel assured that I am not going to the Russian authorities and report what you told me. My objective is the welfare of Finland. In your case, you may have the welfare of Russia in mind when I confide in you. That's the difference. I really don't want this conflict to come between us. I'd like to keep our relationship on a personal basis rather than a professional one. To me, it is not important whether we confide in each other or not regarding professional matters."

"But, it is important to me, Timo, because to me, as a woman, I want and need your trust completely and in all matters. In the hope that I can make you understand that you can trust me, I am willing to confide a matter to you that I would not reveal to any other person whom I didn't know for a while. Do you understand, Timo, I want you to trust me."

"I do understand, Elena. What is it, then, that you want to confide in me?"

Elena moved closer to Koskinen and in a low voice, almost a whisper, she said, "Timo, I am a member of an underground group that wants to overthrow or get rid of Stalin. Lieutenant Valentnikov is also a member of the group."

Koskinen drew a deep breath and the blood drained from his face when he heard this.

"My god, Elena! You are telling me the truth?" Koskinen was in a state of disbelief, if not of shock. This lovely, beautiful young woman a member of the underground and constantly in danger of being unmasked with all of its unthinkable horrors.

"Elena, I find this hard to believe and accept but if it is true, then I have even more respect and admiration for you. I promise your confidence will not be violated. You can trust me on that. But, I don't think we should go any further in discussing this right now and here. Can we meet somewhere, just you and I, in privacy? Perhaps some out of the way hotel?"

"In Russia, Timo, there is no such thing as an out of the way hotel. The NKVD has every hotel and hotel room monitored with some sort of listening or recording devices. I have a better suggestion. I have friends, a couple, husband and wife, who will let us use their apartment. They both work during the daytime, so we'll have plenty of privacy. They are members of our underground group. I have a key to their apartment which we have used from time to time for meetings between two or three of our group; no large numbers."

"That sounds just fine," Koskinen commented. "When and where?"

"Tomorrow, sometime about eleven in the morning. You will have to take a bus there. An Embassy limousine or even a taxi might just stir some curiosity in the neighborhood, something we don't want or need."

"Where is the apartment?" Koskinen asked.

"I cannot draw you a map or write out instructions for obvious reasons if you are stopped and searched. You are to write nothing. Just listen and remember. You are now on Kropotkinski Street. You will walk a short distance to Komsomolski Avenue and get the number twelve bus going southwest to Tolstovo Street. The bus driver will call the name out. You get off there and walk two blocks to Number 963, the number of the apartment building. You go into the vestibule and you press the button for Apartment 227. I will be there to let you in. If I don't let you in within a few moments, then leave at once and walk back to the bus line and take a bus back to the Embassy street. I always say, 'anything can happen.' So we have to always be on the alert and adjust our actions as circumstances require. If you have any suspicion that you are being followed, just keep on walking as if you are a tourist and gradually head back to the bus. I will understand and I'll be in touch later with you."

Elena arose from the sofa and prepared to leave.

"What are the names of the couple who own the apartment?" Koskinen asked.

"You need not know now," Elena replied. "I'll tell you when you are at the apartment. Just remember, Tolstovo Street, Building 963, Apartment 227."

Elena was wearing a very plain but well made and stylish dark brown checkered suit. To Koskinen, as he eyed her, she looked stunning and appealing.

"You are wondering why I am not wearing the usual Russian dress that is drab and looks like a sack cloth," Elena chuckled.

"Well, even if you were wearing a sack cloth, you would look good to me," Koskinen bantered.

"I bought this suit in Finland when I was there on the trip during which you first met me. I am wearing it to show my affinity for things Finnish."

"Good for you," Koskinen said laughingly.

Elena donned her coat and fur cap, gave Koskinen a quick kiss and left. Koskinen immediately felt lonely and looked forward to the next day when he would see Elena again.

At dinner at the Embassy that evening, Finnish Ambassador Peltonen sauntered over to the table occupied by Koskinen and some of the others of the trade mission and addressed the group. "Gentlemen, we are expecting the American Ambassador Harrison Hayes and a couple of the American trade mission people here for dinner on March 13. Please keep that evening free. The purpose of the get-together is to get acquainted and to discuss possible common trade issues and possible cooperation on those matters between our two countries. If you have any problem with being here, let me know sometime tomorrow. In the meantime, enjoy your evening." The Ambassador went to another table to repeat the announcement. Koskinen felt he could use the intervening days trying to learn more about the underground movement. The possibilities of working with the underground people to accomplish his mission were not lost on him. That night he slept little as he turned over and over in his mind all of the things Elena had said to him that evening.

At about 1015 hours the next morning, Koskinen left the Finnish Embassy for his rendezvous with Elena. He had informed the Finnish Ambassador's Aide, Kalle Nevakivi, that he would be going out for a while. He did not say where he was going and Kalle did not ask.

As Koskinen walked to Komsomolski Avenue to take the bus, he was mindful of Elena's caution to be alert to anyone whom he thought might be following him. Koskinen, from time to time, glanced quickly, almost unnoticeably, about him. There were a few people on the street and an occasional motor vehicle, but no one and nothing that stirred his suspicions. He understood, of course, that if someone was, in fact, following, that person would not be blatantly obvious. The police agent could be the middle-aged, frumpy woman wearing a babushka and carrying a market basket or the fellow dressed in working-man's clothing and, generally, unkempt in appearance. And it was very possible that a second agent could take up where the first left off in order not to create any suspicion. Koskinen quickly came to the conclusion that it was futile to worry about being followed. He would simply have to assume the risk and refuse to become paranoid about the problem. He would, of course, still use caution and still remain alert, but that was about all he could do.

The two people at the bus stop boarded the Number 12 bus when he did. A man and woman, middle aged, who seemed unrelated as far as Koskinen could determine. He asked the bus driver in the best Russian he could muster up to let him know when they reached Tolstovo Street. He would then see if either one or both of the passengers who got on the bus with him would leave. Also, Koskinen, however, knew that, in itself, would not mean that either one was an agent.

The neighborhood of this stretch of the bus route was one primarily of apartment houses with some street level shops on the main avenue. To Koskinen there was nothing attractive or distinctive about the buildings. All were drab and of the same light mustard color exterior plaster. Small, slender trees planted at infrequent locations along the Komsomolski Avenue were the only evidence of any attempt at landscaping.

"Tolstovo," the bus driver barked out as the bus pulled to a stop.

Both Koskinen and the man who had gotten on at the bus stop now got off. Koskinen decided to use a ploy that almost any child would use. Instead of going down Tolstovo Street, he walked down the main avenue with the man walking several meters behind him. When he had gone about a half block, Koskinen stopped suddenly and reversed his path and began walking back to Tolstovo Street. The man continued to walk along the avenue. Koskinen did not know if he was a police agent but if he had been he could hardly have done anything but continue in the direction he had been walking. Koskinen walked back until he reached Number 963 apartment building on Tolstovo Street. There were several pedestrians on the street, but they were of no interest to Koskinen. Who they were or what they were no longer mattered to him. His thoughts were on Elena. The admonitions of General Mahlgren not to get involved with a Russian woman under any circumstances primarily for security reasons, were not forgotten by Koskinen, just unheeded, ignored. Passion had replaced good judgment and common sense.

Koskinen pressed the button for Apartment 227. In a few moments the entrance door buzzer sounded and with a click the door opened. He walked up the stairs to the second floor of the three storied building. He saw Elena standing in the hallway outside the apartment. Walking down the hallway a short distance to Elena was, for Koskinen, like walking through a tunnel with a light at its end that spelled release from cares and stress.

Elena took Koskinen by the hand and led him into the apartment and closed the door. They embraced.

Elena whispered, "I'm so happy that you are here. I have been anxiously awaiting you."

Koskinen replied, "And I'm glad to be here with you."

They put their arms about each other's waist and walked to the living room where they both sat down on the large chaise lounge. For several minutes they engaged in amorous caressing with tender expressions of endearment.

Finally, Elena said, albeit reluctantly, "Timo, I think we should talk about a few things, don't you?"

"Yes, Elena, I suppose you're right." Koskinen didn't sound very convincing.

Elena moved slightly away from Timo and leaned back into the corner of the lounge so that they could talk more at arms length.

"Timo, I have confided in you about our underground movement. I would, of course, not have done so had I not had complete trust in you not to expose us. I have not talked with the leaders of our movement about disclosing this to you as I am a great risk even from our own members if information about us should get out to the wrong people through you." Elena looked directly at Timo and Timo thought her eyes had a rather hard and cold look so different from a few moments ago. But, he understood her fears and concerns. If he were in her position, he might have similar feelings of uncertainty.

"I understand, Elena. I want to again assure you that you can trust me. In a sense, I'm in your camp. I think we have the same goals." Timo talked calmly, quietly and, he hoped, reassuringly.

Elena continued, "Now, about you. Putting all that I know about you and what you have said, from time to time, I have come to the conclusion that you are here in Russia on some covert mission. The facts that you have a pseudonym, that you are with Finnish Intelligence and that you may stay in Russia after your trade group returns to Finland, all lead me to that conclusion." Elena paused a moment to see if Timo might dispute her conclusion. He did not. Elena then continued.

"Frankly, I would like to know why you are here in Moscow. I mean, truthfully, what your objective is. I am not trying to trap you, Timo. I am curious to know if perhaps we can be of help to each other. I mean, whether our underground and you may have some common purpose which, perhaps, can be coordinated."

Timo felt he was in a very uncomfortable predicament. Here was a young woman whom he loved, admired and respected, with whom he had been intimate and who had, with sincere trust, confided in him. How could he possibly not answer her under those circumstances? If he did not answer her question he would, in effect, be telling her he did not trust her. Yet, his mission was so important and so dangerous that he retained strong misgivings about telling anyone about his mission who did not already know about it in their official capacities and those were very few persons.

"Elena, let me answer you by saying that, yes, my mission is secretive at this point. I have been sworn by my superiors to not disclose that mission to anyone. Even the members of the trade group with whom I came to Russia do not know what my objective is. So, if I do not disclose it to you at this time, you are no exception. And please understand that it is not that I distrust you. I trust you or I would not be here even with my deep feelings for you." Timo stopped talking as he could see that Elena appeared somewhat crestfallen.

Timo went on. "Perhaps, we can approach it this way. Can I meet with your underground leaders or some of them? When I speak with them, meet them personally and get a better picture of what the underground is all about, then I am sure I can open up and reveal what my purpose is in being here in Moscow. Why don't you ask your leaders if they will agree to that? Frankly, I am anxious to meet with them. You can assure them that I am a Finn, that I am interested in protecting my country from any threats from the Soviet government and so I'm not going to give out any information about your group that might harm it or keep it from accomplishing whatever it is you want to accomplish."

Elena brightened up on hearing this.

"Yes, I think that can be done," Elena replied. "It might be the way to resolve your hesitancy. In fact, that might be accomplished sooner than you'd expect." Elena had a sly look on her face. Timo observed it, but failing to grasp its meaning, passed over it.

Elena glanced at the clock on the wall. "It's getting close to noon. I didn't have any breakfast and I'm getting a bit hungry. I'll make some sandwiches for us. Is that alright with you, Timo?"

"Yes, of course."

Elena arose and went into the kitchen. Timo followed her.

"By the way, Elena, when are your friends expected home?"

Elena answered while busying herself getting bread, butter and sausage from a refrigerator which had the appearance of being one of the first models made with its heavy, bulky refrigeration unit sitting atop the food containing box. The manufacturers name and place had long disappeared.

"The husband usually arrives here at about two in the afternoon. His wife about four-thirty."

"I probably should leave before the man gets home." Timo said this more in the form of a question than in an expression of intent.

"No, I wish you'd stay if you have the time. I'd like you to meet him and have him meet you since you know now that he is one of us."

"I'd be happy to meet him. What are their names? Can you tell me now that I'm going to meet him?"

"Yes. His name is Sholom Lozovsky. His wife's name is Fani. Her maiden name was Shtein."

"They sound Jewish. Are they Jews?"

"Yes."

Timo was silent, as if turning over in his mind what, if any, implication there might be in this information. Finally, he asked Elena, "Do you think they can be trusted?"

"You mean because they're Jewish?"

Timo felt uncomfortable in having asked the question, but having done so he felt compelled to answer. However, he had some subjective and inherent misgivings about taking Jewish people into his confidences. He had never had a personal adverse experience with a Jewish person. It was just something inexplicably intrinsic.

"Elena, I have friends and acquaintances who are in business and they have all told me that you cannot do business with a Jew on a handshake; that everything must be spelled out in writing, that they have loyalties only to their own people and certainly not to any Christians or Goyem as I believe they call them. So, you can understand my doubts. I hope I have not offended you by my question."

"No, you haven't." Elena looked at Timo and smiled reassuringly, "Sholom and Fani are fine people and completely trustworthy. There have been occasions when they have been severely tested and they have never betrayed our cause. You don't have to be concerned about them." Then Elena added, "Timo, I think I have come to love you. I would not expose you to a risk that would endanger you." Elena's voice and the expression in her eyes showed a deep tenderness that stirred a profound passion in Timo.

Timo, already standing close to Elena, put his arms about her, drew her to him and gently kissed her on the mouth. Elena responded willingly with her own amorous pressing of her lips to his while caressing the back of his head.

"Elena," Timo whispered softly, "you don't know how much I have missed you, how much I have longed to hold you and love you."

"I felt the same way with you, Timo."

They continued for a few moments to kiss, to hug, to caress, oblivious to everything but to their own feelings and of each other. Then, without a further word and as if with mutual assent, Timo led Elena from the kitchen to the bedroom. Sitting on the bed, they began to slowly remove each other's clothing. The flush of primordial ecstasy quickly loosened any inhibitions or restraints either Timo or Elena may have had. Their wants, their needs, their desires soon found divine expression in consummate pleasure.

Resting her head on Timo's shoulder, Elena said, "I should not do this, Timo. You are a married man. But I cannot help myself because I want you so much."

"Yes, Elena. I am married but I love you. I have given up trying to resolve or understand my conflicting feelings. When I am not with you, I think of you constantly. I said to myself, 'When I see you, I shall be your friend and not your lover,' but then when I am with you my resolve is as nothing, as you can see."

They lay quietly on the bed as if in meditation and savoring the intimacy with each other. Elena turned to Timo and, smiling, said, "Those sandwiches are getting dried up. And I'm hungry again. Let's get up and eat."

Timo chuckled at the abrupt change of subject and went into the kitchen where they ate, drank coffee and talked until 1315 hours.

"Sholom should be home soon," observed Elena, again glancing at a wall clock. "I think I should clean up the kitchen and straighten up the bed."

"I'll help you," Timo volunteered.

"Oh, no you won't. I don't trust you in the bedroom." Elena laughed at the intimation. Timo was amused and understood the hint. He replied, "I'll read the newspaper in the living room."

Shortly before 1400 hours, Timo heard a key being inserted into the entrance door to the apartment. He assumed and anticipated that it was Sholom Lozovsky. Apparently, Elena had heard it also and had gone to greet the man. Timo, from his position in the living room could not see into the entrance vestibule but he heard Elena say, "Sholom, there is someone I'd like you to meet." Elena, with Sholom at her side, walked into the living room.

Upon seeing the man, Timo was instantly surprised and shocked. He didn't wait to be introduced.

"Elena," Timo said in Finnish, "this is the gentleman who got on and off the bus with me this morning and who followed me down the avenue but had to continue on when I turned back."

"Yes, that's true." Elena seemed to enjoy her plan to take Timo by surprise.

"Sholom, this is Antti Salonen who is in Moscow with a Finnish trade group." Elena had not forgotten to use Koskinen's pseudonym.

"Antti, this is Sholom Lozovsky whose apartment this is."

Apparently Koskinen still had a perplexed look on his face. So, Elena felt it necessary to explain.

"Antti, Sholom accompanied you on your trip here without your knowing it. This was planned when I informed him that you would be coming to visit me at his apartment. This was not because we doubted or did not trust you. It was because we wanted to be sure that you were not being followed by the NKVD agents. If you had been, then Sholom would have warned you not to come here. We don't want to draw the attention of the police to this place. Do you understand?"

"Yes, it is quite understandable," Koskinen replied. "But how would Sholom know if I was under surveillance. I presume the NKVD don't wear identifying clothing or badges."

"Sholom has become an expert in sensing the presence of NKVD people. There are little things that give them away and that most people would not notice even if they were looking. He can explain this to you better than I can, perhaps at some later date. For now, Sholom is probably ready for some lunch. We can sit and talk while he is eating." Elena spoke in Russian to Sholom who nodded in agreement.

While they were sitting at the kitchen table, Koskinen had an opportunity to more closely observe Sholom Lozovsky. Even if Koskinen had not been told that Lozovsky was Jewish or had not been informed of his Jewish sounding name, Koskinen would have concluded that he was Jewish. To Koskinen there was something about a Jewish person that tagged him or her as being a Jew. Koskinen could not put his finger on specific characteristics that distinguished a Jew from others in the absence of Jewish religious adornments. As Koskinen often had remarked to his Christian friends, "It was just something about them."

Lozovsky was a man of medium stature, neither slim nor stout. His face was quite thin and angular with prominent cheekbones and a high forehead although where the top of the forehead ended and the top of his skull began was difficult to determine because the hairline had receded to such a degree that all the hair that remained formed a horse shoe design from long gray sideburns, up around the ears and then to the back of the head. As Koskinen would have expected in a Jew, Lozovsky's nose was conspicuously protuberant. But it was the eyes deeply set under bushy eyebrows that caught and concentrated Koskinen's attention. They were like pieces of black coal which had, as yet, not been touched by flame or fire; inanimate, devoid of expression, cold and so totally black that Koskinen was unable to perceive any pupil. Koskinen was used to judging people, for the most part, by what he could discern in the eyes. By that criterion, Koskinen was at a loss to appraise and categorize Lozovsky. Even Lozovsky's facial muscles seemed inert except while he was chewing his food. Lozovsky seemed such an enigma to Koskinen that he felt he should ask questions of the man in order to determine if he should disclose his true mission to him. But, first he asked Elena in Finnish, "Elena, how long has Mr. Lozovsky been involved with the underground?"

"To my knowledge, about two years," Elena replied.

"Why did he decide to get involved with the underground?"

"From what he has said, he was one of the many young Jews who joined the Revolution movement in its early stages even before the overthrow of the Tsar in 1917. As you may know, Jewish men and women alike were discriminated against and oppressed under the Tsarist regimes and they regarded Lenin's promise of equality for all workers and oppressed people as a means of freeing themselves of the biases and prejudices against them as Jews. However, he became disillusioned several years ago with the way Stalin was running things contrary to the basic principles of Communism. An added factor, apparently, that made him decide to join us was the arrest and disappearance from time to time of some of his friends and, especially, one of his nephews, a son of one of his sisters."

Elena paused and then said, "I think you should ask him if you want more information. I really don't know much more than what I have told you. I can translate for you." Elena and Timo had continued talking in Finnish and although Timo knew some Russian, he felt it was not adequate for lengthy conversations.

All this time, Lozovsky had continued eating and saying nothing. Occasionally, he would look at Koskinen and Elena conversing and then revert to looking down at his coffee cup. Koskinen judged Lozovsky to be in his late fifties which would place his date of birth in the early 1880's. Yes, Koskinen figured, he could have been involved with Lenin and Trotsky in the first years of the 1900's.

"Yes, I think your suggestion is well taken. I would like to ask your friend a few questions."

"And he may have a few questions for you," Elena added, indicating that there was some curiosity on both sides.

"Tell Mr. Lozovsky that I am on a very sensitive mission for my Finland government, that I may want to work with your organization, but before I reveal my mission and before deciding to become involved, I must know with whom I am dealing and therefore I'd like to ask him some questions. Ask him if he's willing to answer them." Koskinen continued to observe Lozovsky closely for any clues that might disclose his emotional nature.

Elena spoke for a few moments in Russian to Lozovsky. The latter nodded his head in affirmation and said a few words in reply while looking from Elena to Koskinen.

Elena turned to Koskinen. "He says he's willing to answer your questions although he reserves the right not to answer a specific question or questions."

"Good," Koskinen said.

Lozovsky went to the stove and poured himself another cup of coffee from the pot that had been simmering. He looked at Koskinen and then pointed to the pot in a gesture that Koskinen understood as asking if he, too, wanted more coffee. Koskinen thought that if he shared in drinking coffee together, it might help to relax the seeming stiff and hesitant relationship between the two of them, sometimes the result of a language barrier. Koskinen offered his cup to Lozovsky who, still unsmiling, poured the coffee.

To further soften the rapport, Koskinen spoke a few words in Russian in a friendly way. "Thanks, Mr. Lozovsky. The coffee is good. I hope you understand my situation. I do not speak a very good Russian. Elena will help."

Lozovsky nodded and Koskinen noticed a slight loosening of the man's facial expression evidencing some warming up.

Lozovsky went to a kitchen cabinet and got out a bottle. He turned to Koskinen and Elena. "You want vodka in coffee?"

Elena declined. "No, thank you, Sholom."

Koskinen, still pursuing a better rapport, said in Russian, "Yes, but just a little bit."

Lozovsky poured about a tablespoon full into Koskinen's cup and then what Koskinen thought was a very generous amount into his own cup. That, Koskinen thought, should help to relax Lozovsky. Lozovsky returned to the kitchen table and said to Koskinen, "What do you want to know?" The conversation that followed was in Finnish and Russian with Elena serving as interpreter.

"Mr. Lozovsky, you are a member of the underground movement to get rid of the Stalin government?"

"Yes," replied Lozovsky.

"Why did you join the underground?" Elena had already given Koskinen a brief overview of Lozovsky's reasons but Koskinen thought he should hear the details from Lozovsky himself.

"My joining the underground was not something that was an impulsive act. It was the result of many years of disenchantment with the Soviet government under Stalin." Lozovsky closed his eyes for a few moments as if he were revisiting and reliving the yesteryears of his life. Then he resumed his monologue.

"I must go back to my early times if you are to understand me." Lozovsky suddenly seemed eager to talk about himself, to unveil his past, to unburden himself of some unrequited deeds of bygone times.

Koskinen was not particularly interested in listening to a long dissertation of Lozovsky's past life, but he had asked a broad question and he now had little choice but to be attentive, at least for a while. To cut Lozovsky off might very well offend him and, furthermore, Koskinen reasoned, he, Koskinen, had wanted to loosen up Lozovsky and he had succeeded in doing so. So Koskinen could not really complain. Besides, he thought, Lozovsky just might reveal something of importance.

"Yes, go right ahead, Mr. Lozovsky," said Koskinen nodding his approval.

"I was born in Petrograd in 1879, March 2nd to be precise. My father was a small contractor for food supplies. Because he was Jewish he was constantly harassed and persecuted by the Tsarist police known as the 'Black Hundreds.' However, almost every Jew was, at one time or another, subjected to an anti-Semitic virulent form of abuse by the Tsar's authorities. Using the Jewish religious rituals and practices as a pretext, the Jews were accused of all sorts of crimes such as drinking the blood of Christians. The pogroms were horrible. Some Jews, in order to avoid this religious persecution, joined the Russian Orthodox church and displayed an icon on the outside of their homes. Thereafter, they were no longer persecuted. But my father would not do this as a matter of principle and so he and our family continued to be tormented by the Black Hundreds. I respect my father for this. He did not subvert his religious beliefs for expediency." Lozovsky paused and took a sip of his coffee. Elena asked him if he wanted it reheated. He said, "No." Koskinen had already emptied his cup while listening to Lozovsky.

"When Lenin came along with his ideas of equality of the masses and his appeal to overthrow the oppressive Tsarist government, many Jews, especially we younger ones, rushed to support him. He promised us a freedom we longed for but had never known under the Tsars. In fact, in 1903 I became a Bolshevik. I was a student at the Petrograd University and all of the Jews there, men and women alike, became active in the Bolshevik movement. I guess I became fairly well known to the leaders under Lenin like Lev Kamenev and Yakov Sverdlov because in 1905 I became a member of the Petrograd Bolshevik Committee. By 1912 I had become a member of the Central Committee and the Russian Bureau of the Central Committee. Stalin was a member also at the time. I got to know him quite well, at least I thought I had. Later, it came to me that I hadn't known his real self at all. I misjudged him completely. But I was not alone in this."

At this point, Koskinen looked at Elena and raised his eyebrows slightly that sent a message to her that she should advise Lozovsky to get on with his answer to Koskinen's question and to avoid a lot of detail.

Taking the hint, Elena addressed Lozovsky, "Sholom, Antti has only a limited time to spend with us. I think you should try to keep your answer as short as possible."

Lozovsky nodded. "I understand. I have just a little more ground to cover to give him an answer."

Lozovsky was disclosing more about the early events of the Revolution than even Elena had heard. Elena turned to Koskinen with an expression of astonishment. She said, "I find I am enthralled by his story. I would like him, really, to tell us more detail. I wish you could stay longer."

"Well, alright," Koskinen replied. "Let him go on."

Lozovsky continued. "You should know that if it were not for the Jews, the Revolution could very well have failed."

"Is that so?" Koskinen looked surprised.

"Yes, that is true. Almost all of the activists plotting with Lenin and later with Stalin to overthrow the Tsar were Jews. They provided the core of the intellectuals, the ideologists, the writers, the propagandists, the recruiters and even the instigators of violence where necessary. I personally knew many of them. There was Yakov Sverdlov and Lev Kamenev, whose name was really Rozenfeld, whom I have already mentioned. There was, of course, Lev Trotsky, a Jew, and also Grigori Zinoviev, Grigori Sokolnikov and a score of others." Lozovsky had changed remarkably from a very silent, taciturn person when he first met Koskinen in the apartment to now someone very garrulous, virtually talking himself out of breath. Koskinen had to admit to himself that it was an interesting articulation of a link to the past. But he was still waiting to know why Lozovsky joined the underground. Koskinen knew he had to exercise patience, either that or to politely leave. The latter, he realized, was inappropriate under the circumstances. So Lozovsky talked on.

"You should also know that it was also Jews who were primarily instrumental in arranging the arrest and ultimate death of the Tsar and his family. The Jews were Yanker Yurovsky, Lev Sosnovsky, Pinkus Vainer and Goloshchekin. They were all good Bolsheviks like me.

"I could go on and on describing how Jews permeated the whole structure of the Russian apparat from top to bottom, from confidants of Stalin to heads of the Cheka, the GPU and the NKVD police as well as the operators of Lubyanka prison where the tortures of people arrested took place. Yakov Agranov, Matvei Berman and Karl Pavker, all Jews, were prominent in the operation of that prison of no returns, the place of horrors.

"You would think that by appointing Jews to high places in the government and surrounding himself with Jewish advisors that Stalin loved Jews. In fact, towards the late 1920's and early 1930's, I became aware that Stalin was intensely anti-Semitic, but he never came right out and said so. But his actions of the last few years demonstrate his contradictory perversity. Almost all of the Jews I have named and many others I have not named have been arrested and shot on Stalin's orders in the last few years."

Koskinen interrupted. "But, Mr. Lozovsky, I understand that many non-Jews, that is, Russians, Ukrainians, and others have also been arrested and either executed or sent to labor camps. Would it not, therefore, seem that Stalin was not necessarily seeking out Jews for extermination? Wasn't it really indiscriminate persecution?"

"Yes, you could say that," Lozovsky replied. "But, the fact remains that most of the Jews in high places were demoted, then arrested and physically disposed of and their places taken by non-Jewish Russians."

"How is it that you survived?" Koskinen asked politely.

"A few of us old timers have been spared, that is, up to now," Lozovsky said. He did not show any visible signs of concern about his future. "Several years ago I saw what was coming. At the time I was teaching mathematics at a local public grade school. I resigned and took a job at a small factory here in Moscow running a tool machine. Stalin, not being well-educated himself, resented people better educated and I knew that it was just a question of time before university professors and school educators would feel his dislike. Some of that has already started. Some of my educator friends have disappeared.

"The trouble with Stalin is that he has always seen his government leaders and advisors as threats to his power. Therefore, he must get rid of them.

"He has done this with the military. Every high-ranking officer, from the General class to lower level officers, have been arrested and shot. So now we have no or few competent and experienced military officers to lead us if war comes to Russia. The Generals, you see, were threats to Stalin or so he imagined. A few years ago, more than forty thousand commander and junior officers were expelled. Those destroyed by Stalin were General Tukhachevsky, Uborevich, Yaker, Primakov, Kork, Yegorov, Dybenko, Blyukher, just to mention a few. Stalin, you see, is destroying the Communist Party and at the same time the very freedom from oppression which we Jews had fought for and for which we joined in the revolt against the Tsar. We Jews, today, are worse off than we were under the Tsars. We have nothing, no hope here in Russia." Lozovsky's scowl evidenced his bitterness as well as his determination to fight back. He reverted to his mood of silence.

Koskinen expressed a thought that had bothered him almost since Lozovsky had begun talking. "Mr. Lozovsky," he said, "would you have joined the underground if there was no anti-Semitism?"

Lozovsky regarded Koskinen and then smiled faintly. He quickly perceived that Koskinen (Antti Salonen to him) was testing his motives. Lozovsky thought for a long, perhaps cautious, moment. Then looking straightforward at Koskinen, he replied, "Probably not, Mr. Salonen." Lozovsky replied with a look of indifference to the effect his reply might have on Koskinen.

"So, you are in this because you want to save the Jews in the Soviet, is that correct?" Koskinen spoke with some testiness in his voice.

"Yes, I suppose you could say that," Lozovsky answered. "Is there something wrong with that?" Before Koskinen could comment, Lozovsky added, "You see, Mr. Salonen, I am no different from any of the great masses of people in Russia under the Tsars. Everyone, from peasants to small shop owners, from small town people to big city people, from Jews and non-Jews, we were all oppressed and neglected by the Tsars. The royalty cared nothing for the people, the ordinary people. But the Jews were especially oppressed and harassed. They wanted so badly to get away from the oppression and the oppressors. And, as I said earlier, Lenin gave us a promise and a hope of accomplishing that. Mr. Salonen, if Stalin is removed, it will benefit the Jews and if it benefits the Jews, it will also directly benefit the rest of the Russian people. I answered your question whether I'd be in the underground if there was no anti-Semitism. That is a silly question, if I may say so with no intention of offending you. There was and is anti-Semitism. And even if we get rid of Stalin, we Jews will still face anti-Semitic feelings. All getting rid of Stalin will do is to relieve the oppression against Jews and allow them the freedom to go about their lives and business without harassment. Do you understand?"

"Somewhat." Koskinen was not ready to concede acceptance in full of Lozovsky's reasoning.

"By the way," Lozovsky interjected, "now that I have disclosed myself to you, can you tell me the real reason you are here in Russia besides trade matters?"

Koskinen felt he had to answer. But he now felt comfortable in doing so. He felt assured that Lozovsky was honest and sincere and could be trusted. After all, the underground could very well be able to help carry out his mission. Koskinen had concluded that he could not carry it out without such help.

"I'm here, Mr. Lozovsky, to try to save Finland from being taken over by the Soviets and losing its independence and freedom."

Lozovsky saw immediately the similarity to his own motivation. "So, you are, in a sense, fighting for Finland as I am fighting for the Jews."

"No, not exactly," Koskinen argued. "Finland is a nation, a specific geographic and political location, a clearly delineated place on the world map. The Jews are not a nation. They are spread about the planet and living in many nations. Finland is not a culture, nor is it a religion. As a nation it contains within its borders many diverse cultures and religions. The Jews, wherever located, have one religion, with some division into sects. Their religion and their culture are intertwined. But, perhaps, this discussion of who is fighting for whom or what, should be dropped. It's of no consequence."

"Well, then," Lozovsky inquired, "how do you propose to save Finland?"

"I am on the same mission as your underground; by eliminating Stalin. It is my mission to find a means of accomplishing that objective. I would like to work with the underground. It must be accomplished as soon as possible."

"Do you have any ideas at all on how you will go about eliminating Stalin?" Lozovsky asked.

"I have some ideas," Koskinen replied, "but how effective or workable they are I do not as yet know. I have to get some information and form my plans based on what I learn may be opportunities."

"Alright." Lozovsky had again become more animated. "Either Elena or I will talk this over with some of our leaders with a view to inviting you to a meeting. That should not take more than a few days. In the meantime, Elena will remain your sole contact. By being able to visit your Embassy she is in a good position to act as liaison and to keep you informed." Lozovsky turned to Elena. "Is that alright with you?"

"Yes, of course," Elena replied, hiding her exuberance to the idea of acting as an intermediary to her lover.

"Then perhaps I should leave now," Koskinen suggested, feeling that nothing more could be accomplished at this meeting.

"Yes, but we must be careful," said Lozovsky. He arose from his chair at the kitchen table and asked Koskinen and Elena to follow him into the living room. Once there, Lozovsky went to one of the two windows overlooking the street and parting the curtains slightly studied the activity on the street.

"Hmm, I don't see anything suspicious. I think you can safely leave, Mr. Salonen."

Elena continued to translate. "Sholom wants me to remain here for a while after you leave. He thinks your being alone will attract less attention." She looked at her watch. "It is now 1515 hours. Sholom says the bus will arrive at the end of our street at Komsomolski Avenue at about 1530 hours. It will take you back close to your Embassy. If you leave now you will be able to catch the bus. I'll be in touch with you." Elena extended her hand to Koskinen and he took it and gave it a gentle squeeze. Elena smiled warmly.

Koskinen put on his coat and bid goodbye to both Lozovsky and Elena. As he stepped outside the door to the street he gave a quick, furtive look up and down the street. There were just an elderly couple walking slowly in a direction opposite to the one he would take to the Avenue. Other than those, the street seemed deserted. It was cold, damp and dreary outside and considerably more windy than when he had arrived. The wind blew against his face and he began to feel chilled as he walked hurriedly toward the intersection of the street with Komsomolski Avenue. He had a few minutes before the bus would arrive assuming it was on time, a risky assumption in Moscow.

Koskinen arrived at the bus stop and found no one else waiting. He felt somewhat relieved to be alone. At least, there was no one else who might be an NKVD agent. With his hands in his coat pockets, Koskinen pulled his coat more tightly about him. The sun was already beginning to go down and the chill seemed to get more penetrating. Ten minutes passed and still no bus. It was 1540 hours and Koskinen, knowing from what he had heard about transportation schedules being generally ignored by bus drivers, began to think that maybe the bus had arrived early and had gone on. Perhaps he should return to the Lozovsky apartment to telephone for a taxi. However, he quickly dispensed with that idea since the taxi driver would probably have to report to the NKVD where he had picked up his fares and where he had taken them. In spite of the fact that he had only been in Russia a short time, Koskinen had already found negative and not very complimentary ideas about how things were run in Russia. Most of the information he had even before arriving in Russia had been gleaned from casual remarks by those people in Finland who had either been in Russia or had talked to someone who had been. Koskinen could not, at the time, be sure that what he heard was true, an exaggeration or false. So, uncritically, he accepted what he heard as fact. Time and experiences would prove what was true of Russia and what was not. Koskinen had just about decided that he had missed the bus when he heard its horn and saw it approaching his bus stop. He stepped slightly out into the roadway and waved to the driver as the bus drew near. He did not want the driver to not see him and not stop. That would have been a catastrophe. Koskinen's fears and concerns about the bus dissipated immediately when the bus stopped and he was able to climb aboard. He told the driver where he wanted to get off and then relaxed in one of the seats. There were only a half-dozen other passengers and these seemed quite indifferent to his presence on the bus.

During the return ride Koskinen turned over in his mind the whole episode at Lozovsky's apartment. He thought of Elena, what a very dear and lovely young woman, and thinking of Elena he coincidently thought of Anna, his wife. He wondered how she and his boys were doing. A sense of guilt came over him. He had been unfaithful to her and he felt he had forsaken her. He loved Anna. He knew that. He should never have allowed himself to get involved with Elena. His involvement, Koskinen could foresee, could lead to complications and disarray in his personal life. Nevertheless, he was in too deep and there was no way out. Elena was now intricately a part of his mission. At this point he could not abandon Elena without abandoning his mission regarding Stalin. Besides, he really did not want to give up Elena. He loved her too. And Elena was here in Russia and Anna was in Finland. If he was careful, Anna would never know about Elena. Then Koskinen started to think about Lozovsky. The man intrigued him. Lozovsky was a complex character. Although Koskinen had come to feel comfortable about confiding his mission to him, there was still lurking in the back of his mind the persistent and perverse question of whether any Jew could be trusted completely. Even so, Koskinen realized, it was a risk he had to take if he were to penetrate the underground movement. He had concluded that if the underground people were well organized and determined rather than merely a patchwork of disconnected dreamers, then he was in luck to have perhaps found a means of accomplishing his mission to eliminate Stalin. It could be the answer he had been groping for in what, up to now, had seemed to Koskinen an almost insurmountable impasse.

Koskinen's musings on these matters were abruptly interrupted by the bus driver calling out, "Kropotkinski." Koskinen got up hurriedly and off the bus before the driver might decide to drive off because he didn't move fast enough to please the driver. Koskinen had settled earlier on the idea that one could not be sure of anything in Russia.

After the bus had departed and Koskinen had walked a few yards towards the Finnish Embassy he glanced quickly about for anyone who might appear suspicious. There was no one else on the street. Koskinen had been in Russia only a short time and yet he was already acquiring the mind-set of a native of the country. Almost since the moment he had crossed the border from Finland into Russia he had sensed the atmosphere of fear, suspicion and distrust that seemed to him to permeate the very fabric of Russian society. From all that he had seen and heard he had come to believe that he, too, had no choice but to trust no one and to be on his guard constantly. The thought that he had to live like that from day to day was abhorrent to him. The fear of government was totally absent in Finland. Koskinen understood clearly now, if he had not earlier, why his mission was so important to him, his family, his country. If the Soviet system came to Finland, life would become intolerable, unbearable. He must do what he can to see that it never happened.

As Koskinen neared the Finnish Embassy building, he heard the sound of an automobile approaching him from behind. He turned and saw a black limousine coming slowly along the street. It passed him and then stopped several feet ahead. As Koskinen drew alongside, a man in a heavy dark coat and wearing a typical Russian fur hat stepped out of the auto and motioned to Koskinen to stop. The man addressed Koskinen in Russian. Koskinen understood him.

"Sir, I beg your pardon. I am with the police. Can I talk with you a moment?" The man reached into his coat pocket and pulled out what appeared to be a shiny police badge and held it up for Koskinen to see.

Koskinen had stopped walking and, looking at the policeman, said, "Well, what is it that you want to talk to me about?"

The policeman replied, "We are looking for someone, probably a male, who we think lives in this neighborhood who has engaged in criminal conduct and you understand that we have to stop people in making our investigation." The policeman was friendly and courteous, but somewhat gruff. The policeman did not explain what the criminal conduct was and Koskinen did not ask.

Koskinen said with a shrug of his shoulders, "I'm sorry, but I cannot help you. I haven't seen or heard anything unusual."

In apparent disregard of Koskinen's disclaimer of information that might help, the policeman continued. "Could I ask who you are and do you have any identification?"

Koskinen regarded the policeman for a moment with some annoyance. "Yes, my name is Antti Salonen and I am with a Finnish trade delegation staying at the Finnish Embassy. This is my passport for identification."

The policeman examined the passport which Koskinen had handed to him and turned a few pages slowly. Looking at the photograph of Koskinen (Salonen) and then at Koskinen, the policeman smiled and commented, "You are better looking than in the photograph." He then returned the passport to Koskinen.

"So, you are going to the Embassy?"

"Yes."

The policeman paused a moment and then looking at Koskinen, sharply said, "Could you tell me where you have been?" The policeman's voice had the sound of a command.

Koskinen retorted quickly and firmly, "That is none of your business!" He was becoming irritated at having been stopped and questioned.

The policeman's face flushed with anger, but he controlled himself and continued to speak politely. "It is our business when we are investigating criminal conduct." He was not used to being told to mind his own business.

"Well, I will not answer your question or any further questions. Now, if you please, I will proceed to the Embassy." Koskinen started to walk past the policeman.

The policeman persisted. "You know I could arrest you for your refusal to cooperate with a police investigation."

Koskinen stopped, turned and, looking directly into the policeman's face, said harshly, "Yes, you could arrest me, but you would be violating diplomatic rules if you did and that might provoke an international incident."

"So, will little Finland attack our mighty Russia if I arrest you?" The policeman's voice was sarcastic. Nevertheless, he apparently recognized that there was some truth to what Koskinen had said. "I will let you go this time, but we shall be watching you!"

"If that happens, our Ambassador will take up your harassment with your Foreign Department." Koskinen then strode away, leaving the policeman standing and visibly fuming.

Although he appeared unruffled by the encounter, Koskinen, inwardly, was shaken by the experience. He had no doubt that he had avoided a very ugly situation, one that very possibly would have destroyed his ability to carry out his mission. Had he been arrested and taken to police headquarters and questioned, the whole facade of his connection to the trade mission could have been exposed as spurious. And thereafter it could be expected that he would be under constant surveillance making it impossible for him to function in the necessary secrecy.

Koskinen was also aware that the police might watch him anyway. The Russian police did not need a pretext to do so. He had to be careful not to lead the police to the underground organization. The thought that he might unwittingly place Elena in danger and at the mercy of the NKVD frightened him. Koskinen decided he would tell Elena about the incident with the policeman when he next saw her. She should know about it so that she, too, could be wary and exercise caution. She might have some answers to the predicament.

At dinner at the Embassy that evening, Koskinen was noticeably quiet and given to very little talk with the other people at his table. Eino Partola, a member of the trade mission, finally addressed Koskinen using his pseudonym.

"Antti, I cannot help but notice how quiet and morose you are. Is there something wrong?"

"No," Koskinen replied with a forced small smile. "I was just reviewing in my mind some of the day's events. I am quite alright, thanks." Partola did not press the subject any further, but from time to time cast a worried look at Antti.

After dinner, Koskinen retired to his room rather than remain with the others to have an after dinner drink of Lakka liqueur and conversation. He lay down on his bed, stared at the ceiling while all sorts of thoughts poured through his mind. Elena, Anna and the children, Lozovsky, General Mahlgren, the Russian policeman, and back to Elena. How he wished she was lying next to him. He would find her so comforting. After about an hour and a half of this self-inflicted punishment, Koskinen arose and, still in his street clothes, went to the reception room where he found an old copy of the Sanomat newspaper to read, anything to dispel his chaotic thoughts and relieve his stress. He read a few lines about a railway accident near the port of Turku in southwestern Finland and then put the paper aside before finishing reading the article. His mind wandered back again to the same things he had thought about while lying in bed a short time before. For a moment he thought he would join the others in the dining room who were still drinking and talking. He could hear their laughter, but could not hear what they were talking about. Perhaps, he thought, a glass of vodka might calm his nerves. But, he gave up on the idea. He was in no mood for any conviviality. Besides, he felt completely exhausted. The brush with the Russian police had had a debilitating effect on him, more than he had at first realized.

Koskinen returned to his room and changed into pajamas and lay down once more on his bed. He pulled the bed covers over himself and in a short time fell asleep.

Later that night, he didn't recall the hour, he awakened abruptly and sat up in bed, his heart pounding. He had just experienced again the strange dream about the seagull. In his dream, he was walking on the farm of Anna's parents. The field of grain had been harvested a few days earlier and the residue left on the ground had attracted large numbers of seagulls from the nearby bodies of large lakes. The seagulls were flying about wheeling this way and that while all the time screaming at one another. Some of the birds were on the ground pecking at seeds and chaff. Koskinen, in his dream, saw a particularly large gull flying near him, close enough for Koskinen to see his red eyes staring at him. The gull for several minutes continued to swoop and dive and wheel, always drawing closer to Koskinen who had stopped walking to watch this bird. Suddenly, Koskinen heard a rifle shot and the large gull fell almost at his feet bleeding profusely from the breast and clearly staining the feathers bright red. Koskinen, in his dream, stepped back startled and then he saw the bird get to its feet and, with great effort, fly off a short distance when it quickly turned and flew with great speed directly at Koskinen. Koskinen could hear the resounding beat of the powerful wings and the rush of air as the bird dove at him, eyes piercing, mouth open screeching and his feet extended with large talons aimed at Koskinen's face. Koskinen threw his arms up to protect his face while shouting, "I did not shoot you." The bird's talons struck Koskinen's arms, ripping holes in the cloth and penetrating to the flesh.

The large seagull abruptly dropped to Koskinen's feet and, still bleeding, died. And as Koskinen looked at the bird, it seemed to evaporate and was no more. It was then that Koskinen sat up in a cold sweat. This was the second time he had had a dream about the seagull. If it had any significance, he was unable to explain it. He simply did not know its meaning. What did these dreams portend, if anything? Were they connected somehow to his mission? Koskinen lay back again on his bed, but remained awake for what seemed an agonizingly and interminably long time. It seemed to him that his day had been a series of danger signals. There was Lozovsky, the Jew, to whom he had confided his mission but with an innate feeling that maybe the fellow could not be trusted. Then there was the incident with the police officer who, when opposed, had become belligerent and threatening. And now the enigmatical and possibly symbolic recurring dreams of the seagull. Finally, weary and fatigued, Koskinen fell into a fitful sleep. In the morning when he arose, he was still exhausted both emotionally and physically. He recognized that if he was to be able to function and carry out his mission, he had to work at regaining his composure and his confidence by ridding himself of his fears and doubts. Elena might be of comfort, but he had to resolve these dilemmas himself. He began the process by eating a hearty breakfast of oatmeal, Russian rye bread, Finnish aamupala juusto or cheese and some fresh fruit

CHAPTER 8

After Koskinen left the Lozovsky apartment, Elena turned to Lozovsky and asked, "What do you think of Antti Salonen?"

Lozovsky pondered a few moments before answering. Elena, by her question, was compelling him to collect his perceptions and to consolidate them into conclusions and he was not certain that he was ready to do that.

Finally, "Elena, I have only known him a short time, but from what I have seen and heard, he seems to be someone who can be trusted." Lozovsky shrugged, indicating that was the best he could say. "What do you know about him?"

Elena then recited how she had met Salonen, their dinner together and their conversations. She said nothing about spending the night with him. If Lozovsky guessed that there was that sort of omission in her story, he did not express it.

Elena continued, "Antti did tell me that he is in Finnish Intelligence and that he had a mission beyond trade discussions with the Soviet authorities."

Lozovsky raised his eyebrows. "If that is the case, then I think we can trust him. If he is connected with their Intelligence, then he would not be a Finnish Communist or a Communist sympathizer. The Intelligence people would not have him in their department if he were."

"Yes, you're absolutely right. Antti told me that his sole purpose is to save Finland from being taken over by us, that is, by Stalin and his administration." Elena seemed relieved that Lozovsky had accepted Koskinen.

Lozovsky commented, "You know, Elena, his name is probably not Antti Salonen. The Finnish authorities would not send him on a serious and secretive mission such as he is on and not cover up his real identity. They'd want to make certain that we did not have a file on him provided by our agents in Finland. But, what his name is doesn't really matter as long as we know what his objective is in being here and that he can be trusted. Do you agree?"

"Yes, of course," Elena replied. She had no intention of disclosing Salonen's true identity and Lozovsky's dismissal of its importance assured her that it was not necessary.

"What do you suggest we do next?" Elena asked. She had her own idea, but wanted to hear from Lozovsky.

"I think we should discuss with some of our people whether we should have Salonen meet with them to determine how, if at all, we can fit him into our plans. Why don't you do that, Elena? You're more free to move around than I am. You can keep me informed. Is that alright with you?"

Elena nodded in agreement.

Lozovsky looked at the clock on the wall. "Fani will be home in a short time. Do you want to wait for her?"

"No, I think I'd better get back. I've been gone longer than I think is wise. You know, there is someone in every office who wants to know where you've been and what you've been doing, especially if you've been gone for several hours."

Lozovsky nodded understandingly. He knew the system. As a further thought on the matter, Lozovsky said, "Perhaps it would be best if you could contact either Viktor or Yosif. Either one can make an immediate decision without having to get in touch with the other for approval."

"I'll see what I can do," Elena answered as she left the apartment.

The next day Elena made it a point to visit the Finnish Embassy. For the most part, she was free to visit the Embassy and the Soviet trade departments since, as an interpreter, it was her job to know about projected conferences between the trade officials. The authorities did not impose a rigid scrutiny of her activities as long as they were satisfied that she was going about her duties. She was, however, expected to observe what was transpiring at the Finnish Embassy and to report on any unusual business activity. In keeping with that covert objective, Elena's superiors were happy to have her visit the Embassy as often as possible without being obtrusive or creating suspicion on the part of Embassy personnel.

On the other hand, the Embassy had given her clearance to enter the Embassy whenever she felt her duties required it, but with the proviso that she was limited in her movements within the Embassy to the dining room, parlor and conference room and, of course, the ladies powder room. Offices of the Ambassador, Chief Secretary and Deputy Secretary were open to her upon invitation only by those officers. She was at liberty to seek out and talk with members of the trade delegation as part of her recognized duties.

Upon arrival at the Embassy this day, Elena asked the receptionist to contact Antti Salonen and to let him know she was here and would like to discuss the trade matters. It was ten o'clock in the morning and Koskinen was still in his room when the telephone rang and the receptionist announced that Elena Marikova was in the waiting room and had asked to see him.

"Tell her I'll be right down," Koskinen instructed the receptionist.

A few moments later, Koskinen arrived at the waiting room and greeted Elena.

"Ah, Miss Marikova, good morning. It's good to see you. May I take your coat?" After helping Elena remove her heavy coat and hanging it in the adjoining coat room, Koskinen asked Elena, rather formally, "What can I do for you?"

"I wanted to talk with you about your trade schedule so that I can coordinate my time."

The formality of the conversation between Elena and Koskinen was a deliberate affectation for the benefit of the receptionist for whom there was to be no hint of any clandestine relationship.

"Perhaps we can talk in the conference room," Koskinen said as he took Elena by the arm and led her down the hall to the room. Koskinen closed the conference room door and he and Elena had the privacy both wished for. They embraced for a few moments, delighting in the intimacy. They then sat down on a sofa and turned to talking about the previous day's events at the Lozovsky apartment.

"I know that there is an underground organization and that you are a part of it," Koskinen began, "but I really know very little about it and if I am to become involved, I must know its size, how it operates and most important, what its plans are to overthrow the government by removing Stalin from the scene. Can you enlighten me on these things, Elena? And I again promise complete confidentiality. You can trust me."

"Yes, I know I can trust you," Elena said. "I'll try to answer your questions and you, too, Timo, must be assured that I shall be truthful."

"Of course, Elena,. I have not assumed anything else."

"Well, then, let me begin by saying that I was recruited to join sometime after my father and brother were arrested and taken from my mother and me."

"Who recruited you?" queried Koskinen. "Was it your soldier friend?"

"No," and Elena laughed, "no, in fact, I recruited him. No, it was a friend of our family who knew that Mother and I were very bitter about my father's and brother's disappearance after their unjustified arrest and totally false charges against them. Of course, every family who has had a loved one arrested is bitter, but the family friend knew I was ready to take revenge. Nevertheless, our friend was very cautious and, gradually, over several months touched on the matter of joining an underground cell."

Elena continued, "I was very hesitant at first because, as you know, if you are discovered, you will end up being shot as an enemy of and a threat to the nation. But, as time went on, the idea began to appeal to me and I finally told our friend I would join and so I became a member of the Leningrad cell and have been ever since."

"I assume, then, that there is a cell in Moscow also," commented Koskinen.

"Yes, of course," replied Elena.

"How many cells are there throughout the Soviets?" Koskinen asked.

"I have no information on the number but there are cells in most of the larger urban areas. The location of the cells for Leningrad, Moscow, Smolensk and Kaluga are known to all of us. Any others are known only to a few of our leaders. You can understand why the locations should be kept secret. There is always a chance someone might disclose the information unintentionally but in a moment of loose talk."

"Of course, I understand. Generally, how many members are in a cell?" Koskinen persisted in seeking information.

"The cell in Leningrad has seventeen. Moscow has, I believe, about thirty. The others, from what I hear, may range from six or seven to a dozen or more."

"I guess the important particular for me," said Koskinen, "is how you plan to get rid of Stalin and take over control of the country."

"Timo, I'd rather not disclose what I know of the plans. It is not that I don't trust you. After you left Lozovsky's apartment yesterday, Sholom and I agreed that I was to contact one of our leaders and ask whether we could or should bring you to a meeting with some of our people here in Moscow. If he agrees, then we'll go to a meeting and I'm sure you'll get some of the answers to your question on plans." Elena added, "Sholom and I believe you can be of help to us in any case and I'll certainly urge our leaders to arrange such a meeting." Elena looked apologetic in demurring to answer Koskinen's question.

"What puzzles me, Elena, is how your group of underground plotters has managed to survive this long without the authorities knowing about you and arresting everyone involved." Koskinen shook his head to emphasize his perplexity.

"It requires money," Elena acknowledged.

"Do you mean that your organization is bribing some official to look the other way?"

"Yes, several officials."

"Then, the next question is: 'Where does the money come from?' Bribes are not cheap." Koskinen was unremitting in his quest for the facts about the underground.

Elena hesitated in answering Koskinen's question. She finally opted to disclose the information.

"Our money is provided by an outside source which is as eager as we are to liquidate Stalin." Elena disliked being evasive with Koskinen, but felt it to be her duty to reveal very little of the collaborators of the movement. Koskinen, she felt, would get his answers in due time.

Koskinen did not press further for an answer. But he knew that besides Finland there were any number of foreign governments who would like to see Stalin dethroned. Germany, Poland, Hungary, Bulgaria, perhaps also, Estonia and Latvia came to his mind.

"By the way," Koskinen inquired, "how do you communicate with members and leaders of your cell and with those cell members in other cities without being caught by the NKVD? Telephones can be tapped, letters can be intercepted and your members can be kept surreptitiously under surveillance. I'm really quite interested and fascinated." Koskinen looked at Elena and observed that she was getting uncomfortable with his pointed and sharp questioning. He decided that he would discontinue his interrogation at least for the present. Nevertheless, Elena sought to answer Koskinen's question.

"We have a somewhat elaborate system with people who have different occupations and various lifestyles, but who have one thing in common: they have had one or more family member or close friends who have been arrested and either executed or sent off to some labor camp where they usually die from overwork, not enough food or disease. Every one of our people hate Stalin and his henchmen so intensely that they are willing to risk their lives to see them all dead. Our people are loyal to our movement. We have no question about that."

Koskinen began to see a quality in Elena that he had not known existed. She was still a gentle, very feminine person, but she now revealed a steely, purposeful, focused determination and resolve to support and to commit to a cause she deemed to be just and righteous. There was a display of intensity in Elena that Koskinen immediately came to admire and respect. Koskinen was attracted to women who possessed a soft and delicate beauty, who were refined, who had class, as he often commented to friends, and who were vivacious, yet not overbearing. He did not find it incongruous that he was also attracted to women with strong personalities, who were intelligent and fearless on issues of importance, women with "backbone" as it were, women who were willing to stand up and support their beliefs in what, to them, was right. In Koskinen's opinion, women with these qualities if they loved, they loved fiercely, passionately and, above all, with loyalty, constancy and singleness of heart.

For Koskinen, Anna, his wife, had all of these qualities and as he came to know Elena better and spent more time with her, he was arriving at the conclusion that she, too, had these qualities he so much esteemed. Koskinen had gained strength of character from Anna in their long marriage. Even now his own resolve was strengthened by the manifest determination of Elena.

Elena continued to explain the communication within cells of the underground movement. "The driver of the truck who brings bread and other bakery to the Embassy here is one of us. You should know that the bakery he drives for here in Moscow is the headquarters for the entire underground movement. The bakery is where our leaders work and where small groups meet to determine and decide on policy and activities. I will be here when he makes his delivery in the morning two days from now. I will give him a verbal message to take to our leaders at the bakery concerning inviting you to a conference with them. There is never any message in writing as you can well understand under the circumstances. The bakery supplies most of the foreign legations here in Moscow. The driver delivers twice a week. I know his schedule. So, you see, that is one example of how we communicate."

"Yes, I understand," said Koskinen. "You can say in your message, Elena, that I would very much like to talk with them."

"Timo, while I'm here, I think I should talk to a trade mission delegate about some trade matters. If I can report something to my superiors, it will help me to legitimatize my visit here."

"Good idea, Elena. Let me find out who is available. Before I do so, though, I'd like to see you where and when we can be less businesslike."

Elena understood Koskinen's hint for privacy.

"Yes, I think that would be nice, Timo. I'd like that. I'll try to make arrangements for a hotel room in some out of the way place, but still on the bus line. When I come here again in two days, I'll let you know." Elena moved closer to Koskinen and took his hand in hers while looking at him warmly.

"What about Lozovsky's place?" inquired Koskinen.

"Well, first, I think it would be nice if we spent the night together and we can't do that at Lozovsky's. The other concern is that while I know Sholom would not mind, nevertheless, he is with the underground and I don't want to impose any needless risk on him which might occur since you are with a foreign delegation and subject to possibly being watched."

"I could also be watched if I went to a hotel with you and you would be at risk," observed Koskinen.

"True, but having an excuse would be easier and more plausible. Even the NKVD understands why two adults, male and female, go to hotels for privacy." Elena laughed at the ingenuity she had just thought of.

Koskinen chuckled. "Alright, you win. I'll get one of the trade negotiators if I can and you can talk with him." Koskinen left Elena in the conference room while he went to the receptionist and gave instructions to locate and have a trade delegate meet with Elena. Koskinen then retired to his room where he proceeded to write a letter to Anna and their children. Koskinen continued his caution. The letter said only that he was well and that the trade mission was being transacted. Koskinen could not be certain his letter would not be censored by the Russian authorities.

At eight in the morning two days later, Elena appeared at the Finnish Embassy as she had promised. The receptionist had just come on duty. Elena asked her to contact Antti Salonen.

"He might still be sleeping," remarked the receptionist.

"Ring him anyway. We'll wake him up if he is," countered Elena laughingly. The receptionist did so.

"Tell Miss Marikova I'll be down in a few minutes," Koskinen said upon being informed of Elena's presence.

When Koskinen entered the reception room and greeted Elena, Elena immediately took him by the arm and virtually pulled him to the corner of the room to be out of earshot of the receptionist. Koskinen had fully dressed in anticipation of Elena's early arrival, but was surprised at the seeming urgency expressed by Elena's action.

"Antti, I'd like to have you take me to the area of the Embassy where deliveries are made. I don't want to miss the delivery man from the bakery. You understand."

"Yes, of course. Follow me." Koskinen led Elena down the corridor to the dining room, then through the adjoining kitchen to a door which opened on a rear yard of the building. Next to the door was a small storage room containing bags and boxes of food items. This room also had a door which, at the moment, stood open. A wooden platform extended a few feet from the outside door to several steps down to the unpaved ground.

No one was as yet in sight in the rear yard so Koskinen and Elena stood just inside out of the cold and waited for the deliveryman. A chef was in the kitchen preparing breakfast for the Embassy personnel. He regarded Koskinen

and Elena with obvious curiosity, but merely said in Finnish, "Hyvaa huomenta."* The chef had never met Koskinen but assumed that he and Elena were part of the Embassy people.

After waiting about fifteen minutes and both growing increasingly impatient, Koskinen and Elena heard the sounds of a motor vehicle coming down the driveway alongside the Embassy building.

"I hope that's your bakery driver," said Koskinen. Elena looked out of the door window as a medium sized box truck entered the rear yard.

"Yes, it's him," exclaimed Elena. She opened the door to the platform and stepped out. Koskinen followed. The truck driver swung his vehicle around and backed up to the platform. Koskinen saw a large bodied, heavyset man alight from the truck cab and walk to the rear of the truck. He looked directly at Koskinen and then back to Elena. His facial expression indicated that he was uncertain of what to make of Koskinen's presence. He neither greeted them nor did he give any sign of recognition of Elena. The driver had decided to exercise caution since Koskinen was a stranger to him and he wasn't sure why the stranger was with Elena.

Elena spoke out in Russian. "Good morning, Akmal."

"Good morning," the driver responded in an indifferent manner as if greeting someone, perhaps a stranger on the street.

"Akmal, this is Antti Salonen from Finland. He is alright." Elena's assurance was accompanied by a wink to substantiate acceptance of Antti.

"Before you deliver your bakery order inside the Embassy, I'd like to talk with you a few minutes. Perhaps we can sit in your cab." The driver nodded his head in approval, but still said nothing. He went to the cab door on the passenger side and beckoned to Elena to enter.

"Elena, I'll wait for you in the conference room. There isn't room in the cab for all three of us. Besides, you'll want to talk to him privately."

"That's fine. I'll meet you in the conference room in about fifteen minutes." Elena descended the platform steps and walked to the cab and climbed in. The driver, Akmal, got in on the driver's side.

"I'm sorry if I appeared not to know you," Akmal said, "but for all I knew, this fellow, Antti, might have been an NKVD. Who and what is he, by the way?"

"That's what I want to talk to you about," Elena declared.

Elena began, "Antti is a member of the Finnish Intelligence supposedly here on a trade mission with a Finnish trade delegation. However, he was sent here to get rid of Stalin through one means or another. The Finnish government is of the opinion that Stalin wants to ultimately take over Finland and they feel that that won't happen if Stalin is gotten rid of. Do you understand, Akmal?"

"Yes and no." Akmal looked skeptical. "How do we fit in?"

"He might be of help to us and us to him. He should meet with some of our people, certainly with Viktor and Yosif. This is where you come in. I have to arrange a meeting through you. When you get back to the bakery later I want you to give this message to either Viktor or Josif or both. Tell them that Elena has a friend from Finland who needs help or wants to help get rid of Stalin. He's with Finnish Intelligence and his government has sent him here for that purpose. Tell them that I got acquainted with him some time back when I was acting as an interpreter for a Soviet trade group and I have gotten to know him well enough to vouch for his honesty and trustworthiness."

Akmal said nothing, but nodded as he appeared to be losing some of his skepticism.

Elena continued, "Sholom Lozovsky has interviewed him at Sholom's apartment and has concluded that Antti is reliable and authentic and can be trusted. Tell Viktor or Yosif that. They respect Sholom's opinion. Tell them to set a time for a meeting with Antti. They will give their answer to you and you can bring it to me when you come here again in three days. I'll meet you here in the morning as I did today. Is this alright with you, Akmal?"

"Yes, I'll give them your message and return with theirs." Akmal broke into a broad, toothy smile revealing strong yellow teeth with three or four gaps of missing teeth. His face was clean shaven with a thin black moustache. His countenance evidenced a blending of Mongolian and Iranian prominent cheekbones, pug-nosed, large brown oriental-type eyes, all wrapped in a lined tawny skin. Akmal was a big man, but by no means obese or paunchy. On the contrary, he appeared muscular and athletic, a man who had lived and worked much of his life in the open.

When Elena first entered the underground movement, she was introduced to Akmal who was already heavily involved. Elena was immediately impressed with his presence and took a liking to him. He was quiet, reserved and unobtrusive, almost to the point, she thought, of being bashful. Although his behavior was modest and gentle, Akmal was in no respect servile. He had the characteristic common to all underground members, namely, tough, determined, courageous, and intensely focused on their cause.

Akmal spoke a dialectical Russian which, through his contact with "true" Russians, had been modified sufficiently to be understood by the latter. In talking with him, Elena learned that he was a native of Ubekistan, a Soviet Republic and from the village of Chimkent about eighty kilometers north of the Uzbek Capitol of Tashkent. He told Elena he had been drafted into the Soviet army at age twenty-three, had served five years before being discharged. During the last two years of his stint he had served in a unit stationed in Podolsk, a place a few kilometers south of Moscow. When discharged, he had no money and decided to stay and find work in Moscow. He had driven truck in the army and quickly found a job driving truck for a company manufacturing boots and shoes. The company was State owned and operated and, like many State companies, was inefficient and non-profitable. He was, he said, frequently paid in boots and shoes which, for the most part, were either mismatched or defective or both. He had described for Elena a closet full of boots and shoes only a few of which he could wear. He finally got disgusted after about a year on that job and left to take work in the bakery where he was now situated.

When interviewed for the driver job by the bakery owner, the latter apparently perceived that Akmal had little or no loyalty to the government and was disgruntled with his experiences in the army and at the shoe factory. The owner must have felt that Akmal would be a good candidate for the underground. Akmal got the job. He was sufficiently naive for some time in not recognizing that something nefarious was going on at the bakery. That innocence was abruptly terminated when he was stopped one day by the NKVD and questioned about the bakery. Akmal told Elena that he was taken to a small district office of the police. The interrogators used rubber truncheons on him to get him to give the answers they wanted. He was bleeding and in pain. But he could not tell them anything because he did not know anything except that the bakery people made bread and other bakery products and everyone worked hard and long hours doing so. The police examined his truck thoroughly and found nothing except bakery products. The police finally, after several hours, let him go. On the way out of the building one of the policemen cursed him and gave him a solid punch to the head for good measure.

When Akmal got back to the bakery he told the owner what had happened. The owner had visible evidence that Akmal had suffered a beating. The owner gave him the option of quitting his job because of his experience with the police or to stay and run the risk of one or more repetitions of NKVD inquiries. Akmal said he didn't hesitate. "I stay," he told the owner.

Akmal related to Elena that at that time he did not know the bakery owner's feelings about the government but, "I am a simple man and I speak my mind. I told the owner that I did not like the way the government did things and how it treated its people." He said that the owner then told him that the bakery was the headquarters for an underground movement to get rid of Stalin and change the government. Akmal had said, "Good! I join you!" He was immediately accepted.

After getting Akmal's assurance that he would take her message to Viktor or Yosif and bring an answer back in three days, Elena left Akmal and returned to the conference room of the Embassy where Koskinen awaited her. He was sitting on the sofa and browsing through a book he had selected from many on the book shelves lining one wall of the room. He looked up inquiringly as Elena entered the room.

"Did you accomplish what you intended?"

"Yes, Akmal has agreed to get the message to the people at the bakery."

"Are you sure you can trust the fellow?"

"Of course." Elena seemed surprised that Koskinen should ask. "Akmal has been tested several times and proved to us that he is very dependable. In fact, we could hardly operate without him. Frequently, he is the only one who can get messages to and from cells."

"How is that?" questioned Koskinen.

"All messages of our movement are oral. There is nothing in writing. If the police stop him, there is no evidence. Akmal can always say he is just delivering bakery goods."

"Timo, dear, I cannot stay. I'm expected at the Trade Ministry. However, I'll see you at about 1800 hours. I've gotten a room at the Zolotoe Koltso Hotel near the Ministry building. Room 209. Just walk into the lobby and come upstairs, the second floor."

"What about the hotel clerk? I will have to say who I'm visiting."

"That's alright. He knows me. I've been there several times. I gave him a few rubles. He won't say anything."

"Oh! You've been there with your other boy friends?" Koskinen feigned jealousy.

"No, I've stayed there from time to time when I have been on assignment in Moscow. And anyway, even if I did have a boyfriend there, it shouldn't bother you. It would have been before I met you." Elena, as she said this, looked at Koskinen with a sly, artful facial expression. "After all, Timo, I am single and have no wish to be celibate." Koskinen had to admit to himself that he could not expect that Elena would or could suppress her life force any more than he could or anyone could for that matter.

"I was only trying to be funny," Koskinen said. "By the way, how did you get here and how do you expect to get to the Trade Ministry building?"

"The Trade Ministry had one of their chauffeured autos bring me here. They told me to call when I was ready to return and they'd send the car for me."

"Well, Elena, let me suggest that our Embassy provide you with a car and driver to take you back. Is that alright with you?"

"Yes," replied Elena, "I think that would be alright."

"The driver is Finnish," advised Koskinen.

"That's fine," Elena said.

"You know, Elena, I'm so happy that you are here on assignment to the Finnish trade mission, but I am curious why you have been assigned to us in the first place. We, here, have our own interpreter and translator who is Finnish but speaks fluent Russian." Koskinen had been perplexed about that for some time even though it had been mentioned before. He felt that it was timely and necessary to ask that question again.

Elena replied, "It's very simple, Timo. The Russian authorities don't trust your translators and want one of their own in on any transactions." Elena paused, "I don't believe they are singling out Finns. Our government assigns interpreters to all governments which are represented here when an event is thought to be of sufficient importance."

"Yes, now I understand. I'll meet you in your hotel room at 1800 this evening." Koskinen left the room to arrange for the Embassy auto and then returned to the conference room where Elena was waiting. In about twenty minutes the limousine pulled up at the front entrance. Koskinen and Elena embraced and kissed for a few moments and then parted.

"See you this evening." Elena waved goodbye.

After Elena had left the Embassy, Koskinen proceeded to the office of Ambassador Peltonen. In the reception room the Ambassador's secretary, Marjatta Ilomaki, was on the telephone when Koskinen entered. While awaiting the secretary to finish her phone conversation, Koskinen walked casually about the room examining the pictures hung on the walls. On one wall were framed certificates of recognition, citations of honor and awards for one service or another granted to the Ambassador. The Ambassador's name was no stranger to Koskinen, as Peltonen was well known throughout Finland as the longtime head of the Valmet Company, a huge manufacturing complex headquartered in Helsinki. The company manufactured trucks, busses, locomotives, ships, papermaking machinery, power engines and numerous other items even including wall clocks and hunting rifles.

There was also a wall citation acknowledging Ambassador Peltonen's service as Economic Minister in the cabinet of Prime Minister P.

E. Svinhufvud. The Ambassador had served from 1931 to 1934. The Svinhufvud government was intensely conservative and anti-Communist. Consequently, when Peltonen was appointed in March 1937 as Ambassador to the Soviet government, the latter was less than cordial in giving the appointment its blessing, but that fazed neither the Finnish government nor Peltonen. Svinhufvud had been replaced in March 1937 by A. K. Cajander as Prime Minister, a Social Democrat. Nevertheless, the Cajander government, under the influence of the Socialist leader, Vaino Tanner, was equally anti-Communist. Koskinen understood that Cajander needed a seasoned businessman experienced in foreign trade matters to represent Finland in the Soviet Union and had, therefore, gone outside of his party to appoint Peltonen.

Marjatta, the Ambassador's secretary, interrupted Koskinen's musings saying she was now off the phone.

"What can I do for you, Herr Salonen?"

"I'd like to see the ambassador if he's available," Koskinen replied.

Marjatta went to the Ambassador's door, knocked and entered. In a moment she returned.

"Ambassador Peltonen can see you, Herra Salonen." Marjatta was at once polite and officious, someone who realized that she was a secretary of an Ambassador.

"Ah, Antti, how are you this morning?" The Ambassador was at all times urbane, genteel, almost courtly, yet not pompous, pretentious or arrogant. He welcomed Koskinen warmly and beckoned him to sit down beside his desk.

"What can I do for you, Antti?"

"I think that what I have to say and report will be of considerable importance to you. It certainly is for me."

"Yes, go on. I'm interested."

"You know what my mission here is."

"Yes."

"You are aware of that young lady, the Russian interpreter?"

"Yes. She's quite attractive."

"Her name is Elena Marikova. She lives in Leningrad, but is assigned from time to time to Moscow. She's been assigned to the current trade mission of ours."

"Yes, yes. What about her?" The Ambassador sounded as if he wanted Koskinen to come to the point.

"She's a member of an underground group dedicated to the elimination of Stalin." Koskinen paused to give emphasis to his revelation and to discern its effect on the Ambassador.

Ambassador Peltonen, who had been leaning back in his chair, upon hearing this from Koskinen, immediately straightened up, an expression of astonishment and intense interest on his face. For a moment he said nothing while he seemed to sort out the implications of what Koskinen had just divulged. Then he exclaimed, "That is remarkable, Antti! How can you be sure that it is not leading you into a trap?" The Ambassador in speaking, was careful to use Koskinen's pseudonym although he knew Koskinen's real identity.

"I'm absolutely certain that this woman is genuine, Mr. Ambassador. I met her in Finland when she was serving as a translator for a Russian trade group and I have had the opportunity to get to know her well. I have no doubts about the authenticity of her membership in the underground. I have also met, through her, another member, a Jew by the name of Lozovsky."

"I assume you know what you're doing, Antti, but just be very cautious, very careful. You know, to us men beautiful women most always seem genuine and authentic. We tend not to look beyond the beauty and to test for sincerity."

"Something more, Mr. Ambassador. She will introduce me to some of the leaders of the underground. They operate in a bakery here in the City." Then Koskinen smiled slyly. "And you should know that the fellow who delivers our bread is also a member of the underground group."

The Ambassador raised his eyebrows and chuckled. "It seems that you've gotten yourself pretty much involved already with these people. Well, if it's the real thing, then I think you've struck on something that may help you in your mission. I, frankly, did not think you could carry out your mission alone. I think you should follow through on this but if the Russian authorities discover what you are up to, we may have to disclaim any knowledge of your mission. But, we won't abandon you. When are you supposed to meet the leaders at the bakery?"

The question went unanswered, for at that moment Marjatta, without knocking, opened the door and rushed in, her face flushed with an expression of panic.

"What is it, Marjatta?" The Ambassador asked softly.

"I just received a call from the police saying our driver, Juhani, was in an auto accident and that he and a woman with him were at the police station."

"Where is the police station and who is the woman?"

"It's a station near the intersection of Smolenski Bulvar and Lyovshinsky Street on the way to the Russian Foreign Trade Building."

"And the woman?"

Before Marjatta could answer, Koskinen spoke up. "The woman, Mr. Ambassador, is the interpreter. She was here this morning to see us about the trade discussions. I talked with her and I arranged for our driver to take her back to the Foreign Trade Ministry rather than have her call for a car from the Ministry."

Koskinen turned to Marjatta. "Did the police say either of them were injured?"

"They said they just had some bruises, nothing serious. But they did say that they would hold both of them until tomorrow noon while they finished their investigation. They said there was no point in anyone coming to visit now. They did say that we should arrange to have the auto towed back here in the morning."

"Did they say how it happened?" the Ambassador inquired.

"They only said another car was involved, but they did not go into details."

"Marjatta, get the police station on the telephone. I still want to talk to them, personally." The Ambassador was visibly disturbed. As Marjatta left the office, he turned to Koskinen. "If they keep them overnight, I'm sure the police will question both Juhani and the woman. I hope your lady friend has the strength to say nothing about the underground and you. Police questioning can be quite severe, you know."

The Ambassador's telephone rang. It was Marjatta.

"I have a policeman on the phone."

Peltonen asked Koskinen to take the telephone and translate for him. The Ambassador had only a smattering knowledge of the Russian language.

Koskinen picked up the telephone and spoke with the police officer on the other end of the line.

"This is the Finnish Embassy and I'm speaking on behalf of the Ambassador. Do you understand me?"

"Yes."

"You have a man and a woman who were in an auto accident a short time ago?"

"Yes."

"Are either injured?"

"No, only some bruises."

"Why are you holding them overnight?"

"We are required to investigate the accident. We want to ask them questions."

"Can we talk with them now?"

"No, not until we have completed our investigation."

"When do you expect to finish your investigation?"

"Probably by noon tomorrow. You can come and pick up your chauffeur at that time."

"What about the woman?"

"She is Russian. We'll see that she is taken care of."

"Do you have the other driver?"

"Yes."

"We would like to talk with him. We want to make our own investigation. Will you hold him until noon tomorrow?"

"He is Russian and we have jurisdiction over him. We cannot allow you to interrogate him. We will send you our report in a few days and that should give you the necessary information."

"What condition is the Embassy automobile in?"

"You will have to tow it. The radiator has been damaged so the water flows out."

"Well, thank you, officer." Koskinen hung the receiver down and turned to the Ambassador.

"There is very little we can do right now, Mr. Ambassador." Koskinen reported the conversation to the Ambassador.

"If the police question our driver, Juhani, I am not concerned. Juhani really knows nothing so he can say nothing except that he drives for us." The Ambassador seemed disturbed, however, when he talked about Elena.

"I hope the lady, Elena, can stand up to the interrogator. She has the entire responsibility for the safety of the underground people while she is being held by the police."

"I think she can," assured Koskinen. He was, however, unhappy. His anticipation of spending a night with Elena had been now thwarted by some blundering bureaucratic fools who spent their careers trying to prove that every incident that came to their attention must somehow involve an act of treason against the State. Yet, frustrated as he was, Koskinen's primary concern was for Elena. He imagined all sorts of ill-treatment of her by the notoriously brutal police. They might be beating her, torturing her, even raping her. He wished he could be there with her, to protect her and to insist that she be released. To himself, Koskinen cursed the police, in fact, the whole Soviet system. He was now more determined than ever to rid the world of Stalin. He now had several personal experiences to realize that Russia under Stalin had become an evil, vicious, malevolent society with persecutions even more damnable than existed under the Tsars. Koskinen's feelings must have surfaced even though he tried not to show them to the Ambassador.

"You seem a bit dejected, Antti," the Ambassador observed.

"I am concerned for the lady."

"I can understand. We'll just have to wait until tomorrow, but I think that since an Embassy, our Embassy, is involved in this matter, the police are not likely to do anything drastic to either Juhani or the lady."

Koskinen found little solace in the Ambassador's opinion.

The Ambassador added, "I will go to the police station tomorrow with one of our aides here. However, I think it would be wise for you to remain here. In view of your mission there is no point in calling attention to yourself.

Koskinen nodded his acceptance.

The district police station in which Elena and Juhani were being held was in an old dull-colored wood frame building that seemed from outward appearances to be similar to thousands of other old, dull-colored wood frame buildings in Moscow. Once inside the police building, a visitor got an immediate chilling sense of malevolence permeating the entire structure. It was as if there was some malignant, evil essence inhabiting the building. Perhaps, the feeling that there was something sinister about the building was less attributable to some stygian influence and more to the fear of the police that engulfed a person coming into the building. No one not connected to the police system entered this building voluntarily. The private populace did not regard the police as hospitable hosts.

The district station was located off of the main Smolenski Boulevard on a side street near the Trade Ministry known as Lyovshinsky Street. People on that street generally shuffled by the police station silently and with eyes cast down on the pavement in front of them hoping that they could get by without a cuff to the head from some police officer who might emerge from the building as the pedestrian passed by the door.

Both Elena and Juhani felt some of this trepidation as they were escorted into the building after being driven in a police car from the site of the accident with another vehicle. The Embassy automobile had been rendered inoperable as a result of the head-on collision.

They were ushered into a small room containing an oblong table, some wood folding chairs and two wood benches along one of the walls. There were no windows in the room and light was provided by an overhead hanging electric light bulb without a shade. Nothing was hanging on the walls except a photograph of a smiling Stalin. One of the escorting policemen entered and remained in the room with them. He directed them to sit down on the chairs while he took up a position on a bench and remained silent. Finally, after about five minutes of nothing happening, Elena turned to the policeman and asked, in Russian, "What are we waiting for?"

"We are waiting for an examiner," replied the policeman. Again silence.

Finally, the door opened and in strode, supposedly, the examiner. He proceeded to a chair behind the table and sat down. As he did, he eyed with coldness both Elena and Juhani. Addressing the policeman, the examiner asked, "Why are these two here?"

"They were in an auto accident about a kilometer down Smolenski Boulevard. The man here was driving a Finnish Embassy car. The woman claims she is a translator employed by the Foreign Trade Ministry. She was a passenger in the Embassy car."

The examiner concentrated on Elena.

"You are ...?"

"Elena Marikova."

"You are a translator employed by the Foreign Trade Ministry?"

"Yes."

"Where is your home?"

"In Leningrad."

"What are you doing in Moscow?"

"I have been assigned to the Finnish Trade Mission."

"What were you doing in the Finnish Embassy car?"

"It was taking me from the Embassy to the Trade Ministry near here?"

"The Trade Ministry has its own vehicles. Why weren't you using one of them?"

"The Ministry car took me to the Embassy. I was supposed to call the Ministry when I was ready to return."

"Did you do that?"

"No."

"Why not?"

"The people at the Finnish Embassy volunteered to drive me back. They told me that I shouldn't bother the Ministry, that they'd drive me. I thought that it was very kind of them to do that."

Elena was of the impression that the examiner was more interested in why she was in the Embassy car than in investigating the accident. She began to worry that the entire incident might result in her being relieved of her assignment and sent back to Leningrad.

The examiner continued his questioning.

"What did you talk about while you were in the car?"

"I asked Juhani, the driver, how he liked Moscow?"

"What was his answer?"

"He said he liked Moscow but that he was homesick for Finland."

"What else did you talk about?"

"Just general conversation. I mentioned some of the places in Finland that I had been in while assigned to various government groups."

"Did you ask him where he has driven people from the Embassy?"

"No, I did not. The thought did not occur to me."

The examiner pointed a finger at Elena and, in an intimidating tone to his voice, said, "Young lady, you have a constant obligation to get information for the State about whatever happens among foreigners. Do you understand?"

"How will I know what is important?" Elena was beginning to resent the arrogant fellow on the other side of the desk. She was willing to challenge him.

"Everything is important, everything."

"To whom am I supposed to report this information?"

"To us here at the police district station."

"But I was to report to my superior at the Foreign Trade Ministry. If you want me to report to you, you will have to get the consent of the people at the Ministry."

With this the examiner jumped up from his chair and came around the desk to stand in front of Elena. The examiner's face was livid and took on the appearance of a snarling, cornered wild animal. Shaking his finger in front of Elena's face, the examiner said, "You do not tell me what to do." His voice was low, guttural and the words ground out from between clenched teeth. He meant to be threatening.

"You know, I can have you sent to Lubyanka."

At the mention of the name of the dreaded prison, Elena became alarmed, frightened. This officer standing in front of her had some evil motive for his threatening behavior. He was going far beyond the investigation of a simple auto accident. What that purpose was, Elena could not fathom. She was soon to find out.

During all of this time, Juhani was sitting on a wall bench next to the arresting officer. Juhani did not understand a word of the conversation in Russian between Elena and the examiner, but from the actions and tone of the voices he sensed that the situation was not at all pleasant.

The examiner turned from Elena and towards Juhani and the officer.

"Go outside and take him with you. Wait outside."

The officer and Juhani quickly left the room closing the door after them.

The examiner then pulled a chair in front of Elena and sat down. He eyed her in silence and she returned his look not knowing what next to expect.

The examiner's behavior changed in a moment. The expression on his face softened and the twinkle in his eyes conveyed humor and friendliness. Finally, he spoke.

"Elena, I am sorry if I frightened you. In front of the police officers here, I have to act severe and hard. That is expected of me. But, I want you to know that I have been attracted to you. You are a very beautiful girl. Would you consider being my girlfriend?"

Elena thought, "so that is what this detestable creature had in mind all along." He had threatened her with Lubyanka so that she would do anything to avoid being sent there. She would be only too glad to become his girlfriend. The examiner was smiling as he awaited Elena's answer. Elena saw in that smile a repulsive callousness and an absence of human warmth. She remained silent tying to determine how she should respond.

The examiner interrupted her thoughts. "You know, Elena, if you were my girlfriend, you would not have to worry about sending me reports or being sent to Lubyanka."

Elena thought if she said "No," she could expect some dire action against her. If she said "Yes," it would get her out of the present predicament and then, later, she would see what had to be done to avoid her promise. She made up her mind. She looked at the examiner and smiled sweetly and in a soft, sultry tone, said, "Yes, of course, I think I would like that. You are very attractive, too. But, you have to understand that I live in Leningrad and I'm not always in Moscow."

The examiner was obviously pleased with Elena's answer as he continued to smile.

"I could perhaps arrange for you to be transferred permanently to Moscow."

"No, I could not do that. You see, I live with my mother and she is quite disabled and needs my care. When I am on assignment like this, I have to put her in a home for the aged and disabled until I return. I would not want to abandon my mother to one of those homes. I hope you understand."

"Yes, of course. I have to be satisfied, then, with you as a part-time girlfriend. When can we get together in private? You can come to my apartment."

"I can't tell you that now," Elena replied. "I have to go to the ministry and get my schedule. Perhaps I can see you in a few days. I can call you. By the way, what is your name?"

"Ah, yes," the examiner chuckled, "with all this conversation, I failed to introduce myself. My name is Ivan Snesarev. I am an investigator with the police region. Here, I'll write down my telephone number. You can reach me, generally, at home in the evening."

"You are not married?" Elena inquired.

"No, I'm divorced."

The thought immediately occurred to Elena, "His wife was probably well rid of him. Who could possibly stand him!"

"Could I call the ministry, Ivan, and have them send an auto for me? Perhaps they will also drive Juhani back to the Finnish Embassy."

"I'll call for you," Ivan volunteered, which he did.

"The auto will be here in a few minutes. So, for now, I'll say 'goodbye' and I shall expect to hear from you in a few days." Ivan extended his hand. Elena responded with her grasp.

Ivan escorted Elena to the door, opened it and told the arresting officer, "These people are now released. A Ministry auto will be here in a few minutes. Take them out to the entrance." With no show of emotion, other than a rigid severity, Ivan turned and went back into the examining room.

The driver of the Ministry auto first drove Elena to the Ministry Building and then drove Juhani to the Finnish Embassy.

Elena reported immediately to her supervisor, Petya Chukovsky, a minor bureaucratic official. After Elena had sat down at his desk, Petya observed, "You look distraught, upset."

"Well, I have just been in an accident. I am quite sore all over."

"Did the police investigate the accident?"

"Yes, I was questioned and I told them that the people at the Finnish Embassy volunteered to have their chauffeur drive me here rather than to bother the Ministry to come for me."

"I suppose they wondered why you were in the Finnish Embassy car."

"Yes, but my explanation must have satisfied them."

Elena's superior was sympathetic and solicitous of her well-being. "Would you like to take the rest of the day off? There is nothing urgent and we can deal with the trade conference scheduled tomorrow."

Elena had decided to say nothing to Chukovsky about her experience with Ivan, the examiner and his proposition. She wanted to think more about what to do and, more especially, she wanted to talk it over with Timo Koskinen.

"Yes, I would like the day off so that I can rest up. However, after we have gone over the schedule tomorrow morning, I would like to go back to the Finnish Embassy to see how Juhani is. The poor fellow was frightened terribly when he was taken to the police station. He was also bruised and cut up a lot."

Chukovsky looked at Elena for a long moment. His expression was of skepticism. Why would Elena want to return to the Finnish Embassy? There was nothing she could do for the driver that the Finnish Embassy could not care for. However, Chukovsky said nothing, but agreed for Elena to go.

"I will not need a Ministry car. I can take a bus."

"Well, if a car is available, you might as well use it."

Elena thought, "Chukovsky is a nice fellow. He doesn't live strictly by the rules of the book. I wonder what he thinks of the Stalin government."

Elena left for her room in a nearby somewhat run down small hotel, a place she generally used when in Moscow.

When Juhani arrived back at the Finnish Embassy, he went to the Ambassador's office. He felt the Ambassador would want a report on what had happened. The Ambassador was working in his office and greeted Juhani warmly, but with surprise.

"The people at the police station said that they intended to hold you until tomorrow. However, I'm happy that they released you today. Tell me what happened."

"From here, the lady and I drove down Kropotkinski Street to Lyovshinski Street. We turned left, that is, southwest on Lyovshinski to get to Smolenski Boulevard which leads to the Foreign Ministry

Building. We had just turned to go north on Smolenski when this other automobile coming at a pretty good speed and coming south suddenly crossed over into our lane and struck us head-on. In a moment, everything happened so fast that I do not recall the details, but we were bounced around and ended up in the ditch. I looked at the lady who was in the front passenger side and she was holding her head. I didn't see any blood. I asked her how she was and she sort of groaned out, 'I'm alright.' As for myself, I, too, hit my head and had a headache. I was bleeding a bit from my forehead, but that was all." Juhani appeared still shaken by the experience.

"You were fortunate you and the lady were not more seriously injured. I take it the police came sometime afterward?"

"Yes, about fifteen minutes later."

"What about the other driver?"

"The police put him in the same police car with us and took him back to the police station. He had a strong smell of liquor on him. I think he was drunk. I have no idea what happened to him when we got back to the police station. I haven't seen him since." Juhani sounded convincingly that he had no concern for the other driver.

"Where is our automobile now?" the Ambassador asked.

"As far as I know it is still in the ditch."

"Well, we'll have to get out there right away and get it towed back here. I'll see that it is done. In the meantime, why don't you get cleaned up. If you're hungry, go back to the kitchen and get the chef to make you something. We'll see you later."

Juhani got up painfully from the chair and left for his room on the second floor.

As he was leaving, Ambassador Peltonen said, "Juhani, in the next day or two write up a report on this and give it to me."

"Very good, sir. I'll do that."

Elena arrived at the Embassy the next day in one of the several Ministry limousines. It was about thirteen hours. She asked to see the Ambassador and was told by the receptionist that he was having lunch but was expected in his office in about twenty minutes. Elena waited in the reception room.

About fifteen minutes later, the Ambassador's secretary came into the reception room and told Elena that Ambassador Peltonen would see her. The secretary led the way down the corridor to the Ambassador's office.

"Ah, Miss Marikova, I'm glad you came. Won't you sit down?"

The Ambassador motioned to a leather upholstered chair in front of his desk.

"That was an unfortunate experience you had yesterday. Juhani told me about the accident. From what he described you are both very lucky to have come out of it without serious injury. How are you feeling?"

"Better, thank you," Elena replied. "I came here to find out how Juhani was. He was a bit more battered than I was and he was quite upset at being held in the police station."

"Juhani will be alright. He just needs a rest for a day or two. Would you like to see him?"

"Yes, I think that would be nice."

"I suppose that you would also like to see Antti Salonen." The Ambassador had a knowing twinkle in his eyes. For the moment Elena was startled by this unexpected revelation that the Ambassador knew of her relationship to Koskinen. Her face flushed and she groped in her mind as to how to react and what to say. The Ambassador perceived her discomfort and with a kindly, reassuring softness in his voice sought to relieve Elena's anxiety.

"Miss Marikova, Antti has told me about you and the group you belong to. I know what his ultimate mission is and he thought I should know about yours and how there can be a mutual help in accomplishing both of your missions."

Elena, still surprised, nevertheless did relax. "Yes, that is true, Mr. Ambassador."

"Miss Marikova, I want you to know that all of this will be confidential, only between me, you and Antti. Don't worry, you will not be exposed. Finland's fate may well lie in Antti's and your hands. It is, to me, a very serious undertaking and we must be very careful."

"Mr. Ambassador, I know Antti's real name, but I agree we should continue to use the name of Antti Salonen."

"Fine. I'll keep in touch with you through Antti. You understand I cannot be personally involved except to give your missions my blessings and, perhaps, to work behind the scenes."

"Yes, I understand." Elena arose to leave.

The Ambassador had his secretary page both Juhani and Antti Salonen to come to his office.

"Wait here," the Ambassador instructed Elena. "They should be here in a few moments."

When they arrived, both Juhani and Koskinen showed pleasant surprise at finding Elena in the Ambassador's office.

Elena embraced Juhani and expressed her wish for his well-being. After a few more friendly words were exchanged, Juhani left.

The Ambassador turned to Koskinen.

"I have explained to Miss Marikova that you have told me about her and the movement. Why don't you both use the conference room and talk over whatever it is you want to talk about."

"Yes, we'll do that, Mr. Ambassador. I want to thank you for your interest," Koskinen responded.

The Ambassador added, "We are all co-conspirators now. But we all play different roles. No conspiracy can be successful unless the conspirators have complete trust in each other. There must be no weak link in the chain that binds the conspirators together."

"Yes, sir, that is understood and agreed upon," said Koskinen. Elena nodded her approval.

"Keep me informed," said the Ambassador as Koskinen and Elena turned to leave.

In the conference room and after closing the door, Koskinen and Elena embraced and kissed for a few moments and then sat down on the sofa.

Elena proceeded to relate to Koskinen what had happened as a result of the accident and of the actions and proposition of the examiner.

"The bastard!" Koskinen was enraged and vehement in denouncing the examiner.

"I think you did the right thing in agreeing to be his girlfriend. It bought you some time to decide what to do." Koskinen put his arm around Elena.

"That is why I really came here, to ask for your advice on what I should do to avoid going through with my promise to him."

"The answer is very clear to me, Elena. I don't have to give it much thought. The fellow has to be killed. You won't get away from him by any other measure. He'll pursue you and if you don't give in, he'll send you to Lubyanka. I am familiar with men like him."

"But, Timo, I can't just shoot him or stab him. I'd be arrested and that will be the end of me. I couldn't even say it was done in self defense. Here in Russia women are expected to give in to men and not resist whether they like it or not. I would not be believed."

"Elena, you can poison him with a poison that takes four to five days to kill. By that time, no one will suspect you, not even the examiner."

"Timo, I don't have any poison. What poison are you referring to?"

"It's a very dangerous toxic liquid made from poisonous mushrooms. It's call phalloidine. It damages the kidneys and liver and over a few days they stop functioning. Some people recover, but most do not, especially if given in a strong, concentrated dose. It's used as a rat poison."

"How do you get it, where is it readily available?" Elena asked with considerable eagerness.

"It is sold on the commercial market and is easily obtainable. It's available in Finland. I don't know if it's available here in Russia. However, even if it were available here, I would not recommend going to a store and buying it. Under the circumstances in Russia, the store owner may have to report such purchases to the police. In any case, if there is an investigation after the fellow has died and they determine that the cause of death was poison, the police would likely visit stores to find out who purchased poisons."

At this point, Koskinen could not help but feel great admiration for Elena. When he had mentioned killing the examiner, she had not flinched, protested or expressed any abhorrence of the idea. 'She is quite fearless and I like that,' he mused to himself.

"I have an idea," Koskinen continued. "We have a courier who comes to the Embassy from Finland with various papers and documents. The visits are irregular depending on events, but generally about twice a month. I don't know when the next courier will arrive, but I will ask the Ambassador to wire the Finnish Foreign Office to have the next courier bring several bottles of phalloidine with him in his dispatch case. It will be on the pretext that we have rats here that need to be disposed of."

"Do you think he'll agree?"

"Yes, I think he will after I explain to him our need."

"How is it administered?" Elena was still curious.

"It's mixed with food or in liquid. I have been told that in the manufactured form it is tasteless."

"Hmm! Good, let's do it!" Elena sounded excited and energized by this new challenge as if it proffered a new adventure. But then she suddenly became more sober.

"What do I do in the meantime? I don't want to get into bed with that fellow," and then she added, "at least not while you're around." Her expression was mischievous.

Koskinen disregarded the addendum.

"You'll have to get busy with some minor assignments from your supervisor. And you can always use the excuse that you're having your menstrual period."

"Yeah," commented Elena, "he's probably one of those guys that that doesn't matter to them."

"Listen, Elena. You are a woman. You know or should know how to handle that. I can't advise you on every detail. You can always have a bad cold and a severe case of laryngitis. In this climate, that's a very believable affliction."

"Oh, dear," Elena sighed. "I suppose I'll have to call him and give him an excuse of some kind."

"Well, you have a good one for tomorrow. We are having a conference tomorrow with those two fellows from the U.S. Embassy whom you met with their Ambassador a short time ago. We shall be talking, ostensibly for the record, about trade matters. But, I think it will cover more than that. I'm sure your supervisor will be glad to send you to spy on us. Talk to him."

"But that is during the day. I'm vulnerable in the evening with that monster."

"If he raises the point, tell him you'll be expected to stay for dinner."

"And the next day and the next day, what then?" Elena exhibited some desperation on how to get out of seeing the examiner.

"Well, we'll see what develops. Elena, it kills me to say this because I love you. But you may just have to have an intimate visit with the guy once or twice to prevent worse things from happening."

"Nothing could be much worse," Elena shrugged as if to cast off a repulsive thought. "I hope that courier gets here soon" she added.

"Just don't get pregnant," Koskinen admonished.

Elena said nothing in reply to that. She arose from the sofa and said matter-of-factly, "I'll have to go now, Timo. I'll have to call for the Ministry car."

"What about our private get-together that the accident interfered with?" Koskinen reminded Elena.

"Oh gosh, yes!" Elena threw up her hands. "I completely forgot about it, Timo. I'm so sorry. It is no reflection on how I feel about you. It's just that I've had all this other stuff on my mind. I would love to spend the evening and the night with you, you know that, but could we just put that off for a day or two. I need to rest up from the accident ordeal and to think how I can stay out of the monster's clutches. I'm sure I would not be very good company for you."

"Of course, of course, Elena." Koskinen smiled graciously. "I should never have mentioned it."

"Yes, you should have. Come here, I want to kiss you and tell you I love you."

As they held each other closely, Koskinen said softly, "It seems that we kiss and hug when we say 'hello' and 'goodbye,' but that is it."

"Isn't that enough for you?" Elena asked with a mischievous expression.

"No. Is it enough for you, Elena?"

"No, of course. I was teasing. I remember our night together in Helsinki. It was wonderful. I want to spend the night with you as soon as possible. But for now, I really must go."

Elena called the Ministry from the conference room and requested to be picked up by one of the Ministry vehicles. She and Koskinen then went to the reception room to await the arrival of the limousine.

After Elena had left the Embassy, Koskinen went to the Ambassador's office and made an appointment to meet with the Ambassador about an hour before dinner that evening. Then he went to his room, sat down on a sofa chair and began to read a Finnish magazine. His mind soon wandered off to dwell on recent events and with it came a sense of despondency. He felt disheartened, dejected. Things were not going very smoothly. He appreciated that he now had a means of accomplishing his mission through the probable intervention of the Russian underground movement. But Koskinen finally realized that what was bothering him was that he could not spend more time with Elena. So much of his contact with her seemed to be at formal, official meetings, not very satisfactory. But then his mind would occasionally revert to Anna and the children and he would experience an intense conflicting emotion. With his interest in Elena how could he be fair to Anna. And with his marital attachment to Anna how could he do the right thing by Elena. Could Elena be wasting her time being involved personally with him. She was such a nice young woman. Perhaps, he should break off his emotional ties to her. He mused that that was what he should do. But, he couldn't. He didn't want to. Besides, he was involved with her in the underground. He would just have to see how things turned out. Koskinen prided himself on being a man of principle and when the time came in the future he would do the right thing by everyone.

When he met with Ambassador Peltonen before dinner, Koskinen related the experience Elena had had with the police examiner and the dilemma with which she was faced.

"Elena and I have talked this over and have come to the conclusion that this police examiner must be gotten rid of and the best way to do it is through poisoning. If this fellow persists in forcing himself on Elena there is a risk he will discover the existence of the underground."

Ambassador Peltonen smiled and commented wryly, "It sounds like a good practice run on getting rid of Stalin."

Koskinen continued, "Mr. Ambassador, I'd like to request that you have your next courier from Finland bring several packages of dried phalloidine, a rat poison. Can you do that?"

"Yes, I suppose I can. I'll have to call headquarters and have them arrange it."

"Will you instruct them that it must be dried phalloidine and that it should be placed in the courier's dispatch case?" Koskinen was insistent on the specifics.

Koskinen went on to explain how the poison worked by delaying the fatal effect by four or five days instead of hours as in the case of other poisons.

"When is the next courier scheduled to arrive?" inquired an anxious Koskinen.

"Probably in a week or ten days," answered the Ambassador. "I'll find out when I call."

"Will you be calling tomorrow, Mr. Ambassador?"

"Yes, I'll see to it."

"Elena will be here tomorrow when those two fellows from the U.S. Embassy arrive. She is to sit in on the meeting." Koskinen knew the Ambassador would not object in view of the role Elena was taking in Koskinen's mission.

The Ambassador nodded his approval. He arose from the chair behind his desk.

"How about joining me for dinner, Antti?" The Ambassador facetiously added emphasis to the name, Antti.

"Very well, sir. I shall be glad to."

At the dinner table, the Ambassador and Koskinen were joined by the leaders of the Finnish Trade Group, Vaino Tanner, the Social Democrat and Juho Paasikivi.

The Ambassador opened the conversation by saying, "Gentlemen, though we're in Russia we try as much as possible to maintain our Finnish culture and eating habits. Our chef is a Finn and he likes to surprise us at each dinner with a Finnish item or two. Let's see what he has for us tonight. I hope you have your appetites with you." The Ambassador smiled congenially.

The waiter brought the first course. Individual bowls of carrot soup.

"Carrot soup!" Paasikivi exclaimed in mock dismay. "I thought we were to get Russian caviar."

"If you like it, I'll see that you have some for the next dinner," Ambassador Peltonen offered graciously.

"No, I was just joking," said Paasikivi. "Frankly, it tastes too fishy for me."

As the group at the Ambassador's table was eating the soup, the Ambassador addressed the two lead trade officials, "How are things going on the trade negotiations?"

"What trade negotiations?" said Paasikivi in an undisguised display of disgust. He continued as if an invisible store of exasperation within him had suddenly been unlocked and vented through a torrent of reproachful words. "Yes, what trade negotiations? They are not interested in talking about trade matters. We had one meeting with Litvinov* and all he would talk about for two hours was Finland giving a thirty-year lease to the Soviets of the Suursaari Island and other islands in the Gulf of Finland. Litvinov keeps talking about needing the islands to protect Leningrad from a German attack through the Gulf."

"What was your answer to Litvinov?" Ambassador Peltonen asked.

"We told him," and Paasikivi motioned to Vaino Tanner, "that we would take it up with our government when we returned to Finland but that it was our guess that the request would be turned down."

"Do you think it would be wise to turn the proposal down?" Ambassador Peltonen had a concerned look on his face. "It might be better to lease the islands rather than risk the Soviet army coming in and taking them and a lot more of Finland while they're at it."

"We know Stalin," replied Tanner. "If we grant him this proposal, he'll be back with another and another until he gets control of large areas of Finland and we'll never get it back."

"I agree. We just have to stand up to these demands and say 'no.'" Paasikivi was adamant.

Juho Kusti Paasikivi was sixty-nine years of age. He had been Finnish Representative in Stockholm, Sweden since 1936 and for about eighteen years prior to that had been actively managing one of the largest commercial banks in Finland. He was a member of the Conservative Party and was very familiar with Russian history and knew the Russian language. His policy in regard to Russia was one of conciliation rather than confrontation and provocation. Nevertheless, he was staunchly against yielding Finnish sovereignty in any part to Russia. He represented Finland well.

Vaino Tanner, on the other hand, was a Laborite and an outstanding leader of the Social Democratic Party. Under his dynamic leadership the Cooperative movement had grown in influence both in the political arena as well as the economic in Finland. Tanner was a tough-minded, solid and outspoken Finn. The Russian government had no great love for Tanner. Even though he represented the working class, the Russians viewed his past conduct as anti-Communist. He had, in fact, managed to suppress any Communist influence in the labor movement.

The waiter brought in the main dish for each. Cabbage rolls and Aaland Island potato cakes with a side dish of beet-herring salad. Everyone at the table agreed that the smell was exhilaratingly delicious. Russian bread was served along with a bottle of red wine.

"Well, what is to take place on trade matters, if anything?" Ambassador Peltonen returned to the subject matter.

"We hope to talk about having Russia send us mineral raw materials in exchange for finished goods, consumer as well as industrial products. We're leaving the preliminary conversations on that to the experts we brought with us on this trip." Tanner looked at Koskinen and smiled.

Koskinen, up to this point, had listened to the discussion and had said nothing. Now he said, "Ah, yes, the experts." He drew himself up like a rooster, puffed out his chest and looked around the dining room in aggrandized self-importance. The group chuckled, for they understood Koskinen's trade "expertise" and his mission.

"How long do you think you'll be here?" the Ambassador continued in his questions.

"Probably for a week more. It is hard to say exactly. It depends on how long and often Litvinov wants to talk about all sorts of issues."

The wine bottle was passed around and, except for Koskinen, each filled a wine glass at his plate. Koskinen said he'd wait for the coffee.

"By the way, Antti," Tanner said, turning to Koskinen, "how is your mission coming along?"

"I think it's making progress, but you understand, I cannot talk about it, at least not at this time. It's a difficult matter and much depends on unexpected opportunities that come along. Sometimes I wonder whether God is not guiding me step-by-step. It is amazing how things evolve in entirely unanticipated ways. I guess one of my jobs is to recognize the opportunities and exploit them." Koskinen had no intention of revealing anything about the underground to the two Finnish trade leaders. The fact that the Ambassador knew was enough, he felt.

The group having finished with the main dish, the waiter now brought in the dessert, a selection of hot raisin-prune soup and Finnish sour cream cake. All at the table took some of both. Coffee was served steaming hot.

"Your chef is to be complimented," said Tanner, addressing the Ambassador.

"Yes. I'm glad you have enjoyed your dinner. Something has to be enjoyable on your trip here," replied Peltonen, recognizing the frustrations being experienced by the two trade leaders over the political situation.

At the end of the meal, Peltonen invited the trade leaders and Koskinen to his office where they could talk in privacy and relax in large, overstuffed chairs. The office room had an atmosphere of luxurious coziness with its paneled walls, plush carpeting and decorative wall hangings.

As they settled down, Peltonen went to a wall cabinet containing liqueurs and other bottles of various alcoholic beverages. He took out a bottle of Lakka, a liqueur made in Finland and popular with Finns as an after-dinner ambrosian. The Ambassador passed a liqueur glass to each.

Tanner raised his glass of liqueur in a toast.

"Gentlemen, I toast to the success of Timo Koskinen's mission. The future of Finland rests in his hands!" The trade leader used Koskinen's name believing it safe to do so in the privacy of the office.

In a rejoinder, Koskinen, still holding his full glass, said, "Sir, if Finland's future depends solely on me, then I suggest that Finland should prepare for a war with the Soviet Union."

Tanner and the others looked startled at Koskinen's forthright and foreboding prophecy.

Tanner interposed, "Timo, I was really exaggerating and being extravagant with my language. Of course, Finland's future depends on many factors, including diplomacy, preparedness for war, and the determination of our citizens to fight for their continued freedom and independence." Tanner chuckled in realizing that Koskinen had taken his words seriously.

Tanner went on to say, "However, if you succeed in your mission, you will become a legend in Finland for all time."

"A dead legend or a live one?" Koskinen quipped.

"A good question, Timo. Perhaps I should consult my crystal ball to get the answer," Tanner laughed.

"And if I fail in the mission?" Koskinen persisted. "What then?"

"Your name will just not appear in the schoolchildren's textbooks."

"Oh, that would be terrible!" Koskinen sounded sarcastic, yet good humored.

Tanner said, surveying the others in the room, "Seriously, we have been bantering here, but the matter is of extreme importance and, if Stalin lives, the probability of a Soviet invasion of Finland is very high. We Finns are very stubborn and unyielding on matters involving our independence. Those are characteristics that could cause us much grief in the long run. It is up to political leaders to determine where the line is between reasonable compromise with honor and capitulation with humiliation and degradation. A proud people like we Finns will probably tolerate the first, but never the second." Tanner articulated his opinion with a trace of the firebrand he could be at times.

At this point, Koskinen excused himself. "I've had a busy day and I could use a little rest. I foresee another busy one tomorrow. I've enjoyed the evening with you gentlemen and I'm sure I'll see you again, perhaps at breakfast tomorrow morning." Koskinen shook hands with the other three and went to his room.

Tanner said, "He's a nice guy. I like him. I think he'll succeed."

"I certainly hope so," Peltonen remarked, but with less conviction than expressed by Tanner.

In his room, Koskinen wrote a letter to Anna. As usual, he could say little except the unprovocative mundane things. He had not heard from Anna and he did not know if Anna had received his letters. He had little faith in the Soviet postal system. He decided that the best way to handle communications to and from Anna was to have the Embassy request the Foreign Ministry in Helsinki to call Anna and inform her that he was alright and, in return, let the Embassy here know that Anna was also well and to so inform him. The Embassy generally made several telephone calls to Helsinki every week anyway. The next day the representatives from the United States Embassy would be coming. It would be a busy day. Koskinen was weary. He retired early but before falling asleep, he had a forlorn feeling of homesickness for Anna.

Elena was admitted to the Finnish Embassy at about eleven in the morning of the next day. Shortly thereafter, Bill Chance and Gene Wagner arrived from the United States Embassy. They were greeted by Kalle Nevakivi, the Ambassador's aide. Chance and Wagner were escorted to the conference room. Elena remained in the reception room.

"We were advised to see Antti Salonen. Will you let him know we are here?" Chance addressed Nevakivi.

"Yes, of course. I shall have the receptionist locate him," replied the aide politely as he turned and left the room.

Alone in the room, Chance turned to Wagner. "I suppose our first task will be to find out what the Finns have in mind to get rid of Stalin. Since they have so much more at stake to succeed than the United States, I presume they have already formulated a course of action. We'll have to discuss what part, if any, we're to take. What do you think, Gene?"

"Yeah, I agree with you. And we decided not to mention the underground at the bakery, right?"

"Yes, at least until we know something about the Finns' plan."

Koskinen on his way to the conference room to meet with the Americans passed through the reception room where he saw Elena.

"Ah, Miss Marikova. I was not aware you were here. Are you here to see me?" Koskinen was taking care to display only a professional relationship with Elena when in the presence of others.

"Yes. I understand that you are having a trade meeting with some people from the United States. My foreign ministry asked permission for me to attend. Permission was apparently granted because I'm here."

Koskinen had an amused twinkle in his eyes. "Well, that's fine. You are welcome. The Americans are in the conference room. I'll go in and talk with them for a few minutes and then I can call you in."

Elena nodded her assent and Koskinen proceeded to the conference room.

Chance and Wagner spoke no Finnish, but they did speak some Russian. Koskinen addressed them in Russian as best he could with his limited knowledge of the language.

"Welcome, gentlemen. I'm glad to meet with you. I know why you are here and you know why you asked to meet with me."

"That is right," declared Chance.

"I don't speak fluent English or Russian," Koskinen informed the Americans. "That young lady in the reception room can translate for us. She speaks some English as well as Finnish and Russian."

Chance reacted in annoyance. "How can we discuss matters of great importance to both of us if she is present. This is not a meeting about trade. Don't you have someone in this Embassy who speaks English and can translate to and from Finnish?"

"Yes, of course we do. The aide who met you when you arrived speaks English quite well, but I'd rather have the young lady with us. I have reason's I'll explain. I presume you are here to talk about what might be done to get rid of Stalin, is that right?"

"Yes, and for that reason we must be very careful how we talk about this and in whose presence. The lady out there I take it is Russian. It doesn't seem very safe to talk these matters over in front of her." Chance acted incredulous that Koskinen (Salonen) would even propose such a thing.

"Well, let me have her come in here. I think you will be convinced that I am right after you listen and speak with her." Koskinen seemed to the Americans very confident and assured.

Koskinen stepped out to the reception room and took Elena aside and spoke in a soft hardly audible voice.

"The Americans, as you know, were sent here to cooperate in eliminating Stalin. I have asked that you attend our meeting, but I have not told them why and have not mentioned your being in the underground. They object to your participation, fearing that because you're Russian you cannot be trusted. I want you to come in and explain your membership in the underground and that you share their mission just as you do ours. They will have to know about it if they are to help and you have to convince them that you can be trusted. So, take off your coat and come in with me."

Elena said, "Sure," and followed Koskinen to the conference room.

"Gentlemen, this is Elena Marikova. You have met her before. She was at dinner with you here a few evenings ago."

Wagner's face seemed to light up as he smiled and beamed. "Oh, yes. I'm glad to see you again, Miss Marikova. I was impressed with your beauty the other night." He took Elena's hand and in courtly European style, bent over slightly and kissed the back of her hand. Chance looked at Koskinen and rolled his eyes at the Wagnerian extravaganza. Chance had been through this kind of display by Wagner on previous occasions. He knew he would admonish his assistant later but he also knew it wouldn't do any good.

"Shall we all be seated?" Koskinen motioned to the chairs around the conference room table.

Koskinen turned to Elena and asked her to explain to the Americans the existence of the underground and her part in it.

Elena faced Wagner and Chance and in somewhat unpolished halting English began to recount her activity with the underground movement.

"Gentlemen, I welcome the opportunity to talk with you about this very important matter. I have known Antti Salonen for some time and I am now collaborating with him on his mission here in Russia. I know what his mission is. It is to eliminate Stalin, to topple him from his position of power by one means or another. I also know what your mission is, to help however you can to accomplish that objective. Antti has told me about you."

Elena paused, still looking Chance and Wagner directly in their eyes. From their facial expressions, Elena detected considerable interest and astonishment on their part in what she was relating. Without eliciting any comment from them, she continued.

"There is an underground organization in Moscow the purpose of which is to rid Russia of Stalin. I am a member of that underground." Again Elena paused to observe the effect on Chance and Wagner. Chance said nothing, but he seemed to have brought his outward expressions under control. He now sat stony-faced. Wagner, on the other hand, showed his reaction more graphically. His eyebrows rose and lowered almost rhythmically, eyes opened wide only to change to squinting and back again, mouth twisting in various convolutions. But, he too said nothing, only listening intently.

"Our underground has cells in some other cities," Elena continued. "We have our methods of communication between us. Our organization is very loose in the sense that there are no officers, but it is tight in the sense that we know who everyone is and that each can be trusted. Every member has lost some loved relative or dear friend or associate to Stalin's purges. Every one of us is outraged that one man has such power to decide who shall live and who shall die. I have lost a father and a brother whom I have never seen again after their arrests."

Elena stopped talking, feeling that she had said enough to convince Chance and Wagner of her authenticity and sincerity.

Chance now spoke up. He appeared to be more relaxed and assured. Elena seemed to him to be genuine, honest and straightforward.

"What are your organization's plans to carry out your purpose to get rid of Stalin?"

"We have a number of alternatives, but our decision on which to use depends entirely on the opportunity offered to us. I think we are ready to act the moment the proper circumstances present themselves."

"That doesn't tell us very much," Chance commented. "I don't know how we can be of help unless we have specific plans as a basis for whatever we decide to do. I think you understand that."

"Yes, I do understand, but I'm not in a position to discuss specifics. For you to get answers on plans and how you can help, I think you should meet with a couple of our leaders at the bakery which you have previously visited."

"Oh, you know of our being at the bakery." Both Chance and Wagner were astounded that Elena not only knew of their mission, but of their visit to the bakery.

"It seems," Wagner volunteered, "that more people know about us than we have had reason to believe."

"Miss Marikova, you probably know that a young man stopped us while Gene and I were out walking near our Embassy and guided us to the bakery. The young man and the people at the bakery already knew about the mission we are on. That surprised us because we had been especially careful to guard against that information being publicized. So, can you tell us how you and your organization learned what we are in Russia for?"

"No," replied Elena, "that is something I cannot divulge. Again, you might ask the top men at the bakery about that."

"Well, I think we'd be willing to talk with one or more people on the matter. I presume that you will make arrangements for the visit."

Elena nodded her approval. "I'll contact them at the bakery and let you know the arrangement. I am advising that Mr. Salonen also visit but not at the same time as you. We don't want to arouse any suspicions with more than one or two people visiting there at any one given time. I shall get word to you at the United States Embassy within a day or two."

"Is there anything else you gentlemen would like to ask at this time?" Koskinen asked of Chance and Wagner through Elena.

"No, not at this time," Chance answered.

"Well, then," Koskinen said, "why don't we have lunch?" Koskinen spoke through Elena.

"That sounds like an excellent idea," Wagner exclaimed with enthusiasm.

"Will we get to talk with the Ambassador during lunch?" Chance asked.

"No, I'm sorry," Koskinen replied. "He and the trade mission people are meeting with the Russian trade representatives. They should return here about 1530 hours."

"Unfortunately, we'll have to leave after lunch," Chance said and then added, "We should all remember that we, too, are on a trade mission as far as people around us are concerned."

"We haven't forgotten. There won't be any slips of speech," Koskinen reassured.

As a consequence, there was small talk during lunch with an occasional reference to trade between Finland and the Soviet government and the possible effects on the United States. For those who might overhear, this group was indeed on a trade mission.

After lunch as Chance and Wagner were preparing to leave with their chauffeur, Wagner addressed Elena.

"Can we drive you back to your trade ministry building?" His invitation was accompanied by a big, friendly smile.

"Thank you, but I have to remain here for a while to go over some matters with Mr. Salonen." Elena glanced at Koskinen in a manner that told him to agree.

"Yes, I'll see that she gets back," Koskinen said supportively. Wagner looked disappointed.

As soon as Chance and Wagner had left, Elena and Koskinen went into the conference room, closed the door and sat down next to each other on the sofa. Elena was anxious to tell him something. Koskinen could perceive that she was upset.

"Timo, that police examiner called me at the trade ministry this morning. He wanted to see me this evening."

"What did you tell him?" Koskinen reacted with irritation at the very mention of the policeman's persistence.

"I told him I was assigned to come here and didn't know when I would be free."

"Well, that was a good excuse."

"But, I can't keep making excuses. He'll get suspicious. He asked about tomorrow evening and I told him I didn't know what my schedule would be. I told him this was a busy time because of the trade negotiations going on."

"Well, how did you leave it. Are you supposed to call him back or what?"

"I didn't say anything definite. I really don't know what to do."

Koskinen thought a few moments.

"Maybe you could get admitted to the hospital for a few days from the effects of the accident."

"Ha! That's a laugh," Elena remarked. "In this city, you have to be an emergency case to be admitted to a hospital. Like bleeding to death or with a burst appendix."

"Perhaps I could stay here while the trade meetings are being conducted." Elena was desperate for a means to avoid the police examiner. "It sounds believable because I have to participate at early morning and late evening conferences and it would be a matter of convenience for me. I think I could get my supervisor to approve it."

"It's a possibility, but I don't know if the Ambassador will go for it. I'd have to discuss it with him when he gets back this afternoon." Koskinen didn't sound very hopeful that the Ambassador would approve.

"While we're waiting," Koskinen added, "why don't we talk about our next moves with regard to my working with your underground."

"The next step," Elena replied, "is for you to talk with some of the leaders at the bakery. They'll have some ideas, I'm sure. I'll let you know when they'd like to see you. I have the thought that when our members travel about, if, at times, you are with them, being a Finn, that will help to provide legitimate explanations for their coming and going. That is, perhaps, one way in which you can be helpful."

"That doesn't sound very exciting," Koskinen observed.

"It's a lot safer." Elena wanted to envelop Koskinen in a protective coat. "We don't expect you to come here and risk your life to save Russia. We have appointed ourselves to do that."

"I did not get sent here to save Russia," Koskinen reminded Elena. "I was sent here to save Finland. If I do that, then saving Russia is a worthy by-product. But, of course, I have added my own rescue mission." Koskinen smiled impishly.

"And what is that?" inquired Elena, knowing full well what the answer would be.

"To rescue you and get you out of this accursed country."

"If we get rid of Stalin, I won't need to be rescued. Russia will be saved."

"Russia will never be saved," Koskinen declared. "The Russian psyche, the Russian essence feeds on oppression and tragedy. Subjugation and tolerating it has been a way of life for generations of Russian people. Whether a city dweller or a farm peasant, whether an illiterate factory worker or an intellectual university professor, almost everyone under the Tsars in the past and under Stalin today was and is a vassal, a serf in the broadest sense. There is in Russia absolutely no understanding of what it means to be free and independent. There is no experience with it. What is wrong with the Russian people that they are so submissive, so docile, unassertive, so non resisting? I do not include you, Elena, and your underground people, but you are so few."

Koskinen shook his head in sincere and utter disbelief that a people would tolerate such an abysmal life circumstance. He knew that historically the Finnish people had been under the rule of foreigners, first the Swedes and then Russia. But, those foreign governments had not been oppressive and cruel and had allowed the Finns considerable self-governance. The Finnish and Russian conditions were totally different and, to Koskinen, the difference was explainable by the dissimilarity of the character of the two people.

"Well," said Elena, "if we accept what you say is true, then we in the underground are wasting our time and effort because even if we get rid of Stalin, we will not get the active support of the people and the oppression will continue under some other despotic ruler who, in turn, will also be tolerated. Is that your conclusion?"

"I don't want to discourage you, but I can't help but think that that might be the case." Koskinen sounded apologetic for his opinion. He had not intended to deflate Elena's enthusiasm for her cause.

Koskinen added, "That is only my opinion and I think we should continue to fight for what we think is right and for what we believe in."

It was shortly after this conversation that Ambassador Peltonen returned to the Embassy. Koskinen spoke with the Ambassador in the latter's office as soon as the Ambassador had removed his coat and hat in his office. Koskinen explained the predicament Elena was in with the police examiner and her request to stay at the Embassy for a few days and nights. The Ambassador did not require more than a moment to give his answer.

"We can't allow that, Timo, even though I'd like to accommodate Elena's request. I have to think of impressions and, if the Russian government learned that we were permitting one of its employees to stay with us, they might get a wrong impression and question what our motive might be. It could very well lead to the underground being exposed and even your mission might be compromised. I shall have to say 'no' to Elena's request. However, she's welcome to visit us during the daytime."

Koskinen returned to the conference room and informed Elena of the Ambassador's decision. Elena shrugged her shoulders in resignation to her disappointment. She was not the kind of person to fret over what she could not control.

Koskinen offered a suggestion. "If the guy calls you, why don't you recommend that you have lunch together in some small restaurant in the neighborhood. That may mollify him until the courier arrives with our tasty mushrooms."

"I can try that." Elena was not convinced that it was the panacea to solve her problem.

"I have a further idea, Elena." Koskinen looked mischievous. "I'll get a taxi and I'll go with you to your apartment. You'll remember we had a date to spend the night together."

"That's agreeable with me." Elena seemed lifted from her cares at the prospect of time with Koskinen. "But, the police examiner might discover your being with me. You know how these police are. They spend time either trailing you or sitting outside a home watching to see who comes and goes."

"I'm willing to take that risk. How about you?" Koskinen inquired gently of Elena.

"I am willing as long as I'm with you." Elena embraced Koskinen affectionately. "Besides, we might not have to go to my apartment. We can try to get a room at that small hotel I had reserved for us the other evening, but had to cancel because of the accident. We can have the taxi take us directly to it. I would guess they have a vacancy."

"Good! Let's do it!" Koskinen, too, had shed his glum feelings at the prospect of being with Elena on an intimate, close relationship instead of the ever present serious business of plotting Stalin's removal.

"There comes a time, Elena, when all of us have to put aside the grim pursuit of what we have destined for ourselves in order to find a few moments, at least, of joy, happiness and love in a simple bonding with another, but special, human being. Unless we do that, we cannot survive in this world of interminable conflicts. I do not envy a Stalin or a Hitler. In their positions of ultimate power they no longer have any refuge, any sanctuary, any haven in which to find true rest and security from their tremendous burdens. I surmise that in spite of all of their public displays of bravado, each must live in a perpetual storm cellar of fear for his survival."

Elena listened to Koskinen admiringly and with approval. The depth of his thoughts struck a chord in her own feelings.

Koskinen called for a taxi and informed the receptionist that he would be away from the Embassy for the night. He did not elaborate with details. Proceeding in the taxi to the small hotel that Elena had in mind, they were fortunate to find an available room. They registered as husband and wife under false names. If the clerk at the hotel desk doubted the veracity of the registration, especially since they had no baggage, he did not show it. The clerk had been through that not uncommon practice of customers many times before. Hotel rooms, after all, provide the havens that Koskinen had so eloquently articulated. In that plain, unadorned and inconspicuous hotel room, Elena and Koskinen found the peace, quiet and love for which they yearned. The police examiner was furthest from their thoughts.

CHAPTER 9

Four days after Bill Chance and Gene Wagner had been at the Finnish Embassy, Chance and Wagner were having lunch at the United States Embassy with Ambassador Harrison Hayes and his Deputy, Fraser Addison. They were discussing the ominous rumors from Germany. According to sketchy intelligence, Hitler was on the verge of annexing Bohemia, Moravia, and the Lithuanian City of Memel.

Wagner commented, "You can't really blame Hitler for wanting these areas. They are all predominantly German populations and they probably should be a part of Germany."

Ambassador Hayes countered, "If you use that reasoning, Gene, then every aggressive nation like Germany can say, 'This area or that area is made up with a majority of our people,' and then justify going in and taking that area. That can apply not only to racial makeup but to political or ideological concentrations. For example, Stalin could infiltrate a country with Communists and then say, 'Well, there are a lot of Communists in this or that country, so we'll take it over.'"

"Yeah, that's why governments throughout Europe and even the United States are concerned about Stalin. They rightfully fear that he wants to spread the Communist ideology throughout Europe to begin with. And then he'll march in and take over." Wagner was not to be denied his beliefs.

Wagner continued, "There is another possible example. When Hitler came to power, there were about five hundred thousand Jews in Germany. According to the information we have, about two hundred fifty thousand have left Germany through last year, 1938. Hitler could say, 'There are Jews who have fled to Holland, Belgium, France, and so forth and we have to get rid of the Jews. So, we'll go into Holland,

Belgium and France in order to rid them of Jews,' and if that is his philosophy, he'd be right."

"Aren't you carrying your reasoning to an extreme, Gene?" The Ambassador chuckled at what he thought was somewhat ridiculously illogical.

At that moment, Rose Arlov, the Ambassador's secretary, entered the dining room and approached the table where Chance was seated with the others.

"Mr. Chance, there is a telephone call for you. The person is waiting on the line. Can you take the call in our office?"

"Do you know who it is?"

"No, he wouldn't leave his name. He said that he wanted to talk to you personally."

Chance arose from his seat, excused himself from the group and followed the secretary to the Ambassador's office. Chance couldn't possibly imagine who was calling him.

"Bill Chance here."

"Mr. Chance," a gruff, masculine voice spoke in Russian, "you can come and pick up the cake you ordered tomorrow at 10:30 in the morning."

"With whom am I talking?"

The caller abruptly hung up without further conversation and identification. Chance stood for a moment puzzled by the message. Then in a flash it dawned upon him. Someone in the underground bakery had called to tell him to meet at the bakery in the morning. The caller had used a discreet way of informing him in the event someone else had tapped into the phone line.

Chance returned to his colleagues in the dining room. In a low voice he told them of the message of the anonymous caller.

"I assume it was to advise me of a meeting at the bakery tomorrow morning. It was something we talked about with Elena at the Finnish Embassy four days ago. She probably set this meeting up for us. In any case, Gene and I will be at the bakery tomorrow morning. Right, Gene?"

"Yes, of course. I think it will be exciting." Wagner sounded ebullient.

Deputy Fraser Anderson spoke up. "I think we should review the guidelines on just what the parameters are for you as agents of the United States in possibly working with these underground people."

"I think that is appropriate," Chance replied. "But we will not commit to any action on our part without first discussing it with you both."

The Ambassador interjected his thought. "I think the basic guideline is that we shall help to bring down Stalin without in any way compromising the United States government. It is a matter of how far we think we can go and still be able to claim to be innocent of efforts to bring down a foreign government."

"It comes down to judging the specific proposal of the underground and we'll just have to wait and see what they have in mind," Chance remarked. The others agreed.

"In any case, pick out a cake that isn't overly sweet," Addison said laughing.

Outside the dining room and after Hayes and Addison took their leave to go to their respective offices, Chance turned to Wagner. "Gene, let's take a walk past the bakery. We won't go inside, but I think we should take a little more detailed look at its outside. What do you say?"

"Sure, we haven't much to do, anyway," Wagner replied.

The weather the last part of March in Moscow was still cold and somewhat a bone-chilling damp. Chance and Wagner dressed accordingly with heavy coats, gloves and fur hats.

As they walked down the street towards the bakery, Chance remarked to Wagner, "I still cannot understand how the underground people found out what our real mission is. There has to be someone in our Embassy who managed to discover it and who passed it along to the underground people. Frankly, I have no idea who it might be, but it could be any one of the local staff."

"I haven't been able to fathom it either," said Wagner, "and as far as I know, neither Hayes nor Addison has been able to discover who it might be." As they drew near the bakery building, an elderly man and woman emerged from the shop carrying bags of baked goods. A middle-aged woman was entering and through the shop front window could be seen several customers at the store counter.

"They seem to be busy enough," Wagner observed. "The bakery is undoubtedly a legitimate business and appears to be well-established."

"That's right," Chance agreed. "It's not 'just' a front for a covert operation."

As they had observed on their initial visit, the bakery was housed in a plain stucco building of two stories. The store front was made up of a large window behind which on a shelf were poster boards containing descriptions and prices of the products available at the shop. The second level front had three narrow curtained windows.

Chance and Wagner walked to the rear of the building and observed a truck standing in the rear yard. There were two doors which they surmised led one to the street level bakery shop, the other to the second floor. There were two windows on the second floor overlooking the rear yard. They, too, had closed curtains. In addition to the truck, the rear yard appeared rather cluttered with rusty, discarded baking equipment, empty wood barrels and boxes and several dilapidated garbage cans.

"Not very tidy," remarked Wagner. "I hope their operation inside is more sanitary than this outside."

"I suppose we'll find that out tomorrow," countered Chance.

The pair resumed their return walk to the Embassy, but hurrying to get out of the cold.

When Chance and Wagner arose the next morning, they found that there had been a light snowfall during the night, probably an inch or two. The new white cover gave the city a fresh clean look that reminded Chance of the scenes portrayed on some of the Christmas cards he and Melissa had received. Although he had been busy since he arrived in Moscow and had been mentally occupied with the thoughts, the ideas concerning the mission for which he and Gene had been sent here, nevertheless, Melissa and their children were always in the background of his mind. Especially in the evenings when he would have gone home from his office in the State Building, he now missed being greeted by Melissa and having the give-and-take banter with the kids at the dinner table. Perhaps, working with the underground people would facilitate the project and, hopefully, accelerate its accomplishment. That thought brought some comfort to him.

* * * * *

Chance and Wagner left the Embassy shortly after ten a.m. and headed for the bakery. A light snow was still falling intermittently. There were a few pedestrians and an automobile or two on the avenue. Both Chance and Wagner kept a lookout for anyone or anything that might arouse their suspicions. Although they had been in Russia only a short time, they had already adopted, subconsciously as it were, the rule to look over their shoulders when outside the confines of the Embassy. Looking over one's shoulder had at this time in the Soviets reached the level of a cultural custom among the citizenry. Foreigners quickly acquired the habit. The environment of fear and suspicion that permeated Russian society was not a pleasant experience for Americans accustomed to the constitutionally guaranteed freedoms.

Just before entering the bakery building, Chance looked up at the second story and thought he saw the curtain in one of the windows part ever so slightly as if someone was behind it observing the street. Since he could not be certain, he said nothing to Wagner. He surmised, however, that it would be the better part of wisdom for the underground group to have a lookout whenever they have a clandestine meeting or other activity in the building.

The customer service part of the shop had neither a customer nor the clerk present when Chance and Wagner entered. However, the thumping sounds generated by their vigorous stomping on the floor to knock the snow from their boots brought the clerk from the back room. Chance and Wagner recognized the young lady as having been behind the counter when they had their first and previous visit to the bakery. The clerk, on the other hand, gave no indication that she remembered having seen them before. She spoke in Russian.

"Gentlemen, what can I do for you?"

"We are from the United States Embassy and we are here to pick up our cake."

At that moment there entered from the back room the young man whom Chance and Wagner recognized as the fellow who had accosted them on the street and brought them to the bakery on the earlier occasion. The young man nodded knowingly to the clerk as if to acknowledge that it was safe for her to proceed accordingly with the two Americans.

The clerk then said, "Gentlemen, Boris will take care of you."

Boris then addressed Chance and Wagner, "Please come with me." He motioned to the door to the back room. He had a congenial smile as he directed them. Chance remembered that smile from the earlier contact with Boris. Chance thought the young man intended it to be disarming. Under the circumstances, however, Chance concluded that it was a mask to disguise a web of intrigue.

Chance and Wagner walked around the counter and through the doorway to the back room, led by Boris. As they walked past the young lady, Wagner gave her a wink. The young lady blushed. The back room was an expansive area where the baking was done. At the moment there were two employees at work. The young man led them to a door on one side of the room which opened on stairs to the second floor. Chance and Wagner following the young man ascended the stairs which, at the top, opened to a small room with one curtained window. The room contained two cots, each with blankets and a pillow, a small table on which stood a lone, half-burned candle in its holder. Hung on the wall was a picture of a smiling Stalin. The picture startled Chance. It was not consistent with an underground group intent on killing the dictator. Under each bed was a pot, which Chance understood, served as a nighttime toilet.

At the far end of the room was a door which opened to another small room. The young man led Chance and Wagner into this second room, also with a curtained window and two iron framed folding-type cots with mattresses, blankets and pillows. It had no table, but had two plain wood kitchen chairs next to each of the cots. An identical picture of Stalin adorned the wall.

As Chance and Wagner entered the second room, they heard low, muffled voices seeming originating in another room. The young man, still smiling, beckoned Chance and Wagner to the door which must open on a third room from which the voices emanated. The young man knocked three or four times on this door. Chance heard the scuffled scraping of a chair being moved, a creaking of the floor as someone in the room moved about. The door opened. Standing in the doorway was a short, stocky man whom both Chance and Wagner immediately recognized as Petrov, the baker whom they had met on their first visit in the back room of the bakery.

Speaking in Russian, Petrov said in his low, husky voice, "Come in, gentlemen."

The room into which Chance and Wagner now entered was much larger. Chance estimated, double the size of the two smaller rooms together. Seated at a table were three other men. All outfitted in baking uniforms, white aprons, white shirt and white trousers. The three men arose as Chance and Wagner entered. Boris introduced them. Pointing to each, successively, he said, "This is Mikhail, Nikolai and Demyan." Gesturing towards Wagner and Chance, Boris said, "Here are Gene and William."

Turning to Chance and Wagner, Boris said, "All these people have been briefed. They know about you. They very active in our movement. They can be trusted."

When they first entered the room, Chance and Wagner had immediately noticed not only the men at the table, but two curtained windows, one presumably facing the street, the other the rear yard. Standing in front of the street side window stood a slim woman with her back to the group in the room and, apparently, looking out of the window. Her face was not discernable to Chance and Wagner.

After the introductions to the men, Chance looked at the woman and then to Boris. The expression on Chance's face was quizzical as if to ask, "Who is the woman?" Before Boris could respond, the woman turned and looked directly at Chance and Wagner. She was smiling mischievously. Both Chance and Wagner almost simultaneously gasped in total disbelief.

"Oh, my god!" uttered Chance in a low, whispered tone, but loud enough for all to hear. "Sofia Kameneva!"

Wagner also spoke her name, "Sofia!" It was indeed the translator at their United States Embassy.

Sofia walked towards Chance and Wagner.

"Hello, Bill! Hello, Gene!" Her friendly smile had broadened to a grin that implied that she was enjoying their surprise. She extended her hand and grasped each of theirs in succession.

Chance recovered from his shock sufficiently to ask, "Sofia, what are you doing here?"

Sofia replied, now laughing, "I was asked to come and translate for you." She was being quite facetious.

Wagner spoke up in English. "You are part of the underground?" He was incredulous.

"Do you think that I would be here if I were not?" Sofia was still amused by the startled expressions on both Wagner's and Chance's faces.

Chance quickly drew a conclusion. "It was you, then, who informed these people about our real purpose in being here in Russia."

"Yes, that is true." Sofia became serious. "I thought they should know because you can be of help, perhaps, to each other."

"You could have asked us first," Chance declared somewhat accusingly.

"Yes, I could have, but I was afraid you would say 'no.'"

"How did you discover what our real mission is?" Chance queried.

"I will tell you later. Right now, these people are anxious to get on with their business with you. They are uncomfortable being here too long. You know, the police. I will translate for you. It will be easier and quicker for everyone."

Sofia turned to the men and told them they could begin their discussion with Bill and Gene and that she would translate. Boris invited Chance and Wagner to be seated, which they did.

Petrov was the first to speak. Sofia translated to English.

"Those whom you see here are but a small part of our organization, but we are providing much of the leadership. The two men you saw downstairs doing the baking are also among the leadership. They are Viktor and Yosif. They provide a cover in case the authorities come in. They are working at baking, you understand."

Petrov spoke slowly, deliberately in his basso voice. Neither Chance nor Wagner said anything, but listened intently. Chance perceived that behind Petrov's words was a very determined and strong personality. Petrov, he could see, was someone to be taken very seriously.

Petrov continued, "All of us feel so strongly that we must get rid of that monster, Stalin, to save Russia that we are ready to die to get it done. And we hope we can get it done without having to forfeit one life of our group. We have plans and alternate plans. This is where you can help." Petrov paused.

"How can we help?" inquired Chance.

"We ask that your United States through your Ambassador here arrange a dinner or party to honor Stalin either because of the great things he has done for the Soviets or because of some event with which he is closely related. The reason we can leave to you."

Chance interrupted, "How will having a dinner to honor him lead to getting rid of him?"

There was unanimous laughter from all of the Russians present in reaction to Chance's question. Chance looked confused. He turned to Sofia. "What did I say that is so funny?" Sofia translated his question for the Russians.

Petrov replied, "Ah, I can see that you don't know Stalin. He's a great lady's man, a womanizer. He never leaves a party or a dinner gathering without taking some female back to his apartment or to his dacha. He is constantly looking over the women at the party or dinner and when he is attracted to one in particular, he will send her word through one of his aides that she should join him during a social time after the dinner. The woman might be somebody's wife, but she can't refuse. In fact, she had better not refuse. And if her husband protests even slightly, he's likely to be on his way to Lubyanka the next morning. When the dinner ends, the woman goes with Stalin."

Again Petrov paused to let the Americans digest what he said.

Chance then asked, "But how does that get rid of Stalin?"

Petrov continued, "At the dinner in Stalin's honor we will have one of our very attractive women at the gathering."

Chance interposed, "Stalin may select some other attractive woman. In that case, you will have gained nothing."

"Yes, we know that's a risk, but we know Stalin. Our attractive woman will lure him, seduce him by playing up to him, by giving him attention, by making eyes at him, by doing whatever women do to tempt men. Stalin's ego is such that he'll fancy himself an irresistible Roman Adonis and give her all of his attention."

"I think Adonis was a Greek," Chance corrected Petrov.

Petrov laughed in good humor. "Alright, Greek. Who cares?"

"Do you have a woman in mind?"

Petrov glanced at Sofia. "Yes. Possibly Sofia here or possibly the young lady you met at the Finnish Embassy. There are a couple of others. But Sofia and the woman who currently serve at the Finnish Embassy are the most trustworthy."

"How is the young woman to get rid of Stalin?"

"She'll poison him. She will know how to do it."

"What happens if she's suspected and arrested?" Chance was insistent on getting specific answers to his questions.

"She'll have cyanide capsules with her."

"You mean she'll commit suicide."

"Probably, yes."

Chance shook his head at the disquieting scenario just described by Petrov. Wagner sat silently, but looking quite glum. To him, possibly sacrificing beautiful women like Sofia and Elena for the sake of saving Russia or the United States or any country was the most absurd, nonsensical and grotesque proposal he'd ever heard. There must be other ways to save countries.

That thought caused Wagner to ask Petrov, "You said you had alternative plans. What might they be?"

"One plan is to ambush Stalin some night while he's being driven to his dacha just outside the city. However, that is extremely risky. He has bodyguards in cars both in front and in back of his car. We would bomb his car and then machine gun his bodyguards as they got out of their cars."

"That sounds more like a sure thing than the poison plot you described," commented Wagner.

"The problem," explained Petrov, "is the difficulty getting our ambush party into position without being discovered. There are guards all along the route that Stalin follows to get to his dacha. Those guards are stationed as soon as police headquarters is informed that he has decided to travel to his dacha. William, I'd prefer to try the dinner method that I described a short time ago. Will you try to get your Ambassador to go along with the idea and let me know of your success or failure to convince him? But do your best to convince him to give the dinner. It's the best way for this project."

"Alright, yes, I'll certainly try," Chance said.

"Can you let us know in a few days if you'll go along with the idea? Arranging the dinner is all we ask of you. We'll do the rest. The Russian authorities will never know of your involvement."

"I hope that's true that no word will get out." Chance looked directly at Sofia when he said that.

"How do we let you know?" queried Chance.

"Let Sofia know and she'll get the information to us. In fact, Sofia will be your liaison to us. That will keep you and your government in the background as much as you wish."

"If I mention to the Ambassador Sofia's part in discovering our mission, I hope she'll have a job at our Embassy. He doesn't look too kindly on spies in the Embassy or on the Embassy staff."

"We'll rely on you to be persuasive. You have a mission to accomplish and I'm sure that your Ambassador will understand that this is the best way for you to accomplish it. Now, I think the meeting should end. Thank you for coming, Gentlemen. Boris will see you out. Don't forget to pick up a cake before you leave. We have to keep appearances legitimate. But wait just a few moments until we look outside to determine if the area is clear, that is, nothing suspicious."

Petrov turned to one of the three men who had sat silently throughout the meeting. "Demyan, check on the outside." Demyan went to the windows facing both the front and rear of the building. After a few moments he reported that the street and yard were seemingly clear.

Chance and Wagner shook hands with all of the men present. As he was leaving the room, Chance addressed Sofia. "Sofia, when you get back to the Embassy, I want to talk with you."

Chance and Wagner, guided by Boris, retraced their steps through the two rooms, down the stairs and through the baking room. They waited in the baking room while Boris ascertained whether there were customers in the store. He raised two fingers toward Chance and Wagner to indicate there were two customers. Five minutes later, he motioned to Chance and Wagner that it was clear for them to enter the customer front shop. They went quickly to the customer side of the counter. The young lady presented them with a box containing, she said, "the cake you ordered." Chance paid her several rubles and he and Wagner left the building and began their walk back to the Embassy. It was then close to the noon hour. In time for lunch and a piece of the cake they had just bought. There was little conversation as they hurried their steps in the cold and biting wind. But Wagner did muse out loud, "I wonder what kind of cake it is."

When they arrived back at the Embassy they checked in with Helen, Deputy Addison's secretary. Wagner went to the kitchen and gave instructions to the chef to serve the cake for dinner that evening. He and Chance then joined Fraser Addison for lunch.

"How did your meeting go?" Addison asked.

Chance replied, "Very well, but Gene and I would like to give a report on the details when we can all get together with the Ambassador present and have a discussion. There are a few things which need to be decided."

Addison understood that Chance did not want to talk further about the subject at that time and so did not persist in questioning. After lunch, Chance and Wagner went to Chance's room where they relaxed and talked casually about the events at the bakery.

Wagner raised the issue that was uppermost in both of their minds. "What do we do about Sofia?"

Chance was silent for a few moments as he thought about the question. "I think we should wait until we have talked with her. My inclination is to do nothing except to report to the Ambassador and Fraser about her being in the underground. I think I agree with Petrov that their suggestion to have a dinner for Stalin is the best way to accomplish what we were sent here to do. Sofia is important to us for that purpose."

Wagner said, "I suppose we should tell her to quit spying on us."

"We can tell her that, but there is no need for her to continue to do so since she knows everything and we're going to be using her as information liaison with the people in the underground."

"Golly," Wagner exclaimed, "I hate to think of Sofia or that gal at the Finnish Embassy being used as bait for Stalin. Can you imagine what would happen to them if they're caught?" He gave a shudder. "Maybe an ambush would be better after all."

"Well, we'll talk with Hayes about arranging dinner. If he says 'no,' an ambush may have to be used or some other alternative." Chance lay back on his bed and Wagner stretched out on the sofa. Both gazed at the ceiling and understood that they were part of a portentous event that was getting closer to being played out.

Sofia arrived back at the Embassy about four p.m. and after going to her room to freshen up contacted Chance on the Embassy phone system.

"I'm back. When would you like to see me?" She sounded so sweet and friendly that Chance, still annoyed at her spying, nevertheless suppressed any stridency in his own voice.

"Can you come to my room in about ten or fifteen minutes? Gene will be here, too."

"Yes, I'll be there."

Sofia knocked gently on the closed door to Chance's room. Chance opened and greeted her with, "Come on in, Sofia." Chance acted friendly and nonchalantly. He intended to dispel any tenseness that Sofia might feel under the circumstance. Wagner helped. He went over to Sofia and gave her a hug. She responded with an irresistible smile.

"Damn him," Chance thought to himself. "This is not time for personal affections."

The three sat around informally. "Can we send for some coffee or anything else for you?" Chance asked of Sofia.

"No, thanks. I'm fine."

Chance got to the point. "You know we were totally surprised at seeing you at the bakery today."

"Yes, I'm sure you were."

"The reason we want to talk with you is because we'd like to know how you found out what our real mission is in being here. It's a serious matter of Embassy security as I'm sure you appreciate."

"Yes, of course I'll tell you. It's quite simple. You were heard talking about it, about eliminating Stalin."

"We did not talk about it when others were present. We have been very careful and circumspect about discussing it."

"Apparently not carefully enough," Sofia commented.

"Did you overhear us talking between ourselves?" Chance asked.

"No, I did not, but someone else did."

"Who could that be?"

"You remember that fellow Kovalenko who asked for asylum in the Embassy and later was found dead from poisoning?"

"How could I possibly forget?" Chance replied.

"His room adjoined yours and from what we know you left your door to the hallway slightly open. You and Gene were talking about your mission to get rid of Stalin. Kovalenko was passing your room and heard you talking and heard enough words to cause him to stop just outside the door and unseen by you to listen to your conversation. He heard enough to convince him of your real purpose in coming to Russia."

Chance and Wagner both looked dismayed.

Sofia then added, "Bill and Gene, I am going to reveal something the police would love to learn about, but never should." Sofia's demeanor had become very serious. She talked is a subdued voice.

"Yes, we'll promise." At this point, Chance would have agreed to most any request so anxious was he to get more information about the circumstances involving Embassy staff and security.

Sofia proceeded, "When Kovalenko surmised that you both were here to assassinate Stalin, he decided, for some reason, to tell Yakov Strinovsky about it. As you know, Strinovsky was Director of Embassy Personnel. We assume that he told Strinovsky because Strinovsky was a Russian and a Jew and therefore must be loyal to Stalin. However, Kovalenko chose the wrong person to confide in." Sofia paused.

Chance asked, "How so?"

"You will be surprised by what I tell you," Sofia continued. "Strinovsky was a member of our underground." Sofia waited for the information to strike Chance and Wagner.

Chance spoke up. "I am absolutely flabbergasted, astounded. The Embassy must be a sanctuary for the underground."

Sofia smiled, "No, not quite that." She continued her recitation. "Strinovsky told me that Kovalenko had said to him that he was going to the police with the information about your Stalin project and that he would use it as a bargaining tool to get the police to release his wife and son from prison. Kovalenko was desperate to get his wife and son back and out of harms way. Strinovsky told me he argued with Kovalenko and tried to dissuade him from doing it. Strinovsky knew that if Kovalenko went to the police with the story, it would trigger a big police investigation that could damage not only your mission, but also the underground. Strinovsky decided on his own that Kovalenko had to be killed when Kovalenko refused to budge from his intent.

That is why you found Kovalenko dead from poisoning. Strinovsky was swift to carry out the killing."

"But Strinovsky himself died by hanging. Why did that happen?" Chance was shocked by what he was hearing. At the time the events occurred he never dreamed that there were these ramifications.

"Strinovsky told me that shortly after the police were here to investigate Kovalenko's death he received a telephone call from the NKVD ordering him to come down to their headquarters. They wanted to question him about the things going on in the Embassy. You know, like other Russians working at foreign Embassies, Strinovsky had to have the approval of the police and the police expected the Russian employees to report to them from time to time. Strinovsky told me that he was fearful that under NKVD pressure he might be forced to tell about the underground. Strinovsky knew, as we all know, that once the NKVD gets its focus on you anything can happen. You can be treated kindly or you can be tortured to tell things or to confess to things that may or may not be factual. Strinovsky was a person who would do nothing to harm the underground movement. He hated Stalin with a passion as we all do. He believed that the underground was the only answer to get rid of the dictator, the monster. He did not tell me he was going to take his own life to avoid having to go to the NKVD, but that is what he apparently decided was his only recourse. He is, in my opinion, a hero, a great man."

When Sofia had finished, Chance and Wagner remained silent for some moments. Finally, Chance said, "Well, what you have told us explains a great deal. Gene and I, as well as the Ambassador, have been puzzled over the deaths of Kovalenko and Strinovsky. By the way, Sofia, who else among our staff of locals are in the underground?"

"I shall tell you because we are all in this together. We are all working towards the same goal. Yuri the waiter, Gregor, the chauffeur and Ludmila, the telephone operator, are all members of the underground. You must keep this confidential, please. I would ask that for now, at least, you not let these people know that you know." Sofia looked earnestly at Chance and Wagner. Chance looked at Wagner and both nodded their assent to Sofia's request.

"Well, we certainly aren't going to tell the police. But, Gene and I feel we should let the Ambassador and Addison know about all this.

Is there some reason we should not?" Chance searched for an answer from Sofia.

"I am concerned," Sofia replied with a worried look on her face, "that they will want to fire the underground people who work here. The police will learn of it and investigate why so many at one time and that may very well disrupt our organization. We may have to go into hiding and after a while it will become difficult to regroup, to get the organization together again. It would be best if nothing is done just now to disturb the status quo."

"I would agree with you on that point, but I think that we can inform the Ambassador and Addison and recommend that they do nothing, take no action except to arrange the dinner in honor of Stalin."

"Well, I'll have to leave it to your judgment, but it would be terrible if the Ambassador did not take your recommendation."

What to do posed a dilemma for Chance and Wagner. They were perplexed and tormented by the delicate position they found themselves in. As employees of their government they felt, on the one hand, duty bound to keep the Ambassador informed. On the other hand, they were aware of the risks in keeping him informed. Their position was not enviable.

"Gene and I will have to talk and think about what to do, Sofia. We'll certainly do what we think is best for all concerned. In any case, we'll take the matter of the dinner up with the Ambassador and let you know of his decision as soon as we can."

"Very well. That's all I can expect. Thanks, Bill and Gene," Sofia said. "Is there anything else?"

"No, we'll probably see you at dinner and you can share the cake with us." They all laughed good-naturedly.

Sofia arose to leave. Chance and Wagner saw her to the door. Wagner then said, "Sofia, I'll walk you to your room."

"That's fine," Sofia smiled graciously.

"Gene, I'd like you to stay here. We have things to talk about. I'm sure Sofia can find her way to her room." Chance was annoyed.

"I'll be right back, Bill. Only take a moment," replied Wagner cheerfully. Chance shrugged in resignation and turned back into his room, clearly showing his chagrin. It was still difficult for him to take Wagner's womanizing in stride.

When Wagner returned to the room after approximately ten minutes, Chance asked sarcastically, "Did you get a big kiss and a hug?"

"Of course, why not? It tends to liven up our existence here." Wagner was quite jovial.

"You know, Gene, it would be nice if you could stick to business and forget the women for a change," remonstrated Chance with Wagner.

"By the way, Gene," Chance added, "you should change your prejudice about Jews. There is one, Lozovsky, who is risking his life for a cause, and another, Strinovsky, who has given his life for the same cause. It proves some Jews have more to their character than just making money."

Replied Wagner, "I'll need more than two Jews to change my mind. However, I have no doubt that there are some Jews who can put the interest of their country over their own interests and the interests of their own kind."

"Sit down, Gene, and let's talk about how we should handle this matter of Sofia, the underground in our Embassy and the plan to give a dinner in honor of Stalin."

"I'll defer to your opinion, Bill. What do you think we should do?"

"I think we have to meet with the Ambassador and Addison to tell them that we met with the underground leaders and they suggested the dinner and their method of enticing Stalin. I think we have to tell them about Sofia and the others who are in the underground while working here for us. Then I believe we should recommend that nothing should be done about our staff. We can suggest that they call in Sofia and the others and tell them to stop the spying or be fired."

"What about telling them about the deaths of Kovalenko and Strinovsky?" Wagner inquired.

Chance replied, "I don't think it's necessary to tell them about that right now. We can tell them later. What is your opinion?"

"I agree with you on all points, Bill," Wagner said. "I just hope the Ambassador will go along with the idea of the dinner."

"Well, I'll see if I can arrange a meeting with the Ambassador and Addison for some time tomorrow. I'll let you know." Chance closed the discussion on that note.

Later that afternoon Chance, through Rose and Helen, the secretaries of the Ambassador and Fraser Addison, scheduled a conference at nine-thirty the next morning in the Ambassador's office.

Bill Chance slept fitfully that night. In fact, he slept very little. His mind kept racing through a rehearsal of the day's events, what was said and what should have been said but wasn't and by whom. Then, intermittently, his mind switched over to the impending meeting with the Ambassador and Addison, what sort of presentation he should make and what reactions from them he might expect. Was he doing the right thing in telling them about the underground among the Embassy personnel?

Chance got up from his bed a couple of times, turned on the light and started to read a magazine thinking that might help to calm his tortured mental activity. It failed to do so. Finally, exhausted at about four o'clock in the morning, he fell asleep on the sofa where he had been perusing the magazines.

When he arose in the morning in time for breakfast, Chance met Wagner in the dining room and complained about his sleepless night, Wagner replied that he had had the same problem.

"I couldn't get to sleep either," Wagner grumbled. "I lay awake worrying about Sofia possibly being used as bait to lure Stalin into taking her to his dacha. That would be terrible."

"Well, somebody has to do it." Chance wasn't very sympathetic and was in no mood to commiserate with his lovesick assistant.

"Maybe I should be excused from the meeting this morning," Wagner said. "I don't see Sofia here for breakfast. I ought to really check on her. I'd like to talk with her also to see if I can get any more information from her."

"About what?" Chance said. "She told us everything we needed to know."

"Well, you can never tell. If I'm alone with her, she may add to what she told us."

"Then go ahead. I can handle the meeting by myself." Chance wanted to avoid an argument with Wagner. Chance knew well enough that Wagner had more on his mind with Sofia than talking about the underground.

At a few minutes before nine-thirty, Chance entered the Ambassador's office. Rose told him to go on in as Deputy Addison was already there with Ambassador Hayes.

"Good morning, Bill," greeted both Addison and Hayes. "Where is Gene?"

"Good morning, gentlemen." Bill Chance took a seat. "He has another matter to take care of."

After a few minutes of small talk about the weather and other inconsequential items, Ambassador Hayes addressed Chance.

"I presume you wanted to tell us about your meeting yesterday."

"Yes. It was interesting and had a surprise or two."

"Really. Tell us about it." Ambassador Hayes expressed considerable interest in his voice.

Chance proceeded to describe the details from the time they entered the bakery building to their entry into the third room with the leaders of the underground movement.

"When Gene and I entered this room, we noticed a woman standing at a window with her back to us. We could not determine who it was. Then she turned around and faced us. We were both surprised and shocked. It was Sofia Kameneva, our Russian translator."

"Sofia Kameneva!" Deputy Addison exclaimed. "I can't believe it, a member of the underground."

Ambassador Hayes grimaced. "An undergrounder in our midst. She has to go!"

"Mr. Ambassador, please, not so fast. Please hear the rest of the story." Chance became alarmed at the hasty, impulsive decision of the Ambassador. If Sofia were fired, Chance felt the mission he and Wagner had been sent to accomplish could be jeopardized.

"Mr. Ambassador and Deputy Addison, what the leaders of the underground have suggested as a plan of action could help us achieve our mission with the least involvement of the United States and with virtually no possibility that even our small involvement will be detected by the Soviet government. Sofia is a very important part of that plan and she should not have her status here disturbed because she is so important."

"Well, you'll have to explain." The Ambassador was placing Chance on the defensive and, in a sense, telling him he had to convince the Ambassador to change his mind about Sofia.

Chance proceeded to relate what the leaders of the underground proposed, namely, to have the United States give a dinner in honor of Stalin and to use it as an opportunity for some woman of the underground, perhaps Sofia, to entice Stalin to take her to his dacha and to there give him poison.

"It sounds ghoulish, I know," Chance said. "But Gene and I were sent here to help get Stalin eliminated as a matter of unwritten policy of the government which we represent. As much as we may be repelled by this plan, we have no choice but to do what we can to carry out that policy."

Ambassador Hayes became quiet, thoughtful and his agitation seemed to have vanished. Finally he said, "Yeah, I guess you're right, Bill. What is your opinion, Fraser?"

"I think I'd agree with Bill. Sofia hasn't done us any harm up to this point even though she has been in the underground movement for a while, apparently, I don't believe that letting her remain here will cause any harm to us, especially if we keep all this confidential." Deputy Addison seemed relaxed and assured.

"Furthermore," Addison added, "if you want my opinion about holding a dinner for Stalin, I'd say, 'Yes, let's do it.' It may be the answer we're looking for."

"Well, I can't proceed with a dinner without getting the approval of Washington. What do I tell them is the reason?" Ambassador Hayes asked.

Deputy Addison answered, "I'd just tell Washington that the idea of the dinner will promote better relations with Stalin who, after all, is the Soviet government. Tell Washington we're at a point where we need to boost our good relations. Stalin may be on the verge of tuning out the United States in favor of working with Hitler to divide up Europe between them. And that is not in our best interest."

"I'll call Secretary Roth today and explain to him and see what he says. But, I'm not going to say anything about women and poisoning and so on."

"That's right," agreed Addison. "That's not a part we would be involved in anyway."

The Ambassador stood up to signify the end of the conference. "Bill, I'll let you know as soon as I get a definite answer from Washington. It may take a few days. You know what the bureaucratic process is back there. In the meantime, you and Gene can carry out your trade mission activities." The Ambassador and Addison laughed at the reference to Chance's and Wagner's cover. Chance smiled.

"I appreciate what you and Gene are doing." There was a warm and friendly exchange of handshakes. Chance then left to find Wagner.

Chance knew where he'd find Wagner. He walked down the corridor to Sofia's room, knocked on the door and waited. Sofia opened the door. She wore a dressing robe and appeared to be slightly disheveled.

Smiling, she said, "Hi, Bill, won't you come in. Gene is here."

"No, thanks, just tell Gene ..." Before Chance could finish his sentence, Wagner appeared at the door. He had removed his shirt and tie, but was otherwise dressed. He looked carefree and happy.

"Bill, if you don't want to come in, I'll meet you in your room shortly. Is that alright?"

"Yeah, I suppose so." Chance was matter of fact and not at all amused. "I'll see you both later." Chance turned and retraced his steps down the corridor.

"I guess he's not very happy that you're here," Sofia commented as she closed the door behind them.

Wagner put his arm around Sofia's waist and they embraced and resumed their affectionate intimacy.

* * * * *

As usual, Elena stopped by the Finnish Embassy and met with Koskinen. It was the same day that Bill Chance received the anonymous telephone call at the U.S. Embassy instructing him to come to the bakery the next morning for a meeting. Koskinen had not seen Elena for two days after he had left the small hotel where they had spent the previous night together. When they parted, they were relaxed and happy. The time they were together had seemed to both to bond them closer to each other.

When Koskinen met Elena at the Embassy his first words to her were, "I have missed you these last two days so very much. Not being with you each day distresses me."

"I feel the same way about you, Timo." Koskinen thought Elena looked so fresh and beautiful.

It was difficult for either of them to think of anything else but their feelings for each other. But, there was business to be considered, serious business to which they had to give total concentration. They both recognized that.

"Akmal brought me a message from our leaders yesterday," Elena said. "They request that you meet with them at the bakery three days from now at noon."

"Fine, I'll be there," Koskinen promised.

"Akmal will be here about eleven-thirty to pick you up and take you there in his truck."

"We might be stopped by the police. That would be awkward." Koskinen was worried about that possibility especially since Akmal had been checked from time to time by the police.

"That shouldn't be a problem. Tell the police that Akmal delivers bread to your Embassy and that you had to go to a certain part of town and Akmal agreed to take you part of the way. Then, if you think the police are following the truck, just get off somewhere near some shops. Akmal will continue on without you and we'll set up another meeting date. You can go into a shop, buy something and then, eventually, take a bus or taxi back to the Embassy."

"It sounds quite simple. Alright," said Koskinen, "I'll meet Akmal here. Have you any idea, Elena, what will take place when I meet with your underground leaders?"

"No, I haven't. You'll find that out when you get there."

"Will you be there?"

"No, and I must tell you why."

"Yes, why?"

"I received a call from that police inspector yesterday. He wanted to see me that evening. I told him I couldn't but to keep him pacified, I took your advice and made a date to have lunch with him. That was before I heard from Akmal about your meeting at the bakery on that day. Now, I don't know how I can get out of it." Elena shrugged as if resigned to the fact that she could not risk giving another excuse to the policeman.

Koskinen became plainly irritated. "That bastard has really complicated things!" He thought for a moment, then said, "I think you will have to contact him and tell him with firmness that something has come up that you didn't anticipate and you have to cancel the date. Make him understand that your schedule is a busy one and that it is subject to changes over which you have no control."

Elena did not reply, but she looked skeptical.

"Not only that, but I have a need for you to be at the meeting to translate for me. I don't speak Russian well enough to be able to handle the conversation from a number of people."

Elena plainly showed that she had little enthusiasm for calling off her date with the investigator. A courageous woman in many risky situations, she nevertheless was extremely fearful of the policeman who was pursuing her.

"Well, I'll do what I can to cancel the date," Elena said, "But he'll more than likely want to arrange a date for the very next day. This predicament can go on and on. You know, Timo, this guy is a real danger to me. I can't keep turning him down much longer. I wish that courier of yours was to be here soon. The sooner, the better."

"Elena, I know it is easy enough for me to say this, but you're going to have to stand your ground with this---this---," Koskinen searched for a non-swearword.

"Monster," Elena filled in the word that she thought might best express Koskinen's opinion about the policeman.

Koskinen laughed, "Alright, I'll accept that description. I wish you'd stay for lunch, Elena."

"Yes, I think I can. It will be served in about an hour, is that right?" inquired Elena.

"Yes."

Koskinen then came up with a suggestion. "Elena, you are supposed to be translating for our trade mission in negotiations with their Russian counterparts. In order to support your work here, I think you should know something about the status of the negotiations. You may have to use that information to justify your being here so frequently."

"Yes, that is a good idea," Elena observed.

"While we're waiting for lunch, I'll try to get one of our trade negotiators to sit down with you for an update on their efforts at working out certain provisions in a trade pact. Is that alright with you?"

"Certainly."

"Wait here and I'll see whom I can trust enough with you." Koskinen smiled at Elena.

The receptionist informed Koskinen that Petri and Eino were in the building.

"Page Eino. I'll talk with him on the house telephone."

When Eino Partola responded, Koskinen outlined what he had in mind. "Can you see our Russian translator for about a half-hour to bring her up to date on the trade negotiations?"

"Sure," Partola replied. "I'll be down in a few minutes. Where shall I meet her?"

"In the conference room," Koskinen replied.

Koskinen rejoined Elena. "Eino Partola will talk with you. He's one of our negotiators. Remember, refer to me as Antti Salonen."

Elena chuckled at the reference to the pseudonym.

When Partola entered the conference room, he recognized Elena.

"No need for an introduction, Antti," Partola said. "I have seen this young lady here before. Glad to see you again, Miss Marikova."

"Call me Elena. It's easier."

As they all sat down at the conference table, Partola addressed Koskinen.

"I have some news for you, Antti. It just came to my attention from Petri who had spoken to the Ambassador late last evening."

"Yes, what is it?" Koskinen was naturally curious.

"Paasikivi and Tanner are leaving tomorrow to return to Finland."

"Let me guess," Koskinen ventured. "They haven't gotten anywhere in resolving the demands of Stalin for concessions by Finland. Am I right?"

"Yes, you're quite right," Partola replied. "According to what Peltonen told Petri, Paasikivi and Tanner are disgusted and disappointed. They're going back empty-handed. They see no purpose in staying any longer. They never got to see Stalin to present their views and Litvinov persists in demanding that Finland give the Soviets a thirty-year lease to the Suursaari Islands and be allowed to fortify them. Paasikivi and Tanner told Litvinov that they'd discuss the demand with their government but indicated that Finland would refuse, probably, because of the Russian-Finland Treaty of 1920 which forbade any militarization of the Islands. Apparently, the Treaty has little meaning for Stalin. So they're leaving."

"What about you and the other trade specialists who came with Tanner and Paasikivi?"

"Petri and I will be staying for a while. Mikko and Raimo will return with Paasikivi and Tanner."

"What is the status of the trade negotiations? What has been accomplished, if anything, up to now?" Koskinen inquired.

"Petri and I have been discussing the request of the Soviet government for Finland to build military ships in exchange for oil from Russia. The trade's representatives for the Soviets want quite large ships because of the threats in the world today. We're trying to convince them that building large military ships could take several years depending on the number they order. In the meantime, the perceived threat from Germany may present itself long before the ships are completed. We are trying to get them to see that smaller and faster boats are more practical for operation in the Baltic Sea. The Soviet Admiralty agrees with us, but Stalin wants the big ones. So, we'll have to continue our negotiations to see which side wins."

"Well, I'm going to leave you two. I think, Eino, that you might go into detail on the trade negotiations, that is, who the representatives of the Soviets are and the amount of money involved and some of the proposed contract terms. Elena should know these things because she is to attend some of the sessions with you and the Soviet reps."

"That's fine. I have about an hour to do that," Partola said.

"Elena, when you finish your 'class' with Eino, have me paged by the receptionist."

"Yes, I'll do that," Elena responded.

Koskinen then left and went to his room. If Paasikivi and Tanner were leaving without any decision on the political process involved with Stalin's demands, it could only mean that it was imperative that his mission to eliminate Stalin had to be carried out soon, no more delays! It was obvious to Koskinen that Stalin was intransigent about demanding a piece of Finland. It would be only a matter of time before Stalin in his crafty and ruthless way would fabricate a reason for invading Finland and taking by military force that which the Finns would not give him. Perhaps taking even more than his original demands. Koskinen, thinking along these lines, became gripped with anxiety. Events might move so quickly that he might not have time to accomplish his mission.

When Elena finished her tutorial session with Eino Partola, she had the receptionist ring Salonen on the house telephone. Elena made it a conscious discipline to use Koskinen's pseudonym when in doubt as to whether a person knew his real identity. Koskinen said he would be down in a few moments.

Koskinen and Elena were again in the privacy of the conference room. Koskinen, still very much concerned over what he envisioned as a serious and ominous turn of events with Paasikivi's and Tanner's departure for Finland without some sort of compromise with Stalin, addressed Elena unusually forcefully and with a sense of urgency.

"Elena, as you heard from Eino Partola, Paasikivi and Tanner are leaving. Stalin is apparently adamant in his demands for Finnish territory. The Finns aren't going to give in to him, so he may very well decide to send his army into Finland to take what he wants. I am of the opinion that if we are to eliminate Stalin, we must do it very soon."

Elena listened and then replied, "Timo, I think you should express these thoughts to the underground when you see them in a couple of days. They may have some ideas. I know they'll agree with you on the need to get the thing done expeditiously. I certainly do."

Elena stayed until after lunch at the Embassy. Later and as she was leaving in a taxi for the Trade Building, Koskinen said to her, "Elena, if you have to have lunch with the police investigator, have lunch and nothing more, promise."

Elena replied, "Timo, I can promise but I still have to play the game as it is presented to me. I don't want to do anything beyond having lunch with the guy. You must know that. So, I'll do what I can." She smiled her usual sweet smile and then left the Embassy.

The next two days were not happy ones for Koskinen. Between agonizing over the detested lunch Elena might have with the policeman and the urgency of getting action to accomplish his mission, Koskinen worked himself into a condition of considerable mental stress. He inquired each day of the Ambassador's Secretary when the courier from Finland was expected. The secretary could only tell him that it would be "any day now." It seemed to Koskinen that everything was moving much too slowly.

Koskinen was relieved when Akmal arrived at the Embassy to take him to the bakery. He felt that at last something was happening. In as good Russian as he could command, Koskinen greeted Akmal in an amiable way. Akmal, in turn, was most affable in giving Koskinen a hearty embrace. Koskinen, Akmal knew, would be working with the underground and that made him no longer a stranger but a comrade and partner in a dangerous undertaking.

"You wait in cab," Akmal said while motioning to Koskinen to his truck. "I deliver bread here and then we go."

Koskinen did as directed and climbed into the truck cab. Akmal delivered several bags of bread to the kitchen and then climbed in next to Koskinen, started the motor and off they drove.

They had driven about four blocks in the direction of the bakery when Koskinen looking into the side rear view mirror observed a black limousine following closely. He nudged Akmal and pointed with his thumb to the rear. Akmal looked into his side mirror and confirmed what Koskinen was seeing. With a sardonic grin, Akmal turned his head slightly towards Koskinen and said, "I no take you to bakery now. They follow. Not good. I take you to street with shops. You get off, go into antique shop, then if alright, take taxi or bus to bakery. Alright? I tell boss you be late."

"Yes," Koskinen nodded in agreement. He knew it would be unwise to have the NKVD led directly to the bakery and arouse suspicion. In Russia, Koskinen knew black limousines were always equated with the NKVD. High government officials also rode in black limousines but the ordinary citizen always presumed the limousines' occupants were NKVD agents unless told otherwise.

Akmal drove to the vicinity of the Belgrade Hotel on Smolenskaya Square where he stopped to let Koskinen off. Akmal was imperturbable. The police had stopped him before this and found nothing. They would find nothing this time.

Akmal then gave instructions to Koskinen. "You go to antique store down the street and call taxi from there. Tell taxi to go to Pysmoy

Street off Novinsky Boulevard. That will be bakery." Akmal then drove off before Koskinen could ask questions. Koskinen wanted to know the significance of the antique shop. Maybe, he thought, the answer would come from people working in the antique shop.

Koskinen observed that the black limousine did not follow Akmal this time. Instead, the limousine stopped where Koskinen had alighted from Akmal's truck. Koskinen felt uneasily that whoever was in the limousine was keeping a watchful eye on him. He walked a short distance to the street level antique shop and entered. The shop keeper greeted him with a smile of welcome.

"I just want to browse a bit," explained Koskinen. "My wife loves antiques, especially those from Russia." The shopkeeper made a sweeping motion around the shop with his arm to encourage Koskinen to look around.

As he browsed through the items on display, Koskinen kept quickly glancing towards the street in front of the shop. In a few moments he saw the black limousine pull up. Two men alighted and came directly into the shop. They wore long black coats that reached almost to their ankles. Fur hats adorned their heads. To Koskinen they appeared grimly businesslike, unsmiling and intimidating. Koskinen knew that he was their object and that he was about to be questioned by the pair.

One of the men went off to the side of the shop with the shopkeeper while the other fellow stood near the entrance and kept an unflinching and vigilant eye on Koskinen. Koskinen was unable to hear what the man and the shopkeeper were talking about, but he observed the shopkeeper nodding in agreement. Koskinen tried to act nonchalant as if he was not involved in whatever the two limousine occupants had in mind. He continued to browse through small antique items laid out on tables, occasionally looking up to see what was happening. The policeman with the shopkeeper then turned to his partner and then to Koskinen. The policeman, if that he was, motioned to his partner and called to Koskinen to follow him into a back room. Koskinen did so with the other policeman behind him. The back room was littered with an apparent disorganized collection of antique items but they managed to locate three chairs.

The fellow who had been talking with the shopkeeper was seemingly in charge. He showed an official badge of some sort to Koskinen.

"I am with the NKVD," he said in Russian. "My partner here also."

Koskinen forthwith produced his Embassy identification certificate and showed it to the NKVD men. The lead officer took it, read it and handed it back to Koskinen with an indifferent shrug.

Koskinen with an indignant bearing asked, "Why am I brought into this back room? What is it you want?"

"We know from your papers that you are with the Finnish Embassy. However, in spite of that, will you agree to answer a few questions?"

"That depends on what you ask," retorted Koskinen.

The two NKVD men wore dark suits under long, heavy black coats. Their fur hats were without any police symbol that was normally attached to the front of police hats.

"We have stopped that truck and driver from time to time. We think there may be something suspicious about it, but we have never found anything illegal about the truck, its contents or the driver. Nevertheless, we think there is something that needs continual surveillance. We don't as yet know what it is. Perhaps you can help."

"I don't know how I can help you," replied Koskinen. "All I know is that the driver and his truck deliver bread and other bakery goods to our Embassy about twice a week."

"Why were you in the truck?"

"Our Embassy auto was in an accident a few days ago and is being repaired. The only transportation I have is by taxi. This morning when the bread truck arrived, I asked the driver if he could give me a ride to this part of the city and he agreed to do so. That's all there is to it. It's very simple." Koskinen was thinking that he was telling a good story. He was watching for its effect on the NKVD men. Their faces were expressionless and their eyes cold as they regarded Koskinen silently for a few moments. Although Koskinen knew that he had diplomatic rights not to be questioned or detained, he felt extremely uneasy in the presence of the NKVD men. But he tried not to show his disquietude.

"We don't believe you, Mr. Salonen," the lead officer blurted out in stabbing bluntness.

Hearing that insolent and disparaging remark, Koskinen reacted immediately with wrathful indignation. "I have said all that I am going to say. If you don't believe me, then that is your problem. I intend to leave this room now and if you restrain me, you will be creating a diplomatic crisis." Koskinen realized that in refusing to cooperate further, it could lead the NKVD men to conclude he had something to hide. But, he had to take that risk. In the short term, his story, he felt, had been credible and plausible.

Koskinen arose from his chair and returned to the main shop where he continued to browse among the antiques. He would browse until the NKVD men decided to leave the shop and drive off. This they did promptly after Koskinen had left the room. Koskinen turned his back on them as they passed through the shop and, therefore, did not notice the glaring, menacing looks they cast at him.

Koskinen was apprehensive. He had become anxiously concerned about the blunt, acrid assertion of the NKVD fellow that he did not believe Koskinen's explanations. In Koskinen's mind, questions arose: Did the NKVD have some information about the underground? Did they have an inkling of his relationship to it or the nature of his real mission here? Or did they lack any knowledge of anything about the existence of the underground and his possible part and were just bluffing? Koskinen reasoned that if the NKVD had developed any intelligence on the matter it would be conducting far more aggressive and direct action. They would not be following the bakery truck intermittently in the hope of discovering something. Nevertheless, Koskinen knew from his own intelligence background and experience that the NKVD must have some suspicion but had, as yet, not uncovered anything of substance to warrant action. However that might be, Koskinen now knew that he had a signal warning him, Elena and all others involved in the movement to exercise intense and disciplined caution in whatever was said or done from here on.

As Koskinen continued to browse, the shopkeeper came to him to express himself about the incident.

"Good sir, I want to apologize and tell you I'm sorry that you were subjected to this harassment in my shop."

Koskinen turned to the shopkeeper. "It was not your fault, so you need not apologize."

"Nevertheless," the shopkeeper continued, "it is an imposition on my customers and I don't like it, but there is nothing I can do about it. I hope you understand."

"Yes, I do." Koskinen then introduced himself. "I am from the Finnish Embassy. My name is Antti. I came into your shop to look for something for my wife when I return to Finland."

"Ah, for your trouble here, I want to give you something for your wife. Wait here a moment." The shopkeeper went into the back room and after about five minutes returned with a small object in his hand.

"I have here for your wife a small icon of the Virgin Mary. These paintings were made before 1917, the year of the Bolshevik revolution. They were forbidden to be made or used thereafter. You know, religion was banned under our Communism." The shopkeeper went on to explain, "These small icons were often carried by soldiers in combat as a means of assuring their safety. I have acquired several of them, but, of course, I don't display them."

"Well, I thank you very much for this generous gift. It must be quite valuable."

"Someday, yes. Not now. Something has value only if someone wants it and can buy it."

"By the way," Koskinen asked, "what is your name?"

"It's Leonid."

"My wife will be most grateful to you for this fine gift, Leonid. Now, before I return to the Embassy, I'd like to stop by a bakery and buy some wonderful Russian pastries. Is there a good bakery nearby?"

For a short, but noticeable moment, Leonid stared at Koskinen quizzically as if he was trying to pry open some hidden meaning in Koskinen's inquiry about a bakery. It was as if Leonid wanted to ask Koskinen something but feared to do so lest it might reveal too much about a subject better left unexplored. "Yes, there is a bakery in the vicinity but not within walking distance."

Koskinen sensed that Leonid wanted to talk but was hesitant to speak up. He was going to be late for the meeting at the bakery, but Akmal would explain that and, hopefully, those at the bakery would wait for him. Koskinen thought it would be worth the extra time to talk with Leonid, at least for a short time. He decided to lead him to talk.

"We in Finland," Koskinen began, "find it difficult to understand how one man can make decisions that affect the lives or deaths of thousands, even millions of people and no one raises a finger in protest. The people are like sheep."

Koskinen paused for a reaction from Leonid. Leonid smiled wanly. He was a small, thin even fragile statured man who, like so many others, seemed to live in a state of permanent fear of the police in a police state. As Koskinen would learn, Leonid might appear to be weak physically, he was, however, a lion of courage and intrepidity regarding his opinion of Communism and the Communist government.

"Yes, I agree almost all of our Russian people are like sheep. There are a few, however, who are committed to revolutionizing the revolution."

"What do you mean by that?" Koskinen asked.

"The Communist revolution ousted the Tsar in 1917," explained Leonid. "Now there are those who will try to oust the Communists. In other words, a new revolution."

Koskinen began to feel that Leonid might know more than he was willing to reveal.

"How do you know that there are those who will seek to oust the Communists?"

"Antti, doesn't history prove that when people are oppressed they will eventually rise up to cast off their oppressors? Isn't that, in fact, the rallying cry of the Communists? 'Rise up, workers of the world against your capitalist oppressors!'"

"Do you have grounds for believing that there is such a movement in existence that wants to overthrow Stalin?"

"I have heard through various sources that there is. After all, the masses need leaders who operate in small groups, at first."

"Have you told the police about this?"

"Of course not!"

"Why not?"

Leonid did not reply and turned away.

Koskinen decided not to question Leonid further. It had, nevertheless, been a short but interesting conversation. Besides, he had to get to the bakery.

"Leonid, I'll have to get a taxi. You can tell me how to get to the bakery."

Leonid turned back to face Koskinen. "How did you get here?"

"The fellow who delivers bread and bakery goods to our Embassy volunteered to drive me in his delivery truck and I accepted."

Leonid said nothing for a few moments, but studied Koskinen intensely. The stare made Koskinen uncomfortable.

"What's the matter, Leonid?" Koskinen finally asked in order to break the silence.

"Was he taking you to his bakery, perhaps?"

For a moment Koskinen did not know how to reply. He was startled by Leonid's direct question as if Leonid had some intuitive perception that had pierced the veil concealing the real purpose behind the emphasis on the subject of bakeries.

"He might have. I had mentioned to him that I wanted to stop at one." Koskinen was still not sure of Leonid's political sympathies and felt that his responses had to be kept intentionally vague. It seemed that the two men were testing each other through a sort of fox and goose game.

Leonid then inserted another surprise for Koskinen.

"It is sometimes difficult to get a taxi here. You have to wait a long time for one to come. I would like to do this for you. I will drive you in my small delivery truck to the bakery. I mean the bakery where your deliveryman is employed. It is one of the better bakeries in the city."

"But you have your shop here," Koskinen said. He still harbored a feeling of some uncertainty about Leonid and was not entirely receptive to Leonid's offer.

"I can close the shop for an hour or so," Leonid replied reassuringly. "You know, 'Out to lunch.'"

"Well, alright. I appreciate what you're doing." Koskinen felt he had no choice but to accept the offer.

As they drove off and through the streets, both men kept a sharp eye out for any automobile that appeared to be following them. They saw none that caused any suspicion.

When they arrived at the bakery, Leonid parked his truck in front of the shop. He said, "I'll go in also. I would like to treat myself to some good pastry."

For Koskinen, Leonid wanting to come into the bakery was entirely unexpected. He was in an unfortunate dilemma. How could he possibly go into the bakery meeting while Leonid was at his side thinking they were both there to buy bakery goods. He was anxious to rid himself of Leonid at this point.

"Leonid, I want to thank you for bringing me here. It was kind of you. But you needn't wait for me. I want to walk about the neighborhood a bit after I leave the bakery. I'll get a taxi back to the Embassy."

Leonid shook his head in agreement.

When Koskinen and Leonid entered the bakery, they saw no customers but there was a young lady busying herself behind the counter. She looked up as they approached the counter. Koskinen in looking directly at her thought he saw an ever so slight raising of her eyebrows as she looked at Leonid. Koskinen was puzzled by it. Well, he thought, perhaps Leonid was here before and the clerk recognized him. With that he dismissed his concern.

"Young lady, did your driver Akmal get back here yet. I'm from the Finnish Embassy and he drove me to this gentleman's antique shop. We'd like to buy a few pastries."

The young lady said, "I'll see if Akmal has returned. If he has, would you care to talk with him?"

"Perhaps just to say 'thank you' for giving me a ride."

The young lady excused herself and went into the back room. In a few moments, she returned followed by a young man in bakery uniform. When the young man saw Leonid, he exclaimed with a big smile, "Ah, Leonid, it's good to see you again. We have a meeting going on. Do you want to stay and listen in?"

"No, I have to get back to the shop," Leonid replied.

The young man turned to Koskinen. "I presume you are Antti Salonen."

"Yes."

"We have been waiting for you. Akmal reported what had happened and that you would be late. My name is Boris." He extended his hand to Koskinen and they shook hands.

Koskinen must have appeared perplexed about the relationship of Leonid to Boris and the bakery. Boris sensed it and, smiling, explained.

"Antti, you have been in good hands. Leonid is one of us."

Koskinen exclaimed, "My god, now I see how it all ties together. Akmal telling me to go to the antique shop and Leonid here suggesting I come to this bakery for my pastries."

Leonid spoke up. "I was not so sure of you at first, Antti, but I put it together also. Akmal driving you, your mentioning a bakery and the fact that you are with the Finnish Embassy and knowing how the Finns feel about Russia. I then came to the conclusion that you were probably working with our underground."

Boris interrupted, "Well, everything worked out alright. I think Antti and I had better get to the meeting before some customer comes in. Besides, our people have been waiting a while."

Koskinen shook hands again with Leonid.

"Thanks for your help, Leonid."

"I'm glad to do it for a co-worker."

Koskinen and Boris then went into the back room to attend the meeting.

"It's on the second floor. Just follow me."

Although Koskinen did not know it, Boris followed the same route that he had guided Bill Chance and Gene Wagner a few days before.

Immediately upon entering the third room, Koskinen saw Elena sitting at a table with several men. He was both stunned and elated. Elena had not contacted him to say that she had managed to get out of her luncheon date with the police investigator. But, apparently she had. "Good girl," Koskinen thought. He wondered how she did it. They both exchanged warm smiles.

The men at the table had arisen from their chairs to greet the new arrival. Boris introduced everyone. "This is Antti Salonen of the Finnish Embassy. I have mentioned him to you and what his mission in Russia is." Boris turned to Koskinen, "Antti, this is Nikolai, Mikhael and Demyan. They are part of our leadership. And, of course, you know Elena here. She will translate for us and for you. She is a very trusted comrade. Please be seated, all of you." Boris took a seat at one end of the table.

Boris addressed his remarks to Koskinen. "We wish to welcome you and express our appreciation for your participating with us." Boris, as always, wore his perpetual smile. "We do not and cannot afford to waste a lot of time in our work, so I shall get to the point of our meeting immediately. We would like to know if you have any plans to take care of Stalin. We have our own proposals but we'd like to hear what yours might be."

Koskinen looked at Elena as she translated what was said. He pondered Boris's question that had been put to him. Finally, he replied, "No, I have no specific action in mind. My government sent me on a mission but did not tell me or help me how to accomplish it. I have been left to work out a plan on my own. Fortunately, through Elena I have met you people and you may be the means to accomplish my mission. I expect to participate with you if you will have me."

"We were hoping," said Boris, "that you could join the heads of your trade mission when they meet with Stalin to discuss trade terms. That might provide an opportunity for you to carry out his assassination on the spot."

"I have to tell you," Koskinen replied, "our trade mission leaders are returning to Finland in a day or two precisely because they could not get an audience with Stalin personally. They have not been able to visit with him and there were no arrangements made to do so. They are quite disappointed as I am. They have little to show for their trip here. Two of the trade specialists and I shall remain here."

"Do you have any suggestion?" Boris probed.

"Perhaps," answered Koskinen. "Why don't you set up an ambush of Stalin when he is on the road to his dacha? In my opinion, that has a greater probability of succeeding than a one-on-one confrontation with Stalin."

"We have that as one of our alternate plans," Boris replied, "but Stalin travels with a heavy amount of police as guards. The police comb the woods on either side of the road when they know he is coming. The risk is very great for many of us. We'll probably use it if other measures fail."

"What plans do you people have in mind?" Koskinen was inquisitive, as well as anxious to get something going.

Boris still carried on the conversation. The other three men sat at the table silently, listening to the dialogue stone faced and imperturbable. As Koskinen looked at them, there was little question in his mind but that these men were tough, determined and courageous.

"We have proposed to the representatives of the United States that their Ambassador give a dinner in honor of Stalin. At the dinner we shall have a young lady who will try to attract and seduce Stalin. If Stalin likes her, we are counting on him asking her to go to his dacha with him after the dinner. At the dacha, she will then place poison in his drink and that will be it. That is our plan." Boris leaned back in his chair to await Koskinen's opinion. He relished the thought of Stalin's demise. Also, the simplicity of the plan pleased him.

"What part do I play in this?" Koskinen asked. "Surely, you must have something for me to do."

"Yes, we have planned your part subject, of course, to your consent. You are to see that the young lady leaves the dacha safely. We chose you for this because of your diplomatic status. There is a certain amount of immunity from challenges and from arrest that foreign diplomats have. We can use that immunity in our plans."

"Have you chosen the young lady for this endeavor?" inquired Koskinen. "I have to know whom I'm supposed to rescue."

For a moment Boris was silent and did not reply. He seemed reluctant to give Koskinen the name. After the pause, he said softly, "Elena here has volunteered."

Koskinen appeared thunderstruck as if not comprehending immediately what Boris had just said. Yet, he had heard precisely the answer given to his question by Boris. Koskinen looked directly at Elena and in a totally incredulous voice said softly, "You have volunteered for this arrangement?" He spoke in Finnish.

"Yes, Antti," Elena replied in Finnish.

"Why?"

"I joined this underground movement to help bring about Stalin's downfall to avenge the disappearance of my father and brother. This now is my opportunity."

The Russian men at the table sat looking on but understanding nothing of what was said in the Finnish language.

"Trying to carry out this plan could end in your arrest and certain death. I hope you realize that. You must not do this, Elena. You must tell these men that you will withdraw your volunteering. Tell them that I have said you are needed at the Finnish Embassy. If you don't want to tell them, I will." Koskinen was earnestly pleading with Elena.

The Russians by now must have guessed what was going on between Elena and "Antti Salonen."

Boris addressed Elena. "It seems that Antti is opposed to your participating in our plan. We didn't understand what you and he were saying, but it was obvious. Elena, if you feel that you want to or must withdraw from this, you can do so. We cannot and would not force you to undertake it. We realize there are risks and dangers."

"No," Elena promptly replied. "I will do it. If I don't do it, some other woman will have to do it or the plan will have to be dropped." Elena turned to Koskinen.

"I am going to do it, Antti. Besides," she added with a carefree toss of her head as if the whole business was of no great consequence, "you will be there to save me." Elena laughed.

Koskinen didn't see it as a laughing matter, but he knew that Elena had made up her mind and that there was little to be accomplished by insisting that she give the whole thing up. At any rate, the United States might not agree to hold the dinner and, if that happened, the issue would become moot.

"Have you worked out the details of how I'm to get Elena to safety?" Koskinen asked Boris.

"Yes," Boris replied, "you and Elena will be invited to the dinner along with Ambassadors or representatives of various governments having Embassies or legations here. You will be Elena's escort to the dinner. We shall see that you and she shall sit as close to Stalin as protocol permits. She should be in a place where she can flirt with Stalin and where he can see her."

Koskinen interjected, "This is all assuming that there will be dinner."

"Of course, but we feel confident that the United States will agree to do it." Boris smiled graciously. "We shall go ahead with our plans on that assumption."

"Then what happens?" Koskinen queried. He had become dubious about the plan now that Elena was to be involved. In fact, he was aware of a sudden strong feeling of disenchantment with the idea of disposing of Stalin. Was it worth risking Elena's life to attempt possibly an unsuccessful assassination of Stalin? If he had to choose between saving Finland and protecting Elena, there was little hesitancy that he would choose Elena. That was how Koskinen felt at that moment.

Koskinen looked at the men at the table. He saw them sitting back in relative safety, smug and self-assured, while they decided to send a young woman out on her own on an extremely dangerous venture. He was deeply resentful. These men, he thought, were placing the fate of Russia, Finland, Europe, perhaps the world on the shoulders of this young, lovely woman. It was an unbearable thought. At the moment, he was at a loss as to what to say short of telling them to go to hell. That is what he wanted to tell them, but he had to consider Elena. He could not abandon her. He could not just simply walk away from the whole project. He had little choice, he knew, but to listen to the rest of the details.

"If all goes well," Boris elaborated, "Stalin will invite Elena to his dacha for the night. By the time they leave the dinner party Stalin will be feeling the influence of vodka. From what we have heard, Stalin usually sits in a small parlor in the dacha drinking and talking with his female companion. Somewhere in time, he will suggest that they go to bed. In the bedroom, he will continue to have more drinks. Then they either will have sex or he will pass out before that happens. During all this time at the dacha Elena will have to determine the opportunity to place the poison in one of Stalin's drinks."

"And what is the plan to rescue her?" Koskinen was impatient for more details. He kept looking at Elena every few moments clearly showing his concern and his disapproval of her participation. Koskinen's reaction to the plan was not what she had expected. She had anticipated that he would be very favorable to her part in the project. That he was not was disturbing to her. Her carefree expression up to this point now disappeared. She became solemn and somewhat dispirited.

Boris continued to outline the plan. "When Stalin invites Elena to his dacha, she will tell him that she will go, but that she is scheduled to be at the Finnish Embassy early in the morning for translating trade talks. You will be present when she tells him this. You will identify yourself as part of the trade mission and will confirm what Elena says. You will say that you will be happy to pick her up with your Embassy car at his dacha in the early morning."

"Suppose he does not go along with my suggestion, what then?" Koskinen asked.

"He will … Stalin is not stupid. He understands what must be. He will be satisfied in having a female companion in his bed for the night. That is what matters to him."

"How do I get to the dacha without being arrested or shot?" Koskinen asked. "I understand from what people at my Embassy have said that the dacha is about twenty miles from the Kremlin and that the route is guarded by several thousand police agents. Is someone going to notify them to allow me to proceed?"

"We shall ask Stalin's aide to pass the word along that you are from the Finnish Embassy and should be allowed to pass through once you have identified yourself. And they will be instructed to allow you to return with Elena."

"Do you have that kind of influence with Stalin's aide to get him to do that?" Koskinen expressed astonishment.

Elena, who had been translating all this conversation, suddenly interrupted and spoke in Finnish to Koskinen, "Antti, do you remember the Lieutenant who was with me when we got on the train at Leningrad, Lieutenant Sergei Valentnikov?"

"Yes, I remember him."

"Do you recall that I mentioned that he was one of us?"

"Yes, vaguely."

"Well, his new assignment in Moscow that I mentioned was as an aide to Stalin."

"A close aide to Stalin is a member of the underground! That is absolutely laughable," declared Koskinen. But Koskinen was not laughing.

"Well, he is the one who will get you passage to and from the dacha," said Elena.

"If there is a member of the underground who is close to Stalin, why isn't he being asked to poison Stalin? Ask that of your Russian friends here."

Elena hesitated to pose the question to the men at the table. Instead she replied in Finnish, "I'm sure, Antti, that they have explored that question and have decided against it."

"Ask them anyway," Koskinen insisted.

Elena did so. The Russians, after hearing Koskinen's question, spoke among themselves for a few moments. Then Boris spoke up.

"Stalin has several aides each having generally different duties. We have talked with Lieutenant Valentnikov and he informs us that his duties are administrative, that is, organizing and maintaining the work schedules of the personnel in and out of the Kremlin who serve the needs of Stalin, that is, the household people, the kitchen help, the security guards and so on. He doesn't get anywhere near Stalin's food or drink, he says. The Lieutenant is a new aide to Stalin. From what he tells us, he was recruited to take the place of an old aide who had defected to the United States Embassy. The old aide was an early Chekist and seemed to think he was on a list to be arrested and shot. Stalin has been getting rid of all of the old Chekists from the early days of the revolution. I suppose he feels threatened by them for some reason. Who knows?"

Koskinen arose from his chair. "It is time for me to get back to my Embassy. When you hear whether the United States will give the dinner, let me know. If they agree to give it, then we can get together again to work out more details on the plan." Koskinen shook hands with the Russians and then turned to Elena.

"I'm going to get a taxi. If you have nothing more to do here, you might join me."

Elena looked at Boris and the others questioningly. "Is there any reason I should remain here?"

Boris replied, "No, go ahead with Mr. Salonen. We'll have another meeting or two on this after we hear from the U.S."

Koskinen bought a bag of pastries and put a call in for a taxi from the neighborhood taxi garage.

Once in the taxi and on the way to the Finnish Embassy, Koskinen put his arm around Elena, kissed her gently and then shook his head as an expression of disbelief and sadness over the involvement of Elena in the proposed plan. Neither of them said more than a few words during the taxi ride. It was not because the taxi driver might overhear them, but, rather, that they both seemed numbed and drained emotionally by the events that had transpired at the bakery. They held hands. There was still that intimacy, their love for each other, their sensitivities attuned to each other's feelings. Neither wanted to do or say anything that would offend or inflict unnecessary distress on the other. Yet, for Koskinen the pain in his heart was already there. A pain that would not be relieved by anything less than a full relinquishment by Elena of her role in the attempt on Stalin's life.

Arriving back at the Finnish Embassy, Koskinen suggested that Elena accompany him to his room where they could have uninterrupted privacy. Koskinen reported in to the receptionist and then led Elena to his room.

Elena slumped into a chair, kicked off her shoes, put her hands behind her head and closed her eyes for a short time. Koskinen had removed his suit jacket and lay down on his bed where he stretched out, took some deep breaths and also closed his eyes. It was the first time that they were able to relax that day. After a few minutes, Koskinen got up and sat on the edge of the bed. He looked at Elena who had opened her eyes and was staring at her hands now folded on her lap.

"Elena," Koskinen said in a low voice, "what need I do to get you to give up this insane idea."

"Timo, we are both insane. Your mission and my mission are identical. We both want the same thing." Elena spoke in a soft almost whispered voice.

"Yes, but you are a woman."

"Do women have less courage or less strength of purpose than men, Timo?"

"No, but they have less physical strength to cope with dangerous situations."

"Women," replied Elena, "don't need the physical strength or brute force that men employ to meet danger. Women have other means that men could not possibly employ."

"I suppose you mean physical allure, enticement and sexual appeal."

"Yes. Where men are involved those things are a woman's way of converting an aggressive male into a passive one."

"Apparently, you have not heard of rape."

"Of course I have. It occurs when the woman panics and fights back or screams instead of remaining calm and trying to talk the man out of it or simply submits and gives the appearance of consent. There is far less possibility of being murdered if the woman stays cool and disciplined."

"Elena, the dangers for you in this plan are extreme. The slightest misstep and you could end up in the Lubyanka prison and you know what that means, I'm sure."

Elena said nothing, but shook her head in affirmation.

Koskinen continued, hoping to dissuade Elena. "You have enough to cope with right now with that police investigator on your neck. Don't take on any more problems."

"Everything you say, Timo, is quite right. But I have volunteered. I have committed to undertaking this mission. It is something I must do. I could not live with myself if I did not go ahead with it." Elena looked a bit haggard.

"Timo, I'm so tired and weary over all this. I'm going to lie down on the bed. You can lie next to me if you want. But I may fall asleep."

"Yes, I'm weary too, Elena."

Both lay down, covering themselves with a blanket. Koskinen put his arm around Elena's shoulders and soon both dozed off into a fitful sleep.

When they awoke about two hours later, it was already getting dark outside. They lay quietly for a time. Elena then turned towards Koskinen and kissed him gently. He returned the affection. Their caresses quickly became more amorous and eager, which, in turn, soon became a full-grown passion from which release was mutually sought and found.

As they lay back on the bed, Elena remarked, "I'm hungry."

"I agree," Koskinen said. "Perhaps we're close to dinnertime. Let's go find out."

Seeing the dining room still empty, Koskinen and Elena went into the adjoining kitchen and had the chef make them some coffee. Dinner, they were told, would not be served for another forty-five minutes. They returned to the dining room to await the brewing coffee. Sitting quietly at a small table with Elena, Koskinen resurrected the matter of Elena's participation in the Stalin project.

"Elena, I don't want to harass you or irritate you, but I beg of you to reconsider your commitment. If anything were to happen to you, I would be devastated. Please, for your sake and mine." Koskinen took

Elena's hands in his and his whole demeanor was one of sheer and overwhelming concern.

"Timo, you don't seem to understand. I want to do what I have promised. I would not have volunteered if I did not want to undertake the job. Furthermore, Timo, I appreciate your concern for me and your feelings for me, but, ultimately, we have to consider that you have a wife back in Finland. You are not free to marry me or to even be a companion to me once you return to Finland. If I went back to Finland with you, what would I do there; what would you do? Would I be your mistress-in-hiding? I could not travel in public with you. Would you be ashamed to be seen with me by your friends and co-workers at the Intelligence Section? You see what little future we have with each other. We have to be realistic."

Koskinen was the picture of utter despair and wretchedness. He knew what Elena was saying was true. He was torn between two devotions; devotion to Anna, his wife, and devotion to Elena, his lover. How could he be faithful to both at the same time? Koskinen knew he could love both, but he was also cognizant that society values would not accept that sort of division. It was not he, it was not Elena where the cause of the dilemma lay. It was archaic social rules and restrictions that hampered the freedom to do what nature and the heart demanded. For Koskinen the outlook became more dismal and he felt his depression deepening. He knew it was futile to continue to press the subject on Elena. At the moment, he felt like going into a private corner of the room to grieve and to cry. He was crushed and hopeless.

Suffice it, neither Koskinen nor Elena ate much dinner. The pangs of hunger had disappeared with a rush of pessimism that seemed to overcome their mutual outlooks just prior to their sitting down to the meal.

On the way out of the dining room, Koskinen saw Marjatta, the Ambassador's secretary, sitting at one of the tables with some other Embassy staff personnel.

"Marjatta," Koskinen got her attention by stooping next to her. "Have you heard anything about the courier from Helsinki?"

"Yes, he left Helsinki yesterday. He should be here tomorrow some time. Just when, I can't say. You know how the Russian rail system is."

"Would you let me know the instant he arrives?" Koskinen was anxious to take possession of the poison which he assumed the courier was bringing.

"Certainly," Marjatta said.

Koskinen related to Elena what Marjatta had reported. Elena seemed to perk up at the news. There was now hope of getting rid of her antagonist, the police investigator.

Diverted for a moment from the sense of gloom regarding Elena's part in the Stalin matter to the problem with the policeman, Koskinen chuckled over the thought of Elena poisoning the officer.

"You know, Elena, I never cease to stand in awe of you. A beautiful, gentle feminine young lady not having a problem in poisoning another human person. As if you were going to kill a lamb or a chicken for the next meal."

Elena could not restrain a smile also. The description of her was amusing.

"Timo, I have no problem with it because I don't see these people as human. They are beasts in my mind. Callous, cold, uncaring, selfish monsters. I am going to go to any length to rid our country of them. Stalin is the chief brute; the police investigator is simply an extension of Stalin. There are thousands of these little Stalins running around trying to save their own skins by imitating him. They have no consciences and no scruples. Do I explain myself?"

"Yes, and I agree. Only I wish someone else besides you was doing the work."

"Will you let me know when the courier arrives with the poison? I can then make my arrangements with my passionate policeman."

"Yes, of course. I'll contact you at the trade ministry. If you're not there at the time, I'll leave a message stating that the trade documents have arrived and need to be translated. Is that alright?"

"Yes, that will be fine."

"Right now, let me suggest a procedure that might be followed. This is just a suggestion. If you have already thought out your plan to plant the poison, then do what you think is best." Koskinen then outlined how Elena might poison the police officer.

"Choose a restaurant that I can reach by bus. The restaurant should be one that is quite busy during lunchtime. I want to be there at the same time that you and the police officer are there and I want to be as inconspicuous as possible. I won't be as noticeable if there are several other diners in the room. See that I get the telephone number of the restaurant the day before your date with the fellow. The restaurant should be on a street with other shops. Also, before the day of your date, check on another shop that has a telephone that can be used by the public and let me know where that is. Then, on the day you have lunch together, I shall be at the restaurant. When I see that you have been served your main dishes, I shall go to the neighboring shop and place a call to the restaurant and ask to speak to Ivan Snesarev, the police officer. The restaurant person will page him or come to the table and tell him he has a telephone call. In the few moments while he is gone to take the call you can slip the poison into his food or drink. I shall have hung up and proceeded to get the bus back to the Embassy. Ivan will be mystified by the call, but what does it matter. He should be dead in a day or two. Now, how does that sound to you?"

"It sounds alright as long as he doesn't taste something in his food or drink that will cause him not to eat or drink it."

"The poison is supposed to be odorless, tasteless and colorless. But, we'll make a small amount first to test it and determine if it fits our purpose. Did you have any other idea on how to use the poison?"

"Well, yes," Elena replied. "I thought I might leave my coat in the coat room with some cigarettes in the pocket and then sometime during the meal ask him to go to the room to get my cigarettes. While he is gone, I can then slip the poison into his food or drink."

"That sounds like a good idea," Koskinen acknowledged. "However, you don't smoke."

"He doesn't know that."

"If he is a smoker and he has cigarettes with him, he may offer you one of his. Can you refuse and insist you want yours?"

"I hadn't thought of that," Elena admitted.

"Also," Koskinen admonished, "beginner or first-time smokers in my experience generally show that they're novices by coughing and choking when they make their first draw. He'll get suspicious, perhaps."

"Well, why don't we keep both plans. We'll see how things go once we're at the restaurant." Elena felt that would resolve the issue of what method to use.

"Yes, I agree to that," Koskinen responded.

The next day was eventful. Elena spent part in seeking and investigating the location and layout of a couple of restaurants. The one that she had intended originally was, in her opinion, too small and not busy enough for Koskinen's plan. She decided on the "Central Workers Restaurant" on Ruzheyny Pereulok, a side street shop near the Russian Trade Ministry. It was, she knew, popular with some of the higher-ranking bureaucrats from the Ministry. She also located a shoe store across the street from the restaurant that had a telephone for public use. Ruzheyny Street was just off the main avenue, Smolenski Bulvar, which was traversed by bus and not too far from either the Finnish Embassy or the police station. With the physical portion of the plan established in her mind, Elena waited to hear from Koskinen.

Koskinen that same day was waiting anxiously for the arrival of the courier from Finland. Finally, the courier arrived by taxi at the Embassy at about eight p.m. He appeared ready to collapse from sheer exhaustion.

"I have had a terrible trip," Heikki, the courier complained to Marjatta, the Ambassador's secretary. "These Russian railroads, I have never seen anything so bad. They spend more time standing still than they do moving. And when they do move it is usually to back up to where they've been. They clank. They jerk. I've got a sore neck and back. I think when I get back to Finland I'm going to ask for another assignment."

Marjatta had to stifle a laugh. She could envision what Heikki had gone through. She knew from experience that Heikki had a valid complaint, but she found his description nevertheless amusing.

"I am going to let one of our trade negotiators know you are here," Marjatta said. "His name is Antti Salonen and he has been quite anxious to see you. It's about something you were to bring him, I think."

"Yes, I believe I know," Heikki commented. "It's in my attaché case here and I want to open it in the presence of the Ambassador."

"The Ambassador knows you are here and will be with you shortly."

Marjatta paged Koskinen to come to her office. In a few moments, Koskinen arrived. When Marjatta had introduced him to Heikki, Koskinen had difficulty concealing his heart pounding excitement.

"Did you bring the rat poison with you?" Koskinen asked.

"Yes, I have it in my attaché case."

Marjatta raised her eyebrows in surprise. "Rat poison. I didn't know we had any rats here." It was the first she heard about rat poison.

"Oh, yes," Koskinen replied. "We've had several around our garbage cans behind the building." He felt that his answer was sufficient to dispose of any questions the courier might have.

Heikki explained to Koskinen, "I'm going to leave the attaché case with the Ambassador and you can talk with him about the rat poison. Right now, I'd like to get something to eat after I see the Ambassador and then get some sleep. It's impossible to get any rest on these Russian trains!"

"Yes, I know," Koskinen said. "Marjatta, I'll leave now and see the Ambassador in the morning. Will you let him know?"

Marjatta nodded her assent. "Yes, I shall."

Early the next morning even before seeing Ambassador Peltonen, Koskinen telephoned Elena's supervisor at the Russian Trade Ministry. Upon learning that Elena had not yet appeared at her office, Koskinen left word to have her call the Finnish Embassy regarding a trade schedule. He identified himself only as one of the Finnish trade negotiators. Later in the morning he went to the Ambassador's office.

"I think we have what you want," the Ambassador said in handing Koskinen a small oblong package. "Be sure to keep control of it. We don't want it to get into the hands of our chef by mistake." The Ambassador chuckled over his joke.

"I'll see that it's properly secured, Mr. Ambassador."

"The courier also brought several letters for you." The Ambassador gave Koskinen the letters that were tied together with a string. "By the way, how are you progressing with your mission?"

Koskinen related what had taken place at the meeting in the bakery, including his part in the plans outlined by the leaders of the underground.

"If this plan is attempted, everyone involved will be at great risk," the Ambassador observed. "Please keep me informed as things develop,

Antti. Unless Finland gives the appearance of non-involvement in your undertaking, the whole result could be catastrophic for our country. If Stalin gets word that Finland encouraged his assassination he would be enraged enough to start an invasion of Finland as a sort of punishment. We can't have that."

"I appreciate that, Mr. Ambassador, and I shall keep you informed." Koskinen prepared to leave, anxious to know if Elena had telephoned. Taking the package of poison and his letters, Koskinen went directly to the receptionist desk.

"Have there been any calls from the Russian Trade Ministry?"

"No, none at all."

"If one does come in, will you put it through to me if it's from Miss Marikova? I'll be in my room."

"Yes, of course, Mr. Salonen."

Back in his room Koskinen placed the package of poison and the letters still tied together on the table and then sat down on the edge of his bed. In quickly looking at the top envelope containing a letter he saw that it was in the handwriting of Anna. He guessed there were about a half-dozen envelopes. His mind, however, was for the moment on Elena. He looked at his watch. It was already ten o'clock. Why had not Elena called? Had she been with that damned police investigator all night and perhaps still with him? Maybe she was getting to like the fellow. Or maybe he had forced himself on her. That could be it. Or maybe he was expecting too much of Elena. After all, he was married to Anna. Anna! Oh, yes, the letters. Koskinen got up and went to the table, sat down on a chair and, with his mind still on Elena, maneuvered the string from around the envelopes. He was aware that he had little enthusiasm for reading Anna's letters just then and that his motions opening her envelopes were merely mechanical. Cognizant of this, he felt a sense of guilt. His whole thoughts, he knew, should be of Anna and he should be excited about receiving her letters. Yet, he wasn't. Poor Anna. If she knew about his feelings for Elena, she would be devastated. His few letters to her were bland because of his concern over their being intercepted and read by the Russians. He would write her a more detailed letter and send it back with the courier. Koskinen's somewhat erratic and rambling musings as he sat in his room were quite suddenly interrupted by the ringing of his telephone. It was the receptionist.

"Miss Marikova is on the line, Mr. Salonen."

"Right, thank you. I'll take the call." Koskinen's heart began precipitously to beat faster in a surge of excitement. Elena! At last!

"Hello, Elena."

"Hello. I just arrived at the office and was given your message." Elena was businesslike.

Koskinen stifled any expression of his concern about her and in a voice that he knew was a facade for the benefit of any third party who might be listening, he said calmly and matter-of-factly. "We have received a new schedule for trade talks. Can you come here so that we can discuss it?"

"I think so. I'll discuss it with my supervisor and if he has no objection, I'll come shortly after lunch. If there is an objection, I'll call you back shortly.

"If you want to come for lunch, you are welcome."

"No, after lunch, sometime in the early afternoon. Will you be there?"

"Yes. Alright, I'll see you when you arrive."

When he hung up the telephone, Koskinen had a recurrence of his fears. Elena's unusual insistence upon coming after lunch aroused his suspicion that perhaps she was having lunch with the police investigator. He knew that he could not have inquired of her over the telephone and that neither could she mention it. There were risks in Russia about any conversation on the telephone. He sat down again at the table in a perturbed state of mind and began to slowly open Anna's letters.

"Dearest Timo," they began. "I have missed you so very much. And the children also keep asking when you will be home. I have received your three letters and they have not said much. I understand why, of course." Three letters. Koskinen did not recall at the moment how many letters he had written to Anna. He thought there had been more than three, but he could be mistaken. Anna's first letter continued. "I called your section in Helsinki the day before yesterday to ask if they had any word on how your work was going. I was told that there was nothing of any significance to report. Perhaps this means you will be away a bit longer than I expected. But, your well-being is the most important thing to me. You know I love you very much. The children do, too. Please write as often as you can. My deepest and dearest love to you, Anna."

Koskinen read Anna's other following letters in the order of dates on which they were written. There were five in all. As he put the last letter of a few days ago back in its envelope, he felt terrible, just terrible. He really loved Anna. They had been through a great deal together. She was so caring, so devoted to him. Perhaps he should end his love relationship with Elena. It wasn't right, not for Elena, not for him, not for Anna. Elena was right. But, if he broke off their relationship, it would have to be gradual. An abrupt ending would be too traumatic for both Elena and him. Besides, it could not be done with their having to work together on the Stalin matter. He would have to end their relationship after that was accomplished. That would be when he would be returning to Finland. Anyway, right now, his feelings were all mixed up. He needed time to think how he would resolve all of the conflicts going on in his mind. He put Anna's letters in his carrying case next to some dirty laundry. They'd be safe there. The bag of poison he put in his long winter coat pocket.

Koskinen ate very little at lunch. He was absorbed in his thoughts. He returned to his room to write a letter to Anna which the courier could take back with him. He had ascertained that the courier would be leaving the day after tomorrow.

In his letter to Anna, Koskinen wrote not much more than he had in previous letters. Although this letter would be carried by the courier and would be safe from prying Russian police, nevertheless, he could not reveal what he was doing specifically to carry out his mission. If he wrote such details, he knew Anna would have all sorts of fears and anxieties about his safety. As always, he professed his love for Anna. He said nothing about Elena. He had not quite finished his letter when the room telephone rang. It was the receptionist informing him of the arrival of Miss Marikova.

"Have her wait in the parlor. I'll be down shortly," Koskinen instructed. Putting aside the unfinished letter, he spent a few minutes grooming himself and then went to meet Elena.

Elena arose from her chair in the parlor to greet Koskinen with a hug and several kisses. Koskinen reciprocated but was eager to clear a question that bothered him.

"Did you have lunch with your friend the police investigator?"

"Of course not, why do you ask?"

"Because you could not come to lunch here."

"I could not explain over the telephone. I have to maintain a professional posture in public. I could not come here because my supervisor had asked me to go to lunch with him. He said he wanted to talk about my work with the Finnish Embassy. As it turned out, he wanted to know how long I expected this assignment would last. I told him at lunch that it would last a while yet. He wanted to know whether the Finnish Embassy people appeared to be satisfied with my work. I told him I thought they were. The conversation was over a lot of small matters. I think he just wanted to get to know me a little better. Really, he does not have any other motive. I'm not concerned about him and neither should you be." Elena seemed annoyed that Koskinen did not trust her, but she said nothing. But Koskinen seemed appeased and relieved by her explanation.

"The courier brought our food additive," Koskinen said with a sly smile. Elena also smiled at the description of the poison.

"Is it ready for use?" Elena questioned.

"It's in powder form and can be used that way by mixing with food. The powder can be mixed with water to form a liquid that can be poured in a drink or on food."

"I think we should have some of both so I can use either one depending on the circumstances."

"Yes, that's a good idea." Koskinen admired Elena's pragmatism. "Wait here. I'll prepare them. I won't be long. Then I think we should talk over procedures to be used in our mutual plans for Stalin."

When Koskinen returned, he handed Elena a small bottle with powder and another containing liquid.

Holding the bottles up, Elena asked, "Are you sure that these are adequate to do the job?"

"Yes, it's a very powerful poison."

"Good." Elena placed the bottles in her purse. "Now, you wanted to talk about procedures in the Stalin matter."

"Yes, I think it's important to do so."

Koskinen and Elena spent about forty-five minutes discussing the proposal of the underground leaders. Koskinen again sought to persuade Elena not to go ahead with her part. Elena was adamant that she would go through with her commitment.

"I really don't want to talk about that anymore, Timo. I intend to proceed." Elena showed her vexation. Timo relented and apologized for raising the issue again, but he explained that he was truly concerned.

Koskinen suggested going to a restaurant for an early dinner.

"It will be a change from eating here. The food may not be as good as we have at the Embassy, but it will be a different environment."

"That sounds fine," Elena said with some of her usual exuberance. "There is a restaurant called the Chalet overlooking the Moskva River. It's not very far from here, but you will need transportation. It's off of Turchaninov Street which extends from here. It's a very nice restaurant."

"Have you been there before?"

"Yes, once. I was impressed."

"Well, I'll see if I can get a taxi," Koskinen said. He put in a call and managed to get one. It arrived a half-hour later. The driver knew his way to the Chalet restaurant.

"Can we agree that we shall not talk about the Stalin matter for the rest of the evening? Let's just enjoy ourselves." Elena had had quite enough of serious conversation for the past several days. She welcomed the chance to relax and enjoy some gaiety.

"I agree," replied Koskinen. "It will be good for both of us."

While they had been in the Embassy during the afternoon, there had been a light snowfall. It gave a fresh, clean appearance to an otherwise drab neighborhood.

As they entered the restaurant, they heard the soothing music of a klavikord, a favorite string keyboard instrument of the Russian people. The layout of the restaurant, the somber lighting, the additional lighted candles on the tables, the rug wall hangings interspersed with framed pictures of seascapes and landscapes, even the white tablecloths and napkins all produced a sense of the cozy and romantic.

The hostess, a friendly and indulgent middle-aged lady attired in a long, black dress with a row of sequins around the neckline, conducted them to a table in a corner of the room. Although there were several other diners, the hostess rightfully surmised that Koskinen and Elena wanted some privacy.

After he and Elena were seated, Koskinen had a chance to look about the room. He observed one discordant fixture that did not fit into the otherwise warm, congenial atmosphere. It was a large picture of Stalin on the wall at one end of the room. Koskinen called Elena's attention to it.

"Look who's here," he said, motioning slightly in the direction of the picture. "He's watching us even in this place."

Elena laughed. "It's required. No matter where you would go, there is always the picture of 'Papa Stalin', the kindly leader of our country." Elena was being sarcastic. "Why don't you shift your chair around so that your back is to him?" She was still laughing over Koskinen's apparent discomfort in facing the dictator. However, Koskinen decided to remain at his place. It was, after all, only a picture, he thought.

The dinner and the conversation proceeded smoothly and delightfully. If any thoughts about policemen and the Stalin project lurked in their minds, neither Elena nor Koskinen showed any expression of them. They reminisced about personal matters, their childhoods, their families, their humorous experiences in the past. Some trivial, others more important, as influences on their lives. During the dinner the person at the klavikord continued to play in a soft, subdued manner some Russian folk songs interspersed with an occasional gypsy song. For Koskinen and Elena the occasion was idyllic. Koskinen desperately wanted to hold Elena in his arms and to whisper how beautiful she was and that he adored her. However, in the restaurant he was limited to occasionally stroking her hand in a show of affection. Towards the end of the dinner, he did suggest that they spend the night together at her apartment.

Elena looked tenderly at Koskinen and then replied, "I would love to, Timo, but I cannot be sure that the police investigator might not be watching from an automobile nearby and if he saw me going into my apartment building with a man, he could become very difficult. I think we should wait until he has been gotten rid of."

"Yes, I suppose you are right," Koskinen reluctantly admitted.

As they rode back in a taxi, Koskinen said, "You will let me know as soon as you have arranged a lunch with the policeman so that I can fulfill my part."

"Oh, absolutely, Timo."

The taxi took Timo first to the Embassy and then Elena to her apartment building. If the policeman was watching, he would see nothing to stir his suspicions.

Koskinen went to his room to finish his letter to Anna. He wrote only a few words more that did not say much. He would give the letter to the courier in the morning.

* * * * *

On the same day that Koskinen had delivered the poison to Elena and then went to dinner at the Chalet restaurant with her, there was a flourish of excitement at the United States Embassy. A message had been received that day by Ambassador Harrison Hayes from the State Department in Washington stating that the proposed dinner to honor Stalin had been approved. The message related that President Roosevelt would send a personal message to Joseph Stalin inviting him and urging him to accept. It stated that Roosevelt felt this would be a means and opportunity for the United States and Russia to establish closer and more cordial relations and that such a dinner would focus world attention on the mutual interests of the two countries. The message instructed the Ambassador to work out the details.

By late March and early April 1939, President Roosevelt came to view Hitler and the Italian dictator, Benito Mussolini, as "gangsters." Roosevelt felt that the Neutrality Act that he had signed in May 1937 should be revised because to insist on adhering to it might give the impression that the United States was on the side of Hitler. Roosevelt had developed an affection for Stalin whom he believed had the same goals for the workingman and the downtrodden that he, Roosevelt, had. Roosevelt was of the opinion that "Uncle Joe," as he referred to Stalin, would be influenced to embrace democratic ideology if a one-on-one personal relationship could be developed between them.

Stalin, on the other hand, at this time in late March 1939 preferred an agreement with Hitler over one with the West. He wanted not only to forestall an invasion of Russia by Hitler, but to use such an agreement to grab more territory for the Soviets. It was reported that Stalin would work out some rapprochement with the Western countries only if he could not get an agreement with Hitler.

In the United States there were those, especially in the State Department, who did not agree with Roosevelt's assessment of Stalin and who preferred a Germany dominated Europe to a Soviet controlled one. They felt that Stalin was the greater threat with his intent to spread Communism. Hence, Roosevelt's approval of a dinner to honor Stalin was in accordance with his respect for the Soviet ruler. Neither Roosevelt nor his aides knew that the dinner was a subterfuge for the more sinister plot on Stalin's life. Ambassador Hayes and Deputy Secretary Fraser Addison were concerned about the consequences when and if Roosevelt discovered the true purpose. The Ambassador and Addison talked about the problem when the message first came in.

"I think we have to go ahead with arranging the dinner," Addison said. "Roth (referring to McKinley Roth, Secretary of State) has agreed to the idea of eliminating Stalin. That's why Chance and Wagner were sent here. I think we have to rely on and try to carry out his initial intent. He has not advised us otherwise or notified us to cancel the project. I think we have to implement his mandate and proceed. We don't have a choice."

Hayes listened attentively and after thinking a few moments about what Addison had just said, he replied, "I want Chance and Wagner to come in here. I'll get Rose to page them."

Bill Chance and Gene Wagner arrived in about fifteen minutes. Hayes had them sit down. Chance felt intuitively that something eventful was the reason he and Wagner were called into the Ambassador's office.

"I called you here, Gene and Bill, because I wanted you to know that Washington has given its approval for a dinner honoring Stalin. You will probably want to let your friends at the bakery know as soon as possible."

"I'm not very surprised, Mr. Ambassador," declared Chance. "Did the President approve it?"

"Yes, apparently. He's sending a letter personally to Stalin urging him to attend the dinner in his honor as a way of letting the world know that the United States is a friend of the Soviet Union."

"And tacitly overlooking all the slaughter of innocent people for perceived traitorous acts that are going on just now in the Soviets," added Deputy Addison. He went on to point out that "We have a lot to do to organize the dinner and the program. First, of course, we have to determine if Stalin will accept. Then to work with his people if he does. Much of what we do will depend on what Stalin and his aides want. The date, time, place, the guest list, the speakers, the menu, the gift to Stalin, and so forth. It's a big undertaking, Bill and Gene, and you and a good part of our staff will have to help to put it together."

"Yes," Chance replied, "Gene and I will do everything we can. We'll probably go to the bakery tomorrow and let them know so that they can begin to arrange their own parts in this drama."

"That's fine," Ambassador Hayes said. "I'll get busy immediately and contact someone at the Kremlin, some bigwig, to let him know and have him take it up with Stalin, himself. I guess that's all for now. Thanks for coming."

Chance and Wagner then left the office. Outside in the corridor, Wagner said, "I think we should contact Sofia right away and give her the news. Then let her get in touch with the bakery people to set up an appointment for us. What do you say?"

"Yes, I was going to say that myself," replied Chance. "I think that we should start there."

At the time that Chance contacted her on the in-house telephone, Sofia was busy reading Russian newspapers and writing translations into English for the English-speaking staff of the Embassy. The translations either in summary form or in complete text formed the basis of the advice Ambassador Hayes forwarded from time to time to his government in the United States. Hayes and Addison were primarily and enduringly interested in Soviet government happenings and in the opinions expressed in editorials. They knew that the editorial opinions reflected the thinking and policies of the moment of Stalin.

The information that Sofia gleaned from the several newspapers and magazines enabled her to keep the underground leadership updated on events which might affect the movement in some way. The opportunity to do this came when Sofia would visit the bakery once or twice a week.

Sofia met with Chance and Wagner in one of the small conference rooms of the Embassy. When she first entered the room, Wagner acted in his usual concupiscent manner. With an ingratiating leer he remarked how attractively dressed Sofia was although she wore her usual plain frock. This time Chance ignored Wagner's remark.

"Sofia," Chance said, "we have received approval of the dinner for Stalin from our government in Washington. We think you should notify your underground people at the bakery as soon as possible."

"I can do that tomorrow morning," Sofia replied. Sofia reacted enthusiastically at the news. "We can now move along. This is a big step to accomplishing our objective. I know the people at the bakery will be happy to hear about this."

"How are you going to notify them?" Wagner asked.

"I'll have to go there personally. I don't want to use the telephone. You never know who is listening in."

"Well, I'd like to go with you," Wagner smiled as he said, "if it's alright with you."

"Yes, that will be fine. You're welcome to come along." Sofia sounded indifferent about whether Wagner trod along or didn't.

"I presume that your people will get the news to our Finnish friends and work things out with them as well," Chance inquired.

"Yes, I am sure they will. The Finns will be playing a crucial role in all of this. It is my guess that Boris and some of the others will coordinate everyone's part. But this will develop over the next week or so. We shall know more about it in due time."

"What part are you going to play in this, Sofia?" Wagner asked.

"I don't know as yet. We'll know more of that in time, too. I would hope to participate in some active way. I don't want to sit on the sidelines and watch this important event merely as a spectator. That is not why I joined the underground." Sofia showed by her expression that she was determined to be in the midst of the operation.

After breakfast in the Embassy dining room the next morning, Sofia and Wagner met in the reception room in preparation to go to the bakery. The weather outside was bright and crisp with the ever present snow covering the streets. Sofia and Wagner were dressed accordingly with their long heavy coats and fur headgear. Each wore boots.

The bakery was but a short distance from the Embassy. Sofia clung to Wagner's arm as they walked along and each seemed to be enjoying the other's company.

"I'm glad you volunteered to come with me," Sofia said in a warm, personal tone quite unlike the businesslike, matter-of-fact tone of yesterday during their meeting.

"I'm not a volunteer. I have no choice. I'm your slave." Wagner laughed at his characterization.

Sofia responded with a smile. "Oh, yes. I'm sure of that!" Her meaning was intended as the opposite of what she said.

They were not quite a block from the bakery when the store came into their view. Immediately they both saw two black limousines near the entrance and a couple of civilians standing nearby as if watching something going on.

"Oh, oh!" Sofia exclaimed. "NKVD are in the store. I think we had better turn around and go back to the Embassy. We don't want to get involved with the police."

"I agree," Wagner said. "Do you think they're investigating the bakery?"

"They are not there to buy bread," Sofia replied. "I'll try to find out later today what happened."

"May I suggest something?" Wagner proffered.

"Yes, I'm listening."

"Bill and I can go down there in the early afternoon ostensibly to buy some bread or cake. Perhaps we can find something out. As members of the United States trade group we have immunity from being questioned about why we came to the bakery or from being arrested. Why don't you let us do that?"

"I suppose you can as a last resort," Sofia said. "Boris and some of the others know you, so you won't have any trouble."

When they arrived back at the Embassy, both Wagner and Sofia stopped in at the office of Deputy Secretary Addison. They reported their experience with the two black limousines and the fact that they decided to return to the Embassy. Addison approved of Wagner's suggestion that Wagner and Chance go to the bakery to determine what had occurred.

"I think you have to find that out," Addison said. "If the NKVD is investigating the people at the bakery, then I feel that we have to reconsider our intent to work with them. An investigation could very well turn up the fact that we're involved with them and that could be disastrous to our relations with the Soviet government." Addison raised his eyebrows and shook his head to indicate that he was repulsed by the very thought of the consequences.

After leaving the Deputy's office, Wagner sought out Chance and explained his and Sofia's experience. Chance agreed to go with Wagner to the bakery. Chance didn't like the fact that the NKVD might be investigating any more than the Deputy Secretary did. In fact, Chance agreed that they might have to dissociate themselves from the underground group. "I hope not," he said, "but we'll have to wait and see what develops."

Later that afternoon, Chance and Wagner paid a visit to the bakery. The young lady at the counter recognized them, smiled and told them to wait a moment. She went into the back room and shortly returned with Boris. Boris was dressed in his white bakery uniform and appeared to Chance and Wagner to be his usual smiling and outgoing self. No one else was in the store.

"Ah, Bill, Gene, welcome! What brings you here besides our wonderful bakery goods?"

Wagner thought that if the bakery had been the object of an NKVD investigation, Boris didn't seem perturbed by the experience. Normally, Wagner mused, one would expect to be quite agitated by such a police visit. But, maybe Boris was one of those individuals who were always in control of their emotions and feelings. Always completely self-disciplined.

"We thought we'd visit with you and discuss a matter or two," Chance replied to Boris' inquiry.

Boris, with no further word, motioned to Chance and Wagner to follow him into the bakery back room. They sat down in a small office room off the main bakery operation.

Wagner began the explanation. "This morning Sofia and I were on our way here when we noticed two black limousines parked in front of your bakery. We immediately concluded that you were having a visit from NKVD and we decided to turn back rather than get involved.

We, Bill and I, are here now to find out what happened. Can you tell us?"

"Of course," Boris said. "Why should I keep anything from you? We are partners in a very great venture. Yes, you are right. The NKVD police did visit us this morning. But you should not be alarmed. It was not for reasons that you probably think. I can tell you with absolute certainty that they were not investigating us. They were here to get us to cooperate with them on their project to find out whether there was any covert action of an anti-Stalin or anti-Communism nature being undertaken in foreign embassies and legations. They knew our driver delivers our products to most of the embassies and legations and they want Akmal and one of us to accompany Akmal to strike up friendships with the employees in the foreign establishments and to gradually get them to talk about what, if anything, is going on along those lines in one or another embassy or legation. You know, sometimes kitchen help will talk too much." Boris laughed at the irony of the NKVD proposal.

"So the visit was to get you and some of your help here to spy on the foreign legations or embassies? That is all there was to it?" Chance was a bit skeptical.

"Did you say you would cooperate?" Wagner asked.

"Do you say 'no' to the NKVD?" Boris declared in a voice that implied that Wagner's question was foolish. "Of course, I said 'yes' and that we'd start right away."

"Are you truly going to spy on the various foreign embassies and legations?" Wagner inquired.

"Yes, we'll have to follow through on our agreement to do so. However, we shall report from time to time that nothing of a suspicious nature is going on, especially in the European and North American foreign representations," Boris added. "We have no intention of compromising anyone."

Bill Chance interposed a comment. "When I think of the NKVD unknowingly coming to a Russian underground to get them to cooperate on spying, then I think I have found one of the most ludicrous and hilarious situations I have ever met."

Chance continued, "So you don't think the police were here to investigate and you believe they know nothing about your underground group?"

"That is right," Boris replied. "I feel certain that they are not aware of our movement."

"Well, that is what we are here for. To assure ourselves that we, as representatives of the United States, can still participate with you in the Stalin project without calling attention to the U.S. involvement," Chance said.

Wagner then interjected, "Sofia and I were on our way here this morning to let you know that the United States has agreed to sponsor the dinner to honor Stalin."

"Oh, that's great!" exclaimed Boris in a sudden display of pleasure.

"Will you notify the Finns?" Chance asked. "We should meet with them and with you and some of your people to work out the details of what each is to do."

Boris replied, "Yes, I'll notify them and I'll arrange a meeting for all to get together. Either here or some other safe place."

"Good." Chance got up to leave. "We shall wait to hear from you. Is that right?"

"Yes, it will probably be within a day or two."

Wagner arose and accompanied Chance out of the back room into the store. Before leaving the building, both bought some pasties from the young lady at the counter. Having the pasties validated their visit to the bakery in case they were stopped by the police. Besides, they both liked to eat the pasties.

"They really make them good here," Wagner said.

Upon arriving back at the Embassy, Chance and Wagner reported to Deputy Addison the substance of their conversation with Boris.

After pondering on the information for a few moments, Addison responded. "Well, I think we'll be safe in proceeding with the dinner for Stalin. Apparently, the police are not aware of what is going on behind the scenes at the bakery."

"Yeah," Chance commented, "I'm relieved that the NKVD is not investigating the bakery. Gene and I would like to get this assignment done and get back to the U.S."

"You sound like you're homesick," Addison noted with a smile.

"Perhaps a bit," Chance replied wistfully.

Wagner interjected, "Yeah, I suppose I'd like to get back, too. In the meantime, however, there are some interesting people here."

"Sure, Gene, we know. Sofia!" Chance spoke wryly.

Wagner smiled, but said nothing further.

During the next few days, Hayes, Addison, Chance and Wagner began the process of planning for the dinner. Until they knew whether Stalin would accept the invitation, their planning was primarily in the discussion stage. They expressed among themselves some doubt that Stalin would accept. Nevertheless, the Ambassador took the initial step of contacting Maxim Litvinov, the Soviet Foreign Minister, to have him sound out Stalin informally. If Stalin was agreeable, the plan was then to have the staff of the Embassy and aides to Stalin work out the details of the event. Litvinov himself told Hayes that he didn't think Stalin would be receptive of the proposal, but that he would discuss it with Stalin.

In March 1939, Stalin was in the position of trusting neither the Western democracies nor Hitler's Germany. But he shrewdly recognized that he needed to obtain the understanding of the West of his territorial expansion ambitions while at the same time placating Hitler and dissuading him from invasion of Soviet lands.

During the latter part of 1938 there were already rumors of a Soviet-German rapprochement and a possible mutual non-aggression pact between the two countries. By March 1939, although Prime Minister Neville Chamberlain of Britain was opposed to cooperation with Russia with regard to protecting Poland and Romania against a German invasion, Chamberlain's cabinet was in favor of a British-Soviet mutual linking. Stalin was hopeful of encouraging the British cabinet's favorable view. Thus, he was playing both the German and British cards.

In the United States, the government can be said to have been generally anti-Semitic and, therefore, not greatly moved to outrage over Hitler's persecution of Jews. However, this attitude changed abruptly upon the happening of the so-called "Crystal Night" of November 7, 1938 when organized groups of Germans went on a rampage of breaking windows of shops in Germany owned or operated by Jews and beating Jews. Thereafter, Stalin was viewed as a possible ally in stemming the violent takeover of Europe by Hitler. Nevertheless, the United States was subject to the Neutrality Act of 1937 in which U.S. Congress set forth a policy of non-involvement in controversies among foreign nations.

It was in this context of world affairs that Litvinov approached Stalin regarding the United States proposal to honor him at a dinner. Litinov's argument presented to Stalin was that he should accept the invitation as a means of promoting good relations with the United States while conveying a message to Hitler that any invasion of the Soviets might trigger the involvement of the United States and the cancellation of the Neutrality Act. Acceptance of the invitation might very well change Chamberlain's attitude towards Soviet actions as well as having a positive effect on other European countries who might view Stalin as a threat.

This argument, apparently, convinced Stalin. After a few days subsequent to Litvinov's conference with him, Stalin informed his Foreign Minister that he accepted the invitation. Litvinov conveyed this information to Ambassador Hayes who was as surprised as was Litvinov of Stalin's decision.

Ambassador Hayes was by no means in happy land with Stalin's acceptance. He told Deputy Addison, "Damned, I was hoping he would refuse the invitation. That would have ended the problem of our participation in his elimination."

"No, it probably wouldn't have," replied Addison. "It would have meant that Bill and Gene would have had to find an alternative. As it is, the dinner is our easy way out. We just have to provide the setting for others to carry out the ultimate in hemlock therapy."

When Chance and Wagner heard of Stalin's acceptance, they were ecstatic.

"At least now the end is in sight and we can perhaps soon be on our way home," said Chance.

"Not so fast," Addison had advised them. "It may be several weeks. We have a great many details to work out. The date, the place, the people to be invited, the speakers on the program, the program itself, and so on. We've only just begun. And you're going to have to work out some details with the underground."

Chance and Wagner remained undaunted. They were both certain that their mission would be accomplished shortly. No question about it.

"We have to tell Sofia," Wagner said. "She will have to let the underground know so that they can coordinate their plans with ours."

"Yes, we'll do that right away," Chance agreed.

They found Sofia in her office and broke the news to her.

"That's great." Sofia, too, was delighted. Having said that, she then frowned.

"That means you'll both be leaving here to return to America soon."

"Yes, that's true," Wagner said. "As soon as our mission is accomplished." He became somber. He had developed affectionate feelings for Sofia and the thought of leaving her disquieted him.

"Could I go to America with you? Will you take me with you?" Sofia asked plaintively.

"I don't know, Sofia," Chance answered. "I hadn't given it any thought. If you're serious about it, we can look into the matter."

"I am serious. I don't want to stay in Russia. There is nothing here for me. I don't want to live with this constant oppression. I think you know what I mean." Sofia was earnest, emphatic.

Wagner spoke up. He addressed Chance. "Maybe we can smuggle Sofia out."

"Don't be silly, Gene. That's too risky for everybody. This is not America where people cross borders with Canada or Mexico illegally every day and get away with it. The Russians have their borders sealed and guarded like a concentration camp."

"Which is what Russia really is," Wagner declared.

"Well, I'll talk to Hayes," Chance concluded. "Maybe he can pull some strings to get permission for Sofia to leave."

Chance then turned to Sofia. "Will you get word to the people at the bakery as soon as possible?"

"Yes, tomorrow morning at the latest," Sofia assured Chance and Wagner.

"We probably should meet with them in the next few days," Chance suggested.

"I'll let you know what they say," Sofia replied.

As they were partly out of the doorway of Sofia's office, Wagner stopped and said to Chance, "I'll be with you in a moment, Bill. I forgot to mention something to Sofia." Chance nodded and kept walking. Wagner turned back into the office. He whispered softly as in confidence, "Sofia, don't worry. I'll see that you'll get out of Russia one way or another."

Sofia got up from her chair, walked over to Wagner and gave him a hug.

"Thanks, Gene. I don't expect a guarantee, but it's nice to know you care." She gave him a gentle kiss on the lips. In a not unexpected reaction, Wagner's heart palpitations increased and instantly he yearned to stay with Sofia longer. But, her office was not the appropriate place to express his feelings beyond a few moments. Unanticipated visitors could enter at any time, he knew.

"How about having dinner with me at some cozy restaurant this evening?" Wagner asked, his voice and face unmistakably communicating his desire to Sofia.

"Yes, that would be nice." Sofia reciprocated the mood of the moment.

"We can decide where to go when I see you later," Wagner said. "How about 1800 hours?"

"Fine. In the lobby."

Wagner patted Sofia's face gently and then turned and left. As he walked towards his room he felt a surge of pleasure in his whole being. He would explain later to Chance that he would not be attending dinner at the Embassy with him that evening.

* * * * *

When Elena arrived back at her hotel after the evening at the Café Restaurant with Koskinen, the hotel clerk handed her a message that read, "Please call me at the station tomorrow. Ivan." Elena noted the terseness of the message. However, she reasoned that the police investigator could not get personal in a note that was to be conveyed by a third person stranger. It would not be advisable in view of his position. Elena at first thought of calling Koskinen and telling him of the message but then decided against it. She knew it would be very upsetting to Koskinen who was already upset by her participation in the Stalin plot. Elena went to bed that night relaxed and at peace. She knew exactly what she had to say and do the next day.

The next morning at about ten Elena telephoned to Ivan Snesarev. The duty officer put the call to him in the interrogation room. He was alone at the time.

"This is Elena. I received your message when I returned to the hotel last evening."

"Yes, I called yesterday morning. You must have been gone all day."

"From the hotel, yes. How are you, Ivan?"

"Fine. But I'm getting quite impatient with you. You always seem to have excuses not to see me."

"Well, I have told you this is a busy time for me."

"You're not busy at midnight!"

"No, but I'm very tired at that time or whenever I get back to the hotel late in the evening."

"When, then, do I get to see you?" Officer Snesarev's voice sounded clearly irritated.

"I like you, Ivan, and I don't think we should argue." Elena forced her voice to be soothing. She quickly understood that she had to placate Snesarev. "Look," she continued, "let's meet for lunch on Thursday. That's two days from now. We can meet at the Central Workers Restaurant on Ruzheyny Street. I like it there and they have good food."

"I know where it is." Snesarev sounded a bit more calm. "What time?"

"How about 1300? They're not quite so busy at that time."

"That's alright. Can we go to your apartment after lunch?"

Elena's heart jumped a beat. She knew what Snesarev had in mind and the thought of being alone with Snesarev in her room was absolutely abhorrent to her.

"Yes, that would be nice, but I have to see what my schedule is on that afternoon. Sometimes it changes abruptly. However, I know I have all day Sunday free. Are you on duty then?"

"No."

"Well, let's count on that." Elena thought that if everything went according to plan, Snesarev would be dead by Sunday. If not, then she had no choice but to see him.

"Good," replied Snesarev. "We can talk more about it at lunch Thursday. But no more excuses!" He sounded cordial.

"No, no excuses."

When she hung up the telephone, Elena took a deep breath. "Whew," she thought, "that's over with. So far so good." She immediately called the Finnish Embassy and told the receptionist that she would be there in about a half-hour. Without being asked, the receptionist mentioned that Antti Salonen was in the building. The receptionist had for some time noticed that Elena had always asked for and visited with Salonen. Elena was not surprised. How could anyone not fail to notice?

"If you see him, you can let him know."

At the Embassy, Elena and Koskinen discussed her telephone conversation with police officer Snesarev and how they would proceed at the lunch at the restaurant. They went over the details twice to firmly establish what each was to do. There were to be no slip-ups.

In the afternoon, Koskinen and Elena joined Eino Partola, one of the trade specialists, at a trade negotiation session with a minor trade official at the Russian Foreign Trade Ministry. Their participation in the conferences had been infrequent but at least often enough to maintain an appearance of being part of a team with trade interests.

Deception is a way of life in Intelligence operations, Koskinen had once remarked to Elena. "Either we are deceivers or searching for deceivers in our practice. In fact, that is not much different from what ordinary people practice in their everyday lives. As you grow older you realize that there is hardly a person who does not have a veneer covering his thoughts and inner feelings. Unless a person is totally honest in expressing his thoughts, opinions and his sensibilities, he is practicing deception. And yet, if a person was totally honest in his expressions, he would offend many people with whom he came into contact. That is because most people see clearly, they think, the faults in other people and neither see nor acknowledge their own. Everyone has fears and insecurities but they rarely reveal them, opting instead to act with pretensions of bravado and heroics. So, acting nice to people you despise because of their perceived faults or having a veneer that hides the true you constitute deception. Do you agree with me, Elena?"

"Yes. But I would reason a bit further," Elena replied.

"What do you mean?" Koskinen thought he had circumscribed the whole concept of deception.

"We may see others' faults but we may either ignore them or decide that they're not important enough to mention. That does not mean we are being deceptive. It means we love or care enough for a person to emphasize the positives instead of the negatives. Now I must ask, are we deceiving each other in some way? Are we being truly honest with each other in our relations?" Elena thought the discussion provided an opportunity to challenge Koskinen on a very personal matter.

Koskinen chuckled. He enjoyed being challenged by Elena. "I am being honest with you on important things."

"And you overlook the unimportant, is that right?" Elena had declared.

"Yes," replied Koskinen, smiling in amusement.

"So that proves my point that you either care for me or love me, does it not?"

"Yes," Koskinen had confessed and admitted that Elena had a sharper perception than he had had on the issue of deception.

Koskinen and Elena did not see each other again until the day Elena was to have lunch with the police investigator. They had decided to name that day "Pay Day." A day when Ivan Snesarev would be compensated and duly rewarded for his malevolence, for his cruelty and brutality. It was Elena who had suggested the name and she and Koskinen laughed over it. They thought that the name was a stroke of genius.

Koskinen slept fitfully during the night before Pay Day although at times he would slip into a deep sleep. It was during one of those times when he dreamed of a seagull attacking him from behind. He did not know of the seagull until he heard the beating of the wings and the piercing screech of the gull's cry a moment before he felt the gull's claws penetrate his scalp. With another shrill cry, the gull flew off and disappeared. The dream pain was so intense that Koskinen awakened abruptly. He immediately knew it had been a dream but it was a traumatic one. Koskinen did not dismiss it lightly. This was the third or fourth time, he wasn't sure how many, that he had the seagull dream. He lay awake in a sweat and breathing heavily, at first, from the dreaming experience. He calmed gradually and thought about the seagull dream. Was it an omen? He seemed to discern a pattern in its occurrence. It apparently came to him just before some significant event, an event sometimes of violence. Koskinen was puzzled. He did not know why this should be. Finally, he drifted off again into his fitful sleep. In the morning when he arose, he did not feel rested. To the contrary, he felt exhausted, depleted. But he was to have a busy day ahead. He could not stay in bed.

Elena and he had agreed that if he did not receive a telephone call from Elena by eleven o'clock in the morning, he was to assume that their plan would proceed. By eleven o'clock there had been no call. Although he had had considerable experience in clandestine operations in his Intelligence work and had always acted professionally, coolly and with confidence in a successful outcome, Koskinen on this occasion was tense and unsure of the plan running smoothly. He had to struggle to subordinate these feelings to a more positive outlook and approach. He reasoned that when the time came for him to play his part, he would be able to do so in a resolute, professional manner. He thought that perhaps his uncertainty about the operation was because Elena was involved. In the past there had never been the complication of personal emotional attachments.

At 1215 hours, Koskinen left the Embassy and caught the bus that ran past the Finnish building on Kropotkinski Street and then to Smolenski Boulevard to the intersection with Ruzheyny Street. Koskinen alighted from the bus at the intersection and walked a short distance west to the Central Workers Restaurant. Before entering the restaurant he noted the location of the shoe store where a public telephone was placed. The bus trip and the walk had taken about twenty-five minutes. He walked around Ruzheyny Street a short distance noting the various shops and general layout of the street.

At 1245 hours Koskinen opened the entrance door to the restaurant and entered a short but broad vestibule. At the other end of the vestibule was another door. Opening that door allowed Koskinen to admit himself to the main dining room. A woman met him. She was obviously the hostess.

"Will someone be joining you?"

"No, I want a table just for myself."

The hostess, a menu card in hand, guided him to a small table near the entrance to the dining room.

"Our waitress will be with you shortly," the hostess said, handing Koskinen the menu as he was seated.

Koskinen made a quick survey of the room. There were about fifteen dining tables about half of which were occupied by diners. The room itself was not remarkable. The walls were painted an off-white color with a few pictures of a nondescript nature hung here and there. As Koskinen expected, there was the inevitable and unavoidable large photograph of Stalin hung and framed in a prominent spot in the room. The other diners seemingly took no especial notice of him.

Koskinen looked at the menu. All items were in Russian and some he understood and others he did not. He was not, however, very hungry. When the waitress arrived at his table, he ordered a large bowl of cabbage soup and some Russian dark bread. His main interest was a large clock on one of the side walls. At 1300 hours, no Elena and no Snesarev. The passage of each thirty seconds seemed to him like several minutes. At four minutes and seven seconds after 1300, an unaccompanied man entered and was guided to a table in the middle of the dining room. Koskinen guessed it was the police investigator. If it was Snesarev, he was wearing civilian clothes. Not a bad looking chap, Koskinen thought to himself.

The waitress brought the soup and bread. Koskinen began to eat very slowly in order not to finish the soup before Elena arrived. He had brought a magazine with him and he began to read it in order to de-emphasize his frequent quick look where Snesarev was sitting, if indeed it was him.

At six minutes and eighteen seconds after 1300 hours, Koskinen saw Elena enter. He observed her stop a moment and peruse the people in the room. Her glance fixed for an imperceptible moment on Koskinen but she gave not the slightest hint of recognition. Her gaze then rested on the man whom Koskinen had guessed was Snesarev. She smiled at the police officer and walked towards him. It was Snesarev after all as Koskinen had surmised. Snesarev arose from his chair and greeted Elena by first taking her hand in his and then helping to remove her heavy coat. The coat he draped over his on one of the extra chairs at their table. The hostess who must not have been at the entrance when Elena entered now came to their table and handed them each a menu card.

Elena had chosen to sit at her table so that she faced Koskinen. Snesarev was to her right and facing the room entrance. Elena and Snesarev at first did not examine the menus but talked animatedly. Elena wore a permanent smile as she talked while looking at Snesarev. Snesarev, in turn, had his hand on Elena's forearm in what to Koskinen was a loving touch. Had Koskinen not known the circumstances he'd have become intensely jealous. He continued to slowly sip his soup and break and eat small pieces of bread. Nevertheless, he gave frequent albeit impersonal glances toward Elena. She, in turn, had eyes only for Snesarev. She was, to Koskinen's great relief, playing her role to the hilt. Koskinen could not hear their conversation but it was not important to him what they were talking about.

The waitress was at their table and after quick examinations of the menus, Elena and Snesarev placed an order. Koskinen was getting to the end of his soup when the waitress asked him if he wished anything more.

"No, I'll just take my bill."

In a few moments, the waitress returned with his bill. He paid her and asked if it was alright for him to sit and read his magazine for a few moments.

"Of course, please stay as long as you wish," the waitress replied. She then disappeared into the kitchen.

In a few moments, the waitress came from the kitchen with a tray containing the dishes Elena and Snesarev had ordered.

Koskinen waited until he felt that Elena and her companion were well into eating their food. He thought he saw an eye movement in a direct glance from Elena to him that seemed to say that the time had arrived for him to do his part. Elena's look was so quick that Snesarev could not have possibly noticed any divergence from her attention to him. But, it was her first glance of the afternoon directed by Elena towards Koskinen once she had sat down at the table. Koskinen understood why Elena had not once looked at him during the meal up to that moment. The one look was meant to convey her message.

Koskinen paid his bill and arose from his table slowly, casually folded his magazine and put on his coat and hat, turned and walked towards the vestibule and out of the building. Once outside he walked hurriedly to the shoe store, entered and went to the public telephone. Elena had earlier in the week given him the telephone number of the restaurant. Koskinen placed some coins in the telephone box and made the call. Someone at the restaurant answered.

"Hello. Will you please ask a Mr. Snesarev to come to the telephone? I am a friend of his and I understand he will be at your restaurant with a young lady about this time."

"Yes, if he is here, I'll let him know he is wanted on the telephone."

"Thank you. I'll hold the phone."

Koskinen proceeded to hold his hand over the telephone mouthpiece in order to eliminate any noise being conveyed to the other end. Shortly, he heard a voice on the other end.

"Hello! This is Ivan Snesarev. Who is this?"

Silence for a moment. Then Koskinen, ear to the telephone with his hand still covering the mouthpiece heard Snesarev mutter, "Some goddamned fool is playing games!" Koskinen then heard the receiver on the other end get slammed down. He hung up his own receiver and made his way out of the shoe store. He walked quickly down Ruzheyny Street towards Smolensky Boulevard to catch a bus.

At the restaurant earlier in the afternoon during their lunch Elena had the impression that she was getting along quite well with Snesarev. Snesarev complained in a nice way that he thought Elena was trying to avoid him, that he really did like her a great deal and that was why he may have sounded impatient on the telephone.

"I feel I must apologize if I seemed to be pressuring you, Elena."

"There is no need to apologize, Ivan. I understand how you felt. But I was truly busy," Elena replied.

"Do I understand that right now you have been assigned to translate at the Finnish Embassy?"

"Yes, that is right. For the trade conferences."

"You know, Elena, I have a word of advice. You must be very careful. People who have contact with foreigners are regarded with suspicion by our government." Snesarev sounded concerned for Elena. Elena thought he was different from the person she had met at the police station. He was not at all intimidating. He seemed kind and thoughtful, even gentle. She began to wonder whether she should poison him. He was really not so bad after all. He apparently had a good side to him that she had not suspected. If he was nice to her, Elena asked herself, isn't that all that was necessary?

Even as they were talking, Elena's mind was racing from doubt to doubt. Finally, she got hold of her wayward thinking and realized that she had to go through with the plan to get rid of Snesarev. She could not forever give excuses not to see him. She would have to sleep with him, something he had already hinted at wanting to do. But most important, he was a police official and she had to protect the underground movement. If she continued to associate with him, then sooner or later he was bound to find out about her affiliation with the anti-Stalin group. And she was sure that however much he liked her, if he had to choose between protecting her and being loyal to the government, he could choose the government. No, he had to go!

At about the time that they were halfway through their meal, a man employee of the restaurant came to their table.

"Are you Mr. Snesarev?"

"Yes."

"There is a telephone call for you. If you wish to take it, the telephone is over there." The fellow pointed to a place in the vestibule just outside the entrance to the dining room.

Snesarev looked surprised. "A telephone call for me! Did the person say who he or she was?"

"It's some man. He did not identify himself. He said only that he was a friend of yours."

"Well, I'll take the call. Please excuse me, Elena. I'll be back in a few minutes." Snesarev then walked over to the telephone in the vestibule. As such, he could not see into the dining room.

As soon as she saw Snesarev enter the vestibule, Elena groped into her purse on her lap and brought out the small bottle of poison. As she did this, she looked quickly and furtively around the dining room to see if a customer or employee might be looking at her. No one was watching. She quickly pulled Snesarev's half-filled wine glass close to her chest, unscrewed the cap on the bottle and with her fingers holding the bottle trembling slightly, poured the contents into the wine. She then pushed the wine glass back to its former position, screwed the cap back on the bottle and returned it to her purse. She felt herself breathing heavily and that her face was flushed with the tension and excitement of the occasion. She realized that she had to pull herself together immediately and to act in a normal, unperturbed and relaxed manner. That Elena was able to do so in outward appearance while still seething and trembling inside herself attested to her emotional strengths and discipline.

Elena saw Snesarev walking back to the table, a puzzled look on his face. As he sat down, he said to Elena, "It was a strange call. When I asked who was calling me, there was no answer, just complete silence on the other end of the telephone. It could be one of my officers at the station playing a joke on me. I mentioned to a couple of them that I was having lunch here today with you. Yes, that is probably it. But I won't ask them because I won't give them the satisfaction of thinking they disturbed me." Snesarev laughed over the incident.

Elena's heart jumped when Snesarev said he told his officers that he was having lunch with her. That was not what she expected. If Snesarev died from the poison, the officers might recall the luncheon date and suspect her of having something to do with it. However, outwardly she continued to appear calm and to accept Snesarev's explanation of the telephone call.

"Yes, I guess there are people who get a kick out of doing something like that," Elena said.

Elena and Snesarev continued their lunch. Both continued their conversation about personal things such as their childhood, their education and so on. Snesarev drank the entire glass of wine and ordered another. He said nothing about the taste of the wine. Finally, Snesarev said that he had to get back to the police station. Elena agreed saying that she, too, had to return to her office at the Trade Ministry.

In the vestibule, Elena gave Snesarev a gentle kiss and said goodbye. Snesarev offered to drive her to the Ministry building in the unmarked police car that he had driven to the restaurant. Elena declined, saying she preferred to walk.

As she walked the few blocks to the Ministry building, Elena thought how easily the poisoning plan had been accomplished. All she had to do now was to wait and see if the poison would have its intended effect. She should know within a couple of days. She had to get in touch with Timo as soon as possible. He would be anxious to know how it went. She reported in to her supervisor and then took a bus to the Finnish Embassy. On the bus ride she had time to think of the event and the more she thought about it the more nervous she became. Suppose Snesarev didn't die, but just became ill from the poison. Would he suspect she had tried to poison him? If he did die, would his friends suspect her? If he died, would he first leave a note during his agony pointing the finger at her? Would she be arrested and tortured to make her confess everything? By the time the bus arrived at the Embassy, Elena was quite beside herself. She needed Timo to comfort and reassure her.

Elena was aware that her fears and anxieties were uncharacteristic of herself. Up to now she had always been and felt self-reliant, willing to undertake potentially hazardous and dangerous actions. Had she not volunteered to kill the most powerful and cunning man in Russia? But, perhaps there was a difference between those schemes and intrigues and the Snesarev pest. The former were ventures proposed for future action. They were more or less remote and she was always able to pull out of an arrangement if she wished. But Snesarev involved an action already taken, no longer remote and certainly not one from which she could recuse herself. It was done.

As these thoughts raced through her mind, Elena wondered if she was up to handling the actual confrontation with Stalin. Would she be so fearful that she could very well bungle the project, make a mistake for which not only she but others in the underground would suffer? Was her bravado in volunteering for the risky plan just bluster? She recognized that these self-doubts had to be resolved and eliminated in short order if her commitment to the Stalin plan was to culminate in carrying it out.

At the Finnish Embassy, Elena met immediately with Koskinen upon her arrival. They went into a conference room and closed the door. There was no preliminary embracing or kissing. Koskinen was eager to learn how her part of the plan had gone and Elena was equally as keen to tell him.

"It all went quite well," Elena said. "A lot easier than I thought it would. When Ivan came back to the table after answering your telephone call and not hearing anyone on the other end, he said he thought it was one of his friends playing a joke on him. He said that he told a couple of friends he was going to see me at the restaurant. And that is what disturbs me. If Ivan dies, they could decide I had something to do with it."

"I don't think that will happen. The doctors will decide he had a heart attack. I don't think they'll conduct an autopsy." Koskinen sounded so reassuring that Elena felt much better. Koskinen continued, "Since the effect of the poison does not kill for several days, no one would logically connect you to the death."

"Well, we shall just have to wait until we hear something," Elena concluded.

Koskinen then informed Elena, "Akmal was here this morning and delivered some bakery goods and, at the same time, gave the chef a message for me. It was not in writing but Akmal said he'd be here in three days to deliver again and would like to know if I needed a ride with him. What do you make of it?"

"I am sure he has a message for you from our underground people and you should see him when he returns here in three days. The message he gave the chef for you was intended to be an innocent appearing way of telling you this."

"Aren't you going to see the people at the bakery before Akmal gets back here?" Koskinen inquired.

"Probably not. We prefer not to have too much coming and going of the same people at the bakery. It may arouse suspicions. We use covert means by choice. We go to the bakery only when asked to do so. Akmal may have a message for me at the same time."

"Why don't you use wireless communication?" Koskinen asked.

"We have used it," Elena replied, "but it is very risky. The operators found they had to keep moving about to avoid detection. They didn't want to do that."

Elena changed the subject. "Timo, why don't you spend the night with me. I don't want to be alone after today's experience. I need to have you with me." Elena was still somewhat distraught.

"Sure, I'll do that." Koskinen was only too happy to comply.

After dinner at the Embassy, Elena and Timo had a taxi take them to Elena's hotel.

"I don't think we have to worry about your policeman friend watching for you from his automobile outside the hotel," Koskinen said facetiously. "Even though he is, he won't be around long enough to make trouble."

"Let's not talk any more about him," Elena requested. "I want to get my mind off today's event."

Koskinen not only spent Thursday night with Elena, but also Friday and Saturday nights. Elena needed considerable comforting. Or so she said, and Koskinen agreed with her.

"How will I know if Ivan's dead?" Elena wanted to know.

"You made a date with him for Sunday. If you don't keep the date and you don't hear from him I think you can assume he has crossed the River Styx into Hades," Koskinen laughed over the description.

"I don't think it's funny," declared Elena in a tone of concern. "I'm the one on the front line."

"We're all on the front line, Elena. Only we each have different weapons," Koskinen said in a subdued voice intended to further allay Elena's shaky faith in the outcome of the poisoning.

Koskinen and Elena decided that on Sunday Elena would remain in her room alone and Koskinen would leave early Sunday morning and return to the Finnish Embassy. For them to be seen together on Sunday would suggest that Elena did not intend to keep her date with Snesarev, probably because she knew that it could not be kept. Furthermore, it was decided that she would go to the hotel desk and inquire two or three times during the day whether there were any messages for her. The hotel clerk would then be a witness to the fact that she was at the hotel and awaiting a message. If anyone investigated, Elena could say that she was waiting to hear from Police Officer Snesarev. For Elena, no message could also serve as probable proof that Ivan Snesarev had become a resident of Purgatory. In anticipation of spending a day in her room, Elena brought a bag of sandwich material to her room. On Monday she would go to the Finnish Embassy and have lunch there as well as to see Akmal when he delivered the bakery products.

Elena was not at all worried that her supervisor, Petya Chukovsky, might think she was spending an inordinate and unnecessary amount of time at the Finnish Embassy. Chukovsky liked Elena. He thought she was an especially intelligent, highly motivated and capable young lady. He was quite satisfied with his marriage and had no physical designs on Elena. They occasionally spent their lunch hours together either in the Trade Ministry Building or at a local nearby restaurant. From these visits and during conference times between the two, Elena and Chukovsky had implicitly manifested a mutual disapproval of the government. Nothing was overtly expressed about this. It was just understood. When Elena asked her supervisor if he thought she was at the Finnish Embassy more than she should be, Chukovsky had replied that working with the Finns was her assignment and that she had to use her own judgment on when to be there. Chukovsky said that his boss also left it to his decision to run his department as he saw fit as long as there was no bungling and no complaints from foreign embassies about the people Chukovsky assigned to various duties at the Embassies or Legations. Elena had never had any complaints about her work. That was good enough for Chukovsky.

According to plan, Elena remained in her hotel room Sunday and occasionally going to the clerk's desk for possible messages. There were none. She hardly ate her sandwich material. She intermittently experienced throughout the day peaks of anxiety and valleys of calm. The day dragged. The evening seemed never to come and when it did she thought it still possible that Snesarev might contact her. He might even contact her tomorrow, Monday, but, at least, she did not have to sit in her room waiting. Monday was a work day.

While sitting in her room with no one to talk with, Elena frequently let her active imagination control her thoughts. She thought about how Snesarev might be dying. She allowed herself to create a mental imagery of the agony he would experience, that he might be groaning in pain and rolling about on the floor. He would not understand what was happening to him and that made his anguish all the more intense. Elena conjectured that since Snesarev lived alone, he could call for help and no one would hear him. Having one's vital organs cease functioning properly or normally would result in a horrible, excruciatingly painful death. Elena felt sorry that Snesarev had to suffer, but she felt no remorse. Anyway, it was too late for contrition. At about 2230 hours,

Elena went to bed and almost immediately fell into a deep sleep caused primarily from sheer emotional exhaustion.

In the morning, Elena took a bus to the Finnish Embassy. She made certain she arrived early enough not to miss Akmal who, in turn, never delivered his baked goods to the Embassy at any regular time although it was always in the morning.

Koskinen had left word with the chef to call him when Akmal arrived. Koskinen received the call at about 1045 hours and proceeded immediately to the loading dock at the rear of the building. Elena accompanied him.

Akmal was standing at the rear of his truck unloading bread boxes when Koskinen and Elena approached him. Akmal stopped his work and turned and smiled at the couple.

"I am happy to see you both. I have a message from our bakery. They have called an important meeting for this coming Friday at 1330 hours at the bakery. You are both to be there. It is very important that you attend. The representatives from the United States will be asked to attend also. Do you understand? Next Friday at 1330."

"Is there any preparation we must make for the meeting?" Koskinen asked.

"I don't know. I have related to you only what I have been told. I cannot answer your question." Akmal, still smiling, returned to his unloading work. Koskinen and Elena thanked Akmal and returned to inside the building.

"Well, we shall just have to bide our time until Friday," Koskinen commented to Elena as they walked from the kitchen to the parlor.

"In the meantime, I think we should involve ourselves with Eino and Petri in their trade conferences. There is little else we can do. What do you think, Elena?"

"Yes, that is a good idea. Let me know what their schedules are after you've talked with them."

Later in the afternoon, Elena asked Koskinen, "Do you think Snesarev is gone?"

"I think so, yes."

"If you, on any day, don't hear from me or see me here at the Embassy it may indicate that I have been arrested." Elena had not fully shed herself of her intrepidation.

"I understand how you feel," Koskinen said, "but I think you're worrying unnecessarily. I think you should try to dismiss the whole thing from your mind."

"Easier said than done," Elena replied. "You don't really know how I feel, Timo. It is impossible for you to know unless you have also committed murder."

"In a sense, I have committed murder," Koskinen admitted. "I assisted you, so I am an accessory."

"That may be, but I am the one who administered the poison. If a person who commits murder is never arrested, that person is nevertheless condemned to looking over his or her shoulder for the rest of his or her life. I can imagine that."

"If you feel the way you do and are as concerned as I think you are, then perhaps you should not participate in the Stalin case," said Koskinen. He thought that this might be the opportunity to try to dissuade Elena from participating.

"I shall go ahead with the plan," replied Elena, "but this business with Snesarev points up the fact that trying to kill someone can leave an indelible and permanent scar on your personality and character. Perhaps after I have poisoned Stalin I should get out of the Soviet Union quickly. Once out, I will be able to stop the thought of my arrest. Maybe you can help get me out. It should not be too difficult to get me to Finland."

"I have already thought of that, Elena. However, I have no solution to get it done at this moment."

* * * * *

At the United States Embassy, Sofia proceeded to inform the underground leaders at the bakery of the approval by the United States government of the dinner to honor Stalin. They were elated to get that information, but they had yet to learn whether Stalin would accept. Boris, who was the first to speak to Sofia at the bakery, had an idea.

"I am going to let the NKVD know about this immediately," he told Sofia. "I shall tell them that our driver, Akmal, got the information. They will be impressed that we learned of it before the NKVD did and that will raise their confidence in us and serve to wash away any questions they might have about our loyalty to the government. Is that a good idea?"

"Yes. I think you're a genius, Boris," Sofia replied with enthusiasm.

"We'll do the same thing when we learn whether Stalin has accepted," Boris added.

Boris got on the telephone and called his contact agent at the Moscow headquarters of the NKVD. He reported to the other people at the bakery that the agent was utterly surprised by hearing the information and thanked him profusely.

"We have passed on to them perfectly harmless information but I think we have impressed them with our ability to ferret out information at foreign embassies efficiently and quickly." Boris spoke with pride in his accomplishment.

The other men at the bakery, while generally approving Boris' idea, were more cautious. Petrov, the principal baker, commented, "We must be careful, Boris, that we don't overdo giving the police information. They might get so impressed that they will want to use us as a source of intelligence and that could mean that they would get more involved with us. And that we don't want. We don't want them here at the bakery. So be careful!"

Boris nodded his acceptance of Petrov's advice. But, when Boris mentioned his intention to let the NKVD know whether Stalin accepted the invitation to the dinner, Petrov and the other men working at the bakery said, "No."

Petrov again spoke up. "If you do that, it will, of course, surprise and impress them. But, it may have the effect of upsetting them and making them feel challenged by our ability to get information before they could learn of it through their direct contact with Stalin's office. We want to show them our cooperation, but we don't want to antagonize them. The NKVD people are very jealous of their close association with Stalin."

Boris thought a moment and then nodded in agreement. "Yes, you're right. I was carried away by enthusiasm for my idea. I was letting my creativity affect my judgment."

A week later when Sofia visited the bakery with the news that Stalin had accepted the invitation there was a subdued exultance among the underground leaders working there. They met in the upstairs room in the bakery building to discuss what must now be done.

"We are now at the threshold of the final stage of our plan and purpose," Boris said in initiating the discussion. "The time has arrived when we must plan every detail with great care and be sure that everyone involved knows exactly what to do and how and when to do it." The other three men and Sofia who were in the room agreed. Petrov made a suggestion.

"We should call a meeting here with the two American fellows and with Elena and the Finnish fellow. They should be here at the same time so there is no mix-up in what each must do."

"We can set a date," Boris said, "and Akmal can get the message to Elena and the Finn."

"It is Friday today. How about a week from now, next Friday?" Petrov asked.

"Does anyone have a problem with that?" Boris inquired as he looked at each individual in the room. No one objected.

Boris added, "Unless the date is a problem with the Americans or with the Finn, we'll set the meeting for next Friday at 1330 hours. If there is any change, you will be informed."

The meeting ended and the men returned to the bakery operation. Sofia went back to the United States Embassy to notify Chance and Wagner.

* * * * *

By the evening of the Sunday following the Thursday lunch with Snesarev, Elena had heard nothing from the police officer. She called Koskinen from a public telephone that same evening.

"Nothing new, but curious," she had said. Koskinen understood what she meant. He, too, was curious. He assumed that since Elena had heard nothing, that Snesarev was dead. However, he wanted to be certain.

The next day Koskinen called the police station where Snesarev worked. "This is the Finnish Embassy. I want to speak to the police investigator Ivan Snesarev. I want to thank him for his cooperation and help in straightening out the accident our Embassy vehicle was involved in a short time ago."

The officer who answered Koskinen's call said quite curtly and in a matter of fact tone of voice, "Officer Snesarev is dead."

"Oh, that is too bad. I'm sorry to hear that. I'm sure you will feel his loss. What did he die of if I may ask?"

"A sudden heart attack," the officer on the other end replied. "We are sorry, of course, that he died at a relatively young age, but it provides an opportunity for someone here to get promoted into the vacant position. Is there anything else?"

"No, thank you." Koskinen hung up. He was greatly relieved to have verified Snesarev's death. It would be a relief to Elena, as well. Snesarev was a momentary blurb in their lives that could not be put aside forever. Koskinen would call Elena at work and tell her that the mission had been accomplished.

CHAPTER 10

Two days before the meeting scheduled for the bakery, Koskinen received another letter from his wife. He had been getting about one letter a week from Anna. Most contained information about herself and the children, what they had been doing since she last wrote. She wrote of the weather, the sermon at church, her classes at school, the prices of food items and many other prosaic and, to Koskinen, wearisome details. Koskinen loved Anna but life with her could become, at times, so routine and boring. He hadn't realized that until he had spent time with the exciting and radiant Elena.

In this latest letter, however, Anna wrote that the newspapers had reported that Paasikivi and Tanner had returned from Russia empty-handed, that their mission to negotiate with Stalin about his demands on Finland was a failure. Anna added that the newspapers also reported that Stalin was becoming more insistent that Finland cede some islands in the Gulf of Finland to Russia. Anna wrote that she was proud that Finland refused to cede Finnish territory but that she was becoming very concerned that the Red Army might invade Finland and that then there would be war. She wished that Timo could get home soon before such a war happened.

"More and more people whom I talk with seem to expect that we shall have to fight to keep our independence and freedom," Anna wrote. "It is quite scary. The government is beginning to set up its defenses against Russian invasion. I don't know how a small country like Finland can stand against a huge country like Russia and expect to win."

What Anna wrote in her latest letter made Koskinen understand more fully how very serious and strained the relationship between

Finland and its big neighbor had become. Obviously the people back home were taking the situation much more gravely than the Embassy was.

Koskinen was an intelligent man. He comprehended that when one has lived in Russia for even a short time one begins to accept as a normal political and social environment what those living outside of Russia would be regarded as crisis situations. In a sense, every day in Russia is a crisis for every citizen. "Will I be stopped on the street by the police and questioned?" "Will I or some family member or a friend be arrested and never seen nor heard from again?" "If I complain about a shortage of bread on the store shelves, will someone report me to the police as a subversive threat to the government?" "If some foreigner or tourist stops me on the street to ask for directions, will I come under suspicion of passing secret information to foreign espionage agents?" "Can I express an opinion about anything but the weather without fear of consequences?"

Koskinen realized that people in Russia lived with these fears daily, shrugged their shoulders and accepted them as normal living. Koskinen also understood clearly that this system was what Elena and her underground friends were seeking to abolish. He also understood that Stalin would impose this system on Finland if the Finns did not stand up to him and resist his takeover demands. The Finns were smart, he concluded, to begin to install military defenses against possible war with Russia. Yes, Finland was a David against a Goliath, but David won. Besides, other countries like Britain, Germany and, possibly, the United States would come to the aid of Finland. They would not allow her to fight by herself.

At dinner that evening, Koskinen sat at the table with Ambassador Peltonen and a couple of Embassy staff. He mentioned Anna's reports and concerns to the group.

"I think that the public in Finland is more concerned than they should be," remarked the Ambassador. "I have faith in our government being able to keep us independent through negotiation with Stalin. Nevertheless, I think the government is wise to prepare for an attempt to invade us. Stalin is very persistent about wanting those islands in the Gulf."

One of the staff members spoke up. "Do you think we should hand them over?"

"I don't think we should give the islands to Stalin. But, to pacify him it is my opinion that we should lease them to Russia until the perceived threat from Germany has disappeared. I have made my opinion known to our State Department."

Koskinen then observed, "But, if we lease the islands, isn't it likely that Stalin will then demand more concessions from us?"

"Yes, it's a possibility," replied Peltonen. "We have to be realistic. Russia can take by force whatever she wants and Finland can't do much about it."

A staff member at the dining table then asked, "What would happen if Stalin were to suddenly die?"

The Ambassador and Koskinen exchanged quick glances as if the questioner had somehow uncovered their mutual secret. They quickly both realized that the staff member was just asking a question that might occur to anyone concerned about the security of his country.

Ambassador Peltonen answered. "I think Stalin's death would have a profound effect on the entire international picture. There would be an immense upheaval in the Soviet Union itself as various interests and personalities struggled for power. Finland would be relieved of considerable apprehension since the invasion of Finland would virtually disappear as a threat. Germany might see it as an opportunity to invade the Soviets while the Soviet Union was in chaos. Some Soviets might seek to secede and set up their own independent nations. The Baltic States of Estonia, Latvia and Lithuania, like Finland, would feel less threatened by a Soviet takeover. Great Britain, France and even the United States would no longer be able to count on Russia as an ally to stem Hitler. There could be other effects, China and Japan, for example."

"Golly, if that would be the effect," said the staff member who asked the question, "then it would seem some effort should be made to get rid of Stalin, if you know what I mean."

Koskinen laughed. "Good observation, Esko. Why don't you volunteer for the job?"

Esko, the staff member, squirmed about in his chair uncomfortably but said nothing more. He seemed embarrassed by the position his question had placed him in.

The other staff member said, "It sounds good in theory, but I think it would be something impossible to carry out. Stalin is always surrounded by a small army of loyalty-tested military guards. And his food and drink are closely monitored in both the cooking and delivery process so that no one can poison him …"

The Ambassador turned to Koskinen. "If you wish, I can write a note to your wife to tell her you are quite well and quite safe."

"That would be very thoughtful of you to do so. Anna would appreciate that very much," Koskinen said.

After the staff members had excused themselves from the table, Ambassador Peltonen said to Koskinen, "I'm glad that question was asked. Answering it helped to accentuate the importance of your mission. By the way, what is the latest development?"

Koskinen then told the Ambassador of the meeting scheduled for the next day with the Russians and the Americans and himself.

"Good," declared Peltonen. "We're at least moving along. See me after your meeting. I'd like to know what came out of it."

"Yes, sir. Of course."

* * * * *

At the United States Embassy during the week before Chance and Wagner were to attend the meeting at the bakery there was bustling activity making preparations for the dinner to honor Stalin. But to Chance, Wagner, Ambassador Hayes and Deputy Addison, there was an additional sense of urgency. They discussed it in the Ambassador's office. Ambassador Hayes told the group:

"I received two short memoranda from Secretary Roth within the last two weeks stating that Roosevelt is becoming less tolerant of Hitler as Hitler continues to expand in Europe. Roosevelt is also contemptuous of Mussolini whom he describes as 'that swaggering buffoon.' It seems Roosevelt is beginning to look upon Stalin with a good deal of kindliness. In fact, he continues to refer to Stalin affectionately as 'Uncle Joe.' He thinks he can convert Stalin from communism to democracy by using his personal powers of persuasion. He sees Stalin as doing for the

Soviets what he has done for the United States in his New Deal. That is, providing jobs, health care, help to farmers, education, and so on."

"Health care!" interjected Chance. "Some health care! It's dangerous to your health to live in the Soviets. How many citizens have been exterminated here?"

Ambassador Hayes chuckled. "Yes, I know. I'm sure that Roosevelt knows about the purges that have been going on here for the last couple of years. Either he has ignored them or approved of them. It's hard to know."

"No, I don't think it is either ignoring or approving," Deputy Addison commented. "In order to promote his image as a caring, fatherly leader of the people, Stalin persistently claims he knows nothing of the excesses of arrests, tortures and killings as well as the Siberian camps people are sent to. Stalin makes a practice of expressing outrage about these things and telling the public and the international authorities that he will personally see that the perpetrators of these heinous acts will be punished. Of course, that's a great big act on his part. He knows about what is going on. The heads of the NKVD, the prisons and the camps follow his orders and report to him continuously. We have information about how the system works."

"Yet, Roosevelt expresses horror at how Hitler sends thousands of Jews, Slavs and mental and physical misfits to concentration camps and, at the same time, doesn't blink an eyelash of the same or even worse crimes conducted by Stalin." Wagner pointed out the apparent hypocrisy and inconsistency in Roosevelt's views.

"Well," retorted Addison, "Roosevelt has naively bought the innocence posture that Stalin has projected. That is how I explain the contradictory positions." After a pause, Addison then added, "What I'm saying is that if we are to continue to participate in this endeavor to get rid of Stalin, we had better get moving on it before we get orders from Washington to pull out of it, that is, canceling your mission, Bill and Gene. Roosevelt may have forgotten about your mission, but if someone reminds him of it and knowing how he has come to feel about Stalin, he may just pull the plug on the whole operation. So, at your meeting with the underground people I suggest you pressure them to get ready to act as soon as we proceed with the actual dinner for Stalin."

"Yes, I understand," Chance replied.

"I agree with Fraser," Ambassador Hayes said. "I'm still not overly enthused about this project, but we have gone this far, we just have to push ahead. And, of course, we have committed ourselves to the underground."

"Have any of the details been agreed upon by you and the representatives of Stalin?" inquired Chance. "If they have, then we'll want to inform the underground people."

Deputy Addison answered, "We have reserved the restaurant dining room at the National Hotel. It's not a very large room, but it's big enough for our purposes. It will accommodate about seventy-five people. We have been contacting other embassies and legations and inviting the heads to attend."

"Where is it located?" inquired Chance.

"It's on Okhotny Ryad, about a two minute walk from Red Square and the Kremlin. It is not only convenient for Stalin, but it is one of the better hotels in Moscow. It was built in 1903 and is well respected among both local and foreign officials."

"When will the dinner be held?" Chance continued his inquiry for information.

"Three weeks from now. April 23, to be exact."

"That's a short time for an event such as this," commented Ambassador Hayes. "But both sides recognize that events in Europe are moving and changing so rapidly that it is important to get the message out to all international authorities about the friendly relations between the United States and the Soviets."

"Well, we'll get the information to the underground when we meet with them," said Chance.

On the Friday following this conference with Hayes and Addison, Chance and Wagner left the United States Embassy to attend the clandestine meeting with the underground at the bakery. As they walked toward the shop, Wagner laughed. "You know, Bill, if the NKVD is watching our going and coming to and from this bakery, they must think we are pastry addicts judging by the bags of the stuff we take back to our Embassy."

"Yeah, I suppose so," Chance agreed.

Inside the store's retail front, the young lady who normally waited on customers was there along with Boris who greeted them with his perfected perpetual smile.

"Ah, welcome gentlemen. You are right on time. Come with me." Boris gestured to the door that led to the baking room. There were no other customers in the store at the moment.

Chance and Wagner followed Boris. There were the usual two bakers actively baking. Chance and Wagner surmised, as in the past, that this was a cover if police should enter the store. Boris led them up the rear stairs to the second floor and through the first two rooms as he had done on the earlier occasion. Nothing had changed to this point.

When Chance and Wagner entered the third meeting room, both were quite taken aback by the number of people in the small room. Chance, without actually counting, estimated quickly that there were about twenty persons there. Sofia was there together with a couple of the men who Chance recognized had been at the previous meeting. Except for these and Boris, the others were strangers.

Boris spoke up, "We have here the leaders or their representatives from some of the cells in nearby villages and farm areas. It will take too much time to introduce them to you. However, I shall introduce you to them."

"Comrades, this is Bill Chance and Gene Wagner from the American Embassy. Their mission is the same as ours: to get rid of Stalin one way or another." A couple of the men arose and offered their chairs to the two Americans, which they accepted, believing that this was expected of them.

In looking quickly about the room, Chance observed that the group was diversified in appearance. In addition to Sofia there were three other women. Some of the men looked to be rough and tough characters, others appeared to be of the intellectual class, perhaps teachers, artists, or minor bureaucrats. All of them seemed to be unsmiling with each gaze focused on Chance and Wagner.

At this point, there was a knock on the door. One of the bakers from downstairs had guided the Finnish fellow and the Russian young lady, Elena, to the meeting room from downstairs. Boris welcomed them with his usual smile. He introduced them to the group.

"This, Comrades, is Antti Salonen of the Finnish Embassy and our own Elena. Antti also has a mission such as ours regarding Stalin. Elena has volunteered to carry out our mission. The Americans have agreed to give a dinner for Stalin in his honor. The dinner will provide us with the background and opportunity to get to Stalin. Mr. Chance, do you have any details on this?" asked Boris, turning to Chance.

"Yes." Chance then related the information as to the date, time and place of the dinner. He also urged the underground people present to be ready to execute their plan as soon as possible.

Koskinen was surprised to see in the group gathered in the room Sholom Lozovsky, the Jew whose apartment he and Elena had visited. And he noticed also the presence of Leonid, the owner of the antique shop. He wondered how all these people managed to get into the building without attracting the attention of the police. Chance must have thought the same thing. He asked Boris about it.

"Boris, I'm curious. How did all of these people come into this building and be seen to not leave again without creating some suspicion on the part of the NKVD?"

Boris replied, "Yes, I shall answer you. These people came in one at a time over the last two days. They entered through the rear door a few during the day but most at night. They have eaten and slept here while waiting for this meeting." Boris smiled, "Does that explain it for you?"

Chance said, "Yes, it does. But I can't help but think if the police raided this place just now they would catch the leadership of your underground and probably put you out of business." He looked at Boris with an expression that indicated that Boris might have made a blunder having all these people gathered together at one time in one place. Boris said nothing, but just shrugged his shoulders and smiled.

Koskinen was not only surprised but dismayed to see the number of individuals at the gathering. He turned to Elena and, clearly showing his anxious concern, said, "This is absolutely nonsensical to have all of these people here who will know every detail of our plan. The more people the more risk that the information will get out to the wrong persons." Since he spoke in Finnish, apparently no one else except for Elena understood him.

"These people can all be trusted," Elena replied in a whisper.

"Perhaps," Koskinen was skeptical. "I think you should pull out of this," he continued. He was still hoping he could find a reason to persuade Elena to end her participation as a key person in carrying out the project.

Elena said nothing in response to this, but her expression left no doubt that she was annoyed that Koskinen had raised the issue again. She had, she thought, made it abundantly clear that she would not withdraw from her part.

If Koskinen was reticent to mention his alarm to Boris, Chance, on the other hand, was forthright. He, too, had the same hesitations about the proceedings and he did not equivocate to confront Boris about it.

"Boris, what part are all these people going to play in this operation?" Chance gestured to the crowd.

Boris replied, "I am about to explain the details of our plan. That is why I have gotten everyone together so that each knows what is being done and will understand his part."

"No, Boris, I emphatically disagree," Chance said firmly. "The United States has a crucial part in this and if you expect us to continue to do our share, then I must insist that you tell us first what all of these people are to do." Chance added caustically, "This is a joint endeavor. This is not to be just your plan. I don't want to get into a divisive argument but I must insist."

For the first time Chance noticed that Boris was not smiling. In fact, Boris' stare at Chance was anything but friendly and, suddenly, Chance felt uncomfortable in the man's presence. Chance was immediately aware that he had crossed Boris. Wagner, sitting next to Chance and listening to the repartee, nudged Chance as a sign that Chance had apparently hit an uncompromising nerve in Boris. The remarks Chance made were in Russian and he could hear some grumbling from others in the room. He understood them to be protests against his position.

Boris must have recognized that he could not afford a conflict with the representatives of the United States so he conceded to answer Chance's question.

"These people and others in their cells will form a rescue party in case something goes wrong and it becomes necessary to attack the guards protecting Stalin. We want to make certain that Elena will not be arrested or captured not only for her sake but for the sake of the underground."

Chance recognized that it was inappropriate to debate the issue in front of all of these underground people.

"Boris, perhaps it would be better if we, that is, you, us, Antti Salonen and Elena go into another room to have a more private discussion about this. Elena can translate for us."

Boris thought a moment and then reluctantly agreed. He spoke to the others in the room.

"Comrades, the United States representatives have requested more private discussion. You will please relax for a few moments and be patient while we are in another room." Boris was smiling again.

Boris and one of the other underground leaders, Josif, Chance, Wagner, Koskinen and Elena repaired to the first room off the stairs. As they sat down on the cots in the room, Chance was the first to speak. He was blunt. He felt frank talk was necessary. Events were beginning to close in. There was no time for niceties.

"Boris, I know that you and your comrades have organized and worked hard to sustain your underground and I admire and respect you for it, but, in my opinion to have these people here and their members in their respective cells form an attack rescue group is absolutely foolhardy."

Boris appeared to react with a grim facial expression.

Chance continued, "You yourself have mentioned that when Stalin travels outside the Kremlin he has an army of soldiers lining the roadway, in this case, all the way to his dacha. How do you expect your rescue group to overcome these military guards? They are well-armed and pretty efficient."

At this point, Koskinen spoke up. "I am supposed to pick up Elena at an early hour the next morning at the gate to the dacha. If I have difficulty doing it or if something has happened inside the dacha that prevents Elena from leaving, your sending in your attack and rescue group will, I'm afraid, merely exacerbate a dangerous situation. I really must say that I would prefer if you dropped the whole idea of rescue. You cannot attain the fine-tuning and timely coordination that an operation like this requires."

Chance chimed in again, "We, in the United States Embassy, agreed to work with your underground because the plan to poison the Chief, Stalin, sounded simple and, barring something unforeseen, easy to accomplish. But, what you are proposing, Boris, sounds very complex and hazardous. I think you should have discussed this part of the plan with us before going ahead with it involving all these people." Chance continued to look Boris in the eye while saying this. It seemed to Wagner that Chance was throwing down the gauntlet to Boris. Either do as the United States wants or count it out.

Boris was speechless and in a quandary. He hadn't expected this strong disapproval from both the Americans and the Finns.

"If I go along with you and agree not to use an attack reserve group, then what do I tell all these people out there who expect to take an active part in the plan to get rid of Stalin? They have been waiting a long time for this moment and they may not want to be denied."

"How many men do you have in your movement, your underground organization?" Chance asked Boris.

"We have about fifteen hundred throughout the country."

"That isn't very many," Chance observed. "I suggest you tell them that their part to act as a rescue group has been called off and that they will be asked to secure the Kremlin the moment Stalin has died. A big power play is expected as soon as that happens. There will be politicians and military men both seeking to grab power and the limelight. They must plan to prevent that. There is little point in our disposing of Stalin only to have another dictator take over."

"Yes, that is what I shall tell them. It will serve to placate them. But, you are right. We must be prepared to step in and form a temporary government until elections can be held." Boris smiled and seemed to be infused again with a new energy.

"I thank you for bringing to our attention the need to address the post-Stalin problem. We in the underground have focused so intensely on our objective to dispose of Stalin that we have ignored what we must do after he has gone. I shall tell the people in the meeting room that they will receive instructions in detail about their assignments."

"One more thing," Chance said. "I think you should have the people begin to leave here to return to their homes. The discussion about the dinner, Elena's part and those details we can conduct here in this room with just a few of the key people. Let's include those of us here now, Sofia our translator and a few of your people whom you think will help. Is that alright, Boris?"

"Yes," Boris replied. "You understand that everyone cannot leave here at the same time. It would possibly create suspicion. So some may be coming through this room from time to time as well as leaving by the back stairs."

"I'm sure we can manage," Chance said.

Boris left the room to return to his group to explain the new plan. In about twenty minutes he returned. He was smiling and seemed self assured. "It is done. It is taken care of." Sofia, Viktor, Lozovsky and Leonid accompanied him. The room was small. All of them sat shoulder to shoulder. Josif opened the window slightly to allow some fresh air to enter.

Boris went over the details of what had been planned for the dinner and, if Stalin took the bait, what would then occur. Some of the specifics had been explained at the earlier meetings, but he recited them once more to be sure everyone understood.

Chance raised a question. "How is Elena going to get the poison into the dacha? From what we understand, Stalin usually has visitors thoroughly searched as they enter the dacha. In the case of Elena, she may be searched including even her privates."

Boris answered, "We have arranged for that. Stalin's aide will accompany him. He will have the poison and after Elena is searched, he will see that he gives the poison to her. The aide is one of us. He will not be searched. He is trusted."

Elena, who was sitting next to Koskinen, whispered in his ear, "That is Lieutenant Sergei Valentnikov, my friend whom you met on the train."

Koskinen nodded in remembrance. He smiled slightly as he saw how things were falling into place. However, there was an item that needed to be considered in his opinion.

"Elena will use a poison that she already has in her possession and will fulfill our purpose very efficiently."

"We have a poison which we decided upon," Boris said.

"How long does it require to take effect?" asked Koskinen.

"From a half-hour to an hour," answered Boris. "I don't know the name of it," he added.

"No, that is of no use," Koskinen admonished. "It acts too quickly. We want a poison that will require three to four days to kill. That will give Elena time to get out of Moscow and, perhaps, Russia without drawing attention to herself. We have such a poison. It is called phalloiden. It attacks the kidneys and liver, but the doctors will probably guess it is an acute heart attack. It can be administered either in powder or liquid form."

"That sounds great," exclaimed Boris. "However, we have already given Lieutenant Valentnikov the poison he is to give to Elena."

Elena, who up to this time had been merely assisting in translation of the discussion, now interjected. "I shall bring the phalloiden here in a day or two. One of the men here will see that Sergei gets it and disposes of the other poison so that there is no mix-up. I agree," Elena added, "that the phalloiden is what I prefer to use. As Antti has said, it takes a few days to be effective and that is what I like about it"

"What do you plan to do after this event is accomplished?" Boris asked Elena.

"For a while I have my assignment to the Finnish Trade Mission. It serves as my cover. I shall act as if nothing happened and continue my assignment. Beyond that I have no plans." Elena looked at Koskinen who nodded is approval of her answer.

Turning to Koskinen, whom he knew only as Antti Salonen, Boris said, "Antti, you understand that you are to appear the morning after the dinner at Stalin's dacha to pick up Elena. It should be about seven hundred hours. Elena will prepare the dacha staff for this by saying that she has to be on her trade assignment early that day. Antti, you will call for her with the Finnish Embassy limousine. Is that understood?"

"Yes," replied Koskinen. "If there is a last minute change, how will I know?"

"Before you go to the dacha, you can stop here and find out if there is a change."

Although the thought occurred to him, Koskinen refrained from asking Boris how he or the people at the bakery would know if there was a last minute change in plans.

Boris then addressed Sholom Lozovsky, Leonid, Yosif and Viktor. "Each of you is to contact the leaders of the cells in and around Moscow to help organize seizing the Kremlin once we know that Stalin is dead. We'll discuss the details on this in a day or two. You are to come here for that purpose on notice from me. Is that alright?"

The men he referred to acknowledged their assent. It was time to terminate the meeting and to depart. Koskinen and Elena left first, followed by Chance and Wagner. On the way out of the bakery, each stopped at the customer service counter and bought a package of cake, pastries or bread. Koskinen and Elena walked a few blocks and then secured a taxi for the trip to the Finnish Embassy. Apparently, the bakery was not under surveillance by the police. Neither Koskinen nor Chance and Wagner saw any official auto in the vicinity.

During the following two weeks preparations for the dinner continued at the United States Embassy while the underground people made their own preparations including the proposed Kremlin takeover following Stalin's death. Replies to the invitations to the dinner sent to various embassies and legations in the Moscow area over the signature of Ambassador Hayes began coming in. The Nordic countries, Finland, Sweden, Norway, Iceland, accepted. England, France, Belgium, the Netherlands, Denmark also accepted, as did Canada and certain Central and South American countries. However, Rumania, Slovakia, Hungary, Poland, all felt it too risky to alienate Hitler by attending a dinner honoring Stalin. Rumania had gone so far as to declare that it would not join any anti-Nazi alliance. At the time Britain, France and Russia were discussing mutual defense pacts to help each other as well as neighboring countries if attacked by another European country. Meaning, of course, Germany.

This was not the first occasion for the United States Embassy to have conducted a dinner to honor some important person. The dinner for Stalin, however, presented some unprecedented problems for the American staff. Primarily, almost every minutiae had to be cleared with and receive the approval of Stalin's personal aides. Paramount was the matter of security. Stalin was certain to take no chances with any attempt on his life.

The route from the Kremlin to the restaurant was to be a secret known only to a close aide who would sit with the driver of the limousine bearing Stalin and direct the driver as he proceeded. Cars carrying guards were to follow closely. There were to be guards of the NKVD surrounding the hotel and restaurant building as well as being posted within the building itself. All personnel of the hotel were to be investigated and their loyalty and integrity passed upon. Preparation of the food was to be monitored by special police stationed in the hotel kitchen. The food for Stalin personally was to be sealed in special containers to be opened only when delivered in front of him at the dinner table. What was true of food applied equally to Stalin's drink. Except for the Ambassadors or heads of legations of countries accepting the invitation to the dinner, a list of the names, titles and positions of those who were to attend the dinner from each country had to be submitted to Stalin's aides for approval.

To accomplish these preparations and to satisfy the security requirements of the Kremlin, officials placed great demands on the time and energies of the key people at the United States Embassy. Deputy Fraser Addison and his secretary, Helen Morgan and Rose Arlov, the Ambassador's secretary, worked feverishly far into almost every night and, as the date for the dinner approached, complained of near physical and emotional exhaustion. Chance, Wagner and Sofia, likewise, devoted hours to working out many of the details.

Addison remarked to Bill Chance, "All of us are working our butts off on this project. I just hope it accomplishes what we have in mind. One mistake or one item overlooked can negate everything we're doing."

"I agree with you," Chance replied. "My anxiety level rises as each day passes and as we get closer to the big event. Gene and I worry about how this will turn out. I'm sure the Finns must feel the same way."

"By the way," Addison added as if an afterthought, "we're planning on having the table for the Finland delegation as close as possible in front of the main table where Stalin will be sitting. I understand the young lady, Elena, is supposed to get Stalin's attention."

"Yeah, that's right," Chance replied. "I hope it works. I hope she can get him to take her home with him." Chance appeared to be not very optimistic.

"Well, she's a very attractive girl," Addison observed.

"Yup! You bet!" exclaimed Wagner.

Addison and Chance looked at each other and each smiled faintly as if to say, "What can you expect from Gene Wagner."

In midmorning of the day of the dinner, Addison, Chance, Wagner and Sofia gathered in Ambassador Hayes' office and with the Ambassador went over a checklist of details in order to be certain that nothing that had been planned had been overlooked. Sofia reported that Boris had told her that Elena's particular poison had been given to Lieutenant Valentnikov both in powder and liquid form. The Lieutenant understood when he was to deliver it over to Elena if she arrived at the dacha. It appeared to everyone in the Ambassador's office that no detail had been neglected. Everything was ready to go.

After the meeting, the Embassy chauffeur drove Chance to the Hotel. Chance wanted to verify that all details were in order and ready there also. When Chance arrived at the hotel, Stalin's guards were already positioned both outside and inside the building. Some were in military uniform, others in plain clothes. Chance had no trouble in identifying those in civilian dress as part of the police apparatus. They just looked officious and arrogant. Chance had to identify himself several times in order to enter the building and to move about once inside. A plainclothesman was at his side constantly as he checked on details and asked questions of hotel and restaurant employees. Chance was particularly interested in the seating arrangements.

As Chance moved about the main dining room with the presumed police agent tagging along, he tried to appear casual and nonchalant in checking the country name cards at each table. He was, however, primarily interested in locating the position of the table for the Finnish party. To his satisfaction, Chance noted that the table designated for Finland was in the first row of tables immediately in front of the head table but a bit to the right of where Stalin would be seated. Chance hoped that Antti Salonen would have the presence of mind to have Elena sit facing Stalin directly and in such a way that Stalin and Elena would have unobstructed eye contact between them. After cursory inspections of other areas of the facilities, Chance returned to the United States Embassy assured that the plans would move smoothly once the dinner was underway.

The diplomats and members of the staff of the United States Embassy who were to attend the dinner were in formal attire. All were scheduled to be at the hotel early so as to be on hand to receive the representatives from other embassies and legations as the latter arrived.

Dinner was scheduled to be served at 1930 hours. For the hour before dinner, cocktails, punch and other liquors together with a bountiful table of hors d'oeuvres were available to the arriving guests.

The Finland delegation was the first to arrive promptly at 1830 hours. Sofia quickly took Koskinen (still known as Antti Salonen) aside and advised him where the Finland table was and to be sure to seat Elena facing Stalin where they could see each other. Koskinen nodded his understanding and returned to the Finnish group who was standing around with drinks in hand and some munching of the food tidbits. Other delegations kept arriving. As they did, the plainclothesman checked them against their list of invitees. Socializing among the various and diverse delegations was generally jovial and always cordial even when language difficulties occurred. Almost all delegations had their Russian translators with them. Sofia and Elena were accepted into the gatherings of this type as reasonable and necessary as well as admissible adjuncts to a successful party.

In the background of the socializing could be heard the soft toned music of a quartet of musicians. Three violins and one concertina accordion. The music provided a calming effect to what might well have been rather tense moments when one diplomat or another inadvertently mentioned the purges going on in the Soviet Union for the past two or more years. Such a diplomat quickly knew he had erred when his comment was met by a stony, silent embarrassment on the part of the listener or listeners. The topic was not one for a congenial gathering to honor the man whom everyone knew was responsible for the purges. Each country represented had its own agenda or reason to ignore the brutality of Stalin in order to curry his favor.

It was an altogether gala, festive affair although considerably ostentatious with the formal wear and display of expensive jewelry both by the ladies and some of the men. Among the latter were those who were not at all reticent about wearing medals attached to their jacket kerchief pocket. Neither the United States nor the Finland staff wore such accoutrements of the ego.

It was planned that notice would be given to the guests when Stalin left the Kremlin in his limousine. The guests were then to go to their respective tables and be seated to await the entrance of Stalin. It was but a drive of a few minutes from the Kremlin to the hotel.

After a drink or two and a few nibbles of the hors d'oeuvres, the guests were becoming anxious and impatient for the arrival of Stalin. A plainclothesman was seen suddenly hurrying to Ambassador Hayes. He whispered something into the Ambassador's ear. The Ambassador immediately rang a hand bell to get everyone's attention.

"Mr. Stalin is about to leave the Kremlin and will be here shortly. Ladies and gentlemen, will you please go immediately to your tables. When Mr. Stalin enters the dining room, we shall all stand and clap our hands in laudatory respect and honor. We shall resume our seats after he has been seated. Mr. Stalin shall at no time be approached in order to shake his hand or to speak with him unless you first request it through one of the agents in civilian dress."

Some grumbling could be heard at this last instruction as the guests sauntered to the tables.

Said one diplomat, "Good Lord, you'd think we were going to assassinate him."

Another remarked somewhat resentfully, "I came here hoping to speak with him personally about selling the Soviets some destroyers."

"Yes," said another, "I understand he's interested in buying a battleship for use in the Gulf of Finland." The diplomat laughed at the absurdity of the idea. "There isn't enough room in the Gulf to turn a ship that size around."

Generally, however, the room of people was silent as they were seated and were anticipating the imminent arrival of Stalin. There was an occasional barely audible whisper between a couple. A military officer in uniform was standing just inside the door to the dining room. He kept turning to look beyond the doorway apparently to determine when Stalin arrived. Suddenly, the officer stiffened, turned to the guests in the dining room and, in a loud voice, made the announcement that Stalin was about to enter the room.

Many of the guests in the dining room, including Koskinen, Chance and Wagner, had never met with or seen Stalin close up. Nevertheless, they were not entirely unprepared for their first view of the Soviet leader. They had heard him described by embassy and legation officials who had had close personal contact with him. All in the room arose and stood with their eyes directed to the doorway. It was as if there was anticipation of seeing at once a curiosity, an awesome human being, a great leader, a malevolent barbarian or, depending upon one's ethical and moral standards, a Satan or a god.

To Bill Chance and Gene Wagner who were familiar with Russian history and Soviet government issues as a result of their jobs in the Soviet section of the U.S. State Department, Stalin had all of these characteristics. He was either a brute or a benefactor at any given time regarding any given issue important to the interests of the United States.

To Koskinen, on the other hand, Stalin personified but one earmark, namely, a venomous, virulent evildoer whose lust for power and domination threatened his, Koskinen's, country. Koskinen could never be persuaded that there was anything good about Stalin.

Yet, when Stalin entered the room that evening accompanied by some high officials these preconceptions seemed, at least to Chance and Wagner, to vanish with the provocative proximity of Stalin in person. They saw not a dynamic, charismatic personality but a rather thin man who, in appearance and dress, was much like an ordinary Russian peasant.

The tables for the United States staff were directly in front of the head table and afforded Chance and Wagner a close view of Stalin. Chance later remarked that he was close enough to Stalin that he "could hear him breathe." As Stalin walked to his place at the head table Chance observed that Stalin was astonishingly short. Chance estimated about five-feet three or four inches. He also noticed the deeply pock marked face and dark brown eyes and that Stalin seemed to carry his left arm and shoulder as if they were permanently stiff or impaired. Chance had heard the story that Stalin had told others that his arm had been injured when he was a young boy when a horse and wagon struck him, threw him to the street and then the wagon wheel ran over his arm.

As the evening wore on and Chance and Wagner focused their attention on Stalin they later agreed that Stalin appeared to be more the warm, fatherly and congenial person than they had expected. He certainly displayed nothing of the cruel, inhumane, unscrupulous demagogue that they had heard some portray him as. There was no evidence of vanity or ostentatiousness. To the contrary, he appeared to be a simple, down-to-earth person dressed as he was in his customary plain brown military coat and dark trousers stuffed into leather boots. No wonder, Chance and Wagner remarked, that President Roosevelt liked him and called him "Uncle Joe." Yet, Chance and Wagner both knew what they observed in Stalin that evening was superficial and that beneath the veneer was a cold, vengeful and mordacious tyrant who had visited enormous pain and suffering on his own people.

Even as they gave their attention to Stalin, Chance and Wagner also closely watched Koskinen and Elena at the next table. Would their plot to seduce Stalin work? Would Stalin take the bait? An intriguing game was being played out in front of them. They realized that the game would be won or lost within the hour. They were sure that Koskinen and Elena had the same sense of anxiety as they had, perhaps even more so because of the role the Finns and Elena had in the drama that was unfolding.

Koskinen, quite normally under the circumstances, was indeed anxious about the outcome of the evening's plans. But his concern was not that the plot might not succeed. Rather, his concern was that it might succeed all too well. Koskinen had fallen in love with Elena and his heartfelt hope was that she would not be selected to go with Stalin and be subjected to whatever Stalin did with his women. In short, he hoped the whole project would fail before it even started. There would be other alternatives to saving Finland from the Russian hordes.

Elena had intense but ambiguous emotions. At one moment she was determined to proceed with her part in the plan. The next moment in looking at Stalin and knowing his position of power, she felt a sense of panic, of wanting to get up and leave, to run anywhere. Then she thought of the other people in the underground and how they depended on her to help carry out their mission to save Russia by ridding it of Stalin. With these thoughts, she managed to suppress her misgivings and to regain her courage to go ahead. Elena knew what she had to do to get Stalin's attention.

Partly through the main course of the meal, Elena arose from the table as if she had to attend the ladies' room. Instead of walking directly to the rear of the room where the ladies room was situated, she walked around her table to the space between her table and head table where Stalin sat. This brought her immediately in front of Stalin who, at the moment, was talking jovially with Ambassador Hayes to his right. As she passed in front of Stalin, their eyes met. Elena's eyes lingered on his just long enough to convey her interest. It was a look that is difficult to describe but which most men, unless very naive, would recognize instantly as suggestive. At the same time, Elena expressed a faint but yet noticeable closed-lip smile which together with other subtle body language was intended to stimulate Stalin's interest. Elena continued on her way to the ladies room. She acted nonchalant, but her heart was pounding. She had her back to Stalin as she walked to the rear of the room past other tables of dignitaries but she could feel his eyes following her. She would know for certain whether she had sparked Stalin's interest when she returned to her table.

Koskinen watched intently as Elena played her role and he saw indeed Stalin's eyes following Elena as she walked away from in front of his table. Koskinen knew instinctively that Elena had captured Stalin's attention even though Stalin continued talking with Ambassador Hayes as if no distraction had occurred.

By observing Stalin, Koskinen knew when Elena was returning to the table. Stalin was evidently watching someone approaching the front of the room from the rear. Koskinen did not have to turn to see who it might be. He correctly guessed that it was Elena. This time Elena came directly to her table. Koskinen thought Elena was quite cunning. She had no intention of overplaying her hand. Elena knew she had gotten Stalin's attention. The next step was up to Stalin.

The dinner finished, the next hour was spent in the tedium of speeches. Speeches praising Stalin for one thing or another made by those who, representing their respective countries, sought some favor or another from Stalin and his regime. Speeches that were inherently dishonest and perfidious in their contexts concerning Stalin and his accomplishments. Speeches that, as Wagner expressed later, could well be forgotten even before one left the hotel dining room.

While the representative of Belgium was speaking, Koskinen observed that Stalin beckoned to an aide or guard who had been standing behind him during the meal. The aide or guard bent down while Stalin whispered something to him. Koskinen noted that the man glanced quickly in the direction of Elena and just as quickly looked away. It was obvious that Elena was the subject of Stalin's whispers and that the aide or guard was intent on locating and identifying her. Both Koskinen and Elena knew then that the seduction of Stalin was working. It was only a matter of time before Elena would receive an invitation to join Stalin.

Chance and Wagner also noticed that Stalin was evincing interest in Elena. Others of the guests not being attuned to a plot would not have noticed the subtle hints of the game being played.

A few moments after having conversed with Stalin, his aide or guard left the dais and quietly came to Elena's table and handed her a folded note. The aide or guard then immediately returned to his position behind Stalin.

Elena opened the note and read it quickly. It was in Russian language. The handwriting was irregular and scrawled as if written in a hurry and in a cramped position. It was brief, terse and, Elena thought, quite businesslike. It was an invitation, but read more like a command.

"Mr. Stalin invites you to a small social gathering at his dacha tomorrow at 1900 hours. His chauffeur will call for you an hour before at the Finnish Embassy. You may remain overnight if you wish."

There was no signature at the end. The note asked for no reply. Elena understood that she was expected to accept the invitation and that she was expected to remain overnight at the dacha. After reading the note, she looked at Stalin and his aide. Stalin was no longer looking at her, but the aide was. Elena nodded her acceptance even though it was an unnecessary gesture.

Elena slid the note over to Koskinen. The plans had to be changed. They had counted on Stalin inviting her for the night of the dinner. It was his usual and customary practice to select a woman from a gathering to accompany him when he left the gathering.

"Get Sofia to get word of the change to your people immediately," Koskinen instructed Elena in a whisper out of the side of his mouth.

With the dinner and speeches at an end and with guests standing around in small groups conversing prior to leaving, Elena walked over to Sofia at the United States table and appeared to chat with her in a casual way. No suspicion could possibly be aroused under such circumstances.

"Meet me in the ladies room in a few minutes," Elena said softly in a barely audible voice as she left the group for the restroom. Sofia waited a reasonable time and then followed. Although there were numerous ladies in the room, Elena and Sofia managed to find an inconspicuous corner to be relatively alone. Elena quickly told Sofia about the contents of the note and asked her to get word immediately to the bakery people. Sofia should let Chance and Wagner know and perhaps they could drive her to the bakery. One or more of the men would be there even at this late hour.

"Don't worry about it," Sofia advised Elena. "Let me handle it. I know what to do."

Elena asked no questions. She knew Sofia was competent to carry out whatever was required. The two then left the ladies room and proceeded separately back to their own group.

Outside the hotel the limousines and taxis were lined up each moving slowly and stopping at the entrance to pick up their respective dignitaries and guests. Koskinen and Elena took a taxi to Elena's hotel. They had decided that the change in the plans allowed them to spend the night together. Elena felt she needed some comforting; Koskinen was always ready to provide it. They were careful not to discuss any underground plan. The room could very well be bugged.

Ambassador Hayes, Deputy Addison, Chance, Wagner and Sofia all managed to squeeze into the Embassy limousine. Once at the Embassy Sofia telephoned the bakery from Addison's office. Boris answered. Sofia informed him that Elena had received the coveted invitation but that her visit would be the next day at 1900 hours.

"Good," Boris commented. "We'll make the necessary adjustments."

Chance and Wagner were jubilant about the results of the evening.

"Well, Stalin took the bait," Wagner enthused.

"Yeah, we're on our way, but the biggest hurdle is still in front of us," Chance philosophized.

Sofia was equally enthused and more optimistic. "It's virtually done. I know Elena. She'll get it done."

"I hope so," Chance said rather abstractly.

Deputy Addison, who was in his office with the others when Sofia made her telephone call to the bakery and who had said nothing up to this point, was less enthusiastic and more apprehensive. He commented now, "Whether it succeeds or not, I just hope no one in the Soviet leadership, Molotov, for example, finds out that the United States is implicated in this plan. All hell will break loose if that is discovered. I think the Ambassador is also quite concerned." Hayes had left them when they returned to the Embassy and, after checking for messages in his office, had returned to his personal suite of rooms in the Embassy building.

Koskinen and Elena were sitting quietly in her hotel room. They were not exultant about the fact that Elena had succeeded in getting the invitation from Stalin. On the contrary, they were both somber as the time of reckoning drew closer with the reality of its attendant risks. They did not talk about the plan for fear of possible eavesdropping, but they talked about their feelings and concerns obliquely.

"Are you afraid?" Koskinen asked softly and tenderly.

"I don't know if I have fear," Elena replied. "But I have a great deal of anxiety."

"I can understand. I do too," Koskinen admitted.

For some time as the plan developed and with Elena seemingly inevitably and irreversibly involved, Koskinen had felt the need to turn to his spiritual faith for support and reassurance that God and not he, Koskinen, was in control of events and his and Elena's safety. He had, whenever alone, prayed silently to see that God was good and that since God was a higher and all-present power, no evil could touch those whose cause was just and right. The thought had occurred to him that God, being all-good and protective against evil would also safeguard Stalin. He dismissed that idea abruptly with the rationalization that Stalin was the devil incarnate and God had the power to destroy the devil and would do so by assisting those who were carrying out His will.

"Do you believe in God, Elena?" They had not discussed the subject before this.

"I don't know, Timo. I really don't know what I believe in. I don't pray to God or to a god. I'm not consciously aware of a spiritual power."

"Didn't your parents talk to you about God when you were a young child?"

"They may have on infrequent occasions, but I don't remember. They were not devoutly religious."

"Were they atheists?"

"Oh, no. I'm sure. They just didn't practice a religion with any regularity."

"Do you feel you missed something very important in not having a religious faith?"

"Timo, one doesn't miss what one doesn't know about. I have been brought up in a Communist society which denies the existence of God on the ground that religion and the churches are tools of the capitalists to keep the workers and farmers suppressed."

Koskinen shook his head in disbelief at what he heard Elena say. He wanted to pursue the dialogue further but did not do so for fear that the discussion would lead to talk about the underground and why Elena joined if it was not to get rid of an antireligious system. He would talk with her about it under other circumstances. Instead, he put his arm around her as a gesture of protection, comfort and endearment. There was little further conversation as they both agreed that the events of the evening and of those to come the next day seemed like a dream world, unreal and illusory. Now that the event was upon them that they had planned for and that had been the major key and focus of their lives for the past several weeks and months, they found it difficult to comprehend the reality of its enormity.

Koskinen slept little that night. Elena, on the other hand, although tense and anxious, slept soundly from sheer emotional exhaustion. After a breakfast of coffee, bread and cheese, Koskinen left Elena's hotel room about midmorning and took a taxi to the Finnish Embassy. Elena remained behind to prepare for her visit with Stalin. As the time ticked by she was becoming more jittery and apprehensive. She was having doubt about her ability to carry out her mission. It was one thing to poison an odious police officer and quite another to kill off the powerful head of the Soviet union.

When Koskinen had arrived at the Embassy, he immediately called Bill Chance at the U.S. Embassy and spoke to him in Russian of which both had limited knowledge and which was the only language with which they could communicate. Chance knew no Finnish and Koskinen knew no English.

"Mr. Chance, can you verify that I am to pick up Elena at Stalin's dacha tomorrow morning? That was the original arrangement before the change in the time of Elena's visit."

Chance replied, "Let me turn you over to Sofia. She has been in touch with the bakery people and they have probably been in touch with Stalin's aide, Sergei Valentnikov who makes the arrangements."

Koskinen was transferred to Sofia. In response to Koskinen's question, Sofia said, "I have been in touch with our people and I was told that they would make the adjustments in view of the change in expected time. We didn't talk specifically about your picking Elena up, but I am assuming that everything is the same. I think to be safe you should tell Elena to contact Lieutenant Valentnikov as soon as she can after arriving at the dacha and tell him to be sure to instruct the guards to let you through."

"Thanks, Sofia. I'll do that."

"Good luck, Antti," Sofia used the pseudonym for Koskinen.

Elena arrived by taxi at the Finnish Embassy about 1400 hours. Koskinen greeted her.

"Lunch is over, but can I get you something to eat from the kitchen?" Koskinen asked.

"No, thanks. I have no appetite."

Elena sat down on the sofa in the reception room. To Koskinen she seemed listless, apathetic, emotionally drained.

"I know you are under great stress, Elena, but you must try to pull yourself together. You must appear eager, enthusiastic and of high spirit. I understand Stalin expects his women to be that way. The women have to make Stalin feel he is their most desirable man. He is a very vain person and you have to play up to that characteristic in him."

"I loathe the fellow. I'll try not to show it," Elena replied.

"For your own safety, I hope you will not show it," Koskinen advised. He then recited his conversation with Sofia and the need for Elena to get in touch as quickly as possible with Valentnikov.

Koskinen and Elena spent the time before the arrival of the Russian limousine in small talk but mostly in silence.

"I guess I'm like a soldier before going into battle," Elena remarked eventually. "A soldier doesn't want to go, but he goes because he is a soldier and he dare not show cowardice or weakness. He goes because it is expected of him and because he owes a certain allegiance to his fellow soldiers to be in the battle with them."

"You're right," Koskinen added. "The loyalty to his immediate companions is sometime, I would say most of the time, far greater than loyalty to his country. A soldier may not even know or understand the issues or the reasons he is involved in fighting his country's war. But he does understand that the fellows next to him depend on him to do his best when the battle is drawn. However, in our case I think we do understand what the issues and principles are in this mission. Isn't that right, Elena?"

"Yes, of course." Elena seemed to recover some of her spirit. Just being with Koskinen at this time of intense gravity was soothing to her. She knew that he was concerned for her and would help her if the need arose. She knew that he was brave, courageous.

A few minutes before 1900 hours, Stalin's chauffeur arrived in his limousine. Earlier, Koskinen and Elena had gone from the reception room to the small conference room for more privacy. The receptionist now came to the conference room to announce the chauffeur's arrival.

"Tell him that the young lady will be outside in a few moments," Koskinen instructed the receptionist.

Koskinen and Elena arose from their chairs and hugged each other in a strong embrace as if never to let go. They looked into each other's eyes and the silent message for each was of love and devotion. They kissed tenderly and Koskinen whispered, "I know you will be alright, my love. I'll be praying for you and waiting for you tomorrow morning. Remember, I love you." Koskinen felt a tightness in his throat as the emotion of the moment overwhelmed him. He fought back tears.

"And I love you, Timo. I may have to make love to that beast, but even then you will be in my thoughts. I must go now."

They reluctantly released each other from the embrace. Elena wiped tears from her eyes.

"You know we are acting as if we shall never see each other again and that is silly and not true," Koskinen said softly. "Come, I'll go to the car with you." Koskinen carried Elena's small overnight bag and placed it in the limousine next to Elena. He squeezed her hand, gave her a nod of reassurance and closed the limousine's door. He stood and watched the car drive down the street until it disappeared. With a heavy heart and a feeling of fear for Elena's safety and well-being he turned and reentered the Embassy building. He went directly to his room and lay down on his bed. He had had a terribly sleepless night and he wished he could now go to sleep and block out all of the anxiety he felt, but he could not do so. All sorts of thoughts about Elena's predicament raced through his mind. She would be caught, arrested and tortured. No, she would be successful and he would pick her up in the morning, safe, sound, smiling and exuberant. No, they would find the poison on her and that would be her ending and his too. Try as he would, Koskinen was unable to control his thinking. Finally, he got up from the bed, paced the floor, looked out the window as if to see Elena returning although he knew better, sat down on a chair, picked up a magazine but made no attempt to read. "This is hell," he thought. He lay down on the bed once again and, in a state of mental exhaustion, finally did go to sleep.

Koskinen passed quickly into a deep sleep. He began to dream and in his dream he and Anna were young and they were standing on a large rock outcropping on the Peltola farm where he had first met Anna. He had his arm around Anna's waist holding her tightly. From the rock they could see the bluish green waters of the Rautavesi, the large body of water that extended for many kilometers north and south of the City of Vammala. It was a beautiful sunny day and Koskinen felt at peace holding his dear Anna. With his arm he turned Anna to face him and they kissed ever so gently. Anna whispered, "I love you, Timo." And Koskinen responded softly, "And I love you so much, Anna." They kissed again.

In Koskinen's dream, the face of Anna disappeared and Koskinen found himself seeing the face of Elena. He was holding her and he was saying, "I love you, Elena." And Elena replied, "I love you too, Timo." Nothing else had changed. They were standing on the large rock overlooking the Rautavesi. As in the nature of dreams and the dreamer, the chimerical transfiguration from Anna to Elena did not startle Koskinen. He continued to sleep. In his dream, Koskinen perceived no conflict or incongruity in the confluence of his two separate lives.

Suddenly, as he was holding Elena, they both heard a sharp, shrill scream and the rush of beating wings. They looked up in time to see a large seagull swooping down on them as if to attack them. Koskinen put up his arm to ward off the attack and the bird passed just above his reach. They could see the gull's piercing red eyes and its opened mouth emitting one scream after another. The gull turned and again swooped down on them. Elena and Koskinen had to crouch low to avoid the bird's sharp talons. Strangely, this gull had feet like those of a hawk.

"The seagull wants to kill us," Elena said in a panic. "I have to get out of here."

"No, don't go!" Koskinen entreated Elena.

But as the seagull passed closely over them again and was turning to come back, Elena stood up and ran toward a row of trees nearby. Koskinen sought to grab her but could not.

"Come back, come back, Elena," Koskinen cried out, but Elena kept running.

The seagull changed its direction and began a swift pursuit of Elena and disregarding Koskinen completely. In a few moments, the gull reached Elena and landed on her head with such force that it knocked her to the ground. Elena lay stunned on her back and the seagull, its wings flapping violently and its voice screaming, pounced on Elena and began to tear at her face with its talons. It took but a few seconds for the seagull to shred Elena's face into a bloody and unrecognizable human feature. Koskinen ran over to her and was shocked at the sight. "Elena, Elena, my beautiful Elena! Where are you?" He lay down on the grass besides her and took her to him all the time crying and wailing, "Elena, Elena, come back, come back!" But Elena was gone and Koskinen lay on the grass alone whimpering. Elena, like Anna, had disappeared.

Koskinen awoke abruptly. He was trembling and sweating. The dream had been so realistic, so violent, so abhorrent. He was shaken to the core.

"My god," he said to himself, "I have these dreams of the seagull always before some terrible event. What does this one portend? Could it be a warning that Elena is or will be in some horrible, evil situation?" Koskinen was devastated but realized it was too late for him to do anything to get Elena to turn back from her mission.

During the drive to Stalin's dacha neither the chauffeur nor Elena said much of anything to each other. Elena felt alone and isolated but it was this sense that seemed to be a source of reviving courage, determination and self-discipline. She had been on her own many times before and she had always confronted and successfully resolved whatever the immediate problem happened to be. She now faced the greatest of challenges and her confidence in herself was quickly being restored. She was amazed at her resiliency. It was as if she was looking at herself through the eyes of another person and perceiving a transformation from the depths of doubt to the heights of spiritual strength. Maybe, she thought, there was something after all to Timo's reference to God. She would explore that idea later with him.

Breaking the silence, Elena leaned forward from her rear seat in the limousine and asked the chauffeur, "How much further do we have before arriving at the dacha?"

"About five kilometers. We should be there in about ten minutes." The chauffeur was polite and well-spoken. Elena thought he was a decent sort just doing his job. Nothing more was said. The silence returned.

As the limousine wended its way through the streets of Moscow, Elena gave little heed to the route that was being traversed or to the neighborhoods through which she was passing. She was intensely absorbed in her thoughts of what lay ahead for her, of what would happen when she arrived at the dacha. She was totally detached from the immediate world outside of the limousine. At the moment, that world was remote and irrelevant. Her thinking had become exclusively focused on her survival in the unknown, unpredictable and uncertain surroundings that would soon present themselves. Elena was vaguely aware that she had pushed aside her interest in saving Russia from a tyrant. Right then her interest was in herself, her own well-being.

She was abruptly aroused from her cerebral musings when the limousine came to a halt. She looked out and saw a fence and a gate in front of which stood several armed guards in military dress. The guards were apparently familiar with the driver, but one of the guards questioned him briefly about the passenger.

"This young lady is the invited guest of Comrade Stalin. She is expected. Haven't you been notified?" The driver was obviously irritated by the questioning.

"Yes, but we have to make sure. You should understand that." The guard was equally annoyed with the driver whom he felt should know what the guard's duty was.

The guard motioned to other guards at the gate to allow the limousine to pass through. As it entered the compound, Elena observed that the driver was proceeding slowly along a paved road that was formally and generously landscaped on either side with bushes and trees in elevated rock settings. She also observed that a large two-story house stood several hundred meters at the end of the road. "This must be Stalin's dacha," Elena surmised. The limousine stopped at the entrance to the building. She saw several guards at the entrance and others positioned around the dwelling. With all this security Elena felt trapped. There was no way out, no escape from the place except by the permission of some person in authority. She hoped that that person might be her friend Lieutenant Valentnikov. She would soon find out.

Elena alighted from the limousine. A guard stepped forward and took her valise and told her to follow him. The guard was a nice-looking young soldier, quite well-built and muscular. Elena felt his immediate interest in her. The thought quickly came to her that if she smiled at him and showed a reciprocal interest he might just become a help to her if needed. One could never tell. So she practiced a brief seduction on the guard. He, in turn, reacted with a warm, knowing smile. But there it ended as the guard put the valise down and turned Elena over to an older woman who had apparently been alerted to Elena's arrival and was waiting for her in a large anteroom off the entrance.

"I am Valentina Istomina, the housekeeper here. I am required to inspect you. Please come with me." Istomina led Elena to a small room about the size of a large clothing closet off the anteroom. Istomina carried Elena's valise with her.

"You will completely undress," Istomina instructed.

"Undress?" Elena was surprised and somewhat embarrassed. "Why?"

"For security reasons," Istomina replied in a matter-of-fact voice.

Elena made no effort to disrobe. Instead, she asked, "Are all people who visit here required to go through this kind of inspection?"

"Yes, those who are strangers visiting for the first time, both men and women," Istomina responded. "You will please undress," she persisted impatiently.

Elena thought it best to comply. To protest would only result in creating an attention-getting scene. She hung each garment over the only chair in the room. Istomina inspected them in a quick, superficial manner. As Elena, still astonished, knew: what contraband could be found on a plain dress and the usual simple undergarments? She wore no jewelry in which a poisonous pill might be suspiciously hidden. Istomina felt inside the linings of Elena's shoes, hat and coat and found nothing. She then had Elena bend over and quickly gave a visual inspection of her privates.

"Good, you can get dressed again while I go through your valise." Istomina proceeded to dump the contents of the valise on a small table and to examine each item in a cursory manner. To Istomina it was all very routine judging by her demeanor. To Elena it was a humiliating, unpleasant experience.

"How long have you been a housekeeper here?" Elena asked in a low soothing voice hoping to disarm the undercurrent of a perceptively adversarial relationship between the two women.

"Since shortly after Nadezhda's death," Istomina answered, still exhibiting indifference while referring to the demise of Stalin's second wife in 1932. "I was first employed as a waitress here and then promoted to head housekeeper. On occasion I do these physical inspections."

Valentina Istomina was not an unattractive woman in Elena's opinion. Elena estimated that she was probably in her early thirties. She was about five feet six inches, still rather slim in figure, with raven black hair, large black eyes sent in a high-cheek boned face, delicate thin nose, and a thin-lipped mouth which, at the moment was quite unsmiling. Elena wondered why Stalin had women visit him when this Valentina was living in the same house with him. Perhaps, Elena conjectured, like so many men who had wives at home there was still a need for diversity for something new to nourish their eyes. Elena got the feeling that Valentina resented these visits by other women but that there was not a thing the so-called housekeeper could do about it.

Elena did not dwell for long on these thoughts. She had other concerns to think about.

"What do I do next?" Elena asked Istomina.

"I will show you to your room. You are expected to stay overnight."

"But then what do I do?" Elena searched for answers. Istomina must surely have gone through this before and knew the ritual.

"Comrade Stalin is not here yet. We do not know just when he will be here, but he usually brings with him a few important people in the government. He will let me know whether you are to join in the party and at dinner and, in turn, I'll let you know. Comrade Stalin may want to see you privately after he arrives. I cannot predict just what he will say or do. In the meantime, after you have settled into your room, if you wish to walk around the dacha, Comrade Stalin's aide, Lieutenant Sergei Valentnikov will be your guide."

Elena gave no sign that Valentnikov was her friend. She concluded that the Stalin entourage did not know that the Lieutenant was a member of the underground. She felt safer.

From what Elena observed of the building, this was no ordinary dacha. It had the amenities and luxuries that few, if any, other dachas possessed except perhaps those of high officials in the Communist Party. This dacha noticeably had indoor running water and indoor lavatories and bathing facilities. The dachas of millions of workers were generally shacks of one or two rooms with water and lavatory outside. Water was from a well and pump and the outhouse provided the sanitary facilities.

The Stalin dacha had several sleeping rooms and larger rooms for social gatherings and entertainment. The furnishings were generally plain and without pretense. Stalin was not given to ostentatious display either in his person or in his surroundings.

Elena knew from her own experience in Leningrad that it was typical of Russians that when Spring came, whole families left the cities to head by bus or train to the outskirts where they had their dachas. There they had their vegetable gardens and a place in the countryside where the children could romp and play outdoors. The dacha was usually a part of a cooperative dacha community or village. It is where the workers could relax from the factory toils and have fun with family, friends and neighbors. Shashlyk or barbecue parties and samovar tea parties along with dancing and singing were part of the dacha lifestyle. When the colder weather again arrived, the dachas were closed up. Most had no heating facilities.

In contrast, Elena observed that Stalin's dacha was a year round facility. Elena had earlier learned that Stalin had two dachas. This one was about eight kilometers from the Kremlin and was known as Kuntsevo. The other dacha called Zubalovo was further from the Kremlin and, after his wife's death, rarely visited by Stalin. Kuntsevo became his permanent home.

After lying down on her bed for several minutes to relax and catch her breath so to speak, Elena decided she would have Lieutenant Valentnikov give her a tour of the place. Under the guise of a tour she would have the opportunity to talk with him and have him transfer the poison to her. She had wondered how that was to be done. The answer was easily provided.

Leaving her bedroom for the anteroom, Elena noticed several men in civilian dress seemingly loitering about at various places within the building. She assumed that they were security people, perhaps from the NKVD. She decided to ask one of them where she might find the housekeeper. The housekeeper would know how to contact Lieutenant Valentnikov. She was about to approach one of the men when Valentina entered the anteroom. Elena stopped her and asked if she could arrange to have Lieutenant Valentnikov guide her around the facility as Valentina had suggested. Valentina instructed her to wait in the anteroom and she would find the Lieutenant and have him report to Elena. Elena sat down on one of the chairs in the room and waited. She noticed that within moments one of the civilian dressed men sat down within a few feet of her saying not a word, but his eyes roving first to the ceiling, then the floor, then to her and then back to the ceiling, the floor, and to her. Elena thought the fellow's actions were quite ridiculous, but nevertheless, he made her uncomfortable. She thought he might at least be friendly and say something. Why was he scrutinizing her? Was this process routine in Stalin's dacha or did they know something that compelled them to watch her closely? She hesitated to strike up a conversation with the fellow. To her great relief, in about ten minutes Lieutenant Valentnikov entered the room.

The Lieutenant was in military uniform and, to Elena, looked quite handsome. His expression was serious and unsmiling and he gave no hint that he knew Elena. He gave a furtive look at the man sitting near Elena and then walked over to Elena and bowed slightly and stiffly.

"Miss Marikova?"

"Yes, and you are Lieutenant Valentnikov?"

"I am. Valentina Istomina sent me to guide you around here."

"Thank you!"

"We should start immediately. It is getting dark soon and we shall have to walk around outside rather quickly."

Elena arose and followed the Lieutenant. As she passed the seated man she looked at him quickly and saw that he gave her a cold, hard and, seemingly, menacing stare. She left the anteroom gladly and with the Lieutenant leading passed through the front entrance door, down a few steps and to the outside ground.

The Lieutenant began the tour by talking about the history of the dacha while leading Elena around the periphery of the building. Elena noticed several military and civilian dressed men stationed around the building and on the further grounds. There was, she mused, very tight security at the place outside as well as inside.

"Over there is the vegetable garden that supplies Comrade Stalin as well as the staff," the Lieutenant said in a voice just loud enough for some of the security personnel to hear.

"Are there any poultry being raised here?" Elena asked likewise in a voice that could be heard by others nearby.

"No. Comrade Stalin doesn't like to be awakened in the morning by roosters crowing."

The Lieutenant went on, "At the rear there is a picnic area. When the weather is warm, Comrade Stalin likes to have social gatherings there. Musicians. Dancing and so on."

As they proceeded along the rear of the building there was a considerable space between the security men. The Lieutenant suddenly took a firm hold on Elena's arm and drew her near to him. In a tense and urgent voice he whispered in Elena's ear, "We must get out of here as quickly as we can. I think we have been betrayed!"

Elena whispered in return, "Do you mean our mission has been exposed to the security people?"

"Yes, I think they are waiting for us to reveal our hand and then they will arrest us."

"Who could have done this to us?" Elena had become very anxious and worried.

"I don't know for certain, but I think it was Boris at the bakery."

"Boris! My god!" Elena was incredulous, shocked. "How are we to get out of here?" Elena was not in panic, but she recognized the urgency that had suddenly presented itself.

"Do you have the poison?" Elena asked.

"No."

"What did you do with it?"

"I put it in a bottle of Georgian wine that Stalin keeps in his room. As his aide I was able to get into his room."

"How do we get out of here?" Elena persisted.

"Can you get sick? You can stick your finger down your throat and cause vomiting. You can groan as if in pain. I may be able to get a car to get you to a hospital, but we don't go there."

"What if they send for a doctor instead?"

"Leave it to me. I'll do what I can. When we get back in the house, after a few moments you can get sick. Do you understand?"

"Yes. Why didn't you wait until I arrived before getting rid of the poison? I might have decided to try to use it as we planned. There is so much at stake."

"There was no use in waiting. Besides the danger in having it in my possession was very great. Under the circumstances, I thought it best to dispose of it and still possibly get to Stalin anyway through the Georgian wine he loves."

"Well, it's done," Elena said. "Let's go inside and see if we can arrange to get out of here. That bastard Boris. He should be killed." Elena was angry and disappointed that all the planning that had gone into the mission was now about to come to nothing.

"How did you find out that we had been betrayed?" Elena asked still in a whisper.

"Akmal, the bakery driver came here yesterday under the pretense of delivering bread. He had never delivered here before and the guards would not let him in. He asked for me and I came out to the gate. I told the guards that there must have been some mistake, that someone,

I did not know who, must have ordered the bakery goods. I said as long as he was here we would take some and to let him through. The guards first searched the truck and inspected Akmal and found nothing. So they let Akmal in. While unloading, Akmal told me that the whole underground was in great danger, that Boris had turned out to be an NKVD agent. He did not say how that was discovered, but he said that you and I had better escape from here immediately. Then he left."

"Akmal is a brave fellow coming here to this tiger's lair," commented Elena. "He could have ended up shot or in Siberia."

"Apparently, the word about the underground has not been spread to all of the security people. Probably only a few at the top have been informed and they want to keep it limited until arrests are made. They have to be careful themselves," said Valentnikov.

As Elena and Lieutenant Valentnikov rounded the corner of the house and walked back to the entrance, floodlights suddenly came on lighting up the building and the grounds around it. Elena was startled.

"That happens every evening when it begins to get dark. It's another security measure," Valentnikov assured Elena.

At that moment there was a bustle of activity by the guards at the entrance gate. Elena could see them brushing themselves off and primping their uniforms.

"They've gotten word that the boss will arrive in a few moments," Valentnikov commented.

"You mean Stalin?" Elena asked.

"Yes, and that means it will be more difficult to escape from here. Stalin usually wants me next to him!" the Lieutenant replied in a worried voice.

"Do you think he knows about us, our movement?" Elena felt herself getting alarmed. She felt she was in a trap with no way out.

"I don't know," Valentnikov replied. His voice revealed that he was tense, anxious. "I am guessing that he doesn't based on my experience here. The police are afraid to tell him about plots against him or the government until they have caught the plotters. They want to be able to show him that they've done their job. They are aware that their heads might roll if they tell him about plots not yet solved. He expects them to solve these things immediately. But, you can't tell with Stalin. He's an expert at making you think he's your best friend while he's adding your name to a list of people to be shot."

"Whew!" Elena exclaimed while shaking her head slightly in an expression of hopelessness. "I guess we're stuck. We'll just have to play along." Then she added, "You said you put the poison in Stalin's bottle of wine in his room. If it was that easy, why have we gone through all these elaborate preparations with me trying to seduce Stalin?"

"I can't explain all of the details now," Valentnikov continued in a hushed voice, "but I did mention it to Boris and he said, 'No,' He felt it would be too risky and maybe Stalin would never drink the wine, possibly throw it out. I think I know now why he didn't want me to do it. He was all along an agent for the police and he didn't want Stalin killed. I think he thought my method just might be too successful. But, let's go inside now before Stalin arrives."

Valentnikov and Elena joined the three interior security guards who had gathered at the entrance door to await Stalin's arrival. In a few moments Stalin's limousine and two others drove up to the entrance to the dacha. Stalin and three important-looking officials entered the building. Stalin at once noticed Elena and smiled at her, walked over and took her hand in his.

"Ah, pretty one, I'm glad you could get here. I shall see you later." Stalin then proceeded into a parlor room followed by the three stony-faced officials.

In the few moments that Stalin had stopped to say the few words to her, Elena had the opportunity to see close-up the man who ruled the lives of millions of Soviet citizens and who had climbed to the top post in the government by deceit, intrigue and the murder of those who had fought and worked alongside him to establish a Communist country. Elena knew that much about Stalin and little more about him personally.

Elena knew that Stalin was of short stature, but now standing next to him she was astonished at how really short he was. She observed that he wore a plain, gray tunic with a single medal of some kind. His hair was dark and coarse. He had had smallpox as a child and this had left pockmarked scars on his face. When he smiled, Elena noted that his teeth were quite yellow. To her she immediately felt his friendliness and cordial approach. When she looked into his eyes, however, she saw a steely cold expression that was almost hypnotic in its effect. In spite of that, Stalin did not give the appearance of being a tyrant. Elena thought he was more the benign grandfather type. She, nevertheless, did not allow herself to be duped by Stalin's kindliness. She was aware that with one spoken word or with the stroke of a pen he could have her arrested, sent to a labor camp, or have her executed.

What unnerved Elena more than anything else was that she didn't know whether Stalin knew or didn't know of her membership in the underground. With the reported disclosure by Boris of the underground movement and the probable destruction of the movement through the arrest of the members, she felt all the more a compelling reason to kill Stalin. If the members of the underground were to die, as surely they would if exposed, she did not want them to die for nothing. They had organized and planned for months for this avenging moment. They must not be unfulfilled. But she now lacked the poison. She could persuade him to drink the wine into which Valentnikov had put the poison. Yet, he, Stalin, might insist that she drink along with him. If that happened, she knew that she too would die from the effects of the poison.

Lt. Valentnikov interrupted Elena's thoughts. "I would suggest that you go to your room for a while. Comrade Stalin and his friends will probably spend some time drinking. Dinner is usually quite late but you never know when. There is no reason for you to sit around here with the guards watching you constantly. If you're hungry, I'll bring you some bread and cheese and a cup of coffee. It will satisfy you until you are called for dinner."

"Yes, I am a bit hungry," Elena replied. "I'll be at my room as you suggest."

Two of the security guards had dispersed to parts of the building. One remained and kept eyeing Elena. He was sitting on one of the couches seemingly looking at a magazine which had been on a nearby chair. It was obvious to both Elena and Lieutenant Valentnikov that he was peering over the magazine to regard Elena. It made her very uncomfortable and she was glad to leave for her room while Valentnikov went to Stalin to determine if he was needed for anything.

Elena lay down on the bed and her thoughts again turned to her predicament in the dacha. Should she abandon her mission or try to find some way to carry it out? How was she to escape if the police knew about her connection to the underground?

She had been in her room about ten minutes with her mind occupied when she was startled to hear and see the door to her room open slowly and quietly. There had been no knock or a voice request to enter. Elena saw the security guard who had been watching her enter the room and close the door behind him. Judging from the look on the guard's face, Elena sensed that something dreadful was about to happen to her. Fear came upon her almost immediately.

The guard had a lustful leer and a sardonic grin on his face. It was all too apparent to Elena that the fellow had some sort of sexual intent. He was a muscular, physically powerful man. She knew it would be impossible to fight him off. She was also aware that if she created any commotion by struggling or screaming that it would bring others in the dwelling running to her room and that there might be questions which would very possibly disclose who she really was.

"What is it you want here?" Elena tried to sound businesslike and stern, but she was sure that the guard could discern the trembling in her voice.

The guard said nothing but continued to express in his face his salacious intent. Elena had sat up and swung her legs over the edge of the bed and was on the verge of standing up when the guard sat down besides her, put his arm about her waist and held her down. He then pulled her tightly to him and said in a low guttural voice, "Pretty one, I have been watching you. You are very beautiful. I want to make love with you." He was breathing heavily and his eyes seemed to sparkle with a carnal passion.

"I cannot do that. I am here as the guest of Comrade Stalin. I am sure he would not approve of what you are doing." Elena's voice was tremulous and raspy from the dryness in her throat brought on by an intense fear.

"He won't know about it," the guard said in a very assured voice.

"If I told him what you did, you would be shot immediately."

"I don't think you will say anything to Comrade Stalin or to anyone else," the guard replied while still holding Elena firmly.

"How can you be sure that I shall not report you?"

"Because I would let Comrade Stalin know who you really are and then you would be the one to be shot."

"What do you mean? Who am I?"

"You are a member of the underground and you are here to assassinate Comrade Stalin. That is who you are!" The guard's eyes narrowed and, to Elena, appeared threatening and cold.

Elena was stunned by the blunt accusation of the guard even though she had earlier surmised from the guard's action that he might know. For the moment she said nothing but her heart was pounding and her head throbbing from the tension of the moment.

"Comrade Stalin probably knows anyway. So, your telling him about me will be nothing new to him." Elena was seeking information about what, if anything, Stalin knew.

"Comrade Stalin does not yet know about you and your fellow traitors. If he did, you would not be here, rest assured."

The guard was beginning to pull at Elena's blouse to expose her breasts. In her state of indecision she did nothing to stop him except to make a feeble effort to push away his hands. The guard had become increasingly aggressive. He quickly began to fumble with Elena's skirt in an attempt to remove it. Elena resisted more strenuously as the guard, failing to remove the skirt began to grope underneath it. Elena tried to push him away and to squirm out of his grasp, but the fellow was too strong and too intent on having his way. Elena became angry and in a low but firm voice told him to stop but to no avail. The guard managed somehow in the struggle to unbutton his trousers and was prepared to commit rape. At that moment, Lieutenant Valentnikov opened the door and entered the room carrying a plate of bread, cheese and a cup of coffee which he had promised to bring to Elena.

Lieutenant Valentnikov instantly sized up the situation as Elena, seeing him, cried out, "He knows about us!"

Lieutenant Valentnikov threw aside the plate he was carrying, quickly reached into his back pocket and took out a medium-sized hunting knife from its leather sheath. The security guard was momentarily taken by surprise at the unexpected intrusion. In that moment the Lieutenant made a decision. Taking a few steps, he was upon the security guard. The guard, seeing the knife in Valentnikov's hand, took his hands from Elena and threw up his arms to protect himself. It was a gesture too late. With all the strength he could command, Valentnikov plunged his knife into the neck of the guard severing the guard's jugular artery. The guard groaned and fell backwards, blood spurting, gushing from his neck wound. Fortunately, none got on Elena who had pulled away and stood up as the guard released her before he was stabbed. The blood, however, covered much of the bed and the floor near the bed. The guard, with another groan, died instantly.

Elena, the young lady who had coolly poisoned the police inspector and had, without hesitation, offered to poison Stalin, now stood shocked by the violent scene in front of her.

"My god, Sergei, what do we do now?" she exclaimed seemingly overtaken by anxiety.

Valentnikov was, himself, highly stressed by the enormity of the implications of his action against the guard. However, he realized that they had to move quickly. It would not be long before the security guard would be missed and a search to find him undertaken. Valentnikov gave Elena instructions.

"Go to the reception room right now. Be sure to act as if nothing had happened. Wait for me there. We have to get out of here as soon as we can."

"What are you going to do?" Elena asked in a tremulous voice.

"I'm going to set fire to the place!"

"No! You can't do that! You'll be caught!"

"Don't argue! Go! Take your pocketbook, but leave your suitcase here. Now go!" The Lieutenant was adamant. Elena left.

Lieutenant Valentnikov moved with haste. He took the oil lamp from the table, poured most its contents on the body of the guard and the remainder on the bed linen. He took a couple of matches from his jacket pocket, struck them and threw one on the guard and one on the bed. The Lieutenant always carried matches with him. He was forever lighting the cigarettes that Stalin smoked.

The flames began to take hold and to spread. Valentnikov stepped out of the room, closed the door and walked hurriedly to the parlor where Stalin and his officials had gathered to talk and drink. Stalin and his guests looked up casually when Valentnikov entered. Stalin immediately gestured by a wave of his hand that indicated that the Lieutenant was not needed and should leave them. Valentnikov knew that by appearing at Stalin and his group he could always say that he was nowhere near the fire when it was discovered. Valentnikov proceeded to the reception room to find Elena. She was alone and sitting reading a magazine. He sat down beside her. It would, they both knew, be only moments before the fire would become apparent to everyone both in and out of the building.

"Why did you kill him?" Elena asked in a strained whisper.

"If I had not, he would have arrested us and that would have been the end for us. As soon as everyone starts running around to contain the fire, we'll grab one of the cars and make a break for it."

"What about Stalin?" Elena had their mission in mind. Even at this moment, she felt reluctant to abandon it.

"We'll have to forget it. There is nothing we can do about it unless I just go back and shoot him. I am not going to do that. We have to think of ourselves right now." The Lieutenant's expression was grim and determined.

Elena and Valentnikov could smell smoke. They could hear some shouting as guards and staff people came running through the building. Some security guards from outside the building burst in looking wild eyed. One of them asked in a loud urgent voice, "Where is Comrade Stalin. We have to protect him!"

Valentnikov replied, "In the parlor!"

Valentnikov took Elena's hand and briskly led her to the outside of the building. There, too, security police were running about in a seemingly uncoordinated effort to do something about the fire that now could be seen burning in the room where the body of the guard lay. Two of the outside guards had obtained a garden hose and were preparing to direct the water toward the fire. If there was any other firefighting equipment, it was not evident although Elena and Valentnikov could hear shouting questions from some guards, "Is there any fire hose? Where is it? Are there any fire extinguishers inside? Go in and see!"

It was obvious to Elena and Valentnikov that there had been no fire drills or training of any kind for just such a situation that was now occurring. To the two, the scene was one of utter chaos.

"This is our chance. Stay here a moment. I'll be right back," the Lieutenant directed Elena.

Valentnikov ran over to the entrance gate to the compound and shouted to a couple of the security guards who stood at the gate doing nothing but watching the fire and the other guards running about.

"Open the gate so the fire engines can come right through! They can't be delayed!"

Valentnikov was unaware that anyone had called for a fire department, but he used the normal expectation that it had been done as a ruse to get the gate opened. The guards recognized Valentnikov and his authority and promptly opened the gate and left it open.

As Valentnikov hurried back to Elena, Stalin and his guests surrounded by security guards came out of the building. Stalin's limousine drew up, Stalin and his guests entered and were whisked away through the open gate and down the road. Several security guards entered a second limousine and quickly followed.

There were several other limousines kept on the dacha grounds. Valentnikov was familiar with them and the fact that their ignition keys were always left in the cars after the hired chauffeurs had either lost or misplaced the keys thus rendering a particular limousine temporarily inoperable. Valentnikov and Elena got into one of the limousines, started up and drove to the open gate.

"We are following Comrade Stalin," Valentnikov said to the guards. The guards again recognized the Lieutenant as Stalin's aide and did not question his statement. They waved him on through. Both Elena and Valentnikov breathed a bit easier, but both knew there were unpredictable dangers still ahead.

"So far things are working out for us," observed Valentnikov.

"But wait until they find the guard's body. It is in my assigned room and the police are going to be hot on my trail to question me about it." Elena sounded pessimistic. As they drove she kept looking back from her passenger seat next to the Lieutenant.

"Shall we go to the United States Embassy and ask for protection there?" Valentnikov asked Elena.

"No," Elena replied, "from my experience with them, they don't want to become involved any more than they have. If we sought safe haven with the Embassy, we might be turned away. If they took us in, we might later be handed over to the Soviet police. It's not safe to go there."

Elena paused momentarily in thought. "I would suggest that we go to the Finnish Embassy and ask for asylum. They know me and I have a friend there who will do anything for me. The Finns are alright. They have been standing up to the Stalin government for some time. Anyway, they're quite deeply involved in this mission as it is." The thought of Timo Koskinen at the Finnish Embassy seemed to have a calming effect on her.

"Good, we'll do that. I know where the Embassy is," Valentnikov also felt somewhat assured.

"You know what I'd really like to do, Sergei?"

"What is that?"

"I'd like to go to the bakery and settle with that bastard, Boris. I would take personal pleasure in killing him. That son-of-a-bitch ruined all of our plans."

"I feel the same way, Elena, but I don't think it would be wise to go to the bakery just now. The place is probably alive with NKVD people."

"Yes, of course, you're right, Sergei. I wonder what Boris is doing and where he is."

"He's probably at NKVD headquarters celebrating his role in exposing our movement," Valentnikov speculated.

"It will be interesting to find out how our people discovered that Boris was the traitor," Elena mused. "Someday he'll get his. One of our people will get to him and he'll be dead on the street." Elena was bitter and frustrated.

* * * * *

On the evening of the day that Elena left for Stalin's dacha, a number of the members of the underground gathered at the bakery to review the plans to converge on the Kremlin as soon as they received word that Elena had carried out her mission. This was the moment for which they had all been working, organizing, planning and hoping. Almost all had to live with the fear of being discovered, arrested and almost certainly put to death. These bold, courageous and idealistic men and women had always been ready to sacrifice themselves and their families to bring down that ruthless tyrant, Stalin and the henchmen who carried out his orders. They were gathered now for the final act in a play that had as its theme "Justice and Freedom."

The usual leaders and motivators were at the bakery along with a dozen others who represented the underground cells located in and around Moscow. There were Viktor, Yosif, Petrov, Sholom Lozovsky, Boris and the truck driver, Akmal. Members of more distant cells were to come in later to support the Kremlin takeover.

Most of those present gave evidence of being nervous, tense, anxious, and under stress. They were fidgeting and walking about aimlessly. A few stoic individuals were content to sit and tap a finger on the table or a foot on the floor. There was little conversation and what there was consisted of small talk irrelevant to the main concern.

Viktor, Yosif, Lozovsky, Boris and two other men were sitting at a table. After considerable silence, one of the men asked, "Where is Kameneva? Shouldn't she be here?"

Yosif replied, "No, Sofia is at the U.S. Embassy. The officials there did not want any of their employees or those working at the Embassy to be involved here tonight. The Americans are always very careful as they can be about their relationship with Stalin."

"How about that Finnish fellow?"

Yosif continued to answer. "He's going to pick up Elena tomorrow morning at Stalin's dacha. He should not be here for that reason."

After more silence, Viktor said quite abstractly, "I certainly hope our plans succeed. So much depends on its success."

Boris, with his usual smile, commented, "I don't think it will succeed."

Viktor stared at him sharply. "What do you mean?"

"Just what I said. I don't think it will succeed." Boris' smile had turned into a smirk.

Yosif joined in. "On what basis do you say that, Boris?"

Boris was casually evasive in his answers. "No basis really. I just think that the NKVD knows all about our plans and about our movement."

Viktor, looking hard at Boris, said, "Boris, how could they possibly know unless someone had informed them?"

"That is true," Boris responded. "You have many people in the underground. Anyone or more could have talked."

"Boris, even if one of our members did talk to the police, how would you know about it? You must have gotten your feeling that the police know about our plans from somewhere," Yosif persisted.

Boris' smile had disappeared. He remained silent choosing not to answer Yosif's question. His face had become flushed and he averted the eyes of the men at the table by glancing down at his hands. The others at the table looked at each other inquisitively, each wondering whether the others had the same question he had. Finally, Viktor in a firm, demanding voice said to Boris, "Boris, look at me!" Boris did so.

Viktor then said, "Boris, did you inform the NKVD?"

"No, of course not! Why would I do that? I have been in the underground for a long time and worked hard." Boris, still flushed, had become agitated. He realized that he had said too much and he now felt trapped. He did not sound convincing to the others.

"I don't think you're telling us the truth, Boris!" Viktor was very stern. "I think you've been in contact with the NKVD."

"That is not true. I have not been in contact with them." Boris was insistent.

"Take off your shirt!" Viktor commanded Boris.

"Why?"

"I have a reason. Now do as I say!" Boris complied.

"Now raise your arms over your head!"

"No! I won't do it. This is ridiculous!"

"Yosif, Sholom. Raise his arms!" Viktor was plainly angry at Boris' refusal to do what he was asked.

Yosif and Sholom moved around the table to where Boris was sitting, each grabbing one of Boris' arms and forcing him to raise his arms.

Viktor came to where Boris sat and peered closely at both armpits. Under the left armpit Viktor found a tattoo. It read: GPU 1037.

"Ha! So you were a member of the Main Political Administration. I suppose you are now one of the NKVD, the Peoples Commissariat for Internal Affairs."

"Yes, In 1934 I was a member of the GPU. When it was reorganized in that year as the NKVD, I resigned. I did not like the things they did."

"Put his arms down," Viktor directed Yosif and Sholom. "I don't believe you, Boris. Once a police agent, always a police agent. I know how the police work." Viktor's voice rose.

The others in the room seeing and hearing the commotion at the table came over to find out what was happening.

Lozovsky, visibly stunned by what he was hearing, said, "Boris, you never told us that you had been a member of the old GPU. If you had, we probably would not have allowed you into our organization."

Boris was shaken by the sudden hostility directed to him. He had thought he was secure in the respect and affections his peers in the underground had for him. Yet, he understood that everyone was on edge and could be provoked at the slightest hint that something might go wrong in carrying out the plans.

"I did not tell you because I did not think it was important since I no longer belonged."

Petrov, who was one of those who had come over to the table, gathered that Boris was being accused of betraying the movement. He spoke up. "I have often wondered why we were able to meet here so frequently without any interference from the police. It would seem obvious to any numbskull that with all the comings and goings here that something unusual was going on and, yet, we had only rare and indifferent visits from the police."

Someone from the group injected his opinion. "Sure! That's understandable. They had someone planted here giving them information. The less they interfered, the more information they received to use against us."

Lozovsky added, "There were really only a half-dozen of us who met here regularly and who knew precisely what was going on in the organization. I am one of those and we all know who the others are. Viktor, Yosif, Petrov, and Boris. If the police were getting information, it would have been from one of us. Look, I'm willing to let all of you examine me." Lozovsky removed his shirt, raised his arms and several of the men examined his armpits for a police identifying tattoo. They found none.

The others whom Lozovsky named did likewise. None had any tattoo marks of the police.

Viktor again turned to Boris.

"Boris, no one believes that you're innocent. However, we'll wait and see what happens. If the police attempt to break in here, you will be shot immediately. If we get word that we have failed in our mission, you will be killed."

Viktor turned to the others standing about. "Is that your decision too?" They all shook their heads in agreement.

Viktor then added, "Some of you go down into the cellar and bring up the guns and ammunition. If the police try to come in, we'll be ready for them."

Viktor then directed Petrov and another man, pointing to Boris, "Tie his hands behind him. You'll find some heavy twine in the storage chest."

Boris exclaimed, "Viktor, why are you doing this? I have not betrayed us." Viktor did not reply. Boris' hands were tied behind him as he sat on a stool.

During meetings of the underground at the bakery it was standard procedure to have one or two of the members on the second floor as lookouts at the window overseeing the street. One of the two now serving as lookouts came down the stairs hurriedly and rushed into the room where the group had gathered. The man was obviously excited.

"There are several black limousines just now coming together and parking about halfway up the street."

"Are any people getting out of the cars?" Viktor asked.

"No," the lookout replied. "The cars are just sitting there."

"They're police!" Viktor concluded. "They know about us and they'll soon be moving in on us."

Viktor made a quick decision. Turning to Akmal he ordered, "Akmal, take the truck right now and get to the dacha and let Lieutenant Valentnikov know that we have been betrayed and that he and Elena are in danger. There is still some bread in the truck. You can use delivery as an excuse to get in. Use the road past the cemetery. The lookout has seen the police limousines at the other end and none towards the cemetery. Get going!"

"So, Boris, you have informed on us. We now have the proof." Viktor glared angrily at Boris.

Lozovsky rose from his chair and, hatred in his eyes, snarled, "You bastard, you son-of-a-bitch, you have betrayed us." Stepping over to

Boris, Lozovsky punched Boris on the head, snapping it back with the force of his blow. Boris cried out in pain and in terror.

"You are doing to me the very thing that we have accused Stalin of doing. You have accused me and you are going to kill me just because you think I am your enemy. I say I am innocent, just like all those people Stalin has had arrested and executed merely on a suspicion." Boris' voice had risen to a scream as he pleaded for the others to believe that he was blameless, without fault. He went on as the men stood silently, glaring at him coldly and unmoved, pitiless.

Boris in desperation implored the group further. "You cannot kill me merely because I said that I did not think our plan would succeed. That was only an opinion."

"No," Lozovsky interjected. "You are a policeman. You have the proof on you. We trusted you all this time and you have been giving our plans to the NKVD." Lozovsky was furious.

Petrov joined in. "We haven't seen the police for months and now, when we are about to carry out our objectives, they are here. Someone must have told them and that someone is you!"

In an outburst of rage, others in the group hissed epithets at Boris, denouncing him and shaking their fists. Someone called out, "Kill him! Get rid of him!" The emotions of the mob spirit now controlled everyone.

Someone from the group stepped up with drawn pistol and pressed it against Boris' head. Lozovsky quickly pushed the man's arm aside.

"No, shooting is too good for him. There is no pain. We think of all the individuals who have been tortured at Lubyanka and Lefortovo. I have a better idea for this stukachi.* We'll put him in the baking oven!"

There was immediate, gleeful laughter. "Good idea! Good idea! Let's do it!" were the exclamations.

Boris, his face white and his eyes bulging with fright, cried out, "My god, no, no! Not that!"

Lozovsky stuffed a rag in Boris' mouth so his screams could not be heard. He directed one of the men to tie Boris' ankles together. This was done. Two or three people in the group protested feebly that that was not the way to treat Boris. But their opposition was ignored by the majority.

Lozovsky and a couple of men picked Boris up and carried him as he struggled and twisted over to the large commercial bread baking oven. They shoved him in head first and closed the door. Viktor, the baker, then turned on the gas and the pilot light. A crematorium had been created.

The weapons, which had been brought up from the cache in the cellar, lay at one side of the room. Viktor gave the order.

"Men, take a weapon! We have to get ready for the police assault when it comes." Most of the weapons were submachine guns. The men filled their pockets with loaded magazines. Viktor and Yosif directed the men to different positions, some at the second floor windows, others at the street level and a couple in the customers' sales part of the building. Those on the second floor could see the black limousines partly up the street. At first there was no movement. After a wait of about a half-hour, the limousines began to move slowly toward the bakery. One of the men on the second floor called down the open staircase, "They're coming!"

Viktor pulled the master switch to turn off all the lights in the building. Each of the men waited, tense with expectation of an assault by the police.

The men on the second floor saw the cars stop. They observed five or six men get out of each of the six limousines. They seemed to be carrying weapons as they moved quickly to different positions to surround the building.

The men on the first floor of the bakery got descriptions of what was going on outside from a member at the foot of the stairs to whom the information was relayed from those at the windows on the second floor.

There was a loud banging series of knocks on the locked door to the customer retail room. A man with a booming voice called out, "Open the door! We are the police. We know there are many of you in the building. We know you have weapons. Throw your weapons down and come out. You will be treated fairly and humanely. The building is surrounded." He repeated this again.

There was no response from the group inside. Several men muttered to no one in particular, "Yeah! We'll be treated humanely. In front of a firing squad!" Each member of the underground in the bakery building was aware that he would receive no mercy if captured. Each thought of his family and feared the worst; that families were being arrested because of association with an underground group member. This thought made each man more determined to fight his way out of the predicament or to die trying.

For a few minutes there was a lull when there was a sound neither inside nor outside the building. Then suddenly there was a sound coming down the street that most of the underground members recognized and the sound froze their hearts. It was the clanking sound of an army tank. They knew at once that the tank was being brought in by the police to blast them out of the building unless they surrendered.

Viktor thundered at the top of his voice for all to hear, "Anyone who attempts to surrender will be shot on the spot! We are going to fight to the end. We are all condemned anyway and they will show us no mercy if we are captured. Do you understand?" Viktor did not expect an answer as long as he had made himself clear. He knew his people understood. They were all tough, determined individuals. But he thought it was necessary to say what he did in case anyone wavered.

One of the men, Mikhail Dumanko, walked swiftly to Viktor. "Viktor, do you have a large crowbar somewhere?"

"Yes, down in the basement. Why?"

"I'll stick it into the tank tracks and the tank will not be able to move." Mikhail, a young burly fellow of about six feet was flushed and eager with excitement over his idea.

Viktor replied, "You won't last ten seconds out there. They've got people around the building who will shoot you down the moment they see you."

"Viktor, we'll die one way or another. Let me try."

The young man descended to the cellar and in a few moments returned carrying a heavy, four foot crowbar. He also carried a submachine gun on his shoulder. Without hesitation he moved quickly to the retail customer room where two of the underground were crouched ready to fire if the door were broken down. Mikhail told the two men what he planned to do.

"Cover for me when I go outside. I will run to where the tank is. You will both have to come outside with me and spray all around to force the police to stay down behind their vehicles. Do you understand?"

"Yes, we'll do it," the two men agreed.

They unlocked the front door. The policeman who had bellowed for everyone to come out and lay down their weapons was no longer there. The two members stepped outside and immediately began firing their submachine guns in the direction of the limousines and down one side of the building where Mikhail was to run toward the tank. Mikhail followed the two men and after thirty seconds of their blanket gunfire ran down the street toward the tank.

Evidently, the tank crew either did not see him in the nighttime shadows or mistook him for one of their police for they did not fire at him. The tank had come to a standstill, the crew apparently awaiting orders. Mikhail ran up to the tank and deftly shoved the crowbar between one of the treads and a sprocket wheel. The crowbar was firmly wedged and, if it held, Mikhail knew the tank could not move any further.

As he was placing the crowbar, Mikhail heard some shots and some bullets struck the tank, but none hit him. As he finished his work, he jumped behind some bushes lining the street and waited for the crew to open the tank hatch and come out to determine why the tank would not move.

As he lay in the dark with his gun at the ready, Mikhail's thoughts, even at this moment of intense concentration and focus on the tank, journeyed to his family, his parents, brothers and sister and he wondered if they had been arrested because of his activity in the underground. It was well known that if a member of a family was arrested on charges of conduct against the State or was identified as a member of a subversive group, the family of that person was more likely than not to suffer arrest or other punitive action by the police even though they might be entirely innocent of any wrongdoing.

Mikhail's digressing thoughts were abruptly ended by the start-up of the tank engine. The tank, however, had been immobilized by Mikhail's crowbar. Unaware that Mikhail was lying in wait, the tank hatch cover opened and two crew members climbed out and started to climb down off the tank to determine why the tank was unable to move. Mikhail opened fire and killed the two tank crewmen. Quickly he came from the bushes, jumped on the tank and fired his weapon down the open hatch. Mikhail knew that anyone inside the tank could not survive as the bullets ricocheted from one side to another. The job done, Mikhail jumped from the tank and back behind the bushes. His heart was pounding with the excitement of having successfully met the challenge he had set for himself by eliminating the threat of the tank.

As soon as Mikhail had started firing at the crew of the tank, he drew a volley of gunfire from police in the area of the bakery. He again remained unscathed. Mikhail knew he now had a choice. He could leave the scene and head back to his family to determine how they were faring or he could stay and help his companions. By engaging the tank he had already served his friends well and they would understand that he was not abandoning them, that he was not a coward. Only for a moment was he torn between two loyalties. He decided to stay. His comrades were facing right now a threat to their lives. His family might not be facing any imminent danger. Mikhail made his way cautiously back toward the bakery.

A firefight had begun. The police were firing a fusillade of rifle and submachine gun bullets at the windows of the building. In the dark they were not always accurate. It was the inaccuracy that enabled the men in the building to fire back from the windows at the police outside. The police were easy targets identified by the flashes from the barrels of their weapons. The screams of pain from the police agents hit by the gunfire testified to the effectiveness of the men defending themselves in the building. However, the defenders themselves were limited by the darkness and some police were able to get to the front and back doors of the bakery and to begin to smash them in. As the police broke down the doors and started to enter they were struck down by a barrage of fire from the underground members guarding the doorways.

Mikhail had maneuvered himself to a position behind the limousines from which he was able to fire on police using the cars as cover. He thought he had cut down several of the police but in the darkness was not certain.

Inside the building, the defenders had up to this point successfully kept the police at bay. Yosif was, however, worried. He sought out Viktor.

"We can't stay in here forever," Yosif said. "Sooner or later the police are going to bring in reinforcements and maybe another tank. We have to fight our way out. We'll then have to disperse, each one on his own. What do you think?"

"I guess you're right," replied Viktor. "Go and tell the men to get ready. Tell them to fight their way up to the cemetery about a half-kilometer up the road. We'll meet there and decide what to do next. But, I agree, we'll have to disperse. We have no place to go as a group."

Yosif quickly went to each man instructing him briefly on what action to take. While three men went out the front door and began to fire in a diversionary tactic, the others, two at a time, were to go out the back door and make their way to the cemetery. Any police encountered at the vicinity of the back door or on the way to the cemetery were to be immediately engaged and shot down if possible. Each man was to take as much ammunition with him as he could and that would not burden his actions. A man at the second floor window overlooking the rear yard was told to fire at random as each two men exited the rear door. This was done and the police were pinned down. The first two men made it out successfully. However, the flash from the automatic weapon revealed the second floor man's position. A rifle shot well aimed at the flame by a policeman instantly killed the fellow at the rear window.

Yosif realized that it was pure folly to send two members out at a time. They could be picked off too easily. He decided that the whole gang should go out in one offensive charge firing their weapons as they went. He conferred with Viktor about this strategy. Viktor immediately agreed. Some of the men would storm out the front door and turn and join up with those swarming out of the rear, being careful not to fire on their own people. The change in tactics was put into effect immediately. The men were grim, determined and resolved. Each was aware that in the next few moments he was destined to die, be wounded, captured or survive to another day.

One of the men voiced a nervous joke. "Viktor, shall we turn off the oven?"

Viktor chuckled even at this tense moment. "Nah! We'll let Boris bake for a while longer until the police find him."

Yosif shouted the order. "Ready, men! Let's go!"

The men poured out of both doors simultaneously, firing at the presumed positions of the police surrounding the building. Three of the men fell when police returned fire. Their companions could not stop to pick them up. They pushed on, firing to the sides. Two or three more men fell to police fire. The rest finally got out of the area where the police were stationed. At the cemetery the survivors gathered clandestinely among some of the taller tombstones.

One of the men spoke up to no one in particular. "I think some of us should go back for those who may be wounded. We can't let them fall into the hands of the NKVD."

"I would not advise going back," Yosif answered the man. "In any case, if they're still alive, they have been already captured and arrested. It's too bad, but that's the way things are."

Viktor spoke up. "Let's have a head count and then we must disperse." Viktor quickly counted eleven of the original eighteen. He ascertained that, in addition to himself and Yosif, those present included Petrov, Mikhail and several others.

Viktor declared, "I guess our friend, Shalom Lozovsky, didn't make it. He's not here."

Viktor then admonished the group. "Comrades, we cannot remain here. The police will be all over this place hunting for us. We shall break up into pairs and leave. Keep your weapons and ammunition. You may need them. I cannot advise you where to go, but I suggest you stay away from your homes. It appears the NKVD knows about our underground and who is a member. They'll be watching your homes waiting for you to return. If you have a friend or relative in a small village or remote farm, go hide at their place if you trust them. You can go to Moscow and try to get lost in the crowds, but you can't take your weapons into a city, you know that, I'm sure."

One of the men asked, "How do we get together again to reorganize?"

Viktor answered, "I don't know the answer to that just now. I can tell you, it will be quite a while before we can start up another underground movement. My bakery is gone. I can never go back there."

Another man muttered, "The baked bread might not taste too good."

Yosif said, "Alright, Comrades, pair up and let's get out of here. Be very cautious. Hide during the day and move by night for a few days.

We'll try somehow to contact you sometime in the future. The best advice is to lay low for a while. Good luck!"

Viktor and Yosif paired. As the others were hastily choosing partners, a Comrade asked Viktor, "What about our families, our wives and children?"

"Comrade," Viktor replied sympathetically, "We are all in the same situation. It is up to you whether you want to visit them, but it is suggested you not do so for a while, I cannot tell you how long. You might want to visit a friend or relative who can visit your wife and family to bring word that you are alright. Do you understand?"

"Yes." The Comrade seemed satisfied.

"Before you leave, Comrades," Yosif said, "Viktor and I want to assure you that we are not hardhearted about the Comrades we have lost. We all grieve for them. But, you must understand that, unfortunately, there is nothing we can do for them." The Comrades nodded understandingly. They then began to leave the cemetery.

As the last pair left, Yosif turned to Viktor. "We have lost everything, Viktor. I wish I'd have been shot instead of one of our Comrades." Yosif was saddened, depressed. Viktor, too, was despondent. Both men had been among the original organizers of the underground movement to rid the country of Stalin. They had sacrificed much to bring the movement to the point where it was ready to consummate its objective, its purpose.

Their families had suffered because of frequent absences of husband and father and because the loyalty to the movement took priority over loyalty and attention to the family. Both men were gruff, tough individuals of whom no one would suspect of having an intense idealism concerning the nature of what their country should be. They believed in a form of democracy and correctly concluded that with Stalin at the head of the government it would be a concept impossible to achieve. Both men were bakers by trade and now their business and livelihood were gone. Like the other survivors in the underground they were aware that they were hunted enemies of the State. They knew too well that the NKVD was relentless in the pursuit of all who were considered traitors of the Soviets.

The people in the underground were an independent lot. They were the kind who refused to be mastered by authorities unacceptable to them. Although it cannot be gainsaid that most people despise and hate tyranny and the tyrants, the underground Comrades were different in that they were resolved to do something to correct it. Passivity was not part of their characters.

As Viktor and Yosif started down a dirt path from the cemetery through a wooded area, Yosif remarked, "I wonder what happened to Elena and Lieutenant Valentnikov."

Viktor replied, "We're bound to find out soon. The police probably knew about them even before Elena went out to Stalin's dacha."

Viktor continued, "I have a cousin on a farm about thirty kilometers from here. I think we should head for his place. We may be able to find safety there for a while."

"Is he part of a collective?" Yosif asked.

"Of course, is there any other kind of farming these days? But the other farmers probably have no idea of our underground. They won't be suspicious."

"But the head of the collective will ask questions. That's one of his jobs," Yosif said.

"We are going to have to take new identities," Viktor suggested.

"But we don't have papers to show a new identity," argued Yosif.

"We'll think of something," Viktor replied wearily. "Let's get there first."

The pair now maintained silence, occasionally stopping to listen for any unusual noise.

* * * * *

Elena and Valentnikov drove in the direction of the Kremlin. If stopped, they could say that they were in Stalin's entourage and following his limousine. They intended, however, to turn off just before the entrance to the Kremlin and follow Znamenski Boulevard and Prechristenka Avenue to the familiar Kropotkinski Street of the Finnish Embassy.

They turned onto Kropotkinski Street and saw the outside lights of the Finnish Embassy building. The practice of the Embassy was to floodlight the building for security reasons during the dark hours.

Elena gave a sigh of relief. "Thank goodness," she exclaimed. "Now we'll be safe for a while at least."

She had no sooner uttered those words when she and Valentnikov saw the headlights of a car coming slowly toward them from the other end of Kropotkinski Street. As the car got closer, it seemed to move astride the center of the roadway to seemingly block Valentnikov from driving past it.

Valentnikov tensed and remarked to Elena, "I think we're in trouble. Get ready to make a dash into the Embassy. This may be the NKVD."

The other car, a black limousine, stopped in front of the entrance to the Finnish Embassy even as Valentnikov and Elena almost simultaneously drew up. In the light from the Embassy building Elena and Valentnikov saw four black suited men come out of the black limousine and walk rapidly the few steps to the Valentnikov auto. The men were burly and very grim and businesslike in appearance. Two of the men went to the driver's side; the other two to the passenger side of the Valentnikov auto. "We are the police. Show us your identification!"

Valentnikov hesitated, then reached into his pocket and handed the identification paper to the policeman.

"Ah, you are Lieutenant Sergei Valentnikov, an Aide to Comrade Stalin, I see." The policeman smiled, but the Lieutenant thought the smile was insidious rather than friendly.

"And who is this young lady?" the policeman asked pointing to Elena.

"She is an interpreter at the Finnish Embassy here. She stays here at times." Valentnikov replied, trying to outwardly portray a sense of calm, but inwardly having a feeling of foreboding.

"Young lady, I'd like to see your identification paper."

Elena brought the paper from her pocketbook and gave it to the policeman.

"You are Elena Marikova from Leningrad and you are an interpreter."

The policeman reached to his inside pocket and drew out a small notebook. He instructed his fellow officer to get a flashlight from their limousine. When the other officer returned with the light, the first policeman who seemed to be in charge, ordered him to hold the light on the notebook. The leader turned the pages slowly, at times stopping and running his finger down what seemed, from what little Lieutenant Valentnikov could observe, a list of names. The policeman after a few moments closed the notebook, but held it up and shook it at Valentnikov and Elena.

"Do you know what this is?" the policeman asked addressing both the occupants in the car.

"No, of course not! How could we?" Valentnikov responded.

"Well, I will tell you," the policeman smirked. "It is a list of members of an underground organization of traitors who want to overthrow our government."

The policeman paused, looking at both Valentnikov and Elena to let the statement's implication take its effect. It had its intended effect. Both Valentnikov and Elena felt their hearts pounding with trepidation. They both knew what the policeman would say next and they both knew they were trapped.

The policeman, with an exultant air, said, "Sergei and Elena, your names are on this list!" The policeman acted like a cat which had just caught a mouse and had finished playing with it.

"You are both under arrest. My men will handcuff you!"

Lieutenant Valentnikov's reaction was instant. With all the force he could muster from his position sitting at the driver's wheel, he struck the policeman in the face with his clenched fist and shoved him against the other policeman at the door. While jumping out of his car, Valentnikov called to Elena, "Make a break for it!"

Elena, however, could do nothing. The two men on her side of the car already had her arms in their firm grips.

The policemen were shouting. Valentnikov was shouting. Valentnikov and the two policemen were struggling on the street. Valentnikov, young, athletic and strong, was a match for the two older policemen. They were having considerable difficulty subduing him. The leader of the police who had done the talking in the first place called out to one of the policemen restraining Elena, "Come over here and help us with this bastard!"

The third policeman had drawn his revolver and was trying to take aim on Valentnikov while avoiding hitting the other policemen. There was a shot and Valentnikov stopped struggling. He cried out in pain with a bullet in his left upper leg. He began to bleed profusely.

The noise of the struggle and the shot brought the military guards of the Finnish Embassy as well as some of the staff from inside the building to the street to see what the ruckus was about. Among them was Timo Koskinen. Elena saw him and cried out, "Timo, Timo, help me!" The policemen still guarding her, slapped her across the face and told her, angrily, to be quiet.

Koskinen rushed over to where Elena was sitting in the auto. His face livid with rage, he grabbed the policeman's arm and spun the fellow around and away from Elena and hissed at him through clenched teeth, "If you do that again, I'll kill you!" Then, in the next breath, Koskinen added, speaking in the face of the policeman, "Release that lady right now! She is an employee of the Finnish Embassy. You can't arrest her!"

The leader of the police group came over to Koskinen now that Valentnikov was subdued. "What is the problem here, Mister?" he said to Koskinen. His voice was stern and demanding.

Replied Koskinen heatedly, "You have arrested this young lady. You cannot do that! She is an employee of the Finnish Embassy."

"And who are you, Mister?" The police leader was sarcastic.

"I am a Finn and connected with the Embassy," replied Koskinen still infuriated at the way the police were handling Elena.

"Well, in all respect to your diplomatic status, Mr. Finlander, this young lady is a Russian citizen and we have jurisdiction over her. The Finnish Embassy has no jurisdiction even though she serves as an interpreter for you. She is being arrested because she is a member of the underground organization bent on overthrowing our government and assassinating Comrade Stalin!"

"Officer, that is ridiculous. I've known this young lady for a long time and I can assure you that she is not a member of any underground. Now, will you please release her?"

"No. If what you say is true, she will be released after questioning at police headquarters."

Koskinen knew what that might mean. The questioning of people could be very severe when conducted by the NKVD.

The police leader had become perturbed and irritated by Koskinen's insistence. "Mr. Finlander, this young lady will not be released. We shall keep her in our custody. That is final! I might add that you are not in a very good position to insist on anything. We have information that someone in the Finnish Embassy is implicated in the underground organization." The policeman had not asked for Koskinen's identification and was, apparently, unaware to whom he was talking.

The policeman guarding Valentnikov approached the police leader as the latter turned away from Koskinen. "Sir, the Lieutenant is bleeding badly. Perhaps we should take him into the Embassy and call for a doctor."

"No!" the police leader answered. "If we take him into the Embassy, he can ask for asylum protection and they'll probably grant it. Put a tourniquet on his leg and we'll drop him off at the hospital. You will stay with him and after he's treated call us and we'll send a car to bring him to headquarters."

The policeman removed Valentnikov's belt and used it as a tourniquet. This done, he helped the Lieutenant to his feet and into the limousine. Elena was placed into the police car as well. One of the policemen was instructed to drive the Valentnikov limousine to police headquarters.

As Elena walked to the police car, Koskinen, who stood close by said in Finnish, "Remember, I love you. We'll do what we can to get you out of this."

Elena said nothing, but nodded her head to affirm that she had heard him. To Koskinen, Elena appeared crushed, her face mirroring a sense of hopelessness and resignation to her fate which she expected to be not very pleasant.

As the cars drove off, Koskinen stood in the street watching them disappear in the darkness. He felt absolutely wretched. He was anguished, his heart heavy and aching. He became tormented by the realization that he had been unable to help his beautiful Elena. He returned to the Embassy building along with other staff members who had been at the scene. All were saddened by what they had witnessed. Many had come to know Elena and to have an affection and admiration for her. They talked in somber tones among themselves about what might happen to Elena and Lieutenant Valentnikov. They all knew that the NKVD had a reputation for harsh treatment of people held for questioning.

At first, Koskinen had the urge to go to Ambassador Peltonen's room to ask for his help in getting Elena released, but on second thought, it was a late hour and he felt constrained to impose on the Ambassador at that time. He decided, reluctantly, to wait until morning.

Koskinen went to his own room, but with no thought of sleeping. He was too agitated. Instead of lying down, he sat in one of the chairs and closed his eyes as if to block out everything but Elena and her predicament. His thoughts drifted, however, to the question of how the police had come to the information about the underground and in such detail that they even had a list of the members. It was obvious to Koskinen that someone within the underground organization was an informer for the NKVD. In his misery, he wondered who it could have been. It could have been anybody, but none of those he had come to know seemed likely to have been an informer. Each was dedicated to the mission of getting rid of Stalin or so it seemed. His speculation on the subject was to no avail. He had not a clue to the person who might have been an agent for the police.

It was a long night just waiting for the morning office hours in the Embassy to arrive. But morning came eventually and when Koskinen left his room to go to early breakfast, he felt physically and spiritually drained. He was exhausted.

Immediately after breakfast Koskinen went to see Ambassador Peltonen. He sat down at the Ambassador's desk.

"I've come to talk with you about last night's incident outside the Embassy."

The Ambassador spoke up in a solemn but kindly manner. "I was aware of the disturbance outside, Timo, but I did not think it wise or appropriate for me to go out. There is nothing I could have done and it would only have left me open to an accusation of participating and cooperating with the underground. I hope you understand."

"Yes, I understand," Koskinen replied, "but is there anything you can do to get Elena released?"

"I would think not," the Ambassador answered shaking his head sorrowfully. "Elena is a Russian citizen. That prevents me from filing any protest. And it gives the Russian police the right to deal with her."

"Well," persisted Koskinen, "can you find out where they have taken her?"

"Yes, I can try that much. I'll have to work it through the Soviet Foreign Office. I'll call them shortly and see what I can find out. I'll let you know the minute I learn anything."

"Thank you, sir," Koskinen said gratefully. He then left the Ambassador's office and waited in the reception room. He spent the time in agonizing over what ordeals Elena might be experiencing. He conjured up all sorts of tortures until he was beside himself in desperation.

About two hours later, Koskinen heard himself being paged. He walked quickly to the telephone switchboard operator.

"Do you have a message for me?"

"Yes, the Ambassador wants to see you in his office."

"Thank you!" Koskinen's heart was pounding with excitement as he walked hurriedly to the office, knocked and entered.

"Have a seat, Timo." The Ambassador was unsmiling, serious.

From the expression on the Ambassador's face, Koskinen knew at once that the news would not be good.

"Elena and Lieutenant Valentnikov have both been transferred from NKVD headquarters to Lefortovo Prison. I must tell you that from the information I have, Lefortovo is probably the worst of the prisons around Moscow, although none of them are pleasant resorts."

"What do you mean by 'the worst,' Mr. Ambassador?" Koskinen felt faint. He guessed at what the Ambassador implied, but he wanted to hear the details.

"I mean that at Lefortovo some very severe and harsh treatment is meted out to prisoners. I don't want to go into detail."

"Mr. Ambassador, I would like your permission to go to Lefortovo to see Elena and the Lieutenant and perhaps get them released."

The Ambassador replied, "I don't think it would be wise. In the first place, I don't believe that you'll get to see them and, in the second place, you probably have been implicated as a participant in the underground. They seem to know who was active in the underground. You could be arrested yourself."

"I'll take that chance, Mr. Ambassador, but I do want to go." Koskinen's voice sounded urgent.

"I can't give you permission under the circumstance but, on the other hand, I can't stop you if you insist on going."

"Thank you, Ambassador Peltonen."

The Ambassador added, "If you get arrested you will cause us a lot of embarrassment to get you released under the diplomatic immunity rule. You understand that?"

"Yes, sir."

With that, Koskinen left the Ambassador's office and proceeded to his room where he changed from casual to more formal dress befitting one with diplomatic authority.

Koskinen hired a taxi to take him the eight kilometers to the prison. Lefortovo Prison was a short distance from St. Peter and Paul Russian Orthodox Church just west of the Youza River.

Koskinen was admitted after showing his diplomatic identification papers to the guard at the prison gate. Once inside the prison, a security officer led the way to the prison administrative office. Walking along the corridors of the building, Koskinen noted that they were kept quite clean and had an odor of disinfectant. On either side of the corridors was a series of rooms with closed windowless doors. All was quiet from the rooms.

The security officer showed him into an outer office room of the administrator's offices. While Koskinen sat on a bench awaiting the administrator, the security officer stood nearby. Koskinen asked the officer, "Where are all the prisoners kept?" The officer ignored the question and Koskinen gathered that the officer preferred not to talk with him.

Within a few more minutes, another security officer appeared and announced to Koskinen that he was to come with him to see the administrative officer in an adjoining room.

"I am Major Dushenov. I understand you're attached to the Finnish Embassy. Your name is Antti Salonen?"

"Yes."

"What can I do for you?"

"I understand that you are holding an Elena Marikova and a Lieutenant Valentnikov. I would like to see them and I would request their release." Koskinen's voice was firm and demanding.

The Major's face mirrored his surprise. Wives of husbands who were detained at the prison often came to plead for their husband's freedom. Generally, such pleas were not granted. However, a foreign diplomat asking for the release of Russian prisoners was very unusual.

The Major was respectful in his answer.

"The individuals you mentioned are suspected of conspiring with other people in planning to assassinate Comrade Stalin to overthrow the government. These are very serious matters and, if proven, they will result in severe punishment. That sort of activity will not be tolerated. I hope you understand."

"I understand what you are saying," replied Koskinen, "but they are not members of any underground group."

That reply drew an irritated rejoinder from the Major who had a list of the underground members on his desk in front of him.

"At this time," the Major stated, "you cannot see or visit with the prisoners. They are being interrogated."

"How long does the interrogation last?" inquired Koskinen. "I can wait."

"It all depends on whether we get truthful answers. Generally, interrogations last several days. It all depends on the answers we get from the prisoners."

Koskinen was stunned by what the Major said. He had hoped to be more effective. He had hoped his diplomatic status would cause the prison authority to relax or make an exception to its rules.

Major Dushenov then asked Koskinen, "You are from the Finnish Embassy. What is your interest in these prisoners?"

"Miss Marikova is a translator who has been assigned by your government to our Embassy. She has done a very good job and we have all come to respect and to like her. She is a very nice person and, frankly, we are interested in seeing that no harm comes to her. We would like to see her released so that she can continue to work with us. As far as Valentnikov is concerned, we all know that he is a good friend of Miss Marikova."

The Major was stony-faced as he listened to Koskinen whom he knew as Salonen. He stared coldly at Koskinen and began to tap his fingers on his desk as evidence that he had become quite perturbed. He waited a few moments after Koskinen had finished his answer. Then in a harsh, accusing voice the Major said, "Mr. Salonen, we have extensive information about the traitors who were plotting against our government. We have a dossier this thick about them." The Major spread his fingers to indicate a thick file.

The Major continued, "Mr. Salonen, there is no point in your coming here trying to fool us with lies about these people. I suggest that you return to your Embassy and wait for us to release your friend, Miss Marikova. When we have completed our investigation and interrogation we'll send her back to you. If she was only nominally involved with the movement, possibly as a translator for you, then we will not hold her. In any case, you will get to see her whether she is guilty or not. You will be kept informed. We understand your interest."

Koskinen arose from his chair and prepared to leave. He thought he'd direct a blunt statement at the Major before departing.

"Major Dushenov, in all respect to you, you may be aware of this prison having a reputation for brutal treatment and torture of prisoners. We hope that our interest in Miss Marikova will spare her from that kind of treatment."

The Major smiled, "Yes, I know about what is said of us. It is a falsehood spread by certain enemies of the people. I can assure you, Mr. Salonen, that we do not treat prisoners other than in a very humane manner. We don't pamper them of course. No prison does. On occasion, a prisoner will appear bruised. That is the prisoner's fault. He or she becomes violent and has to be restrained. Now, good day, Mr. Salonen."

The security officer who had been standing by in the Major's office during the conference escorted Koskinen out of the office and back along the corridors. In the return walk, Koskinen asked the officer, "Where are the interrogations conducted?"

"In the basement," the officer replied and by his expression, Koskinen gathered that further conversation would not be welcome. However, he did ask the security officer to call a taxi. The officer directed one of the guards at the gate to do so. The security officer remained with Koskinen until the taxi arrived and Koskinen left. Koskinen had the impression that he had been under scrutiny at all times while at the prison. "What an unpleasant environment Russians had to live in," he thought.

As he drove back to his Embassy, Koskinen had a heavy heart. Poor Elena. What must she be undergoing in that prison? He hated to think about it. There was no limit to the torture that the police could and would subject her to. Koskinen imagined the worst and the more he imagined, the more miserable and dejected he became. His thoughts became unbearable.

Upon his arrival at the Embassy, he reported to Ambassador Peltonen.

"I am not at all surprised that you were not able to see Elena and the Lieutenant. I certainly wish I could help but it would just not be appropriate for me to intervene in a matter concerning a Russian citizen. No country appreciates another country's interference in the sovereign actions of the first country."

"Yes, I know, I know," replied Koskinen dispiritedly. "But, I was hoping against hope that I, myself, could do something."

"You're very fortunate you were not arrested when you were at the prison. If the Major said that they had a very extensive dossier on the underground organization, then the NKVD and he know about you. I would think that they had decided to do nothing at this time about you, us and the United States in order to avoid an international crisis. Nevertheless, I expect I may receive an order sometime soon from the Soviet Foreign Office to have you leave here and to be sent back to Finland. You know, persona non grata."

The Ambassador continued, "I wonder who in the underground betrayed the group."

"I'd like to know that too," said Koskinen. "Whoever did it was very clever and did a thorough job. All of our efforts have been wasted and all of our plans have gone for naught, damn it!"

"I guess that all you or any of us can do is to wait and see what happens," the Ambassador advised. "I would again suggest to you, Timo, that you not hope for too much. The people at Lefortovo Prison are a mean, heartless and brutal bunch. They're capable of every conceivable form of abuse. That's their reputation."

"Well, thank you anyway for your understanding, Mr. Ambassador," Koskinen said as he turned to leave the office.

"If I learn anything, Timo, I'll let you know immediately," Ambassador Peltonen said compassionately.

Later that day as Koskinen was pacing around the Finnish Embassy aimlessly and distraught, he met Eino Partola, the Finnish Trade Specialist who was still on the job.

Partola stopped Koskinen to talk with him.

"I understand that Elena and her friend the Lieutenant have been arrested and are now at Lefortovo Prison."

"Yes, that is so," Koskinen confirmed glumly.

"Gosh, I've been told that's a hell hole," Partola remarked.

"Yes, I suppose it is," Koskinen responded.

Partola went on, "I've heard that interrogations can last hours at a time, day after day, with beatings and maiming. They cut prisoners, mutilate them, even gouge out eyes, in order to break them down and get them to confess to crimes and to inform on others. In one case, I was told that …"

Koskinen interrupted Partola's vivid descriptions. "Please, Eino, that's enough. I don't want to hear anymore. I am going through hell as it is."

"I'm sorry. I didn't mean to upset you. I just thought …"

"That's alright, but let's drop the subject," Koskinen again sought to put a halt to the very disturbing conversation. Koskinen then abruptly walked away, heading for a conference room.

At dinner the next day, the Ambassador told Koskinen that he had heard from the United States Embassy inquiring about the outcome of the planned mission of the underground. Peltonen said he had brought Deputy Addison up to date and that the Deputy was shocked.

"We'll be keeping in close communication with each other," Peltonen said. "Apparently, they now are worried that their involvement in the plot to get rid of Stalin has been made known to the NKVD and the Russian Foreign Office and there may be a huge fallout in the U.S.-Russian relations. Frankly, we're in the same predicament. However, I'm hoping that the situation in Europe with Hitler getting more aggressive and with Stalin aware that he needs the good will of the United States, England, France and us, as well, this whole business of the plot will blow over and Stalin will do nothing about it except, of course, punishing the Russians involved."

Koskinen did not reply except to shake his head in general agreement.

* * * * *

At the United States Embassy, the day after Elena was scheduled to visit Stalin at his dacha, Bill Chance and Gene Wagner were sitting with

Deputy Fraser Addison in the latter's office awaiting some words as to the success or failure of the mission. Sofia joined them from time to time to learn if any report had come in. Although all were concerned about the outcome, Sofia was especially anxious about the welfare of her friends in the underground. Additionally, her own future was at stake. If the mission failed and the NKVD discovered her role in the plot, her very life would be in danger.

There was no telephone call, no information of any kind about the event during the entire day following Elena's visit.

"I'm getting worried," Wagner remarked that evening at dinner in the Embassy. "We should have heard something."

Chance also was increasingly fearful, but he tried to give the appearance of patient assurance. "The delay in our hearing about this doesn't mean that something went wrong. It may be too soon to get the information. I think we should wait until tomorrow before we panic."

Sofia came in during the meal and sat down with Chance, Wagner and the Deputy. She was obviously nervous and apprehensive. She nibbled at a muffin but ate nothing else.

"I have no appetite," she responded when Wagner asked her if she wouldn't like to order some food.

Sofia suggested, "Maybe we should call the Finnish Embassy. They might have some information. That Salonen fellow was to pick Elena up this morning."

The Deputy replied, "That's a good idea, but let's wait until tomorrow. If we haven't heard by the afternoon, we'll give them a call."

They were all quite glum during the rest of the dinner. Little else was said. Sofia sat twisting her dinner napkin in an expression of nervous concern.

Wagner said softly and kindly, "Sofia, calm down. There is nothing to be done this evening." His advice was better than his example.

Wagner added, "If something went wrong, Sofia, we'll see that you're protected. That's a promise."

Sofia smiled wanly. At this point she was skeptical.

Two days after Elena was to have visited the Stalin dacha there was still no word about the outcome. In the late afternoon, Deputy Addison called Bill Chance, Gene Wagner and Sofia into his office.

"I think the time has come when we should take some action to find out what happened in carrying out the plan. It is now almost two days and we have heard nothing. I'm going to call the Finnish Embassy to see what they know and I wanted you all here when I did so."

Addison asked the switchboard operator to get Ambassador Peltonen on the line. After a few moments, Addison was talking with the Finnish Ambassador.

"Ambassador Peltonen, this is Deputy Fraser Addison of the United States. We haven't had any word how things went on our project. Could you tell me if you have any information ... you do have? Well, tell me about it."

Chance, Wagner and Sofia watched Deputy Addison closely for any clues that might indicate how things had gone. They observed Addison grow very serious.

As he listened to Ambassador Peltonen, Deputy Addison had a few comments that to the others in his office indicated that things had not gone well.

"Good god!" Addison remarked several times. "That's terrible! That's awful!"

"We'll have to discuss here what we shall do now," was the Deputy's final comment before he hung up.

The Deputy turned to Chance, Wagner and Sofia. "Things have not turned out well. The mission has failed. Elena and her Lieutenant friend were arrested by the police as they were about to enter the Finnish Embassy two evenings ago. They are now at Lefortovo Prison. They are being interrogated!"

"Oh," gasped Sofia. "That is absolutely terrible for us and for Elena and her boyfriend. Lefortovo is one of the worst of a number of prisons. How did it happen that they were arrested?"

"The Ambassador said that he does not know," answered Addison.

"The NKVD must have planted an informer in our organization. How else could they have known about us?" Sofia was obviously shaken by the news.

"Poor Elena! What that poor girl must be going through! I know those beasts. They're sadists. They'll torture her beyond any human endurance. And Lieutenant Valentnikov. He's finished. He'll be shot if they haven't done so already."

Wagner again sought to reassure Sofia.

"Sofia, perhaps we can help Elena in some way. Let's think about it."

Sofia, however, was inconsolable. Tears had come to her eyes as she thought of Elena.

"Well, is there something we can do?" Wagner addressed the others.

There was silence as they all thought about it. Finally Addison spoke.

"I don't know what to suggest. But, even if we could do something, the question is whether we should. It is my own feeling that we are in this thing deep enough already and that we should keep our distance from this point on."

Wagner remarked, "If the NKVD already knows about our involvement with the underground, then the damage is done and trying to help Elena won't add anything to worsen the situation."

"It just might make things worse," responded Addison. "We have to think about our relations with the Soviet government, with Stalin. I sympathize with Sofia and her concern for Elena and at the risk of appearing callous, I have to say that the political issue is far more important than one or two lives. I have to say that and as experienced State Department employees I would think you'd have to agree."

Chance, who had been listening and contemplating up to this point, added his view.

"I have to agree with Fraser. We have had a minor role in this whole debacle up to now. We can only hope that the Soviet government will recognize that it is in its best interest to ignore our past and promote mutual good relations."

Wagner expressed the thought, "Maybe if I went to the prison personally and pleaded for Elena's release they might just do that."

"No, the Finnish Ambassador said that they tried that and it didn't work."

"Gentlemen," interrupted Sofia, "I don't think anything will help at this point. Elena has probably already been abused. The prison people don't waste any time in getting down to interrogating and the torture process."

Deputy Addison observed, "I'm afraid that Sofia here will be arrested the minute she steps out of the Embassy's confines. We can't allow her to be subjected to the kind of treatment they give at Russian prisons. What do we do?"

Wagner suggested, "Bill and I will be going back to the United States shortly, I presume. I think we'll have to smuggle Sofia out of the country. She wants to go to America anyway. Isn't that true, Sofia?"

Sofia nodded affirmatively.

"Well, start thinking about it. In the meantime, we'll have to wait and see what happens in the next few days or so," Addison advised. He added, "Sofia, don't go outside. Stay in the Embassy."

Chance, Wagner and Sofia left Addison's office feeling sorrowful and dejected with the realization that the project to eliminate Stalin was finished and unsuccessful.

****

For Timo Koskinen at the Finnish Embassy each day without some word about Elena was a continuous, unrelenting torment. He did not try to conceal his anguish from the others of the staff. Employees at the Embassy had, from early on, been aware that there was more than a professional relationship between Elena and "Salonen." It was accepted without snickering or snide gossiping. It was not unusual for individuals away from family for long periods of time to acquire lady friends or man friends while serving at foreign posts.

However, Salonen's suffering over a "girl friend" seemed so intense and deep that staff members commented among themselves that the relationship was obviously more than a casual, transient one. They wondered about Salonen's wife.

Koskinen had been receiving letters from Anna, his wife, almost weekly. At first, he responded with regularity, but his letters to Anna had lately become more infrequent and the contents more detached from any expression of affection and personal interest. Koskinen, himself, was aware that Anna in Tampere, Finland, seemed increasingly remote and that his feelings for her considerably diluted because of his concentration on Elena. He was not so sure that once back in Finland the old loving fervor for Anna would be restored. That thought bothered him, but not enough to compel him to change anything with Elena.

Indeed, now with Elena in prison his whole being ached for Elena. Anna, at the moment, safe in Finland, was inconsequential.

A week passed and still no information about Elena. On the twelfth day after the arrest of Elena and Valentnikov, Ambassador Peltonen received a telephone call from NKVD headquarters. The caller was terse. The interrogation had been completed. The police would be bringing Elena to the Finnish Embassy tomorrow at eight in the morning. Would the Ambassador have someone at the Embassy entrance to receive her?

"Yes, of course," Ambassador Peltonen had replied. He was not a little surprised and taken aback that the police were bringing Elena to his Embassy but he didn't argue the point with the NKVD caller. Nothing had been said about Lieutenant Valentnikov and the Ambassador felt it would be imprudent to ask. The Finnish Embassy was not supposed to be concerned about Russian citizens, especially those arrested for a possible violation of Russian law.

Ambassador Peltonen immediately sought out Koskinen to give him the news. Koskinen told the Ambassador, "I'm very relieved to finally get some word and happy that Elena is to be brought here but I have a great fear of what condition she will be in. Perhaps, Mr. Ambassador, we should have a medical doctor here when she arrives just in case there is a need."

"I don't think we need to have a doctor present. I can call one of the doctors who treats our people and alert him to stand by if needed," the Ambassador decided.

"Alright, I'd appreciate that," said Koskinen.

"I suppose that they're bringing her here because of the fuss we made over her arrest and imprisonment," the Ambassador conjectured. "I don't know what we're expected to do with her once she's here."

"Perhaps we can get her to Finland," Koskinen offered.

"If they'll allow her to leave Russia," the Ambassador added. "We'll have to think about this."

Although very concerned about Elena's condition and well-being, Koskinen was considerably relieved to learn that he would see Elena the next morning. The stress of the past few days together with the lack of meaningful sleep had taken its toll and Koskinen, exhausted, lay down on his bed and almost immediately fell into a deep sleep. While in this profound state, Koskinen dreamed that he was on the shore of a great lake whose opposite side could not be seen because of the huge expanse of the water. He dreamed that he was on a long jetty extending out into the lake and seemingly into infinity. He walked on and on unendingly with no other living creature about. When he had started out from the shore, the day had been clear and bright, but now as he walked he perceived that mist was arising from the lake and gradually closing in on the jetty. In his dream, Koskinen heard a shrill scream coming from above him. He stopped and looked up and as he did so a large bluish gray and white seagull dropped at his feet. It lay on its back with feet extended to the sky, its eyes still open staring vacuously, its bill partly open. Koskinen bent down and examined the gull more closely. It was dead. Koskinen shuddered. He felt ill at ease in the presence of the dead gull. He turned to go back to the shore, but the mist had enveloped the jetty and him entirely so that he was uncertain as to where the next step would lead him. The dream abruptly ended and Koskinen slumbered on until his alarm clock rang and awakened him at 0600 hours. He remembered the dream and it brought to his mind the other times when he had dreamed of the seagull. Koskinen had sought to find meaning in the dreams. He came to the tenuous conclusion that each dream portended some significant event, even a cataclysmic one.

After dressing, a quick cup of coffee and piece of Finnish bread in the dining room, Koskinen went to just inside the entrance door to the Embassy building. It was 0730 hours. He stood waiting, waiting. At five minutes before the 0800 hour he was joined by Ambassador Peltonen, Kalle Nevakivi, the Ambassador's aide, the Ambassador's secretary, and a staff woman with nurse training.

The 0800 hour came and went. About twenty minutes later when the group had begun to comment that perhaps a mistake had been made, they saw a black limousine coming slowly down the street toward the Embassy building.

There was a stir of excitement among those gathered at the doorway.

Someone said, "This must be it!"

Koskinen opened the door and, followed by the others, went to the gate where two guards stood watch. The limousine drew up to the gate, stopped and two men in black coats got out, one from the driver's side, the other from the passenger side. The driver came over to the group and in an authoritative, arrogant voice asked, "Who is in charge here?"

"I am Ambassador Peltonen." The Ambassador stepped forward to meet the driver.

The driver produced a sheet of paper along with a pencil. "You are to sign here that you have received Elena Marikova and that you assume all responsibility for her."

The Ambassador took the paper, then handed it to Koskinen. "Will you read it and see if that is what it says?"

Koskinen, hands visibly shaking, read the paper for a few moments. "It seems to be alright and is confined to acknowledging receipt and full responsibility for Elena." He gave the paper back to the Ambassador, who then signed it.

The driver then motioned to the other men and ordered gruffly, "Bring her out!" The fellow opened the rear side of the door of the limousine and said something in a low voice to the person inside the rear of the car. Without a word Elena alighted from the automobile. There was an audible collective gasp from the reception people at Elena's physical appearance.

She wore a dark blue beret on her head. One side of her head from the top under the beret to down to her jaw line was covered with a thick bandage held on by generous amounts of adhesive tape. Both hands were bandaged and she walked unsteadily and gingerly as in pain and with hesitation before each step as if reluctant to take the step because of the pain in doing so. To all present, Elena was obviously in great distress.

The driver of the limousine and his companion got into the car and drove off with considerable speed. They had, apparently, brought no bags or the pocketbook belonging to Elena.

Koskinen and the lady nurse stepped forward to help Elena into the Embassy building. Once inside, someone produced a wheel chair for Elena to use. She accepted, nodding gratefully. Strangely, no one, including Koskinen, had uttered a word of greeting or of anything else. Everyone, apparently, recognized the occasion as somber and without need for words.

Finally, Ambassador Peltonen spoke up with a gentle and soft voice directed to Elena. "You are very welcome here, Miss Marikova. We have arranged a room for you while you are here with us. After you have rested, I would like to have an informal chat with you, perhaps tomorrow. You will take your meals with us, of course. We shall also see that you get fresh clothing and, for that matter, whatever else you may need."

Elena replied, "Thank you, sir. I am most grateful for your help and hospitality." Koskinen noticed at once that her voice was weak and tremulous, not the strong and focused voice that she had had formerly.

The Ambassador added, "I think our nurse should accompany you to your room." Turning to Koskinen he said, "If you want to go to her room, you should feel free to do so."

"Yes, I would like to do that if it is not too much of a strain on Elena," Koskinen replied.

Elena overheard the conversation and said in a very weak voice, "It will be alright for Timo to visit with me." Elena had forgotten to use Koskinen's pseudonym. It did not cause a stir among those present.

When Elena arrived in her room, she was helped by the nurse from the wheelchair to a cushioned, upholstered chair in the room. Koskinen stood by while the nurse examined the bandage dressings on Elena's face and hands. The nurse went on to remove Elena's slippers which she wore when she arrived at the Embassy. She wore no sox or stockings, but her feet were bandaged also.

"When were these dressings applied?" the nurse inquired.

"Last evening," Elena replied.

"Well, they are secure, so we'll just leave them in place for the present. Call me if you need me," the nurse said as she left.

Elena and Koskinen were then alone in the room. Koskinen walked over to Elena and taking her gently by the shoulders as if she were some fragile flower, bent down and tenderly kissed her on the lips.

"I have missed you and worried about you so much since you were arrested, Elena dear, my dear, dear Elena." Koskinen's voice cracked, his throat tightened and there were tears in his eyes. "What have they done to you?" His look at Elena expressed total compassion.

In almost a whisper, Elena said, "Timo, I have been through something worse than hell."

"Yes, I can imagine."

"Timo, you will not like me anymore. I am not the same person you knew before I was arrested." Elena spoke in a low monotone. She appeared exhausted even at this early hour of the morning.

"No, that will never happen, Elena my dearest. I shall love you always no matter what has happened and no matter how you are." Koskinen was sincerely grieving. "You are tired. Why don't you just rest and be quiet? I'll sit here beside you."

"I'm tired, but there are a few things I would like to tell you."

Koskinen then and there decided that whatever Elena told him he would not make a big thing out of it or show any shock or horror. He instinctively knew that to show acceptance of her condition would be reassuring and comforting to her. So he steeled himself to listen.

"Timo," Elena began, "those beasts have mutilated me." Elena paused for breath as if disinclined to proceed. Koskinen sought to help her tell her story.

"In what way, Elena?"

"They cut off this ear." She pointed to the bandaged side of her face. And she looked at Koskinen to see his reaction, to see if there was any revulsion on his part. His expression was one of sympathy and tenderness and to give her help, he replied, "We have good restorative surgeons in Finland. I'm sure they'll be able to do something for you."

Elena smiled wanly and continued. "They also pulled out my fingernails and toenails. The pain was unbearable. It still hurts so badly." Elena held up her bandaged hands.

"Those animals! Those bastards! If I could only get my hands on them!" Koskinen was enraged. But he controlled his anger in order not to unduly excite Elena.

"What else, Elena?"

"The first two days I was there for interrogation. I was raped several times by different men. I couldn't fight back because they held me down." Koskinen just shook his head in dismay.

"When they were mutilating me and raping me, they were laughing and making vulgar remarks."

"Anything else, Elena?" ... as if there could be anything else.

"No, that was it. That was more than enough?"

"What about Lieutenant Valentnikov?" Koskinen inquired.

"I have heard that the day after our arrest he was interrogated at the prison as I was, but he was beaten and tortured and then taken to a certain room and shot. That is all I know." Elena's voice was still hollow and dead sounding.

"Well, Elena, even though our mission was not accomplished, you are still alive. You'll get better as time goes on." Koskinen was still trying to demonstrate optimism for Elena's sake.

"I am alive, yes, but I think that perhaps death would be preferable. I am so depressed and discouraged. I have thought, even now, of suicide."

"No, you must not say or think that way, Elena. There is hope and there is love, my love."

"Timo, you have been so kind. Yes, knowing you love me does sustain me. I hope it is enough to keep me going."

"Why don't you rest now? I'll stay here with you. I'll awaken you for lunch."

"Alright." Elena got up and hobbled her way to the bed and lay down, closed her eyes and soon fell asleep.

Koskinen watched her closely, grateful that she was with him, but sad that this lovely young lady had become such a tragic figure as a result of being brutalized. Soon, likewise exhausted from lack of sleep, Koskinen, too, dozed off. It was then about ten-thirty hours.

About an hour later, Koskinen was awakened by a knock on the door. The nurse entered carrying some clean clothing for Elena. Koskinen and the nurse decided to let Elena sleep through lunch. They could always get something from the kitchen later for Elena when she awakened.

At lunch, Ambassador Peltonen invited Koskinen to join him at the dining table along with Kalle Nevakivi, the Ambassador's aide. The Ambassador inquired about Elena.

"How is she?"

"She's sleeping, poor girl."

Koskinen proceeded to relate what Elena had told him about her treatment at Lefortovo Prison and her disfigurement.

As he listened, Ambassador Peltonen shook his head from time to time as if finding it difficult to believe the description. Both he and Nevakivi were horrified. They had heard stories of torture and mistreatment at Russian prisons, especially at Lefortovo, but, then, it had been impersonal and distant. Now, with Elena at the Embassy, the terror pervading Russian society was brought home in stark reality.

"Can you imagine what will happen to us if Russia invades Finland?" remarked Nevakivi. "I shudder to even think about it."

"We shall have to fight them for every inch of our soil," Koskinen retorted. "That is why it is so unfortunate that I was unable to accomplish my mission here. The elimination of Stalin would have solved the problem. I thought we were on the verge of success in working with the underground. Somebody informed on us. I wish I knew who it was."

"Maybe someday we'll find out," Nevakivi offered.

"It will be too late," Koskinen said in a tone of resignation.

"I still have to resolve the problem of what to do with Elena," the Ambassador mused. "I suppose I could contact the Soviet Foreign Office to request that she be allowed to go to Finland."

"Yes, if we can get her into Finland, that would be an answer to her medical and emotional problems," Koskinen said.

The Ambassador looked at Koskinen and smiled. He was aware that Koskinen had his own emotional entanglement with Elena. But, he said nothing.

After lunch, Koskinen went back to Elena's room and sat and watched over her. She was still sleeping, but very restless and, occasionally, groaning as if having a bad dream. At about mid-afternoon she awakened, at first very drowsily. She saw Koskinen and held out a bandaged hand to him. He came over to her bed and sat down beside her and gently grasped her arm.

"Timo, could you ask the nurse if she has something for pain? And I am a little bit hungry." Her voice was almost a whisper and Koskinen thought that, in spite of hours of sleep, Elena still was obviously weak and exhausted.

"I'll be back shortly," Koskinen said as he arose to leave to comply with Elena's requests.

He found the nurse and reported Elena's need for counteracting the pain.

"I have something that might help," the nurse responded. "I'll also look at her bandages. They may need to be replaced. It probably would be best for you to not be in the room when I do so. It may not be a pretty sight and Elena may prefer right now that you not see her condition."

"Yes, you're right. In the meantime, I'll put something together for her to eat," Koskinen replied. "When you're through, come into the kitchen and let me know."

About forty-five minutes later, the nurse appeared at the kitchen. Koskinen had heated a bowl of potato soup and was ready with a tray of bread, butter and a few pieces of makkara (Finnish sausage).

The nurse was somber and appeared worried. "Elena is not in very good shape. That ear wound is very bad. She needs more medical attention than I can give her. I'm afraid infection will set in unless she receives the proper care."

"I'll talk to the Ambassador. We'll have to get her into a hospital as soon as possible," Koskinen said. He, too, now became worried. He returned to Elena's room with the tray of food. He said nothing about the nurse's concerns and his own. There was no need to alarm Elena. Instead, he spoke a few encouraging words. As she ate, Elena said very little except to repeat her gratitude for the hospitality shown her by the Finnish Embassy.

In a sort of casual, offhand way, Koskinen remarked, "I wish we knew who it was that informed on us and ruined our plans. I keep reviewing all the people I've met and come to know during this project and I can't come up with anyone whom I would suspect might be guilty of giving information to the police."

Elena looked directly and intensely at Koskinen. To Koskinen, her visage had suddenly transformed to reflect a dark, virulent recollection of her recent ordeal.

"I know who did it, Timo."

Koskinen, not expecting that answer, was startled.

"You know?" He was incredulous.

"Yes."

"Who?"

"Lozovsky!"

"Sholom Lozovsky, the Jew?" Koskinen's surprise was overwhelming. "How do you know that, Elena?"

"I'll tell you, but let me finish eating first." There was no further conversation while Elena ate what she could except that Koskinen kept muttering to himself, "Lozovsky, Lozovsky! I can't believe it."

Finally, Elena put aside her tray and moved laboriously to a chair. She began to relate about Lozovksy.

"After Sergei and I were arrested we were taken to NKVD headquarters where we were registered, our photographs taken and some general questions asked about where we were born, our education and so on. Then we were taken to Lefortovo Prison. Sergei and I were separated and I did not see him again. It was still early in the day. I was taken to a room where I was interrogated. There were three men in the room. One of them was Lozovsky. I was very surprised, but he was not dressed like the two policemen and I, at first, thought he was a prisoner like myself and to be interrogated. When I entered the room, I saw him and he saw me. Neither of us gave any sign of recognition nor did we say anything that would have indicated we knew each other. However, I found out very soon why he was there." Elena paused to catch her breath and to gather some strength to go on.

Koskinen said, "Elena, if it is too much for you to talk about this, then don't do so. You can tell me about it some other time."

"No, I'd like to tell you now."

Elena proceeded slowly. "The interrogators would ask me questions about the underground and who was involved. I, at first, told them some general things about the underground, things they probably already knew. The interrogator would turn to Lozovsky and ask, 'Is that correct?' Whenever I gave an answer Lozovsky would answer 'yes' or 'no,' mostly 'yes.' At the end of the first two hours, the interrogators asked Lozovsky what else they should ask. He made some suggestions. I don't recall what they were."

Again Elena paused, rested a few moments and then continued. "The first day of interrogation went well. That is, the interrogators were respectful. There was no abuse or roughness. I was taken to a cell which I had to myself. I was still very fearful but thought that maybe I was to be treated differently from what I knew about how they abused prisoners. However, from time to time I heard screams which I knew were coming from other prisoners. I could hear them screaming, 'No, no, stop it! Don't do that, please, please!' and some more screams. It was terrible. That first night, a police officer, a young fellow, came to my cell. The guard let him in and then closed the cell door. The officer was soft-spoken. He said he had seen me and was attracted to me and that he'd like to make love. I told him 'no.' He insisted and finally grabbed me and put me down on the cot and ...!" Elena hesitated. "He raped me. I didn't put up any resistance. I knew it would be useless to do so. But, Timo, I never consented. You must understand that." Elena seemed on the verge of crying and was overwrought at reciting her ordeal.

"I do understand, dear Elena. I do not criticize you or hold it against you." Koskinen was inwardly beside himself with sorrow for Elena. But he decided to let Elena judge whether she wanted to continue.

"The next day, Timo, things were for the worse. I was questioned for hours until I was on the verge of collapse from exhaustion. Even then, they took turns questioning me. They had me stand most of the time. I had no food except some bread and cheese for breakfast and some potato soup and bread in the evening. Lozovsky was present again that second day. When I refused to tell them who was in the movement, they shouted curses at me, slapped me in the face and threatened to shoot me. I still refused. That evening, another officer came to my cell and raped me. It was awful, Timo."

"Do you want to go on like this, Elena?" Koskinen's concern for Elena was increasing.

"Yes."

Elena took a deep breath and continued. "The third day was the beginning of the torture. To make me talk about who was in the underground they tied my wrists and ankles to the chair I was sitting on. Then they started to pull out my fingernails. The pain was so excruciating that I must have passed out several times. They revived me each time with cold water. They were laughing and joking as they worked on me. They continued to curse me and threaten me. After that they released me from the chair, threw me on the floor and the two men, different ones this time, raped me. They laughed and told Lozovsky to go ahead with me. But Lozovsky said, 'no.' They urged him to rape me but he continued to decline."

"He had some morals left," Koskinen observed sarcastically.

"That evening Lozovsky came to my cell. The guard let him in thinking he would do what the others did the nights before I suppose. But he didn't. Instead he came in and started to cry. He said he was sorry that he was forced to be a part of my torture. He pleaded for my understanding and said he never thought they would treat me so badly. I asked him if he had been informing the police about the underground. He said he had and that he had been doing so for several months. I asked why he had betrayed us. He said that the police had been watching him and his apartment and that they knew that his apartment was being used for underground meetings. The police told him that he and his wife would be arrested and punished severely unless he became an informer in the underground. He said that the police also told him unless he did as he was told, every Jew in Moscow would be arrested and either shot or sent to labor camps. Lozovsky confessed to me that to save the Jewish people as well as himself and Fanni, he had agreed to the police demands. He said he told the police who was involved with the underground, where each member lived and he told them of our plans to assassinate Stalin by the use of poison. You can see, Timo, why our plans failed."

"So," Koskinen summarized, "Lozovsky betrayed us in order to save himself, his wife and the other Moscow Jews. Why didn't you tell him to leave your cell, to get out when you saw the extent of his betrayal?"

"I did," replied Elena. "He was sniveling and groveling to the extent that I was disgusted. I told him I despised him and would kill him if I could. I told him he was responsible for many lives lost. I told him to get out of my cell."

"Do you know if Lozovsky is still at the prison?" Koskinen asked.

"He was there the next day when they interrogated me and continued to torture me. But, after my mutilation ended, I did not see him again."

"Did you ask Lozovsky about Valentnikov?"

"Yes, I did. He told me that Sergei had undergone questioning and had been shot for his role in the underground."

"The poor fellow!" Koskinen remarked.

"Did they tell you why they were sending you here to the Finnish Embassy?" Koskinen was curious.

"Yes. They said that by sending me here in my condition that they would give a message to this Embassy not to ever again get involved with plots against the Soviet government. They said that other foreign Embassies would get the message through word of mouth. I'm an example of what can happen if they get involved."

"Well, Elena, you need medical attention for your wounds. We'll see that you get to a hospital."

"Frankly, Timo, I don't trust Russian hospitals and Russian doctors. If the police want me dead, the doctors will carry it out, otherwise they too, will be arrested."

"Well, we shall have to take that chance," Koskinen said. "The nurse said that we don't have the facilities here to give you the care you need. I think if the Finnish Embassy says it's interested in your well-being, the doctors may do what they should as professionals."

"I guess I have no choice," Elena said in resignation. "I'm going to lie down again, Timo. I'm tired."

"Of course, I'll stay with you while you rest. I will, however, first see that arrangements are made for you to visit a hospital Then I'll be back here."

Koskinen had the nurse accompany him to see Ambassador Peltonen. The nurse could describe Elena's condition and the need for medical attention. After listening to the nurse and Koskinen's plea for the Ambassador to call the hospital, the Ambassador suggested a different approach.

"I think we should get Dr. Fodorov, the doctor whom we call in when someone here needs medical attention, to come over and take a look at Elena before we send her off to a hospital. I don't like the idea of her going to a hospital here. There has been some information circulated that doctors have been ordered to kill certain patients through poisoning or otherwise. If Dr. Fodorov can treat Elena here, it will be much safer for her. She is a lovely person and I, too, don't want her to be subjected to further abuse." Koskinen and the nurse agreed.

The Ambassador forthwith got Dr. Fodorov on the telephone. The doctor replied that he would be over that evening. Koskinen returned to Elena.

"Elena, the doctor we use for medical problems here at the Embassy will be over to see you this evening. The Ambassador felt that it would be best to have him evaluate your condition and decide what to do."

"Is the doctor a Russian?" Elena asked.

"Yes, of course."

Elena did not look very happy to learn that.

"We consider him quite capable and learned in his profession," Koskinen said noting Elena's skeptical look and wanting to assure her that she would receive good medical advice and treatment.

Elena said nothing further, seemingly resigned to whatever befell her. Koskinen was aware that the zest and vital force that formerly distinguished Elena was no longer evident. He hoped its absence was only temporary.

When Dr. Fodorov arrived that evening at the Embassy, Koskinen met him at the door and escorted him to Ambassador Peltonen's office where both the Ambassador and Koskinen described Elena's ordeal and her physical condition. The doctor shook his head in dismay.

"I am not surprised at what you are telling me," the doctor commented in Russian which Koskinen translated for the Ambassador. "In our medical circles we have known about these tortures by the police. Even some doctors have been subjected to it and have later disappeared. I speak to you in confidence when I say that I'm sorry that the underground has failed to rid us of our tyrant. Right now Russia is in the grip of a universal paranoia. The Russia I love has become a charnel house, a house of death." The doctor shuddered at the thought.

The doctor was a tall, quite lanky individual. He possessed sharp features accentuated by a Leninisque goatee and pince-nez glasses. He is, Koskinen thought, the epitome of dignity and reserve that one would expect of a professional and learned person. The doctor wore a dark, somber suit that was neatly pressed unlike the loose fitting, baggy garments worn by most Russian men. Koskinen surmised that the doctor was in his early sixties and was a product of the Tsarist era when coarseness, crudity and vulgarity were shunned by the upper classes and the educated.

The Embassy nurse guided the doctor to Elena's room where he proceeded to examine Elena's wounds, to clean and re-bandage them. He spoke gently and reassuringly to Elena.

"You will be alright, Miss Marikova. You will take some time to heal, but you must be patient. I will leave some morphine with the nurse in case you experience a great deal of pain. I am going to prescribe cod liver oil and you are to take a tablespoon with each meal. That is, three times a day. This will help to protect you from infection. You will continue to take it until your healing is complete. You should drink plenty of milk each day. I am also going to ask the Ambassador to arrange to have you brought to my office every other day for violet ray treatments. Violet rays stimulate blood circulation which encourages healing faster. Do you understand?"

Elena nodded and replied, "Yes."

The doctor turned to the nurse. "You understand what must be done?"

"Yes."

"And I suggest that you change the bandages daily," the doctor advised the nurse.

The doctor left the room to return to the Ambassador and Koskinen while the nurse remained behind to comfort Elena.

In the office of the Ambassador, Doctor Fodorov discussed Elena's condition and the treatment he had prescribed.

"Miss Marikova is not in very good condition, both physically and mentally. She is devastated emotionally. She is in an extreme state of fear and panic and that will retard her physical healing. She needs to be in an environment where she can feel safe and secure. Here at the Embassy helps, of course, but she is still in Russia. She should be hospitalized, but I hesitate to recommend that."

"Why?" asked Koskinen.

"First, she will certainly not feel safe and secure there," replied the doctor, "and, secondly, while the treatment in a hospital is better than what I can give in my office, our hospitals do not have the trained surgeons and the up-to-date equipment to repair the injuries sustained by Miss Marikova. People don't realize how primitive medical care in Russia is compared, for example, to that in Germany and the United States."

"Well, then," Koskinen said, "perhaps we could send her to Finland." When he said this, he looked at the Ambassador. Peltonen showed no reaction.

"Yes, Finland has a very good medical system," Doctor Fodorov observed. "It is on a par with Germany in that respect."

Ambassador Peltonen spoke up. "Don't you get discouraged trying to practice medicine here, Doctor?"

"Yes, I do, but what can I or anyone do about it?" The doctor shrugged his shoulders and then answered his own question. "Nothing. We don't even try to suggest any sort of change because the government might construe it as an anti-government expression and you know where that would lead. We'd end up like Miss Marikova or worse."

After Doctor Fodorov had departed from the Embassy, Koskinen and Ambassador Peltonen sat for several minutes in the latter's office without speaking. They seemed to be mulling over the entire predicament in which they found themselves with regard to Elena. Finally the Ambassador broke the silence.

"I think, Timo, what we shall do is to follow the doctor's medical advice for the next ten days or so while I see what can be done to get Elena to Finland."

Koskinen was startled by the Ambassador's suggestion about having Elena go to Finland. He had not expected the Ambassador to go to that length. To Koskinen it was obvious that the Ambassador was deeply affected personally by Elena's adversities.

"How do you expect to do that?" Koskinen asked. He was elated that the Ambassador had picked up on the suggestion he had made earlier.

"First, of course, I'll have to discuss it with our authorities and if they approve we can then issue her a visa. However, we'll have to arrange for the Soviet government to issue a passport to her. That may be very difficult to do. But, we have to try, don't we?"

The Ambassador paused as if to review in his mind the propriety of the procedure he had just outlined. Then he added, "I think it would be best if we not mention our plan to try to get Elena to Finland to her. I think you'll agree that we should not raise her hopes if we cannot get it done. It would just add to her disappointments."

"Yes, I agree," replied Koskinen.

"Timo, why don't you undertake to arrange for Elena to go to the doctor's office for her violet ray treatments? You should also make the appointments with Dr. Fodorov. I'll keep you informed about how things go in getting Elena to Finland. The nurse will keep me informed as to Elena's physical condition."

"Thank you, Mr. Ambassador. I appreciate your interest in this very trying matter." Koskinen left the Ambassador's room and made his way directly to Elena's room. As he quietly let himself into the room he found Elena sleeping. He sat down in a chair and watched Elena for any signs of stirring because of pain or discomfort. As time passed, Koskinen dozed off. He was awakened by Elena groaning and preparing to sit up on the side of her bed.

"Are you in pain?"

"Yes."

"I shall call the nurse," Koskinen volunteered. "She can give you some morphine."

"No, please Timo. I would rather endure the pain, at least for a while, than to take that stuff."

"You should have some food. I can get you something from the kitchen."

"No. I'm not hungry."

"You must eat if you are to get better. I'll see what there is and I'll be back shortly."

Elena did not offer further resistance. She felt too weak to protest.

******

For the next week, the Embassy staff gave special sympathetic attention to Elena. Her ordeal was almost the exclusive subject of conversation. The nurse faithfully changed bandages and saw to it that Elena took her cod liver oil. She also kept her clean by daily sponge baths. The cook made special broths and other foods that were tasty to encourage Elena to eat. Koskinen outdid himself spending all his waking hours with Elena. Every other day he accompanied Elena in the Embassy limousine to Dr. Fodorov's office where she was examined by the doctor and received violet ray treatments.

The doctor had equipment which he explained was a Master Violet Ray High Frequency Wand which was passed over Elena's body as it gave off the rays.

"It will help the healing process," the doctor said.

Elena said she felt better after the treatments. Koskinen was skeptical of the effects of the rays, but as long as Elena felt better, he was pleased and said nothing. He was of the opinion that nature was doing its normal healing and not the rays.

By the end of the week, the bulky bandages around Elena's fingers and toes were no longer necessary and only light bandages were applied to protect the exposed, sensitive flesh. The loss of the ear, however, remained a problem. The wound was still oozing fluid and infection was always a threat. The nurse and the doctor gave it especial attention and care. It was, however, the emotional scarring that soon became evident. As Elena began to feel somewhat better physically, she became more aware of the disfigurement. She was disturbed and embarrassed by what the wound would look like when no longer bandaged. She knew she could not wear a bandage forever. She thought people would stare at her and even try to avoid her because her condition would make it difficult for them not to show pity. And Elena did not want pity. Even with all her pain and her rape and torture still vivid in her mind, Elena, like many women, had her pride.

Above all this emotional turmoil in which she found herself, Elena feared that she would lose Koskinen's love because he would find her affliction repugnant and odious. Although she perceived his devotion to her now during the present trying times, she believed that once she had recovered he would then leave her. That thought troubled her but she did not reveal her fears to Koskinen. She knew she would never beg or implore him to not leave. She would never whine or grovel. She had her pride and her fortitude would return whatever her physical condition.

At the end of the week, Ambassador Peltonen called Koskinen into his office.

"Timo, our Foreign Office has approved granting a visa to Elena so that she may receive medical treatment in Finland. I'm sure you're happy to hear that. The Soviet Foreign Office sent me an application form for a passport which Elena will have to complete and return for processing. I'll give it to you and you can have her fill it out."

"Knowing how the Soviet administration works," Koskinen said, "it could be months before we hear back from them."

"No, I think they'll act on it quickly knowing that we're interested," the Ambassador replied with candid assurance.

Koskinen was afraid that while they were awaiting action by the Soviet authorities on Elena's application for a passport, he could be ordered out of the country as a persona non grata for having participated with the underground in a plot to get rid of Stalin. In fact, he thought it strange that such action had not already been taken. Governments generally don't put up with foreign embassy personnel who try to overthrow the host government. Such foreign diplomats or staff are ordered to leave the country immediately. The Soviet government must know about his involvement since Lozovsky had probably told them everything. Why was he, Koskinen, being allowed to stay even this long? It was a puzzle to Koskinen. The Ambassador had remarked about it as well when he spoke with Koskinen.

Another surprise occurred when a few days after Elena's application had been submitted to the Soviet Foreign Office, a courier or messenger from that office arrived at the Finnish Embassy to hand deliver Elena's passport. When the Ambassador informed Koskinen about the prompt receipt, Koskinen, while pleased, was further perplexed.

"Either you have tremendous influence with the Soviet Foreign Office, Mr. Ambassador, or there is some treachery going on."

"Well, don't worry about hidden meanings, Timo. Elena has her passport. That is what is important."

"I suppose you're right, Mr. Ambassador." In spite of this admission, Koskinen remained considerably alarmed.

"I would suggest that you get yourself ready to accompany Elena on the trip to Finland. Your mission is over and there is really nothing further for you to do here."

"Thank you, Mr. Ambassador. I'll do that."

The Ambassador continued, "I think you should have the nurse or one of our staff women buy some new clothing for Elena. We can pay for it out of a contingency fund. In the meantime, I'll call Dr. Fodorov and ask him if and when he thinks Elena is ready or will be for travel."

"Mr. Ambassador, I'm sure Elena appreciates all that you are doing to help her."

Ambassador Peltonen nodded. "Of course, I want to help. She's gone through hell." He then added, "I would suggest that you take the train to Leningrad and our legation there. I will arrange to have a limousine take you and Elena from Leningrad to the border and then on to Helsinki. Does that sound alright?"

"Yes, that's fine. An automobile gives us some options at the border."

"Well, don't go crashing through the border gates. You'll create a diplomatic crisis if you do that." The Ambassador appeared quite serious in his advice. "I'm willing to stick my neck out for Elena, but I don't want my head chopped off."

"I understand." Koskinen smiled at the allegory.

When Koskinen broke the news to Elena, her response was somber.

"I'm afraid to leave here, Timo."

"Why?"

"You don't know these people. They are sinister and cold-blooded schemers. What they give they can take away in a moment. They have a cunning purpose for everything they do. I don't trust them. Here in the Embassy I'm safe. Outside, I'm not."

"Elena, you need better medical attention than you can get here. Furthermore, you must realize that you cannot stay here forever. I'll be with you the entire trip." Koskinen spoke gently and, he hoped, persuasively.

"I appreciate that, Timo, but you can't hold off a half-dozen of these thugs if they decide to yank me out of the train or the auto."

"Elena, it's a chance we must take and it might as well be sooner than later." Koskinen found himself pleading with Elena.

"Well, I guess I have no choice. I suppose I'll have to pack a bottle of that fishy tasting cod liver oil."

"Yes, you should." Koskinen was relieved that Elena had resigned herself to leave.

For the following several days, some of the Embassy staff busied themselves buying some clothing and a traveling bag for Elena, arranging for train tickets for her and Koskinen and making up a small medical kit containing extra bandages, adhesive tape and a small bottle of cod liver oil. Morphine was not included. Koskinen spent a good part of each day walking with Elena within the Embassy compound and sitting and talking with her until she tired and expressed a desire to rest.

In the course of one of the conversations Koskinen mused, "I wonder what has happened to the other people in the underground. I hope they got away in time. Viktor, Yosif, Boris, Petrov, Akmal. They were all fine human beings. And all the others."

Elena had her memory suddenly jogged. "Oh, I forgot completely to tell you that Akmal told Sergei that it was Boris who had betrayed us. Obviously, no one suspected Lozovsky at the time."

"What let them to believe it was Boris?" Koskinen asked. "I can't imagine Boris being a traitor."

"I have no idea how they came to think Boris was the culprit," replied Elena. "However, I'm sure that they thought they had good evidence. Our people would not accuse someone of wrongdoing and punish him without having solid proof of the wrongdoing. After all, that kind of trial without proof is what we were fighting against."

"What you're saying, Elena, is that Boris and Lozovsky are both informers for the police."

"Well," Elena responded, "I personally saw Lozovsky but I don't know about Boris. I wasn't there. But, mistakes can be made when people are angry. I accepted the accusation against Boris until I saw Lozovksy with the people who interrogated me. I hope Boris is alright."

"Yes," observed Koskinen, "he could have been shot by his own people if they were convinced he informed on them."

On the latest visit to Dr. Fodorov, the doctor told Elena she could travel, but to be careful not to re-injure the ear wound.

"You are fortunate to have Mr. Salonen to travel with you." The doctor admonished Elena to take her prescribed doses of cod liver oil. "And don't be afraid to have help in changing your bandages. You'll be alright."

Koskinen had not written to his wife, Anna, for the past two weeks. He was preoccupied by his concerns for Elena. On the day before he and Elena were to leave for Leningrad, Ambassador Peltonen asked Koskinen about notifying Anna.

"I shall be glad to telephone our Foreign Office in Helsinki, Timo, and have them contact Mrs. Koskinen to let her know you're leaving for Finland. Would you want me to do that?"

"No, Mr. Ambassador, I appreciate your offer, but, under the circumstances, I would prefer to call my wife when I arrive in Helsinki."

The Ambassador guessed that the "circumstances" Koskinen referred to was Elena.

At dinner that evening, the entire staff gathered in the dining room and, with one of them playing an accordion, sang the Finnish National Anthem and then a spokesman said farewell to Elena on behalf of the staff.

"We Finns," said the spokesman, "admire and respect the kind of courage that you have demonstrated. Cowardice is not in our nature even as it is not in yours. We are survivors and so are you. With these qualities that you have shown you will be welcome in Finland."

Elena was deeply moved by the sentiments expressed by the staff. She arose at the table for a moment and said, "Thank you so much for your kindness and help since I have been here. I shall never forget you." She then sat down while the staff applauded respectfully.

After dinner Koskinen helped Elena pack her new traveling bag and finished packing his own. Both he and Elena were extremely tired, primarily from the stress and tension knowing that the next morning they would be leaving the Embassy. Koskinen went to his own room and soon was asleep.

Koskinen was awakened by his alarm clock at 0600 hours and quickly went to Elena's room to awaken her. He found her already dressing.

"I did not sleep much, Timo, so I decided to get up and get dressed."

"We have to be at the train station at 0800 hours," Koskinen said. "We'll have some breakfast and then leave. I'll see you shortly. Are you feeling alright?"

"Yes."

At breakfast Koskinen and Elena sat with Ambassador Peltonen upon his invitation. The conversation was quite naturally about the common interest of the underground movement and the Finnish mission to get rid of Stalin.

The Ambassador remarked, "While it is true we didn't eliminate Stalin, you should not consider that the mission failed entirely. Your underground, Elena, has demonstrated to the Soviet authorities, the NKVD specifically, that an opposition group can organize and exist in a system that prides itself on its ability to suppress such movements before they gain influence among the citizenry. They have to fear that such a movement can arise again and, perhaps, even gain control of the government. A vicious system such as there now exists in the Soviets cannot subdue and subjugate a people forever. We saw that in the 1917 revolution of Lenin."

Koskinen observed after listening to the Ambassador that "until Lenin came along with his Bolshevik organization, the Russian people must have thought that the frequently cruel Tsarist system would last forever after centuries of rule."

"My point is," the Ambassador persisted, "that there was an eventual change and your underground may be regarded as a harbinger of such a change. So don't feel that you've lost."

Elena commented, "It's good of you to say that, Mr. Ambassador, but it is my opinion that until Stalin is dead there is little, if any, hope that there will be a change in our system of government. Even at his death, there is the danger that another ruthless tyrant will come to power. I cannot, at this moment, believe another underground movement will form."

Koskinen interrupted this conversation by calling attention to the time. "I think we should get ready to leave. Juhani must be waiting at the gate to drive us to the railroad station. Elena, you have all of your papers, your passport, visa, your medical records?"

"Yes."

"Good! Well, Mr. Ambassador, we shall say 'Good bye' and thank you for all you have done. I'm sure our Foreign Office will let you know when we have arrived."

"Yes, I'm sure. And our legation at Leningrad has been notified of your coming and will also let me know when you arrive there. I wish you both a safe journey. I'll accompany you to the door."

As Koskinen had guessed, Juhani, the Embassy chauffeur was waiting at the gate and standing at the side of the limousine.

With another exchange of farewells with the Ambassador, Elena, Koskinen and Juhani got into the automobile and departed for the railway station. It was about ten kilometers from the Embassy to the Moscow Station. Very little was said during the ride. Both Koskinen and Elena appeared to be in deep thought and Juhani was the epitome of Embassy driver decorum. He spoke only when addressed.

When they arrived at the railway station they found many soldiers gathered in groups but very few civilians in the station. Koskinen surmised that the soldiers were being transported to various parts of the country and as for civilians Elena mentioned that very few were permitted by the government authorities to travel from one city or village to another. Some of the soldiers stared at them as if they were some sort of novelty or curiosity.

"I suppose," commented Koskinen to Elena, "that the only civilians they see at railway stations are those being sent to Siberia or some labor camps. They are probably wondering how we can be traveling independently."

"Who cares what these poor devils think. These soldiers are treated with no more consideration for their lives than anyone else living in this hellish country." Elena sounded bitter and Koskinen thought to himself that she had every right to sound that way in view of her experience.

A gate separated the public waiting area from the platform where passengers were to board the trains. At the gate stood a uniformed security agent who checked any civilians who presented themselves to enter the platform area. Koskinen showed his Finnish passport which stated his diplomatic status. He was passed through quickly by the agent. Elena showed her citizen identification card issued by the government to all Soviet citizens. She also presented her passport.

"Are you going to Leningrad?" the agent confirmed of Elena. He was gruff, grim and businesslike.

"Yes."

"That is your home?"

"Yes."

"What is your work?"

"I am a translator in the Finnish language."

Koskinen was waiting for Elena on the other side of the gate. He was concerned about the interrogation by the agent.

"You and this fellow here are traveling together?" The agent pointed to Koskinen.

"Yes."

Koskinen intervened. "We are traveling together because I am going to the Finnish legation in Leningrad. This young lady has served as a translator at the Finnish Embassy here in Moscow and her duties have ended and she is going home. There is nothing more to it than that. If you keep asking these questions, we shall miss our train." Koskinen was getting perturbed.

The agent apparently did not appreciate Koskinen's intervention. His face acquired a sour expression and he said nothing for a few moments as he seemed to think about what he should do next. Finally, he spoke to Elena. "You can pass through but we'll keep your passport. You will get it again when you arrive in Leningrad."

"If you keep my passport here, how will I get it when I arrive in Leningrad?"

"I'll give it to one of the police who will be on the train. He will know who you are."

Koskinen and Elena decided that the matter was settled and were glad to have been passed through by the agent. They proceeded down the platform to the train to Leningrad which was already waiting, its locomotive hissing and blowing out white steam. Koskinen and Elena walked hurriedly to where a conductor stood just outside a car door.

To make certain that they were in the right place, Koskinen asked the conductor, "This train is going to Leningrad?"

"Yes."

With that, Koskinen and Elena boarded and found a seat in the mostly empty car and settled down for the trip.

"Well, Elena, we've gotten through one more obstacle. There will be others, I'm sure, before we cross over to Finland. We'll just keep at it." Koskinen tried to appear unworried about the final outcome of the trip for the sake of Elena's peace of mind. Within himself he was very apprehensive. The Russian authorities were capable of unpredictable malevolence.

There was not a great deal of conversation between them. Koskinen and Elena were happy just to be with each other even though both were aware of the uncertainties that might arise. In the course of the ride to Leningrad, Koskinen mentioned his infrequent dream experiences with the seagull.

"It seems," he said, "that whenever I have a dream about the seagull something catastrophic or violent happens soon afterwards. I don't understand it. The dream seems to be a warning. The last time I dreamed of it, the seagull died at my feet. That never occurred before. And then came the failure of our mission and all of the happenings to you. The seagull in my dreams seems like a bird of ill omen. It is, to me, something supernatural that defies explanation."

Elena listened in rapt interest.

"Yes," she said, "it does seem strange. People, humans, have always tried to understand and interpret their dreams. How do they arise? What is their purpose or function? I guess to comprehend dreams you have to know how the brain works. Who knows? Perhaps our whole existence is a dream. We pass from nighttime dreams into daytime dreams. Right now, Timo, I believe I'm perhaps dreaming a nightmare."

Koskinen nodded. "Yes, it's all very complex, isn't it?"

They fell into contemplative silence.

The Finnish Embassy kitchen staff had bagged some sandwiches for them in the realization that food was not available on Soviet trains. And, if it was, it would be hardly edible. So, about the noon hour, Koskinen and Elena shared the sandwiches of cheese, glad to have something to nibble on as well as to take up their time.

The Soviet train was no exception to the rule of expected stops at unexpected times and places. The conductor had collected their tickets and he and some policemen came down the aisle from time to time, apparently to check on people and things. Both Koskinen and Elena had short, fitful naps during the trip. These did them little good. At the time they arrived in Leningrad, they were very tired. Ever present was their fear that at any moment something ominous could occur that would dash their plans. Nothing untoward did happen on the trip to Leningrad. As the train pulled into the station, the policeman who had been assigned to the trip handed Elena her passport. He said nothing except, "Be careful, behave yourself." Elena thought he had a friendly smile as he turned and left.

As Koskinen and Elena alighted from the train with their traveling valises, a young man approached them.

"Are you, by chance, Timo Koskinen?" The young man spoke in Finnish. Surprised at the use of his true name while in Russia and somewhat suspicious, Koskinen did not admit to his identity, but replied, "Who are you?"

The young man replied cordially, "I am Toivo Sorvali. I am here from the Finnish legation to drive you and the young lady to the legation. We were given your and the young lady's descriptions so I had no difficulty in picking you out."

Koskinen smiled and said, "Yes, I am Timo Koskinen and this is Elena Marikova. You'll forgive me if I appeared to be hesitant to identify myself without knowing who you were."

"Oh, I understand," replied Sorvali. "We are in the Soviet Union." He chuckled pleasantly.

"Come, I'll show you to the automobile."

During the short ride, Sorvali carried on a cheery conversation. "I understand you are both on your way to Helsinki."

"Yes," Koskinen responded.

"You will be staying with us at the Legation for a few days?" Sorvali asked.

"We would like to move on as soon as possible," Koskinen explained. "Miss Marikova needs medical attention."

Sorvali nodded as if he had heard about Elena's ordeal. However, he made no comment. What, he must have thought, can one say to a person who has had such a horrific experience.

Instead, Sorvali said, "I understand our First Secretary, Paavo Leino, will discuss aspects of your trip from here to the border. I may be driving you."

When they arrived at the Legation building, First Secretary Leino greeted them. Koskinen had never visited the Finnish Legation in Leningrad before this and was surprised that it consisted of two older one story wood frame buildings that appeared to have been converted from private residences. It was surrounded by a wood fence with a guard gate at the front.

"It's not very impressive," Koskinen commented to Elena.

"No, it certainly doesn't attract attention. Except for a sign next to the gate and a Finnish flag flying over the building, you would not suspect that it was a Finnish agency," Elena replied.

"You have been here before, Elena?" asked Koskinen.

"Yes, when I had to help prepare Russian groups going to Finland for trade or other purposes. I know First Secretary Leino."

After the usual exchange of social amenities, Secretary Leino said, "One of our staff will conduct you to your rooms. If there is anything you need, let him know and we'll do what we can to meet it. You know everything is scarce here in Russia."

"When can we get on our way?" inquired Koskinen. "Elena needs medical attention."

"I'll discuss that with you tomorrow morning. I suggest that for now you both get some rest. Our dinner will be at 1830 hours. Please come and join me."

"Yes, we'll do that. Thank you." Koskinen was hungry but decided not to ask for anything to satisfy him until dinner.

Koskinen and Elena were conducted to their separate visitor rooms by a staff member. Both soon fell asleep, utterly weary from the train trip and the constant stress of fearing some official Russian intervention.

A knock on their respective doors awakened both Koskinen and Elena. The staff member who had conducted them to their rooms called out loudly enough to be heard through the closed doors. "Dinner will be served in a half-hour." Koskinen and Elena both responded with "Thank you." They were both hungry and looked forward to a meal of any kind.

At the dinner table with Secretary Leino, Koskinen related the experience he had had with the Russian underground in Moscow including his contact with the staff at the United States Embassy. Secretary Leino took in every word with evident acute interest.

Elena described how Lieutenant Valentnikov had been informed by Akmal that Boris was the traitor and how at Lefortovo Prison she discovered that it was Lozovsky who betrayed the movement.

"Obviously, the wrong man, Boris, was accused," the Secretary remarked. "The group must have punished him some way. It would be unusual if they did not. Did you find out if they did punish him?"

"No," replied Elena. "Perhaps some day we shall learn."

The Secretary at the end of dinner suggested they repair to his office.

"It is still early in the evening. If it is alright with you, perhaps we can discuss your trip to the border now instead of waiting until tomorrow as originally planned."

Koskinen looked at Elena. "Are you up to doing it now, Elena?"

"Yes. If I get tired, I'll let you know."

"Good!" said the Secretary. "Follow me."

The Secretary's office was anything but pretentious. A roll-top desk and a half-dozen plain wood chairs with tie-cushions on the seats, two metal floor lamps with stained parchment shades, a dark lamp and a well-worn light-blue wall-to-wall rug made up the essentials.

To describe First Secretary Paavo Leino is to describe a stereotypical bureaucrat. The Secretary, Koskinen judged, was in his fifties and had probably spent all if not most of his working life in government employment, the sort of jobs that require no self motivation or the exercise of initiative or a critical analysis of issues or problems. Such lower level jobs require only that you live by rules expounded by others and follow orders without question. Any attempts to use independent judgment is frowned upon by one's superiors. Koskinen was aware, of course, that he, too, was a government employee, but he was by no means a stifled bureaucrat. In his work in the Intelligence Section he had to use initiative and to be resourceful.

The First Secretary was a pleasant enough fellow, in Koskinen's opinion, but he had a bland, ordinary personality. There was nothing dynamic or charismatic about the man. He was, however, businesslike and efficient. When he spoke, he articulated well and precisely. No waste of words and no drift off to irrelevancies. He was, apparently, capable of maintaining his focus on the issue or problem at hand.

"The day after tomorrow we shall drive you to the border. So, tomorrow will be an opportunity for you to rest up for the trip. Sorvali will drive our limousine. He is competent and knows the roads in this area. I have been in touch with our Foreign Office in Helsinki and they have advised that you not attempt to cross the Russian border station leading to Viipuri."

"Why?" Koskinen asked.

"The customs agents and security guards at that station are known to be very tough. They examine and question everything in detail. With them there is always the risk that they will find some flaw in a passport or in identification papers and either detain you for hours or refuse to allow you out of the country."

"What do you suggest?" Koskinen inquired.

"The Foreign Office recommends that you go to Terijoki from the Russian border," the Secretary replied.

Elena spoke up. "Terijoki? I never heard of it. Where is it?"

Koskinen sought to explain. "Yes, I know about it. It is a small village off the Gulf of Finland somewhat south of Viipuri. It is known as a very beautiful beach resort. It is just a few kilometers from the Russian border."

Koskinen then asked the Secretary, "How do we get to Terijoki without first crossing the border?"

The Secretary replied, "There is a group of men in Terijoki who have organized to smuggle people from Russia into Finland, people who for some reason fear to go through the Russian border stations. They are usually Russian people who are being hunted by the Soviet police for their opposition to the government. The men in Terijoki hate the Russian government. They leave Terijoki by boat, small boats, and arrange to pick up the person or persons to be smuggled at a point on the Soviet side of the shore. When they're about a half-kilometer from the shore, they cut the boat motor and row the boat the rest of the way to shore."

"How do they know we're coming?" Koskinen asked.

"We have short wave radio communication. Sorvali knows the men and they know him. He's worked with them before this with a few smuggled people."

"Are there Russian patrols along the shores?" Koskinen asked.

"Not at night, generally."

"Is there any barbed wire or are there land mines on the Russian side along the shore?" Koskinen continued.

"There are no land mines in that area as far as we know, but there is wire. However, the underground has cut some holes in it and have restored it after they've gotten people through it so that the holes are not noticeable."

"After we get into Terijoki, assuming we do, where do we go from there. That is, how do we get to Helsinki?"

"The Finnish organization will pass you along to some small villages or farms for the first day or two. After that you will be met by some Finnish authorities who will either drive you to Helsinki or put you on a train for Helsinki."

Koskinen then motioned toward Elena. "Can you get a doctor or a nurse to come here tomorrow to change bandages and generally give Elena an updated examination for her physical condition? This should be done before she undertakes this trip to Terijoki."

The Secretary replied, "Yes, of course. I'm sure that we can do that. We have a doctor who takes care of our Legation staff when needed. If we can't get him for some reason, he has a nurse who has always been very accommodating."

"I'm glad to hear that," Koskinen said. He was somewhat relieved of his concern for Elena.

"Is there anything else I can take care of for you?" Secretary Leino asked.

"I can't think of anything other than I'd like to talk tomorrow with Toivo Sorvali, your driver. I just want to go over some things with him."

"Fine. I'll make him available during the morning."

"Do you fully trust him, that is, his loyalty to Finland, to the Legation and to the underground?"

"Yes, of course. Why do you ask?" The Secretary was puzzled by Koskinen's question.

"Well, we just don't want any more Lozovskys!" Koskinen said with a bitterness in his voice.

"You're safe with him. He has helped us and the Finnish underground on the border for some time. Furthermore, he despises the Soviet regime."

"So did Lozovsky." Koskinen could not help being sarcastic. "Well, we'll accept your word, Mr. Secretary. But, I still want to talk with him tomorrow morning."

Elena and Koskinen spent the rest of the evening sauntering around the small confines of the Legation and talking in the reception room. Elena said she was feeling better although still very much traumatized by her appearance. Koskinen persisted in giving her encouragement and solace and to urge her to turn to God. Her travails had readied Elena to turn to a higher spiritual power.

"I want to turn to God to give me the strength to endure my fate. But I feel so hypocritical doing so when I have rejected God for so many years."

"God welcomes those who turn to him in meekness and with supplication no matter how long they may have denied him. There is the story of the prodigal son in the New Testament of the Bible. It is the story of a young man who left home, was profligate and wild and when all his money was gone from riotous living came home with a fear that his family would reject him. Instead, he was welcomed by his father who forgave him and bestowed his love on his long lost son. So that tells you that God is Love and Love does not reject you but helps and aids your needs."

"I'll remember that," Elena said simply.

The next morning after breakfast Koskinen and Elena met with Sorvali. The driver brought out a map of the region and traced the route they would be following. The trip would be made at night and Sorvali explained the landmarks along the way. He also explained what Koskinen and Elena were to do when they arrived at their destination. They would be met by one or more of the Finnish men who would then take over and guide them. Sorvali would then leave and drive back to the Legation.

* * * * *

At the United States Embassy Bill Chance and Gene Wagner were making unhurried preparations to leave to return to the United States. Once they learned of the failure of the mission they had no purpose in remaining at the Embassy. However, they shared with Ambassador Hayes and Deputy Fraser Addison a concern for their Chief Translator, Sofia Kameneva. They were all cognizant of Sofia's predicament as a result of the disclosure to the NKVD of her membership in the underground. Finnish Ambassador Peltonen had described to Hayes what had happened to Elena after her arrest outside the Finnish Embassy. Ambassador Hayes had told Addison, Chance, Wagner and Sofia of Peltonen's description. They were all shocked.

"If Sofia steps outside our Embassy, she'll be arrested and then she is as good as dead," Wagner said.

"I agree," Chance added. "Sofia has said she wants to go to the United States. The answer to protecting her is for us to find some way to get her out of Russia and on her way to America."

"We have to take her with us when we leave here. She can't remain in the Embassy here forever," Wagner remarked.

Deputy Addison had an idea. "Perhaps we should change her identity. Give her a new name. Give her a United States passport under that name and make up a Soviet visa for her. We can claim her as a member of our diplomatic staff. She'll then have safe passage."

"Excellent idea, Fraser," enthused Wagner.

"We can fabricate the necessary forms for passport, visa and other identification papers," Addison suggested. "In a sense, Sofia will become an American citizen employed at our Embassy and now returning to America. It should not be difficult. Of course, there is always a risk, but it should be negligible compared to Sofia remaining in Russia." Addison seemed confident his plan would work.

Sofia eagerly adopted the idea. "Just think, I shall become an American overnight." She laughed and then added, "I'll take the risk."

Chance and Wagner also agreed that the plan was probably the best possible to get Sofia out of the country. However, Chance was more concerned than Wagner.

"There is no record in the hands of the Russians that Sofia, whatever name we give her, ever entered Russia as an American diplomatic staff member from the United States."

"I am counting that the Russian border agents won't know that and will assume that she had previously entered with proper authority," Addison replied, seeming not fazed by that problem.

Chance stated, "I'm assuming we'll be traveling by train to one of the countries on the western border of Russia."

Deputy Addison answered, "Yes, of course by train. Going by automobile is out of the question. Where would you stop overnight? Where can you count on getting gasoline for the car? Where can you be certain of getting food? In addition, some of the roads out in the country are practically just cow paths. Also, out in the country you could be set upon by robbers and you might be murdered or badly beaten. If you become ill for any reason, there are no doctors or hospitals around the countryside to call upon for help. No, the train is the only practical way."

"And they're terrible," added Wagner. "You can sit in nowhere with a mechanical breakdown for days."

"Well," Chance summarized, "I think that the train under the circumstances is the best way." He added, "I suppose our destination should be either Estonia or Finland?"

Deputy Addison said, "I would recommend Finland. Estonia is quite unstable at the moment. I have reports that Germany wants to make a non-aggression pact with Estonia. If that happens, I think the Soviets will send its troops into the country to protect its flank there. The Baltic States of Estonia, Latvia and Lithuania are very important to the Soviets if Germany should attack the Soviet Union. As you know, I've talked from time to time with Ambassador Peltonen of Finland and in the course of these conversations he mentioned that crossing the border with Finland on the Viipuri route hasn't presented any problem with diplomatic personnel. Finnish couriers come and go all the time."

"But, isn't the Soviet concerned about the proximity of Leningrad to the Finnish border and isn't the Soviet government demanding some sort of concessions from Finland so as to protect itself against a German invasion of Finland to attack and get a foothold in Leningrad?" Chance queried the Deputy.

"I don't know for sure," replied Addison, "but even if that were true, Finland is the only fairly safe and certainly the most stable country on the Soviet western border."

"Alright then," Chance concluded, "we'll take the train to Viipuri. I should think we can leave in a week."

"Why not sooner?" asked Wagner. "I'm ready to go now and I'm sure Sofia here is ready to leave within two or three days."

"Well, a week will give us time to prepare documents for Sofia and to undertake other preparations," said Addison.

"Alright, then it is agreed," said Chance, "train, Viipuri, one week. Thanks, Fraser."

As Chance, Wagner and Sofia left Deputy Addison's office, they agreed that they felt relief that decisions had been made to start the process going that would take them back to the United States.

"We have to travel light," Chance pointed out. "We can't be tied down with a lot of stuff." He added, "Once we reach Helsinki we can buy whatever basics we may need."

The next few days were spent packing and eating and sleeping. Ambassador Hayes had apparently endorsed the plan implicitly. Deputy Addison had informed him of the details of creating papers for Sofia. The Ambassador had not objected although he did not express manifest approval. The Ambassador had to protect himself from political criticism. Addison, an old hand at the Embassy, knew the rules of the game, so to speak.

It was now the last week of May 1939. Chance and Wagner had first arrived at the American Embassy in Russia on March 14, 1939. They had not known how long it would take to accomplish their mission to get rid of Stalin, but had assumed that it would not require more than a couple of months if at all. As the days and weeks passed, they realized that this was an unrealistic expectation. Now that the mission had failed and there was little or no hope that it could be revived, both Chance and Wagner were relieved that the matter had been resolved although not successfully. They could now return home.

In the almost three months that Chance and Wagner had been in the Soviet Union much had changed and was, in fact, rapidly changing politically in Europe and in the Soviet Union itself. The events were disturbing to the officials in the United States Embassy in Moscow.

The most ominous change occurred when on May 3, 1939, Stalin fired Maxim Litvinov, the moderate, pro-western Soviet Foreign Minister and appointed Vyacheslav Molotov. Molotov had a reputation for being hard, uncompromising, cruel and ruthless. He was one of the original leaders of the Bolsheviks in 1917 and was an early member of the Politburo. His loyalty to Stalin was unquestioned. For the most part, he was hostile and confrontational in his dealings with representatives of other countries including the United States and Finland.

Shortly after Chance and Wagner had arrived in Moscow, Hitler occupied Czechoslovakia territory and Lithuania had transferred its Memel area to Germany. The Soviet government was accusing Estonia and Latvia of committing abuses against Russians in their respective countries and was moving troops toward the borders of those countries. In April 1939, negotiations between Finland and the Soviets broke down when Finland rejected the Soviet demand for cessation of certain islands belonging to Finland although the Soviet government did not threaten Finland with any military action if concessions were not made.

Intelligence reports coming to the United States Embassy in April 1939 indicated that Stalin was seeking an agreement with Hitler for mutual non-aggression and the carving up of European nations between the two. Such reports, when received, created a stir of anxiety not only among the countries that might be carved up but in the United States as well. The United States government was of the opinion that such an agreement between the Soviets and Germany would lead to an immediate outbreak of war. England and France would most certainly be involved.

In view of all of these circumstances, Chance and Wagner felt it was time for them to leave Moscow and return to the United States. Deputy Addison agreed with them.

"It's only a matter of time before we have an inevitable war on our hands," Addison said to Chance and Wagner.

"If things continue as they seem to be going with Hitler and Stalin, I think you're right," Chance commented.

Three days after this conversation in Deputy Addison's office the Deputy called Chance, Wagner and Sofia into his office.

"I have Sofia's new identification papers. She will be known as Rose Murphy during the time you are on the trip and until you cross over into Finland. She can then resume her own name."

"I think these documents should get you through border inspection, Sofia," said Deputy Addison. "They look pretty authentic."

Addison turned to Chance. "Bill, we've given Sofia the job title of Chief Clerk. Perhaps you should be creative and tell her what her duties are in case she is asked either along the way or at the border. You might also describe some interesting features of Washington also in case she is asked."

"I'll do that," Chance replied, "but those Russian guys at the border probably never heard of the Washington monument or what the White House looks like."

"I'll be alright," Sofia spoke up. "I've seen some picture books around here of the United States. I think I can answer any questions about Washington or New York City and other parts of the country. But, I agree with Bill that those people at the border probably aren't smart enough to ask those kinds of questions."

The evening before the day of departure, Chance, Wagner and Sofia had dinner in the Embassy with Ambassador Hayes and Deputy Addison.

"Sofia, what do you plan on doing when you get to the United States?" the Ambassador inquired.

"I have no plans. I have some money saved up and I'll have to live on that for a short time until I can determine what to do. Incidentally, I appreciate your converting my rubles to American dollars, Mr. Ambassador."

Chance then offered, "We'll help Sofia get settled. She can stay at our home for a time. I think we can find her a job at our section. We always need Russian translators."

"What about your relatives and friends?" the Ambassador asked. "I'm sure they'll want to know what happened to you."

"In my situation I cannot worry about my relatives and friends. Besides, in this country people disappear overnight and relatives and friends have learned not to inquire about them. However, if anyone contacts the Embassy about me, you can tell the truth and say I left for America. I think they'll be happy I managed to get out of Russia."

"Do you think you'll miss Russia?" Addison asked Sofia.

"Yes, of course. I love my country. I love its culture. But what is going on in the Soviets under Communism is intolerable to me. Stalin is an evil man and he is destroying everything in Russia that I hold dear." Sofia's voice choked up and those at the dinner table could see that she had become very emotional about the subject. No one further pursued that direction of conversation.

At the end of dinner, goodbyes were said.

"If I don't see you tomorrow, I wish you all well on your trip. If you get into any difficulties and you think we can help, try to reach either me or Fraser or our office in Leningrad." The Ambassador was obviously concerned.

The next morning, May 27, the three travelers left the Embassy at 0800 hours and were driven in the Embassy limousine to the Moscow railroad station. Deputy Addison accompanied them for the reason as he said, "To help make it look diplomatically official."

In addition to light baggage, Chance, Wagner and Sofia each had a paper bag containing four sandwiches and some fruit which had been prepared by the Embassy kitchen staff. They were all aware of the uncertainties of the availability of food on and along the train route.

The railroad station lobby was crowded with soldiers apparently destined for some military post.

Wagner remarked, "If the railroad didn't have soldiers to transport, the trains would be virtually empty. I guess the ordinary citizen doesn't do much traveling."

"Except to Siberia," Sofia added in a low voice.

At the gate entrance to the train platform they said goodbye again to Deputy Addison and, after showing their diplomatic identification to the uniformed guard at the gate, they passed through the gate and proceeded, without untoward incident, to the train for Leningrad. Their tickets indicated first class seats. Guards on the platform directed them to a car for first class passengers. The trio found a vacant compartment in the car and took possession. Other compartments were being taken by military officers. The three diplomats did not see any civilians in the first class car.

In accordance with the customary procedure of the Soviet railway system, security police came through the cars checking identification documents and examining with meticulousness the shelves and seats of compartments. One of the security police came to the compartment occupied by Chance, Wagner and Sofia.

At the very moment that the policeman stood in the compartment doorway, Sofia was startled and her heart began to beat rapidly with her sudden anxiety. She recognized the young officer as one of her classmates at school. She did not utter a word and tried to give no outward sign of recognition but she thought to herself, "Oh, oh, he'll know I'm not Rose Murphy and now what will happen?"

The security policeman in a quick glance at the three occupants showed by his facial expression that he immediately recognized Sofia. Sofia saw a slight smile by the officer and knew that he recognized her. The policeman said nothing except to ask for identification papers of each of the three. When he examined Sofia's papers he at first appeared puzzled and then with a broader smile and looking at Sofia intensely, handed back her papers and said calmly and courteously in Russian, "Miss Murphy, I wish you a safe trip." He then proceeded down the aisle of the car.

Sofia knew at once instinctively that the security police officer had decided to allow his classmate to proceed under the false identification. She sighed in relief and relaxed.

"What was all that about?" Wagner asked. Wagner sensed something unusual had occurred between Sofia and the security officer.

Sofia explained, "He is a classmate of mine. He recognized me and knew I was not Rose Murphy. I guess he decided to go along with my game. I don't think he'll report me or take any action to reveal who I am."

"Wow! I hope not!" Wagner was apprehensive. Chance agreed.

"What is his name?" Chance asked.

"Andrei. I don't recall his last name. We were both in a group of students who got together during lunch breaks and had lively conversations and gossips about everything and anything. We joked and laughed a lot, but that was before the serious Stalin purges began in 1938. Andrei was a very nice fellow. I liked him a lot, but nothing serious ever developed between us. I can't picture him as an NKVD type. He must have needed a job badly."

Wagner commented, "It sounds like he remembers the good times with you and the group and he'll probably not reveal your true identity. There are still some people in the NKVD who are still human apparently."

"When we get into Leningrad I think we should go to our office there. We have to change trains and the train from Leningrad for the border doesn't leave for about three hours after we arrive in Leningrad. What do you think?" Chance addressed Wagner and Sofia.

"I think it's a good idea. There is no point in wandering around the city aimlessly especially with Sofia here with us," Wagner agreed.

Sofia likewise gave her assent with a nod of her head.

The train to Leningrad was uneventful, long and boring to the three travelers. They did not see Andrei again but the train conductor appeared several times and was apparently also bored. He tried to start up a conversation with the travelers but neither Chance nor Wagner nor Sofia were willing to talk with the conductor. They were exercising extreme caution about talking with any stranger. They rid themselves of the conductor by claiming that they had to get some sleep.

The train arrived in Leningrad about 1100 hours the next day. During the trip the train or the locomotive had had several breakdowns and the delays for repairs had added hours to the schedule.

Sofia said, "I don't have any faith in a Soviet train keeping its schedule and arriving as promised at its destination."

The train had stopped from time to time at small villages or farms either because a stop was scheduled or because of a breakdown. It was on such occasions that the three travelers alighted from the train and bought fruit or cakes from the local entrepreneurial farmer or farm wife. However, they did not rove about but remained close to the car with their compartment. They thought wandering around away from the train would attract attention to them.

When their train finally arrived in Leningrad, the three were dismayed to learn that the one daily train to the Russian border and transfer to a Finnish train to Viipuri had already departed. The delays incurred on their trip from Moscow had disrupted the schedule of the three travelers.

"We'll have to go to the United States legation here and ask them to put us up for the night," said Chance. "We don't have much choice."

Their arrival by taxi at the legation took its Chief Officer, Melvin Scope, by surprise. Chance explained their predicament. He introduced himself, Wagner and Sofia. In introducing Sofia, Chance used her true name, Sofia Kamineva.

"Certainly, we can put you up for the night," Scope said graciously. "We always have a couple of rooms held open for visitors." Scope was a congenial man, easygoing, and apparently unruffled by emergency events.

"Would you please come into my office. I would like to talk with you in private."

Once in the office, Scope closed the door and requested his guests to be seated. Sitting behind his desk, Scope looked directly at all three.

"I have something to tell you which may alter your plans," Scope began. "Yesterday, I received a telephone call from an official of the Soviet Foreign Office inquiring whether a Sofia Kamineva, a Soviet citizen, was either expected here or was here or had passed through. I told them that I did not know such a person and did not expect one of that name. I asked why they wanted to know. The official told me that Miss Kamineva was a member of an underground movement and that she was wanted by the Soviet government for treason." Scope paused to let the information sink into his listeners' minds. He then continued.

"When you introduced Sofia Kamineva just now, I was shocked since I immediately recognized the name as the one mentioned by the Soviet official."

"Yes, I am the Sofia Kamineva referred to by the Soviet official." Sofia was quite calm. "I would expect that the Soviet authorities would want to capture me. I was a member of the underground movement dedicated to ridding Russia of Stalin. We were betrayed and now I am on the run and hoping to get to Finland and then on to the United States."

The Chief Legation Officer continued, "The guy at the Soviet Foreign Office said that if Sofia Kamineva came to the legation or if we learned of her whereabouts, I should inform him immediately. They suspect that she'll try to escape the country and might come through here since she was attached to our Embassy in Moscow. They think she would naturally gravitate to the Americans for protection."

"Well, what are you going to do now that Sofia is here?" asked Chance.

"Of course, I have no intention of reporting to the Soviet government." Scope expressed indignation at the very hint that he might inform on Sofia.

"In a way," Scope added, "perhaps you're fortunate that you missed the train to the border. I'm certain the Soviet police have notified the border inspectors to be on the lookout for Miss Kamineva. The Viipuri route is a main line and is fairly heavily guarded."

"Well, then it seems that we have to find a crossing that has no guards," Wagner concluded.

"Yes," the Legation Officer agreed, "that would seem the logical alternative to consider."

"We'll need an automobile obviously," Chance added.

Except for confirming her identity, Sofia had sat listening to the discussion of the others. She appeared stoically unconcerned about the threat to her safety.

Wagner, who was always obsessively observant of Sofia anyway, noticed how composed and undisturbed she appeared to be upon hearing that the NKVD was actively seeking to hunt her down.

Wagner addressed Sofia, "Sofia, you seem not to take this information seriously and what Mr. Scope is saying directly affects you. I am not criticizing you, but you might have a suggestion as to what action we need to take."

Sofia smiled in appreciation of Wagner's concern for her welfare. "Of course I'm anxious about this disclosure, but I'm not in a panic because of it. When you live all your life in Russia and, as you grow up, have listened to the stories the elders relate, you get to understand that the Russian people long ago learned to live with the oppression of tyrants, whether a Tsar or a Stalin. Those of us who try to change that expect merciless retribution if we fail and we have now failed."

Wagner listened quietly. He felt a sense of love for Sofia and her fortitude and serenity in the face of a very real danger to her life. But he gently persisted, "Sofia, what do you suggest?"

"I agree with you, Gene," Sofia answered. "We cannot go to Viipuri. We must find another crossing." She turned to Scope. "Mr. Scope, the Finns are in the best position to know about places to cross without too much risk. Perhaps, if you could contact their Legation here, they could tell you."

"That's a good idea," Scope said. "However, I shall visit the Finnish Legation personally rather than call them on the telephone. In Russia we cannot know if our telephone lines are being tapped. I'll arrange to see someone there tomorrow. I'll then let you know what was said. In the meantime, relax and get some rest. You'll be having dinner with me at 1830 hours."

In the afternoon of the next day, Chief Officer Scope called Chance, Wagner and Sofia again into his office. He was smiling and appearing quite confident.

"This morning," Scope began, "I visited and spoke with the head of the Finnish Legation. I asked him about crossings other than the border crossing leading to Viipuri. I did not mention your names. He told me that the safest place to cross would be at a place just inside the border on the Russian side and on the shore of the Gulf of Finland. He explained that a group of men from a place called Terijoki in Finland and just up the coast from the border have been helping to smuggle people out of Russia. They come by boat, pick you up and take you to Terijoki." Scope paused to see what effect, if any, his statement would have on those sitting in his office.

Chance asked, "How do we contact these Terijoki people to let them know we want to get out of the Soviet Union?"

"We have to work through the Finnish Legation. They have a short wave radio they use for just something like this. They'll make the arrangements as soon as we let them know when you're ready to leave."

"I would suggest that you proceed to make the arrangements. We'd like to leave as soon as possible." Chance turned to the other two. "Is that right?" They nodded their agreement.

CHAPTER 11

Two days after Chance, Wagner and Sofia had arrived at the United States Legation in Leningrad, Koskinen and Elena arrived at the Finnish Legation. Neither party had known of the travel plans of the other and so were unaware of each other's presence nearby.

At breakfast with First Secretary Paavo Leino the day after their arrival, the Secretary in a casual, cursory way mentioned to Koskinen and Elena that there were three people at the American Legation who also wanted to avoid the regular Russian border station and would like to go to Terijoki by boat.

"Who are the people at the American Legation?" asked Koskinen.

"I don't know," replied Secretary Leino. "The Chief Officer of the Legation was here yesterday to arrange for them but he did not mention who they were and why they wanted to avoid the border."

"That's strange," Elena mused. "I wonder if they could be our underground friends who were at the American Embassy in Moscow."

"I suppose they could be," Koskinen conjectured. "However, right now we have our own problems and we can't worry about them."

"I'll be contacting the men at Terijoki by radio and let them decide how they want to handle the two parties," the Secretary said.

"In the meantime, you'll have to stay indoors. It would be risky for you to go out in the streets."

During the morning, Koskinen and Elena met with Sorvali, the driver, to discuss the trip to meet with the Terijoki men. Later in the day, the medical doctor who serviced the Finnish Legation personnel arrived and treated Elena's wound.

Before Elena could explain how she acquired the wound, the doctor exclaimed, "The NKVD I presume."

"Yes, you're right, doctor," Elena declared.

"Those bastards!" The doctor was obviously outraged. "I've seen what they can do much too often!"

"How am I doing?" Elena asked.

"You are doing alright, Miss Marikova. But, I'm sure you realize that you have a severe wound and it will take time to heal. There is no infection and that is a good sign. I'll just put a clean bandage on and you keep taking your cod liver oil."

Koskinen was waiting outside Elena's room and inquired of the doctor as he left about Elena's condition.

"She'll be alright, but she has to keep the wound clean. Here, I'll give you some extra bandages in case you need them on the trip." The doctor then added with a look of anguish on his face, "It's just terrible what the police do to people. If only we could somehow foster a rebellion by the people. But, Russians are so passive." The doctor shrugged and proceeded to leave.

That evening at dinner, Secretary Leino reported to Koskinen and Elena that he had tried to contact Terijoki by radio, but up to that moment had been unable to establish any.

"I'll try later this evening. I'll let you know immediately when I do," the Secretary said.

After dinner, Koskinen accompanied Elena to her room where she lay down on the bed seemingly quite exhausted.

"I understand," Koskinen remarked, "that the Secretary is doing what he can, but this thing seems to be dragging so slowly. I'm concerned about you, Elena."

Elena spoke softly, wearily, "Don't worry about me, Timo, I'll be alright. Just be patient. Things will work out. We're safe here." She then dozed off. Koskinen sat in silence. He felt so alone even with Elena there with him. He just felt angry and frustrated. Everything seemed to have gone wrong from the moment Elena had been arrested at the entrance to the Finnish Embassy in Moscow. He couldn't see how fortunate they were to have come this far in their escape plan without further trouble from the police. All he knew was that his life and the life of this beautiful young woman had been changed forever by the monstrous acts of the beasts who ran the prison in Moscow. He swore to himself that someday he would seek and get revenge. He would hunt them down and kill each and every one of them. He lay down next to Elena and soon fell asleep in utter fatigue.

Early the next morning even before breakfast, Secretary Leino called Koskinen and Elena into his office.

"I finally made contact with the Terijoki men. I explained the situation and they said they would send two boats down to pick up you and the group at the American Legation at the same time."

"Did they say when?" Koskinen asked anxiously.

"Yes. Tomorrow night at 2300 hours."

"Good! We'll be ready." Koskinen turned to Elena. "Is that so, Elena?"

"Yes. I'm ready for anything," Elena said. She seemed resigned to accept whatever befell her.

"I'll notify the Americans so that they can get ready also. Both cars will have to use the same route, I'm afraid," advised the Secretary.

"What is the weather prediction for tomorrow night?" inquired Koskinen.

"So far as we know," the Secretary replied, "it will be dark, no moon, and no rain."

"Sounds good," Koskinen observed.

* * * * *

That same day, Leino sent Sorvali over to the American Legation to convey the information and plans for departure the next night. After listening to Sorvali, Chief Officer Scope called Wagner, Chance and Sofia into his office.

"This is Toivo Sorvali from the Finnish Legation. I am going to ask him to repeat what he just told me about the arrangements to get you to where you will be picked up and carried by boat to Terijoki, Finland. It is important that you hear it for yourselves." The Chief Officer introduced Sorvali to the three travelers. Sorvali spoke in belabored English.

"Our Legation has arranged with some men in Terijoki to pick you up at a point just inside the Russian border and take you to a village called Terijoki. There are two people who have just come to our Legation from the Finnish Embassy in Moscow who, like yourselves, want to enter Finland to avoid going through Russian customs. There will be two boats, one for you three and one for the Finland couple." Sorvali paused for a moment.

"When do we leave?" Wagner asked rather tersely.

"Tomorrow night," replied Sorvali.

"Spell out the details for us." Chance was persistent.

"Your legation will have to provide you with an automobile and driver. He will drive you over to the Finnish Legation where our automobile, driver and the two individuals will be waiting for you. You will then follow us to the point where we shall meet the Terijoki people. We are to meet them at 2300 hours. We shall have to leave our Legation at 2100 hours. You are to be there at 2030 hours."

Sofia was inquisitive. "Who are the two people who will be escaping with us?" she asked.

"I am not at liberty to tell you right now," Sorvali answered. "You will get to meet them when you arrive at the Finnish Legation tomorrow night."

Sorvali continued, "Your car and our car will proceed to the point I mentioned. Either the Terijoki men will already be there or we shall have to wait for them. In any case, they will use a small pen light to let you know of their presence. From that moment they will be in charge of you."

"Will you wait in the cars until they come in case they're not there when we arrive?" Wagner asked.

"We may or may not," replied Sorvali. "It depends on how nervous I get." He chuckled mischievously. "No, really, usually we don't wait. It's too risky with two automobiles sitting there. They can be seen. You people can hide in the bushes near the shoreline. You won't be noticed."

"Suppose a Russian patrol comes along. What do we do?" Wagner continued his interrogation.

"There is usually none," Sorvali answered.

"But suppose there is one?" Wagner was adamant in trying to get answers.

"Then you'll have a fight on your hands, I guess." Sorvali was cryptic. "We'll supply you with some Finnish hunting knives."

"That's great," observed Wagner sarcastically. "The three of us will have to fight armed patrols with knives."

"The men from Terijoki have guns. They'll help you."

"If they're there!" Wagner retorted.

Sorvali was beginning to show some annoyance and irritation with Wagner's inquiries.

"Look, Mister, this whole operation can be very dangerous. You must decide whether you want to take your chance to get out of Russia or stay here. Believe me, if I drive I'm risking my neck too, but I'm doing it to help you and the others. If you don't want to go, say so and I'll report that to our Legation Chief."

"No! No!" exclaimed Chance. "We do want to go. Gene, here, was just trying to get information. That's all!" Chance felt he had to intercede to placate Sorvali.

"What shall we bring with us?" Chance asked.

"Just the clothes on your back, your identification papers and a small carrying case of personal articles. There is not a lot of room in the Terijoki boats."

"Yes, we understand," said Chance continuing to mollify Sorvali.

"Alright, I'll be leaving now," Sorvali said. "You'll take care of your transportation from here to the coast."

"I'll take personal charge of that arrangement," said Scope. "These people will be at your Legation promptly tomorrow night."

Sorvali left, a bit peeved still.

Later that same day while Chance, Wagner and Sofia were sitting between meals in the Legation dining room, Wagner turned to Chance.

"Bill, it's foolish for both of us to accompany Sofia on this trip. Why don't you just go on in the normal way to cross over to Finland? I'll stick with Sofia and help her. There is no point in you taking the risks."

"That's considerate of you, Gene. I appreciate what you're saying, but I want to go along with you and Sofia. We both undertook the mission to get rid of Stalin and I'll see the operation through to its conclusion. Sofia is part of that operation and I don't feel I should abandon her now. Do you understand?"

"Yes, but … " Wagner didn't finish his sentence. He didn't know what else to say. He knew Bill Chance and understood there was no point in arguing with Chance's decision.

Sofia broke in. "I feel terrible exposing you two friends to this sort of risk just for me. Perhaps I could just join the two people at the Finnish Legation and go along with them. That would be a threesome just as we are."

"I know," Chance said, "but the Finns may have different plans and schedules from ours. I think we should just proceed as we originally planned. That is, all three of us to keep and work together."

Nothing more was said on that subject.

All three spent a restless night. There was on again, off again sleep for each. The next day the three kept to themselves except at meal times. There was little conversation among them. They took comfort from merely being with each other. Without talking they could share common feelings, common anxieties, a bonding with each other that they could share with no one else because no one else had their past and present concerns for each other's welfare.

Sofia remained quite stoic during the time waiting to leave the Legation. She was realistic. She understood that if she was captured she could expect to be raped, tortured, disfigured and either shot or sent to some labor camp. She had realized, along with other members of the underground, from the moment they had joined together that they faced a horrible ordeal if captured. Knowing that the Soviet police were hunting for her left her little choice but to take the risk of going to the rendezvous with the Terijoki men.

Chance and Wagner were not as imperturbable as Sofia. Their lives might not be at stake as was Sofia's, but the consequences if they were caught by the Russian police in the act of smuggling out of the country an underground traitor could be far-reaching. True, they were diplomats with diplomatic immunities. As such they were representatives of their country and their country, the United States, could be placed in a very embarrassing position by their actions. In fact, engaging in an illegal act could very well compromise their immune status and even cancel it out. Chance and Wagner realized that. Still, they felt they had an obligation to Sofia not to abandon her at this moment. They had promised Sofia to try to get her to the United States and they were both determined to see it through.

At the Finnish Legation, Koskinen and Elena spent a good part of the day of their scheduled departure socializing with First Secretary

Paavo Leino. Doing so helped them to push the perils of their approaching border escape to the back of their minds. They talked, rather, of the storm clouds that seemed to be hovering over the Soviet-Finnish relations and the possibility of the Soviets sending its military to invade Finland.

"If they do that," Koskinen declared, "we shall fight them to the last Finnish man and woman!"

"That's very brave of you to say that," the First Secretary responded, "but what would you gain except a lot of crosses in cemeteries. You know very well that Finland, a small nation, is no match for the monstrous Soviets which has an endless supply of men as cannon fodder. The Soviets have more soldiers than Finland has bullets. It would be crazy to resist."

"If we die," Koskinen commented, "we shall have shown our utter contempt of the Soviet Communistic system. The world will know about it and applaud it. We shall have demonstrated our strong Finnish character, our sisu.* We shall never submit to the Soviets."

Leino countered, "Finland was under Russian rule from 1809 to 1917. There was no dying to the last man and woman during that time."

The First Secretary had suddenly become uncharacteristically adversarial. Koskinen thought to himself that Leino had deliberately prolonged the discussion, any discussion, in order to keep Elena's and his, Koskinen's, mind off the impending escape. Koskinen appreciated what Leino was doing primarily for Elena's sake and so he abetted the purpose.

"Yes," Koskinen retorted, "but that was under the Tsars and, for the most part, they didn't occupy Finland. Instead, they allowed Finland considerable autonomy."

"That's true," Leino admitted.

"And besides, the Tsars were royalty and when they oppressed the people they did it with class." Koskinen chuckled at the incongruous observation. Leino smiled likewise at the absurdity.

And so the conversation continued from one subject to another obviously intended to use the time that seemed to drag on before the need to depart. During all of the conversation, Elena was mostly silent, only occasionally making a comment. Koskinen, however, thought she was listening to the small talk and helping to divert her mind from the later undertaking.

During lunch and dinner sitting at the table with the First Secretary, Koskinen and Elena ate very little. Perhaps, it indicated that with all the effort to turn the attention away from the imminent flight from Russia there was a deep sense of apprehension and even of a dark foreboding.

After dinner Koskinen and Elena sat on her bed in her room. They held each other tightly in an emotional closeness that lovers everywhere could have understood. Yet, this was different. This mutuality of feeling between Koskinen and Elena was born out of a uniqueness of experiences from the very beginning of their relationship. It could not be duplicated under any circumstance in the lives of anyone else. They each seemed to understand, without voicing it, that they would not be able to be alone together again for some time and that these moments were especially precious.

"Remember, Timo, whatever may happen I love you deeply and forever," Elena whispered.

"Yes, Elena, and I love you too and also forever." Koskinen felt a tightness in his throat and could not hold back the tears that welled up.

At 2030 hours, Koskinen and Elena went to the Legation reception room and met with Toivo Sorvali. Koskinen carried a small hand bag containing his and Elena's personal items and the bandages for Elena.

"The people from the American Legation should be here shortly," Sorvali stated. "As soon as they arrive, we should get on our way." Sorvali appeared somewhat tense. He had assisted in smuggling people out of the Soviet Union on several earlier occasions. Each time he experienced nervousness. It was his feeling that for each event that was successful he was just that much closer to the time when his luck would run out. It was anticipation of the probability of the latter which caused his stress.

At 2040 hours, the American group arrived at the Finnish Legation. The driver and his three passengers alighted from the Legation limousine and were admitted by military guards to the building. It was their intention to go over the plans and obtain last minute instructions. Sorvali met them at the door entrance. He was plainly annoyed and irritated.

"You're late," Sorvali growled. "We have to leave in fifteen minutes if we are to make connection with the Terijoki people." Without waiting for an excuse or explanation for the delay, Sorvali said, "Come, follow me to the reception room!"

As Chance, Wagner and Sofia entered the room, they immediately saw Koskinen and Elena who, in turn, saw them simultaneously. There was a momentary gasp of shock and surprise from each. Then excitement broke loose.

"Elena!" cried out Sofia.

"Sofia," exclaimed Elena as she arose from her chair, walked quickly to where Sofia was standing and quietly hugged her. They both began to sob. Chance and Wagner shook hands warmly with Koskinen.

Finally, Elena said, "I'm so happy to see you and to know that you, too, have decided to leave Russia. It's so good that we are all going on this venture together. I'm just praying that nothing will happen to interfere with our getting away."

"You poor dear, Elena. I heard what happened to you. It's wonderful to see you again. I'm sure everything will turn out alright."

Sorvali, who had witnessed the reunion of the two groups and reluctantly tolerated it for a few minutes, finally spoke up. "Things will not turn out alright if we don't get started. This operation has to function on time. We must meet the Terijoki people precisely when they arrive in their boats. They're very skittish and they won't wait for us if we're not there. Now, listen carefully what I have to say and do exactly as I say." Everyone remained standing.

"I shall lead the way," Sorvali began. "You Americans and your young lady will follow me at a reasonable distance so as not to create suspicions. I shall have my lights on for most of the trip, so you should have no trouble following. You can keep your lights on as well. Above all, don't lose sight of me! I cannot stop for you to catch up and I will not turn around and look for you. I shall keep an appropriate and reasonable speed. Going too slowly or too fast could attract police attention if the police are around. We shall finally come to a dirt road that cuts through some woods and runs parallel to the shoreline. The shoreline will be about three hundred meters from the road. When we reach a certain point on the road I shall turn on the parking lights only. They will be sufficient to see the road for a short distance ahead. When we enter the dirt road, your American car is to keep close behind me and you are to turn on your parking lights when I do." Sorvali paused. "Are there any questions so far?" He waited for Elena to translate the Finnish to English. It took a few moments. As soon as the translations were completed, Sorvali quickly resumed his instructions.

"At a certain point I shall stop my car. You are all to get out including the American car. While you wait, we shall turn our cars around in a clearing so that we are prepared to drive off when we have to. The American driver–by the way, what is your name?" Sorvali asked the driver for the first time.

"Robert."

"Alright, Robert. Robert will wait by the cars while I guide you to the rendezvous point. We are going to have to walk a distance of about one hundred meters to make contact. There is to be no talking. You are to keep your hand on the shoulder of the person in front of you so that you don't lose contact in the dark. We'll meet one of the Terijoki men and he'll take over and guide you to the boats. I will leave you at that point. Is this all understood?" They all shook their heads in affirmation. However, Koskinen added a question.

"What do we do if a Russian patrol happens to come along?"

"We don't expect any, but if by chance one comes along it is generally not more than three or four Russian soldiers. I am going to give each of you, the women included, a six-inch Finnish hunting knife. You are to use them on the patrol. You are to be quick, catch them by surprise and cut their throats."

Chance and Wagner looked at each other with raised eyebrows. This was something they had not counted on.

"I might add," Sorvali said, "if a patrol comes along while you are with the Terijoki people, they are well armed with automatic weapons and they'll finish off the Russian patrol quickly."

Again, Sorvali paused. "If there are no further questions, then let's get going."

At this moment, First Secretary Leino appeared, grasped the hands of the escape people and quickly said 'goodbye.' "The best of luck to all of you," he said.

Each of the groups got into their respective limousines and began to slowly move away from the Legation building. It was dark with no moonlight. The only lights were occasionally from houses or other buildings along the Leningrad streets. These were dim and merely added to the eerie feeling the travelers had as they wound their way toward the outskirts of the City. Except for an infrequent taxi and a few pedestrians, there was a remarkable lack of activity on the streets and avenues.

For a while the two limousines proceeded along the principal thoroughfare, Nevsky Prospekt. In the daytime and with an unworried, carefree agenda, one could stop to admire the important and beautiful buildings along the avenue such as the former Imperial Library, Alexander Theater and the former Anichkov Palace. In fact Leningrad had long had a reputation for its luxurious palaces and beautiful public buildings and as an educational and cultural center.

The City had been founded in 1703 by Tsar Peter the Great and was the capital of Russia until 1917 when the Communists moved the capital to Moscow. The City had been originally named St. Petersburg and, in 1914, renamed Petrograd. When Lenin died in 1924, the City was named after him. The City lies along the Baltic Sea at the eastern end of the Gulf of Finland. Too close to Finland for the comfort of Stalin.

Neither Elena who had been a long-term resident of Leningrad nor the others in the two-car caravan were thinking about Leningrad's beautiful buildings and culture as they drove along. Their minds were on the potential hazards of their trip. Proceeding at a steady pace they could see that they were passing from the intensely built area as the houses and other buildings became fewer and further apart. Even in the darkness they were able to perceive the silhouette of open farmlands. The cars had left the well-paved City thoroughfares for the bumpy, poorly maintained two lane roadways in the countryside. The American car was following about six or eight car lengths behind the Finnish automobile.

The parties had traveled about two kilometers out of the City proper when Robert, the driver of the American vehicle, noticed in his rear view mirror another vehicle approaching at a rapid speed.

"Some car is coming up very rapidly from behind," Robert announced to his three passengers. Hearing this, Chance, Wagner and Sofia became tense.

"Could it be the police?" Wagner asked, knowing that no one in their auto had the answer.

"I wonder if Sorvali sees it," Chance said.

Within moments the speeding car drew abreast of the American auto, then passed at a reduced speed. The occupants of the American car observed the strange vehicle pass Sorvali's auto, blink its lights and then slowed to a halt up ahead in such a manner astride both lanes that neither the Sorvali car nor the American car could pass by.

Three men appeared from the strange vehicle, one of them carrying a flashlight, and walked toward Sorvali's lead car.

"I think we have trouble," Sorvali declared in a low, but calm voice.

Back in the American car, the driver and the occupants could see by their car headlights what was happening.

"They look like police," Sofia said. "If they are, then we know what to say," she added.

Two of the three men walked up to the Sorvali car, one on each side. The third fellow continued to the American car.

"We are police," announced the officer to Sorvali in Russian. Koskinen quickly translated, "You will please all get out so that we can identify you," the officer commanded in a stern, gruff voice. The third officer made the same announcement and command.

All alighted from their respective vehicles. The third officer ordered those from the American vehicle to walk over to the other group. All seven of the occupants stood as a group in the glare of the automobile headlights.

The apparent superior police officer showed his badge of authority to the civilians.

"We stopped you because we want to know why you are on these roads late at night. Who are you and where are you going?"

Elena translated from the Russian and answered the officer in Russian. She was unruffled and spoke clearly and with restraint.

"This car is from the Finnish Legation and this one is from the United States Legation. These people you see here are diplomats and employees of the Legations. We are all going to Finland and the Americans are going on to America. We are all friends as many people in the foreign Legations are. We have finished our tours of duty and we are driving to the border customs station and then to Viipuri."

The Russian superior officer listened silently and when Elena had finished her explanation, he grunted, "Hmm! Let me see your papers!"

Chance, Wagner and Koskinen as Salonen produced their diplomatic certificates. Sofia showed her identification as Rose Murphy and Elena handed the officer her passport. The officer addressed Sorvali and Robert.

"Where are your papers?"

Sorvali and Robert produced their identifications as Legation employees. But Sorvali said, "This man and I are merely drivers. We are returning to our Legations after we have completed this trip." This was also translated from the Finnish by Elena.

With the various identity papers in his hand the superior officer bent in front of the headlights of Sorvali's car to read them. After what seemed an interminable time, the superior officer turned toward the group still standing in a cluster.

"Our job as police is to stop suspicious looking or acting vehicles or people and determine if there is any cause to hold them. Listening to your explanation of who you are and your purpose in traveling at this hour has convinced me that there is no need to hold you. As far as your papers are concerned, they seem to be in order. The inspectors at customs will look at them more carefully. That is not our job. I hope you understand." The officer sounded sincerely apologetic.

The officer returned the papers to the individuals concerned. He saluted the civilian group. Then he and the other two officers got into their car, turned it about and proceeded in the direction from whence they had come.

"Whew! That was close!" remarked Bill Chance. The others agreed.

Sorvali addressed the group before they returned to the automobiles.

"We shall be continuing along this road. Just before we reach the border, I shall make a sharp left turn to the dirt road running parallel to the shore and which will lead you to the Terijoki people. Understood?"

"Yes," came the whispered response from the gathered individuals.

The migrants continued on their way. There was silence in both automobiles. No one cared to talk after the harrowing experience with the police. Nevertheless, in spite of that episode, Elena soon fell asleep, her head gently cradled in Koskinen's arm.

Koskinen felt that Elena had saved them all by her convincing explanation to the police of who they were and their purpose on the trip. As usual, Koskinen saw again Elena's steely resolve.

An hour passed as the cars rolled through the countryside of open fields and occasional groves of trees. It was now 2230 hours. The police had delayed them and Sorvali had thereafter speeded up to make up for the loss of scheduled time. In a few moments, he slowed and turned onto an almost invisible dirt road that began off the main road, ran through an open field and finally entered a strip of woods. When Sorvali's car entered the wooded area, he turned off all but his park lights. Robert, following closely, did likewise. The cars bounced and rocked and groaned as they drove slowly over holes, along ruts and protruding rocks. The passengers marveled how Sorvali knew where the road was at times.

After ten minutes of this, Sorvali stopped at a clearing, turned off the lights and said to Koskinen and Elena who had been awakened by the jostling of the vehicle. "This is as far as we go by car. You will now get out and we shall start our walk to meet up with the Terijoki people."

Robert had driven the American car up behind the Finnish auto. Sorvali walked to Robert's car and repeated what he had just said to his own passengers.

"Before we start the walk, Robert and I will turn our cars around so that we're ready to leave." Sorvali turned to Robert. "You will stay with the cars and wait until I get back."

"What if someone comes along?" Robert asked.

"I don't think anyone will, but if you hear someone approaching, hide behind some trees or bushes. In that way you won't have to answer questions. If someone is still around the cars when I come back, we may have to use our knives."

Sorvali and Robert then proceeded to position their cars facing in the return direction. Sorvali returned to his charges. In a low voice he said, "We shall walk about one hundred meters and we then should meet our boat men. Now, follow me. Each of you keep your hand on the person's shoulder ahead of you. You are not to talk under any condition. If we meet a Russian patrol, we may have to use our knives. Keep them ready."

The group then began their walk in a single file. In the dark, Koskinen could see little. He thought it was like the blind following the blind. He had his hand on Sorvali's shoulder. Elena followed behind Koskinen. Sofia, Wagner and Chance followed in that order. There were frequent stumbles and all were breathing heavily. Chance concluded that it was as much from the emotional stress of the occasion as from the physical effort. His heart was pounding from excitement.

The path they were following ran close to the shore. All of them could hear the water lapping nearby. Insects would all too frequently buzz around them occasionally stopping for a bite or sting. They were each attuned to listening for any unusual noise that might indicate an approaching Russian patrol. Every so often Sorvali would stop to listen. Hearing nothing he would resume his walk. Tall trees bordered both sides of the path with underlying brush growing right up to the edge. There were no lights from distant buildings to be seen although it was late and lights in a building, if any, could have been turned off.

Sorvali stopped once more. This time he used his flashlight to flash its light just once in the direction of the shore. About five meters ahead a responding light flashed once. Sorvali resumed his walk to a clearing revealing a small beach. He stopped again. Someone approached him. A few words were exchanged in very low tones. Sorvali turned to Koskinen.

"This is one of the Terijoki men. He will take charge of all of you now. Do as he says. I am now going to leave you. Good luck and God bless all of you."

Sorvali then walked past the file of the other six. Whispering as he slowly walked by, "You are now in the hands of the Terijoki men. Good luck!"

The Terijoki man then quickly went to each in the group and whispered, "Just follow me and don't talk." He spoke in halting English.

Returning to the head of the file, the Terijoki fellow took Koskinen by the arm and led him across the short beach and into the water. The others followed. If there was any fear at this point, it did not show. Each person knew instinctively that what they were now doing was the next to the last step to freedom. Whatever fear surged in them had to be suppressed. There could be no panic, no paralysis, no going back.

They waded about five meters into the water, getting increasingly deeper as they went ahead. When the level of the water had reached their knees, they suddenly saw two long boats almost side by side. Koskinen could not estimate their length in the dark, but they appeared to be adequate to hold the group.

The water they were wading in was icy. Koskinen and Elena were directed by the Terijoki man in the water to one of the boats while he directed Chance, Wagner and Sofia to the other. With the help of the fellow in the water and the strong hands of a man in each boat, the escapees managed one by one to climb into their respective boats. There were two Terijoki men in each boat including the fellow in the water who quickly pulled himself into the boat occupied by Koskinen and Elena.

Once in their boats, the escapees began to shiver. They were wet to their waists and the crisp wind blowing across the water added to their misery. Yet none complained.

Each boat had a large, powerful outboard motor. It also had oars. The standard practice of the Terijoki men in the smuggling process was to use the motors when in the open water and to silence the motors and to row as the boats either approached or left the beach shore. The men were always aware that the slightest noise carried over the water to anyone on or near the shore.

Each boat carried several blankets for the comfort of the passengers who always came aboard wet and cold. Koskinen and Elena sat huddled in the middle of their boat. Koskinen had wrapped two blankets about Elena and held her tightly to himself. He could feel Elena shivering. For the moment, Koskinen did not use a blanket since without one he was free to protect Elena by putting his arm around her.

The American boat moved away first and led the way, the Finnish boat following closely. In each the two Terijoki men pulled mightily on their oars. They were strong, husky fellows who had been on several similar missions and knew what to do.

They had gone only a short distance from the shore when one of the men rowing in the Koskinen boat carelessly allowed his oar to slip out of the oarlock with result that it banged with a loud clattering noise against the side of the boat. The other Terijoki man rowing in the boat growled in a low voice, "Matti, for Christ sake! What are you doing? You'll get us all killed!"

The men in the American's boat also stopped rowing as they all listened tensely to ascertain whether their positions had been revealed to people on the shore. They heard some voices and shouting coming from an area of the nearby shore. They all immediately sensed that they had been detected and that any further rowing would be foolhardy. The men in the boats hastily pulled their oars into their boats and prepared to start the outboard motors for an emergency getaway.

As they did so, there was gunfire from automatic weapons directed from the shore towards where the sound of the oar had come. It was dark still and the people on the shore with the guns were unable to see their targets. Nevertheless, the noise had given them some clue.

The first volley of shots either whizzed over their heads or hit the water in the general area of the boats. There was a second and more prolonged volley. The man standing up at the rear of the Koskinen boat trying to start the motor suddenly fell to the bottom of the boat.

"God damn! I got hit in the arm!" He grasped at his left lower arm.

The other Terijoki man jumped to the motor and began to pull on the starter rope. Just as the motor started up, another volley of automatic weapon shots came across the water. Elena screamed and then groaned.

"Timo, I've been shot!"

"Where, Elena? Where?" Timo was panic-stricken.

"Here, Timo, here." Elena was groaning and trying to stifle her anguish. She pointed to her side. Koskinen could see her point, but could see little else in the dark. He followed her hand to a point on the blanket which was wrapped around Elena. Koskinen felt a warm wetness and knew immediately that it was blood.

By this time the powerful outboard motor had caught on and was pushing the boat ahead at high speed. As soon as the boatmen in the boat with Chance, Wagner and Sofia saw that the other boat was able to get away on its own, they, too, roared off full throttle.

Koskinen shouted to the boatman operating the motor, "How long will it take to get to Terijoki?"

"Half hour!"

Koskinen felt so absolutely helpless with Elena in his arms. There was nothing, absolutely nothing he could do for Elena. He could not remove the blankets to see how badly the wound was. The spray of water coming over the bow of the boat was drenching everyone on board. Besides, whatever the seriousness of the wound, he could do nothing, so why look at it.

Elena continued to moan and occasionally cry out in pain. Her suffering tore at Koskinen's heart as he continued to cradle her in his arms as best he could.

"Elena, hang on!" Koskinen urged Elena in a soft, modulated voice. "Hang on, Elena, for me, for us" Koskinen was desperate. Elena might be bleeding to death.

"Timo, I feel that I'm going to die. I feel so terrible."

Koskinen could barely hear her above the noise of the motor and the rush of water past the boat.

"You'll be alright, Elena. We'll be in Terijoki shortly. Then we'll get you to a doctor. You'll be alright."

Koskinen noticed that Elena was breathing quite rapidly. He felt her forehead and cheeks. They were cold and damp. Although the cold and wet face could be due to the weather and spray, Koskinen knew enough from his experience that Elena was in shock. He maneuvered himself to a sitting position on the floor of the boat and then gently lowered Elena's upper body to his lap while her legs remained on the boat seat. He had once heard someone, perhaps a doctor, say that this is what is supposed to be done for a person in shock. It allows the blood to flow to the heart more easily.

The two boats continued to speed towards Terijoki. In the other boat, no one had been injured. At the first shots, all of the occupants including the boatmen had quickly thrown themselves to the floor of the boat. They heard Elena scream and knew that she had been hit by a bullet. As soon as the firing ceased, one of the boatmen pulled in the oars, while the other started up the motor. The boatman ran the motor at idle while awaiting the boat with Koskinen and Elena to also start up. The boatman was determined not to abandon his friends and Koskinen and Elena. If the latter could not start up, he would get all of them into the one functioning boat. That proved unnecessary.

About twenty minutes later, a few lights could be seen in the distance. At first they were small and barely visible. But as the boats continued on their approach, the few lights grew brighter. They would soon be in Terijoki. For Koskinen their arrival seemed an eternity. Elena was still moaning. Her breathing had slowed somewhat.

Both boats docked almost simultaneously, one on each side of a pier. One of the boatmen in the American's boat quickly jumped out, tied the boat up to the pier and ran to the nearest house just off the shore. The light in the house was still on. He banged on the door repeatedly. In a few seconds an occupant of the house opened the door. The woman was obviously startled by the banging, but she immediately recognized the boatman.

"Come in, come in, Emili! What is the matter?"

"Quick! Call Doctor Jarvi. We have two badly wounded people. He must get over here whether he is in his nightclothes or not."

The woman's husband had appeared from another room and had heard Emili's urgent order. The husband was already on the telephone making the call. The contact with the doctor was accomplished.

"The doctor will start for here immediately," the husband said. He added addressing Emili, "Tell the people to bring the wounded ones here." That invitation proved unnecessary. Koskinen appeared at the door carrying Elena in his arms. The wounded boatman also entered the house supported by another boatman.

"Where shall I put this young lady," Koskinen asked, his voice reflecting his despair.

"Take the wet blankets off and place her on the sofa. I'll get you another blanket to keep her warm," the woman of the house directed.

Chance, Wagner, Sofia and the boatmen all crowded into the living room. Sofia went over to the sofa and, kneeling on the floor, spoke softly and endearingly to Elena while stroking her head. With the water spraying into the boat and with the turmoil created by the gunfire and her being wounded, the bandage over Elena's ear cut had come off revealing the gaping wound. It was not a pretty sight, but Koskinen, Sofia and the others were more concerned with Elena's gunshot wound. Elena had lost an obviously considerable amount of blood. It was also apparent that she was in deep shock. She was still moaning. Her eyes were shut and her face had become very pale with a bluish tinge. Her breathing had become slow and labored.

Sofia looked at Koskinen and their expressions betrayed their thoughts. Elena would probably not survive.

In about ten minutes, Doctor Jarvi entered the house. The doctor moved rapidly. His attention was focused on Elena. The wounded boatman was ignored. His injury did not appear life-threatening and the bleeding from his wound in the arm had stopped.

"Can you place this young woman on a bed?" the doctor asked. The boatman carried Elena into another room, a bedroom adjoining the living room. There with Sofia present, the doctor removed Elena's upper garment to expose the gunshot wound. It was a small nasty hole from which blood was still oozing. The doctor felt Elena's pulse. It was very weak. The doctor shook his head indicating that he felt Elena's condition was hopeless. He placed a gauze pad over the wound and taped it. He went into the living room and spoke to the gathering in a low and somber voice.

"I don't think the young lady is going to make it. She has lost too much blood and she is still bleeding internally. I cannot do surgery here. I do not have anesthesia and equipment to do it. The young lady should be in a hospital, but even if she could be taken there, I don't think she would survive the trip. I am sorry. I'll give her some morphine to ease the pain."

Koskinen spoke up, his voice trembling. "Doctor, I am a very close friend. I would like to be with her."

"Yes, of course, go in. It will be alright."

Koskinen walked into the bedroom accompanied by the doctor. Sofia was still next to the bed on which Elena lay. She moved aside to allow the doctor to administer morphine. That being done, Koskinen sat down on the bed and held Elena's head. Tears were streaming down his face. Momentarily, Elena opened her eyes and, seeing Koskinen, she whispered weakly, "Please don't cry, Timo. I have known love for you and that will go with me and you forever."

Koskinen bent down and kissed Elena. He was choked up, but managed to say, "Elena, Elena, I love you so. I love you. I love you."

There was a flicker of a smile on Elena's lips. She closed here eyes. A tear appeared at the corner of each eye. Her breathing stopped. Koskinen knew that Elena had passed away. His beautiful Elena had left him. He immediately broke into uncontrollable sobbing. Sofia came over and put her arm around his shoulders to comfort him, but she could say nothing that would help. Koskinen was inconsolable. He sat for several minutes holding Elena and caressing her face. His despair and feeling of loneliness were overwhelming. Yet, he wanted to be alone with his grief.

Koskinen walked past the others in the living room as if in a daze. He seemed to see no one as he walked towards the door, went out into the dark and staggered down to the beach and the pier where the boats were tied up. He had left the little carrying bag containing his and Elena's personal items in the boat when he had carried Elena to the house. He stepped into the boat, picked up the bag and then sat down on the boat seat. He continued sobbing and holding the bag close to his chest as if the bag still contained Elena's life within it. Then in a low almost inaudible voice of great sadness, as if talking to someone and yet no one, ""Why, oh God, why all this to this beautiful, courageous girl? Why, God, why?" Koskinen kept thinking and muttering these words over and over again.

Koskinen was gone from the house where the others were gathered for about a half-hour. Sofia became increasingly worried. She had known of the fond relationship between Koskinen and Elena. Elena had spoken to her several times of their feelings for each other, but Sofia had not realized until now the depth of their affection. She was surprised by the emotional intensity displayed by Koskinen over Elena's passing.

Sofia excused herself from the others and went outside to look for Koskinen. She went directly to the pier and found him sitting in the boat. She stepped down into the boat and sat down next to him. She put her arm around his shoulders as an offer of comfort and to demonstrate that she shared his grief. For a few moments neither said anything and then Sofia spoke softly.

"Antti, please come back to the house. It's cold out here." Sofia was still unaware of Koskinen's true name. However close she and Elena had been, Elena had never revealed to her the true identity of Koskinen. Elena had kept well the secret.

"I know how you feel, Antti, but it's not good to be out here. Please, now, come back."

"Alright, Sofia." Koskinen had stopped sobbing. Then he added with resignation, "My name is not Antti Salonen. It is Timo Koskinen. That was just a cover name while I was in Russia."

Sofia was unconcerned. "I'm glad you told me. It doesn't really matter. You're back in Finland now and that whole business of wanting to assassinate Stalin is over with. It's done."

They got out of the boat and proceeded to walk back to the house. Koskinen still carried the small carrying case.

When they reentered the home, the husband went to Koskinen and led him into the kitchen to be away from the others.

"Sit down," the husband said, motioning to a chair at the kitchen table. The husband sat down on one of the other chairs. He reached over the table and offered his hand to Koskinen in a gesture of friendliness. Koskinen accepted and they shook hands.

"I am Martti Virta. The others tell me you are Antti Salonen."

"No, that was a false name I used in Russia. My name is Timo Koskinen."

"I am so sorry about the young lady."

Koskinen did not reply. He looked absently at his hands on the table.

Virta continued. "I have called the fellow who handles funerals here in Terijoki. He will be over shortly to pick up the young lady." Virta paused so as not to sound too businesslike by explaining all of the details in one breath. Virta realized that with Koskinen's present emotional state there was a need to discuss the details gently and delicately.

"In the morning we shall make arrangements for a funeral. Sofia asked me to ask you if you approved of interring Elena in our cemetery here."

"Yes, of course." Koskinen nodded. "I shall pay for the costs of the funeral and the cemetery plot. And a marker." Koskinen, still deeply in grief had, nevertheless, come back to reality. There were matters that had to be taken care of.

"Your friends," Virta went on, "want to stay here for the funeral. That should be two days from now. I shall arrange in the morning with some of our neighbors to each take in one of the group for those two days. They are very nice people and they will do that. Mrs. Virta and I would like you to stay with us if you would care to."

"Yes, I am grateful to you," Koskinen said.

There was noise out in the living room. Some furniture being moved. Some people talking.

"That must be the funeral fellow. If you will excuse me," Virta said. "I'll leave you to take care of matters. Do you want to come into the living room or stay here?"

"I'll stay here," Koskinen replied. He could not bear to see Elena being carried out of the house.

After Elena's body had been removed, Chance and Wagner went with one of the boatmen to the latter's home for what remained of the night. Sofia and Koskinen stayed at the Virta's home. Sofia slept in an extra bedroom and Koskinen tried to sleep on the living room sofa. They had been given bed clothes by the Virtas.

Koskinen was physically exhausted and emotionally drained, yet, he could not sleep. Elena was on his mind totally. As he tossed and turned on the sofa trying to find a comfortable bodily position, he began to have a feeling of bitter resentment against everything and everybody Russian for what had happened to his Elena. What started as a spark of anger became a transcendent fire of virtual hate for all who had used her for their own ends while failing to shield and safeguard her from a betrayal that led to her torture and death. The leaders of the underground should have detected the duplicity of Lozovsky who was informing on the movement to the police. They failed to do so because blinded by their sense of self-importance and power. Koskinen felt an urge to return to Moscow to seek out, find and punish those blundering leaders. Koskinen's mind was raging from one violent thought to another. He would return and blow up the Kremlin with a powerful bomb. Or, he would go about methodically blowing up police headquarters and offices in Moscow. Even as these thoughts raced through his mind, Koskinen knew they were unrealistic. But it somehow helped to ease his pain to fantasize.

At daybreak, Koskinen arose, put on his clothes that were still somewhat damp from the drenching boat ride. Then without awakening the others he let himself out of the house and walked to the beach. He stood on the shore looking out over the expanse of water and he felt suddenly and quietly at peace. Observing in the distance, a brightening horizon and hearing the gentle lapping of the waters, he felt a part of primitive nature and that his thoughts of Elena would somehow be carried out to embrace her wherever she was now.

In the increasing light of day Koskinen saw several seagulls flying over the water in sharp and swooping turns. As he watched their movements, one seagull hovered near him and then landed on the beach a short distance away. The seagull stared at him for a few moments, then waddled towards him, when almost at his feet, stopped and seemed to Koskinen as if he was trying to communicate some message to him although Koskinen could not interpret what it might be. The seagull then flew off across the water. Koskinen followed the gull with his eyes until he could see the gull no longer. Koskinen thought back to the several dreams he had had of a seagull who always seemed a precursor of some malevolent event.

After some time, Koskinen returned to the Virta house where he found the Virtas dressed and busy making breakfast. Sofia was still sleeping. Although deeply grieving, Koskinen felt compelled to be gracious and to talk small talk with the Virtas. Neither he nor they mentioned at that time the events of the night before. They would do so later.

That day, the day before the scheduled funeral was spent by the escapees visiting with one another. Chance and Wagner came over to the Virta home to spend some time with Sofia and Koskinen. The talk was primarily about the events leading up to their escape and their experiences they had with the underground.

"It's a shame we failed to accomplish what we had set out to do, but that's the way it is," said Chance. Even before leaving the Soviet Union he had become resigned to their unsuccessful mission.

Koskinen added unhappily, "And it's a shame that Elena died for nothing." He spoke in his broken Russian which Sofia translated for Chance and Wagner.

Sofia contributed her view. "Elena," she said, "did not die for nothing, Timo. True, we did not dispose of Stalin and his henchmen, nevertheless, Elena brought hope to many who felt that with her energy and vivaciousness she could be a forerunner of better things to come in the Soviet Union. I know she had that effect on me. Of course, I'm appalled at what happened to poor Elena." Sofia shook her head in dismay.

Wagner observed, "I'm just amazed that the rest of us didn't get killed the way those bullets were flying around us. I looked at the boats and they each have at least a half dozen bullet holes in them." Wagner was incredulous.

Chance addressed Koskinen through Sofia. "I understand that you've offered to pay for the funeral. Gene and I talked it over and we'd like to help."

"Well, that would be nice of you to do so. I have no idea what the cost will be."

At this, Mr. Virta spoke up. "Elena was a fighter for freedom and against a vicious government. In a way, her fight, had it been successful, would have helped Finland. I intend to take up a collection from people in this village in honor of this young girl. We shall buy her a marker for her grave."

Koskinen was touched by this outpouring of generosity. Tears welled in his eyes. He had to control himself from crying. He got up and walked into the kitchen for a few minutes to compose himself. He wished he could be alone and yet he realized that he would just brood and that would not be healthy. After getting control of his emotions, he returned to his friends. It was a somber group.

The remainder of the day was spent in general conversation. The Virtas provided lunch and dinner for the escapees with the help of some of their neighbors. For the night, rather than spread the visitors to one family, the boatman and the Virtas decided to keep sleeping arrangements the same for their visitors, that is, Chance and Wagner with the boatman and his family and Koskinen and Sofia with the Virtas.

The following morning funeral services were held at ten hundred hours in St. Olaf's Lutheran Church in Terijoki. The word had spread about the death of Elena, a leader of the Moscow underground. The villagers turned out in great numbers to pay their respects and to honor Elena whom no one in Terijoki had heard of two days before but had now become an icon of the resistance movement overnight.

The people of Terijoki were rugged farmers or fishermen who believed in freedom from government impositions and in independence of the individual. Their admiration for those who opposed Stalin provided the motivation for the boat trips to smuggle people out of Russia.

St. Olaf's Church building was small with pews for about one hundred worshipers. It had been built in 1478 at a short walking distance from the shoreline. Koskinen knew of the reason for the church to have been built close to the water.

In the early history of Finland there were few roads or even paths through the heavy woods that blanketed much of Finland. Travel on land was difficult. Finland being a country of many lakes it was only natural that the inhabitants adopted a practice of traveling by boat to visit neighboring farms, the occasional store and to go to church. It was common in the era in which St. Olaf was built to see entire families dressed in their fineries converge on Sundays in their boats on the church shore, two or three men rowing in the rather long and substantial boats. The practice continued for several centuries up to and through the 1800's when roads began to be built.

St. Olaf was similar to the church in which Koskinen and Anna had been married near Tyrvaa in the central part of Finland. As in that church, St. Olaf's walls were of thick stone that had enabled it to withstand the rigors of time. Inside the church were the usual straight-backed wood pews resting on a wood floor under which were interred a number of the early inhabitants. The pulpit was built high above the pews so that the preacher could look down on all of his parishioners in one sweep of the eye. At the back of the church building was a special small room for pregnant women whom custom prevented from sitting with the rest of the congregation.

There was no hearse in Terijoki. The coffin in which Elena lay was brought to the church on a small flatbed truck. Several men carried the coffin inside the church and placed it on supports near the altar.

The cover was removed. Elena lay in peaceful repose, the missing ear wound covered by a small, fresh bandage. One of the women in the community had donated a dress to replace the blood soiled one worn by Elena when she was carried ashore by Koskinen.

The June morning weather was cloudy, chilly and dry. Those who had gathered outside the church including Chance, Wagner, Sofia and Koskinen began to slowly file into the church and to take their places in the pews. Front benches had been reserved for Elena's four companions, the four boatmen who had smuggled them from Russia and the Virtas. Many of the villagers where unable to get into the church as it filled to capacity. Some managed to find standing room at the back of the church near the entrance door. An organist played soft dirge music while people were entering the church. When the church had filled, the Reverend Otto Arola entered dressed in robes, stood for a few moments before the coffin and then proceeded to the preacher's podium where he began his eulogy.

Koskinen sat with his hands folded in his lap. He felt absolutely miserable and woebegone. He appreciated the outpouring of respect being demonstrated by the Terijoki people for Elena, but he wished he could just be alone with her, to have just one moment to say goodbye. So engrossed was he in the flashes of memories of the times he had spent with Elena that he heard nothing of what the preacher was saying.

Sofia was sitting beside him and felt his suffering. She reached out and held his hand. Koskinen did not respond, but entranced with his eyes closed he thought he heard the voice of Elena. His heart pounded, his throat tightened. Tears gathered in the corners of his eyes and rolled down his cheeks. He felt Elena's presence in spirit and he recalled her last words of love for him.

Sofia leaned close to him and whispered, "Timo, please. You must stop torturing yourself. Elena is with us as we think of her." She squeezed his hand.

Koskinen opened his eyes and, in doing so, he seemed to come to the realization that these were the moments of parting with his Elena.

The preacher had ended his eulogy and the people began to file past the open coffin. Chance, Wagner, Sofia and Koskinen sat waiting until the last and then they, too, stood before the coffin and looked down for the last time on Elena. Sofia began to sob and Chance and Wagner tried mightily to control their heartfelt emotions but tears rolled down their faces also.

Koskinen had become so drained that he could no longer shed tears. Before the ushers closed the coffin he asked that they leave him for a few moments to be alone with Elena. They respected his wishes and withdrew to the rear of the church. Koskinen leaned down and kissed the forehead of Elena and whispered, "Goodbye, my darling." And then he removed the wedding ring that Anna had placed on his finger when they were married and taking Elena's left hand, he placed the ring on her ring finger. To Koskinen, he was now joined and forever united with Elena, his love. He then turned and walked out of the church. The ushers came and closed the coffin and, acting as pallbearers, carried it to a horse-drawn wagon for a short journey to the church cemetery on the hill overlooking the church grounds. Chance, Wagner, Sofia and Koskinen as well as some of the villagers followed on foot. It was a relatively short walk.

At the grave site, Koskinen and Sofia stood near the cavity that had been dug in the earth and into which Elena's coffin would be lowered. The ceremony was brief. The Reverend Arola said the usual and customary words consigning Elena to the earth. Koskinen stayed during the lowering of the coffin, but left before the earth was deposited on it and the grave filled. One of the villagers had fashioned a temporary wood cross with Elena's name on it. This was driven into the ground at the head of the grave. People began to leave. Koskinen was sitting on a bench just inside the cemetery gate when Sofia caught up to him. He was staring into space. Sofia sat down next to him and again took his hand as a sign of comfort.

Koskinen spoke up in a sort of dull monotone, "At least Elena's lying in the free soil of Finland."

"And you can visit here from time to time, Timo," Sofia added.

"Yes. And I shall do so."

Then they arose and began a slow walk back to the Virta home with Sofia holding Koskinen's arm. Chance and Wagner had gone ahead. They felt it would be an inappropriate intrusion for them to walk with Koskinen back to the Virta home. Sofia could provide the needed solace.

While they walked back, Chance and Wagner spoke of Koskinen's devotion to Elena.

"It's apparent that he really loved that girl," Wagner observed.

"Yes, he was very involved with her and she with him," Chance remarked. "I wonder what will happen when he returns to his wife."

"There will be some difficulties, I imagine," Wagner said.

"Well, at least neither of us got that involved, did we?" Chance smiled and looked knowingly at Wagner. Chance was aware that Wagner had a crush on Sofia. Wagner said, "I refuse to answer on the grounds that it might tend to incriminate me." Then he chuckled.

Chance and Wagner spent the rest of the day at the Virta home with the Virtas and Sofia and Koskinen. Both lunch and supper were somber affairs. In the evening, Chance and Wagner returned to spend the night at the home of the boatman, Paavo and Sinikka Manninen. They learned that the boatman who had received a bullet in his left forearm was not badly wounded and was doing well. The bullet had passed through the muscle and had fortunately not damaged any bone. The doctor's prognosis was that the boatman would have some future problem due to the development of scar tissue. The boatman was willing to settle for that considering what had happened to Elena.

The morning following the day of the funeral was scheduled for the departure of the escapees. They were to take the train from Terijoki to Viipuri and then transfer to a train for Helsinki. Chance and Wagner arranged to meet Sofia and Koskinen at the train station at 830 hours. After bidding the Manninens goodbye, Chance and Wagner walked to the station.

At the Virta home after an early breakfast Sofia and Koskinen also prepared to take leave. However, at daybreak and before breakfast Koskinen had arisen, dressed and walked to the cemetery. On the way, he picked some marsh violets to place on Elena's grave. Arriving at the grave site, Koskinen stood staring at the wood cross and down at the fresh mound of dirt. Then he knelt, placed the violets on the grave and sobbing slightly whispered, "Nakemiin,* Elena, my love and darling, Nakemiin." Then he slowly arose, turned and walked sadly back to the Virta home.

As Sofia and Koskinen were saying goodbye to Martti and Aili Virta and thanking them for their hospitality, Mr. Virta put his arm around Koskinen's shoulders. "Timo, I want to assure you that we'll take proper care of Elena's grave. She was a brave young lady. We shall not neglect her. The gravestone should be ready in about two weeks. We'll see that it is properly placed. When, not if, you visit here, please stay with us. You are most welcome." His wife, Aili, nodded her head in approval.

Sofia sat with Koskinen both on the trip to Viipuri and then to Helsinki. They talked very little. Sofia judged that Koskinen wanted to be with his thoughts. She herself was doing some thinking about her future. Up to now it was assumed by herself and her friends on the trip that she would travel to the United States with Chance and Wagner.

As the train sped towards Helsinki, Sofia for some time looked out of the window and observed the countryside. The farms appeared so well

maintained, so orderly. At the stations at which they stopped along the way, Sofia was impressed by their well cared for building and their cleanliness. The passengers getting both off and on were well groomed and well mannered. To Sofia there were obviously no peasant-types as in Russia. Some of the people she observed standing at the small village stations were laughing while talking with others. This was something she rarely saw in Russia where people were generally glum and appeared dispirited.

Sofia made an abrupt decision. She turned to Koskinen and took his hand.

"Timo, if I were to stay in Finland and not go to the United States, would you be able to find me a job in your Intelligence Department?" Sofia spoke in Russian.

Koskinen was startled. "Yes, I suppose so. But, why the change?"

"Well, I was thinking that America is so far away. I really love Russia and maybe things there will somehow change for the better. Not only that, but I am concerned about the relations between Finland and the Soviet Union. They are not good and maybe there will even be a war between them. I think maybe I can be of some value in an Intelligence Department with my knowledge of Russia and Russian ways."

"Perhaps you can. But you'll have to learn the Finnish language, at least the basics. It is a very difficult language."

"Oh, I'm good at languages. I should be able to pick it up rather quickly. What do you think? Should I stay?"

"I'd like to see you stay, Sofia. But, it is your decision to make. I'll have to talk with my chief about possibly hiring you."

"Good! I shall stay in Finland. I shall tell Bill and Gene. They'll be surprised but they'll understand."

Koskinen was unprepared for Sofia's change of mind. His thoughts were racing about what to do with Sofia for the first few days.

"I'll be going to my home in Tampere, Sofia. Under the circumstances, I don't think I should bring you home with me. I hope you'll understand." Koskinen smiled at the obvious.

"Yes, I do, Timo."

"I'm sure that the Department can find someone on the staff with whom you can stay temporarily until the job situation is clarified. We'll see what happens when we get to Helsinki."

When the train was about a half-hour from Helsinki, Sofia walked forward a couple of seats to make her announcement to Chance and Wagner of her change in plans. She motioned them to join her in the vestibule of the car, which they did.

"Bill and Gene, you both have been so wonderful to me that I hate to tell you this. I have decided not to go to the United States but to stay in Finland." Sofia paused to see the reaction.

Wagner was taken aback. Chance was phlegmatic. Chance was that sort of person. Generally, he did not make an issue of another's personal decisions. In this case, he assumed that Sofia, an intelligent adult, knew what she was doing and had thought the consequences out. In contrast, Wagner wanted explanations.

"Sofia, what made you change your mind?" Wagner asked. He was dumbfounded.

"There are several reasons, Gene and Bill. First, I don't like to be so far from Russia."

"I would think that you'd want to be as far away as possible," Wagner remarked somewhat indelicately.

"I feel safe here in Finland," Sofia replied. "In addition, I believe that I can be of some value to Finnish Intelligence in Intelligence matters. It appears to me that Finland is at a very precarious point in its relations with the Soviet Union."

"Do you think you can save Finland from a Soviet invasion all by yourself?" Wagner was sarcastic.

"Now, you're being silly, Gene. Of course not. But I have considerable information that they might be able to use."

Wagner persisted. "Like what?"

Chance interceded. "Oh, cut it out, Gene. Sofia has made her decision. We have to respect it. Come on, let's go back to our seats. We can talk more about it when we're in Helsinki."

Chance judged that Wagner's harshness resulted from his infatuation with Sofia and his disappointment that he would not be able now to see her after he returned to Washington and she had a job there. Wagner, Chance thought, had not accepted Sofia's decision very graciously.

When Chance and Wagner returned to their seats, Wagner remarked wryly, "Maybe Sofia changed her mind because she thinks she can take Elena's place with Koskinen."

"I don't think that's it. If Sofia thinks that, she's fooling herself. You can see how deeply affected he was by Elena's death. I thought he was going to die of grief. In fact, I feel sorry for his wife. She's going to have a rude awakening. Actually, the guy shouldn't have allowed himself to get involved."

"Oh, come on, Bill. He'll get over it. And Sofia will be there to help him forget. You know how we men are."

"Speak for yourself, Gene. Anyway, we have to begin to think about how we can use in our jobs what we have learned from our experience over here. In my opinion, our mission was not entirely a failure. We have gotten insights into the way the Soviet government operates which we couldn't have acquired sitting back in our offices in Washington. As a result, we should be able to be more effective in our work and in our advice."

"Yeah," replied Wagner. His thoughts were still on Sofia.

When Sofia rejoined Koskinen, he asked, "Well, what was their reaction?"

"Bill was alright. He didn't raise any questions. But Gene, I guess, was a bit upset."

"I think he is quite fond of you." That is all Koskinen said. Sofia could see that Koskinen did not want to talk. She respected his feelings. There was little conversation during the remainder of the trip.

Sofia did, however, offer one observation. "At least these trains don't break down every few kilometers as they do in Russia."

Koskinen's reply was, "There is little, if any, corruption in Finland siphoning off money intended for repairs and maintenance and putting it into the pockets of officials."

"Yes, in Russia corruption is a way of life. That is how many people survive. It's really terrible." Sofia shook her head in disapproval.

The train arrived at the Helsinki railway station at 1500 hours. Koskinen immediately telephoned his headquarters to announce the party's arrival. He asked for and was put through to General Mahlgren.

"Timo, welcome back. We expected you a few days ago and were worried that something may have happened to you. Ambassador Peltonen has been keeping us informed about how your mission turned out. It's quite late in the day. Why don't you go to a hotel for the night and see me in the morning, say about 930 hours. I'll have a couple of the staff in my office and we'll talk about your venture."

"General, I think you should know that two American Embassy men and a lady Russian translator are with me. They made the trip with me under very extreme circumstances. The Americans are headed for the United States. The young lady is seeking asylum here in Finland."

"Well, have them stay at the hotel. We'll take care of the expense. We will want to speak to all of them, especially the Americans before they leave. Will you tell them that?"

"Yes, of course. Thank you, General."

Koskinen returned to his waiting friends and explained his conversation with the General.

"That's fine," Bill Chance said. "I guess we are all pretty tired. Timo, you lead us to the hotel. Tomorrow morning, Gene and I will have to arrange for travel to the United States and I'll want to contact our office in Washington."

Koskinen guided them to the Hotel Klaus Kurki, one of the better hotels in Helsinki. Koskinen felt they were all entitled to stay at an upper grade hotel after their ordeal, each with their own room to restore a sense of privacy that had not existed for a considerable time.

In the evening, after dinner, Koskinen called Anna from his hotel room. He had delayed calling her until he had rested for a while and to give himself time to adjust to the idea of talking to Anna again. He had to be careful about the sound of his voice. Anna would detect it if he sounded other than anxious to get home to her. Koskinen realized that he was just not ready to resume with Anna where they had left off. Too much had happened since he had left her at the train station three months ago. Koskinen was aware that he must put Elena somewhere in the back of his mind. Not to forget her. That would be impossible. But to not dwell on her almost to the exclusion of any other thoughts. That would not be easy and Koskinen at this point was not sure that he wanted to relegate Elena to the back of his mind. He still yearned for her. He still grieved and felt lost without her. How could he possibly have normal relations with Anna feeling this way. Koskinen felt in a terrible quandary. He felt trapped. But he had a duty to perform. It wasn't that he didn't love Anna, but things had changed.

"Anna, it's me, Timo." Koskinen tried hard to sound enthusiastic.

"Where are you?"

"In Helsinki."

"Oh, thank God, Timo. I hadn't heard from you for some time. I called your headquarters and they said that they had heard nothing after you left Moscow. I have been terribly worried. How are you?"

"Fine, except for a little wear and tear."

"When will you be home?"

"Probably in a couple of days. The General wants me to give a report. I'm sure we'll spend most of tomorrow on it. If I have to be here more than two days, I'll call you. How are the children?"

"They are doing well. They miss you. We have all missed you."

"Well, I'll tell you all about my trip when I see you." Koskinen knew that would not be so. There would be certain omissions.

After the telephone call, Koskinen lay down on the bed. His mind raced from one memory to another and to his present situation and back to memories. He was disturbed by his ambivalent feelings about Anna. He knew that it was not right to feel that way. Anna had done nothing to cause his emotional change. Koskinen was honest with himself. He was still in Terijoki.

The next morning before the meeting in General Mahlgren's office, Chance and Wagner telephoned to their respective families. Chance called his secretary, Charlene, in his section of the State Department and instructed her to inform Secretary Roth that he and Wagner were on their way home but were not certain as to the date of their arrival.

Promptly at 930 hours, the four met in General Mahlgren's office. Present were the General, Colonel Lars Blomquist, Colonel Anders Lindforst, Captain Helena Annala, the Russian Specialist and two translators, one for the Americans and one for Sofia. Their interviews had to be translated to accurate Finnish. In addition, two stenographers were present to write the questions and answers as spoken. Each was to spell the other as the session proceeded for most of the day.

During the break for lunch, Koskinen spoke with Mahlgren about the possibility of hiring Sofia on the Intelligence Department staff.

"I think, General, she can be of great help in understanding the weaknesses and strengths in the Soviets, in what is transpiring now. She also knows who among the key government people might by sympathetic to us and be of help to us."

"Let me think about it for a day or two, Timo. I may want to interview her separately. In the meantime, we'll pay her expenses here and give her some spending money. I'm aware that in working in the underground she was indirectly helping us. I think that we should exercise some benevolence towards here. I'll let you know of my decision."

"Thank you, General." Koskinen felt the General would decide favorably. The General understood Sofia's situation. The General was businesslike, efficient and sometimes coldly deliberate, but Koskinen, from experience, knew that he could be compassionate.

The interviews were not completed by the end of the first day. The General perceived the presence of the four who had just come from Russia as an opportunity to get credible information possibly not otherwise available.

"Mr. Chance and Mr. Wagner, I know that you are both anxious to return to your families, but I would appreciate if you could stay one more day. You could probably provide me with a better understanding of how the United States Government views the happenings in Europe. Our Ambassadors in various countries don't always get the best information for us."

Chance and Wagner readily agreed but on condition that the United States Embassy in Helsinki gave the General permission to interview them and for an Embassy representative to be present at the interview if the Embassy so desired. Chance and Wagner, as well as the Embassy personnel, realized that Finland was oriented towards the Western countries both politically and culturally and was a highly probable ally of the Western nations, especially of the United States.

The United States Embassy promptly gave consent to the interview and, at the same time, made arrangements for Chance and Wagner to travel home. They were to go by boat to Stockholm, Sweden and thence to England and, finally, by ship to New York.

That evening, the four friends had a farewell dinner at the hotel. Only they were present. Addresses were exchanged between Chance, Wagner and Koskinen and the Americans gave Sofia their office addresses. The Americans gave Koskinen and Sofia the general invitation to visit them in Washington and Koskinen expressed his hope that Chance and Wagner would someday return to Finland. All realized that it was more than likely that they would not see each other again after the Americans departed.

"I think," Chance observed, "that our experiences in the last few months will change our individual lives forever. None of us shall ever be the same."

"I have no doubt about it, that what you say is very true," Koskinen said.

"I agree," Wagner added. "A visit to Russia is like going to another planet. It is not like going to England or France or other Westernized countries. Russia is so pathetically different." He looked at Sofia and smiled. "Of course, there are exceptions."

"Thank you, Gene," said Sofia in a mock condescension. She also smiled coyly.

On the fourth day since they had arrived in Finland, the day Chance and Wagner departed for America, Koskinen and Sofia were further interviewed by General Mahlgren and his staff. Upon the conclusion of those interviews, General Mahlgren informed Koskinen on his decision regarding Sofia.

"Timo, I have decided to hire Sofia. I agree that she might be of considerable help to us even though she does not speak Finnish. I'm sure she'll pick it up quickly. She's a bright young lady. If it doesn't work out, however, we can always find her a job somewhere. She won't be abandoned. Furthermore, you'll be kept informed."

"Thank you, General. I'm sure Sofia will be very happy to learn of your decision." Koskinen was himself pleased with the General's decision.

"I don't want to keep you in Helsinki any longer at this time, Timo. I know you'd like to get home. Your assignment in the Tampere office will continue and in a week or two we'll have you come back to discuss the operation and the projects for your office. In the meantime, we won't bother you. Take a good rest."

"Yes, I could use it, General." Koskinen wasn't so sure that returning home would prove restful and peaceful.

Koskinen stayed in Helsinki another night. He called Anna and told her he'd be leaving for home the very next morning and mentioned the time of his arrival. Anna was delighted, exuberant.

"I am looking forward so much to seeing you again," she had said. "I'll have the children here, too. We'll all celebrate your coming home, Timo. I love you."

"Yes, Anna, that's nice. I love you, too." Koskinen tried to sound eager. He resolved to get himself mentally and emotionally attuned to the kind of happy homecoming Anna and the children expected.

After talking with Anna, Koskinen and Sofia had dinner together. Koskinen had earlier suggested to Sofia that they do so and Sofia had accepted it as a fitting beginning of a new way of life for her. She had been informed of her hiring by General Mahlgren and she felt overjoyed at the thought of settling down in Finland.

Koskinen took Sofia to the Ravintola Kreisi on Boulevardi Street. Sofia expressed her excitement about her new job in the Finnish Intelligence Section. She and Koskinen spoke in Russian with each other.

"I am going to have to teach you Finnish," Koskinen volunteered with a smile that encouraged Sofia to place her hand on his while saying, "I'd like that, Timo."

"I shall be coming down to Helsinki from time to time, Sofia. We'll get together for lunch or dinner when I do. In the meantime, a telephone call to you to see how you're doing is something acceptable to you, I hope."

"Of course," Sofia replied.

As they were finishing dinner, Koskinen remarked, "Sofia, this restaurant is where Elena and I had our first dinner together. I had met her on the train from Tampere to Helsinki, actually she boarded the train at a place somewhat south of Tampere called Hameelinna."

Sofia looked startled. "Timo, why did we come here? It brings back memories. You must stop torturing yourself about Elena. It isn't healthy for you. We can all think of Elena and remember her even while we are going on with our lives."

"Well," Koskinen replied in a sad subdued voice, "I suppose with the passage of time I'll begin to dwell less and less on Elena. Just now, however, her terrible passing is still so much on my mind, Sofia."

"I understand. Perhaps next time we can go to a different restaurant." Sofia was a bit irritated. She had accepted Koskinen's invitation to dinner with the thought that she might help divert him from his grief and here he was deliberately memorializing it.

"Perhaps I made a mistake coming here," Koskinen admitted. "I'm sorry. I have probably ruined the evening for you."

"No, Timo, you haven't ruined anything. If coming here will help you, then I'm all for it." Sofia had quickly gotten over her peeve. Timo thought Sofia was a great young lady with considerable strength of character.

After dinner, Koskinen and Sofia walked back to her hotel. When they reached her room Sofia invited Koskinen in but Koskinen politely refused.

"Thanks, Sofia. But I'm going to head back to my room. I'm quite tired and I think I need some rest. You'll forgive me, I hope."

"I understand. I'm tired too." She gave him a gentle kiss on his cheek. Koskinen took her hand and, bending slightly, kissed her hand and said "goodbye." Sofia was smiling and so, too, was Koskinen. They held hands for a few moments and then slowly let them drift apart. Koskinen took a couple of steps in walking away when he suddenly turned back before Sofia had fully closed the door.

"Sofia," Koskinen called to her. "I have forgotten something."

Sofia reopened the door fully. "What is it, Timo?"

"I have that small handbag I brought back with me. It contains some of Elena's things. Could you keep it for me until I decide what to do with it?"

"Yes, of course I'll keep it." Sofia saw little point in remonstrating again with Koskinen about his continuing obsession with Elena.

Koskinen went to his room a few doors down the hall from Sofia's room, retrieved the handbag and returned with it to Sofia.

"Thanks, Sofia," Koskinen said as he handed over the bag to her. "Good night, sleep well."

"Goodnight, Timo." Sofia closed the door. Koskinen returned to his room happy that he had managed to preserve safely the few items that had belonged to Elena. He could not have possibly taken them to Tampere and Anna.

In the morning, after a breakfast of bread and coffee in the hotel restaurant, Koskinen walked to the railway station and at 840 hours boarded the train to Tampere. He had brought nothing with him except the clothing he wore. The few personal items of his had remained in the bag he had left with Sofia. He had deliberately left them in the bag as a symbol of his still strong feeling of closeness to Elena. His things and Elena's together.

Koskinen dreaded having to meet Anna at the Tampere station. He just knew that she would sense a change in him try as he would to conceal it. He should have bought a newspaper at the Helsinki station. Reading it on the trip would have relaxed him and gotten his mind on something other than Elena and Anna. So he sat staring as the train moved along so engrossed was he in his thoughts.

When the train arrived at the Tampere station, Koskinen was one of the last to get off. Perhaps an analyst might say that it was a subliminal attempt to delay meeting Anna as long as possible.

Anna was the first to see Koskinen as he stepped from the car. She walked quickly, eagerly towards him smiling happily. Then he saw her and walked to meet her. They embraced and Anna's innate modesty was discarded for the moment as she kissed him fervently. It didn't matter that there was a crowd of people at the station.

"Oh, Timo, Timo. I have missed you so." Anna was crying. "I was so worried about you while you were gone."

Koskinen held Anna and returned the kisses. "I have missed you, too, Anna." Koskinen was surprised that he felt a considerable resurgence of affection and endearment for Anna at that moment. This was after all the woman he had loved, married and had children with. At that moment, he decided that he would do nothing to hurt her and that meant putting Elena to rest.

Koskinen and Anna took a taxi to their home. On the way Anna remarked that he had brought no bag with him.

Koskinen chuckled. "When you hear about my trip from Russia, you'll understand why."

The Koskinen children were at the house when Anna and Timo arrived in the taxi. The children overwhelmed their father with hugs, kisses and expressions of joy at his return. Anna set about immediately preparing the homecoming meal.

Anna said, "Timo, the sauna is hot. You can go in while I'm getting the food ready. There are clean clothes laid out for you on the bed."

"Ah, yes, a sauna. They don't have them in Russia. I don't know which I missed the most, the family or the sauna." Koskinen winked at the children to indicate that he was joking.

At the dinner table the conversation was primarily about Anna's and the children's activities while Koskinen was gone. Neither Anna nor the children pressed Koskinen to talk about his experiences in Russia although they were anxious to hear about them. They knew from reports to Anna from the Helsinki office that the Stalin mission had failed. To talk about it now might be unpleasant for their husband and father. Koskinen himself did not offer to describe his experiences.

"We'll get together again in a few days and I'll tell you all about my trip. I just need a little time to settle down and get readjusted."

The children did not remain long after the dinner. They sensed that their mother and father might wish to be alone. After the children had left, Anna and Timo sat at the dining table talking for about twenty minutes. Anna carried the conversation with small talk about relatives and friends. Anna decided to forego washing the dishes for a while. She could get at them later.

Arising from the table, she went over to Timo.

"You must be tired, Timo. You've had a long trip." Anna took Timo's hand. "Come with me." Timo arose unprotestingly.

Anna led Timo into their bedroom where they sat down on the edge of the bed. Anna had intense feelings of wanting to express her love with her husband. It had been a long time. She assumed that Timo had the same feelings. It had been a long time for him, too, she thought. She began with unbuttoning his shirt. Timo was very quickly aroused. For the moment, Elena slipped to the back of his mind.

In spite of the passion, Anna thought she noticed subtle changes in Timo's expression of affection. He seemed somewhat less amorous, less ardent. Nevertheless, she did not become concerned. She attributed it to either his weariness from his long trip home or, perhaps, to her imagination. She dismissed the matter summarily from further thoughts.

Later in the day when Anna and Timo again sat at the dining table sipping coffee, Anna asked, "Would you like to tell me about your adventure in Russia?" She laughed at the reference to an "adventure." She was merely trying to make light of what she presumed was a very unpleasant experience for her husband.

"Oh, I can tell you some of it. There is too much to cover, however, at one sitting. There were some good experiences and some that were very painful."

Timo began by describing the police state atmosphere in the Soviet Unions and of the harshness of life of the average citizen. He cited some examples of his being followed and of the fear of arrest that seemed to grip almost every Russian individual. He spoke of the prisons in Moscow and of the tortures that took place in them. He related about one woman in the underground movement had been arrested, imprisoned and tortured and had her fingernails and toenails pulled out and one of her ears cut off before the prison police turned her loose.

Anna shook her head at hearing these things. She found them incredulous.

"We in Finland have heard stories about this, but they are so extreme that many, like myself, have treated them as the usual rumors that grow with each retelling. But, Timo, you more than confirm the truth of what we hear."

Anna paused and then commented, "I hope we never have the Russians take over Finland. That would be horrible. That poor woman and others like her must have suffered horribly."

"Yes, I'm sure she did." Timo did not elaborate. If he said nothing more, Anna would suspect nothing. "I'll tell you about the underground some other time when we talk about how things went with my mission but that is enough for today."

The next morning Koskinen went to his office in the Finlayson Company complex. He was greeted with joy and fervent warmth of feeling by Kirsti Rantala, his secretary. The immediate conversation was general, intermingled with light humor and laughter. Kirsti brought Koskinen up to date with the details of the office operation since he was gone. Nothing of great significance had occurred.

Kirsti knew her job and had been able to run the office efficiently in Koskinen's absence.

Koskinen went into his private office and closed the door to be alone for a while. He sat down at his desk, fingered its edges as if to get used to being there again. He perused some reports and other papers in a cursory way, put them aside and turned in his chair to gaze out of the window. He was soon lost in thoughts as he contemplated his situation with the family and his work.

Koskinen had the feeling that he was about to resume the old routine that he had followed before leaving on his mission to Russia. He was not sure that he liked that idea.

EPILOGUE

When Timo Koskinen returned in the middle of June 1939 to Tampere, Finland from his assignment in Moscow he found that nothing had changed. There was Anna, his house, the familiar streets, the Finlayson Company complex where he had his office. There was Kirsti Rantala, his secretary. There was even the same guard at the company entrance gate.

Then there were the friends and acquaintances who greeted him with a degree of adulation that surprised him. It was as if he was some sort of hero although all that the people knew was that he had been away on a secret mission. However, the flattery was short-lived and the daily routine resumed for everybody. To Koskinen it was like he had never been away.

If the familiar surroundings at home had not changed in the three and one-half months that he had been gone, Timo Koskinen had changed. He was no longer the steady, composed, imperturbable, self-disciplined person that had been his lifetime trademark. Anna, the children, Kirsti and even those not close to him very soon became aware of the change. Koskinen seemed almost always angry, irritable, resentful, and quick to take umbrage at others' innocuous remarks.

Koskinen was conscious of the change in himself. He was by no means a shallow, superficial person who might look in a mirror and see only perfection. Since his return he felt restless, a sort of tempestuous turbulence burning uncontrollably inside him. He knew the cause. He understood that it arose from his recent experiences in Russia. It came down to Elena. He could not shed himself of his longing for her. She was on his mind constantly. He felt grief and guilt. Had he done things differently she would still be alive and with him. Sofia

632

had counseled him against torturing himself but her well-meant advice went unheeded for the very simple reason that Koskinen didn't want to let go of Elena.

The change in Timo Koskinen was having a devastating effect on his marriage. Anna was bewildered by it and could no longer treat it as inconsequential. Timo never mentioned Elena and Anna never once suspected that there might be "the other woman." Her Timo, she was confident, would never be unfaithful to her whatever his other faults might be. On several occasions, when the opportunity arose, Anna asked Timo what was wrong, what had caused the obvious change in him. Koskinen consistently replied that he was aware of the change, that it had nothing to do with her, that it was probably due to some of the horrible things he had witnessed and experienced in Russia and that Anna should just give him time to adjust.

Even with that explanation, Anna remained perplexed. To her the love between husband and wife was something that endured forever and was impermeable to erroneous influences or the temptations of the flesh. She failed to understand why, whatever bothered her Timo, his love for her seemed affected by it.

It was Koskinen who first suggested that maybe he and Anna should separate for a while so that he could better resolve his problems in the quiet of his own living quarters. Although Anna tearfully tried to reason with him saying that they could and should resolve them together, her pleas were to no avail. Koskinen knew that if Anna and he were to work out the problems together he would have to reveal his involvement with Elena. And this he could not bring himself to do. The easiest way out of the dilemma was to leave the home. Anna had no choice. Left alone she cried incessantly as she saw her family, her world disintegrate. She turned to her religion, her faith, her God to find solace, but found little comfort.

Two months after his return, Koskinen moved into a small apartment near the center of Tampere. Both he and Anna knew that even if they were eventually to reconcile, their marriage would never again be the idyllic relationship it had been.

Even as the private world of Timo Koskinen had changed, the several months following his return to Finland and the return of Bill

Chance and Gene Wagner to the United States saw the political turmoil in Europe grow more threatening.

Incredibly, on August 23, 1939, Russia and Germany signed a mutual non-aggression pact between themselves. Two days later Great Britain and Poland signed an alliance in which Britain guaranteed military action if Germany invaded Poland. On September 1, Germany invaded Poland. World War II had begun. Finland immediately declared its neutrality.

The non-aggression pact between Germany and Russia was nothing more than a politically expedient amicable veneer covering a fundamental hate for each other and the political systems and ideologies each represented. The Soviets knew Hitler had designs on Russia and feared that he would attack Leningrad by sending troops through Finland which Finland could not oppose even if it wanted to.

Intelligence reports landing on Koskinen's desk hinted at an increasingly menacing posture on the part of the Soviet Union towards Finland. There was little question in Koskinen's mind that it was inevitable that the Soviets would invade Finland. He wanted to do something to help his country prepare for it. When he learned that on October 9, a delegation would be going to Moscow to negotiate a peaceful agreement, he called General Mahlgren and offered to be part of the group. The General turned him down with the excuse that the Russian leadership now knew of his part in the underground and that he would be arrested and, thereby, create an incident.

On October 9 and again on October 23 and November 13, delegations from Finland led by Juho Paasikivi traveled to Moscow to attempt an agreement that would satisfy the Russians that Finland would not allow German troops to use Finland as a route to attack Russia. Each time Foreign Minister Molotov persisted in demanding of the Finns a thirty-year lease of the important port of Hanko on the Southern Finnish coast, the right to station Russian troops on and near Hanko, the demilitarization of the Finnish Karelian frontier with Russia and the ceding of certain islands in the Baltic Sea to Russia.

On December 1, Soviet troops invaded Finland's Karelian Isthmus. On that day the Soviet government established the Democratic Republic of Finland. Its headquarters was in Terijoki. The so-called Winter War had begun.

General Mahlgren immediately ordered Koskinen to transfer to Section Headquarters in Helsinki. The General told Koskinen that he could bring Anna if he liked. Koskinen demurred saying that Anna had to keep her job as a teacher in Tampere schools.

Koskinen knew that any thought he might have of visiting Elena's grave in Terijoki was impossible now. He thought of how ironic it was that Elena who had hoped to escape from Russia and to live in the freedom offered by Finland and who had been buried in Finnish soil was now back in Soviet territory.

Shortly after Koskinen settled in the office in Helsinki he began to visit with Sofia frequently. They had dinner often together and Koskinen stayed overnight with her in her room from time to time. Their experiences in Russia made them feel they had much in common and their fondness for each other quickly developed over the days.

Sofia knew of Koskinen's obsession with Elena but she hoped that time and her own living and vital presence would help Koskinen to ease away from letting the memories dominate his emotions. Koskinen explained his separation from Anna. As a consequence, Sofia felt free to visit with Koskinen.

General Mahlgren explained to Koskinen that the transfer to Helsinki was intended to assure that Koskinen would be readily available to carry out any mission that might be devised to disrupt the Russian military efforts against Finland. Koskinen was invited to attend strategic planning meetings held daily between the Intelligence Section and representatives of the military leadership. The people at these sessions were all too well aware that the small Finnish army of primarily volunteers could not hold out indefinitely against the vast, unlimited numbers of Russian soldiers. It was clear that there was a desperate need for desperate action.

Back in the United States, Bill Chance and Gene Wagner implored the Secretary of State to urge President Roosevelt to send substantial aid to Finland. They understood the urgent needs of the Finns.

Roosevelt expressed sympathy for the Finns. He personally wanted to do everything possible to help Finland but his advisors, including the Secretary of State, opposed any sending of the military supplies requested by Finland. They did not want the United States to get involved in European squabbles. Their opposition prevailed.

Neither Sweden nor other European countries came to the assistance of Finland although, again, expressing sympathy. Finland was on its own in deciding to fight the Russian invasion.

Koskinen was ready to carry out any secret mission assigned to him. His country, Finland, meant more to him than life itself. He also hated the Soviet regime with a fierce and deep vindictive hate for what it had done to Elena.

Herbert Eggie, a retired attorney, has been a frequent traveler to Finland over many years and often remained in that country for months at a time. Mr. Eggie now resides in Wisconsin.